Paragon Exordium

Book 1 of
The Galvorn Saga

Mikel Melwasui

PARAGON EXORDIUM

BOOK 1 OF THE GALVORN SAGA

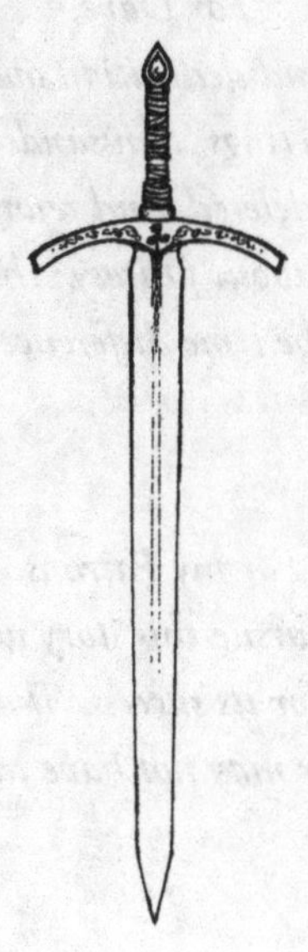

MIKEL MELWASUL

For My Wife,
Whose steady hands, and unshakeable faith in this story have helped
shape its form and soul. Without our long car drives full of world
building, your meticulous attention to character consistency, and
following the rules we designed this story would not be. Thank you for
your patience and commas. (Including the ones on this page).

For Dave,
Whose friendship, time and dedication over the last few years have
resulted in hundreds of meetings, thousands of hours, and hundreds of
thousands of words formed, deleted, and rewritten to form a unique story
that embraces what we love about fantasy. Thank you for putting up with
the time difference.

For my Patrons,
Whose support freed me to pursue this story with the time it required and
proved to me the potential for its success. Thank you for your names and
personalities which may or may not have inspired a character or two.

For Everyone Else,
Sorry I couldn't fit you on the page; I'll get you next time.

AUTHOR'S NOTE

This is an apocalyptic story. This book is written for adults but contains no cursing or sexual overtones. There is intense violence and some mild gore. Additionally, there are references to sexual assault and off-screen suicide. As a film, the story would likely be rated PG-13. It is set in the modern American South and contains regional dialogue consistent with the area.

Enjoy.

SPOTIFY PLAYLIST

We've compiled a recommended music playlist full of songs that inspired our writing or we felt suited the vibe of the chapters written, including a full orchestral theme to Paragon Exordium, You can scan the QR Code if you're interested.

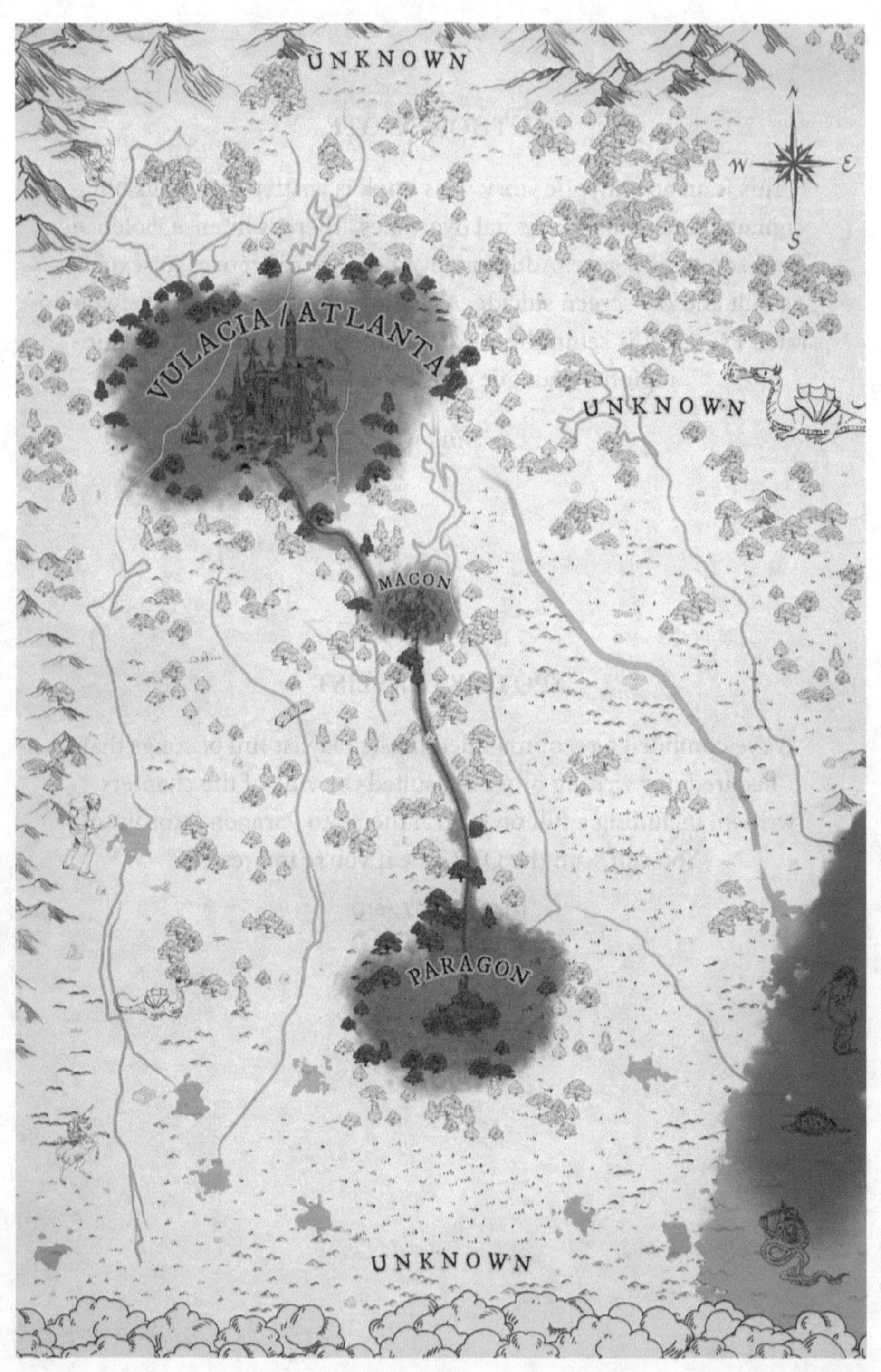

UNKNOWN
N
W E
S
VULACIA / ATLANTA
UNKNOWN
MACON
PARAGON
UNKNOWN

CONTENTS

PROLOGUE

"There are far, far better things ahead than any we leave behind."
C.S. Lewis

The Earth shook, and the sky screamed. Evelyn tore through the living room, scooping up five-year-old Sally and throwing them both under the thick mahogany dining room table.

It had been just an ordinary Saturday; Evelyn had canceled plans with friends to see a movie to make a few extra dollars babysitting Sally.

Sally had been quiet all morning, peacefully playing with her action figures. Then, minutes before the babysitter could get up to make peanut butter and jelly sandwiches, there was a sky-splitting explosion. An explosion so loud and powerful that neither girl could hear their own screams or the crashing of pictures and furniture as the whole building shuddered.

Finally, when her eyes were now dry of tears, the quaking ceased.

"Shh… Hush now, sweetie. It's all right. We're okay. Hush now. Shhh… We're okay," whispered the babysitter to the sobbing child. After a few minutes, the sobs stopped.

Then the screaming began.

More explosions, but nowhere near the volume of the first one. The screech of tires. Gunfire, near and far. But worst of all was the silent absence of sirens. There should have been firetrucks, ambulances, police cars. The city had upgraded all their vehicles in some sort of major business deal, after all. She could not remember the details, but she remembered her parents talking about it. But there were no sirens — only the bone-chilling cacophony of panic.

The babysitter held the power button on her phone down for the fifth time, hoping maybe, just maybe, this time it would turn on.

It had been fine before; charged enough. She never let it go below fifty percent. Never. Tears running down her face, she hurled it out from under the table in a burst of rage. The phone's case protected it but not the drywall, which it dented. Sally flinched in her lap. That was when she noticed the beeping. Half the appliances in the house were beeping, as if they had all been reset.

"I want mommy," Sally whispered weakly.

"Stay here, sweetie. It'll be all right. I'll be right back," Evelyn said as she picked up the little girl from her lap. Sally shook her head with all the violent tenacity of a child, and Evelyn saw tears welling in her eyes. Then she spied a solution. A stuffed rabbit named Basil lay on the floor at the edge of the table.

She must have left him on the table after breakfast.

Sally's babysitter reached out, pulled the floppy brown rabbit to her, and then handed it to the whimpering little girl. Sally took Basil eagerly in her arms, clutching the toy so tightly the babysitter feared she would either hurt herself or break the rabbit. Evelyn could hear her whispering softly to the rabbit as she got out from under the table.

"It's okay, Basil. I'll protect you. Don't cry."

A lump formed in Evelyn's throat as she dashed over to a window. Pulling aside the purple curtains, she saw in the reflection that her auburn hair was an absolute mess.

Click. The lock on the window turned with some effort. The window itself slid open easily. She was surprised it was still intact given the volume of the noise that had accompanied the shaking.

Outside the window, the world was ending. The sounds of the city losing its collective mind filled her with dread as she looked out over it from the third-floor apartment. People were running around wildly below her, some trying to start cars, others trying to get inside different buildings. She saw what looked like a group of filthy homeless men chasing a man down an alley with large knives.

To her relief, the sky was not full of planes or parachuting invaders. *Just strange shining clouds — no, those aren't clouds. They look more like… cracks.* Her focus shifted to the smoke. Lots of smoke rising from all over the city. *What do I do?*

Something else caught her eye. There was a plane; a jumbo passenger jet. But it was not flying peacefully overhead. It was crashing, careening closer to the earth. Closer to downtown. Or what used to be downtown. She could see from the window unfamiliar white stone buildings overlapped with the usual jumble of businesses and skyscrapers, several of which were missing. *That doesn't make sense. How could there be new buildings? Am I hallucinating?*

Evelyn cursed — quietly so the little girl would not overhear. It was all too much. The panicking. The crashing planes. The random new structures. The homeless men with big knives.

Making her way back to the kitchen, she checked under the table. Sally had fallen asleep, Basil clutched in her arms. *She'll be safe here for now, I hope.* she thought as the sounds of chaos still echoed around them.

Before leaving her there, she made sure the back door of the apartment was locked, then ventured into Sally's father's study. Opening the closet door, she found what she was looking for: a safe. The safe was on a high shelf well out of reach of Sally's small, prying hands.

Unfortunately, this also meant it was too high for Evelyn, since she was barely over five feet tall. With no other recourse, she clambered onto a wobbly office chair and snatched up the safe before she could lose her balance.

Once balanced on her own two feet, she turned the safe over and saw the thumbprint scanner and number pad. *Thumbprint first, then Sally's birthday backward.* Sally's father had taught her the first time she babysat.

"Just in case. You never know," he had told her with a reassuring pat on the shoulder. The safe clicked open without issue, showing her what she had come looking for, a pistol. "It's always loaded, so be sure to only point it at something if you're trying to kill it." The salt-and-pepper bearded man had said.

Evelyn tried desperately to get her phone to turn on, but no combination of buttons or chargers worked. She scrambled over and tried her laptop and then Sally's mother's desktop; none of which even flickered. *Nothing to do but wait; going outside is not an option. I'll make sandwiches. I'm not hungry, but Sally loves PB and Js. The best thing for her is to pretend everything is normal.* She was opening the peanut butter jar when she heard movement under the table.

"Miss Ev?" The young girl's voice wilted up from below.

"I'm here. Are you hungry?" *Of course, she's hungry. She's always hungry.*

"M-hmm," came the weak reply, still from beneath the table.

"Do you want to take a seat at the table like a big girl?"

She shook her head.

"Do you want to stay under the table to eat?"

"M-hmm."

The simple noise brought tears to Evelyn's eyes. There was fear in that sound. She could not blame her. She wanted to get back below the table and stay there herself.

"Okay, Sal, we'll eat under the table. That sounds like fun."

A few moments passed in silence while she worked on the sandwiches.

"Where are Mommy and Daddy?"

The question pulled her heart into her stomach. She had hoped the food would be enough of a distraction, but this had been inevitable.

"I'm sure they'll be home soon, sweetie." She tried to hide the fear in her own voice as best as she could. For all she knew, they weren't coming home at all.

"Can you call them?" It was a perfectly reasonable request for a child in her position, but that did not make it any easier.

"I tried to Sal, but the phone isn't working."

Silence.

She waited.

More silence from the girl, but Evelyn thought she heard screaming from inside their building. She joined the girl under the table, handing her a plate with one and a half PB and Js. One for the girl; one for her bunny.

Sally took a bite, holding back tears as she chewed. Halfway through the snack, she asked another question. "Is this a nine-eleven? Pop-pop talks about nine-eleven a lot."

Evelyn did not have a chance to answer. The screaming inside the apartment complex grew louder, joined by gunfire. Then, there came three loud, heavy knocks at the door.

Sally's eyes went big. "Daddy?" Before Evelyn could move, the little girl had dashed out from under the table, running for the door.

Why would her parents knock? They have keys. Oh, no.

"Sally, no!"

But it was too late. The girl's size had made her escape from the table much quicker than Evelyn's. The lock was undone. The door was slowly swinging open but still too fast for her to stop it. Cruel, clawed fingers wrapped around the edge of the frame, pushing the door so it slammed open against the wall.

For a moment, Evelyn thought she was looking at the devil himself. An enormous leathery skinned being who looked green in the unlit hallway stood in the doorway. He wore a strange patchwork of rags over his body and held an abnormally long machete in one hand.

No. A sword, she realized. *Whatever that is, it is not human.* The creature smiled down at Sally — a cruel expression full of rows of bloody, sharp teeth. But it was the eyes of the being that filled Evelyn with the most fear. They were yellow, the same shade you would see on a notepad, the color splintered with red irritation. There was no white in those eyes; only black pupils in a sea of burning yellow.

There was a savage glee in those eyes as they looked hungrily over Evelyn and the little girl. Evelyn's gaze was drawn to the sword in his hand, her mind focusing on the bright red blood dripping from it rather than its bizarre presence.

"You're not Daddy," Sally said in a puzzled voice, temporarily free of the mounting horror seizing Evelyn's chest.

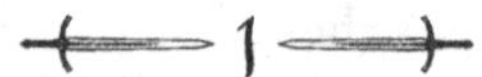

SARAH YOUNG

ocus on your task at hand, Sarah. It's like Dad always says, 'You can't reach tomorrow until you've finished with today.' Sarah Young glanced at her reflection in the scooter's mirrors. She missed wearing make-up; her thin, almond-shaped eyes could have used some eyeshadow.

Looking tired as usual, but it could be worse. I could look tired when I don't feel tired, she thought sarcastically, smiled at herself a second, and then clambered onto the small blue scooter.

Sarah tucked her wavy, dark brown hair up into her helmet so it wouldn't fly in her face as she drove — another on the list of minor inconveniences. Sarah liked to take the time to straighten out those waves in the mornings before she went anywhere. Straightening them made her look more like her mother, and that gave her just a hint of her mother's confidence. But these days, that was impossible.

No time to worry about that, Sarah thought as she glanced down at her list of assignments for the day. *I have to get to work. Still a dozen interviews I need to get through.* Her finger traced the list of names and locations until it found the first one without a checkmark. *Out by the bypass. Cool, I know where that is.*

The scooter's engine coming to life could barely be classified as a purr. It was so quiet. Here, outside her dorm, was quiet. She couldn't see a soul. It felt like she'd been left behind on campus during school break. This changed quickly as she drove. Even if the campus somehow still slept, the rest of the town and its inhabitants were wide awake.

By the time she'd pulled off campus, rolling mostly unopposed down the road, the buzz of the city, beeps of construction vehicles, the frantic barking of dogs, and instructions hollered over the din of tools drowned out the purr of her scooter.

She caught herself about to take a turn towards a grocery store and corrected her turn signal to off. Not that there was anyone behind her to signal to. Still, she checked both ways before speeding back up from her slow-down. Keeping an eye on the road, she avoided one of a dozen large potholes big enough to ruin her borrowed vehicle.

Sarah came to a stop at a four-way light at the turn of a sign by an orange-vested man standing in the middle of the lanes. She looked longingly at a closed coffee shop on a corner as a series of battered vehicles passed by on her left. Around the corner, she spied a pair of moving trucks being loaded down with heavy furniture from the offices they were parked outside of.

The movers made little effort to preserve the finish of the furniture as they loaded it quickly and haphazardly into the backs of the trucks. *They're probably amateurs*, she thought, recalling how many moving companies her mother had her research before finally choosing one to help them move out of the suburbs and into the city when she was in high school.

But that city was states away, in Pennsylvania. She was here in Georgia, at her father's alma mater, and there was no telling what was happening to the north. Or farther south, east, or west, for that matter. Sarah sighed when the traffic director signaled for her to keep waiting as he gave a row of smelly trucks priority. The trucks trundled by, one by one, beds filled with lumpy cargo.

Stink molested the air around her. She brought a hand up, covering her nose. The smell was not unfamiliar; the whole city lingered with it. It'd been getting better, sure, but these trucks were transporting the source, so they did little to make it more palpable.

For some reason, they slowed. The truck in front of Sarah that had been following the other a bit too closely slammed on the brakes. She heard both the driver and the traffic director curse as the truck lurched to a halt. The sudden braking caused a five-foot-long piece of cargo wrapped in a dirty sheet to fall out the back and strike the concrete with a sickening squelch.

Sarah's stomach turned. A man emerged from the passenger side of the truck and made his way over to the spilled cargo. "Gimme a hand?" he asked in a gravelly voice as he stopped over the dark circle of liquid already forming around one end of the poorly wrapped corpse.

"All right, all right," the traffic director replied with a shake of his head. "But you take that end. I can't have bloody hands while directing traffic."

"It's red, ain't it? Might make your job easier," the second man replied as he grabbed the bloody end of the body. Together, they lifted and tossed it back into the truck bed.

Sarah fought back the urge to vomit as the corpse landed among the others with a wet thump. A few seconds later, the trucks were gone, presumably off to the burning pits, and the director was waiving Sarah on. She throttled the gas, eager to be away from the wet puddle of blood that still lingered on the road.

Sarah turned her mind's eye away from the last month of corpses. Away from the haunting face of her mother, her father, her sisters, and her brother who she kept seeing in the backs of those trucks. In every dead face, she saw them. But they were far away. Safe from all this, she hoped.

She wondered if she'd see any of them again. *I doubt the rest of the world is doing as well as we are, thanks to SNW. Most towns don't have a private military organization's training headquarters. They're a scary bunch, but they have been on top of things, working with police and helping with the recovery.*

Wait a second — where am I? She realized she had no idea, as she looked around at the unfamiliar damaged buildings on all sides. *This isn't right. Crap.* She reached into one of the pouches and removed a heavily marked map of the city. *Ah, I should have turned instead of going straight. Ugh. Good thing Mom isn't here, or she'd lecture me for relying on my GPS and not memorizing roads.*

She corrected her course, which took her through a quieter side of town. *Already cleared. Good. At least the worst is over, and there's time for work like this.* Sarah told herself, her mind turning back to her assignment.

It was a straightforward task: visit the different watchmen assigned to posts around the city and catalog the previous occupations of as many volunteers as she could. The hope was that with more knowledge of skill sets, work restoring the city could get done more efficiently.

She was not the only one assigned such a task, but the only one instructed to interview the volunteer watchmen — a task that had consumed her yesterday and threatened to carry into her tomorrow.

Sarah reviewed her list and found she had seven interviews left. So far, she'd spoken with a dentist, two farmers, a welder, three lawn-care specialists, a waitress, and four food-service people with National Guard experience.

Altogether, not quite the set of skills she'd hoped for among those unfortunate enough to be deputized and assigned to the perimeter of the city. She'd found herself wishing there were more soldiers among them.

Much to her surprise, her conversations with volunteers tended to last longer than she hoped. This was partly, she knew, due to her own unwillingness to be impolite and cut someone off when they were speaking. But most of all, it was because they were bored. As it turned out, bored people really liked to hear themselves talk, regardless of how boring they or their lives happened to be. Sarah knew this before, but it still surprised her how much one could say in response to "What was your previous occupation?"

Maybe I should tell people I'm doing a census rather than interviews, Sarah considered as she approached the next set of watchmen. They stood together in the back of a large truck parked by a sign reading *Carriage Hill Rd.*

To be polite, she pulled her scooter to a stop at the sidewalk's edge. Then she placed her small helmet on it and adjusted her glasses properly on her nose before she continued on foot, clipboard and pen in hand.

Beyond the truck she saw the remnants of the elevated bypass that now formed a rudimentary wall of rubble and vehicles around the city. This left a dead space between the town and the woods, a sort of no man's land four lanes wide.

I've got to get new glasses, Sarah thought as the ends of her tattered dress brushed the overeager grass pushing further into civilization. She'd have just worn her leggings and forgotten the messy dress, but it was already getting cold out, and the dress kept her warm.

Good grief, I've walked a lot lately, she thought while stepping over a pile of broken glass. Her gaze turned to the two watchmen she was approaching. Their truck stood only a few dozen yards away at the edge of the barrier, two three-story buildings connected by two rows of empty vehicles.

The beast of a truck loomed over her, twice her height. *No wonder they're using it as a watchtower. I always associated big trucks with dumb frat boys, but it looks like they have their uses after all.*

The men started to notice her approach, one poking the other in the shoulder and pointing back at her. The first man, in sleeveless flannel, was lean with plain chestnut hair and a thin mustache.

"Well, hello there, little lady. How can we help you?" he said with a Southern twang. One covered leg swung over the side of the truck bed, searching for the large tire below for a footrest, as he prepared to drop down to meet Sarah. The older man, in overalls and a camo jacket, spat something brown out of his mouth over the truck's other side.

"Beg your pardon, ma'am, but I'll be staying up here, these old knees o' mine ain't what they used to be," he said with a friendly smile full of dirty teeth. The man's head jerked towards the woods. "Ashe, hold up there, son," he said as he placed his hand on the tan man's shoulder.

"Now come on, Joe—" Ashe began but stopped mid-sentence, adjusting his sunglasses. "What's that?" he asked in a confused tone, staring out away from the city.

Ashe adjusted his position and gripped his sunglasses to keep them from falling off at the sudden change in movement. Straddling the truck bed, he raised a radio to his mouth as he stared out towards the forest several hundred yards away.

"This is Carriage Hill. We got something moving in the trees out here. Thought y'all should know. Over." Both men were armed, from what Sarah could see, so the exclamation did not frighten her despite the strange pitch of the man's voice. The forest, however, did.

The woods were strange. They'd grown unnaturally quickly over the last weeks. An explosion of foliage inched closer and closer to the concrete road and barrier beyond. The growth, too slow to see with the naked eye but unmissable if one looked closely one day then the next.

To make matters worse, the trees surrounded the city. Once upon a time, this made for a beautiful drive in the fall and added a sense of isolationist wonder. These days though, the ever-encroaching foliage only created unease.

Whatever it was Ashe saw emerging from that thick foliage of the woods, though, was out of Sarah's line of sight. But the curse it pulled from deep within his lungs was too loud to miss. Especially when followed by the hushed words, "That's a big snake."

Sarah was not particularly scared of snakes, but the hollow sound of Ashe's words brought every hair on her body to attention and made her take a step backward.

From her position on the ground, she noticed the second man had gone rigid. He white-knuckled his weapon. But he made no attempt to attack the serpent. He simply stood there, still. So still, she realized, that his chest did not even rise or fall with breath. It was as if he'd been petrified.

Sarah's stare lingered on him, searching for some sign of life from the stony man. Someone was yelling something. Her gaze drifted toward the first man. Ashe's body moved, in contrast to the older man. His radio dropped from his hand, forgotten as he raised his rifle.

Bang! Bang! Bang! Bang! The deafening sound of the rifle fire drove Sarah farther from the truck. The gun roared as bullets whizzed through the air toward the creature unseen from Sarah's vantage. Then Sarah caught a glimpse of the incoming nightmare.

The beast's gargantuan body was garbed in scales of deep forest green and splotched with black markings that would hide it in the low light of a dense forest. Scattered among its flaring scales were a series backward-facing, footlong, bony spines, which emerged in lines that ran down its form.

Worst of all were its eyes. The enormous, intelligent eyes grew closer no matter how many bullets Ashe fired. They were like manhole-sized gemstones of kaleidoscopic green and yellow hues surrounding evil, fang-shaped pupils.

The monster's body was at least fifty feet from tooth to tail. The monster's maw was full of fangs the size of a man's forearm, and the head they filled loomed large enough to swallow a man whole without him ever touching a fang. Its open mouth revealed a tongue so deep a shade of purple it was almost black.

Then it struck. The creature burst through the rubble barrier as if it were made of cardboard. In an instant its snout was under the truck's side, which it lifted and tossed violently. Broken glass scattered through the air and landed all around Sarah.

Both men were hurled from the truck bed by the attack. Ashe was the luckier of the two. He struck the ground a few feet from Sarah with a sickening crack of bone. There, he twitched, somehow still consciousness despite the numerous bones that punctured his skin.

The older watchman was not as fortunate. He'd stood immobilized until the moment the monster struck the truck. The blow flung him high into the air with the vehicle. As gravity wrapped its greedy fingers around him in its strong embrace, he screamed, and the snake rose to meet him. The crunch of bones between giant fangs bizarrely emphasized by the sound of the truck as it crashed into the roof of a nearby building. The macabre sound accompanied by a spray of gore brought bile up in Sarah's throat, and the burn of it in her throat was enough to break her shock.

Run!

She tore away from the scene towards her scooter, as only one thought occupied her mind: *Escape!* She glanced back just for a moment. Perhaps it wasn't real, she hoped. She prayed it wasn't real. Maybe, just maybe, if she looked back, it would be gone.

But Sarah's hopes and prayers melted away. She saw Ashe sprawled in the broken glass around him. His right arm dragged frailly at his side, punctured by broken bone. His left arm flailed about in search of his rifle, just out of reach.

The once brave man whimpered like a wounded puppy as the shadow of the snake fell over him. He tried to call out to her to beg for help. But no words came. The beast was done with the first man, and now rose over Ashe, forming an enormous S.

Sarah did not witness what followed. She did not see as Ashe was grabbed by the ankles and tossed into the air like a plaything over and over. But she heard his guttural screams and a booming voice in an unfamiliar language. She did not see him being swallowed, so no image burned into her memory, but the screams did.

Sarah's hair flapped in the wind as she pressed her scooter for all it was worth, helmet forgotten somewhere on the road behind her. She could hear the monster in pursuit. A strange, inhuman gurgle emanated from its throat — more strange, rumbling words followed her.

The instant it was out of sight in her mirrors, she veered towards a small pawnshop with barred windows and doors, which she almost crashed into as she came to a halt. Not leaving the scooter, she yanked repetitively as hard as she could on the doors. To her dismay, she found them locked.

Tears streaked down her face as panic billowed in her mind where it turned into desperation. She kicked at the door to no avail. Her sweat-covered hands clawed at the handle, desperate to get a different result. But the door wouldn't budge.

In her mind's eye, the monster's enormous fangs were already boring into her before swallowing her whole or swallowing her in pieces. She was hit with a surge of nausea, and the world spun around her. She could hear the beast's scales scraping the concrete. The snake was coming, taking its time.

It knows I can't outrun it. A door slammed to her right. A woman dragged a child into a store. *I won't make it back to campus. I have to find somewhere to hide,* she realized as she saw more people throw themselves into whatever building was closest.

They'd heard gunfire, and the panic had begun. Sarah focused, drove back her own panic. *Don't follow a crowd in a panic. They'll kill you quicker than whatever is scaring them,* she recalled her father instructing from a young age.

She saw her salvation: an abandoned restaurant across the narrow street with a glass doorway too small for the nightmare somewhere behind her to fit through.

Behind her, a thunderous, blood-curdling sound almost like laughter clawed through the air. The horrifying noise reinvigorated her, spurred her to point her scooter towards her new hiding place. There were people nearby, screaming, running. But they were like shadows, barely noticeable and irrelevant to her plight. There was nothing they could do for her or her for them.

Sarah crashed her scooter through the door to the restaurant. Hopping off and ignoring her now bruised legs, she slammed the door behind her. Then she turned, and the search for a hiding place began.

The building was unoccupied, the silence of it made eerie by the chaos outside. Chairs and a few tables scattered the floor, doubtless from the tremors that had shaken the world a few weeks ago. Sarah took a step and heard a *crrsshk* underfoot. She looked down and saw broken glass everywhere. Carefully, she made her way towards the kitchen.

She knew it was unlikely anyone out there would survive the thing. *Maybe they'll distract it, and it'll forget about me*, she thought in a moment of sickening weakness. There was no telling when any form of reinforcements would arrive. *Not that they'd make a difference.*

She found herself in the kitchen and paused to catch her breath while she checked the surroundings. Not sure what she was looking for, she scanned the room. Her eyes lingered on an unlit exit sign over a secure metal door at the back of the kitchen.

Uncertainty lay on the other side of that door; uncertainty and an enormous monster-snake. Adrenaline coursed through Sarah's veins with life-prolonging energy. As she breathed, her racing mind quieted and was sharpened by the energy. Help was undoubtedly on its way.

Ashe had radioed for help, hadn't he? Even if he hadn't, there'd been the gunfire and the screams. The thought of Ashe's broken body drew bile from her stomach again.

As she straightened up from emptying her stomach, her mind continued to race.

They're coming. They must be. The police, maybe even those mercenary contractors, FROST, ICE — what were they called…some kind of acronym… SNW. They've been securing the town. Maybe they can help. But those men with the rifles couldn't even make a dent. Sure, they weren't mercenaries. In fact, the older one was too scared to even move… like he was paralyzed… Not out of fear or shock — he hadn't even been breathing. How did it do that?

If the beast had caused the paralysis, why didn't it affect the other guy in the truck or me? She reached up with two pale fingers to adjust her glasses, almost knocking them off, her hands were shaking so badly.

Then a thought struck her: *Glasses?* The idea swirled through her head. The snake had been focused on devouring the older man when she'd fled. *He wasn't wearing sunglasses, but Ashe was and was still moving. It's hardly solid evidence,* a doubtful voice echoed in the back of her mind. *Somehow, that monster has a paralytic effect, though. Solid evidence or not, glasses are the best I have.*

Sarah's mouth was bitter. She spat on the floor, trying to rid herself of the burning taste. *Even if help came with firepower sufficient to damage the beast, how would they fight something capable of incapacitating people with a look? They would need a tank to kill that thing. Or something comparable, like an explosion.* She began tearing open cupboards and flinging open drawers as she searched the kitchen.

But there's no reason for them to send heavy weapons to deal with what could be a faulty radio. What would get them to send that? She racked her brain for ideas. *If glasses work, is glass its weakness? Could I hit it with a car?*

Then she found what she didn't know she was looking for: an industrial-sized bag of cornstarch. An old YouTube video she'd seen late at night popped into her brain. With effort, she carried the bag out of the kitchen, almost dropping it several times as she went. Clumsily, while staying well away from the front door, she began to scoop the bag's contents into the air with a bowl.

"*Sssvlaaaaknnaaa.*"

A rumbling voice shook the walls, huge and abrasive as it slithered out from deep within an enormous throat followed by a guttural hiss at the end of each word.

"*Gulnosss valss siiintass.*"

At first, the words were a garble of unintelligible sounds, but as she listened, they morphed both in sound and dialect until they entered her ears; a twisted, monstrous English. "Liiittle onnee, where aree you hidingss? I can tasste yoou. Your feaar iss in the aiiir. I can smell the magic in your blooood."

An enormous glowing green and yellow eye filled the glass doorway. Sarah froze out of reflex. A terrified squeak caught in her throat. She stood there, once again hoping and praying it didn't see her. The eye blinked slowly and pulled away. Desperate, Sarah pushed the bag off the table and spilled its contents everywhere.

"Your kiind has grown weak! Where are your spells? Your swords? Your bows? Do you thiiink you can stop my feaasting with stoness and powdersss?" The last word came out with a hiss of laughter, which made her bones go cold.

"Thessse morselsss you leave bore me. Whherree is your massster castling? I would know how you deffy my sssigght! If you will not brrring me to herr, I sshall bring your bonesss to her. Know that I am the great basilisk, Shadowfang, small oone. Remember it ssso that you might know your place before you leave this world for the neww." A long purple forked tongue crashed through the glass door and added to the shards already scattered about. It's flickering knocked a chair off a table.

Sarah heard herself scream. *Well, he's not weak* to *glass then.* The thought amused her, but it could have just as easily been the fear. Sarah kicked at the pile of powder, spreading more of it into the air as she backed toward the kitchen.

"Go away," she shrieked in a defiant yet trembling voice.

Shadowfang's mouth pushed at the doorway, which creaked under the force of his size. Sarah snatched a lighter from a basket of them just inside the kitchen door.

The doorway cracked as the beast's maw pushed halfway through. Sarah's arm thrust through the double kitchen doors and pulled the lighter's trigger.

Click.

Nothing happened.

Click. Click. Click.

Still nothing.

Switching lighters, she tried again and was met with a click, which seemed to drown out the groaning of the door. The lighter fell from her hand only to be replaced with yet another before the first could clatter against the ground.

Click. Nothing.

Shadowfang's head was through, scraping against the ceiling. His tongue lashed out and tasted the edge of the cornstarch in front of her. His glowing eyes illuminated the powdered air. A lighter in each hand, Sarah tried again as tears tunneled down the layer of powder on her cheeks.

"Please," she whimpered. She heard sirens in the distance now, but they would be too late.

Shadowfang's mocking chuckle shook the whole building. "Do you take me for a worm, little moussse? I am king among serpents!"

Sarah ignored him. There were two lighters left. She grabbed them and thrust them towards her hunter. A single word sprang from her mouth. It filled the room, as much a hope as a desperate prayer of faith for success.

"Light!" Time slowed, as it seems to do in moments of life and death. Sparks leaped from the barrels of the lighters and expanded into flame. The flame tasted the powder and saw that it was good.

The ensuing explosion threw Sarah backward. As she hurtled through the air, she noticed a strange shine around her; something separate from the fire, like light reflecting off the water. But then, Sarah crashed into the door and was swallowed by blackness.

PETER BLAIR

Peter spat out gasoline. Its sour, acrid taste lingered even as he rinsed his mouth out with water. It didn't take long for the tank to finish emptying into the gas can. Even so, Peter rinsed and spat again.

"I told you it was crooked," a warm familiar voice called to him from where its owner was returning from the open-top jeep a few yards away.

"You're crooked," Peter fired back at the enormous blonde man. Steven Thomas wore the same uniform as Peter. The uniform's standouts were; A black military jacket, military boots, and lightweight plate armor given to all members of their elite private military organization. At first glance, it looked like a standard military black uniform, but anyone with a knowing eye could tell it was all top of the line. It was all brought together by the patch. A patch of a black snowflake behind a red rifle sewn to each shoulder.

In his early thirties, he was only a bit older than Peter but looked every bit a soldier until you got to his face. Steven was not a baby-faced man; his soft features bore the telltale signs of a man in peak physical condition, accustomed to all manner of rough circumstances.

Peter removed the hose from the gas can and sealed the can shut. A shadow belonging to his friend fell over him. Steven's six-foot-six frame towered over his superior officer by roughly eight inches, so when Peter tossed his friend's keys to the truck, he tossed them up.

"That's the last one from this batch, right?" he asked as he adjusted the pistol at his side and picked up the gas can. Steven made a checkmark on a clipboard he'd hoisted from the passenger seat.

"Yup, that's the last from this batch," Steven replied as he opened the metal clipboard and placed the key inside.

Peter passed him the gas can and made his way around to the drivers' side of the jeep. As he climbed into the jeep, he scratched at the multicolored stubble on his chin. *Great, now I'm going to smell of gasoline all day. Nice.*

"Good. Now stop stalling. We've got the top down and the doors off, and it's a beautiful day."

Steven scowled, then proceeded to crumple under the metal bar above and into the jeep. In a moment, he was seated comfortably, with his head poking past one of the metal bar frames of the jeep and a leg resting on a useless step bar by the door.

For a moment, Peter was blocked from taking his seat by a black sword in a mismatched frayed leather sheath. The sword was black from tip to handle with a series of strange, swirling silver symbols along the crossguard. The handle was a hand and a half in length, wrapped in black leather. It was a sword meant for single-handed use but easily wielded with two hands. The second hand would simply overlap with the teardrop-shaped pommel, in which rested a dark red jewel.

Peter stared at the blade for just a moment before he grabbed it and stashed it between the driver seat and the center compartment. Then he clambered into the driver's seat of the jeep, where he adjusted the sword to sit comfortably.

Maybe it's not worth carrying. It certainly garners plenty of strange looks. Peter sighed, reminding himself why he'd decided to keep the obsolete weapon on hand. *It's more than a weapon. It's a tool, and we need to conserve ammo. Besides, people can give you all the funny looks they want — you're the one with a sword.*

Peter stared at their work for a moment before he began to back up the jeep. In front of them, a short line of vehicles parked strategically between three-story buildings on either side of the road — a road that led into town from the bypass, which, strangely enough, had been structured more like an enormous roundabout surrounding the city than a standard bypass.

The city planners for this place must have been one heck of a paranoid bunch, Peter thought. *Then again, is it paranoia if you're right? I mean, they can't have been expecting this, but still… How many cities have such an extensive emergency plan? It's almost as if the founder expected an eventual invasion…*

They pulled to a stop a few moments later to let a caravan of old vehicles trundle past them toward the bypass-turned-wall.

"I still can't believe modern vehicles weren't equipped with some kind of failsafe for an EMP, haven't we been worried about a solar flare for decades?" Peter said.

Steven shook his head. "Whatever this was wasn't a solar flare, or any kind of EMP I know of, it fried things with an active current, but I can't tell what the parameters are yet… I think we could fix most vehicles if we had the time and parts."

Peter watched the last of the cars go with a frown. "I thought Jenni was in the gas-siphoning group with Justin," he said as the last of the caravan passed them.

"She is. Why?" Steven said without a glance up from where he was making notes on the clipboard.

"Because she was driving the green BMW," Peter replied as he turned down one of the streets leading towards the center of town where the college campus stood.

"Maybe transport needed extra drivers?" Steven replied with a glance over his shoulder.

"Maybe. She might have put up a fight though unless Justin volunteered. Those two have been inseparable lately."

"Have you made any progress on the all-hands call you picked up from DC?" Peter asked as he drove the jeep through the damaged streets of the small city. From the state of things, it was hard to believe they'd lost over four thousand residents to the initial chaos of the Shattering. *We're lucky we're isolated and were able to get things under control. DC is probably on fire. We'll probably start getting refugees from Atlanta any day if things are as bad everywhere else as they are here.*

The thought made him queasy, or perhaps it was the sight and the slightly sweet smell of smoke rising over the city from the burning pits. There was no way of knowing what was happening to the rest of the world. Not yet. Not without leaving, and given the state of things, leaving didn't seem like a good idea.

"No," Steven replied. "Nothing. I tried Atlanta too, thinking maybe corporate figured something out, but no. I've tried everything, Peter. Nothing. Short wave radios are still the only thing I can get any kind of signal from." He groaned. "Honestly, Cap, I'm fairly sure every cell tower on the planet was fried. Satellites too. Most of them probably crashed. There's no sign of them now at least."

Peter slowed the jeep as he went around the corpse of a burned-out bus, nodding thankfully to a man who'd paused his recovery work on one of the city's many collapsed buildings to wave them safely around the obstacle.

"Still think it was a solar flare?" Peter asked, curious to see if the smarter man's theory still held.

"At the very least. It would explain the energy spike, the fried electronics, the power outages, the communication blockage, and possibly that," he said with a wave at the translucent cracks that extended across the heavens as though the atmosphere was a piece of glass struck by a savage blow.

"It could be that some other country figured out a flare was coming and attacked at the perfect moment. Although, if I'm honest, Peter," Steven went on, shaking his head, "I don't think anything explains the sky, the sound it made, or the whispers of monsters we've been getting from stragglers wandering in."

"Well, for now, we need to focus on preparing ourselves for whatever comes next," Peter said as he flicked on his turn signal.

"Easier said than done when you have no idea what's coming," Steven replied with a far-off look on his face. *He's still trying to work all this out.*

"True, but this place seems to have a handle on things. The town's emergency protocols are surprisingly detailed, and having the police work with us has been a miracle," Peter replied.

"It's a shame about Chief Bohannon, though. Were you aware he had a child?"

"His boy, Asher? Yeah, he'd mentioned him during drills, I think." The thought of the newly fatherless boy brought temporary silence. He was one of thousands, yes, but having known the father and hearing how he'd died pulling people from a collapsing building not three days ago made the pain of it more personal.

Peter found his thoughts drifting to the night before as he drove. He'd gone to bed physically exhausted. There was no other way to go to bed these days. He remembered dreaming — something vivid, real — but whatever he'd seen in his dreams was now forgotten, as dreams are always eventually.

Peter concentrated the best he could, trying, as the jeep neared their destination, to recall at least some minute details from the dream. An image came to him, slowly, out of focus but recognizable — a scarred gray hand reaching out to him through the fog. Peter concentrated, trying to look past the gray hand to see its owner. But the harder he thought, the thicker the mist grew, until it swallowed the hand entirely, leaving no other memories of the dream behind.

Peter snapped back into the present, alerted by a voice from the radio in the center console. His eyes darted towards the sound, then back to the road.

"Steven," Peter said with an air of command.

Steven also emerged from his distracted state of mind and snagged the handheld radio from where it was shoved in the opening below the car stereo.

"I repeat, I've got incoming! Send help!" came a terrified voice over the airwaves.

"This is SNW Three," Steven said into the radio, anticipating Peter's instructions. "What's your station number."

"Station Seven! Westside!" the voice radioed back urgently, between intermittent swearing. Then the radio stopped but not before Peter thought he heard the sound of gunfire.

Peter yanked on the steering wheel and sent them hurtling around a corner. "That's five minutes out if we press it," Peter called out between warning honks as the jeep sped up along the empty road.

"Station Seven, two SNW inbound. ETA five minutes," Steven spoke into the radio. "Please confirm."

Peter gritted his teeth as he took a sharp turn. *Westside shouldn't be densely populated, but it's a clear shot to campus if the barricade is breached.*

"Station Seven, what's your status?" Steven asked, but no reply came. Even more disturbing was that the gunfire had ceased after a few shots had been fired. "All stations to red alert."

A few moments later, a cop car with flashing blue lights pulled up behind them, and Peter flinched. He fought the urge to pull over or get out of the way, and a new voice came over the radio.

"This is Officer Akena. Is that you in the jeep, Captain Blair?" a woman's firm voice asked.

"Captain Blair and Sergeant Thomas," Steven replied quickly into his radio, holding the metal bar by his head as they rounded another turn.

"Y'all need backup? My partner and I are ready to go," the woman on the radio replied. Steven glanced at Peter, who nodded and took the radio from Steven in his right hand, keeping his left on the wheel.

"Sounds good, officer. Keep the sirens off, though, and don't call any more backup until we know what's going on. I don't want to start a panic or split forces. This could be a decoy, or nothing," he instructed before he passed the radio back to Thomas.

They arrived on the scene too late. Peter stared at where the two men comprising Station Seven should have been. Ordinarily, there would have been a large truck used as a lookout platform parked along the inside of the vehicular wall still under construction. But the truck was instead embedded upside down in the roof of a nearby building.

The wall of cars had a hole in it where something bigger than a school bus had broken through. The ground leading from the hole bore a wide indent that led left into the city and out all the way into the forest. But it was the blood that commanded Peter's attention. It was everywhere on the ground as if someone had been shaking an enormous paintbrush of the stuff violently from side to side.

Steven hopped out of the vehicle and picked something up off the ground: an enormous dark green scale. Peter heard a car door open, followed by cursing from Akena and the sound of a man retching behind him.

"Everyone, back in your vehicles," he ordered, but Steven was already clambering in and held the gargantuan teardrop-shaped dark green scale in his hand. Whatever the scale belonged to was heading towards the university.

Peter grabbed the radio by the antenna, almost dropping it before he brought it to his mouth. *I'm shaking. Need to get that under control*, he realized as he spoke into the device. "All available units, converge on the southern side of campus. Be advised, we have a hostile of unknown size and origin. Execute on sight. O'Cleary, bring the fifty cal."

Then came a sound the likes of which Peter had prayed never to have to hear in this small city: the sound of a building exploding.

RUBBLE

All that filled Sarah's mind was the pain. Pain everywhere. That was a good sign, in a way; if everything hurt, then everything was still more or less intact. Her eyes peeled open only to be greeted by dirt and concrete. Not eyes. Eye. Only one obeyed her order to open.

The right side of her face was pressed against rough concrete, and the disobedient eye was swollen shut. Her left eye wasn't much better. It blinked uncontrollably as it filled with blood, dust, and tears to wash the other two out. It was in this state of pained, blurry vision that she rose from the rubble to her hands and knees. Bits and pieces of the restaurant fell away from her.

She heard voices. Screaming, yelling, calling things she couldn't make out over the ringing. Ringing mixed with blaring sirens. There was so much noise — almost as much noise as pain.

Purple. Why is everything purple? There was a strange pressure in her head where her ears were ringing. Sarah tried to look around but there was too much light. *So many flashing lights. What… What's going on? Where am I?* She looked down. *My clothes are ruined…* A splash of disappointment hit her as she noticed the black watch on her right wrist was cracked. *Oh, no. Dad gave that to me. It was my favorite watch.*

The ringing in her ears wouldn't go away. *I… I have to move. Have to get away. Get away from what? Where am I? I'm bleeding. No. no. no. I have to get help!* She realized she'd collapsed to her knees. Despite her protesting head, she pushed herself up until she was standing. The blurry scene around her slowly came into focus.

There were cop cars all around; three or four, maybe more. Sarah couldn't tell; their flashing lights hurt to look at. She raised her hand to block the pulsing colors and spied a spot where there weren't any.

A black jeep, not far away. She took a step towards it — closer to the four silhouettes moving her direction. They were strange figures: a familiar, scary man in black with an equally dark sword on his back. *Why does he have a sword? Where am I?*

There was an Indian-looking man with incredibly white shoes. *So white. How are his shoes so clean?* she thought as she glanced down at her dirty hands then back up.

Sarah tried to focus on the third figure, an African American policewoman with a stern face. *She's tall.* The ringing continued. *I like her short hair.* The thought puzzled her. It was too normal. Too casual. It felt extremely out of place. Something else was going on; something more important should have been in her thoughts.

Her head was heavy. So heavy. She let it hang and watched her feet shuffle forward. She battled the fog in her mind, tried to figure out why. Why did she need to escape?

A large shadow fell over her, and her entire body tensed. It all came back to her in one terrifying moment, heralded by the dreadful anticipation of her impending digestion. *The snake.*

A deep voice brushed against the ringing in her ears. It was muffled as though speaking through water. This voice was soft, though. Strong, deep, and speaking incomprehensible words like before, but it lacked the bone-crunching power of the basilisk.

Have to warn them… Sarah tried to speak, but only gibberish came out.

Something grabbed her shoulder, and she felt her strength leaving her. She leaned into the grip on her shoulder and began to fall over. A kind face came into view marred with lines of concern; the face of a giant who towered over her. He wore the same clothes as the swordsman, but there was a softness to his face that did not extend to his enormous, muscled figure.

The ringing in her ears continued and drowned out the voice. She felt herself lifting gently into the air, closer to his kind green eyes. *Green eyes… The snake! You have to warn them… before it's too late… before the other eyes come back…* Only gibberish came from her mouth, as she slipped out of consciousness, carried away from the scene by strong arms.

SHADOWFANG

The basilisk woke suddenly but did not move or open its eyes. *Twice now I have woken in a strange place. First, in these small woods full of weak little trees. Now here in this hidden city full of odd humans and their ridiculous buildings. And the caster. She was more than she appeared. Be careful.*

Pain lanced the ancient creature's left eye.

I am injured. How dare she touch me with her filthy magic. Rage boiled in his blood. *There shouldn't be casters for a league. I killed them all.* He waited under the unfamiliar building's rubble and listened for the weaving of spells or the marching of an army. He heard the calls of frightened humans and a new sound, a strange shrieking coming from all sides.

Some kind of new elvish casting? I did not taste elves in the air, though. Perhaps they hid themselves from me… It matters not. They will die. Slower than the humans, but they will still all die.

He heard more unfamiliar sounds above the rubble all over him. Then a familiar smell came through the dust and dirt. *Fear.* It was a smell he knew dearly; it made his mouth water. He smelled strange magic too. Weak, untapped potential. An unfamiliar strand of arcane power in the blood of one of the gathering men. *So many new smells since I came here.*

He took his time, searched for a hint of a curse or spell that might hinder his movement but felt none. His hunger was growing. The few weak humans he'd devoured were insufficient to satiate him. *There must be more, thousands more. Some twisted magic is at work to bring this city to my forest without my knowing.*

All might and fury, he rose from the rubble, ready to feast and seek revenge. The basilisk's anger grew hotter as he realized the pain in his eye was not a minor injury but that he could no longer use his right eye. As the rubble fell away, he heard loud banging and felt the runes in his bones draw on his magic as they protected him from the human's fire and metal. *Fools. Do they not recognize me for what I am? They should grovel before me.*

With his one good eye, he cast his gaze about at his surroundings. Strange buildings, machines, and people were everywhere. All around him were fool-ish-looking humans dressed in blue, standing by strange flashing metal machines like the ones that failed to keep him from entering the city. *There is an unusual variety of colors among these humans. Gooood, more flavors.*

Loud explosions echoed from the hands of the men and women around him. His anger was further kindled as he saw roughly half these human attackers' eyes were guarded by strange dark coverings. *They attack me with useless weapons but guard their eyes against my stare? What wizardry is this?* His enormous, forked tongue lashed out and tasted the air, tasted their fear. *Good.*

There was fear closer than the flashing metal boxes. Shadowfang tilted his head and saw the two of them at the edge of the rubble. *So much variety.* The basilisk stared down at them. Shawdowfang's gaze trapped the one with bright white feet as he looked foolishly back into his eye. *Yes. Know fear. Let it course through your veins. You will all know fear!*

Beneath him, a dark woman raised her strange weapon, training it on Shadowfang's glowing eye. He chuckled. Three shots tore through the air towards him. Then, three inches before striking home in his reptilian eye, they turned.

The bullets curved as if repelled by some invisible force. As his wards protected him, he saw the panic settle into her. *Goood. Fear me.*

Shadowfang struck with the force and speed of a bolt of lightning. His mouth enveloped her companion, cut him off at the ankles with a loud *snap*, and trapped a silent cry of fear caught in the man's throat forever between his fangs. He did not play with this one. There would be time for that in a moment. He swallowed, feeling the man's bones snap in his constricting throat.

The might of the strike knocked her on her backside only a few feet away from the monster's bleeding eye. He was not worried, though. She was no threat to him, and nothing was left of her companion but his shoes. Blood struck the ground around the shoes. Purplish-red blood from Shadowfang's injured eye pooled with the deep red blood that dripped from the fangs, staining the once well-cleaned shoes red.

Shadowfang swallowed loudly, let the sound of crunching bones stir up more terror in his prey. The macabre cracking was delicious to him but revolting to his prey. He watched as the woman scrambled backward before turning over to push herself to her feet to run.

She was moving toward one of the flashing, wailing black machines with a similarly dressed man only a few dozen yards away. Shadowfang locked him in place with the gaze of his eye, so he could offer her no help. "What are you doing? Start the car," she screamed in a strange tongue at the top of her lungs.

Shadowfang understood the words, though. Whatever magic altered them was trivial to him. Delight mixed with anger made the lingering taste of man in his mouth sweeter. *Struggle all you want. There is no escape.*

Clearing the scraps left in his mouth, he swallowed again — loudly, reveling in what he knew would be an overwhelmingly unsettling sound coming from a creature of his magnitude. Then he lowered himself closer to the ground, let his forked purple tongue lash out to stroke the back of the woman's leg, making her stumble. He tasted her hope of escape leaving her as his barbed tongue tore at the flesh of her calf.

Scales ranging in size from a grown man's open hand to that of an arrowhead scraped the concrete and drowned out the screams, sirens, and gunfire all around them. He struck, but the woman threw herself forward in a burst of desperation, barely saving herself from being swallowed whole like her companion. Still, his fangs plunged into flesh with a satisfying squelch.

Shadowfang's rage exploded into pleasure as he realized his newest victim was lodged between his fangs by her attempt to dodge his attack. *Now for some fun*, he thought. He decided to let her die in absolute terror for thinking she could escape him.

He let the blood from her leg run over his tongue. This one tasted different from the one he'd swallowed whole. *Wonderful how the slightest variations can change the flavor.* Blood filled the basilisk's mouth as arm-sized fangs squeezed. By some freak accident, her leg was unbroken. He could tell; he'd broken enough of them before.

The monster was extraordinarily aware of the warm liquid leaking from her leg; he could taste pain in that delicious blood. Shadowfang absorbed her screams of pain greedily, reveling in the terror he struck in those around her.

He made her world spin as he pulled back, making her fall forward with a thud. The snake grinned as she hit the ground, then he slowly lifted her into the air. He was in no hurry; there were no threats to him here. He licked the leg in his jaws. His tongue peeling away skin and coaxing more screams from his prey.

Bang! Bang! Bang!

Shadowfang heard her weapon make a series of loud noises. He chuckled from deep in his throat. *What was she thinking? Did she not know it was too late for her?* He could feel her struggle, twist, and flail, trying to disconnect from her leg. *She attacked her own leg! The fool! She must know how hopeless she is. These fools wear no armor and use weapons made for birds or rodents, not the likes of me. They will learn to fear me. I will show her.*

Shadowfang's tongue twitched at the thought of snapping his head back, flinging his helpless prey into the air, the air filling with delicious screams, before he swallowed her whole and crushed her bones in his throat. It was his favorite way to eat humans. The pathetic thing let out a measly squeak as the ground rose to meet her.

From her place near the ground, Officer Akena's vision was growing dark. Wet, sticky concrete scraped against her head as Shadowfang lowered her, preparing to flick his head back and toss her into the air. He'd give her one last fleeting moment of hope before sending the rest of them a message.

Then, a black boot stepped into Akena's failing line of sight. The officer struggled to look up. A black sword arced through the air above her and then out of sight. Shadowfang did not see the weapon strike, but a split second later, he felt the loss of his prey's weight as the leg came loose in his mouth.

The ruined leg tumbled across his tongue, no longer holding his prize captive. Puzzled, Shadowfang swallowed reflexively. Years of instinct told the basilisk something was wrong, so having already been injured once, the mighty creature yanked his head back and turned to see what happened to his snack.

Beneath him, a huge man dressed all in black had grabbed his prey and hoisted her off the ground. But he was not alone, standing between him and Shadowfang was another man wearing the same blacks, and he had a blade in his hand.

The basilisk was irate. This infestation of humans had to be responsible for his being in this unfamiliar, strange land. Humans had always meddled in things beyond their understanding, ignoring the consequences their actions had on their surroundings.

Shawdowfang had felt strong magic within the city, enough to satiate his hunger for months. It had made him cautious at first, but after three days of seeing no application of arcane skills from the woods, the caution died. The thought of terrorizing and conquering such helpless creatures had enthralled him, and he'd been unable to wait any longer. He had attacked the city after three days of watching it, and, oh, his luck!

A weak young caster waited for him at the edge of the city. He'd toyed with her, and to his surprise, she'd outmaneuvered him. Not outsmarted him. She'd been small and had managed to hide the scope of her powers from him, but she'd killed herself to slow him down. Yes, she'd destroyed one of his eyes, but in time, it would heal. Now, her master would come, and he would kill it as well.

But it was still infuriating. Had she not killed herself, he'd have enjoyed eating her. But now she was gone, and with half his vision. To his shock, she'd been replaced by more helpless fools who saw fit to fling small metal rocks at him.

Now, there was a new surprise. This city was full of them — one after another, each more mouthwatering than the last. *How dare they*, he thought again.

Shadowfang watched as the big man retreated with his prey, raising one of their strange weapons as he fled. The four thunderous cracks that came from it matched its size. *Ting. Ting. Ting. Ting.* Shadowfang blinked his enormous eye. *I felt that! It broke through my wards! Of course, it was too weak to pierce my magnificent scales, though... These two are different from their panicked, flailing kin. These are warriors.*

He turned his attention to the man in front of him, curiosity piqued. *Perhaps a challenge then? He does not meet my eye but watches me, nonetheless. He is strange, but clearly not who I am hunting.*

The man took a hesitant step back, and the sword shifted, allowing Shadowfang to get a good look at it. *A Thalmien blade?* He hissed; the taste of fresh blood still lingered.

Wizard or not, he wields a black Thalmien? It is not the one made for Awan... Did she have the blacksmith toil in secret to make another? Or does this small warrior possess similar hidden knowledge? It matters not. I will know his name so I might list him among my victories.

Keeping his gaze on the sword-bearing man, he let the blonde man carry the wounded human away. *I'll finish them later. They'll be all the tastier, brimming with despair over me killing their champion.* His tongue lashed out, tasted the air, his nostrils taking in the smell of the man. There was magic about him — strange and unfamiliar magic. The sun beat down on Shadowfang and filled him with energy as he addressed the strange city's new defender.

"Whaat havee we heere?"

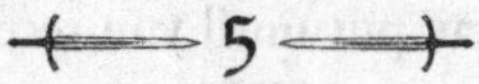

GALVORD

"A re you seeing this?" Peter said to Steven with no effort to hide the contempt in his voice. "It's amateur hour out here. I mean, what are they doing just standing around it?" He gestured to the smoking ruins.

Steven shook his head but gave no reply.

"You're wearing your vest, right?" Peter asked as he took a hesitant step forward.

"Indeed. Why?" Steven replied.

"Because we may need it if half these guys open fire while we're checking that rubble." Peter glanced knowingly at the officers braced against their police cars around the ruined restaurant. The same policewoman who'd followed them there approached from her vehicle, another officer behind her.

"Officer Akena, right?" Peter said, still focused on the smoking rubble.

"Okay. Wow. First of all, rude. We've met several times, Captain Blair. You know my name. You've even approached me about working for your militia boy band."

Peter glanced at her. "Sorry. A bit distracted," he admitted.

"Secondly," Akena replied, almost cutting him off, "none of my fellow officers are going to shoot you. They're following standard protocol — surround the site and wait for instructions. Instructions which, according to the agreement you made with our police force, come from you, *captain*."

Peter grinned. He did remember her. "Glad to see you're alive and well, Officer Akena." He turned to Steven. "Let them know not to shoot us while we clear the rubble, would you?"

Akena shook her head at him in disbelief. "I just told you—" she began.

"I know. And while I may trust that you won't and that you have faith in *your* officers, some of those folks were just deputized the other day. Another reminder doesn't hurt. Besides, Steven's voice provides a bit extra that yours or mine might not." He looked at Steven, who nodded.

Steven took a step closer to the aftermath and looked around at the officers and their deputies before speaking in a loud booming voice. "All right, everyone. Weapons down. Stay put until you receive further instructions." He gestured at Peter and the other two. "We're going to check the rubble. I repeat, weapons down. Deep breaths, everyone."

It took them a moment, but one by one, the weapons trained on the ruins were lowered. Peter didn't relax. He saw something moving in the rubble, a small dusty shape rising from the ruins. *A girl*, he realized as she rose to her knees.

He moved forward, Steven at his side and Akena close behind. Out of the corner of his eye, a shotgun was rising to point at the young woman struggling to get her feet under her.

Peter's head whipped around, and his words lashed out. "Weapons down! Use your eyes! Does she look like a threat?" he demanded. The officer lowered the gun slowly and shakily. Peter fought the urge to stomp over and yank it from its owner's hands.

The girl mumbled incoherently as she got closer, blocking the light of the police cars with her sooty hands. *She's concussed,* Peter realized as she collapsed into Steven's arms, muttering, bleeding, and talking about snakes.

"Steven, get her back to the jeep and see if you can help with the concussion." The big man was on his way before Peter could finish the order, leaving him with Officer Akena and her partner.

"Officer Akena… I'm sorry. I know we haven't met," he said to the man of Indian heritage.

"Harold," the man replied. "Volunteer Deputy Harold Khatri, sir," he said, nervously doing his best to salute.

How are your shoes so white, Harold? Peter kept the thought to himself as he dismissed the salute with a wave. "I want you and Akena to clear the left side while I clear the right. Stay out of the rubble. For now, just look for any other survivors. We'll meet on the other side and create a more detailed search plan from there. Got it?"

"Yes, sir," they replied in poor unison. Peter turned to the rubble. A strange sense of apprehension clouded him. *Something's wrong. What about that scale and the weird tracks?* he thought as he creeped around the rubble. He saw something move out of the corner of his eye.

Peter took another step. Rubble crunched beneath his feet. He paused to get a better look at the rubble. A large, long mound of it shifted. Peter stepped back as a shape more massive than a bus began to rise out of the debris in front of him. He watched in horror as dust and destruction fell away to reveal the head of a serpent large enough to constrict and demolish a semi-truck, lifting into the air. The next few seconds stretched for an eternity.

As it rose through the air, Peter saw that the side of its head closest to him was scorched and covered in ash. Among the burn marks, he spied an enormous, shattered eye dripping purplish-red blood from the various cracks in its brille. He cursed to himself, the words lost to the sound of panicked officers and civilians all around.

It can't see me, Peter realized as he stared at the eye. Then another realization struck him: *I'm going to get shot.* He dove forward into the rubble as gunfire erupted around him. Scrambling forward, he took cover between the remnants of a freezer and some unrecognizable chunk of metal.

For some reason, Peter thought of his sister, Hannah, for the briefest moment. *What would she have done here? Probably try to get its attention, but then what? Now isn't the time to be thinking about your sister, you idiot. Focus.*

He inched slowly through the rubble. Terrified yelling and gunfire drowned out the thumping of his own heart. He rolled behind a charred table and realized his sword was in his hand.

When did that happen? He found himself trying to talk himself into using the weapon. *If I can get close enough, I can stab it. Guns aren't even phasing that thing from the looks of it. Maybe stabbing it will do something. It'll get its attention at least.*

Peter crept towards the monster, bits and pieces of charred destruction crunching under his feet. He caught sight of Harold and Akena, frozen in shock, staring up at the beast. Peter wanted to call out for them not to run, to fire, to do anything but knew if he did, he'd be exposed.

Before he could give the decision further thought, the monster attacked. Its enormous mouth struck towards the ground. In an instant, Harold was gone.

The force of the blow knocked Akena off her feet. *How is it so fast?* Peter thought as he twisted behind a battered fridge. *How am I supposed to fight this thing?*

As he ducked behind more cover, another motion caught his eye. Steven was back at the jeep, yelling into a radio. *Good. He's warning the others… I'm dead. No way around it. I have to stall that thing until backup arrives. If we use enough big bullets, it'll have to go down.*

Bang! Bang! Bang!

The sound of gunfire returned his gaze to Akena. She lay on her back on the other side of the monster, firing her pistol up at it wildly to no avail. *She's not even scratching it*, he realized with a pang of fear in his stomach.

What do I do? He scrambled for an idea, pushed his fear aside as he stalked closer. He saw Akena's resolve break as she scrambled backward as the monster slowly lowered its head to her. Akena managed to get her feet under her, but as she turned, the monster's large purple tongue flicked out and slapped Akena's legs and threw her off balance.

The beast's movements were different from its first strike. It pulled back slowly, rising higher, away from Akena. *It's toying with her*, Peter realized as he came within striking range. He was close enough to count the mottled scales on the giant snake as they shone in the afternoon sun.

The beast finally lashed out. Vicious fangs latched onto Akena's leg with a nauseating *crunch* before it began to drag her into the air. As she was pulled from the ground, she tried shooting again. It had no effect. Peter watched as, in a moment of clarity, she tried to shoot her left leg off below the knee.

Peter winced. He wished he could have told her that wouldn't work, not with her standard-issue bullets and pistol. A strange sound, almost like laughter, rumbled inside the beast, and it began to lower her back down.

What's it doing? Peter wondered as he saw the creature's body adjusting for balance.

Oh… He heard Akena cry out in pain. Something in the depths of his mind called Peter into action. *Last chance to save her. It's now or never.*

Peter dashed forward, under the beast's raised body. As Akena's head reached the ground, Peter swung his sword. The blade passed through her leg with surprising ease.

The strike almost threw him off balance. He had expected resistance when making the cut. As he brought the sword back around, Akena hit the ground with a thud. To his dismay, the monster jerked back out of range of his sword before Peter could bring the blade back around and bury it in flesh.

Peter now stood between the monster and Akena, her blood running down the length of his blade as he held it defensively in front of him. Something told him not to look up at the monster, not to meet its eye.

A realization came to him: he was enjoying this. He knew the thrill of combat, but this was different. This encounter pulled at him, awakened something deep within him that had been locked away out of sight.

He should have been scared. He knew that. He had been scared. But for some reason, now that he stood facing down the monster, he wasn't.

The gut feeling he'd been following boiled over, and a strange energy coursed through him. Every sense was heightened. Colors seemed brighter. The air seemed richer. He even felt lighter. Peter itched to swing at the monster, but something in the back of his mind restrained him — the same odd feeling that had drawn his sword and kept his eyes from meeting the gaze of the monster.

Sure, a giant bulletproof snake just rose out of a ruined restaurant, but a month ago, the sky literally shattered. How is this any more unbelievable than what you've already experienced? Unless this is all a dream… He swept the thought aside. *Dream or not, I'm not getting eaten.*

"Whaat havee we heere?" Words hissed out of the bloodstained maw of the basilisk.

A giant talking *bulletproof snake… Maybe I am dreaming. Might as well talk back.*

"My name is Captain Peter Blair. We have you outnumbered and out-gunned with reinforcements on the way. I don't know who or what you are, but I suggest you surrender."

"Soo, this pathetic city has a defender after alllll. I'd begun to wonder," the gargantuan snake said as its body coiled behind it, moving its exposed under-belly farther out of range of the sword.

He's wary of the sword. Good. With newfound confidence, Peter took a menacing step forward and watched as the snake's head turned at an angle so the functioning eye could stare down at him.

Peter raised the sword and took a familiar defensive stance, the kind he'd use when he sparred with an opponent with a longer reach, something he'd done on many occasions. Sword fighting was excellent exercise, after all. At least that's how he'd been convinced to take it up as a hobby.

Peter made a note of the monster's movement but did not look into his eye. He wanted to — so badly he wanted to — but he couldn't. The strange energy coursing through him demanded he keep his gaze away from the monster's eye.

"I am the basilisk, Shadowfang, of the brood of Aapiepp, devourer of man, elfsbane, king of the forest. Tell me, Peter of Snow, how did one of so few titles come to possess a blooded Thalmein blade? Anssswer quickly, and your death shall not sssshame your warrior'ss honor."

Peter flicked his wrist and sent a spray of bright blood from the blade onto the ground. Behind him, he heard Steven's familiar heavy footfalls approach. The sound overlapped with the noise of Akena struggling to move with one leg. The heavy footsteps paused, and the sound of Akena struggling came to an end.

"Got her," Steven's familiar voice called out from behind Peter. His call was followed by the deafening sound of his Desert Eagle firing off three shots. These shots were different. Peter heard the distinct sound of them bouncing off the basilisk's scales and saw a shimmer in the air before sparks denoted where the bullets struck.

Guns do work. We just need bigger guns. Maybe we can kill this thing.

"Do not ignore me," roared Shadowfang. "Sssspeak! Then meet my eye, and your doom."

In Peter's hand, the black sword seemed to thrum, it was so light — lighter than a sword had the right to be. He redirected his voice to Shadowfang. "Thalmein blade?" he asked, as he raised the sword to eye level, and noted the glow of the basilisk's eye reflecting on the blade.

The eye pulled at him with a magnetic urge. He could feel himself being drawn to stare straight into that enormous, beautiful, colorful eye. The moment passed as quickly as it came, chased away by an overwhelming impulsion to look elsewhere.

"Theyyy will not get faaaar," Shadowfang taunted but made no move to pursue Steven as he retreated with Akena.

Keep his attention.

"I don't know what Thalmein means, but this sword was a gift from a friend. Thalmien isn't much of a name, is it? I should probably rename it now that I'm using it, shouldn't I?" Peter said, eager to keep the creature's attention on him.

Shadowfang hissed a vile wet sound that made blood sprinkle like rain. "That blade has a name that is butchered by your strange speech. It is Galvorn, the forgotten, the all-blooded." The basilisk's muscles tensed. "Others may have forgotten it, but I have not, and it shall be mine." Then Shadowfang struck.

Peter moved faster than he'd ever moved. He threw himself to the side, away from the rubble still on the monster's uninjured half. Behind him, concrete broke with a loud crack as Shadowfang smashed into it. Shadowfang's grisly maw turned toward him, and a giant purple forked tongue flicked out to taste the air.

Blood and other bodily fluids sprayed and would have blinded Peter if he hadn't held his blade in front of his face. The smell of death was palpable, but there was something else in the scent: a strange, sweet, unfamiliar odor nearly concealed by the stench of gore.

"Where did you come from, Shadowfang? What do you want with us?" Peter called out as the beast's muzzle swayed side to side in front of him. As he spoke, he began to distance himself from the jaws. He retreated toward one of the cop cars behind him, abandoned by its owner.

Shadowfang kept coming and closed the distance between them, refusing to let him get far from his reach.

"I do not anssswer to you," Shadowfang responded as he surged forward.

Peter cursed as he again flung himself out of the way. Shadowfang crashed into the police car, and Peter swore. The vehicle looked like it'd been hit with a semi-truck.

He's too fast to strike before he withdraws. I need to limit his movement. Peter gave ground as Shadowfang searched for a chance to kill. The serpent's head shifted side to side. Peter continued his retreat, away from the rest of the snake. Whenever the snake struck, he tried to counter, but he was always a hairs-breadth too slow.

Out of the corner of his eye, he spied an option: two strong brick buildings with an alleyway between. *If I can draw him in, maybe I can limit his movement, or at least slow him down until the real firepower arrives.* He angled his retreat in that direction and led the monster away from the line of police and civilians.

As he moved, he narrowly avoided three cautious strikes from the monster, and even managed to nick Shadowfang with the tip of his sword. As he fled, Peter kept his head on a swivel so that the snake could not use its long body to flank him.

The two danced their dance of death, and Peter found his reflexes amplified. He was able to stay just out of range of Shadowfang's movements on instinct, as if he knew exactly where each blow was going to end before it began.

Despite this newfound advantage, Shadowfang's gargantuan size and speed left little room for a counterattack. After each strike, the basilisk would jerk its head out of range of his sword, but with each exchange, Peter's counters came closer to drawing blood.

It's not leaving any opening. Peter knew even with the adrenaline and strange energy that filled his veins, he didn't have long. Strike. Backstep. Sword block. Jab. Backstep. Backstep. Backstep. Strike. Roll away. Spring up, sword outward.

If I can stay on his blind side, he might use that tongue of his to — Woah. A double-strike rather than a retreat would have been the end if not for strange energy — *see out of reflex. He's trying to keep me on his good side.*

He only uses the tongue when he's out of striking range. Peter grinned as Shadowfang rose high for a downward strike. It was a terrifying image, with the basilisk casting a massive shadow over him. Every muscle in Peter's body told him to run, but his mind held him fast. *Wait for it. He'll strike right after the twitch of the tongue.* As Shadowfang's tongue flicked out, Peter made his move.

Shadowfang tasted the movement in the air and felt the wind from the man's body moving below him. *I know where you are.* Confidence swelled in the basilisk. His tongue retracted, and he struck toward where Peter's body was dodging, tongue safely behind his fangs.

The ground closed in as his muzzle crashed downward as he tried to simply crush Peter with the weight of his head rather than risk swallowing the sword blade first. *If it pierces my hide, it will make a terrifying piece of jewelry for all future kills.*

Then he saw him: Peter Blair, the wielder of Galvorn, the black blade. *What?* Shadowfang realized too late that the man had feinted, moving faster than any man should. He'd baited the great serpent.

Their eyes met. Peter saw the reflection of his gray-blue eyes in Shadowfang's good eye as he painted his sword red. "Noo!" Shadowfang's cry came out as hissing roar. Too late.

No human that the basilisk had ever seen had moved so fast. He was forced to watch the black blade he lusted for tear up through his eye. The pain burned through Shadowfang's mind. Desperate to escape with some remnant of vision, he lurched back, mindless of his surroundings.

The last thing the great serpent saw as everything went red and he tore himself away from the blade were those cold blue eyes. Never again would he use his eyes' ancient power.

Never again would Shadowfang hold a helpless victim in his gaze as it suffocated, unable to move even to breathe when met by the gaze of his eyes. Never again would he revel in watching them as he embraced their motionless bodies and drove his spines deep into their flesh.

For a moment, Shadowfang felt something he had not felt in years: fear. A sensation that had welcomed him into this world at birth. One that he abandoned centuries ago.

What did a basilisk have to fear? They were creatures bred for killing by Awan herself. If they died, it was only after killing hundreds in battle — not slain by one insignificant human. He found the fear in his mind and coiled around it, constricting, crushing it with anger, with rage and utter fury. Shadowfang was wounded, but he was far from dead.

Peter cursed under his breath. Shadowfang was too quick. Peter felt like he was underwater when he met the beast's eye. But the sensation shattered the instant his blade cut up through his opponent's iris. He'd wanted to drive it in, deep, to the brain if possible, but before he could, the monster jerked away, almost taking the sword with him.

Shadowfang convulsed and thrashed. Over twenty-five tons of armored, spiked, serpent spasmed violently. The ground shook under the car-crushing throws of the beast. His monstrous tail connected with a police car as the driver fled and sent the vehicle tumbling, crashing into a nearby building.

Peter ran.

As fast as he could, Peter tore away from Shadowfang's destructive convulsions. The ground trembled, threatening to make Peter fall as he ran, but he was familiar with running on wobbly legs.

Memories of running on wobbly legs flooded his mind, unwelcomed, of how he had learned his legs were weak in the pool, and of how his sister had always pushed him to keep running, to strengthen them; how he had run when she was around, and then stopped when she wasn't; how he had finally taken her advice to heart too late for her to see it; how his legs were steady now. They'd been stable for years. The muscles in his calves no longer threatened to twist around his leg the way they used to. *Focus*, he told himself, trying to push his sister from his mind.

Then the convulsing behind him came to an abrupt, bone-chilling stop. Peter glanced back and saw Shadowfang belly up, unmoving. *He's not dead. I can see him still breathing.*

This observation kept Peter from reversing course. It was too late to backtrack for a killing blow. He was only a few feet away from the sheltered opening between the brick buildings.

If he's unconscious, I should finish him off, he thought as he weighed his options. *Something isn't right. What's he up to? Awfully quiet for such a talkative opponent.* Now that he was no longer within striking range, Peter took a moment to take in the actual size of Shadowfang. The creature was gargantuan.

Peter thought he'd made an excellent retreat until he realized that the end of Shadowfang's tail still lay among the rubble of the ruined restaurant. There was nothing left of the building now. What little survived the explosion was now pulverized to dust by the spasming. Peter even thought he saw the remains of a person impaled on one of the creature's spines near the back of its tail, but if it had been a human, nothing remained but a pulverized hunk.

Then the beast's head turned and righted itself, its body following suit. The whole thing rolled over in a hauntingly reptilian way. Slowly, agonizingly, it turned toward Peter. Shadowfang lay low, belly to the ground. The monster's purple tongue flicked out and tasted the air, finding him.

Peter swore and took an involuntary step back. *Run!* The word filled every inch of his mind and body. It was more than a word; it was a sensation, a command he had no choice but to obey. Before the tongue could pull back behind those killer teeth, Peter had turned on his heel and was in a dead sprint, faster than he had ever run in his life.

The serpent would be on him in seconds. There was no way for him to outrun it. *Get in the alley. Make a kill box. Please, God, let this work,* he prayed in desperation.

"You caan't esscape mee, worm," screeched the enraged apex predator from behind him.

Peter threw himself into the alleyway between the two brick buildings, unsure how far behind him Shadowfang was in pursuit. As he rolled up to keep running, he found himself facing a tall brick wall at the end of the alley. *There's no way out.*

Aw, hell. Maybe I can… Peter thought as he turned back towards the entrance. But there was no time to back out now. Shadowfang approached with reckless abandon, head splattered with gore.

Peter faced the entrance and clutched his black-bladed sword in both hands as he backed farther into the alley. A distantly familiar sensation dawned on him as the serpent slithered forward, scales scraping loudly against the concrete.

This is it. Not dead yet, though. Maybe it'll swallow me whole, and I can cut my way out. Heh, it would probably crush me in its throat. He looked over the sword in his hand. *Always thought I'd die with a gun in my hand, not a sword. Strange.*

The blade still bore droplets of Akena's and Shadowfang's blood sliding along the length. *Death by swallowing it is then. I wonder what Dad would say if he could see me. Probably, 'Just keep the point between him and you, son, and hope for the best.' He'd be right. Even if I miss, it's gonna swallow me and take the sword with me, and that has to do some damage. Just gotta make sure I get past his teeth.*

Then a shadow engulfed him. Shadowfang had reached the alley, and his maw pushed forcefully at the opening between the brick buildings. There wasn't room for his enormous head, so the basilisk pulled back and raised himself up at the entrance. His red-stained head blocked out the low yellow sun. As the sky darkened, replaced by the serpent, Peter's mind flashed back.

He thought about the sky, how it had been bluer ever since that day. How it had cracked like a broken window, jagged white lines scattering across the atmosphere and remaining there. Now, even when the smooth moon rose, its craters no longer visible, those cracks remained, reminding all of what had happened that day.

Shadowfang struck. He forced his way between the buildings in one blow. Bones scraped and crunched against the bricks, but the structures halted his progress. The horrible sound deepened Peter's reflections on the events of the last month that had brought him here. His mind swirled with images of how the world had been so drastically changed in seconds.

Peter remembered the sound had woken him more than the shaking. He was used to loud noises. He had been in firefights and knew what explosions sounded like, but this was more than an explosion. It was like hearing every gunshot and siren he had ever heard go off instantaneously. Peter had felt the sound in his bones; how he hadn't gone deaf was a mystery to him. That sound, that colossal roar, had torn him from his bed with his pistol in his hands where it belonged.

The whole world had shaken as that noise was heard in every corner of the globe. Then it was over as suddenly as it began. Peter's room was left in disaster. His things were everywhere. Even the sword he kept hanging on the wall had been detached and stood embedded in the floor. He had taken it with him as he ran outside to see what was going on.

What he found looked like the end of his world. The sky appeared split open. Red lightning cracked across it in all directions, leaving white scars in its wake. For a time, he thought the sky was trying to tear itself apart. In the distance, he could see a flaming plane hurtling toward the ground, bright jagged lines webbing across the sky around it. They called it the Shattering.

He had leaned the sword against the doorframe and pulled out his phone to see if there was any kind of news. Nothing. Worse than that, his phone was dead. There was no news, no texts or calls from friends or family — only a black screen. He had done everything he knew how to do to turn it back on, to no avail. His laptop had suffered a similar fate.

That left him with one choice: to meet his men at the Basic Operation Execution Training Center; AKA, the Grant Building. As military contractors, it was policy to be prepared for anything. He had taken his motorcycle into town. It was during the drive that he noticed the color change. The world was more colorful than he had ever seen before. Things were brighter; more saturated. He had made it to the safe house, and that was when his work had begun. That work had led him to this moment.

Now a basilisk, a creature of legend, loomed over him, blood dripping from its face as he stood sword in hand with no way out. Sweat trickled down Peter's face. The air felt thick around him.

The sword pulled at him, toward the snake, as if there was a magnet in Shadowfang's stomach. He felt the pull all the way up into his arm; he could no longer tell where his hand ended, and the sword began.

More random images flashed through his mind as Shadowfang forced his way deeper between the buildings. His parents. His sister's funeral. His first crush. His last relationship.

The woman who'd been taken advantage of during the panicking. Her attacker, the tears on his face, the blood on his boots, the gasping crowd, the scared faces, the collapsing buildings.

A giant snake — a basilisk — bearing down; rows of huge teeth, a purple tongue. Blood in its mouth, blood in his mouth, on his face, on its face, on his hands.

The smell of death as a black emptiness descended toward him, surrounded by rows of sharp teeth. He felt a warm moist breath against his skin. He saw the faces of dead friends. He saw his sister again as he stared up into that descending maw. Then a long, thin, sharp point bathed in purple-red blood emerged out of the blackness of the mouth above him.

The blackness stopped its descent. The purple blood dripped away to show silver. *That's a sword,* he realized. The warm awful breath dissipated, no longer flowing over Peter. The stench remained but did not blow in his face. There was silence. No tearing buildings. No scrape of scales over concrete. No deep hissing voice.

Only Peter's pounding heart.

— 6 —

A DWARF BY MANY NAMES

Peter wiped the back of his left hand across his forehead, wetting it with sweat, blood, and spittle. From his precarious position, he admired the fangs hanging over his head just out of reach. *That was close. I didn't hear a gunshot, and that looks like a sword. What's going on?*

Shadowfang's large purple tongue spasmed, went limp, and flopped down in front of Peter's face, reeking of death. Peter took a step back to avoid being hit by it or any falling fluids. His heel and shoulders struck the wall behind him, and he realized just how little room there was left in the space.

With his head braced against the wall, he looked up and saw the light of the blue sky through the barely open space between the basilisk's head and the back of the same wall. *I'm trapped,* he realized as he looked around and found no room for escape.

He stepped awkwardly around the open maw above him and caught sight of Shadowfang's ruined eyes, their once beautiful glow fading as dark blood struck the concrete below.

Peter looked deep into one of those empty eyes, filled with a sense of accomplishment. *He's dead, all right, but how…? What's going on? How can a creature like this even exist without anyone knowing about it?*

An oddly familiar voice interrupted his pondering: "Are you still alive down there, Mister Blair?"

The voice was soft with age but possessed the volume and tone of someone used to people listening to it. A hint of concern mixed with cautious admiration underscored the words. It took Peter a moment to conjure the face that matched the voice. It belonged to a face with dark skin surrounding deep-set brown eyes that radiated wisdom far older than the wrinkles they neighbored.

Peter called out, "Barely. Is that you, Doctor Walker?"

"Indeed, it is, Mister Blair," replied the voice from above. "Can you relocate yourself without injury?"

What's she doing here? Peter wondered as the part-time literature professor questioned him. *This can't be a coincidence, can it?* He'd known the old woman most of his life; in fact, it was she who'd given him the now blood-soaked sword in his hands. He looked down at the sword and saw that he gripped it so tightly his knuckles were white as the bones under his skin, contrasting the blade's dark metal.

"Not really. I could try cutting my way through *Shadowface*, but I'm not sure that's a good idea," Peter replied sourly. "What are you doing here?" he asked as curiosity got the better of him.

"Presently? Given the rather sharp blade embedded in this creature's cerebellum, I'd say I'm saving your life," she went on, taking on the tone of one talking to themself. "Now, let's see, his spines are holding him aloft, which, interestingly enough, haven't resulted in these buildings collapsing..." She paused, then added, "Give me a moment. I may have a solution."

She killed it? How did a little old lady manage that? No, relax. It's Doctor Walker, but why? Why is she here? I must be dreaming after all. He struggled with this as he let his mouth run on autopilot. "The sooner, the better. The stench and view down here aren't exactly to die for."

Dr. Walker had a light, whimsical chuckle at that. Peter continued to stare at the maw of the dead creature above him. The stench of rotten flesh began to claw through the air, lingered in the nostrils, and caused Peter to gag. *I've never smelled something in a dream before. This must be real.*

"I shouldn't think so. Tell me, is there a sweet, honey smell anywhere in the mix?" inquired Dr. Walker, her voice still coming from above.

"Honey?" Peter replied, then braced himself before sniffing the air. Despite his instincts begging him not to, he inhaled through his nose. He gagged. The stench clung to the inside of his nose. She was right — it was faint, but the smell of honey was unmistakably present, mixed in with the rot. "Yes, I'm assuming that's not a good thing," Peter said through a pinched nose.

"Good. You're not in shock then," stated the old woman. "And it isn't necessarily bad, dear boy, but it does require a bit more urgency on my part. Hang tight. I'll have you out in a jiffy."

Hang tight? That's a new one.

The dripping silver blade sticking out the roof of Shadowfang's mouth was pulled back, replaced by a beam of light from above. A second later, a shadow passed over the small opening between the serpent and wall above Peter's head, followed by a light thud on the other side of the wall behind him.

Peter turned his back to the dead beast cautiously, facing the brick wall. *Tap. Tap. Tap.* A series of thumps echoed against the wall; someone was knocking on the bricks. Careful to stay out from under the fangs as much as possible, Peter stepped away from the wall.

The air around the wall began to vibrate and hum. Starting from the ground, a soft glow began to leak through the bricks, forming a six-foot arch. The glow increased in intensity until the bricks within the area of the arch did the unexpected: they disappeared into dust.

What? How? Peter blinked rapidly to keep the dust out of his eyes. The fog of exhaustion that had been creeping into his mind was pushed back. When the dust and his vision cleared into the newly formed archway, a strange little old woman stepped out. *She just disintegrated part of the wall? Talk about out of the frying pan and into the fire. Calm down, Peter. Evaluate the threat.*

Peter stared down at the little woman he'd known as a family friend for years before getting to know her as a professor. He saw features he recognized: she still wore her gray and white hair in a blend of short springy locks that never fell past her chin. She still had a round face, and her ears were still covered by her curls. Her teeth still had a tiny gap in the center of her smile.

The longer he examined her, though, the more he noticed the differences. Her nose was more prominent, taking up more space on her face. Surgery could explain that if it came down to it. But there was more to it. Her face, although familiar, looked a decade or two older than the last time he'd seen it. It was an ancient face. *Sure, it could be makeup, but why?*

Even though she looked older, she radiated energy, as though she'd finally settled into herself. This was the most pressing difference in her strange transformation. Finally, he met her eyes. These, at least, were the same deep brown eyes, almost the same color as her skin, twinkling with countless years of experience.

Peter took it in silently. He made no effort to hide that he was picking her face apart piece by piece in his mind. Dr. Walker remained silent as she waited for him, an enormous pearly grin on her face. Slowly, with all the hesitation due to an old friend, Peter's sword rose to a defensive position.

The dwarf cocked an eyebrow and leaned on her small cherrywood cane, her enormous grin unfazed. "Have I offended you, Mister Blair? Don't tell me I'm that unrecognizable. I see familiarity in your eyes."

Peter's response was equally cautious, the words heavy as lead. "You're not human?" he managed to croak, his voice barely a whisper, sticking in his throat.

Her eyes studied him surgically. The smile finally passed from her mouth, but a trace remained, twinkling in her eyes. "No, I am not, nor have I ever actually been a human," she replied with palpable excitement. "You have no idea how good it is to finally say that."

"What are you then?" Peter still clutched his sword, his pistol forgotten in its holster. *Dangerous for sure, but on whose side?*

"A friend, but more importantly, an ally. Semantics aside, I am a dwarf, Mister Blair, of the nonhuman variety," she replied seriously. "Come now. I understand you are troubled. Tell me what is going through your mind."

She likes talking, so talk. Backup's right around the corner. Peter breathed deeply to center himself. *Focus. Coming down off adrenaline. Keep your wits sharp.*

"You just killed that monster… You've been a family friend for as long as I can remember, and you say you're an ally…" Peter's eyes narrowed. *And even if you aren't, I think I might be more outmatched against you than I was Shadowfang. I don't even know where I was going with this… You scare me.*

"What's going on?"

"Straight to the point then." She paused and stepped out of the opening, motioning him to follow. Peter complied, his eagerness to put some distance between himself and the dead monster outweighed his caution for the strange being.

"Where to begin…? Well, I am… more than just a dwarf. Doctor Walker is just one of the many titles I have chosen after traveling the world these last ten thousand years. My old name is Umindrabo Duridgrihulda: last of the Duridgribuldam, binder of worlds, Allfriend. Last of the faye no longer, a dwarf with some magical talent here to serve as mankind's ambassador, and guide in the new age, PhD."

Peter felt the corners of his mouth twitch towards grinning. Her smile was contagious, so visible was her excitement. "I have more titles, but they are irrelevant or beyond your current understanding. You may, of course, still call me Doctor Walker. It was the name I chose, after all, and the old tongue tends to be a bit laborious," the dwarf added with a bow.

The words finally hit Peter like a bullet; they cemented the reality he now faced. Mankind was far from alone on the planet. Things were about to change in ways he never could have imagined. He had so many questions, but no idea where to begin. *Ten thousand years?* He heard a clang. Peter clenched his hand and found it empty. His sword lay on the ground. The world was spinning.

"Easy now, Mister Blair," Dr. Walker, or whatever her name was, said as she stepped forward and helped him remain standing. With her help, he leaned against the archway and slid down to sit on the ground. She then retrieved his sword and offered it back to him with a bandana she produced from her pocket. "Clean your blade. It has more work to do."

Peter's mind still swirled with shock, so he set to wiping the blood away. The idle task helped settle his pounding heart. As he cleaned, the dwarf produced a glass flask from a pack she'd laid to rest on the ground. There was a strange swirling pattern engraved in the face of the glass vial.

As she moved, she spoke of faye, dwarves, elves, centaurs, orks, magic, and all manner of things Peter could not follow or understand with how his head swam.

As Peter worked to clean the sword, she moved past him into the basilisk's temporary grave. Once the blade was clean of blood, Peter turned his buzzing head to observe the dwarf at work.

Dr. Walker stood on earthy steps, which had grown out of the ground for her. The basilisk's open maw covered her to the knees. *She just made stairs from earth. What else can she do?* After a few moments, she descended the steps. It was then that he noticed her arms.

They were covered in a series of strange white rune tattoos. They had distinct, consistent patterns to them, reminiscent of lines in a book. In her hands, she held the glass vial, which now held several ounces of a clear, thick substance.

She tucked the vile away in her pocket, and he realized he hadn't been listening. "Now, of course, I don't expect you to familiarize yourself with all the fayemaia. That would be quite impossible, really. Even an elf would be daunted with the task considering it is widely accepted not all fayemaia are even discoverable by those of us of the fayelager, which is quite a fascin—"

"Doctor Walker," Peter interrupted.

Dr. Walker flinched as if surprised to hear a voice other than her own. "Yes, Mister Blair? A question, perhaps?"

"Slow down. We've just been attacked by a giant monster-snake, and you're going on about elves and centaurs. It's too much. Focus. What do I need to know right now."

The old dwarf's lips pressed firmly together, and she nodded. "Of course. I digress. No, I don't believe we are facing any immediate threats. Please proceed with your most pertinent questions."

"Are we in danger of another one of those attacking?" Peter said with a look at the dead monster.

"A basilisk? Goodness no. It's a one-in-a-million chance, perhaps a billion… Either way, no, and I plan to take steps to prevent similar attacks," she continued, verging into the voice of a lecturer. "I dare say you utilized a preventative measure of magic yourself a few minutes ago, since you managed to survive."

I was moving faster than I've ever moved… Peter gave her a sideways look as she continued, unfettered.

"Your kind has been cut off from it for so long that there have been some heartbreaking side effects."

"It?" Peter asked, eager to not have another conversation this heavy but confused as to what she was referring to.

"The arcane flow. Did I not mention that? Magic, Mister Blair, magic. Do pay attention." She extended a small, wide hand to help him to his feet. "Oh dear. I'm doing it again. I apologize. So much to discuss…"

As Peter got his feet under him, he caught sight of Steven rounding the corner, Desert Eagle held at the ready. A grin broke through the blood and dirt on Peter's face. He was glad to see an unchanged familiar face.

Why is he alone? Where are all the cops? Peter glanced at his watch and realized they could only have been talking for a few moments despite it feeling like a dissertation. Peter followed Steven's gaze to Dr. Walker.

She really was a spectacle. An old, dark-skinned woman, with a plethora of strange runic tattoos on her arms. She was immaculately clean, her clothing in pristine condition, which only served to highlight how out of place her clothes really were. What looked like a poncho was actually some sort of mottled, green-gray, sleeveless, hooded robe that left the arms exposed.

Peter spoke first. He started with a neutral question to bring a sense of normalcy. "How are Officer Akena and the civilians?" Something about his own voice seemed distant, as though he wasn't entirely there.

"Alive," came Steven's reply. "The girl's concussed. She warned me too late that that thing was bulletproof. Said something about glasses too. Officer Akena is doing as well as she can after what happened to her. We've got a couple of casualties too, but I don't have numbers yet."

Steven scratched lightly at his head. "Your cut was clean, at least. Right below the knee. I'm not sure how she was still conscious when I left her with the other officers, but she was." He gazed up at Shadowfang. "Speaking of, they're securing the perimeter… How'd you incapacitate it? It is incapacitated, yes?"

Peter glanced at Dr. Walker, who gave the answer Steven waited to hear.

"Technically, I thrust a blade into its cerebellum. However, it was Peter who trapped him, making it possible for me to do so."

Steven refocused his attention on the woman. He towered over the dwarf like an elephant to a lion. "Its cerebellum? So, it's not mechanical? Hold on — who are you?"

Peter could see Steven struggling to decide what was more important for him to garner information on, the dwarf or the dead basilisk. *He's going to want to start dissecting it immediately to see if he can figure out what made it bulletproof.*

"Doctor Walker, PhD. I am a dwarf," Dr. Walker restated. "To be clear, Mister Thomas, I am not a person with dwarfism, or whatever the current proper term happens to be, I'm a member of a humanoid race called dwarves. I expect I'll be explaining that a lot in the next few days. I shan't grow tired of it though. It's good to be back in my old skin. Although I had grown quite used to looking more human."

Steven looked to Peter. "Is she serious?" he asked as he lowered his weapon.

Peter nodded at his old friend. "She is."

Steven stared suspiciously at Dr. Walker. Peter could see he wasn't sure how to address her. "What are we examining here, some kind of new biologically engineered super-snake with a set of speakers installed to make it more terrifying?"

Always quick with a hypothesis. Not a bad one though. Maybe that's what it is after all.

Dr. Walker chuckled. "Add blood magic and dragon to the mix, and you're on the right track. No speakers, though. I'm afraid what you heard was its own voice."

"Will there be more like him?" Steven repeated Peter's question.

Dr. Walker's eyes twinkled. "I certainly hope not. Basilisks are a rare breed. Indeed, I'd thought they'd all been hunted by the elves to extinction even before the Therin-Selu. No doubt, this one was slumbering when it was cast, or else I'd have heard some news of it." She shook her head. "In truth, it is an astronomically unfortunate stroke of chance that not only was Shadowfang alive but that he came here of all places."

"We need to figure out what to tell people," Peter said. "World-changing news like this is the kind that causes panic." The three of them took a moment of silence as they weighed their words carefully. The Shattering had killed thousands of people in their town alone, both directly and indirectly, with rioting, panic, and the inevitable diseases if they weren't careful.

The fact that more weren't dead was, in part, due to the town's extraordinarily competent national emergency response plan, a plan that, among other things, had seen power restored to most of the city within the two weeks, which was something of a miracle.

"I think we give the credit to Peter Basilisk-Bane," Dr. Walker said as she waved a hand dismissively, cutting off Peter's response to the last two words. "I know your family's opinion on the use of flattery in warfare. I am not flattering you. This is a new title you have earned. You would be wise to embrace it. It may serve as a sort of armor for incoming events."

This time it was Peter's turn to raise eyebrows. He couldn't deny that he liked the sound of the title, but it hardly did anything to answer his questions. "From my point of view, Doctor, it was you who slew the basilisk."

"I may have landed the final blow, dear boy, but it was you who crippled, captured, and enraged the spawn of Aapep. The title of bane belongs to you. Besides, I have enough titles."

"Perhaps… it would be wise to give Doctor Walker full credit for the kill." Steven pinched the bridge of his thin nose with two fingers. "People are paranoid, easily frightened, distrusting of the unknown or different. To establish trust between people and our dwarven ally, people will need something to base it on."

Makes sense…

Dr. Walker shook her head almost apologetically. "I've experienced more than enough frightened paranoia in my time to know how to deal with it. Besides, Mister Blair is currently a divisive figure. I believe giving him credit will serve to cement him as a hero. People will be more willing to listen to him about trusting me."

The dwarf raised a knowing finger. "Additionally, it could help when dealing with the faye. Those are magical creatures like myself, Mister Thomas. Yes, most of them will think twice before challenging a basilisk's bane, as you know now, killing one is no easy task, especially one as old and feared as Shadowfang."

Steven's brow furrowed in thought, then he nodded. "Agreed. Captain?"

Peter shrugged. "You two seem to have figured it out."

The sound of an approaching vehicle halted their conversation. Peter mentally identified the low growl of a Supacat Jackal.

Perfect, reinforcements. SNW owned a slew of eclectic military vehicles acquired all over the globe. Then the truck came into view; both mounted machine guns scanned the street for potential targets. The Jackal, which brought more than enough firepower to shred a regular vehicle, rolled up to them and came to a stop.

Four familiar occupants exited the vehicle dressed in the same uniforms as Peter and Steven. The uniforms could have been mistaken for civilian clothing if not for the matching patches and equipment. Each had an M4A1 carbine — easy to acquire, maintain, and use effectively.

There was Brandon O'Cleary, a strong wiry man about six feet tall and in his forties. He had a hollow-cheeked face that bore the scars of a man who'd spent his life in fights. The hair on his head was short, dark brown, and receding. A small patch in the middle of it was curiously white. His hazel eyes darted about frantically as he took in the scene.

Curses accented by an Irish tone poured from his mouth as he gaped at the body of Shadowfang, unmissable behind the strange trio.

Next to O'Cleary was Justin Lewis. He was a tad taller and broader than the Irishman, in his mid-twenties, and never without a baseball hat. Today his hat actually matched his uniform: black with the company logo on the front. His face bore a permanent smile cracking through a short beard, unaffected by the scene in front of him.

The third member of the reinforcements was in his thirties, and wore it well. He was of Vietnamese descent and straight black hair pulled into a ponytail. Simon was the same height as Peter, with dark inquisitive eyes. He remained stoic and silent while his companions expressed their horror at the scene.

His focus was not on the dead monster but on the blood covering Peter and Steven. Simon Luu reached into a satchel of medical supplies he carried, withdrawing trauma shears for quick fabric removal should he need them.

The fourth member was a toned woman in her mid-twenties with olive skin. She was Middle Eastern with thick eyebrows. Peter was one of the few who knew specifically where she was from, and he kept that close to his chest per her request. He also knew that she'd been in and out of civil wars from childhood until finally escaping.

Once you knew this, the hardness in her eyes was impossible to miss no matter how well she hid it from those who didn't know better. She went by Jenni, whether in an effort to ditch her old name or out of concern that Americans would be unable to correctly pronounce it was a subject of betting among her fellow soldiers in SNW. Peter had made efforts to discourage this.

To Peter's surprise, her oldest and most trusted companion, a dog named, Hauch, was not at her side. *Why didn't she bring him? He could have been useful.*

Each of them took in the sight of Shadowfang's corpse in their own way — O'Cleary and Justin with a slew of curses, Simon in silence, and Jenni muttering a reflexive prayer — all before they noticed the paradoxically more shocking dwarf. It dawned on Peter that the magnitude of the situation was lost on them.

From their point of view, it was a huge snake and a short, albeit strange-looking, woman. Strange, yes, but not as bizarre as they were about to find out it actually was. It would take more to convince them and others of the scope of the situation. Had Shadowfang not spoken to Peter himself, he'd have probably tried to rationalize a big snake with similar theories as the ones Steven was surely considering.

People are stubborn, critical, angry, and broken. At least I have SNW. At least we're united. Once order had been restored, the recent tragedy brought people together in a way that was hard to believe. Peter stepped forward into the shade as a cloud passed overhead. All eyes focused on him.

"Where's Hauch?" Peter asked calmly as though everything was normal and right in the world.

Jenni blinked at him, her mouth in a frown. "Napping. He's put in a lot of overtime this week. What's going on, captain?"

"That," Peter motioned at Shadowfang's corpse, "is a basilisk."

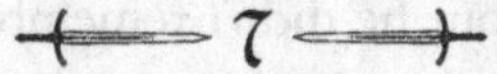

THE BURNING PITS

Without a doubt, it was the smell he hated most. Smell wasn't the right word for the savory, barbecue scent that mingled aggressively with burned hair and bacteria. Shawn pondered the word stench, considered whether it could really describe the gut-wrenching stink that molested the air he breathed. He drove his shovel into the ash-stained dirt at his feet and shook its new contents along the edge of the pit to stave off the spread of flames.

One burning human corpse was more than enough to make anyone gag. They burned thousands, hundreds at a time. Initially, those in charge had tried to burn more to expedite the process, but the fumes and heat were so violent they'd been forced to pace themselves. There was now a limit imposed: no more than two hundred corpses at once.

Shawn rubbed at his eyes, blinked quickly, then held them shut to get moisture back into them. The sting of the smoke made it difficult to keep them open for more than a few seconds at a time. Tears would have been helpful, even though he was sick of crying.

But no tears came. In a way, it was a relief; crying was too taxing.

This must be what hell is like, he thought as he glanced down at the flames as they licked away at the strange bodies huddled together below him, searing them into his mind. Their tangled forms reminded him he was alone.

Memories flashed in his mind: The sky split with a *crack*, and his father lost control of the car. The car rammed into the back of a truck. The front of the roof of the car tore off as large chunks of metal crashed into his parents. His mother did not even have time to scream before she and his father died, then both vehicles crashed into marshy water.

Shawn remembered going under the dirty water, struggling with his seat-belt. The sight of their mangled bodies stole any hope that they'd survived; his mom's airbag hadn't gone off, and his father's hadn't made a difference. Not that it mattered as they all sank into the murky water. He remembered someone else's hands had freed him, but he didn't remember how he got out or got to shore. He didn't remember seeing anything in the water other than bubbles.

Shawn would never hear their voices again; he never got to say goodbye. *They're still down there somewhere. They're not even ashes now*, he realized. *Not with everyone else in the pits.* The thought brought him some small comfort. He wasn't sure if he could handle seeing them burn. *The only family I have left is Aunt Taylor in Atlanta, and she's probably dead too.*

Even if she was alive, there was no way she'd have even thought of him. Why would a teenage boy she hadn't reached out to in seven years be her concern? After all, it'd taken him a week to even remember her.

Shawn's stomach turned. It did that a lot lately. The bile burned in his throat before he could force it back down. It left his mouth and nostrils with the raw burn of suppressed vomit. *Great. More burning. Just what I need.* Heat licked closer to his boots than was safe. He shoveled more dirt into the fire, trying to calm the edges of the flames down. He received a fresh blast of smoke as a reward.

I need air. Fresh air. The young honey-toned boy stumbled away from the pits full of charred corpses — some only blackened bones. Some of the bodies from hours before refused to burn away to make room for others.

At least we don't have to stab them anymore, Shawn thought and winced at the memory of Joseph, the first shift supervisor. He had given out pitchforks at the beginning of the burning and told them to stab the bodies before dumping them or they would explode. This practice lasted for the entire shift. It hadn't stopped until a fireman arrived with the next shift.

Shawn recalled the look of horror on the fireman's face at the sight of corpses being pierced for no reason. For a moment, Shawn had feared the fireman would use one of the pitchforks on Joseph, he had been so heated. Thankfully, he did not, and the stabbing was brought to a quick end, much to everyone's relief. As awful as burning the bodies was, stabbing them first had been worse.

It was hard work; too much for the weak of will or body. *I've been doing this for four days. Has it really been over a month since the Shattering?* Standing a safe distance from the fire, he removed his small canteen of water he'd been given. He took a sip and realized it was all but gone. Frowning, he peered into the canteen and saw only droplets. *Could be worse. I could be tossing the bodies instead of just tending the edges…*

As he lowered the canteen from his eye, he spied a violet, a tiny blooming flower somehow still alive at the edge of where the grass met stomped dirt surrounding the fire pit. "Here you go, little guy," he said to the flower as he tilted the canteen and waited patiently for its last few drops to fall onto the flower's petals.

Then he stored the canteen and pulled his bandanna back over his face with one last gulp of air. It was fresh compared to what he'd just escaped, but hardly identifiable as such to any who might have ventured to the spot for the first time. For a moment, he regretted getting involved, not to the point of quitting or anger, but in the way we so often regret taking on a difficult task, even though we know it must be done.

As he mentally prepared to return to work, he noticed his clothes were crusty from dried sweat. *Great. More chafing*, he thought sarcastically as he resumed working his way around the pit with his shovel. The sound of the fire and machinery around him served as a replacement for music as he toiled.

"Gather round," called a vague voice over the noise of the worksite. There was urgency in this voice. Shawn turned and searched for its origin. The speaker was a man in his early forties with dark curly hair cut short and a round friendly face. It took Shawn a moment to recognize Al in his bright blue button-up shirt and cargo shorts.

He was the first familiar face he'd seen in days. Al was a friend of his dad, or at least used to be. Shawn wasn't even sure how they knew each other. Now it looked like he served as something of a town crier. Al had a way with words; that, or it was just his personality that got people to listen. Shawn tried to do just that as he made his way over to where folks were conglomerating to listen.

"It killed three people. They said the thing's bigger than a bus. Swallowed one fella whole! Captain Blair killed the beast, trappin' it in between some buildings." The small crowd of local workers began to whisper among themselves. Shawn joined the group without any trouble and moved toward the front to hear better.

Al continued. "Apparently, the little lady ain't even human either! No! No! Really! That's what they're saying. Calling her a dwarf. I'm tellin' ya, honest. You'll believe it when ya see her." Al chuckled. "I always thought short folks were human, but I suppose I wasn't right about all of 'em! She's something else."

There were mumbles from the crowd, and a few began to wander off, waving their hands dismissively. "Now, when I say she's something else, I mean it literally, y'all. She ain't human."

A tall, thin man with sunken eyes and a shaved head scoffed. "You expect us to believe a bus-sized snake showed up and got itself killed by those mercenaries, and now there's some fairytale dwarf?" he said as he waved his hand dismissively. "I know a lot of craziness has been going on lately, Al, but we're not dumb enough to fall for such a childish story."

Al raised his palms in surrender. "I wouldn't have shaken a stick at the story myself a month ago, and I don't expect you to just take my word for it." The truck bed he stood in creaked as he adjusted his weight. "But I'm telling ya — you can ask William Shaw yourself if you don't believe me. Captain Blair frogged that snake the mess up."

Frogged it the mess up? What kind of a sentence was that? Shawn wondered as he listened for more information. *A giant snake and a dwarf lady? What? What is going on?*

"Shaw's one of them Snow fellas. Local or not, he's gonna tell the same tall stories they do, Al," called a voice.

The round man nodded. "That's fair. That's fair. Tell ya what — you don't have to believe me. They're having a meeting downtown. Y'all are supposed to wrap up here then get inside the barricade as soon as possible. Then you can see it for yourself."

The crowd began to break into smaller groups and continued to debate whether Al's story was believable. Most people leaned toward the latter. Some checked the time to see how long they had left in their shift. Some returned to work, while others used the interruption as an excuse to catch their breath.

Shawn watched as Al gazed over the group, he noticed the man shove his hands into his pockets to hide their trembling. *He certainly looks scared enough to be telling the truth.* Shawn overheard plenty of excuses from the groups around him.

"He's losing it," argued one man.

"Exaggerating. Always liked a good story," insisted another.

"More likely was a big snake. You know, pythons been coming up from Florida for decades now. Wouldn't put it past that scary captain of theirs to kill one of them and make a big deal of it. Probably got all up and personal with his sword too."

"Sounded like a lot of bull to me till he said Shaw would vouch for him. The man may be one of them mercenaries, but he's a good fellow. Good kids. I can't see him spinning no tales," chimed in another adult Shawn couldn't make out. "We'll see for ourselves soon enough."

There were those among them who, like Shawn, had started to believe it. He saw it on their faces; albeit, they were few and far between. One thing they all shared, though, was a desire to see what had inspired such a ludicrous tale.

Why would they make up something so ridiculous? It has to be real. There's no way they could fake something like what he's saying.

Shawn wished he hadn't come to see what was going on, that his eyes hadn't been opened to the horror that was their new world. Ignorance was truly bliss. He could see the disbelief on their faces sprinkled with fear and anxiety as they considered their already unbelievable circumstances.

Shawn stood there and stared blankly at Al as he processed what he knew. He tried to make sense of it all. Shawn struggled as he realized that claims of dwarves and giant snakes were hardly any more unbelievable than the last month of hell had been. *Perhaps this is hell, and we're all already dead,* he considered.

Shawn didn't think it was, though. Sure, even the air was different; everyone felt it, but no one knew why. They just knew it scared them. But that didn't mean they were in hell. *I think I'd remember dying.*

Shawn's train of thought was derailed by a voice calling out his name. *Who?* He glanced around. His teenage self was just short enough to be disoriented by the crowd. "Shawn!" The word jumped through the air again, calling him towards the speaker.

Al met his gaze and motioned him over. As Shawn approached, the man braced himself with a swallow before asking the critical questions. Their hands met firmly in greeting. Al's voice was soft to lessen the impact of his words.

"Your parents?" he asked. The raw wound was so fresh that this prodding was hardly noticeable, yet, Shawn's throat constricted at the vocal reminder. Al swallowed again at the look on the boy's face, and his own eyes blinked back tears.

The small shake of Shawn's head was enough to bring the back of Al's hand to his own eyes to rub back tears. "One second, Shawn." Al turned back to the crowd and looked for the assigned supervisor.

He spotted a man with a bright green bandana giving instructions. Al managed to wave the man over. "Imma take Shawn here back with me if that's all right."

The man's response was indifference, a common reaction to things now. "Sure. See ya." Shawn glanced at Al upon hearing this.

Al caught the look and explained, "This is no place for a kid, or teenager. Sorry." Al gestured at the fire pits. "How'd you get stuck out here anyway?"

Shawn realized he hadn't spoken with anyone in the last few days. No more than "Over here," "Yes, sir," "Give me a hand with this," and so on.

"After the accident, I went looking for help since my phone wasn't working…" he began. Those first words were the leaks strong enough to break the dam of his silence. "It still only turns on and takes pictures…"

Shawn went on in a croaky voice, "There was so much noise in the beginning. Everyone was running around panicking, screaming, and crashing into things. But there was this girl… yelling for help. She wasn't screaming. Just calling out, asking for someone to help her dig another girl out from some rubble. And everyone was just freaking out around her."

He looked down at his hands covered in bruises and scabs under the ash. "Next thing I know, I'm helping her. Then more people joined in, and we got her free. Then it was on to the next person calling for help." Shawn shook his head. "More and more people. Every time we helped someone, they joined in if they could."

Al motioned for Shawn to climb into the passenger seat of the truck. Shawn complied, the flood of words uninhibited.

"After the deputies and those Snow people showed up and started organizing things, people calmed down. Giving people jobs and handing out food and water helped. They had me marking areas where the dead were ready for extraction, using spray paint and police tape." Shawn wiped his dirty hands on his filthy pants. "Then I almost fell through the floor of an apartment building. That got me moved to collection." Shawn leaned forward until his face was almost touching the A/C vent as it blasted in cold air.

"One of those Snow people — I think her name was Jessica — suggested it. I didn't know it was moving bodies, though." Shawn wrinkled his nose. "I wasn't strong enough for that, so I ended up in cataloging. That was my favorite. No bodies. Just making a list of the IDs collected from corpses."

"Did you know they photographed the ones without an ID?" Shawn didn't give Al a chance to reply as he drove them slowly down the dirt road leading out of the fields towards the main road and the town. "I didn't. I'd hate to be the one stuck doing that."

"Next thing I know, Jessica moved me to corpse transportation. I thought I was going to be driving, but I don't have my learners yet, so that was dumb." He scowled as they made their way through the dispersing crowd at a slow roll. "Instead, I was supposed to help unload. Stupid Jessica. I told her I didn't want to help with more bodies," he added the last bit in a whisper.

His voice returned to normal volume. "When we got to the pits, I saw this man collapse. I went to help him, but people beat me there. Then someone handed me his shovel as he was carried away. He was coughing, like, really bad." Shawn leaned back from the A/C as they cleared the crowded work site and rumbled off the dirt road onto pavement. "I've been doing this since then. Burned corpses are better. At least this way I don't recognize them."

Al was silent for a moment as the truck trundled around a turn towards the town. The encroaching woods obscured their destination from view. When Al did speak, it was in a soft voice. "Well, I'll see to it you don't have to worry about no more corpses."

A minute later, they were within sight of the city. Shawn glanced back out the window, looking into the woods behind them. He was fascinated by the trees and how they had changed in the last few days. The woods were growing, not in a manner which the naked eye might discern from a few moments of staring. Instead, they'd grown since yesterday, and the day before; thicker, taller, and closer to the road.

A localized gust of wind at the edge of the trees drew his attention, barely perceptible. Shawn focused on the movement in the trees. There was no wind anywhere else. *What's moving the leaves?*

He stared deep into the woods, and a leafy green face stared back — a sharp face formed by shifting leaves. It was the face of a woman standing among the trees. Her form was composed entirely of floating leaves.

Shawn blinked, and she was gone. One second, a person made entirely out of leaves was standing there clear as day, watching him. The next, she had vanished. *Where did she go?* The confidence of youth left him with no room to doubt what he saw. There had been a face made of leaves watching him. He'd met its gaze, and it disappeared.

Shawn turned back around in his seat and clamped his mouth shut. He was not sure if he should say anything now that the face was gone. Al turned the truck onto the bypass. Up ahead, a barricade of vehicles had been parked strategically between the buildings, establishing a sort of wall around the town.

Shawn stared at it. He'd lived in the town most of his life, and he'd never noticed how tightly packed the buildings along the bypass were, or how encompassing the woods were around the city. It was as if the city had been built to perfectly accommodate the vehicular additions that formed the barrier. Whatever the reason, be it foresight or blind luck, it made him feel safer.

Shawn watched carefully as they got closer to the construction. It was a massive project, busy with bulldozers and other equipment, hard at work converting the collapsed bypass. After several days it was finally starting to look less like a pile of rubble and more like a wall.

It had seemed silly when it started, but now with these rumors of giant snakes and dwarves, Shawn wished they were building it faster. They approached the "gate" — a pair of semi-trucks parked with bumpers facing out toward the road. This way, they could be moved to make room for incoming vehicles entering the city. He could see the deputies tasked with shooting out tires should an advancing enemy begin to overtake them.

I hope they finish and we get a real gate soon, the teen thought. They wove through a makeshift set of barriers that formed an alternating pattern in front of the entrance to slow down any attackers. Al's truck came to a stop in front of the semis.

Al rolled the window down as a middle-aged brown-haired woman with a rifle approached. She wore jeans, boots, and a flannel shirt, the expression on her face unidentifiable.

"That took longer than I thought," Al murmured, staring at the hood of the vehicle. On it was painted a half circle and three dots, another security step. It made all outgoing vehicles easier to identify at a distance when returning. *Maybe she'll ask me for the password.* The panic-inducing thought caught Shawn unawares as she got closer.

They'd all been told to memorize two, and Shawn could only remember the one he was supposed to use if there was trouble: "How's Fred doing?"

He knew the other one was based on the city's university's motto, *Non Stabit Invictus,* meaning *We Stand in Victory,* but he couldn't remember what it had been changed to. *Stupid password. Come on, think,* he told himself, but his mind still lingered on the face in the woods.

The woman reached the window and greeted Al.

"Hey there." Her round brown eyes reminded Shawn of a bear the way they eyed the truck's occupants.

Al replied with, "Calm invictus, Tara. How are you holding up?"

"It's *com invictus,* Al. Come on. See how easy that is? Com invictus. I swear not a single person has gotten it right all day," she replied, exasperated. "I'm as well as can be expected with a giant snake being dragged into the middle of town, and who knows what else out there."

Al grinned. "My bad. Com. Com invictus. Got it. Always a ray of sunshine, eh, Tara?"

Tara's frown curled into a soft smile. "Who's the kid?" she asked, jerking her head towards Shawn.

"That's Shawn. I used to sell to his dad. They had him out there working the pits. Can you believe that? A fourteen-year-old kid working those pits."

Tara pursed her lips. "Not the worst thing I've heard today. Still, sorry they had you doing that, kid. Stay safe, Al," she said kindly and patted the side of the truck before she turned to wave open the gate.

Not entirely sure why, but strangely emboldened by the woman's friendly voice, Shawn leaned over toward the open window. "There's something in the woods," he declared, his voice coming out shakier than he'd intended. Tara's smile twitched as her eyebrows furrowed. She glanced between the woods and Shawn.

Al spoke up before Tara could reply. "Yup. Sure is. Lot's more things than there used to be according to the folks in charge. Keep an eye out." This seemed to pacify Tara, and Al pulled toward town, rolling the window up as he went. Shawn sat in silence as they drove, disappointed at being dismissed after working up the courage to speak.

Finally, Al broke the silence, speaking in a low tone that reminded him of his principal. "What did you see?"

"I dunno," Shawn said more out of reflex than a desire to deny anything.

The truck came to a stop in the middle of the street, drawing glances from some people tending to repair or salvage jobs nearby. Al shifted into park, sweat glistening on his round face which wore a stern expression as he turned to face the boy, "Shawn, listen, I need you to tell me exactly what you saw. Even if it sounds crazy. Every detail."

He lost his accent, Shawn thought with a swallow as he tried to find his voice. "I… I'm not sure." His dark eyebrows furrowed. "There was a face, in the trees. It was only there for a sec. It…" he paused, trying to put what he'd seen into words. "It was in the leaves. I think it *was* the leaves. But it just sort of vanished. It was watching, though. It understood, I think."

Al searched the boy's face, lips pressed firmly. After what felt like an eternity, he nodded. "Okay, if you remember or see anything else, tell me. You're gonna have to tell Captain Peter too. Luckily, that's where we're heading now."

The gears shifted, and the old blue truck continued towards its destination, deeper into the recovering busy town, as Shawn racked his brain for more details, the image carved clearly in his mind.

There had been something else, something Shawn pushed out of his mind as soon as he'd seen it, but it was making its way back, bringing with it a cold sense of dread. The face had smiled. It locked eyes with him and smiled before vanishing.

8

DARK DREAMS

The sensation of firm ground spread across Peter's back as he gained awareness. He slowly blinked one eye open. The world around him was dark,
full of glowing, swirling mists. The strange mist served as the dim and
only source of light. Even odder was that it shifted about despite the absence of
a breeze. There was no color here; only black and white or shades of gray.

The room was stagnant; a slight chill in the air. Peter sat up slowly, his
palms resting against the cool stone that made up the ground beneath him.
The sensation of the stone was odd: a pressure on his hands and backside that
lacked texture.

Peter looked around and found nothing other than a sword embedded in
the ground near his feet. It took Peter a moment to recognize the sword. Slowly,
as if through water, he leaned forward and grasped the hilt. The instant his
fingers wrapped around the leather handle, he felt a jolt.

An unfamiliar sensation akin to electricity but cold and almost fluid shot
up Peter's arm and through his nervous system and was followed by intense
pins-and-needles throughout his skeleton. As the bizarre feeling subsided, he
realized he'd regained the full scope of his senses. He brought his hand up to
check for injury but found none.

Not only did this chilly place lack color, but it also lacked any kind of smell
or sound whatsoever. Strangest of all, though, was the weight of the place. Peter
felt as if he was covered in an invisible lead sheet from head to toe. He rose to
his feet and was suddenly aware of soft, loose-fitting clothes brushing his skin.
He looked down to see black garments he could not remember donning. *What's
going on?*

The smooth stone under his bare feet made him want to stand on his toes,
but he breathed deep through his nose and pushed the discomfort from his

mind. His mind was foggy as he tried to remember where he was and how he'd gotten there. *I was in bed, finally. I'd finished cleaning the sword, locked my door, and lain down. How did I get here? Am I asleep?*

He felt a shift in the stagnant air behind him and spun around but found only swirling fog and unending blackness. *I must be asleep. Some dream this is, though. I'll have to check the expiration date on those rations.*

Peter pinched himself. *Ow, good.* Not satisfied that he was awake, he punched air. The increased sense of gravity slowed his blow. This only served to further his confusion. *If I'm asleep, I should be waking up now, but I'm not. Maybe a lucid dream.* He focused, trying to will himself into the air, into flight, but nothing happened.

A voice broke the eerie silence behind him; close to him; too close. "What are you doing?"

A woman? Sarcastic and confident, possibly a threat. I need my sword. Peter's hand struck out, and his fingers coiled around the cold leather hilt of his weapon. He flinched, but there was no jolt this time. Neither did the sword move. Peter looked around for the source of the voice but saw nothing.

The tendons in his arms bulged while he tried to yank his sword out of the ground. Still, the blade didn't budge. A snicker mocked him from behind; a thick, silvery voice following on the laughter's heel, far more severe. "You have the right idea, but you have not earned that yet. Give me your title."

Fear poked cruelly at his mind. Peter realized that the emptiness of his environment filled him with dread. There was no echo from the voice, no warmth anywhere, no stars above. No smells or colors. *If this is a dream, it's a rotten one. I should be waking up by now.*

One hand went to his head and ran through his messy hair, searching for some kind of helmet, while the other kept pulling at the sword. *Maybe some kind of augmented or virtual reality. It has to be. Might explain the weight, if I'm in some weird suit.* But he felt nothing out of the ordinary in his search. *This could be something I don't even have a word for. I have to be careful.*

Peter turned to see the speaker, knuckles white from the strain of his attempts to free his sword. A slab of rock that hadn't been there before was protruding from the ground at a forty-five-degree angle. Sitting on the edge of the lump of rock was a humanoid being unlike anything Peter had ever encountered.

Her skin was the color of ash. Long, pointed ears stuck out of her pure white hair, which fell over one shoulder in a tight, thick braid. There were thin white lines that on a human he would have assumed were surgery scars along her cheeks and up the bridge of her nose. They even extended down her neck and into the folds of cloth that covered her chest and reappeared along her arms to her fingertips.

She wore a tattered sheet almost as ashen as she was with frayed edges dyed a deep rusty red, one of the only colors in the whole place. A leather rope wrapped around her left shoulder to her right hip like a sash.

Her large, upturned eyes were the color of amethysts and seemed to glow in the low light. Those eyes tore Peter apart, broke him down from head to toe. *She looks like a ghost.* When she'd finished dissecting him, she scoffed and blew air from her nose, followed by a soft, self-berating chuckle.

"A human, of course. You are a human. Your kind never did know how to mind their own business." The voice set off Peter's survival instincts, but there was nowhere to run, and he was unarmed.

A cruel grin carved across her face. "Scared?"

Peter found his voice, drawing it out of hiding. "Only enough to keep me alive. Where am I?"

She raised a white eyebrow. "Obvious question. It lacks ingenuity. But I asked you your name."

Peter crouched reflexively as the being launched herself from her perch and landed softly, silently, on the ground in front of him. She was smaller than he'd expected, roughly the size of a fifteen-year-old. She barely came to his shoulder. This did nothing to relax him as he watched the way she moved: like a predator.

Peter's muscles tensed, and he took a step back from the sword. Whatever had put it there was stronger than him, and there was no way this girl would have the strength to remove it. He prepared to defend himself. The menacing girl moved slowly but with confidence.

Peter's instincts were confirmed: this creature was dangerous. *She has me isolated, unarmed, and she's relaxed. She has every tactical advantage.* But she wasn't entirely there. It was brief, almost imperceptible, but at times she seemed translucent. It was as if she faded out of existence, anchored to the world around them but constantly slipping away. *Maybe she is a ghost. If basilisks are real, why not ghosts?*

"Last chance," she almost snarled. "This is my third asking. What is your name?"

"Peter," he replied simply. "Is this some kind of augmented or virtual reality?" he asked hopefully.

"It is an alternate reality, yes," came the reply just slow enough to not hide the confusion behind it. The girl stalked closer. She tried to circle him slowly, but he gave ground, not allowing her to get within striking range or out of his line of sight. *Alternate? What?*

"Be still," she whispered, and an invisible force seized him. He felt bound by a rope but saw no restraints. His body did not react to his commands as the being approached, whispering under her breath as she circled, poked, and prodded him. Fear crawled up his spine, grasping him in its open maw, set to devour him. *I can't move. What do I do? What do I do?*

The jabs and her barely perceptible hesitation to answer his question returned him to the theory that this was a dream, or some kind of nightmare. Finally, she stopped in front of him and glowered up at him, her form no longer drifting in and out of translucency.

"My turn. What did you use him on first?" she asked as a scarred finger came to rest on the point of Galvorn's pommel.

Strength returned to his limbs, and Peter felt relaxed slightly. His mind still racing, he replied dismissively, "A traitor."

The purple eyes flashed from him to the sword and back again. "Explain."

The words came quickly enough; the memory still warm embers in his mind, not hidden behind the smoke of dreams. "He was a subordinate named John. Right after the Shattering, there was a lot of rioting, and I caught him and some others raping a woman after having killed her husband for water."

Peter's voice was as cold as steel as he went on. "My men and I executed them to set an example. We weren't about to waste resources keeping them alive. Any other time, and I'd have trussed them up then turned them over to her and whoever her parents are to get justice," Peter said, his mood darkening with the reminder.

"The Shattering?" she replied, clearly puzzled.

Some ghost you are. "That's what people are calling it. A few weeks ago, the sky split, and now dwarves, basilisks, and who knows what else are turning up."

Her eyes widened, and a whisper escaped her lips. "He failed." A look of deep thought came over her face. When she looked back at him, her expression was guarded. "You have used him since then. You must have. Tell me."

The question surprised him. *How does she know that? No, of course, she knows. She's in your dream. That's why this doesn't make sense.*

"Most recently? On the basilisk, and before that… Akena. Her leg was caught in the basilisk's teeth. I amputated it to save her."

Her eyebrows shifted upward and her eyes widened slightly. "Did it have a name? Is it still alive?"

"Shadowfang. No, I took care of it." Something about her eyes told him not to outright lie to her, but if this being knew what a basilisk was, then maybe him having killed one would cause her to hesitate before striking him. "Would you like to hear about those I've killed who fought back? The men and women I've lost under my command? The fights I've survived by the skin of my teeth?"

The amethysts shrank behind narrowed eyelids. "What is your full name? Titles and all?"

Oh, right. "Captain Peter Blair, Basilisk-Bane," he replied, wondering if he should include anything else.

Her face remained impassive, but he could have sworn he saw a hint of a smile in the corner of her mouth.

"My turn," he continued. "I'm owed some answers."

She tilted her head then nodded slightly. The game was simple. Information for information. "What are you?"

She frowned. "I am an Eölin. We are children of the moon."

Eölin. Remember that. Eölin. Ask Doctor Walker about it.

"Is that… a type of elf, like, from the moon?" he asked. She appeared similar to what he'd expected an elf to look like.

Her eyes burned, and the Eölin spat on the ground. "My kind has not been elvish for a millennium. We are Eölin, and you shall call me Jadis." Jadis frowned.

Hedging his bets, Peter asked another question. "Why am I here?"

The approval in her eyes lasted only a second. In one smooth motion, she sat cross-legged on the ground, waving for Peter to do the same. He did.

"You are here because Galvorn is my *aluth-nava*," she explained.

Peter ran a finger along his jaw. "I don't know what that means."

The voice that continued was dripping with condescension. "The sword is my anchor to your world." She leaned in until he could feel her breath against his face, watching him more closely than she had since their conversation had begun. "What do you fear?"

Anchor? She's sounding more and more ghostly. Peter took a deep breath. The air that passed into his lungs was thick and flavorless. Images flowed through his mind as he searched for the proper response. *Don't give too much away. This dream is bad enough without turning into a full-blown nightmare. Give her something she can't actually use against you.* "Failure. Not being able to make a difference," he replied.

Jadis chortled. "Then you have nothing to fear. I believe I have uses for you." Her cruel smile returned. Her eyes glowed as the light faded around them until all was dark, all but those eyes which filled his vision. Then, they too faded into nothingness.

Peter spasmed back to consciousness. The dark room spun around as though he were strapped to the ceiling fan. His blue-gray eyes disappeared as he squeezed them shut to stop the spinning. After an untraceable amount of time, the world stilled, and his mind began to clear.

Peter's heavy breathing returned to normal. He sat up in bed, then slid his legs in their pajamas over the side. Bare feet met the cold floor, bringing a flood of fresh memories. Jadis' eyes and voice flashed in his mind. He glanced at the clock. He'd only been out for a few minutes, but it felt like hours.

He focused on the dream. It wasn't fading and growing foggy as they so often do. He could remember every second of it with terrifying clarity. The strange dense environment closed in around him as the girl watched.

Brisk night air stung Peter's eyes as he opened a window, his chest hair providing little protection from the cold. He began rubbing his arms in response to the chill and felt a twinge of pain. Somewhere in the night, an owl hooted.

There was a small bruise on his bicep, and fear gripped his stomach as he searched for a light. It clicked on, and he stared down at the purple mark. It was one of the places Jadis had jabbed.

Calm down. You could have just rolled over onto something, or it could be from the fight earlier. But Peter knew it hadn't been there earlier when he'd showered and checked for injuries. Sure, he had plenty of cuts and bruises, but this one was too precise, too perfect.

Peter ran to the door, bursting out into the hallway. Down the hall, he spied the light coming out from under Steven's door. He dashed forward, practically colliding with the door as he went to open it. A confused Steven looked up at him from where he was huddled over his workbench. A single lamp illuminated his task.

"Peter?" he asked in a befuddled voice.

"How long has it been since I left for bed?" Peter asked urgently.

Steven shook his head in confusion, looking down at his wristwatch. "A half-hour at most. I've only been here for about twenty minutes. What's going on?"

"Did you hear anyone out here? Any alarms go off?" Peter said.

Steven rolled his chair over a few feet and typed a login into a computer by his workbench. "No, nothing's been tripped. You okay?"

Peter clenched a fist. "Yeah… Yeah, just a bad dream. Do me a favor. Keep an ear out, would you?"

"Sure thing, buddy," Steven replied kindly. "You should try and get some more rest. You look exhausted."

"Thanks," Peter replied and returned to his room, where, rather than try to go back to sleep, he spent the hours before dawn going over every inch of

Galvorn and writing down what he had seen in his dream, searching for some explanation for what occurred.

Was it just a dream? Or is my mind trying to compensate for the stress of all that's happening? It could have been something else, something I have no frame of reference for. I can't rule anything out.

GOOD COMPANY

The light overhead flickered as one of its three bulbs surrendered to age. Sarah's gaze flittered toward the dying light instinctually. "No," she murmured.

The ancient dwarf-woman sitting across from her lowered the glass from her lips. "No?" The professor's voice was aged honey; sharp and sweet with wisdom.

Sarah said, "I'm sorry?" Her voice was sturdy but lacked volume and seemed inclined to trail off.

"You said *no,* dear, are you all right?"

"Yes," came the reply, too quickly.

The older woman smiled slightly, tilted her head, and raised an eyebrow.

"Well, no. I mean, no, it's not. I'm not alright." Sarah's voice shook as it trailed off again. Her head still throbbed on occasion despite the concussion having been dealt with. She glanced down at the scab on her hand. *I'm better, somehow, but it doesn't make sense.* She had survived the explosion and the basilisk with dozens of small cuts, half of which should have been enough to kill her on their own. But they hadn't.

Dr. Walker looked down her nose over the rim of a large pair of spectacles. "Deep breath, little one," came the instruction. The intended irony was not lost on Sarah, who did as she was told.

"I keep hearing its voice, its bone-shaking voice. Every time I try to sleep, I have nightmares about it." Her voice wavered. A small, soft hand came to rest on the back of where her hand lay on the table.

"Shadowfang is dead. To let him haunt you is to give him victory in death where you bested him in life. You are safe, Sarah. Be at peace."

Sarah nodded; the motion helped to strengthen her resolve. "Okay, where were we? We just finished sorting names, right?" she asked, looking down at the piles of notes they'd been sorting through regarding the town's survivors. *I still don't understand why this couldn't wait until morning, or why she needed me to do it here of all places.*

She looked around the small room, a conference room on the first floor of the Grant Building, SNW's headquarters in the town. A clock on the wall read 11:40 PM. *I've been here for two hours now...*

"Yes, dear. I think that completes that task for the evening. I would, however, like to discuss some other things with you if you do not mind," the dwarf asked kindly, but Sarah got the impression refusal was not an option.

"Of course," she replied eagerly, wanting to get to the reason behind the strange meeting and busywork.

"First and foremost, casting is a wonderful, but very dangerous gift."

"Casting?"

"Magic. Magic is the word you'd be more familiar with, although casting is the closest thing to the correct word this language has."

Sarah's voice was now sprinkled with excitement as she replied, "Oh, yes! Please, do."

Dr. Walker smiled and launched into lecture mode. "There is, of course, the tried-and-true method of waiting for one to accidentally use magic, but that has proven rather unideal for detecting if one is in tune with the arcane flow." Dr. Walker's russet eyes twinkled as she reached into her loose robes.

From the robes, she pulled an orb roughly the size of a Rubik's cube, wrapped in a thin cloth. The sphere was crystalline and transparent, but as she unwrapped the cloth and placed it in her naked palm, it began to glow with a warm reddish-orange light that bathed the room with a firelight effect.

The dwarf's old eyebrows climbed knowingly up her forehead at the sight. "As you can see, this little device of mine glows when in contact with my skin. This is simply called an arcane orb. Not very creative, but it doesn't do much to warrant a more original name."

She paused, staring over the glowing orb into Sarah's eyes. "Tell me, Sarah Young, how is it you survived the basilisk unarmed and largely unscathed?"

Curious as she was about the orb, Sarah realized she hadn't gone into the details of what happened with anyone other than an initial sort of debriefing with Steven and Peter. Memories of Shadowfang eating the two watchmen and the bloody chase through the town flooded her mind.

A shiver went down her spine despite being warm, safe indoors, and rested. Still, the dwarf's presence was somehow comforting, so she slowly walked her through her experience. It took some time to get through as Dr. Walker continued to coax details out of her, and the trauma of the event made certain parts difficult to recount.

But the dwarf was patient and kind, despite a barely suppressed excitement. This made talking through it much easier for Sarah. Dr. Walker was especially interested in the final moments of her confrontation, in which, she'd managed to blow up the flour.

"There must have been a gas leak or something. I really didn't expect it to do that much, and I honestly have no idea how I survived," she said, taking a sip of water and eyeing Dr. Walker's contemplative expression.

The orb in front of her continued to glow with that soft orange light. Sarah waited patiently as the dwarf took longer than seemed necessary to ponder her retelling of events. At long last, the dwarf spoke again, tapping a finger gently on the orb. "Would you like to hold it?"

Sarah shrugged and extended her hands hesitantly. The broad-nosed woman smiled and dropped the orb into Sarah's outstretched fingers. Her hands dropped a bit, expecting weight to the strange ball, but it weighed less than an egg despite being twice the size. The orb was warm in her hands, she could feel it emitting a soft pulse.

As it rested in her grip, it began to change; the orange glow fading until, at last, the orb was once again clear. Still warm, the pulsing sensation increased, and then suddenly, the glow returned to green, then shifted to blue, purple, then red, and back to orange.

Dr. Walker let out a small gasp, her eyebrows getting more exercise, furrowing and unfurrowing as the gears in her mind worked overtime watching the orb shift through colors. At last, the orb again became void of color. When it remained that way, she extended a hand and snatched it from Sarah, pulling it back so it vanished into her robes. Sarah watched the spot where it vanished, wishing the woman had kept it out. But the warmth and the pulse seemed to remain in her hands, spreading through the rest of her body.

With an amused twinkle in her eyes, Dr. Walker spoke up. "Different glows indicate different abilities or arcane proficiencies. Magic, in its most basic form, is simply described as energy manipulation. There is a wide variety of magic that can be used. Dwarves and elves can learn to use almost all of them and focus on our preferred school of magic to specialize in, known as casting." She paused, taking a sip of her tea. "Are you following so far?"

Sarah nodded silently, the full implication of what the dwarf was saying dawning on her. She stared down at her warm tingly hands, still wrestling with what was so clearly happening.

"It is different for humans. Your people are limited, first and foremost, by the fact that only a certain percentage of you can even tap into magic at all, and those that can, usually, must master a castology before they can begin to learn any others. The orange glow the orb gave off is indicative of enhancement-style casting, which can vary dramatically depending on the user."

But it gave off multiple colors...

It was too late to point out, though. Dr. Walker was in lecture mode now, and there was no sign she was stopping. Thankfully, she seemed to read Sarah's mind. "However, I have never seen it cycle through the colors like that. It may be broken or altered by the Therin-Selu, but I think it's more likely it is a sign that you have great potential for the use of magic."

She paused to take another sip of tea. "Tell me, Sarah, before the Shattering, did you suffer from any form of disability or abnormality?"

If it's broken, then I don't. That'd be simpler, yes, but when was the last time things were simple?

She didn't have to think long on this, but her reply was distracted. "I'm a hemophiliac, and I mean, my vision has always been terrible, so I've always worn glasses... but I think I need a new prescription, because they haven't been working very well." She removed her glasses and turned them over in her hands. "In fact, come to think of it, I've been seeing better without them, honestly," Sarah explained. She felt as though the old woman's eyes were a telescope into her mind the way she stared at her. Sarah looked down at the healed cuts on her arms. "I should have bled out."

"Consider yourself blessed. The side effects of Therin-Selu on humanity have been, in all honesty, cruel, as unintended as they were." Dr. Walker leaned back in her chair, fiddling with her own glasses. She seemed ancient. How old, Sarah couldn't tell, but it was like looking at an archaic tree that refused to die.

"I'm sorry, Therin-Silu?"

"An ancient, powerful spell cast to remove all magic from Earth. Quite an interesting one, too." She paused. "I've noticed your habit of taking notes. It is only fair to warn you, should you attempt to write the words of this particular spell, you will find yourself incapable of spelling it consistently. I was told it was a strange side effect of its incredible power. But I later learned that was not entirely true, as it can be written out correctly, but only with the proper runes."

Sarah nodded slowly, not sure how else to respond to the idea.

The dwarf shook her head slightly, as if trying to clear it of water. "A topic for another time. As I was saying, you may hear me refer to magic as the arcane flow. That flow is in the air, all around us. It creates its own creatures, and they tend the world." A faraway look took hold of her, pressing her wrinkles together, compounding them into more lines.

"Surely you've felt the change in the air since the Shattering. Her gaze returned to Sarah, but she didn't wait for an answer. "As I said, humanity has always been unique in their connection to magic. The reason for this is a story of some debate, but that is for another time. For now, there are some things you should understand. First, you are not to use it again without my supervision, under any circumstances. You could end up killing not only yourself but everyone around you if you do. Is that understood?" This time she did wait.

"So, the magic fixed my eyes, and cured me?"

"Yes. Among other things."

I can use magic. She's sure of it. It makes sense. How else could I have survived? She nodded her understanding. "Yes, ma'am," Sarah replied, not eager to use it again with or without the dwarf's supervision. Her thoughts wrestled with her miraculous cure and the knowledge that not only did magic exist but that she could use it.

Dr. Walker pursed her lips, her brows furrowing as she chose her words carefully. Sarah got the faint sense that the dwarf was holding something back, but she dared not pry further; her head was already reeling with the information provided.

Walker came to a mental conclusion before continuing their conversation. "Secondly, those who can cast among the human race are strongly bound to its energy. Being cut off from magic had…" She stalled, searching for the correct word. "…consequences. What humanity came to call disabilities or impairments. Essentially, your bodies attempted to compensate for the absence of magic without being aware it was missing. Some, like Captain Blair, have been, in one way or another, able to overcome these disadvantages, and humanity has made incredible strides without the use of magic to compensate for the differences. Your now unnecessary glasses are one such example."

Captain Blair has magic, too? Sarah's head thrummed as she processed what she'd just been told. "So… now that it's back, magic that is… Disabilities are going to start disappearing?"

Dr. Walker frowned sadly. "I do not know. It is possible. It seems to be the case with you two. But you've also both used magic under extremely strenuous conditions — hardly a controlled test. Presently, I can only speculate what might happen." She scowled — a scary expression for one so tiny. "Unfortunately, my memory isn't what it used to be. Dwarves don't usually live as long as I have, and I fear my age is finally catching up with me."

Sarah felt light-headed, a cold sensation settling in her stomach. So much had already changed, and now magic was real? Something dawned on her: *the list!* They'd been compiling lists of the city's occupants. One of those lists was specifically in regard to people who would need special provisions due to disabilities. Sarah looked back at the dwarf and saw the list in her hand.

"Come to think of it," the old voice interrupted her thoughts, "there aren't nearly as many potential casters in this town as I'd hoped." She seemed to have forgotten Sarah was there.

Sarah watched as the dark-skinned woman found a piece of paper she'd been writing on in some foreign language. As the block-shaped letters were carried across the page, Dr. Walker continued to mumble to herself. The words morphed into a language as foreign to Sarah as the writing.

"Any questions, Miss Young?" the old woman asked without looking up.

"I… Are you sure I have magic?" Sarah asked, still not quite believing it.

Dr. Walker nodded, pausing her writing to look down her nose at the girl. "Yes, quite sure. Tomorrow your lessons will begin. You have had a long day, though, so I think getting what rest you can would be prudent."

Sarah nodded and quietly excused herself, trying not to appear eager to depart. With a sigh, she made her way up the stairs to the second floor of the headquarters. There, Sarah found the room she'd been assigned to earlier in the evening. Lost in thought, she paused outside her small room.

As she stood there, thoughts swirling chaotically around her head, she noticed a light under her neighbor's door. Straining to listen, she heard strange muffled clicking noises coming from within. Curiosity and an urge to not be alone got the better of her, and Sarah's pale, shaky knuckles rapped softly on the door.

Sarah's arm was raised for a second knock when the door was almost torn off its hinges. In the frame stood a giant wielding a long blade. A scream caught in Sarah's throat as her eyes met his. Those green eyes were as wide as they could get. Sarah had never seen a more panicked expression on a face than the one on Steven's at that moment.

The scream in her throat retreated to make room for laughter, taking hold of her, rising like a geyser from her stomach. That laugh grew stronger as Steven fumbled to hide the blade behind his back, as if removing it from sight could erase the memory of its existence.

Sarah doubled over, shaking with laughter at the bumbling giant in front of her. It felt good. For an instant, the pain and misery hounding her were pushed aside by mirth. She couldn't remember the last time she'd laughed, especially this hard. She didn't care, all she could do was laugh as it took control of her being.

Steven joined in, unable to separate himself from the contagious hilarity. His booming chuckles mixed with her soft giggles, which only encouraged each other, and were amplified by their attempts to keep quiet in the lateness of the night.

At last, their mirth sputtered to an end. Sarah wiped a tear from her eye and caught sight of the room behind Steven's bulk. It contained a well-lit desk full of small tools and a speaker that pumped soft electronic music throughout the small space. Her stomach hurt with the beautiful pain of prolonged, endured laughter.

"I'm sorry about the knife. I didn't know you were here. I didn't think that was a knock. I figured something was wrong," Steven explained, a hint of panic undercutting his voice. "Everything is all right, isn't it?"

"Oh, yes, everything's fine. Peter insisted Doctor Walker and I stay here at your headquarters for the time being," Sarah replied. "Sorry if I disturbed you. I didn't know I had a neighbor, and I heard some strange sounds." Sarah's voice was warm and strong. She felt comfortable talking to Steven; more so than she did with the rest of SNW, or most people these days.

"Ah, sorry. I'll keep it down. I was trying to figure out Shadowfang's scales. You see, they're nothing like normal reptilian scales. Here, let me show you," he said as he turned his back to her and meandered back into the room.

Sarah smiled. "That would be delightful."

Steven left the door open and allowed her to enter the flat as he made his way to a small kitchen area. Sarah noted his quarters were much larger than hers, which consisted only of a bedroom and bathroom.

"Is tea all right? I have lavender, pomegranate-blueberry, and earl grey," he said as he poked his head back around the corner.

"Lavender please," Sarah replied as she sat down in an oversized office chair next to a workbench and computer desk with two monitors. She noticed images sliding across the idle screen of the monitors of a young Steven surrounded by four girls of varying ages who shared his eyes, nose, and hair. "Is this your family?"

Steven glanced up from the tea he was pouring. "Oh, yeah. Those are my sisters," he said as he made his way over with a warm cup of tea, which he handed carefully to her. As soon as the drink was in her hands, he sat down at the workbench and waved her towards a microscope. "Have a look at this," he said as a prelude to the lengthy explanation of the scale under the microscope.

Together they talked deep into the night. Sarah felt truly warm and safe. For the first time since the Shattering, everything felt normal.

THE KID

Peter peeled his gaze away from the wall of framed photos he'd been staring at. The retraining graduation pictures contained dozens of other SNW agents. Whatever your role was in the paramilitary organization, you were required to go through the basic military training SNW provided. With few exceptions, this was retraining, as the company hired vets.

Thirty-five of those vets he'd seen combat with, only five of which were here in town now. Ten were dead — killed in service before all this. Seven he knew of were in Atlanta, last he'd heard: Leefield, Ian, Alex, Tanner, Alan, Daniel, and Courtney. The rest of the faces on the wall he knew, some better than others, but hadn't fought alongside. *I need to find out if they're alive. It was pure luck I was here when this all started, or maybe the opposite…*

"Morning, Blair. Rough night?" William, the man tasked with the training on Peter's mind, asked. His white teeth broke through dark brown lips as he set a small plate of steaming gray food on the table in front of Peter. "You look like you slept on a bed of rusty nails."

"You could say that," Peter said as he stifled a yawn. Three days had passed since the dream, and he'd barely slept since. "That's the only kind of night we get these days, though, isn't it?"

"At least you're getting some sleep. Jere's been struggling. He misses his shows. Really, kids his age just need routine, I think. Hard to have that these days," William said as he paused near Peter's table.

Peter nodded. "Speaking of, where are the rascal and your wife?"

William smiled. "Up in my office. She finally got him to pass out, and I wasn't about to wake either of them up. I'm lucky enough to have them." He winked. "Might as well do what I can to keep them happy."

Peter nodded again. "Yeah, why not keep them at the Igloo, though? Seems like it might be more comfortable."

William's face took on a concerned expression. "My bar's half rubble. Did no one tell you?" he replied as he continued to pass out breakfasts.

Peter's heart fell. "No, I haven't been over that way yet," he said as disappointment soured his tone.

As their conversation reached a natural end, Peter looked around the room for the first time since sitting down. He noticed a man on his phone, who scrolled aimlessly through a stagnant feed of some kind. He put the phone down, then picked it up again a few seconds later. *Old habits die hard. People are adjusting quickly, though, especially around here.*

His gaze moved on, and he spied Sarah Young, the girl from the snake attack, next to Steven, where they were discussing one of his current projects. She stood out like a beagle in a pack of wolves. *They're getting on well, but what is she doing here?* he thought as he listened in on the conversation.

"It just doesn't make sense," Steven was saying. "We got one short signal before it happened, then everything froze. That's not even how the internet works. We shouldn't be able to access any information if we can't send information." Steven was on a roll, and Sarah was scribbling in a small worn notebook.

Steven waved an arm, and Peter spied Dr. Walker at their table, mostly hidden by Steven's enormous form. Their presence was making some people noticeably uncomfortable, but with Steven with them, that discomfort wavered and died. *Well, that's an interesting group. I'll have to figure out what they're all up to later, not the focus now.* Peter thought as he noticed Simon making his way over.

William passed Simon a plate of the unrecognizable gray meat and sides as the medic sat down. Peter took a bite and nodded good morning to Simon, his squad's combat medic. The gray meat bit back with a tangy spiciness and a slight chicken taste. *Looks like his promotion to chief medical officer is going to have to wait.*

Peter pulled the fork slowly from his mouth. "William, is this what I think it is?"

William grinned a pearly smile and tapped the side of his broad dark nose. "Fried basilisk. We got our portion of the cut this morning, and I figured I'd try it for breakfast. Got a bite to it, doesn't it?"

Simon paused, fork halfway to his mouth. Then he slowly lowered the fork to his plate, brushed the meat off, and took a scoop of grits.

Peter smiled. Simon hadn't made a big deal about it, but he sympathized with the townsfolk who argued against eating meat from an intelligent, speaking creature. While the morality of it was most people's focus, Simon's concerns were in regards to what effects such meat would have on the body.

Dr. Walker, though, assured everyone it would be ripe with nutritional value and that, if they thought it unethical, starvation was their prerogative.

Peter continued to smile to himself and called out to the other table, "Speaking of Shadowfang, Steven, will you be helping with the wall today? You did prove yourself quite adept at lifting and carrying while I was *charming* that basilisk."

"You're really calling it by its name?" questioned Simon.

"You would if it had introduced itself to you, Simon. Besides, that seems to be what's expected of things like this by Doctor Walker," Peter replied.

Simon nodded casually and finished off his plate, choosing unknown side effects over malnutrition.

Steven, having politely waited for them to finish, addressed Peter's question. "I was planning on it, actually. From what Doctor Walker was telling me before you joined us, she's taken quite an interest in the wall's development. She wants to start incorporating magic into our defenses. I'd like to learn how that works."

He's taken to the idea of magic shockingly well.

"And what are your plans for the day, Miss Young?" Peter asked Sarah.

"Well, training with Doctor Walker…" She trailed off, looking contemplative.

Peter would have pressed her for more information, but Dr. Walker cut in. "I'm also planning to examine the pits before they're filled in for a close inspection of what happened," The dwarf said.

From another table, Jenni pipped in. "Whose idea was it to do that? Should we really be filling them in after we found them decorated like that?"

William offered an explanation. "Doctor Gibson's idea. He thinks it'll help morale. People are scared of the pits now."

"What happened with the pits?" Simon inquired.

"You haven't heard?" Sarah replied in disbelief.

Simon pursed his lips, shrugged, and shook his head lightly.

"Something got into them. Cleaned all the bones. I'm talking unnaturally clean. Reorganized them, too, like they'd all been laid to rest. That's not the strangest part, though. A whole lot of flowers and vines sprang up overnight decorating them too. It's a haunting sight," William explained as he sat down to eat.

"Doctor Gibson, is that the guy who calmed everyone down about the girl they found?" asked Peter.

"Sure is," William replied. "There's talk that they're tryna put the brother in charge of the council. He's already on it, despite his protests. You know he's put himself in charge of examining all new arrivals? They're still trickling in here and there, hungry and full of crazy stories about things they've seen in the woods. Some are telling tales stranger than what happened at the pit."

By now, everyone other than William was finished eating. "Who all was selected for the council? I've been too busy to keep up with politics," Peter said, "and it seems like that got put together really quickly, all things considered."

Sarah flipped through her notes before she answered. "Doctor Gibson, Pamela Fritz, Donna Meents, Lieutenant Rory… That's all so far."

"Is it just me, or is it weird how quickly all this is coming together?" Peter began but was interrupted as Dr. Walker stood loudly to her feet. "Sorry to interrupt, but Sarah and I really must be on our way," she said as she led the younger lady towards the exit of the Grant Building.

Where was I going with that? Peter wondered for a moment, but his train of thought was already derailed and moving on. Still trying to retrace his thoughts, he stood and collected his plate.

Simon followed Peter into the kitchen, where they added their dishes to the pile. *Good. Conserving water — nothing wrong with that.*

"Peter, you should go to the filling. I know you want to get things done, but it would be good for the town for you to be there," he said in his usual quiet voice. "At least for one of them."

"They should be doing it all at once. Multiple services are a security risk," Peter replied.

"That may be, but people need to take some time to grieve. It's healthy. Funerals help people move on," Simon said, his head tilted slightly and eyebrows raised.

"Fine. I'll go." Peter leaned against the doorframe to the kitchen, then changed the subject. "What are your thoughts on Gibson, Simon?"

"He's a good doctor and a better man. You'll want him on your side when all this is over."

"Honestly, I doubt I'll still be around when all this is over," Peter said as he eyed the pile of dirty dishes and clenched his jaw.

"You going to run away? That's not like you," Simon jested.

"No, but if what's out there," Peter gestured in the direction of the woods, "is anything like what we've encountered or have been hearing about from refugees, I…" he trailed off.

Simon's gaze was kind. "Peter, I've seen you survive things no one has any right to survive. If anyone is gonna make it through this, it's you."

Peter's jaw clenched. "You know better than anyone that's not what I want."

"It's not, but it may be what other people need."

William appeared behind where Peter stood in the door frame and cleared his throat. "*Ahem.* I know you like to hide in tight places when it comes to snakes, but I cooked him. He can't hurt you."

Peter chuckled and let William into the kitchen. "I wanted to talk to you, William. I was gonna do this myself, but some things have come up. Who's on OP duty today?"

"That'd be Jessica, Eduardo, Smith, and... Let me see now... O'Cleary. Yeah, O'Cleary, since Connors asked to be relieved — wanted to attend the filling. He lost his girlfriend to the Shattering, ya know."

Peter rubbed the stubble on his face. "He hadn't told me that. Here's what I want you to do — there's a young boy named Shawn. He's got deep tan skin — maybe part Native American, part African-American? He's on the watch-volunteer list. Shouldn't be hard to find. Put him with O'Cleary at the southern observation. It'll be good for him. He's got a keen eye, and that's probably the safest of the outliers for him to be at."

"Yes, sir. Will do."

"Thank you. Simon, I'll see you at the filling." With that, Peter departed to tend to his never-shrinking list of errands.

Shawn wiped the sweat from his brow as he thought back on how he'd wound up in a broken car outside the safety of the city walls with an Irishman. Al had taken him to see Peter and the dwarf they called Dr. Walker. He remembered walking into the building he'd heard people jokingly refer to as the Igloo or Icebox.

There had been security — the same man he sat in the car with now. He'd known Al and waved him in without question. It did not take them long to find Peter once inside. He was standing over a flat video-screen table, a black sword strapped to his back and Dr. Walker by his side.

They were looking over a map of the city displayed on the screen with a rendered wall encircling it. With them was an enormous blonde man he later learned was named Steven, who, despite the dwarf's presence, made everyone look short.

Peter paused mid-sentence at the sight of them entering the room. "Al, good to see you. I assume everything went well at the pits. Who's this?"

"This here is Shawn, and he's got something to tell ya." Shawn noticed Al's accent had become drastically less invasive. Peter waited in silence for Shawn to speak, but Shawn found himself at a loss for words.

"Shawn, is it? What is it you need to tell me?" His voice was kind; not what Shawn had expected from a man who'd killed three people in the street to set an example.

"Please, if it wasn't important, Al wouldn't have brought you. You may not believe you saw it — there's been a lot of that going around — but I promise you, nothing is outside the realm of possibility anymore."

Shawn nodded, summoning the courage to speak to the man who'd helped slay a giant snake. "A face. I saw a face. Out in the woods."

"Go on." This time it was the dwarf who encouraged him to speak. There was a look in her eyes that made Shawn wonder if she knew what he was about to say.

"It, it…" he swallowed. "It was made of leaves. Just floating leaves. And it was watching me — well, us. I don't know. It was watching the city, maybe. But it saw me, and it smiled, then it disappeared."

Peter's eyes turned icy. "Professor?"

Dr. Walker was grinning. "Nothing to worry about, Peter. It's only a dryad. There are a few of them keeping watch around the city at my request. I asked them to remain unseen. Shawn, would you come here quick?" She motioned him to her with a surprisingly tattoo-covered old hand.

Shawn walked toward her, and Peter stepped out of his way. She was wearing robes. He hadn't taken much notice of it, but they reminded him a bit of Greek robes he'd seen in history books. From her robes, she drew an orb glowing with soft light.

"Shawn, would you hold this for me." She offered it to him graciously. Shawn looked back to Al, his only anchor in this sea of unfamiliarity. Al looked as confused as possible but shrugged and nodded for Shawn to do as he was told. Shawn took the orb and turned it over in his hands. The glow faded away, and all that remained was a transparent orb, strangely warm in his hands.

Dr. Walker nodded as she spoke. "He is not a caster, but he does possess keen eyes and the wisdom of youth. We would do well to have this boy's eyes facing outwards rather than down to the ground."

"I take it from the ash and smell you've been working the pits, Shawn," Peter said, the kindness returning to his voice.

"Yes, sir."

"Family?"

"Gone, sir."

Peter grimaced. "You're a brave man, Shawn. Thank you for telling us this. How would you feel about joining the watch?"

"You mean at the wall?"

"Yes. If the Professor thinks your eyes are wasted digging pits, I'm inclined to agree with her."

"I… Is it dangerous?'

Peter placed a hand on his shoulder. "No more dangerous than anywhere else right now, Shawn. Perhaps even safer than most. I won't ask it of you if you do not want it, but you may have the ability to make a difference between life and death for someone. That is the risk we all take to protect each other. You may take time to consider it if you so choose."

"No. I'll do it. If it'll help, I'll do it."

"Good." Peter said with a soft smile. "Al can make sure you're shown to the right people. And if you see anything else, I want to know immediately. You understand?"

"Yes, sir."

⟵ — 11 — ⟶

UNEXPECTED VISITORS

S hawn hadn't seen Peter since his new assignment. Sure, he had heard plenty of talk about him, and sometimes, it was more heated than Shawn thought it should be. He'd wondered if the captain forgot about him, but then O'Cleary found him and told him he was partnered with him at one of the tints. It took him a moment to realize the tints were how the SNW members referred to the tinted-windowed vehicles they'd strategically placed outside the city walls to watch the roads for refugees or invaders.

That was where he was now. He sat next to a fierce-looking man with an Irish accent who kept complaining to himself about being stuck with "some scrawny kid," as if Shawn couldn't hear him.

"Oi, lad, you better not be a blindin' dosser. You hear me? If I tell you to leg it, you leg it. Got that?"

Shawn stared at him blankly. "What?"

"No acting the maggot, all right, boyo?" He stared pointedly at the flare gun Shawn was fiddling with in his left hand.

"Oh, okay." Shawn set the flare on the center console. *I can't understand a word this guy says.*

"Does your mom know you're out here? Someone owes her a favor and think this'd be the safest place for you?"

Shawn wanted to ignore him and just sit in silence until this was over. Then he could get back behind the walls. He had not expected this kind of reception after his talk with Peter. *I mean, I'm not some hero. I just saw something in the woods. But this guy won't get off my case.*

"Say again?"

O'Cleary's eyes narrowed in mild annoyance. "Your mom, lad. Did she get you out here? Course, they'd stick me with a waine."

Shawn stared him dead in the face, noticing the strange white patch in the Irishman's short hair. "My *mom* is dead. I watched her bleed to death. She lasted longer than my dad, though. He didn't even get to bleed. Get off my case."

O'Cleary went whiter than his already pale complexion. "I… I'm sorry, lad. I assumed you… Well… Never mind." The apology was heartfelt. O'Cleary was obviously upset with himself for his comments.

"Well, you know what they say about assumptions."

"What's that?"

"Oh, just something my dad used to say. Ya know, it makes an ass out of you and me."

O'Cleary's face broke into a massive grin as he guffawed. "Ha! Your da was a smart one, wasn't he?"

Shawn hadn't thought much about his parents. At least, he'd pushed them out of his mind every time they slipped into his thoughts. A tear slid down his cheek and met a smile. It was a strange feeling.

He missed his parents, but it was good to think about them in a context other than their gory death. As he tried to conjure more happy memories, Shawn stared down the road they were supposed to be watching. "Yeah, he was," he replied as O'Cleary sat there still chuckling to himself.

Movement at the edge of view caught Shawn's attention. Two shapes were moving along the road towards them.

"Shut up!"

The laugh caught in O'Cleary's throat and died. His face went stoic. "See something?"

"Yeah, two somethings. There." Shawn pointed down the road. Two shapes were barely visible, topping the crest of a hill a way off. There was still plenty of time before they got close enough to distinguish.

"Good eye," O'Cleary said. "Use your scope." He gestured to the weaponless scope Shawn had been given. O'Cleary cracked his door open slowly, rifle in hand, looking down the rifle's scope to get a better view.

The sweat on Shawn's brow would have increased if not for the open door letting the cold air in. He recognized the beings for what they were from the briefing he'd received before being given the assignment. *Dwarves*, he thought, but knowing this in no way lessened the shock.

Down the road, the pair of dwarves trundled along at a surprising speed towards the city. The pair each wore an ill-fitting fur hat with large ear flaps and a red star stitched into the front. On their broad faces, each sported beards; one was a foot long and just as wide, with a round bushy shape that reminded Shawn of a fluffy dog.

It was the biggest beard the boy had ever seen. Its only maintenance seemed to be the trimming of the edges to make sure it retained a round shape.

Shawn wondered if the dwarf was wearing the back end of a surfboard covered in brown fur. This same fellow also wore a large green coat, somewhat haphazardly cut down in size to fit him.

Shawn blinked to make sure he wasn't seeing things: glint from within the coat caught his attention. He focused his gaze on the dwarf's chest. There, he saw that the short being wore chunky bits of plated armor beneath the jacket. "O'Cleary, they're wearing armor. Knights' armor."

"I see it," O'Cleary replied quietly, his accent not as strong as before.

A cloak of worry settled on his shoulders. Shawn refocused on the second dwarf. This dwarf was the slightly slimmer of the two. He wore the same hat but not a coat like his travel companion; instead, his armor was adorned with a red scarf fashioned into a cape covered in a stylized floral pattern.

The beard that decorated his face was a few shades darker than the bushy one, but much better kempt and with streaks of white and gray. It was formed into a distinctive, tremendous mustache pulled into two fine points. An unattached, trimmed goatee accompanied the mustache, forming an impressively long Van Dyke-style beard resting over ruddy cheeks. Clearly, this dwarf was the older of the pair.

"What do we do?" Shawn asked, trying to keep the panic in his voice down. *At least there's only two of them. Could have been more of them, or worse, another giant snake.*

"Radio," O'Cleary whispered, his eyes not moving from the target.

Shawn picked up the radio on the center console. The light was off, and no sound came when he pressed the speak button. Turning the knob at the top did nothing to help. Trying to keep his voice from shaking, Shawn said, "It's dead."

O'Cleary's curse was mangled by his accent beyond Shawn's comprehension, but the meaning was obvious.

Shawn grasped the flare gun in his hands. It was surprisingly light, he realized as he dug a purple-labeled flare out of the small bag they'd been stored in. Loading it was a simple task and, seconds later, the flare clicked shut, ready to be fired. Shawn paused, waiting for further instructions.

"Go on. No time to waste." O'Cleary's voice was level, his focus unwavering from the oncoming dwarves. Shawn stepped out of the SUV into the cold air. His hand trembled slightly from both fear and adrenaline. He pointed the flare to the sky and pulled the trigger. It was louder than he expected. The signal shrieked upward, tearing over the treetops and exploding with purple smoke visible for miles.

CHEEKIE BREEKIE

At the Grant Building, Peter held the chunk of basilisk meat out to the dog Hauch. "Good boy. That's a good boy, Hauch," Peter said with a calm reaffirming tone directed at the Belgian Malinois with fading dyed black hair.

"*Plutz!*" Peter barked the command, and Hauch did as he was told, dropping low to the ground. "Good."

Then more softly, Peter said, "*Kriechen.*" Hauch's ears twitched at the soft sounds of his voice, and he tilted his pointed head slightly before crawling slowly and silently forward on his belly until he reached Peter, still keeping his head low.

Peter knelt next to the dog, scratching him behind the ears and glancing across the room to Hauch's trainer, Jenni.

She nodded, smiling. "He's been working hard lately."

"Hauch, *steh,*" Peter said, and Hauch rose silently to all fours. "*Setzen.*" And like the good dog he was, Hauch sat promptly on the ground.

"Good boy, Hauch. Good boy." Peter patted his head and then tossed him the meat at last, which the dog caught eagerly in a set of sharp fangs.

Hauch only enjoyed the treat for a moment before dropping it on the ground and signaling a warning with his stance to Peter. A growl begged to escape from the dog's bared fangs, but he kept silent. *Atta boy.*

Peter, knowing a door stood behind his back, stepped quickly so as to be able to intercept anything coming through the door. Just in time, the door burst open and a man stumbled in.

Peter recognized the man as Rick Gardiner. Rick's face contorted with a look of horror at the sight of the murder-ready dog growling at him. The look weakened as he met Peters' eyes, but Rick did not venture farther into the room while the large dog menaced him.

Peter could smell the sunscreen on the pale man from several feet away. *Probably what alerted Hauch to him,* Peter realized.

Rick's bright yellow soccer jersey made him easily identifiable at a distance. It fit him well despite his build being of one who had until recently, been scrawny. Rick spoke as though the two of them had been in conversation for some time, his words morphed by the strange accent that had resulted from growing up in Australia before spending a dozen years in the southern US.

"Neveh seen anything quite like them before, Pete. Can I call you Pete?" he continued despite the puzzled expression Peter granted him. "Pair of hobo-lookin' bogans, I'm telling you."

"Gardiner!" Peter's voice cut through the man's incomprehensible tirade. Rick stopped mid-sentence, not daring to speak. "What are you talking about?" Peter asked, trying not to grit his teeth.

"Well, it's dwarves, Pete. A pair of them. At the front gate, no less. But they won't let 'em in. There's all kinds of yelling and shouting going on, and they're armed, Pete, sir." He paused at that. "O'Cleary sent me to fetch you, sir, and bring you back to the gate."

Before Rick could go on, Peter was out the door and making his way to the parking lot. Rick followed quickly, explaining the situation.

"A crowd had started gathering when I left, too. Not sure what they're gonna do."

Peter felt for the sword on his back. Finding it there, he grabbed a set of keys from a box by the front door. Gardiner continued following, apparently done with his description.

Knowing Jenni would be making sure the rest of the watch was on high alert, Peter continued toward the exit. After exiting the building and reaching the parking lot, Peter turned to Rick.

"Go find Doctor Walker at the pits. Tell her what's happening and get her to the gates. Now!"

Rick's head jerked up and down in understanding. Eyeing the man, Peter mounted his bike, which roared to life before tearing down the road toward the gates. A siren cleared anyone out of his path that might have impeded him.

It took him a mere four minutes to arrive at the gates, where a restless crowd had gathered. Peter practically jumped from his bike after parking it. The whispers began before he'd even parked, his approach sending ripples through the crowd. Many of the faces bore angry expressions of those not bothering to disguise their disapproval as he approached.

Others let out exclamations of excitement, and for a moment, Peter feared some might start clapping. His presence thickened the already palpable tension. Despite his mixed reception, the crowd parted for him as he rushed at the semis that formed the gate.

As Peter emerged from the crowd, he heard swearing and shouting from the far side the trucks blocked from his line of sight. *Definitely O'Cleary.* There were other voices, too; the words in a language he did not recognize.

A man Peter didn't recognize clambered out of one of the semis at his approach, and a hand extended to Peter, signaling him to stop. Peter noted the rifle in one hand but gave no indication he'd stop.

The man stepped sideways and planted himself firmly in front of Peter. "Hold it right there, Blair. I can't let you pass. This is a matter for the council."

Peter stared at the man in disbelief, realizing the tanned, oily-looking man who stood a head taller than him must've been one of the volunteers enlisted by the police. *I don't have time for this.*

"Get out of my way."

A look of defiance Peter knew all too well passed over the man's face. "Or what? You'll kill me? In front of all these people with your sword?" The man smiled. There was no longer any pretext of civility in his voice. His chest puffed up, and Peter let him slide his free hand over, so both gripped his rifle. "The way I see it, Blair, I'm armed and following orders, and all you've got is a sword, and it seems to me like you might be about to disobey the law."

The man, of course, was mistaken. Peter did have his firearm; it was merely well concealed but in no way inaccessible. Half a dozen ways to dispatch the man passed through Peter's mind before he spoke, grinning with arms raised in a placative gesture.

"What's your name?"

"Gunter Brown," he replied.

"Well, Mister Brown, I have no intention of hurting you, but if those two out there are, in fact, dwarves, then they could be as dangerous as the basilisk, and there's two of them. If you think you can handle whatever it is they're capable of, be my guest. Otherwise, step aside. Maybe I'll get myself killed. You won't have to worry about dealing with me anymore."

Gunter clenched his jaw, eyes darting, the sound of the dwarves' raised voices behind him. Finally, the frazzled man deflated. He turned without a word and signaled the drivers to open the gate.

The semi's engines grumbled to life, causing several surprised sounds to issue forth from the other side of the trucks as well as indistinguishable shouts from O'Cleary. Peter remained where he was as the trucks came to a stop.

Then, into the city walked two dwarves, followed closely by an armed and frustrated-looking O'Cleary. The two dwarves, distracted by the trucks, took a moment to register Peter. Then the one thing he'd hoped wouldn't happen did. They drew their weapons.

"Everyone, stand down." Peter's voice cut through the air at the men and women as they raised their firearms at the dwarves. "Whatever happens, hold your fire. We don't know what they're capable of, and Doctor Walker will be here soon."

Okay. You've got the height and reach advantage. Use it. Peter calculated as he drew Galvorn from its place on his back. He kept the sword facing down, ready for a quick reaction but not in a threatening position.

The dwarves were not carrying their weapons menacingly, drawn as they were. If anything, they seemed jovial. *Then again, for all I know, that may be what they look like when they're angry.* Peter considered.

The skinnier dwarf with the well-kept beard held two identical, single-bladed battle axes by the base of their heads. His posture was relaxed down to the way he held his weapons. The younger dwarf with the sizable bushy beard carried a massive war hammer, one end rounded and the size of a bowling pin, the other a deadly spike. His stance was of a fighter, ready to battle.

This weapon concerned Peter the most. *Axes aren't too different from short swords — easier really since they can't stab. Just used for slicing. But that hammer looks made to shatter blades, and I don't know how quick he is.*

The dwarves approached, then stopped a few paces in front of him, ignoring the crowd of onlookers, most of whom had taken several steps back to make sure they were well out of reach of whatever happened next. Those among them who were armed were slower to follow suit, but a look from Peter served as a sufficient motivator.

Behind the dwarves was O'Cleary, rifle raised. At that distance, there was no way he would miss. Still, Peter suspected that somehow the gun would prove useless against the pair.

The older dwarf took another step forward and spoke in a voice that reminded Peter of bending steel. Behind him, the younger dwarf, whose face still looked to be the human equivalent of a man in his thirties, lowered his war hammer so that the spike on its back carved a large groove in the ground.

"*Zdravst-vuite,*" said the closer dwarf, which caused his mustache to wobble.

Peter blinked. "What?"

"*Zdravstvuite?*"

Russian? That sounded like Russian. Peter grasped for the only four or five phrases he knew in Russian while the other dwarf carved a wide circle around him.

"*Zdravstvuyte,*" Peter replied, playing for time. "I'm Peter. Peter Blair," he added with a finger pointed at his chest.

The dwarf blinked, a puzzled look on his face. Peter patted his chest twice with his left hand and repeated, "Peter Blair."

Understanding dawned on the dwarf: He copied the gesture and spoke again. "Cheekie." A firm smile on his face, he pointed to the dwarf carving a circle in the ground, gestured to himself, and said, "Breekie." He then continued quickly, the words no longer Russian, yet Peter couldn't help but notice the words seemed tainted by a Russian accent.

Peter looked over the dwarf's shoulder at O'Cleary for help, but his friend merely shrugged. As he did, Cheekie removed his jacket, folded it, and placed it outside the ring before returning to stand a few feet from Peter.

The dwarf with the hammer came to a stop. A perfect circle had been dug into the dirt around Peter and the dwarf with the stylized beard calling himself Cheekie. War hammer resting on the edge of the ring, its dwarf clapped his hands together, a glow shining through the sleeves over his arms. He then grasped the handle of the hammer, and a shimmer of light soared up from the circumference of the circle around them.

Peter felt a trickle of relief wash over him. Good. Just me and him then. *They're leaving the rest of them out of it. Means I don't have to hold back, but what are the stakes? My life? Their lives?* But before he could figure out an answer, the younger dwarf with the bushy beard began to speak in a raised voice, booming so all could hear. Peter recognized it as a countdown. *No time.*

The counting came to an abrupt end roughly four seconds later. The smile was gone from Cheekie's face, replaced by a dogged expression. Raising his axes into the air, he slapped them together a few times. The sound of metal on metal tightened Peter's muscles.

Peter gave him a hard look over, revealing strong sinewy arms with a spattering of blue tattoos similar to the white ones Dr. Walker had but only extending from halfway down his bicep to his shoulder with room between many of the runes — a contrast to the tattoos that decorated every inch of Dr. Walker's arms.

The dwarf's armor was now fully on display. It did not shine but was clearly well maintained. It was made of overlapping metal plates, joined by brown leather, and allowed for mobility and protection everywhere but his muscled arms. These were bare, highlighting the tattooed runes. Cheekie watched Peter back with intelligent eyes; the instant it was apparent Peter was finished, Cheekie stepped into a combat stance.

I guess that concludes negotiations.

Peter was not sure what else to do as the dwarf stood waiting, so he mirrored, raising his sword into a defensive position and bending at the knees in anticipation.

That was all it took. The dwarf struck first. Lashing out with the axes lightning fast. The move was expected but quicker than Peter would have thought possible. The strange energy he'd felt during his fight with Shadowfang was back but faint. He barely dodged the blow.

The dwarf did not give him a chance to process what happened. His lunge brought him closer to Peter, and while one ax swung furiously down at him, the other soared in from the side. The second was aimed at Peter's waist, which would bring a quick end to the fight if the blow connected. Galvorn moved freely in Peter's hand, as though pulling itself. Peter let the swing follow through with the pull of the blade, and it crashed into the first ax, then almost seemed to bounce off it as it canceled the attack and moved to stop the other.

Metal clanged against metal, as both weapons vibrated in their owners' hands. The warriors stepped back in unison. Shocked, Peter brought Galvorn up between him and the dwarf. Amazingly, it was unscathed despite the dwarfs' surprisingly powerful strikes. There was no time to examine the sword further or consider why the blow hadn't at least knocked the sword from his hand. The fight was afoot.

"Get'm, Captain Blair!" a voice called out from the crowd, followed by a rabble of supporting shouts. Peter grinned at the dwarf, hoping to unnerve him, but Cheekie only scowled back and brought the axes back around for another unnaturally quick swing. Peter parried, knocking the blades back. *Fast. He's too fast. Not good.*

Cheekie struck at Peter's legs next, forcing him to leap back. He felt the wind of the axes slicing air and just missed him. Sweat trickled down the back of Peter's neck. He barely caught another swing of the ax with the black blade of his sword. The force of the collision threw him off balance, and he stumbled backward and crashed into something hard.

Peter's head whipped around to see who'd caught him, but there was no one there. He'd collided with shimmering air rising from the edge of the circle creating a glass-like barrier. Peter cursed as he saw his opponent pressing the attack out of the corner of his eye. There was no time to concern himself with the invisible barrier.

There was a gleam in Cheekie's eyes as he came at Peter, backed against the border. Peter dove at him, crumpling into a roll, then bringing Galvorn up at the end of the roll to meet the descending ax. *Clang!* He felt the force of the blow travel all the way down his arms as the ax crashed into Galvorn. With his other hand, Peter barely managed to snag the second ax by the handle just below the dwarf's grip.

Good grief, he's strong.

Peter dropped to one knee to try and leverage his weight behind his weapon. This brought him almost eye level with the dwarf. He smelled of iron and unfamiliar sweat. The precariousness of his situation was not lost on Peter. He was trapped between his sword and the ground, with no conventional means of counterattack. Peter felt a weak warning from the energy, but he was too slow to respond. Cheekie's skull smashed into Peter's in a brutal headbutt. The attack threw conventions out the window as Peter's head spun.

His vision went blurry and red. He felt the blow down to his teeth. It muffled his senses, but not the strange energy. That energy now roared through his limbs. He embraced it, letting it guide him, listening to it as it coaxed his movements. It gave orders faster than he could respond. With an effort, Peter shoved himself backward from the dwarf, who stumbled in kind.

Peter's vision was distorted by blood running down his forehead. Luckily, Cheekie chose not to make a follow-up attack. Instead, he raised both axes in the air and made a come-at-me motion with the first two fingers on each hand. For a split second, Peter found the action odd, the dwarf's fingers taking on more of a point than one might expect.

But the observation was quickly dismissed as Peter realized the energy pulsing through Peter's body began to wane. *No. Not yet,* Peter told it. Seizing it with his mind, he rushed his opponent, depending on the energy to compensate for their skill difference. But the dwarf was turning away, his axes already lowered and his back half to Peter. He was calling something out to his companion. Too late.

Peter was in range now. Galvorn arced through the air in a downward swing. There was a cry, and the pointy-bearded dwarf began to turn around. Horror split across his face as he realized he was too late to stop the descending black blade.

Peter saw a shimmer of light at the edge of his vision, and the energy he'd been desperately holding on to spiked in his veins and warned him of something hurtling through the air towards his sword arm. Peter listened, pulling the sword out of the killing arc and throwing his body behind it.

A war hammer crashed into the sword's crossguard and hilt with a *clang*. He felt the bones in two of his fingers snap as his whole body slid back. Cheekie had lost his composure, and axes in hand he charged Peter's left. Peter ignored the throbbing in his left hand so that he could still use it to grip his sword with both hands.

Directly in front of Peter, a new challenger had entered the match. The younger dwarf with the wild bushy beard hefted his war hammer, an expression on his face Peter immediately recognized as rage. They came at him together. Hammer, ax, and knife. There was no time to think. No time for pain. He let the energy, now fully present, take control, blocking, parrying, and dodging faster than he'd ever moved in his life, knowing his survival depended on every movement.

Peter felt more than saw himself being pushed back towards the barrier and crowd behind it making incomprehensible noises. His blocks were growing slower. He was running out of strength. Peter tried to strike back in the onslaught of deadly metal.

He found an opening, and Galvorn tore a cut across the bigger dwarf's arm; too little too late. The moment of exhilaration at having drawn blood back was a shift in focus and all it took. Pain stuck at his mind, causing his grip on Galvorn to loosen. His connection to the energy fluctuated. It left Peter exposed, and Galvorn was knocked from his hand by a blow of the hammer.

The next blow was more painful. Peter felt one of the axes cut across his chest. A cold sensation soon replaced by the warmth of blood. *I'm too slow*, he thought again. Then he heard the crunch of the hammer striking his side. He felt his ribs crack; a volcano of pain erupted in his mind. There was no curse. No wail of pain. Just thoughts swimming in his head.

No, no, not yet. The thought joined the pain as he fell to the ground. The world went from red to black. Pain. All over, pumping the warning that something was wrong to his brain.

Of course, something is wrong. I've been killed. A silvery voice called into his ear through the black, *No, not yet. You will not get off that easily.* But even that faded into nothingness as his brain shut down, trying to protect him from the pain by taking his consciousness.

The crowd was silent, with one exception. At Shawn's side, O'Cleary was cursing up a furious storm, using a splattering of words Shawn did and did not recognize.

Shawn stared in horror at Peter's broken body lying at the feet of the two dwarves. Rage filled the boy's mind and consumed his being into irrational action: He charged. No plan. His only thought was to strike the dwarves as they'd struck Captain Blair before they could do any more damage to the man.

But an iron vice grasped Shawn by the shoulder, nearly tearing him off his feet, stopping his charge in its tracks. Shawn looked over his shoulder to find that his captor was Al. He hadn't even seen the man in the crowd, but there he was holding him back. Al's face was white as a sheet, but his grip didn't loosen as he met Shawn's eyes.

The dwarves slowly raised their heads from staring down at Peter, their attention turning to the crowd. Shawn saw their faces turn pale as their eyes widened and wavered over the squirming crowd as it threatened to become a mob. They exchanged worried looks and quick words.

But the mob was still in shock, undecided on how to react to their divisive, wounded defender. Having succumbed to Al's grip, Shawn watched as a short, mustached man and a heavyset woman broke from the back of the crowd and fled in terror.

Bang!

The sound of a gun being fired was unmistakable. The shot was immediately followed by a scream of pain from the crowd.

"Hold your fire," roared O'Cleary, and the crowd took a collective step back from two people.

The first person was Gunter, the man who'd refused to let Shawn and O'Cleary escort the dwarves through the gate then had argued with Peter. He was an extraordinarily normal-looking man, Shawn realized. He had greasy brown hair, a patchy short beard, and wore jeans with plaid. There was nothing out of the ordinary about him besides the rifle he had aimed directly at the dwarves. Those closest to him gave a wide berth.

Gunter looked as though he'd swallowed a live worm, and it was stuck in his throat. The rifle in his hand aimed straight at the ax-wielding dwarf's chest. "It. It. Curved. I saw it. The bullet curved!" He took a drunken step forward.

O'Cleary was at Gunter's side before Shawn realized he was moving. He'd blinked, and O'Cleary was there. The Irishman's pistol was in his hand, pressing menacingly against Gunter's temple.

"Finger off the trigger. Now," O'Cleary ordered harshly among a slurry of curses. Gunter complied, head cocked to the side under the pressure of the gun jammed against it. "That's it. Put it on the ground."

Gunter's face contorted, horror and rage doing battle for control as he went down on both knees and relinquished the gun to the ground. "They killed one of us, then they curved my shot." He was protesting in a shocked whisper that threatened to boil over into rage.

"Shawn, take the rifle," O'Cleary demanded.

Al loosened his grip reluctantly, and Shawn rushed forward to scoop up the rifle. It was then he caught sight of the second figure moaning from the crowd on the other side of the dwarves. A young blonde woman with dark skin lay on the ground in a pool of blood, not unlike the dark spot forming under Peter. Kneeling beside her was another woman about the same age, wrapping a piece of torn cloth around the bleeding wound in her arm.

Gunter stumbled forward. "I'm sorry—" he began, but O'Cleary yanked him by the back of his shirt. "You don't move, you bloody idiot, unless I say so, or I put what little brains you've got all over the ground."

O'Cleary seemed to be ignoring the dwarves for the moment. "How bad is it?" he called out to the second woman in his thick accent.

"She'll be okay," she replied as she helped the crying woman to her feet.

How did she get hit? He was aiming right at the dwarf, Shawn wondered.

Another woman's voice cut through the crowd like a whip. "Out of the way!" The crowd opened up in response to the voice and out emerged Dr. Walker with a young lady with soft oriental features holding a notebook, and a man in a yellow jersey trailing behind.

"Gonna have to ask y'all to—" the man in the jersey began in a strange accent, trailing off as he saw the dwarves and Peter.

The new dwarves' faces lit up with surprised relief at the sight of one of their own, only to fall once again under Dr. Walker's withering gaze at the scene. She barked an order at them in the same unfamiliar tongue they'd tried to speak to Shawn and O'Cleary in after Russian failed.

The pair stepped back from Peter in unison. Then they each went down on one knee, placing their weapons in front of them. There, they remained with their heads bowed.

Shawn watched as the young girl with Dr. Walker stared shakily down at Peter, who lay on the ground, drenched in his own blood. The cruel reality that the man who'd slain a basilisk was incapable of defeating two dwarves filled Shawn with dread.

Dr. Walker knelt next to Peter's body, rolling him onto his back.

"Sarah."

"I'm here," Sarah replied weakly, already with the old woman at Peter's side.

"Good. Shawn! Al! Come here," she commanded with calm control. Al snapped into action, rushing to their position, but Shawn hesitated.

"What are you doing?" O'Cleary shouted from where he stood with Gunter.

"Saving your captain's life. I do not have time to explain, Shawn."

Shawn cringed. *What do I do? She's a dwarf too.* He looked to O'Cleary for guidance.

"Go on then," O'Cleary shouted at him.

Shawn obeyed, taking up position by Peter's head, next to Sarah and then the old dwarf. Dr. Walker continued speaking in her lecturing voice. "Al, I want you to hold him down by the shoulders. No matter what happens, keep him still until I say so, and when I say so, let go immediately. Shawn, I want you to watch his face. If anything strange begins to happen, let me know. Do you both understand?"

"Yes, ma'am," Al replied politely.

"What do you mean, *strange*?" Shawn asked.

"Anything unnatural. He may twitch and grimace, but if you see a whitening of hair or the skin in his face taking on an irregular color, tell me immediately."

Shawn nodded vigorously. Not daring to ask another question as he was already confused by the answer to his first.

Dr. Walker was on to the next. "Listen to me carefully, Sarah Young. I need you to put what I've taught you to practice."

"Uh, what?" came Sarah's nervous reply. "You haven't taught me anything."

"Have I not? Dear me, it has been a busy week. Then consider this your first lesson. Reach out to and embrace the arcane flow, feel the energy, pull it into yourself. I'll walk you through the rest."

Sarah nodded, her face almost as pale as Peter's. Dr. Walker's voice was instructional, but the urgency in it could not go unheard. Shawn watched as Sarah closed her eyes and seemed to concentrate on nothing. He saw her expression soften as if she'd been searching for something in the dark and had finally found the light switch. She twitched, the color returning to her cheeks. The twitch seemed to pass through her whole body in a wave.

"More. This will take quite a bit," Dr. Walker insisted.

"I... There's so much," Sarah replied, her voice barely above a whisper, a bead of sweat running down her forehead. The old woman's frail hand grasped Sarah's firmly. There was power in the grip but no threat.

"Peter's life depends on this, Sarah. Trust me. If your hold begins to slip, focus it on me," she instructed.

"What? But you said earlier never to direct it at another person unless it was life or death."

From his position next to her, Shawn could feel warmth coming off the girl. He stared intensely down at Peter's puzzlingly peaceful face, fighting the urge to shift closer to the heat radiating from the girl.

"This is life or death, just not yours, Sarah. I don't have the fortitude to do something this serious alone anymore. I need your help. Now concentrate. Whatever you can give me, I can handle it."

Sarah took a deep breath.

Out of the corner of Shawn's eye, he saw her hand tighten in Dr. Walker's grip, and then the heat rising from her vanished.

Dr. Walker did not release her hand, though. Instead, she gripped it tighter. Her own free hand rested on Peter's bloody chest. A white rune tattooed on the back of that hand began to glow purple. The glow spread to Peter, running along his body and coalescing at his injuries.

Shawn's eyes widened. His stare focused on Peter's face, which seemed to wrinkle with pain. The man's eyes flickered open, just for a second, and Shawn thought he saw a trace of amethyst in the gray. He leaned closer, and the gray-blue eyes snapped shut.

Is that normal? It must be. She said unnatural. The purple must've been a trick of the light. Despite his focus, Shawn still could not help but see the change happening just south of Peter's face.

Slowly, the wounds began to close, knitting themselves back together. Skin grew fast over the open wound. In a few minutes, all that was left of the gash in Peter's chest was a long white scar and a torn, bloodied shirt.

Shawn blinked. Not sure what to think. All of Peter's injuries were healed, except for his middle finger on his left hand, where a bit of bone still protruded below the first knuckle. Shawn watched as the bone corrected itself, but the skin above it did not heal.

Sarah leaned forward and stared intensely at the still injured finger. Dr. Walker shook her head. "That's quite enough, Sarah," she managed to pant out, her voice suddenly exhausted.

The last of the glowing energy faded from Peter's body, and he convulsed. "Aaaagh!" Peter's eyes tore open as he let out a blood-curdling cry, jerking out of Al's grip and up into a sitting position. The sudden sound and movement scared Shawn so badly he fell on his backside, a curse of his own escaping his mouth.

Dr. Walker grasped Peter's flailing hands just in time to stop him from striking Sarah across the face. "Deep breaths. That's it, Peter. You're alright. Sarah, tend to him," Dr. Walker said, handing her his hands and rising from his side. The dwarf then turned and addressed the crowd. "Nothing to see here, everyone. Captain Blair is all right. I implore you, go on about your day. There is still much for all of you to do."

The crowd shifted. Some complied immediately, eager to be away from the scene. Some simply turned to whisper among themselves. A teenage boy stepped bravely out of the crowd toward Dr. Walker. "What about them? They attacked him! They almost killed him," he exclaimed, jabbing his finger in the air at the two dwarves who had not moved since Dr. Walker's order.

Dr. Walker's face grew stern. She looked past the boy and addressed all present, speaking loudly enough for everyone to hear her without shouting.

"These are my people. Despite what you have just seen, we are not prone to acts of violence, especially compared to other members of the faye. This was a simple misunderstanding. I assure you they meant Captain Blair no harm. Mark my words, I shall get to the bottom of the misunderstanding and deal with them myself."

She leaned on her cane. "This is a key moment for the future of mankind. Will you open your city as a safe haven for all and establish equitable relations with my people and the rest of the faye? Will the city live up to its name? Or will you cower and lash out at what you do not understand and those who do not understand you? I beg you to think carefully and choose wisely."

The boy lowered his accusing finger, looking back over his shoulder at an older boy with the same nose and eyes as him who stood close by. The older boy took a step forward. "You promise they won't try and hurt us?"

Dr. Walker smiled. "You have my word. They will help us with the troubles we are facing."

The boy nodded. "Works for me," he said, puffed up his chest, and turned to leave as he took his brother by the hand. To Shawn's surprise, the crowd followed his lead. In a few moments, only the dwarves, a few members of SNW, and a scattering of volunteer deputies remained.

Peter made to stand, and Shawn extended a hand. Peter took it, and Shawn felt a jolt run up his arm, almost as if he had touched a live wire. The sensation came and went so quickly he was unsure he'd even felt it in the first place. *I need to get more sleep,* he told himself when Peter didn't give any sign he'd felt the static electric-like zap.

Peter looked down at his ruined shirt and prodded at the fresh new scar among the blood-stained chest hair. He winced and held his left hand in front of his face, looking at the open wound on his finger with a dazed expression.

"That is to serve as a reminder of what just happened. It will heal on its own, but I want it to remind you of today. I hope that it motivates you to become stronger and wiser," Dr. Walker explained. Then, at last, she turned to the dwarves, her eyes glistening with tears. The two kneeling in front of her remained unmoved and wide-eyed.

They began to speak, and Dr. Walker held up a hand for quiet. "There has been enough confusion of words today." She raised her staff with the other hand. This hand had white runes tattooed across the back of it which lit up with a purple glow. Then she brought her staff down so that it struck the ground.

Shawn suddenly felt as though there was fluid in his ears. He swallowed, feeling his ears pop, the sensation of fluid running out of his ear brought his fingers up to wipe it away, but there was nothing to clean. Shawn's brow furrowed. *What was that?* He was about to ask when the dwarves spoke again, and he found he understood them.

"Knowledge and warmth be with you, oh, wizened one," spoke the pair in unison. "We lay our weapons to rest in your presence."

Peter's eyes narrowed at the words, and Shawn heard O'Cleary let slip a soft curse. Shawn met Peter's eyes and tilted his head. He caught his meaning and nodded. Then Peter whispered to him, a look of wonder on his face, "Sarah, too."

It was clear the dwarves were not speaking English, but Shawn and the others understood them. Breekie placed a hand on his hammer head and continued speaking. "This is Foecrusher, my father's hammer and his before him."

Cheekie went next. His twin axes, perfectly balanced, rested on their heads in the same fashion as the hammer. "This is Bloodbringer," he said proudly.

Shawn understood. He knew there were a pair of axes — two parts of a pair that received one name.

Once the weapons were introduced, there was a pause. During this lull, Dr. Walker took and examined each weapon before she placed it back in front of its owner. At last, Dr. Walker's surprisingly firm voice shattered the tension, speaking in Dwarvish.

"Who wields these armaments, and to what end?" Her words came slowly, as though each syllable was pulled from a deep well and Dr. Walker feared that the slightest mistake would cause them to fall away.

A trace of a frown passed over the ruddy-faced dwarf as she spoke, but it only lasted a fraction of a second. The dwarf with the full beard spoke first, smiling broadly, a trace of a Russian accent coloring his words.

"I am called Dalmack Fellhammer, grandson of Fraklim Fellhammer, once Fraklim Bluecoal, and my grandmother, Dronil Fellhammer. I wield Foecrusher so I might guard my companion. I seek the knowledge of combat in hopes I find new ways to defend my clan."

The smile melted away. "I ask that you and yours call me by the name Breekie, though, until a time at which a recent passing no longer brings pain."

When he finished, Dr. Walker nodded slowly and redirected her attention to the second dwarf, the older of the two. This was all the prompting the dwarf with the well-manicured beard needed. Unlike Dalmack, who's gaze was unwavering, his gaze regularly flitted between Dr. Walker and the ground. His voice, like the crunching of gravel underfoot, also contained a hint of a Russian accent.

"I am called Morind Fellhammer, son of Foirn Fellhammer, once Foirn Birchstone, and Linad Fellhammer. I carry Bloodbringer to shield what knowledge I possess until I reach Boguide, where I hope to share my knowledge of forgery in exchange for like knowledge. I also request that you and yours honor me by speaking to me as Cheekie until a time at which the mourning of a lost one no longer pains my mind."

They're using nicknames because someone died? That's weird.

Dr. Walker's eyes danced with excitement, but otherwise, her face remained expressionless. "Tell me, Fellhammers—" She paused, an eyebrow raised accusingly at the flinch Cheekie experienced at her words. "You wish to speak, Morind, son of Foirn, henceforth known to me as Cheekie?"

His reply came in a respectfully apologetic tone. "Only to add to your knowledge what little I might, wizened one."

Dr. Walker's mouth twitched, a grin attempting to seize control. Suppressing the grin, she nodded her consent.

"We are indeed both of the name Fellhammer, but there is no blood twixt us other than that shed in small combat. You see, I am of the Dargelic Mine Fellhammers, and he is from the Faldeic Mountains."

Breekie chose this point to chime in. "Grinstin Mountain to be exact. It is the widest of the four, though not the tallest. He sought out my services as a bodyguard and saw our shared names as a sign of good fortune."

Dr. Walker nodded, a smile having finally fought its way onto her face. "Very well put, unbloods. How long have you been traveling?"

The pair looked at each other, muttering back and forth while counting on their fingers. Cheekie gave the final answer. "Eight and twenty total. Ten and four on both ends of the sky's splitting."

"You have traveled more than you know for such a short time. Come. Let us rest and refresh so you may share what knowledge you have gained in your travels and that I may impart some of my own learnings upon you." She took a deep breath. "But first, I must introduce you to our host. You've met Peter Blair, son of Ann Blair and her husband, Robert Blair, who I gather you assumed was a Dashnival?"

Breekie nodded. "Yes, wizened one. He approached us at the entrance to the town and bore a Thalmein blade. It was not until after I struck the first blow and gave the sign of understanding." He raised a hand and beckoned towards himself with all four fingers as an example. "He continued his attack on me.

With the fight ended, Breekie stepped in to defend me. I offer my shame. I was enraged and retaliated too harshly."

"Dashnival?" Peter asked, his voice cracking.

Dr. Walker answered in English, "It is customary among my people to duel a warrior from a new town upon arrival. It's called the Duel of the Dashnival. This was widely known before Therin-Selu. Peter, you were the first figure to approach them with a weapon they recognized."

She paused and considered her next words. "Dashnival translated literally means ambassador of the blade. A Dashnival is a representative soldier, an honorable position in dwarven custom only given to those whose folks feel represent their ideal way of thinking or acting. The custom is to fight to the first blow, something you could not have known."

She chuckled lightly. "And, unfortunately, the gesture given by Cheekie was easily misunderstood. Had I been here, I'd have encouraged you to participate but informed you of the nature of the contest." She tapped her cane thoughtfully on the ground as she considered the dwarves.

"Was he not Dashnival?" Cheekie asked, still speaking Dwarvish that strangely rang of Russian.

"Cheekie, there has not been a Dashnival among humanity for an eon, although Captain Blair is as close as this city has to one. Much has changed, and much must be relearned, perhaps even rediscovered," replied Dr. Walker.

"Good. Then his ignorance does not dishonor him. He fought well in spite of it. We learned much from these people by it," Breekie replied with a broad smile.

"Oi, before you lot keep talking the sun out of the sky, what should I do with this fella?" O'Cleary asked, jerking a sideways thumb at the now handcuffed Gunter.

Peter looked back and forth between the two. "What did he do?"

"Took a shot at the leprechauns when you went down. It ended up hitting some poor sod in the crowd. If I didn't know better, I'd say the bullet curved. He certainly seems to think so."

"It did. I swear to God it did," grumbled Gunter.

"Did it kill anyone?" Peter inquired.

"No, I think it was a through and through from her friend's reaction. They're both gone now, though. Probably dragged her off to the doctor," O'Cleary replied.

"Well, if no one's dead, let him go. I'm sure he'd appreciate the chance to apologize to the injured," Peter replied.

Gunter sneered but dared not do more than that as O'Cleary begrudgingly unhandcuffed him. "Go on," he said, helping him to his feet by roughly grabbing handfuls of his shirt.

Gunter rubbed his wrists, eyeing Shawn, who still held his rifle. "Kid's got my gun," he said bluntly.

"Give it to him," Peter ordered offhandedly.

Gunter received it carefully then made off towards the hospital, where the injured girl had been assumedly rushed off to.

As she watched him go, Dr. Walker spoke again. "Peter, we have much more to discuss. Would you lead us back to the Grant?"

"Of course."

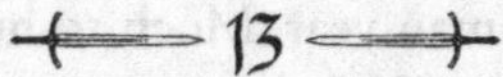

THE HEALER

I *used magic. I healed Captain Blair's wounds. Well, I helped. I think she did most of the healing, really.* Sarah's mind had not stopped racing since they had left the scene, and now she found herself searching for a distraction from all the questions that tumbled around in her mind.

The Grant Building loomed in the distance. Sleek dark steel and tinted glass sharply contrasted with the town and university's federal-style brick structures. Further setting apart the building was the state of it. Compared to most buildings around it, which were marred with cracks and broken windows, the Grant Building remained relatively unfazed by the Shattering. It was not cracked. It boasted no broken windows.

The tall fence around it was unharmed. It looked almost identical to before the world broke, perhaps a little dirtier. Sarah wondered what it would take for this building to look damaged. *Not something I think I want to be around for. Then again, I've been around for a lot I never would have wanted to be around lately.*

Above the fence, an American flag fluttered, brushing against a flag bearing the SNW logo: a snowflake with some kind of gun in the center and the initials SNW below it. Now, both flapped in the wind, which gave the still building some semblance of life.

At the front of the gate was a familiar silhouette. Sarah sat up in her seat to get a better view as the vehicle rumbled forward. She spied the dwarves in the back seat of the SUV looking about with awed expressions at their quickly moving surroundings.

Sarah pulled her eyes from the rearview mirror to focus on the man waiting for them. He was a tall, middle-aged African American with a well-trimmed mustache speckled with white that rested casually below a broad nose. It was the only thing well kept on his person.

His matching sport coat and slacks had seen better days. His loose tie was stained with flecks of blood. *Doctor Gibson.* She recognized him from a health class she'd taken in her freshman year. Much to her surprise, on either side of him stood three armed police officers.

Their SUV came to a stop only a few feet from where Dr. Gibson stood by the gate and guard box barring entrance to the facility. From their vehicle and the one behind it emerged their strange entourage. Sarah exited first, moving quickly to help Dr. Walker out of the vehicle, then she hid her amusement while the other two dwarves took their time exiting. Captain Blair emerged last from the driver's seat.

He looks so intense. I guess he has a right to though.

If Dr. Gibson was in any way surprised, he did not show it. He stood there patiently, twiddling with the right corner of his mustache as he continued to watch the arrivals. Then he saw the large blood-stained gash across Peter's chest.

Dr. Gibson strode forward, waving his left hand at the group of nervous-looking officers behind him. As he moved, he spoke. "I apologize for the escort. I do not want to create the wrong impression, but the rest of the council insisted."

Peter eyed the man carefully as he got closer, not so much as raising an eye to the escort. Before he could reach Peter though, Dr. Walker stepped forward and greeted the tall, dark man with a familiar smile. "Well, hello, Doctor Gibson. How are you this fine evening?"

Gibson put on a wide smile. "Better than I deserve. If you'll excuse me, Doctor Walker." He directed his voice to Peter. "Captain Blair, you shouldn't be walking in that condition. Please let me examine your wound."

Peter stared, unblinking, at the tall man, then grinned. The expression reminded Sarah of a wolf baring its fangs.

"I'm fine. Doctor Gibson, was it?" Peter replied.

The mustache on the doctor's face bobbed ever so slightly as he nodded. "Ah, good. Yes, or Mayor Gibson, if you prefer now," he replied as he came to a halt, his voice laced with confusion. The hands he'd been raising to aid Peter no longer necessary, dropped to his sides.

He stood taller than every member of the small party of people. "Those men are here for my protection, captain. I'm sure you understand why some might think I need protecting?" His tone was prodding; the question not entirely rhetorical.

"I see. Well, as I'm sure you can tell, doctor, I am a bit preoccupied," said Peter as he motioned the members of his group towards the gate.

Gibson straightened himself to his full height, his voice taking on a note of steel. "No, Captain Blair. Unless the city is under attack, you are not preoccupied when it comes to speaking with me. We can put it off no longer. It's time you talked with the council."

Peter's grin didn't waver. "Of course," he said in a voice that sent a chill down Sarah's spine. "But first, let me make our guests comfortable."

"I'm afraid that will have to wait. The council must speak with our new visitors first." Gibson adjusted to a more polite cadence, turning his shoulder to Peter and bending down to one knee in front of the dwarves. "Professor, would you be so kind as to introduce me?"

He's not scared of Peter at all, Sarah thought.

"Doctor Gibson, this is Cheekie." She gestured to the older dwarf. "And this is Breekie," she said with a pat on the taller dwarf's shoulder.

"Cheekie and Breekie?" The pediatrician asked with a raised eyebrow but placid expression. Both dwarves nodded as each of their names were spoken. "Do they speak English?"

"Not yet, but they should adjust quickly."

"Fascinating. Well, would you inform Mister Cheekie and Mister Breekie that my name is Doctor Gibson, and I'd be happy to take a look at that cut on Breekie's arm."

"That would be Peter's doing, but in fairness, they paid him back," Dr. Walker dismissed.

Dr. Gibson's face lost its placidity, replaced by a look of horror, which was quickly put to rest by a steely gaze. "We have more to discuss than I thought. If you all will accompany me to the town hall…"

"Of course, it's not too far from here. Do you mind if we walk? I could use the exercise," said Walker.

Gibson smiled. "A pleasant walk is always welcome."

Behind her, Sarah heard Peter whispering to Shawn, "Here's my entrance card. Head inside and let Steven or William, or whoever's there, know what happened and where we're going."

THE COUNCIL

Peter stood in the town hall's hallway. It was as typical a place as one might expect. Along the walls hung paintings of the town's history, many now cracked or damaged. Small and comfortable benches occupied the rest of the empty wall space. Peter stifled a yawn, as exhaustion beckoned to him like an old friend. He went to put his hands in his pockets and was reminded of the basilisk tooth he'd been keeping in the larger lower pocket of his pants.

He thought over the last hour. He'd been close to death before on more than one occasion. The tooth was a reminder of that. But never had he felt so helpless. His mind had been blank since the fight. He had woken from the blow different. *It's like I can feel beyond my skin,* he thought as he tried to put his state of being into words for himself.

Peter looked over to where O'Cleary sat silently on the bench across from him. The pair had been left behind when the others went into the nearby conference room. O'Cleary looked back up at Peter and unclenched his jaw. "Well, this is a bloody mess, isn't it?"

Peter collapsed onto the bench next to him, the sword strapped to his back, making it impossible for him to sit comfortably. Hands trembling, he undid the straps holding it in place and set the sheathed weapon on his lap. O'Cleary stood and began to pace in front of the conference room doors as he continued to speak.

"Bloody idiots, the lot of them. Especially that Gunter, aye? I about put him in the ground myself before you showed up," O'Cleary stated as he paced and prattled on, his accent exasperated by stress. "He's a troublemaker, mark my words. My mum used to have a word for lads like him. She called them…" O'Cleary's curse brought Peter's attention back to him.

"Your mother said that?" he inquired with a slight grin.

"Oh, aye. My mum said worse than that. She'd have had a right time when those lads started swinging their axes at ya. Woulda torn 'em limb from limb, swearing as she did. Then she'd have sewn 'em back together and cooked up some spaghetti that'd knock your socks off."

"Spaghetti?" Peter chortled the word out.

O'Cleary came to an abrupt stop and turned to face Peter with a wicked look in his eyes. "That's right. Spaghetti. My mum makes the finest spaghetti in Ireland or any of the fifty-three states."

Peter could tell he was walking into a trap by the glint in the scrawny man's eyes. He glanced at the white spot of hair near the front of O'Cleary's scalp for just a moment before he conceded. "States? I thought you told me Ireland was divided into counties?"

The Irishman grinned with satisfaction. "Aye, that's true. Ireland is, but Ireland is the first state of America's fifty-three. What? Did you think a bunch of Brits on a different spot of land would rebel against their dear ol' King George? Nonsense. The founding fathers were all Irish to the bone. All but Jefferson. That man was a bloody Scot."

O'Cleary's expression was unwavering as he spoke, and upon finishing his monologue, his look dared Peter to argue with him. It reminded Peter of a cat you knew had done something you just hadn't figured out yet, and they knew but were unashamed.

"I'm inclined to take you at your word," Peter said with a laugh. "Ha ha. It makes sense that a country that turned out this dysfunctional would have been founded by a bunch of Irishmen."

"I'll let that one slide, cap'n, since there's a twinkle of Irish blood in your veins, if I'm not mistaken. It's the fight in you. Lordy, the way you swung that blade of yours when those fellas were coming at you — I tell you, cap'n, I ain't ever seen a man move as quickly as you did. And to get up from that blow and still be walking and talking?"

O'Cleary scratched at the scruff on his face. "I always did believe in a bit o' magic. Can't grow up in Ireland and not in the back of your head. But I never woulda guessed a leprechaun like your Dr. Walker could bring a man back from that." He spoke as though to himself, but Peter could feel the man's watchful eye.

"Certainly a strange time to be alive. Stranger still to be alive. I'll be honest, O'Cleary. I'm not entirely sure I'm glad she did whatever it is she did," Peter replied.

"Ouch. Now, none of that, cap'n. You can't be quitting on us this early in the fight. We need a basilisk bane if we're gonna keep folks like that lot at bay," he replied, gesturing towards the meeting room.

Peter flinched at the title. *Basilisk-Bane. There it is again. If Doctor Walker hadn't shown up, I'd be basilisk dung by now. Good grief, if she and Sarah hadn't been there earlier, I'd have been killed by two dwarves over a misunderstanding.*

O'Cleary gripped his shoulder. "Do you need some time alone, Peter? You've got a lot to process, and this meeting you're about to be in isn't gonna be no picnic."

"That might be helpful. Thank you, O'Cleary," Peter replied.

O'Cleary shrugged. "I got better things to do then gob on about this and that anyway. Plenty of craic to be had around the town after what just happened." His face grew stern. "You're not gonna go all mentaller once I leave, are you?"

"Mentaller?"

"Crazy. Nuts. You're not gonna go and do something brutal and make me regret leaving you?"

"Ah, no. I'm all out of something brutal for the day, I think."

O'Cleary nodded, his face stoic. "I'll be going then. Should probably get my weapons checked. No telling what this strange air is doing to the things." He stretched as he made his way towards the door. "That idiot from earlier had a clear shot. He may have been right about the shot curving."

Peter hadn't been paying much attention to his subordinate's mumbling, but the last few words yanked him to his feet. "What?" he asked with a raised voice so as not to be missed as the man reached the door. "Did you say the bullet curved around the dwarf he was firing at?"

"Yeah. Was the weirdest thing I ever saw. Well, would be if not for the fellas themselves."

"And you're sure he had a clear shot?"

"My drunken grand-dah coulda made that shot with her eyes closed. Especially with one of our guns, which he had, mind you," O'Cleary replied from the open doorway, looking over his shoulder at Peter.

Peter rubbed at the stubble on his face." O'Cleary, find Steven. He's probably in his lab. Have him check your gun, then tell him to meet up with me."

"Yessir. Good luck."

With that, O'Cleary let the door close behind him as he ventured off with a song on his lips, and Peter was left alone in the hall to await his confrontation with the council.

I've got to be better prepared. That's twice now I've almost died in the last two weeks. Peter ran a finger along his chest. His curled chest hair gave way to smooth skin where the cut had healed over. *They didn't even give me time to change.*

Flexing his fingers, he winced at the pain from his left hand. *As if I needed a physical reminder.* Peter examined his still injured hand, grateful it was the only thing left unhealed and not something more significant. The hand was still usable, and the pain only served as a minor inconvenience.

Peter took a deep breath. The familiar face of his sister, full of determination, paced through his mind's eye. He pushed her out of his mind. *She'd have done the same thing.* He pulled Galvorn from its sheath, letting the tip of the blade rest on the floor as he examined the dull red stone in its pommel. *I have to get stronger. I can't hold back. If I do, people will die.*

Peter weighed the blade in his hands. *Dad always said, too weak to save yourself is too weak to save others. I wonder how bad things are up in DC with him and mom.* He tested the weight and length of the blade, trying to get more used to it. *I'm sure they're fine. If anyone is going to be okay, it's them. No sense wasting energy worrying about them. Focus on the now.*

The sound of a door opening drew his attention. Peter shoved the black blade in the mismatching brown leather sheath he'd been gifted. Out came Sarah, and she smiled awkwardly at him. She was followed by the two dwarves and Dr. Walker, who was speaking in Dwarvish. *Is it just us who can understand Dwarvish now? Or can everyone understand them? How is it I even know that's what it's called?* he wondered.

"How're you feeling, Peter?" The question came from Dr. Walker, who'd just finished saying something about Shadowfang to the two younger dwarves.

"Alive. Thanks for that, by the way. Different though. What exactly did you do to me? Why can I understand Dwarvish?"

The small woman raised an eyebrow. "I thought it was quite clear I used a bit of magic to help you understand," she replied with a dumbfounded expression.

"I guess I was a bit distracted when you did that," Peter replied.

Dr. Walker's lips clenched in a thoughtful expression. "To be fair, I'm not sure how long it will last," she said dismissively. "Perhaps the Babble spell will finally finish breaking. You said you felt different, Peter. Different how, other than the Dwarvish?" she asked and left the Babble comment unaddressed.

Peter pondered the best way to reply for a moment. Then with his thumb and forefinger tracing his jaw, he spoke. "More awake. More aware. It's as though there's some kind of energy at the back of my mind waiting for me to tap into it. I felt it when I fought Shadowfang, but now it isn't fading."

"Well, dear boy, when Sarah and I healed your wound, it may have had some strange side effects. You have an arcane ability. I do not doubt that. I just do not know yet what that ability is other than that it is a passive ability, unlike Sarah's, which is more active."

Peter noticed Sarah's green notebook had appeared in her hand, and she was scribbling away. Cheekie and Breekie appeared content to stand and wait, neither looking directly at Peter even when he gave them a pointed glance.

"On the subject of language, though, you may find you understand spoken Dwarvish, but you will not be able to speak it or read it yet. You see, in the beginning, there was one language. Of course, it developed dialects, which some might argue were different languages among the dwarves or elves of different regions. Still, overall, the 'One-tongue' was spoken universally and understood by all, as it was the only language spoken since the dawn of time. That is the Dwarvish me and our guests have been speaking."

She sat down heavily next to him on the bench. "I'd hoped your increased connection to the arcane would give you an understanding of the One-tongue sooner, but when it didn't, I took things into my own hands."

"Do not worry. In time, your mind will adjust to how speech should truly be. I expect, in a few years, English and all other human languages will have gone the way of Latin."

Peter wasn't sure how to feel about this news. He knew some basic Spanish and a bit more Arabic than that, but the idea that he and the rest of humanity might completely abandon their childhood languages was a bizarre concept.

Dr. Walker waved her cane at him. "Enough yammering. The council is expecting you. No need to keep them waiting any longer." She paused as he rose to his feet. "And, Peter, try not to enter into any life-threatening duels while you're in there." Her tone was playful, and she said it with a broad smile, but as Peter looked into her deep brown eyes, he saw a hint of warning.

Peter grimaced. "I'll do my best, professor. See you back at the Grant?"

"I expect you will. Good luck, Captain Blair. Make your case well." *My case — huh?* he thought, bemused. He nodded to Dr. Walker and stepped into the council room.

The room was well lit. In the center, three long tables formed a U shape with the opening facing him. In the space between the tables sat a single chair, positioned so its occupant would face everyone seated. *Either I'm a potential hire or facing a court martial.*

Around the outside of the table sat the council. There were thirteen of them in all, including Dr. Gibson. *Quite a lot of people are sitting around inside while others dig graves.*

"Captain Blair, thank you for joining us. Please have a seat," Dr. Gibson said from his chair at the middle table, directly across from the chair he motioned to. His voice held no hostility, only formality. Peter moved forward to take a seat as the mayor removed a stack of papers from a folder and arranged them in front of him.

"Why is he armed?" The anger laced question came from a short Hispanic woman five seats to Gibson's left.

Dr. Gibson sighed almost imperceptibly. "For the same reason that several members of this council, including myself, are armed. Because we now live in a world where danger is ever-present and unexpected."

"I made my stance very clear on this, Gibson. The fact that you chose to ignore it undermines this council's authority. It's bad enough this vigilante isn't in handcuffs, but to have him come in here with the same butcher's knife he used to murder people in the streets — do you want the town to take us for fools?" Her voice rose in shrill exasperation.

I know that voice… Where do I know her from?

"That is quite enough, Missus Lucia," chimed in an older woman. "We are here to have a civil discussion with a military leader. You do not begin such a discussion by disarming him and accusing him of murder at the outset. Captain Blair, I do apologize for Councilwoman Lucia's poor beginning to this meeting."

Lucia was fuming, but a hand placed lightly on her shoulder by a familiar ginger man cut off a response. Peter had often seen the man down at the pub signaling for another round.

Rory Effith was every part the humble veteran, from the easy humor and slight skittishness to the airborne decal on his truck. He calmly whispered a few words to the angry woman, words which seemed to calm her for the time being.

"Allow me to introduce myself, captain. My name is Pamera Fritz," the round older woman with glasses and spiky white hair said. "If I might, let us try and start over. Foremost, how are you? We were informed you were badly injured only a few short hours ago."

Peter spoke at last, his tone even and absent of emotion. "I am doing well, thanks to Doctor Walker and Sarah Young's care. I'm sure we have much to discuss, though, so I would not be offended if we skipped the pleasantries."

Dr. Gibson nodded solemnly. "Very well. Please don't hesitate to ask if you are unfamiliar with any of us. That being said, let us cut straight to the point, captain." Mayor Gibson tapped a pen against the papers in front of him. "You are in a fragile position in the eyes of this council."

Dr. Gibson paused to see if Peter wished to say anything before he continued. Peter sat in silence, and his father's advice echoed through his mind as he waited for Dr. Gibson to continue. *Speak softly and carry a hidden stick.*

"There are several here who think you should be kept in a cell until such time as a trial can be held. The crimes you are accused of are as follows," he said, looking down at his paper and pulling on the end of his pristine mustache. "Three counts of murder, assault, and one count of treason." Once again Dr. Gibson stopped. He steepled his fingers, leaned forward, and said, "Do you have anything to say, Captain?"

Peter sat straight in the chair, hands folded in front of him. He looked around the room and observed the faces of those present. They were mostly strangers to him. His eyes passed over Lucia, and recognition dawned on him. *You.* The thought was venomous, but he kept his face impassive.

You're the one who tried to have SNW removed from the town over a parking ticket. You're one of the protestors from when grandad decided to build the training center here. Didn't get you anywhere then and certainly won't matter now. He forced himself to move on, and Peter met the mayor's eyes. "Is this a trial, Doctor Gibson?"

Dr. Gibson leaned back in his chair and sighed. "No, captain. It is not. At best, you might consider this a preliminary hearing."

"On whose authority?"

The question seemed to take the room by surprise. "Why, our authority, of course," replied a teddy bear of a man in a cowboy hat.

"And where exactly do you get that authority? I don't recall voting for any of you," Peter said.

Mayor Gibson frowned. "Are you serious, captain?"

"Completely," Peter replied, keeping his face blank.

A balding scholarly man at the far end of one table sat forward, opening a large book in front of him. "If I might, Mister Mayor?"

"Of course, Doctor Engle," Gibson replied.

"Thank you. Now, Captain Blair," he said, looking down his stylish horn-rimmed glasses at the open book in front of him, "according to the city's bylaws, *Section 11:D*; 'In the event of a national emergency, senior members of the city council are to be elevated to the twelve roles dictated in subsection T.'" One finger followed along as he read. "'Until a time at which the federal or state government may resume authority, this provisional council is to act as a governing body for the city.'" He stopped. "It goes on to detail how a leader — in this case, Doctor Gibson — shall be selected as interim mayor as well as given the individual responsibilities of each council member." He closed the book with a heavy thud. "As you can see, our authority is quite legitimate."

Peter nodded. "Very well. I did nothing that did not have to be done. Those men were employed by my company, and they were dealt with accordingly.

My actions prevented them from doing further harm in a time of chaos and dissuaded others from imitating them."

Peter could feel his blood threatening to boil. He knew he was exhausted, and his patience was stretched to the limit. *Stay calm. You're in control.*

Peter looked deep into Gibson's dark eyes. "If you want to discuss a trial once all this is over, so be it, but in the meantime, there are real threats that need dealing with." Peter folded his arms. "In other words, not guilty."

Pamera was the first to respond.

"Once this is all over? Captain Blair, do not take us for fools. Such a vague condition is too widely interpretable."

Rory spoke, his cheerful voice at odds with the tension in the room. "Perhaps you could offer us some clarity on what you would consider *all over?*"

"The chair recognizes Lieutenant Effith, our senior military advisor."

Lieutenant? That's rich. In all their hurried pleasantries, Peter had never noticed Rory was an officer. He didn't take him for the type. Rory told enough war stories to fill volumes. *If he had called it quits at Lieutenant, then his time in uniform was even shorter than my own.* The irony of the situation almost made Peter laugh out loud.

"When the people of this city are safe from attack, starvation, or other apocalyptic dangers."

Rory did not appear satisfied. "In the meantime, you intend to organize, train, supply, and maintain our fighting force?"

Spoken like a true service academy reject. Peter saw his opening. "Certainly, *lieutenant.* I, a terrible mercenary, would not give up on our town. Unless, of course, with your vast military experience, you would be willing to take up the responsibility?"

Lt. Effith's shocked silence lingered in the room for an agonizing moment before being interrupted by a lanky Big Bird-looking man in a tweed coat. "Do you really believe yourself qualified to undertake such a momentous task?"

"I do." Peter did not bother to learn the man's name. Instead, he smiled softly. It was not a threatening smile; although, there was doubtless those present who took it as such.

"Would you call yourself Caesar and hold us hostage with our own fighting force?" The croaky voice speaking this time came from an Asian woman with short gray hair.

Peter's eyes darkened. "Would you call yourselves Brutus and destroy what we've built by dispatching me?" He noticed smiles flicker across Pam and Rory's faces.

"I don't think you understand the situation. Let me contextualize it for you a bit." A voice in the back of Peter's mind warned him to stop, not to say what he was about to, but he was tired, and the voice was weak. "I could single hand-edly kill everyone in this room without breaking a sweat. That is not a threat. It is a fact. More than that, though, your police force is loyal to my organization. They actively sought us out to organize things when the police chief bravely died in a rescue attempt."

Peter leaned forward in his chair. "I don't know what it says in your bylaws about replacing the chief of police, but I don't think it matters right now. If you were to manage to kill me, you'd lose the support of the officers, not to mention my men." Peter scowled.

"Speaking of my men, you all know what the ones I executed did. I hold my soldiers to a higher standard than that. Most are better people than those three, but who's to say what they'd do if I wasn't here to keep an eye on them."

The air in the room had grown thick and heavy. *You're talking yourself into a corner. Find a way out if you still can.*

Peter raised his hands and sat back. "I do not desire power. If I did, I would not have armed our citizens with SNW weapons. Furthermore, if I did, I would have sought a position on this council. Instead, I have worked with the police to deputize capable people to create a force which I hope will be able to protect this city. That force is yours to lead or choose a leader for." Peter looked around the room, meeting the eyes of one council member after another.

"However, my people will continue to operate as I see fit. Their talents would be wasted otherwise." He took a deep breath. "We are all Americans, are we not? We stand together in times of adversity. No… We're more than that now. We are all human. And we are no longer alone." With those words, Peter stood, reached into his belt, and removed a long white fang, which he tossed on the table in front of Dr. Gibson.

Thud. The sound echoed through the room. Several members of the coun-cil, including Lucia, flinched.

"We do not know what has become of the rest of the world. For all we know, we are all that's left of mankind." Peter's voice trembled a bit at these words. "And my soldiers and I will do what we must and others cannot. If any of you know someone willing or able to face creatures like the one who's fang that was, I will give them my sword and submit to their authority."

"Take your seat, please, Captain Blair," Dr. Gibson said as he took the fang carefully in his hand. Peter complied. *What now? Gibson doesn't even look fazed.*

The mayor spoke as though nothing had happened. "Our second point of discussion with you, Captain Blair, is your encounter with the dwarves. We have talked about the situation with Doctor Walker and the dwarves themselves, and we understand it was a misunderstanding."

The mayor ran a forefinger and thumb over his mustache. "Please understand, we want nothing more than to guarantee safety for the city. Despite your outburst just now, it is my personal opinion that you have proven your loyalty and willingness to die for the people of this city, and for that, I wish to thank you personally."

Outburst? I was perfectly calm. You haven't seen an outburst. Peter inclined his head in acknowledgment, not trusting himself to speak.

The mayor continued, "That said, captain, you must be held accountable for your actions by us, or our authority will be undermined into futility. Do you understand?"

Peter grimaced. *He's got a point. Even if I say I don't want power, I've got it.* "I see your point."

"And as you so clearly put it, you understand why we're incapable of properly holding you accountable due to your position within the city."

Peter raised his eyebrows, the acknowledgment of his point catching him off guard. "I'm sorry?"

"Captain, we cannot hold a fair trial when half the city considers you a hero, and the other half fears the repercussions of such a trial. I realize you are a military man, but I want the record to state that we have not at any point threatened your life," Gibson said sternly. "Nor do any of us take kindly to your death threats, hypothetical or not."

Peter bit the inside of his cheek, trying not to give off any reaction.

"In all honesty, captain, we are at a bit of a loss on how to handle you. I hope you might have some suggestions of your own if you were as concerned with the people's safety as you and Doctor Walker says you are."

Peter chewed on the idea a moment, trying to see the situation from their point of view. *If I were them, I'd have me killed and deal with the consequences, but they aren't me.* "Perhaps some distance would be good for us all," Peter suggested.

"Explain yourself," Lucia snapped.

Peter blinked. He'd almost forgotten she was there, he'd been so focused on talking directly to Dr. Gibson. "I was already considering scouting missions to get a better idea of what the surrounding areas hold for us," Peter explained. "I would be happy to lead one myself."

Lucia leaned back, nodding. "I would accept exile over a trial."

This was the last straw for Dr. Gibson. "Lucia, we have already discussed and decided that Captain Peter is an essential element in this city's safety."

"That was before his outburst," Lucia shot back. A few other members of the council including the birdish man nodded their support. "He clearly cannot be trusted."

Gibson stood up from his chair. "That is enough. You've said your piece. We are here to reach a compromise, and you are hindering that process by not setting aside your own personal biases."

To Lucia's credit, she did not shrink back or lash out. She simply set her jaw and glared silently at both the mayor and Peter.

Gibson turned back to Peter. "Scouting would be wise. There are doubtless people out there in need of our help. Additionally, we would do well to seek out supplies for the city. Does anyone object to Captain Blair distancing himself from the city for a time by way of scouting?"

No hands were raised, but the gray-haired Asian woman did clear her throat before speaking. "Might I make a suggestion?" she asked.

"Of course, Councilwoman Long," Dr. Gibson said.

"If the captain is to set out on an expedition, I believe we should send along one of our own with him to report back on his behavior."

I don't think so.

"Seconded," said Pamera quickly, rising partially out of her seat. Echoes of agreement and raised hands signaled a group majority around the table.

What? Wait, no—

"Very well," Gibson said then addressed, Rory. "Lieutenant Rory, would you kindly select a volunteer for the task?"

"I can do that," Rory replied seriously.

Peter silenced the urge to protest. *You're on thin ice as is, you idiot. Pick your battles.*

Dr. Gibson turned back to Peter. "Additionally, captain, we would ask that all further major undertakings you pursue be discussed with us prior. In an emergency, you are free to act as you see fit until we have selected a new police chief. It is imperative that we have your compliance. Do we have your word?"

"You do."

"Very well then, Captain Blair. We will expect an update on your planned reconnaissance mission by the end of the week. Will that be enough time?"

"More than enough. Have your man report to the Grant Building tomorrow afternoon, and I'll update him on the situation."

"Thank you, captain. You are dismissed."

Peter rose calmly, bowed slightly to the room, and left.

✦ — 15 — ✦

SURVIVAL OF THE FITTEST

Peter sat on the side of his bed with Galvorn laid bare across his thighs. He'd been examining the blade for a few minutes now. *It should be dulled, or at the very least nicked in some way,* he thought as he traced the edge with his forefinger, careful to run it along the flat of the blade.

The sword looked as though it was more alive, sharper, more in focus, as though it hadn't truly been fully present before now. Peter's eyes flitted, and his vision blurred. He pressed his eyes shut, just for a moment, the action a tad painful as if his eyes hadn't been getting enough moisture. *That fight really took a lot out of me. I need sleep. The sword looks fine.* Peter tilted the blade to insert it into its sheath, when something at the tip of the blade moved.

Something tiny, shiny, and dark, almost as dark as the blade itself. Peter tilted the sword, causing the droplet at the tip to slide down the center of the blade.

He reached out and poked the trail of liquid it left behind. The droplet continued its descent as Peter drew his finger to his eye to examine it. *Blood.* Browner than blood should be, but unmistakably blood. He resisted the urge to taste it and be sure. *Where…? The dwarf. I cut him.* The droplet reached the crossguard and vanished.

Peter blinked, wondering if his eyes were playing tricks on him. Then he ran another finger down the path the droplet had taken. It came away clean; not even a trace of blood. He looked back at his forefinger, the lines and ridges of his fingerprint still highlighted in red. *Okay then. That doesn't make sense.*

Fear seeped into Peter's bones — not the usual anxiety that was always passing by before a battle. This was different. An uneasiness accompanying the dark unknown. *No. All fear is the same. A motivator. A tool for survival that heightens the senses,* he told himself, embracing the feeling, leaning into it, allowing his senses to be elevated but remaining calm.

Something was wrong. He tried to focus his gaze but couldn't. The edge of his vision was growing dark, and he felt the weight of his own head as it seemed to pull him towards the bed. He was losing consciousness.

Peter fought to stay awake, slapping himself a little too hard in the face. It worked for a second, and he found himself looking jerkily around the room to be sure he was alone. The room was empty, and the fear threatened to become panic. Galvorn struck the ground at his feet with a soft clank.

No… this isn't right… Peter felt like he was being submerged in thick, soft liquid as his body slumped to the side. Sleep gripped him in a tight embrace before his head even hit the pillow.

Hard, unforgiving ground pressed uncomfortably against Peter's back. The air on his skin tingled strangely as fear settled into his bones. His eyes lurched open, his head shooting up from the ground. Glowing silvery mist swirled away from him as he surged to his feet.

Peter turned around slowly, the mists curling with his movement. He wore a loose-fitting black material that was so light it felt like wearing nothing at all. The hair on the back of his neck stood on end. *I'm being watched.*

Peter reached for the pistol he always kept at his side. *I'm unarmed,* he realized as his fingers grazed the soft fabric on his leg. He got low, making himself a smaller target, as he searched his surroundings for anything he could use as a weapon.

Through the softly glowing mists, he spied a faint red light. Moving as silent as a breeze in the night, Peter stalked closer to the light. The clouds swirled around him, serving as his only cover.

Then he spied it. Galvorn was embedded in the cold stone ground. *Deja-vu,* he thought as he examined the sword. The red jewel in Galvorn's pommel emitted a faint red glow, discoloring the strange heavy mist that permeated the air. Familiarity exploded in his mind. The last vision, or dream, or whatever this was, tore through his mind's eye. He'd foolishly pushed it to the back of his mind where until now it had lingered just out of thought.

"It feels different this time, does it not?" A voice cut through the fog, a voice of liquid silver flowing through the mist. It reverberated as if the speaker stood alone in a stone cavern.

Peter reached reflexively for the weapon he knew wasn't on his hip, then redirected the motion to grasp Galvorn by the handle. He knew only one being that voice could belong to: *Jadis.* Knowing it was useless, Peter gave Galvorn a tug. It didn't budge. Dejected, he let go and turned to look for the voice's owner, mist brushing his skin. *It has no texture. It's not wet or cold, but I can feel it.*

There she was, slipping towards him through the mist. Short and slender, her striking gray complexion and distinct scars almost blended her with the fog. Jadis' face wore a slight grin that was quickly replaced by a scowl. As she approached, Peter thought he caught a whiff of iron in the still air.

Peter found his voice: "It does. I'm not sure how yet, but it's definitely different."

"Shadowfang's blood was stronger. There was more of it. Took you long enough to return, though. I was growing tired of waiting." She stopped next to him and examined Galvorn, forefinger tracing the outside of the pommel as she whispered to herself. After a moment, she stopped and faced Peter. "Dwarf?"

Peter frowned as the unpleasantness of the day's events returned to his mind. A phantom pain lanced his chest, followed by a real one in his still injured finger. He rubbed casually at the spot where his chest had been opened.

I almost died. No, no time for that now. Am I losing my mind? No. Calm down. I'm alive. If I want to stay that way, I need to be careful. Find out more about what you're dealing with here. You're out of your depth again.

"What about dwarves?" he asked.

Jadis frowned back. "Dwarves then. You cut one but did not kill it. Why?" Her voice dripped with accusation. The glow from the sword reflecting in her eyes conjured the image of a panther in Peter's mind. Like a panther blends into shadows, it was hard to tell where the mist ended and she began.

Sometimes when he blinked, she even seemed to fade, just for a moment. Her frown morphed into a glower. "I asked you a question, swordling. Do not waste my time. I have precious little of it."

Peter knew an insult when he heard one. He scowled back. "They attacked me," he replied dismissively. His muscles were beginning to feel more his own, but the gravity here was different. It was heavier, much like a dream; he could feel his movements were slowed. As he stood, he began to flex different muscles, testing the effect of the altered gravity to see if it was really just something in his system.

Jadis' stare bore into him. She was waiting, analyzing him. He knew the look in her eyes.

He'd seen it hundreds of times before. Suspiciousness.

The girl wasn't sure how much of a threat he posed. As he watched, the Eölin stepped back into the mist and vanished from sight.

Peter was left alone with Galvorn, stubbornly unmoving in the ever-present mist. He reached back out and grasped the firm leathery handle of the sword, giving it one last brutal pull, believing it would come loose.

Once again, it remained unmoved. A warning pulse flared in Peter's mind. There was a being at his back, close enough to strike. But he felt no motion, no warning that the creature was making an attack. Peter spun around, ready to defend himself, and found Jadis.

The mist seemed to be retreating from her presence, her flowing white hair now pulled back in a sophisticated, tight braid. Her ragged, gray, stained robes were replaced with a light black material that matched his own clothing. He blinked, and for less than a moment, she seemed to be back in the red-fringed rags.

"Why are you bringing me here?" Peter inquired. *It's been a week since the last time.*

"I am not. Or else we would have made more progress," Jadis replied in an weary voice. "Tell me about the attack."

"Why do you want to know so much about it?"

"To understand what I have to work with. Why I had to reach out with what little strength I have to spare you from death. Now, the dwarves — describe them more. Did they have gray hair? Extensive tattoos? Braided beards?" The space between them waxed and waned as Jadis angled her steps.

"No. Darker unbraided hair and beards. They had a handful of tattoos between them but not many. Why does it matter?" She was closer now, within reach.

She looks so young. Fifteen or sixteen if she were human.

"Because, swordling, you lost to a pair of dwarves, the least combative of the four races." She looked as though she'd tasted something bitter as she practically spat out the words.

Four races? What are the other three?

"Sit." She motioned to two stone rises in the ground with a short stone table between them. He hadn't seen them before, but there they were, sitting cross-legged across from her.

Peter mused over his next question. Jadis asked first, though. "How did you come to possess Galvorn?"

The question froze his thoughts. The way she said Galvorn held something extra in it, though he couldn't quite place what it was. "An old instructor of mine gave it to me as a gift. At the time, I thought little more of it than that. She hasn't said anything about it since the Shattering, though, other than telling me it was wise to wear it."

This caused the Eölin to chuckle softly, a strange sound for a creature who appeared so sinister. "Wise — or perhaps the most foolish thing you have ever done. When this is over, we will see if you live to call it wise as well."

Peter winced. "You don't seem to think I'm going to live much longer, do you?"

The trace of amusement on her face retreated and was replaced by a look of indifference.

"After almost dying to a pair of young dwarf travelers? No." She sighed. "You do not carry yourself like a man not long for this world. Death lingers around you. Your first

bloodshed with Galvorn was the blood of an ally. The elves call that a sign of Naliege,

one doomed to die, a cursed one who bathes in blood. But perhaps Galvorn's curse will

cancel it out."

"Galvorn's curse?" Peter's hands became fists. "Explain."

Jadis' eyebrows rose. "Did your teacher not tell you? You carry a cursed blade. Not with magic or a spell, but by fate. All who have wielded it have died, their names forgotten. Perhaps she did not know. Do you trust her?"

"I trust Doctor Walker as much as I trust anyone who risked their life to save my own. Besides, what choice do I have?"

"Fewer than you know, it would seem. And you cannot be rid of it either."

"Why not? I could easily give it away or leave it behind," Peter said.

"No." She almost hissed the word. Peter saw fear in her eyes. Human or otherwise, he knew the sight of it, but then it was squelched by rage, a rage that stayed in the eyes yet did not carry to her voice. "If you do that, you will die. You are linked to the blade, not as I am but still linked. To separate yourself from it would kill you," she said.

More on that in a moment.

"That reminds me, last time we spoke, you said Galvorn was your anchor to the world, your…" He paused to remember the term. "Aloof-Nava?"

"Aluth-nava, yes."

"What does that mean?"

"It means my soul is bound to the sword and to the one who wields it. That is how I know when you have put it to use."

Peter considered this. The last time he'd been here, he'd woken up with a bruise from where the Eölin jabbed him, but he'd assumed the dream had been his subconsciousness providing a reason for his bruising as he slept, the way one dreams of falling when slipping out of bed. "How do I know this isn't just a dream? That you aren't some figment of my imagination?"

A small smile snuck its way onto her dark face, contrasting the fierce appearance of her scars. *She can't be as young as she looks. Not with how she talks and moves. There's no way she's a teenager.*

"You do not know. Have you not seen things you thought impossible? Why now do you doubt what is real? You could ask when you wake, seek out your doctor and inquire about my kind, tell her you spoke to an Eölin, but she will tell you I am not what I claim to be, that I do not exist. I would say nothing though. She might think you've cracked, or worse — she might try to cut you off from me." Jadis trailed off, but the smile remained, haunting him. "You know better though, swordling. You know I exist."

Peter's curiosity burned away at his patience. He had so many questions. No warning bells were going off as he spoke to her like they had with Shadowfang. Here, he had time to ask. Time to discuss. So why not take advantage of it?

Perhaps Dr. Walker was not entirely honest with him, but by the same logic, he couldn't trust this creature. Still, why not learn what he could and grow stronger for it. The game of questions seemed to have been forgotten, so he pressed his advantage.

"You said if I got rid of the sword, I'd die. From what? Would it be like withdrawals?" It seemed a logical question given what he'd read in mythology about cursed magical items and the adverse effects they have on their users.

Jadis' eyebrows wrinkled. "Withdrawals? Are you so obsessed with the sword that being separated from it would cause your heart to break like an elf and kill you?"

Peter's ears burned. It annoyed him, her condescension regarding matters he lacked a frame of reference for.

She went on: "I thought humans were made of tougher ore than that, but it looks like all one has to do is disarm you, and you will die of fear. Ha ha." This time, her laughter was infectious, pulling a chuckle out of Peter as he considered what he had suggested. Cool mist traced his skin; it was rising slowly now.

Jadis put her mirth in check. "No, you would die because the blade you wield is the greatest one you will ever lay hands on. Without it, you would not have survived what you have. And should you dispose of it, another would find it, and we would seek you out to kill you with it ourselves."

I need to take her out. Peter's eyes flicked over to where Galvorn lay embedded in the rock surface. He leaped to his feet, but before he could take a step, he was interrupted by a lightning-quick backhand to his face, which sent him stumbling backward.

The strike had been quicker than anything he'd ever encountered, just like everything else these days, too fast for him to stop. She was stronger than anyone who looked like a teenager had a right to be.

Peter did not cry out or ask why she'd struck him. Instead, he took up a defensive pose. Despite the power behind the blow, he knew it for what it was: a warning shot. His heart dropped a fraction of an inch. *If she can move that fast and hit that strongly at her size, I'm screwed.*

She stood at ease just out of the reach of his arm. "Do you want to die, Basilisk-Bane?"

Not here, Peter thought. "No," he replied. *Not at the hands of a little girl, no matter how old she acts.*

"Prove it." She signaled for him to attack back with two fingers.

Peter's confidence was shaken. *Everywhere I turn, my foes are miles ahead of me.* A month ago, he'd have dispatched the girl with two quick strikes, but now he found himself hesitating to approach her. *Whatever this is, it can't be real. If it's not real, you can win.* He focused, finding that place in his mind where thought flowed into motion. *Test her. Don't get too close. Get a feel for her fighting style.*

Peter stepped forward and punched downward at her center mass, trying to gauge how she would move in response. She swept his hand aside with the ease of a brushstroke and planted a foot in his chest. The blow felt like a bullet connecting with body armor, a familiar sensation that knocked him on his back.

Mist swirled away from the force of his collision with the ground. The air driven from his lungs, Peter gasped for breath. Stale air stung his lungs. He rolled to the side for more room to get up. It was unnecessary, though. Jadis made no move to follow up on her retaliation.

"What do you want with me?" he asked as he got back to his feet. Despite the strength of her blows, he could tell she was holding back. It was unlike any sparring he'd ever experienced. He felt like a child compared to this almost child-sized opponent.

"Nothing. I do not want you. You are weak, fragile, and naive. But I need you, and you need me." She spoke as though merely stating a fact, then stopped, waiting for him to strike again. Peter feinted to the right but went for a sweep of the legs.

Jadis dodged the attack with ease. Peter grimaced, a low growl in his throat. His slowed movements made the situation all the more frustrating, compounding his sense of helplessness.

Stepping back, Jadis reached into the fog, her hand disappearing from sight.

When it reemerged, she held a sword, one that looked made of glass but the same shape and size as Galvorn. She held it out towards him with a smirk.

Peter took the strange sword in his hand. It was identical to Galvorn in every way except weight and material. *Must be the extra gravity here.*

When he looked up from examining the blade, he saw Jadis now held a sword of her own. Hers was not made of the same translucent material. Its handle was a black spiderweb mesh, the black continued to the beginning of the long thin blade but blended into the standard silver color of steel.

He recognized it as a rapier-like design, with a guarded hilt. At the top of the guard facing outward was a sort of strange outshoot of metal that curved almost to a hook. It was the most unique sword he'd seen other than Galvorn.

"I would duel you barehanded, but your enemies will not go so easily," Jadis said, driving the blade into the ground so the hilt wobbled slightly at her waist. Then, as she pulled her hand from the grip, something came with it. The sword remained embedded in the ground, but a glass-like replica similar to the one Peter held came away in her hand. Now she stood facing Peter combatively.

"You are not taking this seriously, Basilisk-Bane!" The statement was accompanied by a quick jab of her blade toward his chest, which he deflected clumsily. Too clumsily.

Peter felt the tip of the blade slide across his right shoulder. It was an unpleasant, cold, electrical sensation that shot fear to his brain. He looked down to see the magnitude of the wound and found not so much as a scratch.

"Last chance. Prove yourself, or I will draw my real sword and do us both a favor by killing you here, now," Jadis declared.

Enough! The dam of Peter's frustration which he kept so well concealed burst.

The lingering fear which told him to flee was driven away. One thought filled his mind:

Survive. The now familiar sensation of energy from his encounter with the dwarves and Shadwfang surged through him, more robust than before. He focused, concentrating on it, listening to the impulse pulling at him, and he went with it.

"*Antemáklasi.*" The word emerged from his mouth without him knowing what it meant. The result was instantaneous. The last of the dam broke. The energy was no longer just in him; it was all around him. He felt more alive than ever.

The strange pull of this place's gravity was still there, but now it was his tool.

The translucent Galvorn stabbed towards Jadis, lancing out eagerly for a taste of her skin. He felt her next movement. He could almost see it in his mind's eye, but there was no time to conjure the moment. A quick twist of his sword to connect their blades, and she'd be disarmed. Peter did not know how he knew it, how he felt it, but that didn't stop him from following the instinct.

But he was wrong. Jadis did not meet his blade as he knew she should. Instead, as he struck out towards her, she threw herself back out of range, sword held in a defensive stance. Her movements seemed slow now that he felt the energy. No, not slow, they were faster than his, but now they were almost predictable.

For a moment, he felt what she was going to do before she did it; then it was gone as she retreated. *No, she was going to attack. Why didn't she attack?* he wondered as he glared at her standing out of range of an attack without approaching.

"Interesting." Her voice was firm as she spoke, but her eyes seemed to shine with triumph. "Maybe you are worth something." She lowered her sword, turning her shoulder to him as she returned to her seat.

Peter felt his fingers brush the inside of his palm. The translucent sword was gone. The girl looked up at him expectantly, as though he posed as much of a threat to her as a mouse might a tiger. "Take your seat, Blair."

He still felt the invisible energy in a bubble around him. His blood still boiled, spiked with combat adrenaline. He did not take his seat. "You're here because you're dangerous, aren't you?" Peter's voice was cold, no friendly pretense left in him.

She laughed. It was a wild laugh but not as unnerving as Peter would have expected. "Good, you have some fire in you after all. You would have to be a fool to think I am not dangerous. But no, I came here by accident." Her laughter ended as abruptly as it had begun. "If I were your enemy, do you think I would let you live after that attack?"

She leaned forward, elbows resting on a stone table that Peter wasn't quite sure had been there before. "I can help you, Blair. I can teach you to fight, to survive. I can help you grow stronger, to properly use the power you have only just now tasted the potential of. I can make you a true warrior." Her words took on a pleading tone she struggled to hide. She seemed sincere, almost desperate.

"What will it take?"

"Time here."

The mist swirled all around them. Peter still felt the energy drawing on his strength. *Find out more. It doesn't seem like she's going anywhere, and neither are you.*

"Sit. Do something that relaxes you. It will be harder to cut yourself off from it here," she instructed in that tone that rang of an older woman's confidence.

Peter took his seat across from her, a cloud of thick mist rising from the center of the table. Jadis reached into the fog and drew out a long, thin, translucent dagger. Then she withdrew a whetstone and began to sharpen it.

She gestured at the mist with the blade. "Now, you."

Peter reached into the swirling mist.

"Envision what you desire in your hand. Feel its form."

He closed his hand as though gripping his rifle and felt its familiar cold grip. He removed a perfect replica of his refurbished M14 made of the same translucent material as the dagger. He instinctually redirected the barrel so it pointed away from Jadis into the fog. *Would this work on her here? Even if it did, could I hit her?*

The light at the back of the rifle shone light green, indicating it recognized his grip, a perk of Steven's employment. He checked to see if it was loaded. Finding it was, he removed the magazine, which he set on the table.

The mist dissipated, and Peter cleared the chamber of the rifle before setting it next to the magazine. Then he began to pop one bullet after another out of the magazine onto the table as Jadis watched him like an injured wolf.

"What is that? A metal puzzle? I asked you to calm yourself, not fool about with a

child's play toy." Her sarcasm was biting, but Peter resisted the urge to reply in kind. "This is not a toy. It is an M14 assault rifle." Peter reached down and picked up a bullet, holding it out towards Jadis. She took it suspiciously, looking it over carefully as Peter spoke.

As she did, he caught a closer glimpse of the inside of her hand. It bore the same white marks as her face, which extended perfectly down the length of her arm. *Scars, intricate, and precise, what happened to her?*

"That is a bullet," he said, then patted the rifle. "The rifle hurls the bullet towards your enemy at the speed of lightning."

"You used this on Shadowfang?" The question came so quietly that Peter hesitated a moment to be sure he heard it right before answering.

"Yes," he answered aloud.

Jadis whispered something to herself that Peter couldn't make out. Nevertheless, the sound made his skin go cold. Jadis put the bullet to rest on the table and watched Peter reload the rifle.

Peter checked the weapon over and then stood, aiming into the fog. *Blam!* A bullet tore a hole in the mist, but there was no sound of it striking anything. Peter turned and fired in the opposite direction. *Bang!*

Again, nothing. *No walls. If I walked a hundred miles in any direction, would I actually go anywhere? Maybe this is a dream, after all.* He repeated the action two more times to be sure, with the same result every time. Jadis didn't even flinch during the display. Once he was finished, Peter sat back down, removed the magazine, and placed it on the table.

It has to be a dream; this environment doesn't make sense. If we were in a cave, there would have been more echo or the sound of the bullet striking stone. It's too real to be some kind of augmented reality.

"No surprise it did not work on the basilisk."

"What makes you say that?" asked Peter.

"Because if such a weapon had proven successful against a descendant of Aapiepp, then there would have been no reason for you to use Galvorn, who you are so unfamiliar with."

Peter frowned. "Most opponents I encounter are not basilisks."

"Did you try to use it on the dwarves as well?"

"No, I was advised against it by Doctor Walker."

"A wise woman. I hoped you would have at least a basic understanding of arcane war tactics," she replied dejectedly.

"Since I need you alive, I will explain. Basilisks are creatures bred for war, molded by dark means, blood magic, witchcraft, and other dangerous methods. As such, they have been warded like many warriors against certain types of violence."

Jadis began to slowly unload the magazine round by round as she spoke. "Elves discovered early on that a small object hurled with enough speed was an extremely efficient killing method, but an elvish lord named Lanuri saw the destructive danger of such attacks and with the help of a few followers created wards and armors to counter such attacks. This took place during the Garden Wars, which we will discuss later."

She began to line the bullets up in a row, speaking in a soft voice. "Lanuri was captured though, and his secrets were pulled from him, as was his mind. This led to an arms race and the inevitable obsoletion of such weapons." She spoke the words as though referring to a children's book every child knows.

"Your rifle operates with the same methodology. Clever that it does not require magic but is ineffective against most magic users or their allies." By now, she'd laid twelve bullets in a row, a thirteenth slightly in front of them, and two closer to him for fifteen rounds in all.

Mist tickled the back of Peter's neck. Jadis examined her setup before speaking again.

"That moment of fury you felt, the one that helped you feel my attacks before I made them — has that happened before?"

"Yes," Peter replied. There was no reason to hide it.

"It was stronger this time, though?"

"Yes."

"That is because you are an Antemáklasi. I suspected it, but you gave name to it yourself." She paused. "We are running out of time." There was urgency in her voice. "To return, Galvorn must taste blood. I can help you, Blair. You must believe me. You need me to master this power. Quickly, tell me how you survived your wound. I sensed another's magic, but I could not discern its origin."

"Doctor Walker and Sarah did that."

"Are they both human?"

"No, Doctor Walker is an old dwarf. No, old doesn't quite capture it. She's ancient. She's been around since before all this happened. She's the one who gave me Galvorn."

Jadis arched forward, two hands crashing onto the stone slab, knocking over nine of the bullets she'd so carefully laid out. He saw his own reflection in her strange eyes.

"Did she give you her true name?"

Peter could not discern whether her tone held panic or anger. There was undoubtedly more emotion in it than she'd expressed so far.

"Walker," Peter replied as the fog swirled higher around them.

"No. Her *true* name. Her Dwarvish name."

"Oh, yes, and a lot of titles—"

Jadis interrupted, sweeping a hand wildly through the mist, which had begun to grow thicker around them. "I don't care about the titles! What did she name herself?"

"*Umindrabo Duridgrihulda.*" Peter wasn't sure how he'd remembered it so well, but something about the girl's voice brought the memory reflexively into words.

Jadis' face went blank. The mist rose around her, covering everything but her large eyes. Peter's vision darkened. He heard her speak, a muffled whisper, as even her eyes began to fade from view.

"Umindrabo." Jadis spat the word out with a sneer, and then all was mist and void.

THE FORGE

Compared to the rest of the university, the Forge stood out like a soldier in a room full of nurses, large and dangerous. It bore distinctive, high, dark metal arches and windows that contrasted with the old brick buildings of the rest of the university. At a distance, the entrance was indiscernible, but upon closer inspection, Peter saw that the building bore a half-finished look. This was the result of the strange way in which it folded in on itself. It's transitioned from outdoor fountains to courtyard interior, outside, then inside again.

There was something gothic about its structure, but it was far more modern in its material. Students knew it as the university's engineering building. The one-of-a-kind structure came equipped with all the modern necessities as well as a modernized forge and blacksmithing yard.

Peter admired the building thoughtfully as he and Simon approached the entrance.

I wonder how much of a hand Doctor Walker had in this. She must have known it could become more useful one day than any of us could have imagined, and she's close friends with the head of the engineering department. They say the design was a result of student and faculty collaboration, the perfect environment for Walker to suggest some features. Another coincidence in a growing list of strange happenstances.

With the Forge only a few paces away, he could see Steven, drenched in sweat and grime, making his way towards them from the outer courtyard. Steven greeted them with a smile and led them into the building. Warmth washed over them as they passed into the smithy. It smelled of iron, sweat, and the distinct odor of dwarves – a smell best described as a dry stone cave. The sound of men and women hard at work with the clanging of metal and the burning of welding filled the busy room.

Some melted-down metal from ruined cars and made spears to embed on the walls. Others worked to repair damaged tools or hardware. A few stood around what looked like a table of bones; doing what, Peter could only guess. Simon stepped forward next to Peter, his long dark hair pulled back out of his face. He placed his old medical satchel on a nearby table.

He never puts that thing down. Must have been a long morning checking up on folks.

Peter's gaze was drawn to a heated argument. The retired head of engineering was speaking sharply to one of the young dwarves.

Peter had never bothered to spend time at the Forge before and only met Professor Donna Meents once. She'd left quite an impression. The woman sported a full head of crazed, bushy gray hair and a voice like freshly tilled earth. That same voice now rang hot as smelting iron.

Between Donna and the dwarf he recognized as Cheekie, stood Dr. Walker, attempting to quelch the argument. Despite the heat of the Forge, the dwarf still wore his ear-flap hat with the red star tightly on his head.

"Not again," Steven mumbled with exasperation.

Donna's face was bright red, and springs of hair popped out of her ponytail holder as she shook her head in frustration. The shaking of her head brought the new arrivals into her field of view. Her head stilled, and she called out towards them.

"Mister Thomas, explain to this arrogant midget that we have the finest equipment money can buy, and that only a fool could break one of our hammers."

Steven turned to Peter for a moment. "Don't let their bickering fool you. She's thick as thieves with C and B."

Peter arched an eyebrow. "C and B?"

Steven shrugged before striding familiarly between tables covered in bits and pieces of metal, bones, and dark green scales. When he arrived at the animated pair, he took a large forge hammer with a crack down the side out of Donna's menacing hand.

Peter watched as Steven attempted to cool the two workers down.

Movement from the entrance caught Peter's eye. Apprehension turned like a concrete mixer in Peter's stomach at the sight of a familiar face entering.

"There you are," a frustrated Lt. Jessica Martin called out. She was short, with straight short brown hair that fell just past her ears. She wore her black SNW casual uniform with the company logo on each shoulder: a red M4-style rifle in a black snowflake.

We served what, three, four missions together before her promotion? Peter grimaced, recalling multiple accusatory conversations with the woman about her reassignment to intelligence despite her 'personal preference for active duty.'

Beside her strode a tall, broad-shouldered man with a face like a pit bull: sober and clean-shaven.

Peter recognized him as one of the new hires from six months back brought on to work in the security division. He wore no uniform, opting instead for jeans and an athletic shirt with the company's slogan: *Covert. Efficient. Secure.*

She looks even more annoyed than usual, Peter mused. "Hello, lieutenant," he said with as much friendliness as he could muster.

"Don't 'hello, lieutenant' me, cap. What's this about sending out scout teams tomorrow? Good grief, Peter, I know we were planning on secondary surveillance groups, but tomorrow? You could have given me a better heads-up than that. I barely have time to put together a team," she complained, a hint of excitement in her annoyance.

"That's what we're here to discuss, lieutenant. Do you already have a team in mind?"

Jessica grinned. The expression made her look fierce, like a predator that just cornered its prey. "You got me. I want Luu," she said, gesturing at Simon.

"No, I need Simon with me. I'll be leading the Macon-to-Atlanta team. O'Cleary is with me as well."

Jessica's expressions soured, the gears behind her eyes turning. "Fine. Are you taking any of my regulars?"

"Hauch and Jenni."

"Oh, come—" She stopped as Peter raised his eyebrows, a grim expression etched into his face.

"You know Atlanta has to be the highest priority."

She nodded distractedly. "Fine. I want Akena on my team then."

"The police officer? She lost a leg barely a week ago."

"Recovered and walking on a prosthetic leg Steven and Cheekie made from the snake's bones at her request. She's not SNW, but she'll want to go."

"If you think she's up to it, that's good enough for me. Civs are volunteer-based only though. According to the council, we don't have the authority to draft anyone who isn't SNW."

Behind her the big man scoffed.

"Arguing will end soon," a gruff voice with a slight Russian accent said at Peter's elbow, so Peter turned to the brown-eyed dwarf with a shaved head wearing an oversized forge apron, motioning for Peter to follow him. *This one's Breekie, I think.*

"We'll finish this later," Peter whispered to Lt. Martin and followed after the dwarf.

"Cheekie, he is good intended. He think we need Duelma, or even a Borstine clan hammer. Huh-huh-huh." Breekie's laugh came from deep within his belly. "Bah, we do not need these things to craft basilisk. Are you well, Pytor, slayer of Shadowfang? Your wound is mended?"

"I am, Breekie. Thank you. Your English is improving," Peter replied curiously as the others followed.

"Da, is easier, Duelma Umindrabo says many humans still do not know the arcane. Is a simple cast for dwarf to learn your tongue. Is a strange tongue though. Does your wound give panics?"

Peter chuckled. "Ha ha, it is strange. You mean like flashbacks? Seeing the fight in my head?"

Breekie nodded solemnly, concern etched across his face.

"No, this is not my first wound. Helps that it's already healed," Peter explained.

"Good. This is good. I will be wanting to cross your blade again when you learn to fight like dwarf. Huh-huh-huh." Breekie graced Peter with a wide grin. "But you are here for weapons, yes?"

Peter smiled back. Glad the dwarf was eager to get to the point.

"Your English really is exceptional. I am indeed."

"Bah, is strange tulk. Confusing. I would like to speak your Russian more, but Duelma Umindrabo says it is not your people's tongue. But some words you know, I think." He shrugged heavily before patting a tarped table he'd brought them over to stand by.

When he spoke again, his voice shifted, and a deeper, more fibrous sound came from his throat. Despite Peter's understanding, he knew the dwarf was no longer speaking English. "Morind, stop your bickering. The not-Dashnaval is here with his warriors to examine the tools of war we have made for them."

The switch between languages was strange. Peter couldn't help but feel like it would have been less unsettling if he didn't notice when it happened. Most words filtered into his mind with what seemed like vibration.

As though the foreign words contained physical energy beyond that of a typical language when striking his ears, it reminded him of lately when the energy pulsed through him during fights. When he heard the words, he knew they weren't English, but when they reached his brain, he understood most of them.

The room brightened as a door to their left opened and Sarah Young entered with a small group of people, a few of whom wore SNW uniforms, including O'Cleary. The new additions gathered around the table: Sarah, Steven, Simon,

Dr. Walker, Cheekie, Breekie, Jessica, William, and a few others. The dull clangs of metal echoed through the Forge as a handful of men and women continued to work, unfazed by the newcomers' arrival.

"Good, we have much to show." Cheekie spoke with a slightly thinner accent than the broader Breekie. "The dagger first, Breekie?"

Interesting. They use the other names when speaking English.

"Dah, the dagger first. I have it just here *drasa*," Breekie said as he reached into the forge apron he wore and pulled forth a sheathed dagger.

He handed the blade to Peter, who slid it from its sheath eagerly. A blade, slightly curved and seven inches long, emerged. It was eggshell-white from blade to leather-wrapped handle. Upon closer inspection, he realized it was made of bone, smooth and sharp. The round pommel bore a rune carved into each side that consisted of five overlapping lines. Peter held it out and found it perfectly balanced.

"That is a basilisk-fang dagger. It will hold its own against any blade, even your black Thalmein for a time," Breekie said, his eyes lingering lustfully on the black sword.

Peter handed the knife to Jessica to examine, a greedy glint in her eye.

"The sheath also good. Good for washing in *yad*," interjected Cheekie.

"Yad?" Peter asked.

"Venom. It is Russian for venom."

"Does the dagger have a name?

Cheekie's brow furrowed, and he answered. "It is custom of dwarves for the builder to name their creation. But…" He glanced at Breekie. "We thought it was human tradition for wielder to name a blade after it's been bloodened."

"That may have been the case once, but in this area, we will follow your example," Peter replied gracefully.

Breekie stroked his long beard thoughtfully. "Is called Shazal then."

Peter raised his eyebrows curiously. "Is there a translation for that?"

Cheekie and Breekie glanced at each other, stone-cold expressions on their faces, and shook their heads. Dr. Walker spoke up with a mirth-filled chuckle. "Fangblade would be the closest English translation."

"Fitting," Simon said with a smirk from across the table.

"Bah, is but a dagger. Come, we have better to show you." As Breekie spoke, he and Cheekie pulled the tarp on the table off, exposing the table's contents.

Behind them, one of the side doors to the Forge opened, and in stepped council member Lt. Rory Effith, a fiery-headed man with an equally orange goatee. He was ladened with the finest tactical accessories a child could ask for: a totally furnished rifle with the most up-to-date fixtures on the civilian market, a wrist-mounted GPS, lightweight body armor with impeccably clean camouflage, and half a dozen pouches, the uses for which escaped Peter's practiced eye.

Rory proudly displayed several nonstandard velcroed symbols on his front plate. Peter would have written off the entire package as amateurish fantasy if not for a distinctive scrollwork patch emblazoned front and center. *Seventy-fifth Ranger Regiment, and a deployment patch at that. Easy enough to fake, but only a madman would do so in a military town. The chances of reprisal were too high. Maybe this guy has something going for him after all.* Peter made a mental note to dig into it later.

The walking Hollywood poster paused halfway through the door and muttered something to someone on the other side. Peter tensed slightly at the thought of a council member being present for the meeting. *At least it's only this low-threat, walking VA advertisement. I need their support, whether I like it or not. We can't do all this alone.*

O'Cleary leaned over and whispered into Peter's ear in a playful tone, "What's the ginger injury doing here?"

Peter chose to answer for everyone present. *Best not to dress him down in front of his would-be constituents.* "Everyone, this is Lieutenant Rory Effitth. He was recently selected for the city council. Now that he's here, we can get to the point of this gathering," Peter said to the small group. "As soon as our dwarf friends finish going over their progress, that is," he added to combat the wounded look emerging on Breekie's face.

Lt. Rory nodded at the table's occupants as he made his way over, taking up a position at Dr. Walker's side. "Good morning, everyone. My apologies for being late, and for interrupting you, Mister Breekie. Please, continue."

At a nod from Peter, Cheekie reached down to the table and picked up a gladius-style sword, just over two feet long, with a pommel and small crossguard. This sword was not made of metal. It was the same polished, almost glowing, white bone as the dagger. Peter assumed the black material wrapping the handle was leather.

Cheekie handed the blade to Peter with a sparkle of pride in his eyes.

Peter tossed it from one hand to the other. It was perfectly balanced, light as a stick of similar length.

"We have more, but you name this one. Perhaps you trade for your black blade?" Breekie said with a sly look at Peter.

"Unless I'm mistaken, you're offering to trade me something that is already my shared property with Doctor Walker and Miss Young. Or did your elder misinform me of slaying customs among your people?"

"Nyet, nyet, nyet. She is right." Breekie shook his head vigorously. "You had said yes, I would have cursed you for a fool. A Thalmein blade has no better. You must tell us more of yours later. Is first I have seen this color."

Cheekie spoke up impatiently. "Name the bone sword Non-Dashnaval. We have more to show."

Peter passed the sword delicately to Steven. "We'll call it Shadowfang the First," he said with a smirk. "How many more do you have?"

All three dwarves chuckled at this before Cheekie answered. "Is good name. We have twelve. Can make thirty-four. But we could make many more spears instead and arrows." He looked knowingly around at the humans. "Long arms, long weapon, little experience — you will want spear and arrow."

"Very well. Twelve Shadowfangs and as many spears and arrows as you can give me." Peter paused, looking at Dr. Walker. "These will work on what's out there?" he asked with a hint of doubt in his voice.

Dr. Walker spoke up at last. "They will work against most, although the only fayeleger you should do battle against is the orkum. Where these weapons fail, you resort to firearms. Should they fail as well, flee. Should you need to return here, there are protections which Sarah and I have established that will shelter us against most any foe you encounter."

That's the idea. I wonder what kind of protections she's talking about.

"Okay, that's enough. This is a joke, right?" Jessica interrupted, her face almost red with anger. "You don't actually expect us to go out there wielding swords and spears made of animal bones. Really, captain, we all have better things to do than indulge in your hobbies or sit through some elaborate prank." Jessica cursed in frustration.

"No, Jessica, this is not a joke. You weren't there when Shadowfang attacked," Peter shot back. "Guns were useless. Cheekie and Breekie have given us the tools to defend ourselves, and we need to use them," Peter said with a flat voice.

"I'm not leading a handful of soldiers armed just with bone daggers and spears into god knows what. If an M4 and explosives can't do the job, do you honestly think a bone knife will?" Jessica replied, her voice boarding on irate.

"I'm not asking you to. Take your usual load out, but bring some of what we're being provided with as well. This is all hands on deck, Jessica. I need every able-bodied SNW member that we select to be ready to go by tomorrow morning."

"You're insane," the big man who'd come in with Jessica spat out with disgust.

Peter turned to face him.

"Is there a problem, Mister…?" He left his implied question of the man's name to hang in the air.

"Name's Elijah. Elijah Rangsford, Blair." The man puffed out his chest a bit as he spoke.

"It's *Captain* Blair to you, Rangsford. I asked you a question. Is there a problem?"

"Hah! Captain of what exactly, Petey?"

"Elijah," Jessica's voice cautioned the man to restrain himself with the word.

"No, Jessica. I've had enough," he snapped back before staring down at Peter.

"You're mad. You don't have the authority to draft anyone into this. This. madness, *captain*." He spat out the last word as if it were poison.

Peter smiled harshly. Jadis' eyes flashed in his mind. *Buddy, you haven't seen madness yet. No. Think. If you were him, you'd think this is nuts too. Still, insubordination cannot be tolerated in times of emergency. Calm down. Fear is his motivator. Help him direct it. Tell him what he's up against, how deadly the world has become.*

"Do you want to die, Elijah?" Peter asked.

"Are you threatening me?" Elijah replied with a voice brimming with disbelief. *No, you idiot' I'm—* "Who do you think you are?"

"Who do I think I am? I'm the reason you're still alive," Peter shouted back, the limit of his patience for the man reached.

Elijah's face contorted with rage, and he sputtered nonsensically. *Great, he's going to want to fight now — in front of a council member. I don't need this.* Peter followed the man's eyes as he tried to size up Peter. They froze on Peter's hand, which was resting on the hilt of his sword. *When did I do that…?*

In front of him, Elijah glanced back and forth between Peter's hand and eyes several times like a parrot bobbing its head. Peter felt a hand on his raised arm and tore his attention from Elijah to look at Simon, who'd grasped his arm.

Simon gave his head an almost imperceptible shake. Peter tensed then relaxed his grip on the sword.

"You were going to kill me. I was right. You are crazy. I'm out of here. Don't try and stop me," Elijah shouted and stormed off. It was then that Peter realized how quiet the Forge was, all the hammering and welding having halted.

Peter turned back to the table of stunned faces. "I was going to say, if we don't do this, we're all going to die anyway." He shrugged. "Jessica, finish selecting your team and arm them with whatever these two offer you. That's an order."

"If it's all the same to you, captain," interjected Rory, "I'll be leading a party of my own, and we won't be using any of this. Do what you will with your men, but I trust good old-fashioned American firepower."

Dr. Walker spoke up. "Lieutenant Effith, I really must encourage you and the rest of those present," she said with a glance at Jessica, "to at least carry a few of the weapons being provided. You may find they'll save your life."

Effith shifted uncomfortably in his plates like a man who hadn't worn kit in a long time. "Ma'am, we'll be running a reconnaissance mission. We won't be going far, and unlike Captain Blair here, none of us would know the first thing about how to use 'em."

Rory smiled warmly. "If we do run into any major threats, we'll lose 'em in the woods and head back here. This is our country, after all. Wouldn't be the first time a few under-armed Americans took advantage of the woods they call home."

Peter sighed. *Why won't people listen? Fine. If people want to get themselves killed, that's on them. You can't help those who don't want it.* "That's your prerogative, lieutenant, but this isn't ranger school. Your enemy isn't here to assess you, and it certainly won't play fair. Do you need backup?" he asked.

Effith shrugged. "If you've got a volunteer. I've seen what your boys can do on tour. Wouldn't be opposed to one joining up and carrying one of yer bones if they want to." He scratched the back of his neck.

This guy might have some salt after all, Peter thought. "Speakin' of Gunter, put yer cig out and get in here," he called towards the cracked-open door behind him. A second later, Gunter stepped into the building, flicking a cigarette over his shoulder to the ground outside. A smirk etched onto his bearded face.

O'Cleary muttered something venomous Peter couldn't make out.

"Gunter's being assigned to your squad, cap'n. We expect you to return with him intact. Gunter, you're to follow Captain Blair's orders. Is that understood?"

"Yes, sir," Gunter said, still smirking.

Peter drew in a deep breath through his nose, careful to not let it show. Having Gunter around would be almost as trying as facing trial. "You can have one of ours too, lieutenant, so long as you don't get him lost. I'm sure you remember how to spell it." Effith looked as if he had finally caught on to all of Peter's prodding. He adjusted his kit again.

"Hilarious, Captain Blair, but even I can spell lost without LT. That joke has been out of style since you traded your uniform for a fatter paycheck." Peter grinned. At least this guy wasn't completely hopeless.

"Anything else, lieutenant?"

"My team will be heading south. Team Albany. Any objections?"

"None."

"Then proceed," Rory said with a wave of his hand.

Peter nodded. "I think we've done all we can here, for now. I'll continue to go over what our friends have provided us. Jessica, you're leading Team Augusta. Be ready by oh-eight hundred. William, if you're up to it, I'd like you to lead Team Columbus to the west."

The dark-skinned man nodded in agreement. "I'll be taking one of those swords myself if there's one to spare. If this lot says that big snake was bullet-proof and one of these'll stop it, then I'm taking one," William replied.

"Good. You and O'Cleary discuss with Jessica who's available. Follow roads as long as you can. From what we've seen so far from short patrols, terrain has changed.

O'Cleary, I need you to put together my team. Hauch, Simon, and you are already on it. We'll need a few more. Standard recon operations."

"Forgetting about me already, cap?" Gunter interjected. Peter wanted to ignore him but thought better of it. "O'Cleary has good ears, Gunter. He knows you'll be joining us rather than staying behind. Speaking of… "Peter turned back to the rest of the group.

Jessica was already making her way towards the door.

"Jessica, this goes for all of you. Volunteers only. This may as well be a suicide mission. I expected all SNW personnel to volunteer willingly, but it would seem I was mistaken. Use your own discretion." He paused. "One last thing. Steven, you remain here with your own assignments. Understood?"

"Yes, sir." The words were echoed by all present, and they broke to go their separate ways. In a few moments, the sound of working resumed, and only Peter, the dwarves, Sarah, Steven, O'cleary and Gunter remained.

"Steven, you're in charge of operations while I'm gone. I want you to learn as much from our guests as possible. I'm sure you're already halfway done with that."

"About two-thirds done, yeah," the big man said with a smirk.

"Good. Meet with William before leaving and put together a training regimen for the weapons they're providing us. I want every person in the city trained on how to use these things. We will be ready if we are attacked again. If the council gives you any grief, I'm sure Doctor Walker can help smooth things over." He glanced at the gray-haired woman for confirmation.

She nodded. "Absolutely."

"Very well. The rest of you are dismissed. I will see you at oh-seven hundred for a final briefing, prepped for a three-day reconnaissance operation before departure at oh-eight hundred."

With that, Peter and O'Cleary and the two dwarves stepped to the side of the room with Dr. Walker. "Now, Mister Blair, a matter I wished to discuss. I have a member for your party. One of the Fellhammers," she said firmly as she raised a shaky hand to stop Peter from interrupting.

"They both have a greater understanding of the old world than anyone other than myself. I would accompany you, but the city still needs work if it is to be a paragon for all." She sighed. "Sarah's skills are progressing quickly, but she has much to learn. If you take one of them, you will have a proficient arcane user and an experienced traveler."

Peter fiddled with the pommel of his sword, absentmindedly for a moment as he thought. "Can the work that needs to be done here continue with just one of them?"

Cheekie pulled at the tip of his curled dark mustache. "Dah. I can do without Breekie. Maybe faster. Steven Thomas is quick, and work is simple."

Breekie grinned widely. "Bah, Cheekie is scared there is another basilisk in the woods. He would rather stay here safe behind walls than search the world for knowledge," he teased the other dwarf.

"Much knowledge is to be found in an empty cave. You must only look closer," Cheekie shot back, his cheeks growing a bit red.

Dr. Walker grinned back. "I have not heard a Boleshikn proverb in a millennium."

She pounded her cane on the floor twice, her smile disappearing. "It is decided then. Breekie will accompany your team, Peter, as I fear you may be taking the most dangerous path."

"All right, O'Cleary, can you put together the rest of the team?"

"Aye, I'll meet you back here then," O'Cleary replied.

"Good." Peter glanced around as O'Cleary slid out the door. "Doctor Walker, I don't have time at the moment, but there is something I would like to discuss with you in the morning. Can you meet us at oh-six hundred at the north gate?"

"Of course, Mister Blair," The old dwarf replied, her head bobbing up and down. "I'll be there bright and early."

✦— 17 —✦

LINE OF DEPARTURE

Dr. Walker was better than her word. She met Peter and Simon on their way to the gate accompanied by Sarah and the two dwarves, a small box of homemade donuts tucked under her arm.

"Good morning, all." Peter glanced at the two dwarves and Sarah. "Breekie, Simon can show you where to load your supplies." He looked to the other two. "If you don't mind going on ahead, I'd like a word with Doctor Walker in private?" he said, gesturing to a nearby vacated coffee shop.

The others complied, and the two of them stepped inside together a moment later. Peter closed the door softly behind them and remained standing. The dwarf took a slow and deliberate seat at a small table. She looked older than ever.

"Are you all right, Doctor Walker?"

"I've told you before, Peter, you may call me Walker. We both know I have my doctorates, so there is no reason to remind ourselves in private. As to your question, I am as healthy as could be, just finally feeling my age, and yet, feeling younger than ever now that the world is returning to how it should be," she explained.

How should it be? Full of death and fear? No, Peter, come on, you know that's not what she meant.

"How long do your people live? You were old when I met you as a child, and my parents always said you were old when they met you before I was born," he said curiously.

"We dwarves do live a good deal longer than humans, although none of my people have lived as long as I have. The Therin-Selu not only saved my people but in some strange way has kept me alive since it was cast." She took a bite of a donut and smiled.

Peter gave her a moment to chew before replying, "You didn't answer my question."

The dwarf smiled, donut gore decorating her lips. "I believe I'm about ten thousand three hundred and forty-two years old."

Peter's jaw dropped. *Over ten thousand years old?* "How— How have you not been driven mad?"

She shrugged casually. "Hope. Rest. Study. I gave myself things to do and got lots of rest. Decades of it — sometimes centuries. I missed the fall of Rome due to that," she said with a grimace. "In all my years, I have found that exhaustion is the mind's greatest threat to itself. I cannot stress how important it is for one to rest. This is no time for my history though. What is it you wanted to discuss with me?"

Peter's mouth quirked to the side in what was almost a smile. He had so many questions but so little time. "You mentioned before that humans saw through the Therin-Selu in their dreams, that bits and pieces of what we'd forgotten leaked over, and that is why we wrote stories and myths of creatures we thought didn't exist."

"Yes, very astute, as always, Mister Blair." She cracked the box of sweet-smelling donuts back open and offered it to him.

He shook his head, and she shrugged, taking a glistening round treat in her hand and bringing it to her mouth. "Is it possible that something else was left behind — something trapped, over there, or in the spell or however it works? Is it possible not everything came back?"

Dr. Walker frowned a deep and contemplative expression. "No. I do not believe so. Why do you ask?"

"I've been having dreams, visions really. They're so real. There is a girl, well, a creature. She has gray skin with strange scars, white hair, and purplish eyes. It looks like how you described an elf. She seems to know things about Galvorn."

"Galvorn?"

"That's what she calls the sword you gave me," he said and patted the handle.

"A fitting name. Not all dreams are… a peek behind the curtain, so to speak. There are those who know the magic of dreams better than I, but a strange being appearing in them hardly qualifies… I'm sorry, Peter, you wouldn't have mentioned it if there was not more to it. Go on," she said, taking out another donut.

"Thank you. When I asked if she was an elf, she got offended and insisted on calling herself an Eölin."

Dr. Walker's eyes flashed, barely perceptible, but it was there. *Holding out on me, are we, doctor?* Peter continued, "The strangest thing is that I remember every detail. It's not fuzzy or missing pieces like a dream. It's vivid and clear, like a memory. Well, stronger than that even. Oh, the sword is there too, embedded in the ground. She told me it was more than a dream. I seriously cannot express to you just how real it felt, but every time it happens, I wake up when it ends." Peter stopped. Realizing that his voice was becoming heated. "Sorry."

Dr. Walker shook her head. "No need to be. These dreams or visions are obviously bothering you. I have a few questions, and I need you to answer them honestly."

Peter nodded. "Of course."

"Did the creature change forms at any time during these dreams? Did she take the form of a dead relative? Your sister, perhaps?"

Peter was caught off guard but answered quickly. "No, she remained the same being for both dreams. Never anyone I know, living or… deceased."

Dr. Walker's brow furrowed. "Did she attempt to seduce or feed you? A drink, maybe? Wine, or a small fruit perhaps?"

Peter did not blush despite the personal nature of the question. "No. We spoke and sparred a bit. She was much stronger and faster than me, but there was no exchange of anything other than information."

Her wrinkles shifted on her broad face as she thought. "And she did not swear you to secrecy?"

"She suggested I would be dismissed as mad if I spoke of her. She was obsessed with me keeping Galvorn, even threatening to use someone else to kill me if I got rid of it or that I would die regardless without it."

"I see…" Dr. Walker was clearly deep in thought, so Peter waited on her to sort through her mind. A soft scrape on the other side of the wall drew Peter's attention for a moment. *Someone's trying to listen to us,* he thought but did not make for the door.

Nothing he'd said so far would make any sense to anyone who overheard, and if the sound was loud enough to reach his ears, only a fool would have remained there for him to catch. Peter fingered the hammer of his sidearm beneath the table. *And if they remained when the conversation was over…*

"Listen to me carefully, Peter. There is no such thing as an Eölin or dark elves or anything like the creature you've described. They are a fantasy created by humans. There are a few such creatures, to your credit. Nothing could still remain beyond the veil of the Therin-Selu. I would know."

She chewed for a moment, her eyes distant as she considered her next words. "The creature you're seeing is most likely a manifestation of your imagination due to unprecedented stress, exhaustion, and the awakening of new abilities which I have, to my chagrin, failed to address. It may well be that your subconscious is trying to work through all of these changes."

She snapped her fingers. "It's likely even that your mind has created a persona in your dreams. You see, dreams are a place where ancient magic resides as a way of training your mind and allowing your skills to grow, especially if these dreams are preceded by extremely stressful events during which you used this new magic." She eyed him scrupulously and took another bite of donut.

Now that's not something I want someone overhearing, he thought, listening intently for signs of the eavesdropper.

"I do not know all there is to know about dreams, but if it were a creature reaching out from beyond our walls to meddle with your mind as you sleep, I would have sensed it. Darker… well…" She struggled with a thought for a moment, working her jaw distractedly.

"Spirits, demons truly, would have taken a different form had they approached you in a dream, and there would have been" —She paused again, rubbing the back of her hand— "side effects. But do not worry about such things," she said dismissively.

Peter stood silently, stretching his legs, deep in thought. *Stress makes more sense than anything else. The dreams did happen right after Shadowfang and right after the dwarves. It does seem to want to help me get better at defending myself… The obsession with the sword could just be my own dependency on it manifesting with my fear of helplessness.*

It was all possible. Still, Peter couldn't shake the suspicion in the depths of his gut that there was something Dr. Walker wasn't telling him. *No sense in pressing her. If she isn't trustworthy, we're worse off than we thought. Making accusations and division would doom us all just as surely.*

He ran a thumb over the bandage on his finger. *Fine, if she has something she's keeping from me, there's nothing I can do other than wait and watch.* "Thank you, Doctor Walker. Let me know if you think of anything else. Follow up question — what are the new abilities you referenced?"

"Well, Peter, one of the side effects of the Therin-Selu was that many members of humanity developed disabilities. Your legs when you were younger, for example."

Peter's mind flashed back to the dozens of times his legs had given out, or his calves had spasmed so severely that the muscles had moved around to the wrong side of his shin.

"Handicaps, as it were, came about because your bodies were trying to compensate for the severing of your connection to the arcane flow." She spoke as if she'd rehearsed the words a hundred times. "I believe I may have mentioned this before, although maybe that was to Sarah…" She trailed off for a moment.

As she stared off into the silence, Peter raised a finger to his lips, signaling for quiet as he made his way carefully to the door. One hand holding his drawn pistol, he whipped open the door and spun around to the corner he'd heard the noise from but saw nothing.

He was surprisingly disappointed to find no one there, but he did spy a smoldering cigarette on the ground. He cursed in his mind. *I don't have time to chase this down. We need to leave soon,* he thought as he returned to the table, where a contemplative dwarf sat staring into nothing.

"Umindrabo?" Peter said softly.

"Hmmm? Oh, no human has called me that in… Well, I can't remember now. No matter. As I was saying, from what I have seen and heard from Cheekie and Breekie's accounting, you possess passive magic."

Peter raised his eyebrows, knowing the tired-looking dwarf would get to the point in her own time, faster than if he questioned her.

"It's a bit of a different skillset from Sarah and me, who use active magic. Well, most casters, really, but still handy. Unfortunately, I have little experience with passive magic… I'm sorry, dear. I'm rambling, and you must leave soon. I'll be more concise. Just give me a moment," she said with a wave of her hand.

Peter nodded, watching her closely as she devoured yet another donut. "Essentially, your ability will affect you with minor effort on your part. Like your heart beating. You make it beat, but not consciously."

She raised her cane and tapped it on the table. "Humanity is different from most of the faye because magic is a rarity among your kind." She rubbed her temples with both hands. "I'm sorry I've not spoken on this in some time other than what I've been teaching Sarah. I seem to be having more trouble focusing lately," she added.

"Am I in danger of hurting myself?" Peter asked cautiously.

Dr. Walker smiled. Her face glowing with the expression. "No. Not as a result of your ability… Quite the opposite, in fact, if I am not mistaken. Unfortunately, I cannot offer you the same advice or training I can provide to Sarah, or I would. You should be in no danger, but be careful, Peter. Do not fear using it. The more you do, the stronger it will become, and the greater your tolerance for it will be. You may find it drains your energy, though, so do exercise some caution."

She eyed the open box of donuts as she finished speaking but closed it with a slight shake of her head. "Is there anything else?" Dr. Walker asked eagerly.

"No," Peter replied quietly.

"Good. Here, this is for you." She produced a small round silver pendant at the end of a thong of leather. Carved into the quarter-sized medallion were three connected spirals, identical to the symbol at the center of the crossguard of his sword. "This will symbolize that you are a friend to my kind and elves. It will, at the very least, make them hesitate before attacking you."

Peter took it and put the necklace around his neck.

With a close-lipped smile, Dr. Walker clambered out of her seat and made for the door. Peter turned, beat her to the door, and held it for her as she left, then followed her out, making his way to the wall from which he'd spied the cigarette.

Peter sighed. With no real evidence, there was no one to accuse. Besides, none of what he heard would make any sense or be of any real consequence to share. Peter stood and began to follow Dr. Walker towards the gates. *I could deny it if they said something, but there really wouldn't be a point in denying I'm having weird dreams.*

Peter picked up his pace and came up beside Dr. Walker, forcing him to slow again, his boots echoing on the uneven pavement leading to the outer perimeter. He felt a single bead of sweat form on his brow and work its way down the side of his face.

Things had been unnaturally cold lately, but for some reason, today was a typical fall Georgia morning, uncomfortably hot and unbearably humid. The rest of the walk through town was uneventful enough; only a solitary police patrol breaking his solitude. He could see now that his peace was at an end.

The north gate was a whirl of activity in the predawn hours. Even at a distance of two hundred meters, Peter could make out a small crowd gathered near the line of vehicles poised at the opening. He saw several of his own people making preparations and final checks of gear and equipment.

He moved to the front of the gathering. It was a strange sight: four squads, three of which were familiar SNW faces, with a handful of extra volunteers. All three were armed with standard gear and reinforced with basilisk armor enhancement and weapons. This only made Effith's unit stick out even more.

There was a diversity of age among the three SNW groups, but there was even more among Rory's. They ranged from what looked like an eighteen-year-old to a man in his late forties. All were dressed in inconsistent camo, none of it matching. This, of course, defeated the entire purpose of wearing it in the first place, but none of them seemed to mind. They were ROTC, Veterans, and volunteer police officers.

Each of them is braver than most, though. Peter nodded to his company man on the team, who was giving his new basilisk-bone gladius a few practice swings. He was one of the only soldiers there not accompanied by family or friends. In fact, now that he was looking for it, he noticed just about everyone there was saying goodbye to one civilian or another.

William was hugging his blonde wife and young son tightly, whispering words of comfort into their ears. *Been a while since he had to do that, hasn't it?* Peter felt a pang of guilt at the sight. The majority of civilians to volunteer farewells, though, were taking place in Rory's group. Most notable was a thin middle-aged mother struggling with a man no older than nineteen who could only have been her son. She was quite literally trying to pry him out of his uniform and drag him off. This created an awkward tension among those around them as she bordered on screaming, "You're just a boy. Not a soldier. I don't care what you told them. You're just ROTC."

The poor fool should listen to his mother, Peter found himself thinking, but before he could take a step in their direction, the boy planted his feet and grabbed his mother by the shoulders, pulling her into a fragile hug. Her arms flailed for a moment before collapsing into the embrace.

A few paces away, William's son began to cry, driving the knife of guilt deeper into Peter's chest. *I could tell them all to go home. I could just do this myself,* he thought, but logic quickly caught up. *You can't split yourself into four, Peter. Besides, they're all here by choice. You can't take that from them.*

His eyes flitted over the other farewells, and he found himself wishing he had someone to say goodbye to himself. *It's your own fault you're single, you workaholic. Besides, even if Mom and Dad were here, Dad'd be trying to lead a squadron himself, and that'd just leave Mom. And she hates goodbyes. It's better this way.*

Peter's eyes lingered on O'Cleary and the boy next to him, standing awkwardly alone as the groups divided into distinct squads, the civilians and family gathering in a crowd off to the side. *Guess I'm not the only one.*

Seeing his opportunity, Peter made his way through the press to Rory, who'd just finished saying goodbye to a woman almost as ginger as he was.

"Quite the crew you've put together here, LT. Half of them look like they went through Desert Storm, and the rest couldn't find Afghanistan using a smartphone map." Effith bristled, his patience with Peter's jabs wearing thin.

"I know what we're about, captain. I did my time in the sand the same as you. They've earned their stripes, one way or another." Half a dozen wisecracks came to mind, but Peter thought better of it and instead extended a hand.

"We're already too short on good people, Rory. We can't afford to lose any more. If you get into trouble, come right back — no heroics, all right?"

Effith smiled and took Peter's hand. "You have my word, captain." With that, he dropped the handshake.

For your sake and mine, I hope you're right.

"We'll be leaving here shortly. I have a reputation to uphold, after all. Rangers lead the way, captain."

Peter stopped himself from wincing. *Enthusiastic but predictable — one of many reasons I went corporate.* Peter nodded and walked off in search of his own team, ready to be leaving, himself.

As Peter approached his squad, he spied O'Cleary coming his way. At his side, was a familiar light brown-skinned teenage boy dressed up in military gear. *Is that the kid I assigned him for watch duty? What's he doing here?*

O'Cleary quickened his pace to put himself ahead of the boy, telling him over his shoulder to wait. Shawn shrugged, stopped, and pulled a strange metal ring roughly the size of a crown out, which he began toying with.

"Ready to go?" Peter said to O'Cleary as they met in a familiar shoulder-patting embrace, his eyes lingering on the boy.

O'Cleary raised both hands in surrender. "I know, he's just a lad, but he's got nowhere else to be. Captain, his mom and da are gone. Only kin he's got are in Atlanta. Besides, the wain handled himself well when C and B showed up."

"Wain?"

"Yeah, the kid. He's eager to learn, and if he doesn't learn now, he might not get the chance. Besides, didn't the old dwarf-woman say something about his eyes? I could use a spotter with good eyes out there, and we've got everyone else we need."

Peter's eyes narrowed as his friend spoke. He glanced at the boy then back to O'Cleary, his meaning clicking. "Brandon, you can't actually be suggesting we bring him with us. The last thing I need is that boy's blood on my hands right now."

"Leaving him here's worse, the way I see it. Least this way, he learns how to take care of himself. Besides, who's got a better track record than you? Far as I'm concerned, near you is the safest he can get." He paused, rubbing the back of his neck. "He'll be my responsibility. You haven't got to worry about him taking a step outta line. He's got sharp eyes. Even the dwarf says so."

"You said that already," Peter replied, glowering; annoyed but not angry. "I assume he'll just follow us anyway if we leave him behind now, thanks to you."

"Ha ha, the lad might do just that. Then he'd be in real trouble. He's barely a wain anyway, cap'n. Most places, a boy of fifteen is a man already."

"Who else do we have?" Peter asked, chewing on the suggestion.

O'Cleary began counting on his fingers. "Jenni, Justin, Simon, you, me, Hauch, Breekie, and Gunter," he said with a scowl.

"That makes nine with the boy. You gonna take the heat from Jenni?"

"More like six and a half, counting the dwarf and Hauch," O'Cleary replied, smirking. "Transportation's taken care of," he said more seriously, "and I doubt Jenni will have a problem. If anything, she'll relate to the boy."

Good point. Growing up in a civil war-torn country does give her a unique perspective. "Fine. But his blood is on your hands if something happens."

"Right. Like you'd let anything happen to that lad or the rest of us any more than I would," he said with a wink.

As the last of the stragglers trickled into the crowd, Peter took a deep breath. *I should have prepared something. Too late now. Just say what comes to you…* He turned to his squad and the two other SNW formations, and with nods from Jessica, William spoke in a voice just loud enough for all of them to hear.

"I want to thank you, guys. None of you has to do this. There's no payday this time. It just has to be done, and each of you has chosen to see that it is. I wish I could tell you this is standard recon, but it's not. It's as far from standard as it can get."

He ran his eye over them. Some looked excited, eager to be off, but most knew better. Most had the look of those haunted by things to come. Fear of the unknown.

"I don't know what you'll see out there. I wish I did. But we need to seek peaceful options before resorting to violence. If it comes to violence, don't hold back. Make sure you are the one who survives." Peter brought his hands together, popping his knuckles.

"Follow your commander's instructions, stay safe, and most importantly, don't die. I'll see all of you back here in three days."

There was no applause. No *oo-rahs*. Only a silent nodding of heads and the quiet exchange of handshakes and goodbye's as they split to go their separate ways, loading into their mix of jeeps and Polaris MRZR 4 off-roaders. Peter's unit was the first out of the gate and the only one going straight. Five mercenaries, a civilian volunteer, a teenager, a dog, and a dwarf due north into the unknown.

✦ 18 ✦

UNCLE BIL-Y'S BBQ SHACK

Shawn righted the potted plant by the fence then returned to his seat. The nine-member group led by Captain Peter Blair had stopped to rest at *Uncle Bil-y's BBQ Shack* at the end of their second day of traveling. The sun was getting low, and the building offered them shelter and a place to warm themselves.

As they approached the building, they found it teeming with plant life encroaching on the walls and entrance. It took little effort to remove the shrubbery, and they decided to use it to get a fire going. The back of the restaurant, an open area made for outdoor seating and cooking, was fenced in.

At the center of the area sat a covered fire pit. The cover itself resembled a sizable upside-down metal colander with two rods, one of which opened at the top, allowing for more wood to be tossed in, and another opened smaller windows across the metal frame for releasing heat or smoke. From these windows, the faint leftover scent of barbecue drifted into the air as the fire warmed the party.

Seven figures were gathered around that glowing pit; eight counting Hauch, who lay at Shawn's feet basking in the warmth of the fire. Across from him, Peter sat in a small chair closest to the rods, staring into the flames of the open windows in the cover. O'Cleary rested at his side, drinking from a flask he procured with dinner.

The soft light from the fire bathed their campsite in a low glow. The shrubbery covered the fence that surrounded them, cutting off the outside world from the heat and most of the light.

Behind Peter, Justin sat at a table that held his disassembled rifle he was examining. Sitting to Shawn's left was Simon, a plant-patterned notebook in hand being utilized with utmost efficiency. A few steps from Simon, Gunter sat upon a metal chair he'd pulled closer to the fire, the man's stare focused on

Peter. In fact, it hardly ever seemed to waver from Peter. Shawn could not recall having looked at Gunter's bearded face without finding it directed at Peter.

A chilly breeze ran through the gathering, causing people to scoot closer to the fire or tighten their jackets. *I hope Jenni isn't too cold up there by herself,* Shawn thought as he tossed a glance at the roof of the restaurant behind them. After a moment of searching, he found her, still and silent with a rifle in hand and some kind of night vision on her face, looking out into the night.

He liked Jenni, with her dark red hair with black roots showing, tan Middle Eastern skin, and a gap-toothed smile. She was one of Hauch's trainers and had been friendly to Shawn from the beginning of the trip. They all were, really; more than he'd expected.

Shawn fidgeted absentmindedly with his pistol, which he kept pointed at the ground as he continued loading and unloading the magazine. His hands warmed the cold metal. O'Cleary had given it to him the morning of their departure, shoving the heavy weapon into his hands and repeating the safety rules he'd told him with the flare.

Never point at anything you don't intend to shoot. Keep the safety on and finger off the trigger unless shooting, Shawn repeated to himself. *I hope I don't have to shoot it.*

The presence of the pistol comforted him, but the thought of using it made him queasy, or maybe it was the barbecue smell reminding him of the burning pits that made his stomach turn. Another cool breeze caused goosebumps to appear on his arms. Shawn slid the pistol into its holster and leaned closer to the fire, extending his hands out until the warmth of the flames chased away the numbing cold.

The fire popped and crackled, floating sparks and embers up with the smoke into the dark cloudy sky. In the waning light, the story being told by the bald, broad-bearded dwarf, Breekie, in his thick Russian accent continued.

"We buried the old man in his garden." *Sniff.* Breekie wiped a tear from his eye with the back of his hand. "I wish we'd spoken his words. Much knowledge he took with him to the earth, I am sure."

Those gathered around the flames waited in silence for Breekie to contin-ue. Shawn watched a tear slide down O'Cleary's face into his scraggly stubble, which was only a day away from becoming a beard.

Hauch rose from his place at Shawn's feet. As he moved, the transitioning color of his fur, with the dye fading, made the dog look more like a shadow than a living creature. The dog made his way silently around the fire pit until he reached Breekie's side, where he nuzzled at the dwarf's leg.

Breekie's face broke into an enormous grin, and he chuckled quietly and said, "You're not as mean as you'd have me think, are you, dog?"

Until now, Hauch had been avoiding Breekie since the moment they left the city. The first night, it had been hard not to notice the dog meticulously smelling each of the other members of the squad he was unfamiliar with. When Breekie tried for his attention, Hauch had reacted strangely. There was no growling, but his ears had laid flat, and he'd shown his fangs.

This was enough for Breekie, who'd left him alone. Jenni had been particularly perplexed by the behavior, claiming she'd never seen him act that way. Regardless, her encouragement made no difference, and Hauch had stayed clear of Breekie.

Now, Hauch sat calmly by the dwarf, wagging his tail ever so slightly as Breekie petted him.

"How did you find your way to us?" Shawn asked, eager to hear the rest of the story.

Breekie shrugged. "The old man had, uh, a map. On a table. Dah, with big arrows and circles. I think he drew it himself. We followed and found your city." Breekie's eyes went wide. "I do not know your city name. What is it called?"

"Paragon." The words came from Peter, whose gaze was locked on the fire. "I always thought it was awfully haughty to name it that, but that's what it needs to be now — a place we can send people to be safe. No more basilisks or other monsters are going to attack it. Dr. Walker's seeing to that. It'll be sheltered from the horrors of this new world once we're done."

Horrors? Are there more monsters out here like the snake? Wait, duh. That was stupid, Shawn. That's why we're out here. Stupid. Maybe it would have been safer to stay behind after all… Oh, well.

"City's off to a rough start if it's supposed to be an example of the best of humanity," Simon said, just loud enough for everyone to hear.

"Good. Dah, Paragon is a good name," Breekie said.

Across the fire, Gunter stood and crossed his arms. His jaw worked in silent fury as he continued to stare daggers into Peter's chest.

What's his problem? wondered Shawn.

"Sheesh. So, you've gone from paralyzed on the ground, to being in some old man's care, to kicking the captain's tail, to being out here? If I were you, I'd have stayed back in Paragon," said Justin as he lifted his camo hat and rubbed a scarred, freckled hand across his shaved head.

"I wouldn't say no to heading back," called Jenni softly from above them. "It's cold out here."

She's right, Shawn realized. He'd been close to the fire and so enraptured by the conversation that he'd lost track of the cold on his back. He thought of returning to Paragon and found it comforted him despite the emptiness he felt there. *It's nothing like the emptiness out here,* he mused as he glanced out into the darkness of the night.

"Nyet. Paragon is behind us, the world ahead," Breekie replied with a pearly grin. Then he spread his arms. "A king's hall worth of knowledge awaits me with you, I think."

Shawn shifted his seat on the ground, struggling to get comfortable with the number of bruises and scrapes from their trek through the frightening, unfamiliar terrain.

"Knowledge? Is that why you come with us?" O'Cleary blurted.

Simon shot him a vexed look that was impossible to miss.

"What? You're wondering too, aren't ya? It doesn't make sense to me. He left two of his own kind to come with us like a chancer." He paused and looked to the dwarf. "Don't get me wrong, I'm glad to have you. It's just been eating me up wondering why you'd risk it, with you not knowing what's going on anymore than us," the Irishman said.

Breekie's gold-green eyes bore into O'Cleary. "Dah, and because is right thing to do. Helping. Help who needs help. This way, their knowledge will not be lost. It is a sad thing for knowledge to be lost because one was too weak or coward to help. This was my Guelma Folnok's first teaching to me. Your Duelma Umindrabo is of same philosophy."

Shawn stared up at the broken night sky. The scars decorated it, giving off a soft flow of moonlight. "What's a Guelma?" he asked.

Breekie pulled at his round beard contemplatively. "Is tricky. Guelma is like great-grandfather but to all. Same for Duelma. Duelma is like grandmother to all. But more… Chief," he said, chewing each word.

"Cool," Shawn replied, not knowing what else to say.

Breekie raised his eyebrows as he addressed those around the fire. "Come! I have shared knowledge. Is your turn," he said, looking eagerly from face to face.

There was silence for a moment as those around the fire pondered what story to tell a being who was not human and had no experience with humanity.

What would I want to know? Shawn asked himself, grappling with the sheer magnitude of what Breekie did not know about his world.

"We invented airplanes," he blurted.

"Air… planes?" Breekie's response was as eager as a small child's.

"Yeah, they're like big metal birds. We can fly in them, and they're powered by oil."

"These metal birds… are better than wyverns or pegasi?"

"A month ago, I'd have said neither of those exist, so, of course, planes are better. Then again, I have no idea what a wyvern is," interjected Justin, his orange beard seeming aflame in the firelight.

"It's a dragon, I think," said Simon with a shrug.

"Nyet," Breekie insisted. "Nyet, is no dragon. Is Dracolear."

"What?" Shawn asked, inching slightly closer.

"Dracolear. Not dragon, but come from dragons. Wyvern is big lizard — two legs, two wings, long neck. Most can carry two, three men. But more dwarves." He chuckled, amused by his comparison.

"Sounds like a dragon to me," muttered Justin as he continued to reassemble his rifle.

"Nyet. Is much a dragon as you are a dog. Not good dog like Hauch, though," he said with an apologetic look at the hound, which he petted affectionately. "Dragons, much bigger. Smart. Very smart. Can talk. Breath fire. Wyvren just animals. Nyet talk. No fire. Dragon something else." There was no mistaking the fear in his eyes as he spoke. It made Shawn's heart beat faster.

"Hold on. Are you telling me dragons are real too now? You're pulling my leg. Giant snakes are bad enough, but now huge, flying, fire-breathing lizards are roaming about all willy-nilly?" Justin blurted, his face going flush.

Breekie's smile returned. "Huh-huh-huh. Nyet, we no fight dragons. We would lose, all willy-nilly."

Shawn watched Breekie glance at Peter, the dwarf's smile frozen in place, not meeting his eyes.

"Airplanes carry how many?" Breekie asked, his eagerness to move the conversation away from dragons obvious.

"They can hold a couple hundred people, or two if you're in a fighter jet," Justin explained.

Breekie's mouth gaped, he made no effort to hide the shock in his face. "This *is* impressive, but is not a story. I cannot tell you what you do not know since I do not know in return. Is poor exchange. Tell me a history."

"Why don't you tell him how your fearless leader murdered two of his own men in cold blood." Gunter's harsh tone cut through the night like a blade of ice.

Peter didn't so much as flinch. His reaction was more like that of a statue. Shawn wondered if the man had even heard the accusation.

That's true then? he thought. Shawn had been wondering about it for a while. He'd heard the talk around the town during the first days. *Heck, people were still talking about it when we left.* If the stories were true, it happened during the Shattering, an event which somehow now felt like a lifetime ago. *It doesn't really matter though. He helped kill the snake after all. Besides, if those men really were innocent, the council would have done something about him.*

"Now hold on…" Simon began.

"No! If this fella is going to risk his life to help us out, he needs to know what kind of a *man* he's risking it under. *Tell him.*" Gunter's voice rose to a crescendo, then, clenched hands shaking at his sides, he continued coldly, "Tell us all how you killed those men in cold blood, how you can sit here and pretend it didn't happen." His face was red with fury as he glowered down at Peter, who sat still across the fire.

"You weren't there," said Simon calmly, rising to his feet with the grace of a mountain lion.

"*You're right, I wasn't! Else I'd have stopped him killing Keith!*" The shout was loud enough to be heard a mile off. Shawn saw the fells from SNW wince, and Hauch began to bare his teeth.

"Stop your blindin', you thick dosser. You'll bring all manner of manky beasts down on us with your racket," O'Cleary snapped at him.

"What in the hell did you just say?" Gunter asked, having barely lowered his voice.

"He said, stop yelling, or you'll bring whatever's in the forest down on us." Shawn translated, trying not to let panic creep into his words.

"I know what he meant. I'm not an idiot, kid," Gunter shot back, his words softer when he addressed Shawn. Gunter's jaw worked furiously before he spoke again, obviously strained by the effort not to shout. "Doesn't change the fact that Captain Peter here murdered two boys," he said, spitting out Peter's name as if it would poison him.

Shawn met Breekie's gaze across from him. The dwarf looked knowingly at Shawn's hands. It was only then he realized he was clenching the pistol hard with shaking hands. Breekie gave a slight shake of his head and glanced meaningfully at the holster at Shawn's side.

Shawn looked back at Peter. The man's cold, gray eyes pierced straight through him. Shawn froze, unsure what to do. *He should be focusing on Gunter. Why is he looking at me? Oh.*

Peter's eyebrows rose almost imperceptibly, and Shawn slid his gun back into the holster at his side with a soft *click. I should have put it away as soon as things got heated.*

"Like I said. You weren't there, Gunter. I don't know what you heard, but you've been misinformed," Simon repeated.

Gunter redirected his irate gaze towards Simon. "And you were? Go on then, tell them what he did."

Simon watched Gunter carefully before speaking. "We heard screaming inside a shop. William and Captain Peter were the first ones in the building. I was only a few seconds behind them." Simon paused, taking a deep breath before continuing. "A woman's husband was on the ground, skull caved in. They'd killed him over a case of water. Joshua was going through the dead man's pockets, hands covered in blood, when William got to him. Hit him so hard he went through the window. Captain Peter put a round in Kieth's head before he could do anything else to the woman."

Simon didn't so much as flinch as he said it. "I don't have to tell any of you why. The third man, I didn't know, but he tripped over his own unbuckled pants when the captain went for him. He tried to get up and scramble away, but the captain put a bullet in his knee."

Simon's voice was soft. "The captain had us toss the two of them in a closet while I got the story from the woman. It was exactly what it looked like. The one who lost a knee even recorded the whole thing like an idiot, laughing the whole time. We still didn't know what was happening to the world at the time, but we knew communications were down."

Simon shook his head. "Things were too bad for people like that to be left alive. So, Captain Peter had us drag the two of them out into the middle of town." Simon glanced at the dwarf, his expression blank. "He told the crowd what they did and executed them himself. Warning that any similar behavior would be treated the same way until things settled down."

Gunter's face was pale as a sheet. "He had no right. They had rights. You can't just go killing people," he hissed, a strange tremble in his voice.

Justin stood, stretching his arms once he'd clambered to his feet. "If you ask me, they gave up those rights. You knew one of them?"

Gunter's fists clenched tightly at his side. "Yeah, Keith was my exe's brother. He was a good kid. Us and Joshua were drinking buddies. And your captain blew his brains out in the town square."

At least he knows better than to start an actual fight. I don't think Peter would hesitate to kill him. Shawn thought.

"Sounds like he wasn't as good a kid as you thought," scoffed Justin. "Why are you here if you hate the captain so much? I thought this was volunteer work for civvies."

"Oh, I volunteered. They wanted someone to keep an eye on Peter to make sure he didn't go all John Wick on anyone. They knew about my ROTC experience, so when I volunteered, they gave it to me without blinking. Didn't he tell you? This is a banishment trial run. I'm waiting. One slip up, and dear Captain Pete is done," Gunter said, puffing his chest up.

Shawn almost heard the roll of Justin's eyes when Gunter said ROTC.

"So, we've got a kid with us *and* a brat supervisor," said Justin, turning to Simon. "Did you know about this?"

Simon nodded, continuing to watch Gunter closely as the fire died down.

"Nothing to say, *captain*?" The way Gunter said captain made Shawn squeamish every time. He'd never heard someone use a term of rank with so much venomous sarcasm, and it made him uncomfortable.

Peter stood, brushing his hands off on his pants. Galvorn shifted on his back, the jewel in the pommel catching a glint of light from the glowing embers, shining blood red in the dark of night.

"We each have jobs to do. Mine is to eliminate threats. I didn't enjoy killing them. I served with Joshua once, and they were both recruits in my organization." He paused. "But I do not answer to you, and I have no need to justify my actions to you…"

There was no trace of rage or annoyance in his voice. It lacked any emphasis at all. If not for Peter's eyes locked in a contest with Gunter's, Shawn would have thought the man was talking to himself.

Then something moved behind Peter. A shadow shifting in the dark. Shawn almost jumped out of his skin as he scrambled back and to his feet. This flinch was a bolt of electricity through the SNW agents.

Peter's right hand tore the sword from his back loose, and his left hand pointed a pistol into the dark woods. Justin, Simon, and O'Cleary each snapped to a position facing a different direction out of their limited cover. The change was instantaneous and silent. Gunter fell back towards the restaurant and hunkered by the door.

"Jenni." Peter's voice was barely a whisper.

"Nothing. No heat signatures anywhere other than a bird and some kind of rodent in the bushes." Jenni's whisper carried to them from her elevated position.

"Breekie, could there be anything out there that wouldn't give off a heat signature?"

"Heat signatures?" Breekie asked.

"Warm-blooded. I— Crud. Jenni, switch to standard."

"Already there. I'm still not seeing anything."

Breekie stepped forward, scanning the woods from Peter's side. "There are cold things in the night, dah. But I see none… Wait…" The dwarf took another step forward, bracing for combat, then his tight shoulders relaxed, and he lowered his war hammer.

"What did you see?" he asked Shawn over his shoulder.

"A face in the shadows. Like the one I saw back in Paragon. It looked like it was made of wood."

"Is no danger. The boy saw a dryad, huh-huh-huh," Breekie said, the frequent smile he wore returning.

Peter gave no sign of relaxing. "Dryad?"

"Dah, is a... tree spirit. Hard to explain. Good being. She's been following us since Paragon. She likes Shawn, and she's harmless. To us."

He's right, it was like the face I saw before, but this time it was over Peter's shoulder, watching me.

"Come to think of it, I coulda sworn I saw a tree moven earlier," said Justin guiltily, his sidearm starting to lower.

Peter turned back to face the group. "None of you thought to mention this?" he waved a hand dismissively. "Never mind. It's too late. But if you see anything — *anything* out of the ordinary — you say something. We don't know what's out there, and as far as I am concerned, literally nothing is impossible. No matter how strange it might seem right now, say something if you see anything."

"Yes, sir," they all echoed.

"Good. Breekie, should we try and talk to the dryad?"

"Nyet, it will come to us if it wants to. Your jumping scared it. Just don't cut down any young trees," Breekie added with a grin.

"Captain Peter?" Shawn said, after a few moments while watching the man sheath his sword. The scale armor he wore under his jacket did not reflect the glowing embers; although, his eyes did.

"Yes, Shawn?"

"I think I caught a glimpse of it when we were camping last night."

Peter's lips pursed as he returned his pistol to its holster at his side, but he didn't respond. He just aimed a look at O'Cleary that made Shawn's heart fall.

Shawn shrugged, trying to make it seem like it wasn't a big deal. "I didn't realize it until just now. It just looked like a tree — not the same as the leaf lady I saw back home."

Peter winked at Shawn then turned to the woods. "We know you're out there. Why don't you come talk to us?" he called softly into the woods, then said to the dwarf, "I hope you're right, Breekie. It'd be nice to have something friendly out there keeping an eye on us."

A small tree near the edge of the wall moved, drawing the jumpy attention of the mercenaries. Then a strange thing happened: a humanoid shape emerged from the bark of the tree. It was as if there'd been a person painted to look like the tree, and they'd just stepped away.

"She's young," Breekie gasped.

Shawn wasn't sure how he could tell, as the being's face was almost indiscernible; nothing like the woman made of leaves he'd seen before. She had physical features, but they were weak, indistinct. Making her more tree than person. She approached them slowly, feet never rising from the ground. Instead, they moved through it.

"Why are you watching us?" Peter asked in what Shawn assumed was supposed to be an unprovocative tone, but the fierce look in his eyes made Shawn less sure.

The bark-skinned creature tilted its head. Her wooden mouth opened slightly, showing two pieces of wood. *Are those supposed to be teeth? All together like that?* For a moment, nothing happened. Then a voice like bending wood came out in a weak wail.

Breekie lurched forward in front of Peter. "Easy. She's young. I don't think she's manifested a form before," he explained in hurried Dwarvish. The dryad tilted its head at him, it's face doing the best it could to form a confused expression.

"You sure she isn't dangerous, or mad about the fire?" Muttered Justin.

Breekie nodded. "She'd have brought us firewood herself if we'd asked, and she was a little older." The dryad tried to speak again with poor results.

"Tell her to knock that off," Gunter interjected. "It hurts." Next to him, Simon pulled a glow stick out of his luggage, cracked it, and placed it on a table. The crack made the dryad flinch, and Jenni let out a curse from the rooftop.

"O'Cleary, kill the fire," Peter ordered, and the Irishman obeyed by closing the pit's lid. The dryad just stood there.

Why isn't it moving closer? Shawn wondered.

Breekie took a step towards it. "I think is studying us, trying to look like us." *Come to think of it, its nose is looking more real.*

Peter looked baffled. "So, what do we do?"

Breekie shrugged. "Leave it," he growled.

Shawn could tell Peter didn't like that, but it didn't stop him. "All right, everyone relax. Time we got some rest anyway. No sense wasting that light anymore."

Slowly, they all stepped away from the wooden humanoid and began to pack up their gear. Gunter stood in awkward silence. Peter exchanged a few whispered words with Simon while Justin finished reassembling his gun.

Then from the top of the building came Jenni's voice. "Hey, Justin, get your butt up here, and try not to collapse the thing. I'm hungry," she said softly but did not bother to whisper this time.

"Hold your horses, Jenni. I had second shift last night. It's O'Cleary's turn," Justin objected, as he kept a wary eye regularly drifting back to the dryad.

"Shoot, you're right. He's thinner and a better shot than you anyway. Good idea," she teased, her voice shifting as she made her way gracefully down from the top of the restaurant.

Justin frowned, and O'Cleary punched him in the arm, smirking and cackling as he walked past. "There's the crack," he said with a chortle.

Simon turned to Gunter. "The captain knows what he's done. Any more outbursts like that could get us all killed. We are in unknown territory with an unknown enemy. You can report what you want when we get back to Paragon. Understood?"

Simon was smaller than Gunter, but the steel in his voice was enough to convince Shawn that he could probably end him if needed. *He's talked more tonight than both days of walking put together. He and Peter must be close.*

Gunter glanced past Simon, at Peter handing Jenni her portion of food they'd set aside. Then, Peter began to put out the fire, starting by stomping out the embers.

"Understood," said Gunter, not bothering to look back at Simon as he turned to find his place in the shelter of their temporary base. Simon followed behind shortly after, disappearing into the building's maw.

"It's so eerie. Like the whole country turned into a ghost town overnight, or we all Rip Van Winkled twenty years into a desolate future," Jenni said to no one in particular.

"Rip Van Winkled?" Breekie asked curiously, saving Shawn the embarrassment of asking himself.

"Hah, sorry. It's an old fa— legend," she stuttered, "about a man who falls asleep in a magic glade, I think, and wakes up like a hundred years later or something with a long scraggly white beard, and everything's changed, and his wife got old and stuff." She took a small bite of her food, chewing quickly.

"It was my dad's favorite western story. He used to tell it to my siblings and me whenever we had to leave for the next city. That's what all the random growing and ruined buildings made me think of is all," she explained with a shrug. "I drove by here two months ago. There were cars and people just minding their business, and now it's in shambles, and nature's gone and grown up into everything."

Is the whole world like this? Or just us? I miss my phone. I wish I could just use Google Maps or something, but I don't have service, Shawn thought as he realized he really didn't have any idea where they were other than between Atlanta and home.

"Shawn." Peter's voice came to him.

He turned to face the speaker. "Yes, sir?"

"Get up there with O'Cleary. You might as well learn to keep watch too," Peter instructed.

"Yes, sir," Shawn replied and wrapped his jacket around himself. Once his jacket was secure, he climbed the ladder on the side of the building. He went slowly, eager to learn how to make himself useful but reasonably concerned about the dangers of climbing in the dark.

O'Cleary was wearing the same goggles Jenni had been, his head slowly oscillating. It reminded Shawn of a fan, meticulous and slow from side to side.

As Shawn got closer, he realized the man was singing softly under his breath. "They said let grief be a falling leaf, at the dawning of the day." O'Cleary's singing came to a stop as Shawn sat down next to him. "Peter send you, boyo?"

"Yeah… Did he really kill those guys in the street?" Shawn asked quietly.

O'Cleary continued to scan the darkness. "You've seen his eyes, right Shawn?"

"Yeah."

"You know how they feel like they're dissecting you? Like he can see through your skin, into your muscles? That's nothing compared to how he looked at those men. I've seen Peter kill before… When he killed those men, it was different. There was something else there." He shrugged. "Aach, maybe it was just me. Either way, I trust him to keep us alive."

Shawn thought it over, fidgeting with a hole torn in his shirt. *Random… but… I think he's right.* He couldn't remember where he received the hole, which grew as he prodded it. He guessed it didn't really matter now anyway.

O'Cleary glanced over at him and scowled. "What're you doing, lad? You'll only make it worse. Sew that up before it becomes a problem," he ordered.

"I don't know how to sew," Shawn replied, surprised by the instruction. "Even if I did, I don't have stuff for that."

O'Cleary shook his head. "Everyone should know how to sew, especially soldiers." With that, he reached into his bag and pulled out a round container, handing it to Shawn.

Shawn opened the container, and after staring down at it in the shifting moonlight, he plucked out a thread and needle, stabbing his finger in the process. "Ow," he said softly.

O'Cleary looked back over at him, doing a double take. "What are you doing, lad? I'll show you how to use it when we've got some light, you idjit."

Shawn's lips made a firm line as he shook his pricked finger in the cold air.

O'Cleary shook his head, turning back to his watch. "A few pricks won't get in your way. Besides, if you want something done right, it's gonna hurt to get it done."

Overhead, the clouds continued to float casually by, unperturbed by the worries of the lonely boy below who searched the dark for threats beyond his imagination.

—◆— 19 —◆—

ROUTE RECONNAISSANCE

Shawn woke shivering and sore, the nudging of O'Cleary's black boot in his side.

"Wake up, lad," he chuckled softly. "Hah-hah, you missed breakfast."

Shawn sat up quickly. The memory of where he was and who he was with chased the fog of sleep from his mind. "I'm up. Sorry. Sorry. I didn't mean to oversleep." He blinked, looking around at how dark it was. "Did I oversleep?"

"It's all right, lad, waking up with the sun takes getting used to. It's even harder when the sun's hidden behind clouds and fog as thick as a rhino's arse. Here." O'Cleary tossed a trail bar in Shawn's lap. "Make it last, right? Today's the last day before we're 'sposed to head back, but it doesn't look like that's happening," he said, looking pointedly at one of the booths containing Peter and a few others.

Shawn took a small bite of the bar, chewing slowly, knowing it would make it last longer. *It doesn't take much to fill up these days. Getting used to eating less, I guess,* he realized as he finished the bar.

He looked around the restaurant at his fellow travelers. Breekie, Justin, and Peter sat at a table with a large map unfolded before them. Jenni was equipping Hauch for the day ahead with his dark body armor. O'Cleary was now rifling through the cupboards of the kitchen, muttering about coffee. Simon was nowhere to be seen.

"No, but look. We're here. That means Macon is a straight shot. If we keep following the road, we should be there by noon. That has to be where it's coming from," Justin suggested in his baritone voice.

Where what's coming from?

"If the town is still there. We haven't traveled nearly as far as we thought we would have, and on top of that, we haven't seen anyone," added Gunter dejectedly. The words sunk in to the ears of all present. "For all we know, that signal was just some random automated broadcast."

Signal? Shawn's stomach dropped at the realization Gunter was right. *We haven't seen anyone or anything — just woods and ruined buildings. We haven't even seen corpses. Oh. Oh, no.*

Peter nodded. "I don't like it either. We were supposed to be there already. If Macon is anything like what we've seen so far, we can't stop there unless absolutely necessary. In the event there are no survivors *but* there are supplies, we'll send Hauch back to inform Steven of our progress."

Peter drummed his fingers on the table. "Best case scenario? We find survivors, it's their signal, and they're willing to head back to Paragon with supplies. We resupply, rest, and head on to Atlanta. Worst case? Well, there are a lot of possible worst case scenarios right now." He rubbed his growing beard as he leered down at the map. "I'd say, the worst case is no survivors, no supplies, and automatic broadcast. In which case, we head back to Paragon and prepare for a longer second trip straight to Atlanta."

"Geez, captain, you've almost got me hoping for the worst case," said Justin before adding, "I mean, you can't seriously be suggesting we press on without any backward communication? I thought our assignment was to get to Macon then report back in five days?"

Peter shook his head. "Our original target was Atlanta — we have people there — and it's our best hope at figuring out just what's going on. Macon was only supposed to be a pit stop." Peter clenched his fists. "Even if our people aren't there, and there isn't any intel, we've at least got more firepower there… I hope." He shook his head, bemused. "Besides, returning to Paragon now, having learned nothing — that would make this trip virtually worthless."

"And you don't want that, do you, Pete. No, you need to bring something back to the council to bargain with, don't you? And you're willing to continue to risk all of our lives to do it if necessary," said Gunter as he rose from the table, his tone more in-check than the night before.

"Come on, man, you knew what you were getting into when you volunteered, didn't you?" Justin asked, exasperation plain in his voice.

"Really?" Gunter fired back. "You didn't even know what our destination was?"

"Yeah, but I've got a good excuse," Justin replied with a smile like a man who knew his opponent was walking right into a trap. "I'm too lazy to worry about the big picture stuff."

Shawn suppressed a chuckle.

Gunter scowled at the mercenary, choosing to remain silent rather than see what jab Justin might have next.

"Look, the captain has a point. Atlanta is our best bet, and we can't just ignore a call for help. But, captain, they're right. It would be risky to keep going, and we are ill-prepared," Jenni said, tossing a look in Shawn's direction that Shawn assumed he wasn't supposed to catch on to.

Call for help?

"If it's drowning, you're after—" Justin began.

"Don't torment yourself with shallow water," said O'Cleary's with a grin as he turned the corner back into the room.

"What?" asked Gunter.

"He says it all the time. If you're gonna do something risky, might as well go all the way." O'Cleary scratched the white spot in his hair. "I mean, we're already out here, right? Wouldn't making a second trip double our chances of something going wrong between here and there? I, for one, want to know more about that signal, and I wouldn't mind checking on Atlanta."

"You've got to be joking. Have you all lost your minds? We've been traveling for five days and haven't even seen a soul. We haven't even found any corpses. Doesn't that scare you? We should have found something," Gunter said. "With that in mind, you're going to risk moving forward on some random short-range radio SOS playing on a loop?"

"If you want to head back to Paragon, be our guest, Gunter," Justin said with a smirk.

"That'd solve our backward communication issue," chimed in Jenni.

"Hah, I may not like it, but I'm not going out there alone. Not with bodies disappearing into thin air."

"No one's splitting off," Peter said dismissively, staring intensely down at the map.

Shawn finished packing his sleeping roll and shuffled out the back door, eager to distance himself from the conversation and thought of something out there making bodies disappear.

The cold outside was enough to send a brief shiver through him, but not enough to drive him back inside or worry him about the temperature of the day. The sound of movement drew his attention to Simon, who was climbing down from the roof.

Simon nodded at Shawn casually, his dark hair pulled back out of his face.

"I, uh, needed some fresh air," Shawn said, not wanting to admit that the conversation was making him nervous.

Simon smiled, but it didn't reach his eyes, which were searching their surroundings behind Shawn. "Make it quick. I don't like the look of that fog. Something feels wrong out here. Do you feel it?"

Shawn waited a moment, just now noticing the thick fog around them. "Like something's watching us?" he asked in a whisper.

Simon's gaze met Shawn's eyes. "Could be the dryad. She disappeared sometime during the night." He gave Shawn's shoulder a squeeze. "Keep your weapon ready."

Simon started to march back inside when Shawn spoke up. "They were saying something about a signal…?" he wasn't entirely sure what he was asking.

"I'm surprised it didn't wake you," Simon replied. "I picked up an SOS on the radio at oh-six hundred this morning."

Shawn swallowed. "That's it? No details or directions."

Simon shook his head and stepped inside.

The ever-encroaching woods drew Shawn's focus. The fog was entrenched around them, a thick milky mist oozed out from the forest, concealing all but the shadows of the trees bit by bit. Shawn's eyes darted over what few trees he could still see, searching for a sign of the dryad, hoping it was responsible for the growing sensation that he was being watched, which gnawed at his gut.

But he saw no living creature in the mists, only the autumn trees in various states of undress, their leaves scattered on the ground, and swirling mists inching ever closer, turning one tree after another into shadows. Unease turned in his gut more the longer he stared into the unknown. *Don't be silly. It's just plants and moisture,* he told himself, trying to dismiss the sense of creeping anticipation. But the feeling of dread lingered. The trees made strange shadowy shapes in the fog as the sun came and went.

Shawn waited at the edge of the patio, afraid to move lest the sound of his footsteps brought something crashing out of the unknown. *Come on, there's nothing there. You're paranoid,* he tried to assure himself, *but what about the people? The corpses? People don't just vanish. Something must have happened to them.* Images of monsters and burning corpses flashed through his mind's eye.

Maybe they were just like me, staring stupidly into the fog. Shawn took a step back. His heart thundered in his chest, the only sound he heard. The woods were silent. Deathly silent. Panic's icy claws scratched at him, turning him and sending him dashing back into the restaurant.

Shawn slammed into a tall figure. Looking up, he saw O'Cleary staring back down at him, broken ceiling tiles hanging above him.

"Oi, slow down, lad. Did ya see something?" O'Cleary's Irish accent contained a note of concern.

"I— No, no, I didn't see anything. I was just… cold. It's chilly out there."

O'Cleary raised an eyebrow. "All right then, watch where you're going, Shawn. Lots of dangerous stuff lying about," he said then moved past Shawn to the kitchen, where he began to fill a canteen with a water bottle.

Shawn looked around the room. The map and everyone's belongings were packed, and Gunter was standing with Shawn's clear pack in hand. He offered it to Shawn with a small smile.

Shawn accepted the pack, awkwardly holding it in his arms.

"Goes on your back, kid," Gunter whispered slyly.

"Everyone ready?" Peter asked from the center of the room, looking at Shawn.

"Yes, sir," came the chorus of responses, Shawn following the response himself a half-second late. "What are we doing?"

"Pressing on," Peter said as he made his way to the front door. There, he grabbed the closed/open sign and began to draw on it with a large red permanent marker.

Shawn watched curiously as a crude snowflake appeared with five points, the longest of which was at the top.

Shawn couldn't help himself. He needed to know, even if they found it annoying. He had to ask: "What's that?" he blurted, wincing as he did.

"This is a message if anyone comes looking for us. The number of points indicates how many days out we are. The longest one indicates the direction we're heading. In this case, north." Peter capped the pen and stored it in one of his pockets. "Red means we're alive but cautious. Black would mean we've run into trouble."

The mercenary pushed his way through the door, holding it open as the rest of them filled out. He paused for a half-second, staring at the fog, only a few steps from the door, then he strolled forward, the mist swirling around him.

They all followed, gravel crunching underfoot as they strolled toward their vehicles concealed by the fog. Peter was putting a hand on a jeep handle when Hauch's ears went flat, and a soft growl emitted from his throat. Shawn froze. He knew the growl was quiet, but in the deafening silence, it seemed almost like a roll of thunder.

The adults reacted instantly, springing to cover behind half a dozen dead cars and trucks in the parking lot. Even Gunter found a position in the formation with his rifle pointed aggressively at the mist. Breekie remained in the center, looking the most out of place with his war hammer held low at his side.

Shawn watched as Breekie's left arm extended out in front of him, a soft glow emitting from his palm and a blue rune tattooed on his shoulder. The light caught Gunter's attention, and he glanced back to see the dwarf. With an indiscernible yelp, he grabbed Shawn's wrist and yanked him between two cars for cover.

"What in the name of sanity are you doing, dwarf?" snapped O'Cleary. The dwarf gave no answer. Shawn noticed Peter's gaze remained focused on the fog, but the rest of the group was fighting to keep their gazes facing outward and not back at the dwarf with the glowing arm.

They stood like this in silence for a full minute. The fog moved slowly around them, the trees beyond view. From his position between Jenni's legs, Hauch sniffed the air curiously, still looking out towards the fog. Then his ears perked up, his growl coming to a stop. He turned and looked towards Breekie, cocking his head to the side in confusion.

Jenni leaned down and tapped the dog's combat vest once, and Hauch sat. The crew relaxed, but weapons remained at the ready, pointing outward.

"Breekie, what was that?" Peter asked in a low tone.

"Searching." Breekie lowered his arm, and the glow faded away. "We are not alone, but the dryad is gone. And she left us a warning." He pointed to a cluster of strange black flowers at the edge of the road.

All around the group, weapons were lowered. Gunter released his tight grip on Shawn's wrist. Shawn stepped away from the man and sheathed his pistol before rubbing his wrist where Gunter had clenched it.

"Warn a guy before you light up your arm like that, would ya?" Gunter grumbled.

Breekie smiled broadly but didn't say anything in reply.

Justin made his way over to where they'd parked the vehicles, ignoring the cluster of strange flowers.

"Wait," Peter cautioned.

Justin stopped and turned. "What?"

"Breekie, what do the flowers mean?"

"Death ahead," he said with a shrug. "Is more complex, but I am no pointy-eared leaf reader."

"You're sure it's a warning, not a threat?" asked Jenni.

"Dah," he said with a chuckle. "Dryad would not threaten us. Is helping."

Peter stood in silence for a moment, clenching his thumb in his right hand. "Leave the vehicles. We're going on foot."

Jenni turned to Peter. "What?"

"They're loud. We can barely see five feet in front of us anyway," Peter explained, gesturing at the soupy fog.

"You've gotta be kidding. We'll be quicker on wheels, faster escape in case we run into something we can't handle. I'd rather retreat than use this," Justin said, gesturing at the bone-white sword at his hip.

"We should be twenty miles from our destination. Whatever is out there could be used to this fog. Our rides just make us vulnerable," Peter replied firmly. "We're on foot from here. If we're lucky, the fog clears, and we hotwire a car for the duration."

Jenni groaned and slung her pack back over her shoulder.

Twenty miles on foot? I'll have blisters by the end of that. Something is already trying to kill us, and I don't need my feet as an accomplice, Shawn caught himself thinking.

Beside Shawn, Gunter muttered obscenities low enough for Shawn to assume he wasn't meant to hear them. As the rest of the group made adjustments to their packs and equipment, Shawn walked over to Breekie and the flowers. The dwarf's grin had only grown. He looked delighted at the news they'd be walking.

Shawn decided not to ask. *It'd just make Gunter more upset to know he prefers walking.* Shawn bent down to pluck one of the flowers, pausing and glancing at Breekie.

"They're not poisonous," the dwarf said with a raised eyebrow.

Shawn plucked one from the ground with ease. It came up root and all; a solid black flower, from root to its five broad round petals.

"Elves say they are bad luck, but they are just a plant," Breekie said.

Shawn tucked the flower gently into one of his coat buttonholes near the top before returning to the group.

"Hauch, *erkuden,*" Jenni instructed the combat-ready dog as the group began walking down the road. Hauch dashed ahead only a few feet then stopped at the edge of where the mist was rolling over the road. Frozen in place, Hauch looked back, his tail tucked partly between his legs.

"Well, that can't be good," muttered Gunter.

Jenni's face screwed up, her lip curled, and her nose wrinkled. "Hauch, *erkuden,*" she said more firmly.

Hauch seemed to shrink where he was and let out a soft whimper.

Jenni took a few steps forward, and so did Hauch. He continued to stay about ten feet ahead as they all moved forward in formation. O'Cleary grabbed Shawn's shoulder and placed him slightly behind himself.

"Keep up, boyo," he instructed.

As they moved into the fog, the hair on Shawn's neck stood on end. He could still feel something watching him but couldn't see far. Shapes were moving in the fog. Tall, dark scraggly shapes loomed overhead. *Trees. It's just trees,* Shawn repeated to himself over and over. Still, he flinched every time he saw a shadow shift at the edge of his vision.

The world was quiet. The only sounds Shawn could hear were the crunching of gravel underfoot and the breathing of those close by, all of which was muffled by the fog. Nature was silent, as though waiting with bated breath for something to happen.

Tired of staring at the fog, Shawn looked down for a second. The road was gone. It wasn't gravel crunching beneath their feet, it was leaves. *Where's the road?*

Simon bumped into Shawn, almost knocking him over and sending him stumbling into O'Cleary. "Oof. Oi, what're you doing?" O'Cleary growled at him.

His words were muffled, as though fighting through the fog to get to his ears. The leaves at his feet spun in a blur of color. Dizzy, Shawn swayed back and forth. His mind went blank, thoughts abandoning him with his sense of balance. He struggled to stand as the thumping of his heart overwhelmed him. Everything spun. His ears thundered. He couldn't breathe properly. He couldn't see properly.

Firm hands grasped his shoulders, steadying him, bringing the world still. The leaves at his feet ceased their spinning. *Yellow, gold, red, brown — so many colors. The road — where's the road?* A face filled his view — a round face with small dark brown Asian eyes and dark hair. *Simon.*

Simon's mouth was moving, out of focus. His words seemed to be traveling underwater. Something collided with the back of Shawn's skull. Jarring the watery sensation from his mind, bringing the world into focus. He blinked and looked up. O'Cleary was glowering down at him, hand raised from striking him on the back of the head. "There ya are, laddie. I dunno what that was, but it can't happen again. Understood?" he said in a serious tone that reminded Shawn of being lectured by his father.

Simon's grip shifted to his forearm, still supporting him. "Panic attack," he whispered barely loud enough for even Shawn to hear him. Simon raised a finger towards O'cleary "Don't do that again."

Shawn shook him off. And Simon raised his hands to chest level, maintaining eye contact.

"Deep breaths. In your nose, out your mouth," Simon instructed calmly.

"The road. The road's gone," Shawn managed to choke out as Simon handed him a canteen of water.

Behind him, Gunter swore. "He's right. It's gone. When did that happen? I mean, how long have we—"

Simon shot Gunter a harsh look, and he stopped mid-sentence.

"Is he all right?" Peter's voice carried over to Shawn.

"I think so," said Simon. "Small panic attack. O'Cleary snapped him out of it."

"Lad's fine. Just a little nervous, right Shawn?" O'Cleary added a slap on Shawn's shoulder to emphasize his point.

Not wanting to look any weaker than he felt, and already embarrassed, Shawn nodded. "Yes, sir. Sorry, sir. I'm all right, sir," he said quickly, jumbling the words.

At the front of the group, there was a strange, choking whine from Hauch, drawing Shawn's attention.

"Not to increase alarm, but there is something up ahead," said Breekie in a low voice.

"Weapons ready. Shawn, Gunter, keep your fingers off the triggers," Peter ordered, his voice almost a whisper as he stored his pistol and drew Galvorn from its dark sheath. Simon positioned himself at Peter's right elbow, rifle raised, as they all slinked forward. Breekie walked at his left, war hammer raised, ready to strike.

Shawn stepped slowly forward with the rest, trying desperately not to crunch leaves beneath his shoes and flinching every time he failed. His heart was still thundering, but his attention was on the mist all around them.

Ahead of them, Hauch froze, teeth bared and snout pointed forward, a low growl emitting from his throat. *Crunch, crunch, crunch*, went the leaves beneath their feet. There was something ahead of them at the edge of their vision: a large lumpy thing on the ground. Two more steps. It was coming into focus. Another step.

Sonofa—" O'Cleary groaned. "It's just luggage."

He was right. An open suitcase lay sprawled in their path, clothes hanging out haphazardly, a purplish leaf resting on the top of it.

At his side, Shawn heard Gunter let out a massive sigh of relief. Jenni looked down at Hauch, who remained frozen in place with his lips peeled back in a snarl.

"Really, Hauch? Luggage? Come on, dude," she protested.

Ahead of them, Peter took a step forward, as though the pile of clothes might explode. Shawn watched him while the rest of them paused to readjust gear or tie boots.

Why is he gripping the sword so tightly? Shawn wondered as he saw Peter's muscles flinch as he stepped to the side of the pile. The instant his foot touched down, his muscles relaxed, but his arm swung his sword up through the air. At that same moment, a shape burst from the fog.

A hand pulled Shawn back, and he heard the sound of guns being yanked into shooting positions. But it was too late. Galvorn carved through the doe's neck with grotesque ease. The creature's head went flying back over its body, blood spattering the fog as the body crashed to the ground a few feet from Shawn. The head landed with a splat on top of the pile of laundry.

"Breekie?" Peter asked as he strolled over to the deer's corpse and began to wipe the blood on his blade off on its fur.

He knew. He knew that thing was coming. How? Did he know what it was? Shawn stared in silence. *He'd flinched before it got close. If he knew it was dangerous, wouldn't he have warned us? Why did he kill it? He didn't have to kill it.*

Shawn looked over at Gunter. All color had drained out of the man's face, leaving it almost the color of the fog. Their eyes locked for a moment, and Shawn realized Gunter must have been thinking the same thing. *He didn't have to kill it.*

"Dah?" came the dwarf's reply, his broad grin missing from his face.

"Are we alone now?"

Breekie's jaw worked. He adjusted the war hammer, and his shoulder tattoo glowed once more. "Dah. We are alone, much as I can tell."

"Was that really necessary?" Jenni said, wiping blood off Hauch's vest with a bandana.

"Well done, captain," added Justin with a smirk. "You saved us from the mighty doe. We'd have been doomed if not for your quick thinking." He and O'Cleary had a good chuckle at this, and even Peter managed to grin back at him.

Justin gave Shawn a wink. "Ya know what?" he said in his perpetually amused voice. "Why let it go to waste?" He emphasized his point by drawing a massive buck knife and approaching the corpse. A moment later, he was carving it apart with all the skill of a professional hunter. "Which of y'all want to help me carry some?" Justin asked as he removed a leg from the creature.

Breekie and O'Cleary both eagerly volunteered, and each was granted a slab of meat for their willingness.

Shawn found himself speaking as Justin fed a piece of the meat to an eager Hauch. "I can carry a bit," he said, realizing even though he didn't really want to, it might make him look a bit tougher after his panic attack earlier.

Justin smiled weakly as Shawn extended a slightly shaking hand out for some of the venison. "Oh, no, you've got enough to carry, Shawn. Wouldn't want you dropping it if you got dizzy again, would we?" he added with a friendly jab.

Before Shawn could respond, he was cut off by Peter. "All right. We've still got ground to cover. Let's pick up the pace," ordered Peter. "Simon, keep an eye on your compass, the road may be gone, but if we stay due north, we should make it."

Simon nodded. He glanced down at his wrist where he wore a watch with a compass on it. "We're good," he said, pointing in the direction the deer had come from.

Peter grinned and started a light jog forward as the rest of them followed closely. Deeper and deeper into the wooded mist, they traveled, blind to the dangers of the city ahead of them.

20

LEFT BEHIND

Sarah stood with Dr. Walker on the east wall. Vehicles, gravel, and rubble lay crushed and molded together beneath their feet. The citizens of Paragon used whatever they could to build the walls up, strong and tall. Most of it required reinforcing the buildings that already formed the circumference of the city. The trickier part was connecting these pieces to build a wall.

Over the last month, they'd made incredible progress, bit by bit. The city's efforts were doubled after Shadowfang's attack. No one questioned the wall now. No one argued it was a waste of resources. They all knew better.

Looking down into the outside world, she was struck by how still and quiet it remained. The trees were turning, their gold and red leaves reminding Sarah of the burning pits. The trees were silent though; no screaming from dead bodies as heat and gasses strained vocal cords.

The memory of screams while staring into the deep woods haunted her. The rubble beneath her feet crunched as she stepped closer to Dr. Walker. Sarah glanced down at the concrete crushing and molding everything beneath to form this section of the wall. The wall stretched strong and wide; tall ramparts bore brave men in motion armed with guns and bone-tipped spears.

I wish I'd been there when they were debating what materials to use. I would have liked to see the looks on their faces when Doctor Walker explained whatever they used, she could make it work. Sarah looked down at the dwarf. She'd brought her here to fulfill that very promise she made to the council to improve the wall's shortcomings.

It's getting harder for her, all of it, Sarah thought as she shivered, a cold breeze cutting through her clothes, leaving her wishing she'd worn a coat. *It could be the cold or the stress. Then again, she's old. But she's been old for a very long time,* Sarah told herself, watching closely as the frail woman traced four curves connected by an outer circle into the concrete with her rune-covered cane.

A rune on the cane's handle glowed as it carved the concrete like a knife carves playdough. The grooves filled instantly with glass as the cane formed them. Once the symbol was complete, Dr. Walker paused, examining her work.

Sarah found herself running her finger over the intricate swirling patterns she'd copied into the notebook Dr. Walker bequeathed to her. It was green, as deep as a forest glade. She ran her hand over the intricate grooves on its surface. These grooves looped and tangled together to form a kaleidoscopic pattern. If the notebook was a forest glade, these were its shadows. Fingers on her left hand still tracing the pattern of the journal, she began to sketch the symbol below her onto her paper.

The symbol in the concrete was noticeably different from the runic patterns that arched across Dr. Walker's dark skin. There were dozens of these white tattoos. *But they don't look like a tattoo sleeve. It's more like she has pages of an ancient foreign book printed across her skin. There are even coherent lines and breaks between the words. If only I could read them, I could ask why she chose each and every word. No point asking now though. It'd just waste her time.*

Both pages of the tattoos came to an end an inch before the old woman's wrists. There was a finality to it that tickled her curiosity all the more. *Why stop there? It can't be a pain thing.*

Dr. Walker motioned Sarah to lower herself closer to the new symbol.

"This will bind the components within the walls and strengthen them. This is a basic transmutation rune. Not my best subject, but it will get the job done."

Sarah scribbled away in her notebook, writing notes above her drawing of the rune on the page. "Will you be teaching me runes then?'

Dr. Walker smiled warmly. Sarah recognized this particular smile. It was the same one that occupied the soft woman's face whenever Sarah asked something wrong. Her heart dropped slightly into her rather hollow stomach.

"No dear, at least not for a time. And even then, it would be unwise for you to use such things, lest you gain the title of Krel-ka. The use of another race's casting is a bit taboo and can be dangerous. That is why only those who have mastered their own casting and been granted the title of Krel-ka, which means *friend of arcane*, are permitted to study other races' castologies."

Sarah continued to jot down notes as her teacher lectured. "Oh, so you're a Krel-ka then, since you're teaching me how to use the arcane, right?" she asked with a confident smile.

Dr. Walker nodded solemnly. "I was granted the title of Krel-ka at the young age of two hundred seventy-seven," she said proudly. "Prior to the casting of Therin-Selu, I was quite interested in castology, especially human casting methods," she said with a hint of remorse.

She didn't get it until she was over two centuries old? I don't stand a chance then.

"Does human casting use a different set of runes? So far, I've just been tapping into the energy and redirecting it without any kind of filter." *All I've done so far is help her to cast. I want to learn to cast things myself.*

"That is the core of the arcane. The filter allows for more refinement and flexibility, which I believe you are now ready for," she said with a smile. "Human casting involves the spoken word. You have heard the story of Adam, who gave names to all things. There is truth in it. Mankind composed the first dialect."

The old woman tapped the top of her cane thoughtfully. "Man bound energy to that dialect so that they need only speak when using their arcane. This is why when your kind attempted to break the Therin-Selu not long after it was cast, you were cursed with different tongues. That curse is now fading, and the first tongue is returning. Faster for those in touch with the arcane flow."

"However," she added with a raised hand, one finger pointing to the sky, "dwarves were the first to use written words, hence our preference for using runes for casting." She gestured over to the rune in the wall. "We preferred our method to spoken words. You may find yourself speaking the old tongue without realizing it, but the old tongue is not required for your casting. Despite composing a dialect for it, casting in one language or another makes little difference. The words are but a conduit."

I wonder how true that is. If she's a dwarf, she's going to naturally assume her own kind's methods are superior. No, that's silly. She's too open-minded to think like that. Still, everyone has their own inherent biases…

Dr. Walker turned her back to Sarah to examine more of the wall beneath their feet. A leaf crunched under her shoe. "There are also many *schools*, or abilities, of the arcane. Transmutation is one of them. Humans have something of a disadvantage here. Your kind gained the knowledge of arcane late and not from its first source. That is why you must master your first school before I can truly teach you another."

Dr. Walker took Sarah's hand in her right and placed her cane against the glass symbol on the wall with her left. "Your ability is a fortunate one, Sarah. It is known as enhancement and is best when used in tangent with another caster."

At a nod from her instructor, Sarah reached out to touch the arcane flow, to open her mind to just a trickle of it, to channel it through her fingers at first, and then up and down her arms. Sarah could feel the energy in her fingertips now begging to be redirected outward.

Only after you have been able to gain an understanding of the energy will you be ready to release it. She felt she understood it now. She was ready to release it, to use it, so she directed the ethereal energy through the dwarf and into the symbol.

This time was different. This time, Dr. Walker did not cut her off and take control. She simply guided the energy so it filled the rune entirely. It glowed green a moment. Then, the dwarf released her hand, and Sarah cut off the flow of energy. *That's getting easier*, she thought as a warm shiver spread through her.

The dwarf's forehead lined with even more wrinkles. She gave Sarah a moment to catch up before asking, "Any questions so far?"

Sarah thought for a moment. Preferring silence to correction, she chose her questions carefully. "Is that why you've only had me helping you with your casting?"

"Yes, and casting is the correct terminology. Excellent." Dr. Walker shifted her weight to make better use of her cane as she led them to the stairs. "You can use arcane energy to enhance or increase things that already exist. It is a useful ability and a dangerous one, and should you master it, an excellent doorway to other abilities. I wanted to be sure you had a feel for it before pushing you to cast on your own. I wouldn't want you accidentally blowing up another restaurant," she said with a twinkle in her brown eyes.

"I-I didn't mean to. I mean, it wasn't…" Sarah stumbled to find the words. She hadn't thought back to Shadowfang's attack other than when telling Dr. Walker what happened. She didn't like to think about how close she'd come to being devoured. But there it was; it all made sense now. The size of the explosion, and the fire catching at the sound of her voice. "It was just a spark…" The last words slipped past her lips as it all connected. *It was only a spark.*

Dr. Walker tapped her nose gently with a knobby finger, then took Sarah's hand as they moved down the stairs. "Exactly. That's why we've been taking it slowly. Your prowess is rather spectacular, which makes teaching you a bit more complicated."

The look of fear on Sarah's face was emphasized by her tightly squeezed lips.

"Now, now, dear, you're not going to accidentally blow us all to kingdom come just by speaking. You are perfectly capable of severing your connection with the arcane flow at will at this point."

Sarah nodded as relief washed over her. She preferred listening to speaking, and the realization that her words could cause physical destruction terrified her. They came to the bottom of the stairs, and Sarah slowly sat down, trying to hide the wobble in her legs.

"Now, I have been considering a way to make our lessons easier for both of us," Dr. Walker said in an excited tone. If she'd noticed Sarah's dismay, she was ignoring it.

"There was something of a fusion of human and dwarf casting methods back in the day that might help you," she explained, adding, "Rather controversial, though."

Sarah's ears piqued at this. "Anything that can help, please, Umindrabo," she said, trying to use her teacher's proper Dwarvish name.

Dr. Walker smiled wryly. "If the headmasters had known I knew how to do this, they would have been despondent…" Dr. Walker turned to look at the city. She stood stone still in all but her hands, which never stopped trembling ever so slightly, surveying the city full of movement and sound as people went to and fro tending to its needs.

There she goes. Sarah thought, bemused. *These spells — Heh, that's not the right word anymore. Hmm… These episodes seem to be getting more frequent.* Taking her pen, Sarah made a small horseshoe-esque symbol at the top of the page. She used this mark to track whenever Umindrabo began staring silently into nothingness during their conversations. Then she flipped back through the previous pages. There were four on her last page, two on the one before that, and so forth until there were several pages without any marks.

Dr. Walker blinked rapidly, then shook her head side to side as though she'd just emerged from underwater.

"Tradition be blasted, we have the resources we need now. Come, come, let us visit Cheekie at the Forge." Their journey to the Forge took half an hour due to the city teeming with activity. They were forced to make multiple stops to allow for the constant movement of construction equipment or gaunt-looking workers crossing the road, going from one job to the next.

There was no conversation while they journeyed into the city. Dr. Walker seemed deep in thought, which Sarah was content to let continue as it gave her more time with her own. She considered what she learned as she drove the small golf cart the council acquired for Dr. Walker towards the Forge.

If my casting is strengthened by words, but the language is irrelevant, what about the words helps the casting? Is it meaning? I need to ask her more about it. When I said light, I wanted to create an explosion, and… that's what happened. So, is it the thought that forms the spell, and the words just help focus it? Enhancing… What can I enhance? Is it just external things? Or could I make myself stronger by increasing my muscle density?

The questions continued to pile up as she attempted to solve them on her own, not wanting to appear foolish or ignorant — a misguided concern, as she proved to be neither by not attempting to test her powers without proper guidance.

Sarah's mind continued to race as they arrived at the Forge and ventured quickly inside. The warmth of the building brought a sense of relief. Sarah rubbed her hands together, eagerly trying to push the cold from her body.

As usual, the Forge was teeming with activity. Men and women darted about working on various weapons and armors, unlike any Sarah would have expected a few days ago. The sound of labor and constant calls from one worker to another of "Hammer!" or "Set it there!" and so forth made her feel small but safe.

Then, much to Sarah's delight, she caught sight of Steven carrying an armful of staves ready to be converted into boneheaded spears over to a table. She drew his eye with a wave, and he greeted them with a warm smile as he passed the poles off to a skinny, long-haired man with a frazzled look about him.

Steven then made his way over to them, men and women darting out of his way as he passed between workbenches and ovens like the lumbering giant he was.

"Hello, hello! Why, it's my two favorite science saboteurs. Here to show me more acts that defy the laws of nature and physics as mankind so poorly understood them?" he asked with a chuckle. The words might have been sarcastic from someone as intelligent as Steven Thomas. Still, he seemed genuinely excited at the prospect of having everything he knew about science called into question.

Dr. Walker was equally jovial in her response, her grin increasing the wrinkles on her face beyond a number one could reasonably count. "Nothing quite that mind-bending today, Mister Thomas. Although, I was surprised not to see you at the wall for our enhancements."

Steven winced. "The outer wall is a bit of a structural abomination in terms of longevity. I do hope you were able to make significant improvements to it." He wiped large, black-stained hands on the already filthy apron he wore. "Let me know when you start on the eastern or western portions, and I'll be there." Steven cleared his throat, glancing casually down at Sarah and offering her one of his now only mostly black, smeared hands for a handshake. "Sarah, good to see you."

Sarah grasped his hand softly and smiled as the man went on with childlike glee.

"I'm afraid I lost track of time, Doctor Walker. Cheekie has been regaling me with explanations on the workings of transfiguration, and there is so much work to do. He says he can't teach me to use it unless I have some arcane knowledge myself and that you'd be the best one to help determine that, so your timing is truly impeccable."

Steven began to pull on his left thumb, absentmindedly getting it to *pop* as he finished and waited for Dr. Walker's response. "I do understand correctly that human-arcane abilities directly correlate to genetics?"

Dr. Walker tapped the top of her cane lightly. "Thinking about it in terms of genetics is…misguided. Would that we were so lucky to have one as eager and intellectually gifted as you, Mister Thomas, as a caster. Unfortunately, I do not believe you have a caster's blood. That being said, you may come by later this evening, and we can do some tests."

"I see," said Steven, looking slightly crestfallen. The expression did not last, though, and was soon replaced as his grin. "I'll be by later to make sure. Well, even if my blood is not rich with the arcane, I see no reason I cannot benefit from it and make use of it in other ways. I digress, what brings you to the Forge?"

"An admirable perspective. We hoped to make use of Cheekie's transfiguration specialization. You'll be intrigued by this, I believe. Is he present?"

Steven nodded, his green eyes glowing with excitement as he turned and made his way over to the other side of the Forge. There he paused and spoke to a figure out of sight. The words were lost to Sarah in the din of sound, but Steven's face bore a look of amusement.

Then a moment later, a blurry-eyed Cheekie emerged from the corner, tumbling slightly like a man half-sleeping, the disheveled dwarf making his way towards them. The dwarf was wiping at his face with a sleeve as he approached, Sarah noticed that his previously immaculate facial hair was in disarray.

Furthermore, he was no longer dressed in a coat and armor but now sported a heavy, rolled-up smithing apron and oversized sleeveless shirt, which made his tattooed arms visible. His tan arms did not have nearly as many tattoos as Dr. Walker, nor were tattoos as elegantly placed like words on paper; bearing a closer resemblance to an unfinished tattoo sleeve. One tattoo stood out to Sarah on his right shoulder. It was gray and resembled a melting cube.

"Duelma Umindrabo," he said with a bow, his arms balled into fists and crossed over his chest. "What brings you to the Forge?"

"I am in need of your help, Fellhammer. We are to make a wand for Miss Young," Dr. Walker said with authority.

Cheekie's face went pale and his eyes wide as he raised both hands in protest. Steven's face fell from where he stood behind the dwarf when the dwarf's speech switched to Dwarvish.

"Duelma, I assure you, I am no *vismunt*. I have no knowledge of such things, nor would I—"

Dr. Walker raised a hand to quiet him, replying meaningfully in English, "I am not questioning your integrity as a caster, Cheekie Fellhammer, nor is this entrapment. Your response is justified and true. but there is no need for such panic."

Cheekie's face hardened, as he continued speaking Dwarvish. "But, Duelma, it is a crass thing. We would embarrass ourselves and the humans who have shown us such hospitality. I am not so ungrateful as to brand one of them with a cursed object."

"Nonsense. We have no time for traditionalism. A wand will much serve Miss Young, as she has no human teacher by which to perfect her casting."

Cheekie cast a sympathetic look at Sarah upon hearing this but kept shaking his head, finally catching on and returning to his Russian-tainted English.

"Nyet, Duelma. It is forbidden. She would be turned away at the door of any dwarf home, seen as a thief at best by our people. I cannot do this."

Sarah motioned to Steven, who stepped over beside her, looking at her scribbled translation of the conversation in her notebook. Steven gave her a gracious smile and read quickly to catch up.

"We are not within your colony's halls, Morind Fellhammer. Here I am your Duelma. I say it is permissible, and I require your help with it."

Cheekie's face contorted, growing flushed. Whether from the warmth of the room or from frustration or even embarrassment, Sarah could not tell.

"You ask much, Duelma. I learn their tongue, I have forge weapons, armor. Now you ask me to go against my colony's teachings and commit an act some call heresy? Perhaps if Breekie were here, you ask him. He is more comfortable subverting tradition," he replied in his thick Russian accent.

"Morind, what is our kind's greatest calling?"

Cheekie's jaw dropped, and he swallowed as he attempted to regain his composure, mustache wobbling as he did so.

"To gain knowledge, Duelma Umindrabo. For benefiting our kind and the world."

Dr. Walker smiled appreciatively as she pulled out a chair from one of the workbenches.

Sarah stepped forward and helped her into the seat.

Dr. Walker spoke again slowly. "Has Mister Thomas discussed the internet with you, Cheekie?"

Cheekie took a moment to think. "I have heard him mumbling about such a thing with some others, but nyet, he has nyet discussed it with me."

"The internet is a human creation capable of storing limitless information. On it exists more information than exists in all the libraries of Burimm Thond: Vast knowledge collected and compiled by humanity over the past ten thousand years." She looked down her nose at the other dwarf. "All of which can be accessed with a tool you can fit in your pocket."

Cheekie's eyes widened at Dr. Walker's words — brown-green gems full of wonder.

Dr. Walker continued over the hum of work in the background. "Young Miss Sarah is a highly capable caster, a prodigy of a kin with Kelrigh Bright-beard, the light-bringer. I tell you this because humanity is on the cusp of ex-tinction. Sarah must learn to use her abilities. She *must*. And we are duty-bound by not only our greatest tradition but also out of a moral obligation to help those who need it."

Cheekie nodded. The room had grown quieter. Sarah could feel eyes on her — glances, side-eyes, obvious looks away. *Oh,* was the only thought she could muster before the Cheekie gave his response.

"Very well. I bend to wisdom, Duelma. I speak truth. I know not of wand crafting, and I will not leave my mark on it."

"Your wisdom hides behind your youth, Cheekie. So be it. It is a sim-ple enough craft. Do you still have one of Shadowfang's hollow fangs?" said Dr. Walker.

Youth? He looks like he's in his late forties at best. Then again, she's about a millennium old.

"Dah, we have two," came Cheekie's accented English.

Sarah shifted uncomfortably. "Umindrabo, if it's really an issue, I'm sure I can—" Dr. Walker cut Sarah off with a shake of her head.

"It's not, dear, not really. It's complicated. Wands are a bit of a fusion of dwarf and human casting that's considered rather crass by most traditionalists, which, unfortunately, is most of the dwarf-elder council. It is not, however, ex-pressly forbidden or as dangerous as some would have us believe." The last few words were more directed at Cheekie than Sarah as he searched for the fangs.

"I really don't want to cause any trouble," Sarah said.

"You won't, dear. Now, before we begin, do you have any requests for your wand? No," She shook her head. "Wands, plural, let's make it two just in case."

"Well, if they'd be kinda controversial, it'd be kind of good for them to be inconspicuous, right?" She swallowed, trying to ignore the rumble in her stomach. "Could we make one… that would fit in a notebook? There's space in the binding of the one you gave me."

"A wonderful idea, but I do not think there will be room for both. What do you think of the second?"

Sarah pondered this for a bit. "Well, I have a bit of a habit of sticking pens in my hair buns. It could be something not much bigger than that which I could put in my hair. Sort of decorative."

"Prudent," said Steven admiringly.

Dr. Waller tapped her cane lightly. "Indeed. Very well. These wands will also serve as a way to enhance your filtrating. Humans have quite a knack for ingenuity. Even something symbolic could increase the effect as long as it has meaning to you."

"You mean in the design?" Sarah asked, taking off her jacket as the warmth of the Forge became too much for it.

"Yes. A standard wand is simply a long stick with a rune at the butt of the handle. Humans, though, have a habit of making extra changes. I'm sorry. I am being vague. It has been a while since I even saw a proper wand."

Sarah draped her jacket over a chair. "What if it had rifling on the outside to help focus the spell?"

Steven cleared his throat. "Rifling is designed to be on the inside, but those fangs are hollow, so theoretically it could work."

Sarah shifted her feet. "Why not both then? If they're already hollow on the inside…" she trailed off, her mind wandering towards food as her stomach complained of emptiness. She'd been hungrier lately. Dr. Walker told her that was a natural result of arcane use and training, but the last two days, she noticed everyone had been eating less. This didn't help, given their increased activity.

Steven nodded. "Why not? I can show Cheekie what he'd need to know about rifling."

Cheekie rejoined them, toying with his mustache, bringing it to a proper point.

"Good. We make quick with help. I am tired, and food has not brought."

"That's quite all right, Cheekie. We can assist you. I know the runes, and Sarah can provide a boost. "

"Good. We need her here. I knew not or would have asked." He shook his head. "Breekie taught me runes we need, but is much to do for one dwarf."

Steven picked up a thick writing pad and began sketching. "They've usually brought us some lunch about now. Must have been a delay. Maybe the kitchen's lost power again."

I hope not. Things were tense enough last week when that happened. People get snippy when they're hungry, and situations are already stressful, Sarah reflected.

Steven held the sketch he'd made up to Cheekie, who held the fang in his hands. The symbol on Cheekie's shoulder began to glow a soft purple as he grasped the fang and drew it through the hand of the arm with the tattoo. Sarah felt the energy in the air shift ever so slightly.

When Cheekie finished, he raised the bone up for Sarah to inspect. It was split into two smaller pieces, one longer than the other, both thin enough to fit in the binder of a notebook. Black spiral grooves worked their way from stem to tip, except for the base, which remained unmarked. Cheekie handed the smaller wand over to Sarah for inspection, then pulled a small sharp tool from his apron and handed it to the older dwarf.

Sarah took the wand in hand. It was smooth, warm to the touch, and almost imperceptibly light. She glanced at Dr. Walker, looking for some kind of guidance. *That's it?*

Dr. Walker stared back at her. "Well?"

Sarah nodded. "It looks good. Is anything supposed to happen?"

Dr. Walker looked confused, then it dawned on her: "Oh, no, it's not going to shoot off sparks or anything like that, sweetie," she said with a smile. "Give it here, and give me your hand. I am tired already, and hunger does me no good."

Sarah did as she was told, opening her mind to the flow of arcane energy and guiding it into Dr. Walker. She felt it pass through her as the dwarf carved a rune into the butt of the wand. It was over in a moment. Sarah got a closer look at the rune and found it resembled a spark.

"A spark. This wand is to be used for self-defense. All you need is a spark to get you started. Now help Cheekie with the second. He is tired."

Sarah turned to Cheekie, who took her hand and placed it respectfully on his shoulder. The flow felt different this time. Cheekie's connection to the energy was like ice melting. It was different from Dr. Walker's connection but not shockingly so. It reminded her of when she'd helped Dr. Walker heal Peter.

She'd felt something within him then; energy of his own, far different from hers; energy with a strange duality to it that confused her. Cheekie's power was clearer, shifting, and turning constantly. They were done in a moment, and the second wand was placed in her hand.

Steven watched the entire process eagerly.

Sarah hadn't noticed how close he'd drawn to examine it until she entirely disconnected herself from the flow and found him only a few inches away. She turned to Dr. Walker, offering her the second, longer wand.

Dr. Walker carved a circle with a V in the center without asking for Sarah's help this time. "This one you will use for training and all manner of casting. In time, you may want to bind more spells to each, but we are not nearly ready for that yet."

Sarah took both in hand as Dr. Walker offered them to her, holding the shorter of the two more gingerly, not wanting some trace of arcane energy to cause an accident.

"Is that all?" she asked hesitantly. As fascinated by them as she was, she did not feel any special connection to the tools.

"For now. In time, you may find a core for each, but that is a decision and discussion for later. Let us give your new tool a test, shall we?" Dr. Walker said, her eyes ablaze with excitement.

"Here? Now? With all these people? Isn't it… dangerous?" She was suddenly extra aware of how many people there were in the room. *It's crowded. At least two dozen people are working here, and more outside or in other parts of the building. What if I can't control it?*

Dr. Walker seemed to read her mind. "Peace, Sarah. There is no safer place in this city for you to test it than right here in the company of myself and Cheekie. In the unlikely event something should go wrong, we are skilled enough to ensure no harm should come of it." She picked a polished rib off the table. It was three feet in length and smooth to the touch.

"Remember, the wand and the words are not the spell. They only help focus the energy, direct it. You decide what is done with it. When you cast, there must be no hesitation. It could cause the energy to stutter. Make sure your mind is clear and focused on the task. Push the flow through the wand. Allow the rune to help shape it. Any questions?"

A dozen. But no good ones, Sarah thought. "No, ma'am."

"Good. Now, at your own pace, I want you to make this rib grow. Focus the energy on that goal. Speak whatever word you feel best describes the action you desire the energy to undertake. A foot in length should do the trick."

Sarah nodded decisively and took a deep breath, clutching the smaller wand tightly in her hand. She stared at the rib and opened her mind to the flow of arcane energy. Sarah could feel her heart thumping in her chest as magic pulsed into her, spreading through every fiber of her being.

More, a voice in the depths of her consciousness whispered. She listened, nudging the door of her connection open, just a bit wider. That small nudge gave way to a flood. Raw power stormed her every molecule. It needed releasing. It could not stay there; not in her weak, fragile human body. She tried to lead it, like a toddler guiding a lion by its mane.

Her vision blurred as she tried to remember what she was meant to be doing with all this power. *Get it out!* Another weak voice screamed from the recesses of her mind. She focused, sharpening her vision. She felt her hair standing on edge. Steven had stepped away from her, a look of confused curiosity etched on his face as he raised an arm to shield his face.

From what? a passing thought questioned, but it was drowned out by the noise of the energy throbbing inside her.

Then she saw Dr. Walker. Her face was stone as she clasped her hands around Sarah's wrists. Her right hand held a wand pointed down at the bone; her left hung limp at her side. The instant their skin made contact, the white tattoos on the dwarf's arms lit up, glowing white-hot. She felt the dwarf's presence as much as she saw it.

Together, they directed the magic into the rib, willing it to grow to twice its size. She was forgetting something. She knew there was more to this but could not for the life of her think what it was. *Too hot to think clearly.*

Sarah's whole body felt hot. There was still energy. Too much of it. She knew that. Somehow, she could tell that if they poured anymore into the rib, it would shatter. Sarah threw her limp arm towards the ceiling, yanking it from the dwarf's grip.

Everything was ringing. With a mighty effort, Sarah cut herself off from the arcane. But there was still too much to handle, so she sent the energy up and out through the other wand. The ceiling burst above them as if struck by a wrecking ball from below.

Then Sarah was falling back into Steven's arms. She could feel hot tears running down her cheeks. She wanted to tell him not to touch her, that she was sweaty, but she was too tired.

Dr. Walker stood in front of her, her own springy hair a wild mess, a huge grin plastered across her face. Behind Dr. Walker, Cheekie's face bore an expression of abject terror.

Sarah heard voices, yelling, and people running around.

"I'm sorry," Sarah choked out softly. "I didn't…"

Dr. Walker shook her head. "No. No Miss Young. It is I who must apologize. I overestimated your preparedness and underestimated your abilities." She looked up at the ceiling, still grinning entirely inappropriately. "Perhaps now, though, you understand the importance of words in your casting," she said as though everything was perfectly fine and that explained the hole Sarah had just torn in the roof.

✦— 21 —✦

FIRST CONTACT

"Again!" Jadis' voice was hard as her translucent sword, which left a bruise on his shoulder. Peter stooped and picked up the translucent copy of Galvorn. The taste of blood still lingered in his mouth from her last strike. He ignored the pain in his cheek as he rose, blade in hand. The sword in his hand rose slowly, reminding him how much everything here was weightier.

"Quickly now. We do not have time to waste," the white-haired girl taunted as she bounced lightly on the balls of her bare feet. Her ragged robes had been replaced with a tighter, equally tattered violet-colored outfit that did not flow and shift with the mist.

Energy pulsed through Peter's muscles as he strode toward Jadis, deciding to go on the offensive against the short young girl. *I can't keep losing to a teenage girl. She's used to the weight here. I have to find a way to compensate for her speed and strength,* he thought while looking for an opening between the slashing and swinging of the translucent blade humming through the air.

Jadis dodged or deflected every attack, turning the sword's blade away with a light touch of her hand or the flat of the blade. Peter no longer held back, he made no effort to spare her injury. He knew the blade wouldn't do any real damage in this realm, even if he could get a hit on her.

Jadis' leg kicked out with the power of a bull. Peter avoided the strike with an agile sidestep.

"Better. Lean into the energy. Let it control your actions," she instructed and landed a punch on his leg as she dove into a roll under his blade. "You are thinking too mu— Umph."

He caught her with a kick of his own. His foot collided with her stomach, sending her sliding backward. She took the blow like a pro, bending her body to receive it and not letting it throw her off balance. Peter followed it up by bringing Galvorn down in a quick arc toward the drow's shoulder. He felt a shift in the energy and submitted to it. His sword curved through the air and caught Jadis in the side with a thump.

She grimaced. The expression looked at home on her face.

Peter jerked back out of her range reflexively, narrowly dodging a punishing blow that would have met his temple. This time, Jadis actually grinned. The grin was gone in an instant though, swallowed by the mist. *What?*

The mist burst up from the ground a second later, engulfing both Peter and Jadis as the ground beneath his feet shook. He heard her voice as the mist shifted from white to gray to black.

"Kill something better than a deer next, and we'll have more time," she whispered through the dark.

Peter's shoulder shook again as his eyes snapped open. The shadowy form of O'Cleary was crouched at his side, an inquisitive expression on his scarred, patchy, scruff-covered face.

"You all right, cap'n? Not like you to doze off like that," he said in a concerned whisper. "Simon's back."

Peter nodded. Taking O'Cleary's hand as he hoisted him to his feet from where he'd dozed beneath the old oak tree.

Kill something better, Jadis' voice still echoed in his mind as he stretched, adjusting his muscles to the real world.

Peter shrugged off the fog of the sleep with a sip of water from his canteen. *Looks like the opportunity might be closer than I'd hoped. Training is helping, but these dreams are too short,* he thought. Refocusing on the task at hand, he looked out at the road from his position in the trees.

A few hundred yards away was a lamentable barrier of broken trees set up on the road leading into the small town ahead of them. *Ideally, we won't have to kill anything, but if that's what it takes to get stronger, so be it.*

"I'm just sayin' they did a sloppy job. It seems more like the work of some panicked civvies than anything else," Justin whispered to the group.

"Or, it could be intentional. It could just as easily be a trap," countered Jenni.

"Why are we being so paranoid? We're still in Georgia, aren't we? We've all probably driven through Macon once or twice," Gunter grumbled. He glanced at Shawn and their dwarf companion, the only two who seemed to be paying him any real attention. "Well, most of us probably have."

"You're sure no one saw you when you first spotted it?" Peter asked, turning to Shawn.

"Yes, sir. I didn't even go past the tree line," Shawn replied confidently.

"You'd think they'd have some kinda guards at least," complained Justin. "If they're going to go to the trouble of makin' a lazy barrier, they should at least have people watchin' it."

"Again, we don't know that they aren't watching, or that there are even people in there," Jenni pointed out from where she was leaning against an old oak tree.

"There are people," said Simon softly.

Peter gave his new beard a scratch as he turned to the rest of them. "Right, Simon. Go ahead."

"I didn't get to go far. Basic stuff. Nothing reinforced. No Hescos, concertina, or concrete. Looks a lot like what we saw in Koba, or what you'd see deployed — minus the sand, of course." He brushed a loose strand of hair away from his eyes. "But there are definitely people here. I came back because they've been clear-cutting a lot of the trees around the side. I didn't want to risk getting seen at that point, because people were keeping an eye out," Simon explained.

"Then this is our best entry point," said Peter. "Jenni?"

"Yes, sir?"

"We're going through that… barricade to get eyes inside the town. I'm taking everyone but you and Hauch with me. Remain here, out of sight. Expect to hear from us in three-zero minutes. If you don't get something from us in six-zero minutes, come in after us, but send the dog home."

Peter checked his gun, finding it loaded as he expected. "Use your best judgment, but it'll be weapons-tight. If we're engaged, we're falling back to this spot and will need cover. Got all that?"

"Hold up, what now?" interjected Gunter. "Some of us don't speak merc, Peter."

"If we're not back in an hour, she sends Hauch back to Paragon with intel before checkin' to see if we're alive herself," interjected Justin. "If we come runnin' back with guns blazin', she provides cover fire. It's basic stuff. Didn't they teach you anythin' in ROTC?" Justin replied in a haughty tone.

Gunter glowered back but didn't rise to the bait.

"I'd like to send out another R and S cloverleaf five hundred meters both ways around… but I don't think that's realistic," Peter said. "Anyone have any ideas?"

"Uh, captain?" Shawn said.

"Shawn, you've been a big help, but I was asking the people with military experience."

Shawn shook his head and pointed past Peter towards the town. Breekie had exited the woods and was walking calmly across the six-lane highway that separated the town's outskirts from the tree line. He gave no indication he planned on stopping before he entered the city. *How'd he get that far so quickly? Idiot. He's going to get himself killed.*

"What is he doin'?" scoffed Justin.

"Doesn't matter now," Peter growled. "Wedge it out, low ready, weapons tight. ID before engaging. Good luck, Jenni."

"Good luck, guys," Jenni said, gripping Hauch by the collar as the rest of them scrambled to gather their equipment and catch up to the dwarf. Peter moved the fastest of them, crossing four lanes in a sprint before the rest of them could emerge from the cover of the trees. They followed his lead in a mad dash across the open ground towards the poorly barricaded road. O'Cleary barking softly to Gunter and Shawn to keep up.

Peter caught up to Breekie a few strides short of a partially collapsed overpass leading into the city. "What are you thinking, Breekie?" he hissed as they slipped easily along the two open lanes leading through the overpass.

Breekie shrugged. "Much talk by blind builders cannot build a home."

Peter grasped him by the shoulder, pulling him around to face him.

"We're entering a potentially hostile environment. You can't just go dashing off like that."

Breekie's eyes narrowed as a look of indignation came over his face. "Are these not your people? Your allies? Are you not here to offer your help or ask for theirs?"

His English is improving, Peter thought with clenched teeth. "Yes, but that doesn't mean we can just stroll in like we own the place."

"Bah, is too late now. We will be fine. Come."

"No," said Peter tightening his grip on the dwarf's shoulder as he tried to turn away. *They're super submissive to their elders — use that.* Breekie's eyes widened in surprise, and he met Peter's gaze.

Peter released his grip. "Doctor Walker placed you under my authority, and you *will* follow my orders. I will not have my people killed due to a violent misunderstanding."

Breekie's mouth made a thin line, but he gave no indication he intended to interrupt.

Peter continued in a low tone as their allies caught up. "That means you don't do anything without consulting me first. We will not be challenging strangers to bloody combat or rushing off before plans are finished because of some dwarf proverb. Am I understood?"

Breekie's jaw worked for a moment before the wide smile that lived on it returned to its rightful home. "Dah... sir? This is right word?"

Peter nodded, letting a silent sigh of relief escape through his nostrils. *Thank God that worked.*

Breekie nodded eagerly. "Yes, sir. You are Gris-leonc. I follow your wisdom," he said, then clapped Peter on the forearm.

Gris-leonc? Peter wondered as he turned to the group crouched around him. *We need to be careful here.*

"Cap'n?" asked O'Cleary exasperatedly.

"Be ready. Diamond stack," Peter ordered, a grimace in his face as they formed two diamonds that met in the middle with Shawn. Peter formed the top of the first diamond; O'Cleary at his left, Breekie at his right. To Shawn's back left was Gunter, with Simon at his back right and Justin bringing up the rear.

As they moved forward, Peter searched his mind for the energy Jadis was teaching him to use. He knew it was there the same way he knew his heart was beating. It was like adrenaline; it came to him when needed, but his control over it was limited. *Use it like adrenaline. When it comes, lean into it and turn it into a weapon. The sooner I master it, the better.*

They passed out the other side of the overpass and found themselves facing a crude pile of logs and vehicles.

"Is that supposed to be a barricade?" Justin asked quietly.

"I think so," Peter replied as they made their way easily around it. *Unmanned and with no real effort put into it. Could it be a trap?*

Once around the pathetic attempt at a barricade, they entered the town proper. Most of the town's buildings were in such a state of distress that it made Paragon look pristine. Of the buildings that stood, not one bore a window that was not broken or boarded up, nor was their evidence of any electricity working in any of them.

The blacktop beneath their feet was cracked and broken, small green weeds and grass crawling out of its wounds towards the sunlight. Among the spread of struggling vegetation, Peter spied a single tiny black flower trying desperately to escape the weeds around it. The sight of the outnumbered flower sent a cold drop of fear down his back.

Before anyone else could get close enough to see it, he tweaked his pace and crushed it underfoot. *Justin doesn't need to see that with how superstitious he can be. We have enough to worry about without more ominous signs.*

Moving forward along the remains of the road between damaged buildings, it became apparent there were no operational vehicles anywhere on the road. The only vehicle in sight was one burned-out skeleton of an SUV outside a collapsed fast-food joint.

"Where is everyone?" whispered Gunter, the sound of his voice threatening the silence of their surroundings as it bounced off the surface of the damaged walls encompassing them.

"Inside. Look closer. They're in every other building," Peter responded.

They continued forward, remaining in a tight formation.

"We're being watched," whispered Shawn, his eyes lingering on a boarded-up window.

"Ya think?" Justin muttered under his breath.

"Stay calm." Peter firmly directed his words at Shawn as they continued forward. "Third floor. Eleven O'clock. Second window. Fourth window." *We've got four exit options and a dozen buildings we could breach and take cover in. For now, we keep moving.*

"Two on the first floor, two-thirty," replied Simon. Their steps barely registered on the pavement. Somewhere out of sight, the sound of scurrying feet could be heard, followed by a door being slammed shut.

"One, eight O'clock, second window," muttered Justin as they passed a small dark building painted green. "Man, I miss Apaches… or any air support."

I miss satellites, Peter thought as the adrenaline coursing through his body heightened his awareness. *Still, this. This is my element.*

"We're surrounded, cap. This is a kill zone," whispered O'Cleary between clenched teeth. "If these guys are anything like what we saw in Koba, we're in trouble."

"Anyone have eyes on weapons?" Peter asked gravely. *This isn't going to go anything like Koba.* No one replied, but even Breekie's pace had slowed to a crawl.

"Good. Keep moving." *I'm not sensing danger anywhere. What's going on here?*

"Coming out! Hold your fire!" a voice called from one of the buildings up ahead. The sudden sound drew barrels like a magnet towards the building. Shawn jerked his gun clumsily toward the sound, a look of panic across his face. He stared nervously at the brick building from which the voice came.

Peter raised an open palm bringing the group to a silent halt. "Hands where I can see them when you do," Peter shouted back.

Ahead of them and to their right, a white door on the front of a tall old brick building creaked open slowly. Peter kept his eyes moving, looking for any sign this was some kind of a decoy but found none.

From within the door's jaws emerged a lean figure with both arms in the air. He was of a height and complexion similar to Peter, with a smooth face and hazel eyes. He wore green combat trousers, boots, and an unmarked gray t-shirt. On his head sat a large camouflage beanie which slouched slightly in the back.

He took a few steps to clear the door as Peter's rifle followed him, finger off the trigger.

"Turn around, slowly."

The man complied but did so while striding towards them. As he approached, he kept his arms high and turned in a slow circle, which impressively did not hinder his pace.

"Hello there. As you can see, I am unarmed," he called out in lyrical baritone. He came to a stop a dozen paces ahead of them. "I'm afraid you've come at a bad time. People here are already timid, especially at this point in the day."

Peter took a few steps closer, weapon still raised. "Why's that?"

"I'll let Jason explain. It would be best if I were to take you to him. Keep your weapons on hand, though. Things can get dicey where we're going." The man said, his gaze wandering perceptively over them. "I apologize. How rude of me not to introduce myself. My name is Caraticus. Caraticus Whitaker. Who are you folks?"

Still nothing. No warning of any kind. Peter strode forward, slipping his Mk-11e onto his back over his sword and extended a hand in greeting. "Captain Peter Blair of SNW here to help your town in whatever way we can."

THE INNER CITY

Caraticus looked Peter up and down for a moment before taking a step forward and gripping his forearm in greeting. "Pleasure to meet you, Captain Blair," Caraticus said, his eyes drifting over Galvorn on Peter's back. "Your group is well armed for the time. I assume SNW is some form of military organization."

"The Silent Night Warriors, yes. We're an American contractor organization."

Caraticus' brow furrowed as his eyes moved over their weapons. "Ah, have you had much trouble with monsters yet where you're from?"

Peter smirked. "You'd be surprised."

Caraticus nodded, his eyes lingering on the sword. "Perhaps not. What are the names of your companions?"

"Companions? Do we look like—" Justin started with a snicker.

"Justin." Peter cut him off before he could add the impending insult.

Peter half turned to his group. "The long-bearded one is Breekie. The older looking one is O'Cleary," Peter added slyly.

O'Cleary glowered at this, but Peter continued down the line. "I'm sure you can tell which one is Justin. That's Simon, Shawn is the young one, and that's Gunter," Peter said, glancing at his watch. *Still got plenty of time before Jenni makes a move.*

"He's not human, is he?" Caraticus said, knowingly glancing from Breekie to Peter.

Peter frowned. *So much for putting him in ordinary clothes to make him look less bizarre. I should have traded him to center formation.*

"No, but I can vouch for him. Is that going to be a problem?"

Caraticus adjusted a purple braided necklace around his throat. "I wouldn't advertise it. Most folks won't notice since he looks friendly enough, and he's not quite as ugly as our other non-human visitors. Still, people are nervous about outsiders."

Breekie chuckled from between the pair and the rest of the group. "You must've been dealing with elves then. Ugly, beardless beings, elves."

Caraticus raised an eyebrow. "No, no elves, but we have been having a bit of an ork problem that hopefully you can help us with."

Breekie's grin went from amused to savage. "Oh, I think we might help, dah."

"What's an ork?" whispered Shawn to O'Cleary.

"I think it's like a goblin," O'Cleary whispered back, grinning sardonically.

"If you don't know, better to see than have me explain," interrupted Caraticus. "You really haven't encountered any? We assumed everything to the south was decimated."

"You have some here?" Peter asked. *I bet killing an ork would make for a decent training session with Jadis.*

"Not presently, but they'll be back. If you'll come with me, I can introduce you to our leader. Lucky for you, I found you, or you wouldn't be able to get in to see him."

Peter raised his eyebrows. "That is fortunate. Was it you broadcasting the emergency signal?"

The man's eyes shrank by a hair. "Emergency signal? Not something I know about, but maybe Jason will."

"Very well. Lead the way, Caraticus," Peter replied.

Caraticus nodded, a smile crawling across his face.

Peter turned to Breekie. "Breekie, move to center formation and switch with Shawn. No sense in drawing unnecessary attention."

Breekie shrugged, adjusting his grip on his war hammer before repositioning himself between Gunter and O'Cleary.

Caraticus took point, walking only a step ahead of Peter, leading them farther into the city where the state of the buildings improved. Furthermore, the number of sloppy fortifications increased, consisting mostly of piles of trash and broken furniture shoved up against windows, which were now not all boarded or broken. As they ventured forward, Caraticus' presence emboldened the town's inhabitants.

People began to emerge from the dwellings. There weren't many, but on more than one occasion, Peter saw someone staring out a window. It was still quiet out, but the street was no longer bathed in eerie silence. Then they passed a dirt-covered, middle-aged man hammering planks over a window. Of the people they saw, everyone wore the same gaunt, tired expression and were dressed in damaged, dirty clothes.

Peter attempted to strike up a conversation with their guide, eager to create an ally of the man. "An interesting name, Caraticus. Is it biblical?"

"People do seem to think so, but not that I know of," Caraticus said with an easy smile. "I share it with some Celtic war chieftain apparently. Always wondered about it but never took the time to find out more."

"Ah, maybe that's why it sounds familiar. My mother was a professor of military history, so she could probably have told you all about it," Peter replied as the group strolled deeper into the town.

"Interesting," Caraticus replied, but before he could say anything else, an old woman burst out of one of the buildings to their right. Rifles swung in her direction, responding to the sound of her abrasive emergence. She tottered forward, leaning on a weak cane, looking for all the world like a human Tower of Pisa.

Caraticus slipped deftly forward to help her, holding an open palm out toward Peter and his men as he bent over to offer an arm for the frail old woman to lean on. Peter caught the sound of her weak raspy voice: "Nooo, it's not safe for you, boy. Get back inside, please. Get back inside." Peter followed her surprisingly clear gaze to Shawn.

She thinks she recognizes him. The woman continued forward despite Caraticus' protests, but he was helpless to resist her too forcefully lest he injure her fragile body. He looked to Peter, a firm plea for help on the embraced man's face. Peter released his grip on Galvorn's handle, the sword sliding firmly back into its sheath.

"Weapons down, but eyes up. It's all right," he ordered in a tone soft enough for the old woman not to hear. Slowly, arms spread wide, he approached the struggling old woman, intentionally stepping in her line of sight with Shawn.

"Ma'am, it's all right. We're here to help," he said in a soothing voice. For a moment, her eyes lingered on his chest, as if trying to bore through it to see to the other side. Then something gave, and her whole body sagged, her attention going to Peter.

"H-h-help?" she wheezed out as Peter offered her a hand for support. She blinked. "Hello, young man. You're a soldier-r, aren't you?" she said, eyeing his uniform.

"Yes," Peter replied. "Are you all right, ma'am?" he asked sincerely. He felt the tug of Caraticus' eyes as together they helped turn the little woman around.

It's a miracle she's alive. She could easily be in her nineties, and they don't seem to have power in this side of the city, he observed as he walked forward, her weak shaking hand resting on his forearm. "I am fine. But the children — Oh, the children." Her voice began to verge upon hysteria.

"What's your name, ma'am?" Peter asked, trying to calm her down." Her brow furrowed as she considered this, pausing her lamentations about children. "Martie," she said decisively.

Looking up, Peter saw another old woman waiting at the door the first woman had come from. It was impossible to tell at a glance this woman's age. She could have easily been the same age as the first or, for all Peter could tell, her daughter. Either way, she stood in the doorway like a tombstone. Her eyes leered and lips pinched tightly together. A wrist brace adorned her right hand. She said nothing as they approached. Martie mumbled again about the children, but her intelligent eyes didn't leave Peter for a second.

"Here she is, Leta, safe and sound," Caraticus said warmly as the other woman stepped aside to make room for him and Martie. "I'm working on visitation for you," Caraticus was saying, but Leta did not make room for Peter. Instead, she remained directly in his path as the other man helped the woman inside.

"You should leave," Leta whispered.

Peter met her eyes. They were firm, unwavering, but there was a familiar fear in them. Peter knew fear. He knew the shapes and forms it took. He knew the fear men had of him. He knew the look of anxiety before a battle. He knew the dread of pain, the terror of death. This was a fear of things to come, of the unavoidable; a defiant fear of corrupt authority.

Caraticus returned to the doorway, stepping past Leta towards the street. Peter followed. "Sorry about that," the odd man said. "People are a bit worked up after everything that's happened. I think she thought your friend was one of her grandchildren."

Peter watched Caraticus move, searching for the slightest change in gait or a minuscule change to his clothing — any sign of change or that the man had acquired a new weapon. He saw none. Whitaker was much the same other than a minor increase in hurriedness. Peter couldn't fault him for that. *If I were him, I'd want to distance the unfamiliar armed militia from the weak old ladies too.*

"Here we are," Caraticus declared as they turned at a road sign that read *Houst Ave*, which led into a more commercial district of the town. Ahead of them, the road was blocked with a wall of desks and logs stacked tightly together eight feet high at a narrow point in the street.

It was evident at a glance that this structure was not a poorly made barricade resulting from a mad grab for anything that would fit like what they'd seen so far. No, this was put together with care. There was no route around it, and at its center sat a small opening just wide enough for a single person to squeeze through.

O'Cleary and Justin exchanged a look. "IDB?" Simon asked quietly.

"IDB," the two of them replied in quiet unison. Peter pushed the memory of the mission to the back of his mind, focusing on the here and now.

Sitting in front of this narrow entrance was a fat man in a faded polo and poorly fitting brown Carhartt. He rested in a folding chair, hunched over a phone. Behind him, a hunting rifle leaned carelessly against the wall just out of reach. *The idiot would have to stand and take two steps before he could grab that — too much effort to actually be able to make use of it.*

Peter glanced at his watch. *Forty-five minutes until we need to get back to Jenni.*

"Hello, James," called Caraticus as they approached the lazy man.

James looked up slowly from the phone in his hands, soft music emitting from its speakers. *They have enough power on the other side of this to be playing on phones? Why are there people out here then?*

As he saw Caraticus, he tapped the screen, bringing the music to a stop, and stood up. He did not, however, even make an effort to reach his weapon.

Foolish. Not that it mattered though. If we were his enemies, he'd be too late already.

"Carrie?" the man said in a droll base. "Isn't you supposed to be at the square? It's 'bout time to see off the tribute selection." His gaze shifted to the rest of the group.

"Who's this lot? Don't tell me you're trying to bring more strags in. We've been over this."

"I'm on the way there, James. Do these folks look like strags to you?" Caraticus replied in an authoritative yet friendly tone.

James' brow furrowed, sunken eyes drifting slowly across Peter and his friends. "Nah, suppose not," he said, sitting back down heavily.

"James, you'll have to let us in," Caraticus said with a hint of annoyance.

"Oh. Right, 'course," James said before rising and lumbering through the opening behind him. Peter's jaw clenched at the rifle left forgotten against the wall. Through the narrow passage, Peter could just make out the front end of a semi in front of James.

A few seconds later, the truck growled to life, followed by loud beeping as it rolled back from the entrance. "Right, come on then," James called out once the beeping stopped.

With an apologetic look over his shoulder, Caraticus began to make his way through the barrier.

As Caraticus pressed forward, O'Cleary grasped Peter by the shoulder before he could follow. "You sure about this, cap? Feeling more and more like a trap to me," he whispered, eyeing the reinforced buildings that stood over them.

"I know. Be ready," Peter replied just loud enough for the rest to hear him.

Don't underestimate your enemy. Ignorance and ineptitude are easily faked. Peter heard his father's words repeated in his head as he gave the unattended rifle one last bitter look. "We're the experts here, after all," he said to O'Cleary, then entered the barricade.

The barrier was roughly six feet deep, composed of logs and tightly packed debris ranging from pieces of desks to refrigerator doors. Upon exiting out the other side, Peter found himself in an alleyway face to face with the front of the semi, only a few feet to spare on either side.

Ordinarily, he'd have been forced to choose between going right or left around the truck or going back. But James was leaned against the truck blocking the right. With his men behind him, Peter was left with only one exit. He did not like having only one exit. He frowned up at the truck's driver, a thick-set androgynous woman blinked down at him over the steering wheel.

"This way, captain," Caraticus called reassuringly from the passenger side of the vehicle.

He followed the man's voice, and soon they'd all joined Caraticus behind the semi. Once they were through, the truck rolled back without another word from James or a first word from the driver.

Idiots. This would be easily defendable if manned properly.

To his surprise, the city on this side of the wall stood in stark contrast to what they'd passed. It was almost as if they'd stepped back in time a few weeks, the change was so sudden and drastic from the war-torn ghost town they'd been in. The change in smell, sight, and noise were all startling.

The most significant difference was the people. On this side, there was no shortage of people; in fact, men and women with somber expressions were emerging from the surrounding buildings in droves. It was a strange sight to behold. Despite the presence of so many, there was hardly any noise coming from the crowd, only whispers and the sound of many feet.

"What is going on? Why are they keeping people on the outside?" Justin muttered, all humor gone from his voice.

They're all better dressed and fed than anyone we've seen, too. Peter glanced into an office building as they passed by. *And they've got power?* He noted a number of growing reactions to their group. *Why are there people left on the outside?*

We're drawing quite a bit of attention. Curious glances and mutters were being cast in their direction as Caraticus lead them farther into the town. Everyone was going the same way, gathering for something. The more people they passed, the more attention they drew. That was to be expected, but the expressions Peter felt were wrong.

They weren't hopeful, scared, or even indifferent. *What are they muttering about...? Shawn.*

Then it hit him. Among the crowd of men and women, there was not a single person who could have been younger than seventeen. It was Shawn, not his men or Breekie, drawing attention as they moved through the crowd.

Still, even with the strange glances and whispers, no one spoke to them, and no one stopped moving. Caraticus followed the flow of traffic, and thus so did they, until they all turned a corner, finding themselves at the edge of a square filling with people from all directions.

Roughly, three, maybe four thousand, give or take. Now the crowd began to ignore them as it passed, settling in the square. They did not quite squeeze in around Peter's group yet, but they were close enough to make him nervous and were getting closer as more and more civilians appeared. *This is bad. They don't seem hostile, and it doesn't look like they're armed, but if they turned on us, we'd be in trouble.*

Peter did a double take as he noticed three stockades on an elevated platform at the edge of the square to their left. Each stockade contained a figure with a bag over their head, all being entirely ignored by the gathering crowd. On either side of the stockade were men armed with guns, spears, and wearing bits and pieces of ragged medieval-style armor over everyday clothes.

Not just them. Peter searched the crowd and edges of the square. He found over a hundred men armed, not unlike the stockade guards. *Eighty-seven obviously armed hostiles, none of which look like they have military experience.* Strangely, there was no indication of anyone sporting injuries. *They look like they've been under siege if I had to guess.*

Peter continued his search as he walked behind Caraticus, looking for a reason other than their own arrival that the crowd would be gathering. He found it quickly. At the center of the square stood an elevated, round, stone fountain. A wooden rise had replaced the fountain's water, and three men stood elevated atop it instead of being knee-deep in liquid.

Two of the men were armed with pistols and swords and dressed in the now familiar strange conglomeration of chain and plate mail. The third man stood between them, tall with a shaved bald head, facing away from the crowd toward the fountain, looking up at the mismatched fixture that rose from the fountain's center.

Peter followed the tall man's gaze, trying to figure out what was off about the fountain. He recognized the familiar shape of a face. Impaled upon the fountain's primary tall spigot was an enormous head, an inhuman wooden head the size of an oven.

The head wore a short beard made of moss with a cropping of vines, which could only be hair. Its features were too lifelike to have been carved, with black eyes and eyelids that lay open, unseeing. An enormous knot of wood formed its nose, and beneath that, a wide mouth hung open in death.

"Criske," Breekie muttered with a sharp inhale at Peter's side. "That's a Treant."

"What's a Treant?" Gunter asked softly.

A wave followed by a soft whistle from Caraticus distracted Breekie from offering an explanation. Still, Peter could see the anxious curve of eyebrows on the dwarf's pale face. *He's horrified.*

Beneath the wooden head, the tall bald man turned slowly to face the crowd. In his early forties, he wore a long dark jersey underneath a chestnut brown leather chest plate interlaced with a layer of chainmail. On his arms, he wore wooden bracers, the same shade of brown as the head under which he stood.

His legs were garbed in washed-out jeans tucked into clean brown boots. His hooded hazel eyes rested under fading arched eyebrows. His stubby hawk-nose sat over flat, broad lips, which bore a somber expression that did not match his eyes, which sparkled with glee. From his lofted position, his eyes swept over the crowd.

Peter felt warning energy surge through his veins.

"That," said Caraticus as he turned around to face him, "is Jason."

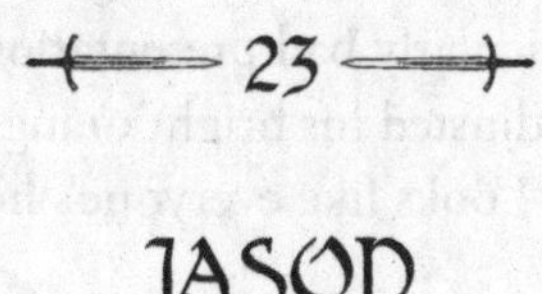

JASON

Caraticus brought the group to a halt at the edge of the crowd. In front of them was a barrier of police tape, behind which stood armed guards. The gathering ended before the barrier.

There was an uneasiness in the crowd; people murmured quietly, shifting their feet and glancing about. Peter picked up on the behavior and wasn't the only one. All of his soldiers were trained to perceive these changes.

O'Cleary worked his fingers up and down his rifle barrel like some deadly guitarist warming up. What, to the casual observer, was meaningless fidgeting, Peter knew as one of O'Cleary's tells. *Not a good sign. A nervous crowd and nervous soldiers make for a poor combo.*

"Wait here a moment," Caraticus said, then paused and added, "this part gets a little weird." Before Peter could respond, Caraticus shimmied between two fidgety onlookers and disappeared into the crowd.

Without his guide, Peter's senses kicked into an even higher gear. Where before he saw furtive glances and not-so-subtle whispers directed at his group, he now saw apprehension and fear. All of that nervous energy was directed toward the makeshift stage, though, not at him and his men. Whatever happened next, Peter was confident he was not going to like it.

Onto the stage walked the most ludicrous thing Peter had seen since departing Paragon. A large African American man with a gut spilling over the front of his pants barely concealed by an orange name-brand shirt big enough to fit three normal-sized men trundled onto the stage.

On his head rested a faded red flat top. Below the hat, the rotund man's face bore an enormous, white-toothed smile and sunglasses despite the overcast sky. On his arms and hands were more jewelry than any one person needed. The grip he held on the loudspeaker made precarious at best by the bling.

Peter heard his own thoughts voiced by O'Cleary. "What the hell?" O'Cleary asked, his voice infused with confusion. Around them, dozens of eyes rolled, but no displeasure was voiced. Nevertheless, a strange, awkwardness had fallen over the crowd. It was reminiscent of once in high school, when Peter's class was being forced to watch a particularly bad presentation about the industrial age.

On the stage, the man adjusted his bright orange shades and spoke into the loudspeaker. "Wassup, y'all? Looks like everyone's here. Cool, cool. Aight, fam, y'all know what time it is."

"You've got to be kidding," spat out Gunter.

"Our leader! The ork tamer, the peacemaker, the treeeee slayer! Give it up for yer boii, Commander Jaasoooon," the man exclaimed.

Peter exchanged looks of shocked disbelief and confusion with the other members of the group, except Justin. The man's face was bright red with a hand clasped over his mouth as he did everything in his power not to burst into laughter.

Amid scattered applause, Jason stepped forward and took the microphone from the man, who quickly hopped down and tried to blend into the less eccentrically dressed crowd. He failed. His bright colors gave him the appearance of a plump peacock among a flock of wild chickens.

Well, that was ridiculous. Caraticus was right. Where the hell did he go? Peter thought.

A loudspeaker in his right hand, looking more like a stork in a sports jersey than a plump peacock, Jason swaggered to the edge of the stage. His left hand grasped the end of a chain hidden in his shirt. In an instant, the crowd fell into muted anticipation. This is what they were compelled to bear witness to. This is who they harbored real fear for.

After a moment of intense silence, Jason addressed the crowd: "I know times are hard. You've all lost things, haven't you? We all have," Jason said authoritatively.

Despite Peter's expectations, he found the man's voice surprisingly soothing, like sliding into a hot bath — unpleasant at first, but the longer you wait, the more you realize it's not so bad, and you begin to relax.

We should probably listen to what he has to say, he found himself thinking, then the pain in his unhealed finger throbbed, burning the thoughts from his mind.

"I lost my wife. She was killed when her car crashed during the breaking of the sky," the man went on.

Peter felt a tug at his elbow. He looked down to find a vexed looking Breekie holding a sharpie. The dwarf motioned for Peter to bend down, so Peter squatted to get closer to his level, not taking his gaze off of Jason.

"Can you focus on my voice?" Breekie muttered in Dwarvish.

Peter took a deep breath through his nose. "Yes, why?"

Breekie continued to speak softly. "I will explain later," he whispered, giving Peter's injured finger a squeeze. Peter felt a cold shock run up his arm as if he'd shoved it in a bucket of ice water. The sensation tore his attention further from Jason's words.

He looked down at the cold rune left by the marker. His head now teemed with thoughts, the foremost of which was how the cold reminded him of Jenni still waiting for information out in the chilly woods. He checked his watch. *We've got time. Morse would be best.*

Turning his attention back to the situation at hand, he noticed his companions all seemed to have relaxed, focused on Jason's speech. He was saying something about two men who stole supplies from a community area. Whatever it was, the man's voice had lost its charm, and Peter was too preoccupied to pay attention, but O'Cleary was nodding along thoughtfully with the words.

"You good, man?" Peter asked his friend. "You hate speeches."

O'Cleary shrugged, his fingers no longer fidgeting, and his eyes didn't waver from the fountain. "He's got some good points," he said like a teenager with headphones on responding to an inquiring parent.

"Does he? Sounds like a lot of posturing to me," Peter prodded, but O'Cleary didn't reply. Of the group of them, only Breekie and Shawn seemed unfazed by the strange speech. Shawn was clearly unaffected as he'd taken a seat on the ground where he'd removed a shoe and was examining his blister-covered feet.

A few moments later, the speech was over and met with a round of applause by those closest to the fountain. Their eagerness to show their approval was in no way subtle. Shawn got quickly back on his feet. The applause spread slowly and weakly through the rest of the crowd before dying pathetically. Lazily the crowd began to disperse, all looking tired and somewhat numbed.

In Paragon, whenever people gathered, the conversation never ceased, but as Peter looked around here, he saw only the lines formed by lips pressed tightly together in silence. The crowd had gone mute as a child who knows if he opens his mouth, he will expose the stolen treat inside. The only speaking taking place was by the fountain where a small group of clean, well-dressed people had gathered around Jason.

Someone in Jason's entourage helped him shakily down from the fountain into a large armchair. A moment later, Caraticus re-emerged from the dispersing crowd, an expression on his face like he'd just eaten a rotten pistachio. His gaze lingered on Breekie for a moment before he addressed Peter. "He'll be ready in a minute."

Peter nodded to him expectantly as a woman a bit on the heavier side, in a bright green shirt with round orange symbols, said something to Jason, gesturing enthusiastically in their direction.

After a couple of handshakes, back claps, and a drink being handed to Jason, the woman walked over to where Peter's group waited. She had a round, flat, soft face, and a short-styled haircut with pink and blue highlights accompanied by plenty of small tattoos.

"He's ready for you, Carrie," she said in a penetrating voice, her highlighter-green eyes probing Peter and his men.

"Thank you, Marah," Caraticus said to the pear-shaped woman as they all walked over to where Jason was sitting in his large out-of-place armchair.

They were mostly well-armed, and all wore critical, condescending expressions. *Great*, Peter thought, sarcasm leaping to his defense.

"What have you brought me today, Carrie?" said Jason with our sigh and an aggravated look from his seat. His voice was taught and tired. "And could it not have waited? Grelnog will be here soon."

"If your speeches weren't so exhausting, it might have waited, Jason," Caraticus said.

Jason's eyes narrowed slightly, and he smiled sarcastically. "I do not enjoy it, but I do what I must for the people."

"Yes, the people are always your concern," Caraticus said facetiously.

"You can't—"

A member of Jason's entourage tried to interrupt, but Caraticus continued over him. "Allow me to introduce Captain Peter Blair, of SNW. He and his men have traveled here to offer us aid in these strange times." Caraticus spread his arms as he spoke. "I thought you would prefer to introduce them to the town and our current… situation."

Jason nodded, standing up from his chair, brushing off the helping hands extended by his companions. He put out a hand expectantly towards Peter, forcing him to take a few steps forward to take it. When he did, Jason grasped his hand harder than necessary.

"Yo, welcome to my town, Captain Peter. Name's Jason Mingledorf, but you may call me Jason, although many people call me Commander Jason." His lips peeled back in a smile that seemed more like a sneer."Despite my protests."

I'm not going to call him commander. He obviously wants me to, but he clearly doesn't have a day's worth of military experience. "Hello, Jason," Peter said, letting go of the grip.

Jason's brow furrowed at this, and he took a step back, looking Peter up and down. "Hmm…" he mumbled like a disappointed talent show judge before returning to his chair. "I appreciate the offer, but we have things under control. And I don't think you know what you're up against." He paused, pulling on his chain again. "Please, you look tired, won't y'all follow Marah to my home and rest?"

Around Jason, his posse bobbed their heads up and down like a bunch of parakeets in agreement.

"That sounds kinda nice, captain," Justin said softly. "We are pretty tired."

Peter frowned and fought the urge to cross his arms or rest his hand on his sword. It wasn't like Justin to rest — criticize, complain, and make light, sure, but not rest. Peter let the comment slide and replied, "If it's all the same, we'd rather hear more about this ork situation."

Jason looked a bit surprised at this and frowned. His entourage exchanged shocked looks.

"Tell me, Peter Blair," Jason continued, "where are you from? Farther south, right? Which means you haven't seen what we've been fighting up here, I imagine."

Peter was starting to get annoyed with this man. He breathed subtly through his nose, masking his displeasure with a grin. "From the South, yes. We're from down the road in the new town of Paragon."

Jason shook his head. "Times have changed since the Breaking, haven't they? Change happens too quick. Names, government — all gone in the blink of an eye." He snapped his fingers to emphasize his point. "And the strong are left behind to pick up the pieces," he said proudly.

Peter shifted his weight. "We've had our fair share of trouble and changes, but I understand you're short on time. I do not wish to waste it on talk of how things have changed. Time for that later. I think it would benefit us all if we discuss the ork problem."

Jason's frown deepened. "You really have a one-track mind, don't you?" he replied. "The orks are something I worked hard to resolve at no small cost to our town." He turned his glare to Caraticus. "Are my methods not good enough for you, Carrie? Been complaining about them to strangers?" he asked harshly.

Before Caraticus could reply, Peter interceded, "I am not questioning your hard work or abilities, Jason," he said, waving his hands in a placating gesture, "and neither has Caraticus. He simply told us you've been dealing with orks."

Jason snorted like a wild animal trying to decide how to attack.

"I would like to better understand the situation for my own peace of mind. Surely you can understand that?" Peter continued. "As a fellow leader, especially."

Eyeing Caraticus suspiciously, Jason replied, "Of course. Of course, Mister Blair. Times are tense, but we are happy to hear that there are survivors among our fellow Georgians, are we not?" Once again, his question was directed outward, not at Peter, seeking the approval of those around him.

"But really, the orks have been— *Haaarruuuummmmmmm!* He was interrupted by the blare — a sound long since abandoned by mankind, yet still unmistakable: a war horn.

"Speak of the devil," Jason growled. "Peter, I must go," Jason said suddenly, rising again from his seat.

Peter tilted his head. "Are you under attack?"

Jason scowled. "No. You mentioned you've had troubles. Has your town had orks yet? I expect not."

Peter shook his head as he matched stride with Jason. "No, no orks yet."

"Good, you can thank us for that. We have been holding them back here. Of course, orks were not our first problem, no. It was a week after the Breaking that the orks came. Our first encounter was a giant tree monster." He motioned at the guards standing at the stockades, and they began to remove their occupants.

They're gagged. Peter noted.

"I was able to defeat it. Of course, then the people begged me to lead them. I accepted, not at first, you know, but they were so desperate for my help I didn't have much of a choice." He shrugged dramatically, continuing away from the stage as his retinue followed closely. "You see, the Breaking gave me power — the power to communicate with these new monsters."

"Unfortunately, I do not have time to explain anything to you right now," Jason said as they reached the edge of the square. Here, several muscle cars were lined up, ready to go. Peter glanced at his watch. *Still got time.*

"We only have a few working vehicles, and as I said, I have business to deal with. I'll leave Caraticus and a few of my men to show you around." He waved at two of his armed men and pointed them toward Caracticus, who stood alone as the rest of Jason's crew loaded into vehicles.

"Maybe we can talk tomorrow," Jason added as he clambered into his car, with Marah taking a position in the passenger seat. Not waiting for a reply from Peter, he slammed the door and revved the engine. The vehicle jerked forward carelessly, music pumping from the speakers.

Nose curled in disdain, Peter turned to look at O'Cleary, whose mouth hung slightly agape. "Can you believe that guy?" he whispered as Caraticus approached with two from Jason's entourage.

"I like him," O'Cleary said in a dull tone, shrugging. Peter glanced at him, eyebrows raised in disbelief.

"This way, captain," said Caraticus. "And, yes, he's always like that," he added in a low voice as two armed men took up position behind them.

INTELLIGENCE

S hawn felt nauseous. At least that was the closest word he had for the uncomfortable sensation he'd felt since stepping into the square. The unpleasant sensation was beginning to fade as Jason pulled away and the crowd dissipated. Shawn looked around at his allies, wondering why they were all just standing there.

Except for Peter and Breekie, the rest of his original companions seemed in a daze. Their expressions was not unlike one someone might have after waking up on the beach, sleep interrupted by a passing cloud. Peter was talking to Caraticus a few feet away.

Carrie, Shawn thought, laughing silently to himself. That's what the bald man had called him. It didn't seem to bother the calm man, though. *I wonder if anything bothers him*, Shawn pondered as he took an absent-minded step away from the group. His bored gaze shifted over the dispersing crowd, searching for something to keep his teenage mind entertained.

He saw a man with a funny mustache and a woman with a weird wart above her eyebrows. *They all look dazed too.* A bored-looking guard. A middle-aged couple was staring at him. A man in a sports hoodie. A woman that looked like a children's book illustration of a teacher. *Wait.* He re-traced the path his eyes had taken, looking for the thing that stuck out to him.

The middle-aged couple was without a doubt staring at him. The man was balding, with sinewy arms and a beer gut. The woman was only slightly shorter than him, with a severe resting face and a beak-shaped nose. They were whispering to each other softly while staring right at him. His allies to his right, Shawn glanced over his shoulder behind him. Nothing. It had to be him they were staring at.

"This staring, is rude, nyet?" Breekie asked softly from beside him.

Shawn flinched, trying to hide it. Not wanting the dwarf to know he'd caught him off guard. "They were doing it first," he replied defensively.

Breekie shrugged. "Dah, and now they come." He pointed out as the couple was approaching shiftily.

"You are hurt?" Breekie asked Shawn out of nowhere.

"What?" Shawn replied, barely listening as the couple made their way slowly through the remains of the crowd towards him.

"Your fingers."

Shawn flexed his hand in response, the dull throb in his fingertips wrapped in bandages almost forgotten. "Yeah, knicked 'em pretty bad with a needle last night. O'Cleary was trying to teach me to sew."

"Is good skill," the dwarf replied in his strange accent.

"Yeah…" Shawn said, trailing off. The couple was getting closer, and it was now evident that the woman was leading the man who did not appear at all eager to get closer to their group. Behind him, Shawn could hear Peter, Caraticus, and the guards discussing something about the city's defenses.

The couple came to a stop a few feet away, just out of handshaking range. The man stood nervously behind the woman, clutching anxiously at one of her hands. His eyes darted between Shawn and the guards to their right.

"Are you with Scott?" the woman asked in a hushed tone, her voice scratchy from years of self-inflicted smoke damage.

"Scott?" Shawn replied, not sure what else to say.

"Yes, Oscar Scott. He sent you, didn't he? He must have," the woman went on. The man pulled on her arm, not forcefully but with an obvious desire to be gone.

"Come on, Shelah. He doesn't know Scott or any of the others," he protested.

"Then what're they doing here?" she shot back. "You know what he said. There's no one else left, only burdens. But they look well enough." The woman took a step forward, wincing as she put her weight on her right foot.

"If you're not with Scott, where are you from? Tell me there's somewhere else," she begged.

But before Shawn could reply, a loud voice cut him off.

"Hey! You two! What're you doing? The speech is over," exclaimed one of the guards that'd been left with them. The man shrunk behind Shelah as the guard approached, gesturing with a long spear.

Wincing, the woman turned to the guard, a thirty-something apple-shaped man with dark skin and misfitting armor. "Sorry, sir. We were hoping these fine folks could get us in contact with Commander Jason. We'd love for him to join us at our dinner table."

"You know the commander is far too busy for socializing. He has a city to protect."

"Well, if he's too busy, then perhaps he could spare our nephew for the evening. We haven't seen him in weeks, and I'm sure wherever it is, he has him—"

"That's enough! Speech is over. Return to your quarters. You know the drill," the guard demanded.

After a brief tour of the city, Caraticus ushered them inside a single-story office building. The sign out front read *Mclaughlin, Neal, and Associates.*

A law firm, I guess. Shawn thought as the large wooden door closed behind them. The guards who'd been following them ever since splitting with Commander Jason stayed outside.

Their group was now alone with Caraticus. The local grimaced as Peter whipped around on him. "What is going on?" he demanded in a tone that made it abundantly clear he was serious.

"Jason doesn't want a bunch of armed soldiers wandering around town until he's had a chance to vet them himself," their guide explained calmly.

Shawn caught Breekie brushing his nose with a single finger at Peter. Peter's eyes narrowed almost imperceptibly. "Makes sense," he replied to Caraticus. "What are we supposed to do in the meantime?"

"Wait," Caracticus replied, pursing his lips and blowing air into his cheeks. "You'll be allowed to leave and look around the town if you want, but you'll have to leave your weapons here. That was the best I could do. I'm sorry," he explained, and Shawn believed him. Peter and Breekie seemed to be communicating silently, so Shawn decided he'd try and help by distracting the man in the beanie.

"Who's Oscar Scott?" he burst out, loudly enough to end up drawing the attention of everyone in the room. Shawn bit the inside of his mouth, cursing at himself in his head for being too loud.

Caraticus tilted his head slightly. "Scott was a bit before my time here. I believe he was a rival for command of the town. A soldier, if I'm not mistaken. He and a number of his followers, apparently several hundred well-armed men, left the city before I arrived." He shrugged lazily. "I'm afraid I don't know much about where they went or what happened to them after they left, but according to Jason, it left the city in a rather vulnerable state."

Caracticus glanced out the window. "It's getting late. I really must be going. I have a number of things that need to be taken care of, and I'm sure Jason will send for you before long."

Peter stepped away from the door, letting him go.

Then the state of the rest of their group finally dawned on Shawn. Simon leaned lazily against a wall. O'Cleary reclined in an office chair behind a desk, his face oddly neutral. Strangest of all, Justin and Gunter both leaned against the desk, not bickering in the slightest.

In fact, now that he thought about it, other than himself, Peter, and Breekie, they'd collectively spoken fewer than ten words since Jason's speech ended. Sure, they were in an unknown environment and silence was standard for Simon, but Justin hadn't reminded Peter to contact Jenni. Gunter hadn't complained once. And O'Cleary? The man hadn't so much as tried to crack a joke or even hum a tune. They were quiet. Too quiet.

The more Shawn thought about it, the more nervous he got. This was wrong. All of it. Only Peter and Breekie were behaving normally, and Peter was clearly unhappy. Shawn's heart began to speed up as he worked himself up towards a state of panic.

"In Dwarvish," Peter said to Breekie in a voice Shawn almost couldn't hear.

The dwarf raised his eyebrows then began to speak in an unfamiliar language to Peter. Shawn's brow furrowed as he tried to place the words, wondering what the dwarf was saying. After a moment, he felt a pressure in his ear akin to being in an airplane. He swallowed, and the pressure popped.

Suddenly, he understood the dwarf's words. Still in a different language, yes, but now he took in the meaning of the earthy, guttural words.

"I am not sure how aware he is of his casting. He must have some idea, but it seems like it's canceled out by pain."

"Just pain?" Peter asked.

The dwarf's mouth shifted to the side thoughtfully. "I could… create a rune that would counter it. It's similar to a bushclar, and I have a rune for that."

Shawn didn't know what a bushclar was, and he was too surprised by his sudden understanding to ask.

"It will take much from all of you, and will draw on your own strengths," Breekie explained as he ran a hand through his beard.

"What if we were all injured? Is there a way to give the pain priority and the rune to act as a backup?"

Breekie nodded slowly at first, then picked up speed and ended with a broad grin. "Dah. Could work. But injuries must be hidden. He may know his weakness."

Peter stepped past the dwarf towards the desk and snatched a sharpie from a cup of pens. "Will this do instead of a tattoo?" he asked, drawing on his skin.

The dwarf frowned, his dark mustache hairs dropping back around his mouth. "It will with the pain, but not as good."

"That's fine," Peter said, tossing the marker to Breekie then sitting down on the ground.

"What are you doing?" Shawn asked quietly as Peter removed one of his boots.

"Being cautious," Peter replied as he rolled a sock off and drew his k-bar. Shawn stepped back, not liking where this was going.

Peter flipped the blade around dexterously in his hand and inserted the point between his first and big toes. He hissed in pain, refusing to let himself make any more noise as he made a small cut. The blade came back bloody, and Peter quickly applied a bit of bandage.

Shawn backed away from Peter while the rest of the group watched in uninterested silence.

"Why did you do this, Dashnival?" Breekie asked in his accented English. "Your finger is already injured."

"How is a leader to lead if not by example," Peter replied, then grinned, the expression savage on his face. "Besides, a little extra precaution never hurt anyone."

Half an hour later, and the rest of them were sporting unimpactful but painful wounds and sharpie runes. They'd swept the house for bugs, tended to their injuries, and regathered. The atmosphere of the room had transformed. Gunter, Justin, and O'Cleary were seething. Even Simon looked angry.

Peter finished speaking to Jenni over the radio and turned back to the group.

"So, that bastard has a hypnotic, magical tint to his voice that makes people go all mellow, how do we deal with that?" Gunter growled.

Shawn caught Peter rolling his eyes at the statement and felt a small sense of relief.

"I'll skin the bloody dosser alive, so help me," O'Cleary was muttering.

"Not yet, you won't," Peter said. "We don't know if he's doing it maliciously or not."

"Don't know that I care if he is or not now, do I, cap?" O'Cleary replied defensively.

Gunter chimed in. "Why aren't you as pissed as the rest of us? Seems to me you'd be most angry of all."

"He is," Justin said. "Look at his eyes. They go gray like that when he's about to kill, or someone actually manages to piss him off."

Shawn looked up at Peter. He didn't react to Justin's statement, but he did meet Shawn's eyes. *He's right. The blue is gone. It must be a trick of the light.* But Shawn knew it wasn't. He could feel the cold heat in the man's eyes; festering, controlled rage.

"Now's not the time to get angry and rash," Peter replied, still staring into Shawn's brown eyes. "We're still in hostile territory without enough information. There's a chance this guy, Jason, is what he says he is, a leader put into power by circumstances beyond his control."

"He killed a treant. Peaceful beings. Was probably coming to ask them to stop cutting and burning its flock," Breekie shot back in broken English.

Peter shook his head. "I'm not saying I trust him, and you won't like it, but I might have killed it also if I were in his shoes. To us, a giant tree person is no less frightening than a basilisk."

"What are you suggesting, captain?" Simon asked.

"We gather more information while we wait to hear from him. Talk to who we can. Learn what we can about this Oscar Scott fellow. About their defenses. About how he's dealt with these orks. I assume orks aren't as friendly as treeants." Peter asked the dwarf.

Breekie went to spit in disgust, but upon seeing the carpeted floor, he caught himself. He swallowed his disgust, but the putrid hate was still in his voice as he spoke. "Only friendly ork is dead ork," he growled.

"Good. Justin, O'Cleary, I want you two to go gather that information. Don't draw extra attention to yourselves. Play it close to the chest." Peter ran a hand over his scruffy face. "Take Gunter with you. Good opportunity to show him the ropes."

Justin and O'Cleary both turned to Gunter with equally wicked grins.

"Can I go?" Shawn chimed in, standing up as straight as he could.

"No. You'd draw too much attention. Same for Breekie and me." Peter paused while the party made for the exits.

"Gentlemen, let's not do anything rash while we're out. Best not to wake the neighbors."

25

SURVEILLANCE

Justin bit his tongue as he was searched. *Mustache and Tubby here might as well just give me weapons. Don't antagonize them, though. Remember what William always says — pickin' on someone makes them remember you. It'd be so easy, though*, he thought as he adjusted his retained pistol, boot knife, and taser while the others were searched. *Simple sleight of hand. Mercenary basics. Too easy. Crap, they didn't take anythin' off O'Cleary. He might win. He can hide a weapon like nobody's business.* As for Gunter, they hadn't even bothered trying to get the man to hide a weapon. What would be the point?

Justin took point for the simple reason that he was outside first. He began to roam down the street. "All right, how many?" he asked O'Cleary.

The Irishman smirked and held up four fingers, counting them down one at a time. "Two knives, a pistol, and a taser. You?"

Justin grimaced as he continued to walk. "I only got three. Should have gone for two blades, but I thought it'd be too much."

O'Cleary nodded. "Aye. Figured our lad, Gunter here, would need a weapon," he said, passing a knife to the newbie.

As they walked, Justin's hand went reflexively to his pocket to pull out his phone. An idle thought skirted its way through his brain *I should message Jenni to see how she was holding up*. His fingers clenched around the device, reminding him of the futility of his instinctual reaction to reach for it. There was no point; the device wouldn't have done anything even if Jenni were the type to be idle while working, which she certainly was not. Justin sighed to himself, letting the weight of the old device slip into its familiar place in his pocket.

They made it a mile without stopping or seeing anything of note before Gunter spoke up. "So, where are we going?"

"Uh…" Justin grimaced. "Jenni or William usually run point on these things." *I hope Jenni's okay. It's chilly out here, and she sure hates the cold.*

O'Cleary rubbed his temple and took point. "Yeah, I bet she does. Have you talked to her yet?"

Aw crap. Not in front of the new guy.

But it was too late. Gunter wasn't about to let it slide. A maniacal grin was already slipping across his face. "You got a thing for Jenni?"

"Shut up ROTC. I didn't say that," Justin began.

"Oh, no, of course not. He'll talk your ear off, but bring up that lass, and his lips get tighter than a leprechaun's grip on his pot of gold." O'Cleary's face bore a hint of genuine anger for a moment. "You'd think the apocalypse would be enough to kick him into gear."

"I— that's not—" Justin tried to protest, then spied a middle-aged woman coming out of an office building. She was of average height and build, with snakeskin cowboy boots and the roots of her gray hair dyed reddish-brown showing from going too long without a new dye.

Thank God.

"Excuse me, ma'am," Justin called out, desperate for a way out of the conversation. *I don't need advice. I'll talk to her when I'm good and ready. Not gonna let a stupid apocalypse stop me.*

The woman paused, a cautious, defensive smile revealing her teeth, stained from years of smoking. A worried look manifested in her increasingly panicked eyes as they flew back and forth over the three men.

"Howdy," Justin began. *Howdy? Really?* "We're new here. Can you tell us a little about what's happened here since the Shattering?" He pointed to the sky to emphasize his point.

The awkward smile still plastered to her mouth, the woman muttered back, but the only word Justin could make out was "Breaking."

"I'm sorry?" he replied reflexively as he tried to decipher what she said. *Good grief. She's got a worse accent than my Uncle Tanner.*

She pointed up at the sky. "We call it breaking, not shattering, ya hear now?"

"Okay, why is the town split up like it is?"

"Only got enough for so many. Them's got nuthin' to offer. Can't be getting none of what us's got," she replied, her defensive smile beginning to break.

"Uh, okay. That makes sense, I guess," Justin answered. *Messed up sense.*

"What can you tell us about Oscar Scott?" Gunter interjected.

The woman's defensive smile broke. Her eyes, full of fear, darted past their group. "I don't know nuthin'," she replied through tightening lips. "I got work to do," she said and brushed past them, making her way towards the pair of men who'd been following them since they'd left the others.

"Too scared to talk with our friends watching," O'Cleary grumbled. "Best if we lose the geebags." This time, O'Cleary took the lead, ushering them quickly from building to building, stopping in shadows, dashing through alleyways. Eventually, they found themselves along the edge of where the interior and exterior parts of the city met. Despite having lost their tails, they still stayed close to the shadows.

Justin was about to suggest they start moving back to a more populous area, when O'Cleary spoke.

"Hold," O'Cleary ordered. "Was that the girl from earlier?" he asked, nodding ahead.

"What girl?" Gunter replied.

"That guy Jason's lass. The pretty one. She just went down those steps."

"You mean the one clearly tryin' to avoid bein' seen or followed? Good eye, Brandon. Must be why you're the sniper," Justin jabbed sarcastically.

"Not to be a broken record, but what now?" asked Gunter.

Justin rolled his eyes. *Might as well have sent us with two teenagers.* "We wait. Then see who, or what, she's tryin' to hide."

The short bright-haired woman reemerged twenty minutes later. She stopped at the top of the stairs leading to the cellar area and took a sip of water from a bottle, swishing it around her mouth then spitting on the ground. She then tossed the container to the concrete and slinked off, still clearly trying to keep from drawing attention.

"Once we're in, Gunter, guard the door," O'Cleary said without giving him a chance to respond.

They burst into the room, sending a man tumbling back and into a recliner. O'Cleary recovered from the collision and was behind the man with a knife to his throat before Gunter could get the door closed behind them.

Jeez, he's fast for an older guy. Okay, establish a baseline. "Name?" Justin asked calmly to the man, who, despite being short of breath and a little flush, looked extraordinarily calm.

"John Buchanan," the man spat back. He had the build of someone who used to be a gym rat but was a few years and a few beers past his prime. His voice came out raspy but firm. "You're not feds," he said as his eyes unshrank, his hand no longer inching toward the inside of his recliner. "I'd already be dead if they hired you."

"Not even close. And if you go for whatever's in your chair, I'll put a round through your hand," Justin replied. *Your good hand, if I'm lucky,* he thought sadistically.

"Try it," O'Cleary growled in the man's ear. "I'm dying tah know what's faster, my knife or his finger."

"You're not with Jason either, or you'd be draggin' me off to him," John said as he showed them his open palms, his right hand wrapped in a bandage.

"Probably," Gunter replied. Justin glanced back and saw him crushing the empty bottle he'd apparently picked up off the ground outside.

"Really?" *Worryin' about litterin' right now. What a wuss.*

"What?" Gunter replied defensively. "C'mon, man, you wanna make the tree people madder?" he added in a low voice before starting to latch the plethora of locks on the door they'd just burst through.

Justin blinked. *That's actually a good point.*

"Can we focus, lads?"

"Yes. How can I help you, gentlemen?" John said with a now surprisingly friendly voice. It was then that Justin really took notice of their surroundings. The cellar was really a bunker. Army crates were stacked neatly from wall to wall. Weapons, ammo, boxes on boxes of MREs.

A corkboard was at the back of the room covered in photos of politicians, celebrities, and places such as Stonehenge, Washington, and somewhere that looked like Ireland, all connected by a series of strings that, if you looked at them right, formed three outward turning spirals.

Next to the conspiratorial display was a lit-up, old fashioned radio set-up.

"You're the one sendin' out the SOS, aren't you?" Justin asked as his eyes worked their way over the room, searching for a hidden door that would lead deeper.

"You picked it up? Is that why you're here?" John began excitedly. "They're blocking everything else. They've been planning it for years. It's the only way to get any sort of signal out. I think it's the only one they can't block. You have no idea what's going on, do you? You can let me go. I'm not your enemy," he said. "I've got no bone to pick with SNW."

"Hold up. How'd you know we're with SNW?" Gunter asked from the door.

"Are you kidding? They've got the best shooting range in the state. I go at least once a month. Least I did before the breaking. Did William survive it?"

"Yeah. And his family. You're a vet?"

O'Cleary began to relax his grip, but the knife was still to the man's throat.

"I was a navy man back in the day. What about the igloo? Always liked that place."

That did it for O'Cleary. He returned his blade to its hiding spot and let the man up. "It's a right shame. Igloo's got a big ol' hole in the roof now."

John shook his head. "That's too bad. Can I get you boys anything? Coffee? Something stronger?"

Justin could see the pain in O'Cleary's eyes at the offer and decided to make it easier for him. "Answers will do for now."

John made his way into the kitchen and opened a cabinet slowly, pulling out a sealed glass bottle of coffee and a clear bag of sugar. Justin let out an imperceptible breath of relief.

"Sure, sure," the man said, cracking open the bottle. "Don't mind if I have some, though, do you?" O'Cleary stayed close to him, but Justin lowered his pistol. "Go for it. What can you tell us about what's happenin' here in Macon? Start with what you were doin' with the lady."

John choked on his drink, sending driblets of coffee over his bandaged hand and down his short, scraggly beard. "Marah and I have, uh, an arrangement. She tells me what that idiot Jason's up to, I make sure she has a place to bug out if Oscar and his merry band show back up."

He took another sip of coffee then poured some of the sugar onto the back of his hand. "You don't want to know about him though. He's just some ex-CIA lunatic using his stash of leftover MK Ultra drugs he puts in the food and water to keep the town in check."

What's he…? The man brought the white substance to his nose and snorted it violently. *Oh no.*

"Whew," the man exclaimed before resuming more energetically. "I can tell you about the bigger picture. About the disciples of Awan. What they're doing in Washington. I don't know how they're blocking everything, but they've known an interdimensional fusion was coming for years."

Oh, no. He's nuts, Justin realized.

"That all sounds interestin', but let's start with small bites, aye? Where are all the wains? Why aren't there any children?" O'Cleary asked carefully.

John scowled. "That? That's common knowledge. Jason needs more leverage and is scared of Scott coming back, so he rounded them up and is keeping them at the town hall. The teens, at least. Anyone under twelve isn't allowed outside. It's too dangerous. One thing we agree on." He smirked. "Well, one of two things. Y'all sure you don't want some of this?" he asked, holding up the bag of white powder.

"You sure he won't talk?" Gunter asked as they were making their way back to the others.

"You think anyone'd believe him if he did?" O'Cleary replied, shaking his head. "The man's bleeding haymes."

"Haymes?" Justin replied.

"A complete mess. Bonkers. Off his rocker," O'Cleary replied.

"Our tails are back," Gunter interrupted, his head shifting to look over his shoulder.

"Don't turn your head. When you turn your head, it alters your profile by eighty percent." Justin murmured to Gunter without turning his own head.

"Oh, aye," O'Cleary muttered back sarcastically as they rounded a corner. "It'd help if we were in plain clothes too. How do ya know, Gunter?"

Gunter flicked his head at a window up ahead. "Caught a glimpse of them in the reflection there. They just barely saw us then ducked back, though."

"Good stuff," Justin answered. "Basic alley sandwich?" he asked reflexively as they approached a space between buildings. Together the three of them rounded the corner.

Justin stepped back under a shadow against the wall as O'Cleary continued forward. Gunter tried to stop, but a firm hand from O'Cleary placed on his arm kept him from moving forward.

Oh, Lord, now for the fun part, Justin thought as his heart pounded. Despite the chilly weather, he felt sweat running down the inside of his arm. Grimacing, he rubbed his arm against his ribs, his and O'Cleary's tasers clutched in his hands. *It'd be a lot easier if I could just kill them. Any second now. Come on. Come on, come on.*

His heart skipped as he heard the sound of approaching, hurried footsteps. They turned the corner just short of a jog, moving past Justin without so much as a glance as they tried to catch up.

Yeehaw! Justin found himself thinking as he closed the distance between them in a single step. *They look like regular civilians,* he thought as the tasers connected with them both, sending them into spasms on the ground, soaked in their own urine. *The kind of people I risked dyin' for, for four years.*

O'Cleary stepped out from his secondary ambush position. Gunter looked stunned over his shoulder. *Stunned. Heh. That's good. Oh, I've got it.* "Shocking, isn't it?" Justin cackled to the frazzled Gunter. *No, no. That was bad.* O'Cleary smirked. *Maybe not.*

"That's great, but what do we do with them now?"

A curse slipped out of both O'Cleary and Justin's mouths in unison as their eyes locked in horror.

Justin, you idiot. You've got to think before doin' things! "I…" Justin trailed off. "Well, first off, we don't tell Peter this happened."

"Agreed." The other two said after exchanging looks.

REPORT

Much to Peter's relief, the tired trio returned after two and a half hours, looking only a little worse for wear.

"Well?" he asked as they settled back into the room.

"Bah, we found out these folks call the Shatterin' the Breakin'," O'Cleary said, putting it in air quotes.

"But other than that, we didn't learn jack," Justin said, coughing a bit into his elbow. "No one wants to talk about Oscar, or Scott or whatever his name is. They're all scared of the worthless guards that tagged along. Could've ditched those civvy idiots easy too if we'd wanted. They're no real threat at least," he said, purposefully keeping Gunter out of his field of view.

"Good that you didn't," Peter replied. *He's hiding something. Either they can't tell me now, or they'll let me know later.*

"It wasn't a total waste. We found out why there aren't any kids around," Gunter said calmly.

"Oh, yeah, well, there was that," Justin replied excitedly, smiling at Gunter. "Just nothing about the defenses, or orks either."

"Apparently," Gunter went on, "Jason was worried Oscar would come back for them, so he rounded up every kid from twelve to seventeen and is keeping them in the town hall where he's staying."

"And get this," Justin said, slapping Gunter on the back and stepping naturally into the flow of information. "Anyone younger than twelve is still with their families, but they aren't allowed outside. No matter what. Can you imagine keeping a bunch of toddlers to middle schoolers cooped up inside for days on end?"

"Anything about why some people are being kept in the outer city without power?" Peter replied.

"Something about them being undesirables, a waste o' resources or something. I couldn't really tell what the lady with the yellow teeth was saying. You, Justin?" O'Cleary interjected, scratching at the white spot in his hair.

Justin shook his head.

"Well, now what?" Gunter asked curiously.

"Now," Peter said, a predatorial curve in his lips, "Breekie, tell us everything we need to know about orks."

ORKS

Two days after they heard the trumpet blast that set Breekie off on a ti-rade of Dwarvish curses, Jason sent for them. During their time waiting, they'd learned nothing useful and were never allowed out of the law office without an escort. So, instead, they'd trained with their blades. Now that the time had come, they'd been escorted to the northern end of town, weapons, and armor untouched.

The buildings that surrounded the town center had all been converted into living quarters, which kept the majority of the town at a centralized point. The farther towards the town edge, the fewer civilians they saw, and the more makeshift soldiers they passed. Here, they found the town's actual defenses, a puzzling conglomeration of intentional, well-established fortifications and chaotic amateurish nonsense.

"They clearly had someone capable of running things here at one point," Justin chimed in. "I mean, what is that?" He gestured ahead.

Jason's train of vehicles was parked near a wall reminiscent of a wooden colonial fort. Large, trimmed logs averaging twenty-five feet with pointed ends were shoved into the ground to form the wall that curved around this end of the city. Cargo containers were lined up along the inside of the wall, utilized as ramparts, which bore a scattering of armed men.

Beyond the wall, they could see buildings in various stages of distress. Most had clearly been torn down to increase visibility. One gas station was even par-tially demolished, an unfinished project in a sea of purposeful destruction.

"Cargo containers aren't a bad idea, though," commented Simon as he eye-balled the wall's decorations. Sparsely scattered heads of various gray-skinned creatures that Peter assumed belonged to orks were mounted on poles. Not far above these poles flew a single flag. It was a dark American flag with the Atlanta

Falcons logo where the stars should have been. Peter fought the urge to roll his eyes at the sight.

"They've got half a dozen perfect sniper-nest positions just sitting empty," O'Cleary growled in disgust. "Even if guns aren't working the same, you could at least have more time to see your enemies coming."

At the centermost point of the wall was a large apartment building, the back of which was marred by a hole roughly the size of an SUV. Jason stood waiting in the opening with his hands on his hips and tapping a foot like some disappointed mother. A large, mangled truck hung, swaying slightly, a few feet above him, suspended by a thick chain that led to a wench on the side of the building.

So much for being in a hurry, Peter thought as he followed the guards up to Jason. *It'd be so easy to drop that truck on him and make it look like an accident.* Jason offered his hand out to Peter to shake.

"Good morning, Captain Blair. I apologize that I was not able to see you sooner, but I have been swamped, and I wanted to take care of two things at once," he explained, shaking Peter's hand with a tighter-than-necessary grip.

Before Peter could answer, Jason turned and entered through the hole. Not in need of any extra encouragement, Peter followed. His six men and the two guards stayed close behind. Once inside, Peter found he was pleasantly surprised at what he saw.

The large foyer's original contents had been completely replaced. Diligently placed throughout the room were large, sharpened sticks protruding from concrete-bag barricades. *Someone else oversaw fortifications on this side. I wonder why they didn't take care of the rest.* Aside from the fortifications, he also made note that the room contained four sets of stairs, one in each corner.

The front two stair rooms were sealed off, meaning the two stairways closest to the city and best guarded were the only way to the upper floors of the building. Nervous looking men with guns and shoddy medieval weaponry were scattered throughout the room.

At the front of the room was a large opening that, at one point, would have contained glass doors, but those were long since shattered and cleared. The opening was now blocked by a wooden gate, bound together with chains and rope, which fed into two open-doored elevators on the right side of the room.

Jason led them to where a collection of men, including Caraticus, and a woman stood at the center of the room with three prisoners. Whether they were the same poor folks from the stockades or new ones, Peter could not tell. Their faces were covered, and their limbs were bound. Jason came to a stop by the woman, and Peter recognized her as the same one he'd seen Jason with after the speech.

Peter tried to remember the name he'd heard Caraticus use for her, trying not to scowl at her bright freshly dyed hair.

Bad idea dying your hair bright like that right now. Makes you stick out… Mary? No… Marah.

"Commander." A lanky man with a long beard stepped toward Jason, addressing him after giving Peter and his men only a slight glance. He gave a sloppy salute that Jason dismissed with a wave.

"Grelnog has returned on schedule?" Jason asked, his eyes on the gate, not looking the lanky man in the face.

"Yes, sir. And he stopped at the golden arch just like always. Two orks are waiting just outside the gate, haven't moved since they blew the horn."

Jason nodded. "Did they say anything? Ask about the tributes?"

"Tributes?" Peter asked.

"Did you not listen to my speech the other day?" Jason asked rounding on Peter, exasperated, and openly surprised. "I have an agreement with Grelnog, the ork warchief. One which took a lot of work, mind you. We give him a tribute of men in exchange for his protection from the other ork tribes. They keep the men as… collateral. Servants, really," the tall man explained, obviously proud of himself and oblivious to the mounting fury concealed by Peter.

You're trading the people you're supposed to protect to the enemy!

Breekie made a strange choking noise, and the sound snapped Peter out of his daydream; wherein, he was running Jason through with Galvorn. Peter's nails dug into his palm as he fought the urge to end the man's life here and now. *Calm. Down. Learn as much as you can. Killing him here just puts you into a firefight with orks ready to swarm the survivors.*

Behind them, one of the bound men struggled with his bonds and was met with a harsh rifle blow from one of his captors.

"None of that," Jason said calmly. "These brave men are ensuring your safety. Do not mistreat them." The man who he'd reprimanded gave him a puzzled look but kept his mouth tightly closed.

"It sounds a bit barbaric, doesn't it? But trust me, it is for the best. The tributes aren't innocents, mind you. Each is guilty of one crime or another that normally would get them thrown out of the city." Jason sighed dramatically. "Which would surely get them killed. This way, they at least survive, even if it is as servants."

"Why not fight?" Peter managed to ask without his voice shaking. Slowly, he released his fist, cracking his knuckles one at a time with his other hand to keep both hands busy.

"We tried fighting." Jason shook his head. "But after my commander's first battle, he and most of the rest of our soldiers slipped away in the dead of night. They took most of our weapons too, the cowards. If it wasn't for Grelnog showing up and listening to reason, we'd all be dead," Jason explained, his shoulders slumping.

"Any idea what happened to the deserters?" O'Cleary piped in.

Jason looked a little miffed at this, but he dismissed the expression and directed his reply to Peter. "I can only assume they were killed by Grelnog or one of the other tribes of orks. We haven't heard anything about them in a month. A shame, really. If he'd come back, I'd have forgiven him," he said unconvincingly with a shake of his head and a shrug. A pair of guards behind him exchanged strange, subtle looks.

Jason went on. "What was I to do? Our guns have been useless against them, and my men who remained... Well, they're hardly skilled enough with sword and spear to do anything more than die slower. Maybe with proper training, we could fight them. But we didn't have time. I was forced to negotiate to bring the fighting to an end. I did what no one else could. I worked with Grelnog."

Jason eyed Peter closely while he rubbed his jaw with one hand. Then he reached into his shirt and softly grabbed his necklace, exactly as he had before beginning his speech. "You're a leader, aren't you?" His eyes narrowed. "You know that sometimes one must sacrifice a few to save the many," he said, his hand resting on the chain of his necklace, his legs wobbling ever so slightly.

Not if you're unwilling to make the same sacrifice or they're being sacrificed against their will. It's one thing to give up one's life willingly and another to have it taken.

"I'm familiar with sacrifice, Jason, too familiar." Peter turned to a new man who'd just appeared and was attempting to stand at attention. "How many orks in total?" he asked.

The man looked surprised by the question and glanced at Jason for instructions. Jason's face spasmed, then he raised his eyebrows at the man. "Well? Captain Blair asked you a question, didn't he, Pierson?"

"Yes, sir. Sorry, sir," Pierson said to Jason before addressing Peter. "Twelve, sir. Thirteen counting Grelnog, but I'd count him twice."

"How are they positioned?"

Pierson bit the inside of his cheek. "Well, we've got two right outside the gate. The other ten, though, are hanging out a couple hundred yards back with the big one."

"Thank you, Mister Pierson," Peter replied. "Commander Jason, I'd like to see if my men and I can take care of these orks for you," he said, trying not to choke on the word commander.

Jason looked slowly around the room. Not meeting Peter's face. "Perhaps I undersold the gravity of the situation. I have worked hard to secure our position with these orks, a race of deadly beings that you have no experience with." He scowled up at the ceiling, not meeting Peter's gaze.

Marah took Jason by the arm. "Would you give us a moment, captain?" she said, pulling Jason back.

Pierson and the others stepped forward, forming a small wall between Peter, his men, and the two as they stepped away, whispering.

As they spoke to each other in low tones, Peter motioned for Breekie, who slid over to his side. "Can you do anything about the orks being bulletproof?" he whispered.

"Depends on armor. If old and weak, aye." The word *aye* was pronounced strangely, and Peter realized it was an attempt to say it the same way as O'Cleary. "But nyet all at once. I am weakened by him," he said, as he glanced in Jason's direction.

Peter nodded back and stood as Jason's wall disbanded, and he returned to their group, his gaze on Breekie for just a moment.

"Very well, Peter. I have heard my people's council, and you don't strike me as the type of person to take no for an answer," he told the room. "You all bear witness to this. I have urged this stranger not to risk his life so carelessly, but he believes he and his men can do what we could not."

Puffing his chest a bit, he continued, "You may take your chances, but I cannot allow the boy to go with you. Here in my town, we shield the young the best we can from the horrors of the Breaking."

I wasn't going to send him out there, you fool. Peter grinned. "I assure you Shawn can handle himself well enough, but don't worry, he'll be remaining here. If you'll give my men and me a moment, commander?"

Jason finally met Peter's gaze. His large eyes glowered down at him as he scratched at a mole on his head. Peter stared back unflinchingly, and after a moment of silence, Jason shrugged. "I'm not going to stop you from getting yourself killed. Maybe if they kill you, I can convince them not to take any further tributes today," he added with a mocking smirk.

Then, arm in arm with Marah, he marched off to the side of the room to talk with the men there.

Peter turned to his group and glanced at his watch.

"We need to let J know something," Justin said a bit eagerly.

Peter nodded then began speaking low and firmly. "Justin, get morse to Jenni. Let her know we're about to engage a nonhuman threat and to remain incog until further instruction. Then I want you to set up your SAW just in case, follow O'Cleary's lead." He looked at Gunter and Shawn. "All of you, O'Cleary. Breekie will be disabling their armor. Breekie, how close do you need to be?"

Breekie furrowed his brow. "Depends. Best? Three yous, worst? One me."

"How long do you need?"

Breekie took a moment to shed his coat, exposing his armor and tattooed arms. "Seconds between. No prep time? Is that how you say?" he asked, tapping one of his shoulder tattoos meaningfully. "If armor is old and they have nyet caster, will be simple. Else? Not so simple."

"Good. If they do, O'Cleary will provide enough distraction for us to get in close. Anything he can look for when you disable a ward?"

Breekie pulled on his beard, then smiled. "I could make small blue flash?"

"That'll work. O'Cleary?"

"Aye, small blue flash, then…" He closed one eye and made a finger gun. "Bang."

"Good. Simon and I will cover Breekie with blades. Any questions?"

Shawn raised a hand slowly. Peter sighed softly and smiled. "Yes, Shawn?"

"What can I do?" the boy asked sincerely.

Peter placed a hand on Shawn's shoulder and glanced around slyly to make sure no one was listening in. "Keep an eye on O'Cleary's back. He'll need to give us his full attention, which means he'll be open to other threats. Finger off the trigger, though. Wait for Gunter to fire first. I don't trust these people, but I don't think they'll try anything. You got that, Gunter? You're to watch Justin's back. And you four are collectively watching ours."

Gunter, looking a little paler than usual, set his jaw, and nodded. "I can do that."

"Anyone else?"

They all shook their heads. The plan was clear and straightforward.

"Good. If all goes right, we take most out before they can get close enough to overwhelm us."

Three against thirteen could go sideways real quick if we don't get those guns working. Jadis' training better be good for something.

Peter braced himself and turned to look for Jason. The man was standing only a short distance off, staring daggers at them as Marah spoke to him in a low voice. Peter ignored the blades and marched towards Jason carefully.

"Thank you, commander. My men and I are ready to go. If you'll allow some of them to set up upstairs to provide the rest of us with cover…"

Jason folded his arms, looking confused. "Did you not hear me? Most of these creatures are bulletproof. Would it not be wiser to conserve your ammo for more traditional threats?"

Peter grinned. "We may have a solution to that. I appreciate your advice, Jason, but we can't sit by and watch our fellow Americans suffer without trying things our way. I'm sure a leader like yourself can understand."

"You're sure you won't reconsider?" Jason asked smoothly.

Peter felt the sting of the cut between his toes flair up, as if the words were prodding at it.

"Positive."

Jason frowned, a bead of sweat running down the side of his shaved head. A moment of silence passed, then the man shrugged. "Fine. Pierson, escort his men upstairs."

Pierson set off toward one of the back stairways, and O'Cleary's crew followed close behind. As they went, Jason extended an arm dramatically toward the gate. Taking his meaning, Peter approached it confidently with Simon and Breekie at his sides.

"All right, Breekie. What are we about to see out there? Doctor Walker gave me a brief description, but I expect you've had more recent experience."

Ding, went the elevators, and with a groan and a creak, the gate began to rise slowly.

Breekie hefted his war hammer, spinning it between his hands a bit. "Vile, violent savage beings. Are different sizes. Big ones worst. Might not attack until they think is challenge. They can take much pain. Sharp teeth, claws. They keep coming until you're dead, so no running, no surrendering. They not animals though. Smarter than they look."

Peter shifted his weight and drew Galvorn, the sound of metal on leather heralding the pumping of adrenaline. "You ready, Simon?"

Simon held his basilisk-bone blade, giving it a quick twirl. "Yes, sir."

"Good. Play it safe. We're guarding Breekie until O'Cleary can take his shot after all."

Simon gave him an unamused look. "Really?" he said, his voice laced with irony.

A breeze brought the smell to them before the gate was half up. It was the all-too-familiar smell of dead flesh. Through the opening could be seen a few rotting ork corpses stripped down to no more than a loincloth.

The creatures' leathery skin varied between different shades of dirty green, gray, and brown. What they lacked in beauty they made up for in diversity of physical attributes. While all were humanoid in shape with two arms, two legs, and necks recently robbed of heads, they differed widely in size and shape.

Peter grinned savagely as the gate clanged to a stop. In front of them was a parking lot leading to a three-lane road. At the edge of the parking lot was a slightly elevated roundabout. On it sat two living orks, relaxing as if they hadn't a care in the world. Despite their supine posture, they were brutal creatures, each wearing a strange conglomeration of clothes and armor that seemed to be held together mainly by duct tape.

The taller of the two wore a jersey of some football team Peter did not recognize draped across him like a sash. Whereas human eyes were white, his were yellow. His pupils were slanted like his sharp teeth, and a falchion rested casually on his shoulder.

His companion's outfit included a torn denim jacket with the sleeves torn off that was taped to a breastplate. This one's eyes were an orange hue, and he was of a similar build to Simon. He held a shotgun in his hands, the barrel of which had been crushed into a makeshift club.

Neither of them made any move as the gate came to a stop. They simply stared at Peter and the crew expectantly.

"Giving them a surrender option?" Simon asked doubtfully.

"Breekie, any idea what they're doing with the men Jason hands over?" Peter asked in a low tone.

Breekie's face filled with contempt. "Eating them," he spat out.

"That'd be a no, Simon."

Weapons drawn, the trio marched under the gate and out of the city proper into the parking lot battlefield. As they moved forward, the orks at the edge of the roundabout exchanged a gleeful look then stood and began to approach, the smug grins on their faces made undeniably sinister by the sharp stained teeth which filled their mouths.

Peter didn't bother to wait for Breekie to make his move. He felt the call of his sword. The energy screamed at him, *Strike now!* He obeyed.

Peter leapt forward like a tiger, closing the gap between them in seconds and taking his prey down with one swift blow. The pent-up rage at Jason's barbarism further fueled his ferocity. Galvorn buried itself in the larger ork's chest before his Falchion could come off his shoulder. The ork gurgled gruesomely, and Peter felt a wave of satisfaction mix into his rage as life left the creature's yellow eyes.

One. Turn. Obeying reflex, Peter turned, pulling Galvorn out of the ork's chest as he did and bringing it to meet the shotgun club, which was crashing through the air towards his shoulder. The weapons met with a cry of metal.

Galvorn tore through the makeshift club, sending a piece of it tumbling through the air. The ork's arm continued its swing, hitting only air. This left the ork's body exposed and his arms wide. Peter brought Galvorn up, leaning into the momentum of his first swing. The strike was true, severing the ork's hands, sending them hurtling through the air still clinging to the club.

The ork shrieked, a monstrous ear-piercing sound, and threw itself at Peter. Stubbed arms reached uselessly in front of a tooth-filled maw that would have made a shark blush. But it was too late; Peter was ready.

He sidestepped and rolled out of the way of the attack. The ork landed roughly on his dead comrade's form. Peter didn't waste a breath, and he brought Galvorn down. The blade embedded harshly in the ork's back and pinned both of them to the ground where it severed the creature's spine.

"Criske," Breekie said as he arrived on the scene with Simon. He wasn't looking at Peter, though. His attention was focused down the road. "Here come the rest. You're gonna let us get a piece, dah?

Peter jerked Galvorn out of the two bodies and gave it a cursory glance. Oily black blood slid down the unscathed blade. *That's new.*

"If you can keep up," he goaded. "O'Cleary?" he called back over his shoulder.

"Aye, cap'n?" came O'Cleary's voice from the windows above them.

"Give their armor a test. The one wearing the blue tie like a belt."

The words had barely left his mouth when the thunderous roar of O'Cleary's rifle echoed through the air. *Crack!* Peter saw a flash in front of the ork he'd singled out. The creature stumbled for a few seconds, and Peter thought he was going down. But he caught himself and continued to charge towards them.

"I'll take the roundabout. You two move left toward that truck. Angle them. Try and give O'Cleary a better shot," he instructed. *We need to spread them out at least. I can handle the brunt of it.*

Up on the first floor of the apartment, Shawn and the rest of SNW watched as Peter put his plan into action.

"Looks like he's trying to split 'em, cocky son of a gun," O'Cleary growled the words, interrupting his humming. "All right. Shawn, keep an eye on the ones that get close to the cap'n. Let me know if you see a blue flash and on which one you do."

"Got it," Shawn said, the words catching on his tongue on their way out. He swallowed, trying to combat his dry throat.

Below, Peter took up a position on the roundabout and drew his pistol. He fired several rounds uselessly at the charging orks just to be sure. The bullets glanced off an invisible force and plunged harmlessly to the ground. To Peter's left, Simon and Breekie dashed toward a truck on the road.

As the first of the orks drew close, Breekie lifted an arm, his hand forming a symbol with his thumb and middle finger touching. A blue shimmer flashed in front of the foremost charging ork, and Shawn clapped his hands over his ears.

Crack! O'Cleary fired again. The ork's head exploded. His body tumbled to the ground, tripping the two orks following closest behind, turning them into a flailing pile of armor and rags. It wasn't enough, though.

The seven still charging split, four turning towards Breekie and Simon, and three still making their way towards Peter. Breekie's spell flashed over the first of the three as it entered his range, and O'Cleary dispatched of him with another headshot.

His companions were wise to the threat now. They avoided the falling body of their comrade and continued their assault towards Peter. Two more flashes and two more shots left only two headed for Breekie and Simon.

Simon and Breekie met these two with weapons drawn. Sword clashed against sword and war hammer shattered spear.

Breekie made short work of his opponent, crushing its chest with his mighty weapon. Then, as Simon held the attention of his foe, Breekie brought his hammer down on its back, breaking its spine.

Meanwhile, Peter parried and struck back and forth with his two assailants. While deflecting a blow with Galvorn, he felt an opening. In one smooth motion, he brought his basilisk fang dagger out and across the neck of one of his opponents. The blood that filled the wound left by the knife's path turned purple and bubbly, not black as before, as it ran down the leathery gray skin of the dead beast.

What was that?

The sight distracted Peter for a moment, and his remaining opponent pushed its advantage, swinging wildly with its battleax. Peter felt the blade graze the edge of one of his pockets. *I need to kill with the sword,* he thought, and he sheathed his dagger.

Taking Galvorn in both hands, he blocked an incoming blow. *They're not nearly as fast or strong as Jadis.* Bending with the flow of energy, he found another opening and struck this ork down as well.

That leaves… Peter glanced around the battlefield. *…three.* The two who'd been tripped by O'Cleary's first kill were making their way towards Simon and Breekie with shields raised to head level.

Behind them, the big fellow was on the move, marching forward with a swagger as he nocked an arrow to a startlingly large bow. At the same time, one of the creatures on the ground at Breekie's feet twisted around. A dagger rose in its hand, aimed for Breekie's gut. Peter was on his way, but he knew he was too far.

"Look out!" he screamed. As he cried out, he felt an arrow enter the space around him. The sensation was a strange one. Galvorn rose to block the arrow, guided into position by the flow of energy coursing through Peter's veins. The block succeeded, but the force of the projectile threw Peter off balance, forcing him to catch himself or fall sprawling on the ground. He lost sight of his allies and heard a small explosion followed by an urgent shout from Breekie:

"I'm out!"

Regaining his footing, Peter made a decision and turned his full attention to the ork he assumed was Grelnog, who was sprinting forward, notching a second arrow.

Over by the truck, Breekie planted his feet in the ground. He'd used the last of the magic he could afford to spare without exhausting himself to finish off his knife-wielding assailant. He hoped the meaning of his shout was clear because their newest opponents were upon them shrieking furiously.

Breekie met his foe's sword with a mighty swing that sent it reeling from its owner's hand. Out of the corner of his eye, he saw the other ork, who wore a leather jacket with plaid sleeves duct-taped to the arms, tackle Simon. Together, the pair hurled past his point of view. With a roar of his own, Breekie brought his war hammer, Foecrusher, around his ork's shield and into the beast's shoulder, shattering the bone.

The ork took a swipe with its open-clawed hand, but Breekie broke that too, then crushed his head. Behind him, Breekie heard Simon scuffling with his ork. Turning to help, he found the beast atop Simon, clawing for a knife at its belt.

Simon's sword lay a yard out of reach, and with one hand, he struggled deftly at the ork's claws, trying to stop them from grabbing the knife. With the other hand, he yanked his pistol from its holster at his belt. He whipped the gun out, pointing it directly at the ork's open maw, and pulled the trigger.

Fire flashed from the muzzle as Simon fired round after round, and nothing happened until the seventh shot. With this spark of flame, the back of the ork's head exploded. Only one major threat remained. Breekie turned on his heel and found Peter clashing blades with an eight-foot-tall, fully armored ork with football pads over his chest plate and a black and red football helmet pressed down awkwardly on his head.

Breekie barreled forward, catching the beast from the side. Not giving him a chance to react, he struck. Foecrusher collided with the ork chief's legs with a gruesome *crack*. The force of the blow tore him forward off its feet.

At the same moment, Peter sidestepped and brought Galvorn up in an arc, the sword tearing through Grelnog's neck before he could hit the ground. Oily black blood arced through the air as body, helmet, and head thumped separately to the ground.

Another softer crack of gunfire drew Peter's attention. *Are there more?*

He turned to face the city where the shot came from. Men were pouring out of the apartment building, cheering and clapping. One stood over the body of the first ork O'Cleary had taken down, unloading a shotgun into the creature's corpse. Peter ignored the cheering crowd and looked up to the window where O'Cleary was stationed. A green laser flash signaled to him that all was clear.

Breekie chuckled as he plopped down on the ground by the dead ork. "That went well."

Peter stepped over to where Simon was clambering to his feet and offered him a hand. Simon took him up on it, and Peter hoisted his friend to his feet. "You all right?"

Simon brushed himself off and winced. "A cracked rib or two. Nothing bad." He looked down at his gun. "Looks like we just weren't using enough bullets."

Peter grimaced. "We'll have to let Steven know. He can do some tests, see if volume or caliber make a difference in beating these wards."

Simon nodded. "Hopefully, both," he said as they were joined by the dwarf. "That's a mean looking cut on your leg. Let me have a look."

Breekie waved a hand up at him dismissively. "I am good. Need to catch my breath," he said as he tore a sleeve off his jacket and began to wrap it around the cut.

"Not good enough. That could get infected," Simon fussed at the dwarf as he helped him into a sitting position, not taking no for an answer. "Fascinating," he said in a low tone. "Lucky you're not human. We have an artery in that part of our leg."

Peter stopped listening as Simon explained what an artery was to the dwarf and began questioning him about dwarf anatomy. The gunfire from the crowd ceased.

They were drawing closer. As the adrenaline drained from his body, Peter felt exhaustion setting in. He wavered a bit, and Breekie tossed him a concerned look. "You good?"

"Yes, the fight just took more out of me than I thought."

"The fight wasn't the only thing," Breekie commented in a low somber tone.

"Meaning?" Peter replied, an uneasy feeling creeping over him.

Breekie looked intently at the approaching crowd and spoke quickly as Simon cleaned his cut. He spoke in Dwarvish. "That Jason, he's a strong caster. I don't think he knows how strong or how exactly his magic works, though. I don't think he knows how you're resisting it, either."

Peter's eyes narrowed. "I had a funny feeling when he was talking earlier. A mix of pain and magic at once."

"Dah. He is weak. He doesn't seem to know his own limits. Very dangerous. When he touches his necklace, he's focusing it. If you start liking him, you may need to give yourself another cut, you know, to help resist," he said with a hint of dark humor.

Peter rolled up his sleeve to check the mark Breekie had put on his arm. Sweat and blood had smudged it. Breekie followed his gaze, and his eyes went wide. "Criske! Is ruined. You may need that extra cut sooner."

Peter scowled. "You can't do it again?"

"Nyet. I need rest," Breekie said painfully as Simon tightened his bandage. "Will the pain be enough?"

Breekie nodded solemnly. "With your ability, I think so. Can't speak for the others."

Back to the approaching crowd, Peter brought his forearm to his mouth, and bit into it hard enough to draw blood. He spat the blood nonchalantly and took a bandage offered by Simon. "When can you get me a new rune?"

"I do not know. Food and rest will help me do it sooner, though," Breekie said, eyeing Peter bemusedly.

"Good. Play along for now. We have the advantage of information here," Peter instructed the pair.

"Well! I seem to have underestimated you, haven't I?" Jason's voice called to them as he approached from the back of the crowd. Caraticus and Pierson were close behind him. Marah, though, was nowhere to be seen.

Jason walked over to Grelnog's head and picked it up with both hands, staining them with dark blood. Behind him, Peter spotted Marah moving through the crowd. She stopped and knelt next to one of the orks Peter had slain, but Peter's view of her was quickly obscured by the masses.

Mirroring Marah's action closer, Peter and Caraticus also bent down to the ground. Peter let Caraticus take hold of Grelnog's bow from where it had been tossed to the side, looking it over critically.

"Fan-freaking-tastic," Peter murmured with a sly smile.

Jason turned to Pierson, extending Grelnog's head to him. "Mount this on the wall with the others." Then he addressed the small crowd, which was busying itself with the corpses of the other orks. "Leave Grelnog's clothes as they are and hang his corpse between the windows at our front gate as a warning to others about what happens when you mess with the humans of Macon."

A soft cry of support came up from the crowd in response.

"Divide their weapons as you see fit among the guard. Double-watch tonight. I'm sure some may come looking for what happened to these here, though without Grelnog to lead them, I doubt they will try anything." Jason stepped over to Peter and put an arm tightly around his shoulder.

"Tonight, a feast! To celebrate our new friends," he called to the crowd.

This was met with boisterous applause as Peter felt the cold grip on his shoulder tighten.

28

ꝒEGOTIATIOꝒ

eter sat at the head of the table, watched the crowd, and didn't touch his food. Two lines moved slowly along the tables that hosted the so-called feast. A few chairs away from Peter, Shawn began to dig in but was stopped by O'Cleary's steady hand as it gripped his bicep, keeping a forkful of dripping spaghetti out of his mouth.

Shawn looked up in confusion and saw that none of his friends were eating. "Don't be rude. We don't know if they'll want to say something before we start." Shawn put his fork down reluctantly.

The room was permeated with the sounds of what Peter could only assume was Jason's own personal playlist. A mixture of rap and pop blared through the speakers on an old CD system. It was louder than necessary, forcing everyone to speak in a loud voice or close whisper.

Over at the head table, Jason and company had already dug into their plates. They devoured their meal greedily, but still, Peter waited. *Caraticus isn't here,* he observed. That did not sit well with him. As capable as he expected Caraticus was, his absence was suspicious.

It wasn't until he saw members of the crowd start stuffing themselves that Peter took a bite himself and nodded to the group to do likewise. The rest of them followed suit, and eagerly consumed the warm bowls of pasta and meat sauce. The meat was like venison, but less succulent. He wouldn't have noticed the difference if he hadn't had venison just the other day. *I wonder what it is, or if I even want to know.*

As the meal went on, men and women from the town took breaks to come over and express their gratitude or ask questions about the state of things. Peter's foot throbbed with each passing moment where he'd sliced it. Looking down at his food, he was reminded of the orks. *He was feeding people to those monsters.*

The thought set his blood boiling and brought out the pain in the cut in between his toes. He isolated the pain in his mind and stored the cuts, bruises, and bites from the last few weeks away. After years of battling his own body for full control, his mind was his stronghold. He tucked the pain away, into a deep corner of his mind where he'd learned to store such things so they would not hinder him. It was within reach should he need it, but for now, it was a distraction best left alone.

His thoughts returned to Jason. Anyone who could tamper with the minds of others was a threat to be eliminated. He reached a decision. Jason's awareness of what he was doing was irrelevant. He was a threat to every living person. A threat to free will.

Peter focused on the crowd as he took another bite of spaghetti. At his side, O'Cleary was talking between mouthfuls of food to an old man in a tattered blazer. Peter waited for a lull in their conversation before he injected himself. "We're simply overjoyed to hear that another town has survived the Breaking. We were beginning to wonder if it was only us and strags left," the old man was saying.

"Excuse me, where's Caraticus? I expected to see him here," Peter said.

"Caraticus? Oh, you mean the Gatherer. That's what most folks call him. Of course, not the commander's crew. They call him Carrie."

"The Gatherer?"

"Yup. He doesn't eat with the rest of us. Prefers to hang out with the strags." The old man shrugged. "Don't know why they haven't got power out there."

"You've lost me."

"Ah, well, you see, uh, strags is what we call the stragglers that live outside the Sanctum," he explained, gesturing to their surroundings. "You know, the inner wall area. Did no one explain this to you?"

"I'm afraid not," Peter replied, taking a swig of water.

"Oh, well, basically, people are only allowed entrance to the Sanctum if they can provide something that would benefit it. It can be anything really — information, supplies, or decent labor. As long as the commander approves." The old man scratched his head.

"Of course, we don't just turn people away. That'd be cruel. But we can't afford to let everyone in, you see, so they get to stay in the outer areas," he explained defensively, air puffing his cheeks as he paused to consider something. "The Gatherer brought you a lot in, didn't he? He didn't explain this?"

"No, why would he have?"

"Well, cause he's the Gatherer. He, uh… How to put it…? Vets? Yeah, he vets people who show up, makes sure they're not a threat and have something to offer before presenting them to the commander." The old man pulled at his collar nervously, glancing at Jason's table. "Wouldn't want to waste the commander's time, right? Ha-ha." He chuckled nervously.

"That's why you call him the Gatherer?"

"Part of it. That and everyone knows if you need something, you go to the Gatherer. He's got this way of finding things."

"I see. Thank you," Peter said and returned to his meal. After another moment, the old man politely excused himself and set off back to his table. He moved quickly and purposefully kept his eyes away from Jason's table.

"Hey, cap," whispered Justin.

"What's up?"

"I was just talking to that pretty brunette. Looks a bit like Jenni, don't she?" he said, jerking his head in the direction of a young Easternly woman who was also returning to her seat. "Anyway, you won't believe this, but I found out what those fellas in the stockades are there for."

"I believe it," Peter replied, smiling.

"I meant you won't—" He paused. "Okay, smart Alec, you got me. Anyway, it turns out two were caught staying out past curfew. Listen to this though. The third was found with rations he kept for himself rather than handing over to the commander's men. Worst of all, it was just a sleeve of Pop-Tarts." Justin cracked a grin. "Can you imagine getting put in a stockade just for not sharing two Pop-Tarts?"

Peter didn't smile back. *He doesn't realize they're being sacrificed to orks. Idiot must not have been paying attention to that conversation. Tell him later.*

"I mean, it's ridiculous, is all," Justin added, his grin souring defensively into a scowl as he watched Peter's expression. "Turns out this dinner is some kind of initiation too. Apparently, they usually avoid talking to newcomers until they've been approved."

Justin shrugged. "Guess we've been approved."

Before Peter could reply, he saw Jason approaching, Marah at his side. The two came to a stop in front of them, looming over Peter and the rest of the table. The few men and women who'd still been talking to the others at the table scurried off at a glance from Jason.

"So, I think it would be wise of you to explain how your men were able to shoot the orks, don't you? It had something to do with him," he said, gesturing to Breekie. "You know people are starting to talk about him, don't you?"

Breekie smiled a wide, disarming grin. Up to this point, he'd been keeping silent around the folks from the town. He'd elected to simply nod and smile whenever he was singled out to be thanked for their aid.

Jason eyed him suspiciously. "I know he can talk. I heard him yell during your fight. What are you, little man? Do you have some strange powers I should know about?"

"I'm telling you; he's not human, darling. Just look at him," Marah said in a hushed voice.

Peter frowned, not eager to reveal Breekie's true identity. To make matters worse, there was no good way to explain his strange accent. Not to mention that addressing his abilities might tip their hand.

Breekie met eyes with Peter and shrugged then addressed Jason. Before he could stop him, the dwarf spoke up. "Is true. I am not human. I am dwarf."

Marah scowled. "Don't mock me. Midgets are still human. You're not a midget."

Breekie chuckled, a soft earthy sound. "Nyet, I am not small human. I am dwarf. We are a different species. Shorter yes, but compact is good. Not all spindly and long and floppy." He chuckled then added with an outstretched hand, "Name is Breekie."

Jason's gaze remained suspicious, but he shook Breekie's hand and let go of it quickly. Marah made no effort to do the same when Breekie offered it to her. Instead, she merely glowered at him. A condescendingly amused smile crept onto Jason's face. "What's with the accent?"

Peter resisted the urge to facepalm, choosing instead to insert himself into the discussion before it was too late. "It's a long story. You'll get used to it," he piped in dismissively.

Breekie shrugged and reached into his pocket, startling Marah, who took a dramatic step backward.

From his pocket, Breekie removed a white discus-shaped stone no bigger than an egg. It had a black G-shape rune carved into the surface with the curls turning in at both ends.

"This I used on orks. Is magic stone. Stops bullets hitting me, and make bullets hit enemy when I point it at them."

Jason's eyebrow climbed up his forehead. "Do… Do all of you have these magic rocks?" he asked.

Peter thought for a moment. *If he thinks we do, he might be less inclined to attack us, but he'd also probably try to take them. Then we'd be trapped if we're playing along with his ability. If Breekie had told me he was going to pull something like this, we could have made more and given them to him and his men to trick them into thinking they're bulletproof.* Frustrated, Peter shook his head. "No, I wish. Unfortunately, just Breekie."

Jason frowned, eyes not waving from the rock. "Can you make more?"

Breekie grinned as usual, but Peter could see the hatred he was keeping tucked in the corners of his eyes. "No, it was gift from father long time ago."

Idiot! Honest idiot. He should have said yes. We could have trick them into false confidence.

"So, there are more of you," Marah murmured.

"Hopefully," replied Breekie, his smile finally breaking.

Justin stood abruptly and interrupted the conversation. "We allowed to get seconds?" he said, looking Jason in the eye.

Jason's brow furrowed, and he glanced around the room, pausing on one of his retinues refilling their plates with pasta. "Apparently," the bald man said dismissively.

"Cool. Anyone else?" Justin asked the table.

Breekie lifted his clean plate eagerly as he made to stand.

"Nah, bro, I got you," said Justin, taking the plate from Breekie.

Marah put a hand on Jason's shoulder. "You should eat more too, darling. I'll get it for you," she said softly, gesturing Jason towards his table. Jason's brow did an impression of a field before planting at this, but he slowly returned to his table. Peter watched Justin and Marah as they made their way through the gathering crowd moving in for seconds over to where the food was served.

They must not get seconds often. Then again, who does these days?

Marah seemed suddenly friendlier now, putting her hand on Justin's upper arm to draw his attention to fresh plates. He turned to face her, and they chatted for a moment. Both were smiling and after a moment laughed lightly as Justin cracked a joke. *Probably something that'd make me roll my eyes,* he thought dryly.

He redirected his attention to Jason's entourage. Carefully, he evaluated the threat level of each of the men and women gathered around him at his table eating eagerly.

Justin returned to the table, a mischievous grin on his face as he absently handed a plate of spaghetti to Breekie with his left hand. Breekie eyed the blue plate thoughtfully and looked back at Justin. "This was your plate?"

Justin shrugged and laughed lightly. "Doesn't matter, does it? They were both cleaned off before I grabbed seconds."

Breekie grinned back and nodded. "Dah, good. Steven does not share plates," he said, taking on a mock somber expression.

Justin's grin grew even more extensive. "Doesn't let his food touch either. I say it all goes to the same place, so why care?" He chortled.

Breekie stroked his beard thoughtfully, his thick accent ever-present. "This is good saying. I will remember it," he said before he eagerly shoveled another forkful of spaghetti into his mouth. He chewed vigorously and washed it down with a drought of soda. The soda caused him to shake his head side to side in the way only carbonation can as his nose wrinkled dramatically.

Peter glanced over at Breekie, who reached over to O'Cleary, pulling his right sleeve up just a bit, enough to show where Breekie had redrawn the rune in sharpie. *Good, he recovers quickly,* Peter thought as Breekie touched the rune, giving it the charge it needed to be effective in canceling out Jason's ability.

That leaves Justin, Shawn, and Gunter, then Simon and I, if he has the energy.

Breekie wasted no time in helping himself to another forkful, then said with his mouth full, "This is gud. Spaghetti? What is Spaghetti?" he whispered to O'Cleary next to him.

"Pasta," growled O'Cleary, his eyes drilling holes in the heads of Jason and the crew sitting around him at his table. "You sure this thing is gonna work?" he said, referencing the mark made on the back of his hand.

Breekie nodded eagerly, still gulping down pasta. "Dah, Dah. Is simple rune. How you say, child play? The cold when working is my trick," he added with a wink.

O'Cleary scratched absentmindedly at the white spot of hair on his head and took a small bite of food. "If I feel it get cold, I'm gonna stab him," he murmured under his breath.

Breekie glanced about eagerly, empty plate in hand. "What is pasta?" he asked. Shawn perked up at this. He seemed to enjoy explaining everyday things that the dwarf found fascinating. "Pasta's used for mac and cheese, lasagna, spaghetti. It's noodles. They're made of wheat, I think."

"Wheat and flour. Sometimes eggs," Gunter added casually.

"You must teach me how to make," Breekie said enthusiastically to Shawn.

"Uh, I don't know how. We just buy it at the store in a box and boil it," he explained apologetically.

"I can teach you," Gunter volunteered. "I minored in culinary arts in college."

Breekie's broad grin stretched across his face, and he raised a fist meaningfully toward Gunter. Gunter looked at it for a moment, then laughing, tapped it with his own fist.

Justin gave off an amused snort as well. "You're catchin' on there, Breek." Then, he turned to Gunter and mocked, "Planning on joining the Navy after you got done learning how to cook then?" he teased.

Gunter leered at him for a moment, then smiled weakly. "Army, but my Dad had other ideas."

Something's not right, Peter thought, pulling his focus away from the banter. There was no warning energy telling him to dodge or draw his sword. This was an older sensation. A warrior's sensation. An almost imperceptible shift in the room's atmosphere.

If asked, he wouldn't be able to pinpoint what set off the sense of dread in his stomach, but it was there, undeniably. And he wasn't the only one who felt it, he saw both O'Cleary and Simon shifting too. The muscles in their faces tensed, just a bit. But that was all it took for men like them.

Jason stood from his table. At his side, the peacock-looking man, Lil' Pape, began to rise, but Jason put his hand on the man's shoulder, holding him in place. The talk and laughter pervading the room died out slowly like a town without food starving to death. Two men who'd been making their way towards SNW's table stopped and returned to their own tables with disappointed looks on their faces. Once the room was silent and focused on him, Jason spoke.

His words were honey to all without the proper protections, Peter could feel it. "You all know how hard times have been. I don't need to tell you again how I lost my wife, or how the disappearance of Oscar Scott with half our able-bodied men and arms put us in a… difficult… situation where I was forced to negotiate with monsters for our survival." He shook his head dramatically side to side.

Jason held up a hand for quiet, despite there being no one to quiet. "I only remind you of these things so that we do not forget what we have gone through as we celebrate our new freedom." He paused, resting his palms on the table in front of him.

"If I had not requested Captain Blair's assistance in dealing with the orks, we would have lost three men who can now live out their punishments among their own kind."

Liar.

He directed his attention towards SNW's table. "Peter and his men defeated a foe which held us captive within our own walls. They have earned their right to bear arms, but in doing so, he and his men have trapped us here," his voice took on a new tone, darker than before, as he continued, "Grelnog's forces will come again. Should the brave members of Snow abandon us as warriors have before, we may all perish."

He stepped away from the table; sauntering towards SNW, as though taking his time. Peter felt his men shift; ready to fight. The movement was imperceptible to the average onlooker but second nature to trained eyes.

"So, I ask you, as one leader to another, Captain Blair, will you not stay with us and defend us? Teach us how to fight! Join me in protecting these people!"

Peter was silent. *Jason's hand hasn't touched his chain since he started talking.*

"Well, captain?" Jason said impatiently. "Will you abandon us to death like our government? Like the traitor, Scott? Or will you stay and fight for me?"

There it is. He doesn't think he needs to. Peter stood, straightening his sleeves as he did so.

"Jason," he said, then looked out at the rest of the town's people gathered at tables. It was only a fraction of the town's populace, but it was enough to witness and back up whatever those in charge wanted them to say about what happened here. "Ladies and gentlemen," Peter added, "my men and I are on a critical mission. One which cannot be further delayed, for all our sakes."

Back turned to the rest of the crowd, Jason smirked. The expression gave him a weasel-like appearance. Peter hated him for it. He wanted to run him through — right there, right now — to use his blood to enter that dream world where he grew stronger. Taking a breath through his nose, he continued.

"However, we will not leave our fellow Americans to the wolves, or in this case, the orks. I offer you two options. You may each choose among yourselves whichever you prefer, including you, Jason," he said, meeting the man's eyes, which began to blaze with rage. *You don't like that, do you? Me giving them power like that. Good.*

"First, you may remain here, and I will send word back to Paragon that you need protection. Hopefully, reinforcements will be sent to help protect you from any retaliation from Grelnog's forces. This should be more than enough until we return from our mission." Peter stroked the short beard making its home on his face.

"The second option, which I think would be wiser, is for me to assign one of my men to take you all back to Paragon. You will have to bring supplies, and it will be a dangerous journey." He raised a finger. "But our city is better fortified, concealed, and armed."

He paused for a second, keeping all eyes on him. "I know they would not turn away those seeking refuge," he said, glancing at Jason. The man's jaw worked furiously. Behind Jason, the men and women of the town were already whispering softly to one another.

Jason turned, a simmering pot of water threatening to boil over. "Turn off the music!" he demanded, sending one of his table's occupants running over to shut the music off.

"Out," Jason snapped at the townsfolk as soon as the music died. There was a collective flinch from their tables, but no one made a move. Jason stomped a foot and brought his hand to his face, sliding it down his chin towards his neck.

Peter grabbed his forearm with his left hand, and put pressure on the bite. He glanced over to Breekie. The dwarf was already dropping Justin's hands and motioning for Shawn to take his now empty hands. Shawn complied, as Jason's hand reached the chain. Peter made a fist with his free hand behind his back for all of them to see. The signal to play along.

Jason took a deep breath and spoke loud enough or all to hear, the rage boiling in his voice. "I said, get out! It's curfew!"

Peter felt nothing. Just the pain in his arm. There was no urge to stand and leave for him. But one by one, the townsfolk stood silently. Then they made for the door. Even Jason's underlings began to rise and move. "Not you," he snapped at them, and they seemed to snap out of their trances.

Some carried on until they reached the doors, closing them behind the others. One particularly large man remained in front of the door and drew a gun from his waistband. The others spread around the room until Peter and his men were surrounded by men brandishing weapons of all kinds. Finally, Jason turned shakily around to face them, hand still resting on its chain.

"Hand over your guns. And the stone," he added, looking at Breekie.

This time Peter felt it. The honeywords dripped into his mind, urging him to obey. For a split second, he was glad he hadn't been sure if they should have risen to exit as well.

He thought about his weapons. It was a good idea. After all, they didn't need their guns here. Peter squeezed his wound. The pain spread like fire up his arm into his brain, burning away the oozing honey, which compelled him to obey. Jason stared down at him expectantly. *Good. He doesn't know.*

"Sure," Peter said, nodding slowly. "Sure, we'll give you our guns."

The man practically glowed with self-satisfied triumph, and it took Peter every ounce of patience he had not to remove Jason's head from his body.

O'Cleary made a face Peter recognized as the one he made when biting down on his tongue to stop himself saying anything in the moment. Breekie was the first to go, offering up the smooth white stone he'd shown them earlier. Jason snatched it out of his hand like a child worried the treat his older brother was offering would be yanked out of reach.

He scrutinized it as his men strode forward and received the weapons handed over none too eagerly by Peter's men. Peter went first, handing over his rifle, then unholstering his pistol and giving it up as well. He made no move to hand over his knife, sword, or second pistol he kept concealed at the small of his back, and the guards didn't press their luck by trying to search him.

Simon, O'Cleary, and Justin followed his example, handing over only their visible weapons, making no effort to reveal or divulge their backups, which they always carried. During the exchange, Jason turned the stone over and over in his hands only a few inches from his face before finally shoving it deep into his pocket.

"Now, to business," Jason said haughtily. "You've caused quite a bit of trouble for me, Peter." Peter's name was uttered with such venom that it reminded him of Gunter during their first encounter.

"From what I can tell, I saved you quite a bit of trouble."

"Of course, you'd think that, you arrogant neanderthal," he shouted as he leaned down and grabbed a cup off the table, turning and hurling it as hard as he could at one of the pale pink concrete walls of the room. It struck the wall hard, shattering violently into a thousand pieces.

When Jason resumed speaking, his voice was erratic but soft, almost babbling to himself. "You have no idea what it took for me to get Grelnog under my control. It was *perfect*. *Perfect*. Wasn't it?" he asked one of the goons at his side.

"Yes, s-sir, commander," the burly man said.

"First Oscar with his ideas, then you, you. You! You and your damn dwarf. Why do you army jugheads always mess things up? Can't you see I have it under control? I did this. I saved this town. Me. Not you. Not any of you."

Despite the man's raging, Peter's other senses gave him no warning to strike or retreat. He could feel that he wasn't personally in any danger, yet.

The fit came to a stop, and Jason repeated the now familiar motion of touching his face then grasping his chain. Marah stood and slid to his side; whispering softly in his ear. Her hand on his shoulder as if to calm him.

"You're right," he conceded. "I can't kill them. Not yet, at least." He turned back to them as if they hadn't heard him, hand on the chain. "You will take the night to consider staying here and swearing yourselves to my service. In the morning, you will report to the fountain where you will announce to the town that you have changed your mind and will openly swear to follow my orders." He turned toward the door.

"Jermaine, take them to the Pound. You too, Michael C," he said to a sinewy, thick-bearded man. Then, leaning on Marah for support, he left the room, followed by a handful of his remaining crew.

"Well? Y'all heard him. Let's git," said Michael in a shrill voice.

O'Cleary looked at Peter and mouthed, "Now?"

Peter shook his head ever so slightly, just enough for O'Cleary.

"We'll be havin, that there sword and big ol' hammer too," instructed Jermaine. Peter and Breekie complied reluctantly, then, together, they all stood in silence — all except Justin, who placed a hand on his stomach and moaned softly. "Overate," he explained with a weak grin.

Breekie patted him lightly on the back, and he flinched. After a moment, he stood painfully, then together they all followed Michael C out the door, Jermaine brought up the rear, his gun pointed menacingly into their backs.

As they made their way through the town, Peter made careful note of the roads and turns, making sure he'd be able to find his way back to the center of town easily. It didn't take long before they arrived at the Pound, a large concrete building with fading blue paint on the walls. Once inside, they were taken through the reception area to the back rooms.

They came to a stop in a long wide room full of kennels. The kennels were made of chain-link fence that rose to the ceiling, small enough for two people to stand or sit comfortably, as unlikely as that was with the concrete floors. They were ushered into them so that no two groups were directly next to or across from each other.

O'Cleary and Shawn went first on the left, followed by Gunter and Breekie on the right, Peter alone in a kennel on the left, and finally Simon and Justin on the right. As their escort made to leave the room, Shawn spoke up.

"Excuse me. Where are all the animals?" he asked, glancing around at the empty cages. The room still smelled of dogs and cats, but there were none to be seen.

Pausing at the doorway, their escorts, Michael and Jermaine, exchanged a look.

"You gonna tell him?" asked Michael lazily, swinging Galvorn.

"Nah, man, that's messed up. What the kid don't know can't hurt him, right?" Jermaine replied.

Michael glanced over, failing to be nonchalant about it. "I mean, not like he can't hear us."

"Maaan, the kid's already having a rough time. We're locking him in a dog cage with the others — you really think he wants to hear that?" said Jermaine. "Come on," he added, rubbing his arms. "It's cold in here," he said, pulling Michael through the doorway with him and slamming it shut behind.

Gunter turned in his kennel to face Peter through the links, a glazed expression on his face. "Well, I guess we're staying here then."

"Criske," mumbled Breekie, whose head barely showed over where the wall of his kennel became chained fence. "That's my bad," he said as he took Gunter by the hand. Then, to the surprise of everyone else, he brought the man's fingers to his mouth and bit down hard.

The glazed look on Gunter's face melted away into wide-eyed horror. He swore violently and yanked his hand back from the dwarf.

"Shut it!" O'Cleary hissed aggressively at the man before he could get any louder. Peter held a finger up to his mouth to make sure Gunter got the point. Breekie took a menacing step forward, and Gunter clamped his mouth shut rather than spew forth more expletives.

Gunter glowered at Breekie. "The hell was that for?" he asked Breekie as the dwarf shuffled through his pockets for something to use as a bandage for the bleeding fingers. He found a scrap of cloth and motioned for Gunter to give him his arm, which Gunter did hesitantly.

Breekie tied off the bandage sheepishly. "I forgot to get you, and am still recovering."

Gunter's face grew pale. "You mean, he—"

"Yes," Peter interrupted. Then after looking around for a camera, when he did not find one, he looked to O'Cleary, who caught his meaning and gave the room a cursory search of his own then shook his head.

"Good. Speak softly and carefully. They may be listening." He looked to Gunter. "Got any lingering urges to do what he said?"

Gunter sneered. "The only lingering urge I've got is to break that jerk's nose."

"Next time, focus on the pain in the bite. You'll feel the effect of his voice, but the pain will cancel it out." Peter turned to Simon, who was trying to get a look at Gunter's bandage from several cages away. Besides Simon, Justin leaned against the side of the kennel, trembling and sweating profusely.

"Simon, signal Jenni. Tell her we're locked up, easy escape, instructions to follow. Justin, you okay?" Peter said.

Justin groaned loudly. "Yeah, just need to sit-sit down," he stammered and plopped down on the ground. His hands wrapped around his stomach.

"You sure?" Simon asked seriously as he sent the message in morse over the radio he'd kept hidden from Jason's men.

"Yup," said Justin through gritted teeth. "Like I said, ate too fast. Nothin' but rations lately. Stomach is just bein' a brat." He waved a hand dismissively. "I'm allergic to cats too, and there's probably been cats here. Don't mind me. Go on."

Simon turned slowly back to face the rest of them.

"If you've got ideas, now's the time," Peter said.

O'Cleary sighed and said slowly, as though the words hurt to say, "We could just leave."

Peter arched his eyebrows, and O'Cleary frowned. "We could. Not saying we should." His hands moved dramatically as he continued. "We could come back, just like Operation Dust."

"Or, we do a Monte Cristo, tonight," Peter countered.

"Or we could just leave altogether and not come back," said Gunter, giving his arm a bit of a shake.

Peter ignored him and looked to Simon, whose focus was on Justin, not the conversation.

"Simon. What do you think? A Monte Cristo or Operation Dust?" *They could be listening.* He added sarcastically loud enough to be overheard, "Yeah, Commander Jason had some good points. We did kind of mess things up for him."

Simon sighed, shaking his head softly and not looking up. "Neither is ideal." His right pointer finger massaged his temple. "I don't like leaving these people like this, but Dust might be safer. Justin, hold out your right arm for me?"

Breekie cleared his throat and raised a hand like Shawn tended to do.

Peter let himself smile a bit and shook his head. "Okay, look, you guys don't have to raise your hands. Breekie, you don't know any better, and Shawn, I know you're trying to be polite, but this isn't a classroom."

Gunter rolled his eyes and leaned against the fence, pulling a pack of cigarettes from his pocket only to find it empty. In a huff, he tossed it to the ground and sat on the cold concrete with his back to the fencing. Shawn nodded enthusiastically, holding his hands apologetically behind his back despite not having done anything wrong.

"Wasn't sure you could see me," Breekie said with a twinkle in his voice. "What is Monte Cristo?" he asked, bringing his hand down to his side.

The only thing necessary for the triumph of evil is for good men to do nothing. Peter repeated the quote to himself silently.

"I'll explain after we decide," Peter said. "I don't like the idea of leaving Jason in charge. If he can get into people's heads and influence them, he's a threat to everyone. As far as I'm concerned, that's reason enough. He needs to be eliminated, unless I hear an argument better than it being safer, we're going with a Monte—"

"Justin—" Simon said in a low, urgent voice.

Thump! Justin's body slumped over, his head striking the concrete floor lazily. Simon rushed to his side. "Captain, get over here," he ordered, leaning Justin up. His skin was cold and clammy despite sweating violently. Justin's head lolled as Simon steadied him, peeling open an eye to check his pupils.

"Hurry," Simon shot out in Peter's direction as Peter made short work of the lock on his fence and pushed open the gate.

Gunter slid off the chain-link fence, trying to get a look at what was happening.

"What's going on?" asked Breekie as Peter tore open the door to a kennel that contained Simon and Justin.

"Turn him over," Simon said, slipping a pair of rubber gloves out of his satchel.

No, no, no, no, no. Not like this.

"Simon?" Peter inquired through the lump in his throat.

"Poison. Hold on," Simon shot back as he pried Justin's mouth open. Justin moaned loudly, his tongue a strange gray hue. "Good. Hold him there," Simon instructed as Peter grasped the redheaded man by shoulder and thigh.

"Something's wrong with Justin," Gunter whispered softly to Breekie who could not see out of his cage. "Peter broke into their cage."

"Hold him still," Simon said as he held Justin's mouth open with one hand then inserted two fingers into the man's mouth.

Justin's eyes shot open as he gagged. "Don't fight it," Simon said firmly. "You've got to empty your stomach." A second later, Justin's dinner was on the concrete floor.

"All right, Peter, I need you to—" before Simon could finish, Justin began to spasm violently, gray foam spilling out of his mouth. In their kennel, O'Cleary grabbed Shawn by the shoulder and dragged him to their gate door, redirecting his attention to the lock.

"Here." O'Cleary put an arm around his shoulder, drawing Shawn closer to the lock, speaking in a thicker accent than usual. "Don't worry about him, lad. Watch me. You need to learn how to do this yerself," he said, pulling a wire out of his sleeve and taking it to the lock.

"Oi! Lad, pay attention," O'Cleary said, slapping Shawn on the shoulder. "Don't you mind dem. He'll be fine."

Shawn nodded shakily, his face going pale.

O'Cleary glowered at him. "You feel all right, don't-cha?"

Shawn's eyes went wide. "Yeah."

From within his kennel, Justin moaned loudly. "Breath, man," Simon ordered urgently.

"Good. Now, we don't have long, and this lock's simple," O'Cleary said to Shawn, going on to explain how the wire could be used to trigger the lock open. He tried to keep Shawn's focus on the lock and not the spasming man a few feet away as Justin's friends attempted to save him from the poison, which ravaged his insides in the dying light.

Simon compressed Justin's chest one last time. Nothing. He stood up, brushed off his legs, and glanced at his watch. "Time of death, seven forty-five." Simon closed his eyes and murmured a silent prayer. Once finished, his hand went to the small of his back, removing a pistol. His other hand pulled a silencer from his satchel, which he attached to the gun. "Monte Cristo?"

"Yeah," said Peter, eyeing Justin's body and reflexively reaching for Galvorn, before remembering it was gone. *How? Why did I let this happen? We can't afford to lose people. Not like this. Not Justin.* Peter banged a fist against the fence wall. *The woman. But was it her or Jason? Doesn't matter. If we hadn't been here, we might have saved him. That makes it Jason's fault. This has to end. Grieve later.*

GROWTH

Well, that certainly explains it," said Steven solemnly as he stared at the sparse shelves.

If we're running this low, how have I been eating just fine? Sarah sighed softly. "Is that really all you've got?"

Belford pulled the freezer door shut. "Just about," he drawled. "Ain't no accountin' for what folks keep to themselves or that goes unreported. Not like we can go round strongarmin' newcomers to give up what they've got." An accusatory gaze lingered on Steven for a moment. Then the old man shrugged, removing his big brown cowboy hat to scratch his bald head.

"Well, we could, but most do of their own accord. Don't misunderstand me, y'all." His gray and white beard bounced as he spoke, reminding Sarah a bit of Santa Claus. *If only he was shorter and just a bit rounder. And jolly. He's not jolly.*

"The snake meat barely put a dent in things. That warehouse you suggested we check had plenty of dried food — enough for now, at least," he said to Dr. Walker. "But our population keeps fluctuating. Every garden or farm nearby is picked clean." He tugged lightly on his beard. "I'm not sure what y'all are supposed to do to help unless you can find us another abandoned warehouse, but Mayor Gibson said to ask." He looked down quizzically at Doctor Walker. "Any ideas, Doctor, uh, Doctor Cleaton?"

"Walker," Sarah corrected.

"Thank you, Raven."

"It's Sarah."

"Oh, right. Thank you, Sarah."

No wonder we're running out of food if he's in charge of rationing. Doctor Gibson's is the first name I've heard him get right since we got here.

"Were the scouting parties informed of this predicament before their departure?" inquired Dr. Walker, not at all fazed by Belford's inability to remember names.

"Unfortunately, not," said Gibson, taking a step closer as he pulled at his immaculate mustache. "That being said, they should be returning soon. Hopefully, before the end of the day, if all went well," he added somberly.

Gibson glanced over at the closed freezer door. "Even if things went well, we cannot rely on what we do not know. So, we must plan for the worst. Should it be too dangerous to venture far from Paragon, how will we feed our people? I had hoped the three of you could help us come up with a solution," he explained hopefully.

Steven rubbed the back of his neck. "I've drafted a broader grid pattern focused on supply recovery. I can implement it once the scout's return, but that's barely a short-term solution. I'll start looking into another idea I have. I've got a bit of time now anyway since weapon production is moving along steadily without me having to be there constantly."

Steven frowned. Then he added, more to himself than those present, "and I cannot, for the life of me, determine the causality between the Shattering and the bizarre blockage of our information technology. Oh," he said with a snap of his fingers. "I realize it's not the ideal season for it, but have we begun any sort of planting?"

"We've planted some corn, and we was considering planting more, but ain't gonna do no good. 'Specially not with things gettin' colder," said Belford.

Steven turned to Sarah and Dr. Walker, his eyes twinkling. "Do you think the two of you can do something to help things along?"

Dr. Walker smiled warmly. "I think Sarah is just the person for such a task."

No! No, I'm not. Sarah's eyes went wide. *I've barely even used the wands since the Forge. What does she think I'm going to be able to do?* Butterflies harassed her stomach, but at the same time, she felt a surge of anticipation. She could feel an urge to cast again, to test her abilities – an urge at odds with her fears of what might go wrong. *She's not going to make me do it myself. And she'll be there to make sure it's okay,* the urge tried to reassure her.

She looked at the woman, who opened her eyes to a world of impossibilities. Dr. Walker looked older and frailer by the day; there was no denying it. Their exercises were taking a toll on her.

She needs more food. Even Steven is looking thinner. That settles it. "I'll do whatever I can to help," Sarah stated firmly.

"Good. That's comforting to hear," said the mayor. "Belford, where—"

Clang! The sound of a door bursting open caused all of them to flinch. Moments later, a spindly middle-aged woman with strands of gray in her blonde bob marched into the room, followed by an exasperated-looking Al.

How does her hair look so perfect? Did someone reopen a salon? Sarah marveled.

"I'm sorry, y'all. She just barged in. Wouldn't stop, and when I tried to stop her, well…" He blushed.

"I told him to keep his hands off me. It's still a free country, is it not, *Mister Mayor?*"

"Ah, yes, Missus Norman. We're quite busy at the moment, could I get you to schedule an appointment at my office?" Gibson said with a note of pleading.

"Where is my son, Mister Mayor?" Demanded the rail-thin woman, her barely in-check anger making Al look like a helpless child behind her despite being four times her size.

"Missus Norman, we've been over this. Your son volunteered to go with the scouting party and had military experience—"

"He went to boot camp for three weeks instead of juvie because he got caught drinking with some friends in high school. The boy has no *military* experience. And you sent him out there with giant snakes and monsters armed with bones?" she shouted sardonically in her shrill voice. "I know I didn't elect you, and I'm not sure who did, but you're in charge, and that means you have responsibilities to the people of this city." Her arms were shaking, but her voice was steady. "You told me they were due back today. Now. Where. Is. My. Boy?"

"As soon as he's back, you'll be the first to know. Now, if you'll please go with Al, he'll escort you to wait at the gate where your son is to make his return." Gibson said, motioning her towards Al, whose face fell at the suggestion. As he gestured her forward, they all made their way out the door.

"If there's so much as a scratch on him, I am holding you personally responsible. Personally! Do you hear me?" The woman continued ranting as Al led her away with effort. The rest of them piled into Belford's truck, so he could drive them to where the corn was planted. The city hummed with life as they rode, thinning in population near the edges when they approached the color-changing trees.

"I'm sorry about that. Missus Norman is really a good woman. She's just worried about her son," said Dr. Gibson absently. No one responded, not wanting to risk jinxing the return of the scouts or perhaps because there was simply nothing to say. Their short journey continued in silence until they passed through the gate, and Belford began explaining their choice of plant, location, and everything he could about how it was doomed to fail.

They endured his prattling for a mile outside the wall before arriving at their destination, a field not far off the road where with tractors set up at its corners and mounted by armed guards. Once parked, Steven helped Sarah and Dr. Walker gingerly out of the truck. Belford continued, unfazed, explaining the planting process and having no success remembering anyone's name.

In front of them were rows upon rows of ready-made earth, but not a single piece of green. Not far from this field, a tractor dredged the ground, in the process of making a fourth field ready for planting.

"Good work, Belford. Thank you," interrupted Dr. Gibson admiringly. "Miss Young, Doctor Walker, I don't know what you have planned, but everyone here is at your disposal," he said, pointing out the workers tending the other fields.

Dr. Walker shuffled forward, teetering slightly as she moved. She reached the edge of the soil and prodded it with her cane. "Hmm," she mumbled and rolled the sleeves of the robes she now regularly wore up to her elbows.

Then the white tattoos began to glow blue. Belford made a strange choking sound at the sight of the glow and took a heavy step back. The glow only lasted a moment, and the sleeves were being pulled back into position.

"Sarah, dear, this is the perfect opportunity for you to push yourself. I want you to do this without my assistance," she said calmly.

"Do what exactly?" Sarah asked, knowing full well what the little woman was about to tell her to do but stalling for time.

"Help them grow," replied Dr. Walker, gesturing at the field. Her eyes held a hint of rebuke, but her voice was gentle. "It's time to push yourself, Sarah. You don't need me for this. Reach out. They want to do it. They just need your urging. Remember, do not hesitate. Focus on what you want to happen and will it so. Oh, and this time make sure to speak your spell," she added with what Sarah thought was a rather inappropriate twinkle to her eye.

Sarah reached up and adjusted her glasses. She hadn't needed them since Shadowfang, but after confirming that they'd canceled out his paralytic effect, she'd gotten Breekie's help adjusting them to her improved vision.

"I— It's too much. It's not just increasing something like a spark or a bone. I can't make a plant grow. It's a living thing, with moving parts, how am I supposed to do that alone? I'm not a botanist. I have a journalism degree," she protested.

"Miss Young, you are not one to shy away from a challenge. Come now, I've known master enhancers with half your talent. You can do this. Confidence is the key to success, after all," Dr. Walker chided.

Sarah blushed. "You're exaggerating to make me feel better."

"No, Sarah. I am not. I tell you this so you might better understand the scope of your own abilities. You possess a power so unlike any I have seen, and you've only scratched the surface of it. Perhaps it is the hopes and prayers of all your terrified kind spread across the world that bolsters you."

"Really? Would that help me?" she asked.

Dr. Walker shrugged. "Who's to say? I'd be a fool to claim I or anyone else know all there is to know about magic. But in dark times, the brightest are given the power to shine." She again poked at the upturned dirt with her cane. "Sarah, there is much you do not know, and much I cannot teach you. This is a thing you must do."

Sarah nodded and knelt at the edge of the dirt. Bolstered by Dr. Walker's words, as carefully as one might remove an expensive kitchen knife from its sheath, she slipped her wand from its place in its notebook.

"Both, deary."

Sarah grimaced and withdrew the second wand. *I can do this. It's just like watering plants. With magic.* She could feel the self-doubt clawing at her chest. *No, calm down. She wouldn't have you do it if she didn't think you could. Come on, Sarah.* She plunged both wands into the soil, opening her mind. The energy waited for her, like water in a lock, powerful and ready to flow through.

She took a deep breath. The energy pushed eagerly at her, begging to be released. She embraced it, feeling it flow through every inch of her being, warm and robust, coursing through her veins, searching for an outlet.

Then it was flaming hot. *Too hot!* "Grow." The word escaped in a mangled squeak. Nothing happened. She felt damp and clammy all of a sudden. She realized she was drenched with sweat.

Sarah unclenched her eyes. Looking down at the field, she saw steam rising from the tilled earth. Steam and nothing else. *I failed.*

"Again," Dr. Walker instructed callously. "Envision the seeds growing. Know the seeds. Command the magic with your voice."

Sarah clenched her teeth, then her eyes. She conjured an image of a field of corn in her mind. Green, tall, and healthy. She saw it breaking the earth and rising, healthy, and plentiful, the leaves peeling back as the corn emerged plump and ready. The magic came back to her.

"Grow," she said, the command almost a shout as it burst from her lips. This time, the energy found its outlet in her wands, flowing through them into the ground where it sought out the seeds planted throughout the dirt. Sarah concentrated on the image in her mind, willing it into existence. The ground shivered, and greenery burst from the orange-brown earth. Small sprouts of corn climbed out of the soil, opened up, and reached eagerly for the sun.

Sarah slammed the door on the flow of magic, cutting the circulation off in an instant. The final traces she redirected into her wands and stored there rather than releasing them into the field of vegetation barely breaking from the soil.

It was then that her hunger truly struck her. Her stomach was gnawing at her, begging for nutrients, and her hands were shaking. She fell back on her rear with a *thump*. Exhausted, she felt like she'd just run a marathon.

Dr. Walker put a hand on her shoulder and squeezed. The embrace warmed Sarah's heart but did nothing to help her hunger or exhaustion.

"You're all right, dear. That was quite a task. Take a moment. Steady yourself. Deep breaths. Concentrate on your surroundings," she instructed calmly.

Sarah did as she was told, feeling the grass on her hands and staring intently at the mass of small corn sprouts, she readjusted her mind to the absence of the flow.

"Witchcraft." The whispered word floated ominously through the air, clawing into the mind of all present. It was followed by a louder declaration: "Witches — both of them. You've got witches doing foul, demonic, unholy witchcraft." Belford's words directed at Dr. Gibson grew into a cry by the end of the tirade.

Dr. Walker left Sarah's side like a billowing storm. "Enough. No. Be silent and hold your tongue lest you say more filth you may come to regret." Her voice was living fire and steel cutting off the man's opportunity to retort. Sarah had never heard Dr. Walker angry before, but the fury was there, a forge fire, contained and controlled but capable of destroying a building if left unchecked.

Belford went as white as his beard, stumbling back in terror as the old dwarf who was half his size marched forward, cane waving menacingly in the air, no longer supporting her.

"Now, hold on," he tried to protest. "Stay back Wit—"

But she cut him off, "No. I said, silence! I will not have a second Salem come of my town due to ignorance and paranoia. Fear is rife enough as it is, and your mindless accusations could start an inferno of a mob that would burn us all to the ground," she shouted. "Your kind are far too prone to panic and have come too far for this kind of regression," she stopped; placing the cane on the ground to steady herself. When she resumed her voice was cold; the heat and fury replaced by strange malice. It made Sarah nervous as she listened.

"What we are doing is magic. There is no denying that. But witchcraft is an entirely different matter which involves consorting with demons. Should there be a witch among us, I will deal with them myself as they should be dealt with, but what we are doing is good and pure. While it might scare you, Belford, and remind you of Hollywood's romanticized misrepresentation of the dark arts, I can assure you it is no such thing. Look into my eyes and ask yourself, do they contain the will of evil spirits?" she said, her unblinking gaze drilling into the man's face, daring him to press the issue.

Belford stared down at Dr. Walker, the fear plain on his face. He swallowed, seemingly unaware that Steven now stood within arm's reach of both of them, ready to pull them apart should things escalate.

"No, ma'am," Belford croaked out in a weak voice.

Dr. Walker turned to Mayor Gibson, who'd gone rather pale himself.

"See to it that no dark rumors of witchcraft are spread, Doctor Gibson. Young Miss Sarah is a gift to this town, the likes of which I could not have hoped for in my wildest dreams. The *last* thing we need is a scared mob trying to burn her at the stake," she said firmly.

"Of course," said the mayor, fiddling with the end of his mustache. He glanced back at the newly sprouted field. "Thank you both. This will help tremendously," he added as he turned and placed an arm on Belford's shoulder.

"Belford, would you leave your keys with Mister Thomas, please? You and I have much to discuss about rationing, and I think a brisk walk back would do us both good." eyes still locked on the little dwarf lady, Belford complied, haltingly handing the keys to the truck over to Steven.

"Mister Thomas, if you would speak to the guards and workers here. Explain the situation and instruct them to leave the corn alone for now. When you're done, please use the truck to drive Doctor Walker and Miss Young back to town," Mayor Gibson instructed calmly.

"Yes, sir," said Steven. Then he made his way towards the crowd of confused men and women gathering at the edge of the field. Meanwhile, the two older men began their stroll back to the town.

Demons and dark magic? Witchcraft? What's she talking about? Sarah wondered. *There's a difference? I thought they were just other words for what we're doing.*

Dr. Walker made her way slowly back over to Sarah's side, where she sat down in the grass. Not far off, she could hear Steven's booming voice gathered the onlookers together.

"How do you feel?" the dwarf asked as if the outburst hadn't happened.

Sarah took a moment before replying, "Good. Hungry, though."

The old woman chuckled lightly. "That's to be expected after what you just did."

Sarah smiled weakly. "Umindrabo, what did you mean about dealing with witches just now?" she asked tentatively.

Dr. Walker sighed heavily. "Ah, yes. Of course, you don't know anything about the dark magics. I'm sorry, deary, I should have explained all of this sooner, but it slipped my mind. It's something most casters learn from childhood not to discuss." She pushed a springy gray hair away from her eyes. "Still, not a subject I relish… but the nature of our time and circumstance are significant enough for me to put aside my own discomfort."

With the end of her cane, she flattened out a small patch of dirt at the edge of the corn sprouts. "If you have questions, do not hesitate to ask them, as I know you sometimes do. I would prefer if this is the only time we discuss these things."

"Yes, ma'am," Sarah said with a frown. *Is it obvious that I hold back?*

Dr. Walker began, her voice in full lecturing mode, "As with all forms of power, the arcane is corruptible, Sarah. This manifests itself in two primary ways. Ways that it would be best kept between us. Understood?"

Sarah nodded eagerly. "Yes, but I do not understand why."

"Good. You will once I am done. The first of these is blood magic. Within the blood of one who knows the arcane, there is power. A power that some learned can be harnessed and used. That is why many casters undergo a treatment that burns arcane energy from their body when they die. Which I really should have mentioned earlier, I now realize."

Sarah's eyebrow rose. "Burned? Is the treatment painful?"

"Yes, burned, or perhaps washed away is a better term. Lest a dark force be allowed to use it. Now…" she paused to organize her thoughts.

That's why I try not to ask too many questions, Sarah chastised herself.

"Ah, yes, blood magic can be utilized by casters or those with no true knowledge of the arcane. It is a ruinous thing, Sarah. It destroys the mind and soul as much as it grants power. Blood of the living is more powerful, but the blood of the dead is often easier to obtain," Dr. Walker explained. "Hence the rituals associated with becoming a caster, rituals I am not capable of performing," she added with a hint of dejection.

That must be why she didn't think to bring it up. "Does the blood of a dead caster… expire?"

Dr. Walker's expression was a new one: a mixture of confusion and surprise.

"I — I don't know. That's an excellent question. I don't believe it's been tested, at least not by any decent folks. Hmm… Well, Sarah, as much as I value knowledge, I do hope that is a question neither of us finds out the answer to."

"Oh. Okay, I'm sorry," Sarah replied.

"No, no, deary, there's no need to apologize. Better to ask me than to be led to the wrong people searching for answers," Dr. Walker replied.

"Do I need to go through the treatment?" Sarah asked hesitantly. "In case… something happens to me?"

"Eventually, if it's not too late," Dr. Walker replied with an unusually eager dismissiveness. "Very good then. Moving on… The second dark magic is witchcraft, a practice so uniquely scarring that it has found its way into your world despite the power of Therin-Selu. It has infiltrated your entertainment and even inspired a religion."

Her cane drew a circle in the dirt. "Belford is right to fear it. But his fears have been abused by Hollywood, twisting his perception. True witchcraft is most simply explained as consorting with demons in exchange for power."

"Demons? Literal, like, from hell, fallen angel, demons?" Sarah asked in awe.

"Yes."

That brings up a thousand more questions. Wait, let her finish, or she never will. You can save those for later. "So, just making sure I have this right — witches… make deals with demons and use them for power?"

"Witches are *used by* them. They offer their powers in exchange for dominion over their host. Although, they may not explain it this way. They will make deals with casters and non-casters alike and are not limited by experience or natural talent in the same way we are," Dr. Walker explained.

"They are incredibly powerful." She looked deep into Sarah's eyes. "They are to be killed on sight. They are dangerous, untrustable, unpredictable, and evil. There is no room for modern idealism or attempts to turn them." She said all this with a cold fury that contrasted how she'd spoken to Belford. "They are creatures bent on power and destruction, uninhibited by conscience, as nothing remains of the host to be saved."

"That's terrifying," Sarah murmured.

Dr. Walker nodded slowly. "They are. Ordinarily, there are people trained for dealing with them. When they are unavailable, casters have been known to submit themselves entirely to the arcane to stop a witch."

"Oh," *that's suicide. That's insane! They'll destroy an entire city just to kill one person? No wonder she was so upset with Belford.*

"How do you identify a witch? Just in case," she asked. *So I can get as far away as possible from one if I meet them.*

Dr. Walker stood slowly and carefully examined one of the sprouts of corn. "Often, their eyes have gone white. Early on, it will be milkier, as though they go blind, but it doesn't take too long for them to go pure white. You know the old saying, eyes are the doorway to the soul?"

"Yes. I've always liked it."

"Good. Possession destroys the body. Eventually, it becomes too much for the host, and their soul is driven from the body, but they often try to hide these traits."

Sarah reached absently to adjust her glasses again, reminding herself for the second time in a few minutes she wasn't wearing them. *Okay, that's getting annoying. I need to do something about that. Witches' souls are destroyed by demons. Then, does that mean…?*

"Is…?" she paused, fearing the answer. "Is necromancy possible?" she asked.

Dr. Walker smiled softly. "You are asking me if it is possible to use magic to bring someone back from the dead."

"Mhmm," Sarah said, wincing at the dwarf's words.

"No. Not for us. Not the way you're thinking."

"What do you mean?"

The sorrowful smile remained on her face. "The soul is not something the arcane flow can control."

"But you just said… Can you not use the arcane to fend off possession?"

"In a way, yes, but once the soul has departed our plane of existence, there is no power that you, I, or any earthly caster possesses capable of returning it to its host."

"Oh. Then in what way can the dead be brought back that I am not thinking?" Sarah asked, rising to her feet and dusting the dirt off her jeans.

Dr. Walker's smile showed a hint of approval behind the sorrow. "Very good. Necromancy cannot restore life as we know it. Yes. But arcane energy can be used to reanimate a body, giving it the ability to speak or move. But it does not retain the ability to think for itself, and once it's connection to the arcane is severed, it will no longer function as an animate object."

"That's horrible, too. Someone could pretend to have brought someone back to life."

"Yes, but the act itself requires so much energy and focus that there is no real point to it. And the caster runs the risk of losing part of themself if they do it with the body of another caster. Then you are overlapping with blood magic," Dr. Walker said.

After a moment of silence, Sarah asked another question. "There's something else, isn't there?" she pressed.

"Heh-heh. Have I become too readable in my old age, Sarah?"

Sarah blushed. "I'm sorry. I shouldn't have said anything. It's just your mouth and eyes twitch a bit when you're trying to decide whether or not to tell me more about something."

Dr. Walker threw her arms up in a dramatic display of surrender. "I tire of such dark talk. But yes, better you learn these things from me and the dangers therein than seek out answers yourself."

"I'm sorry! I didn't mean to—"

"Hush now. Curiosity is nothing to apologize for." Dr, Walker, cut her off. "You are a student. I, your teacher. How am I to teach if you do not ask?"

"Yes, ma'am," Sarah said, biting back the urge to apologize yet again.

"You remember what I told you of divination?"

Sarah nodded, fighting the urge to pull out her notebook and jot everything down. The itch to write had been bothering her for some time now, but she got the sense these things were better off not put to paper. "That it involves the tracing of the arcane flow. It's one of the rarest methods of casting, and it's the least understood."

"An accurate summary. I am not knowledgeable on how, but I do know that divination has been rumored to have been used to speak to the dead. And that it is an unpleasant, dangerous thing. It's not quite necromancy, but still not something to attempt. And there you have it. Witches often claim to have such abilities, actually."

The ability to talk to the dead… How long? How many? How long dead? The questions tumbled through her mind, and she stood there, staring down at the sprouts of corn.

Silence overtook them once more. Sarah sat in the shade of the corn with feet resting in the small border of upturned dirt at the edge of the crop. Dr. Walker poked and prodded at the corn and soil. Sarah could think of nothing more to say. She found that she was too overwhelmed by everything she'd just learned — overwhelmed and hungry, she remembered as her stomach growled loudly.

"Hush, you," she mumbled at it. Then, turning to face Dr. Walker, said, "Thank you, Umindrabo."

"Hmm? For what, deary?"

"Defending me. Teaching me. Giving me books to study. Everything else you've done for us." She gestured at their surroundings. "We could be a lot worse off. If not for you."

Dr. Walker fiddled absently with her cane. "You're welcome, Sarah. Your kind was almost lost to the world once. It would be a tragedy to lose you altogether… Especially with how far we've come. Now, let us get some food and rest. You must do this again tomorrow."

OPERATION CRISTO

Signal Jenni. Tell her we've got a man down and are going for a Cristo. Gunter, Shawn, you stay here," Peter added as Simon began the message. Peter bent down to pull a pistol from Justin's ankle holster, handing it to Gunter. "Shoot anyone who comes through that door without whistling first. Got that?"

"He… He's dead?" Shawn squeaked.

Peter glanced at him through watery eyes, letting a tear slide down his cheek. "Yes, Shawn," Simon said softly.

Gunter took the gun like it was made of solid lead. "Why? W-why would th-they do this?" he choked out, with a look at Justin, not letting his gaze linger on the man's corpse.

Shawn stepped closer, holding the gate lock in hand, tears sliding down his cheeks despite his effort to hold them back. Peter knelt in front of him and repeated his father's words: "Fighting it will alter your state of mind. Let them flow without distracting you. Time for tears later, plenty of time." He pressed Justin's boot knife into Shawn's hands.

"But why? He was kind. Funny. Why would they poison him?"

"Why doesn't matter now. They need to pay for this. Keep your mind clear. We'll be back."

Peter made his way to the door. His steps created no sound on the concrete. The door was a simple metal structure with a round knob and a small wire net window. He grasped the handle and turned slowly. It opened without issue.

The lock clicked softly, and Peter put his ear to the door, listening carefully. After a moment, he glanced back at his crew. *Simon, O'Cleary, and a dwarf. Hauch and Jenni on their way as reinforcements. Oh, Jenni, they were so close. Two guns, several blades, and a bit of magic. Good. Step one, get my sword.*

The door pulled open inward with a small creak as Peter stepped back with it. This left the space open should O'Cleary and Simon need to fire. There was no one on the other side, so Peter took point, knife in hand. O'Cleary and Simon followed with weapons raised and Breekie bringing up the rear with fists clenched, ready to break bones.

Ahead of them lay the long dark hallway they'd been brought in through. Peter knew that at the end of the hall stood a door with unknown contents. At the left bend and then immediately to the right sat a desk. Peter paused and listened carefully.

It was no surprise that he heard the light breathing of a man. He held up a single finger to let the others know as he crept forward like a tiger in the underbrush.

Peter came to the corner and glanced around it. Michael sat at the desk in an office chair, his feet propped up in front of him next to Foecrusher. Galvorn rested on his lap, where he stared at it in silence. Jermaine was nowhere to be seen, but a soft light shone from under the doorway to the men's bathroom on the other side of the room.

Peter got low, stepping lightly forward until he stood directly behind the man. In one lightning-fast move, he grabbed the man and drove his bone blade through his throat, pushing the blade in and then out the front. It was over in one bloody second, not even long enough for the man to scream.

The sound of running water could be heard within the bathroom as Peter slid Galvorn off the dead man's lap. Behind Peter, O'Cleary stood tall. From within the bathroom came a voice and the sound of footsteps.

"I'm tellin ya man, the dirty birds'll be back once all this is—" The door opened, and O'Cleary's gun clicked in the silence, followed by the soft ting of the bullet's casing striking the linoleum floor. Jermaine stood motionless for a moment, frozen by the round red hole between his eyes. Then he teetered and fell backward against the blood-stained bathroom wall with a soft crash, his predictions left unfinished for eternity.

Peter stood up straight, sheathed Galvorn, then grabbed Foecrusher and passed it to Breekie.

"Thank you," Breekie said with a note of apprehension in his voice.

Peter turned back to Michael's corpse. The blood from his neck was a strange bright purple, like the blood from the ork he'd used his poison-laced dagger on earlier. *Purple. Regardless of the original color, interesting. I'll have to tell Steven about that.*

Peter searched Michael's body for weapons. O'Cleary stepped over to the bathroom, where he dragged Jermaine's corpse farther in, out of the way of the door, then reemerged empty-handed. "Nothing on him."

"Here," said Simon gesturing to the desk where a revolver and a hunting rifle sat. Together, they sifted through the weapons. Peter grabbed the corpse and hauled it into the bathroom, careful not to step in any blood. He turned off the light and closed the bathroom door softly behind him.

"I guess they weren't stupid enough to store the rest of our weapons here too. Pity," Peter said coyly. "Heads on a swivel, boys. He said something about a curfew earlier, so I doubt anyone we see on the street is going to be a civvy."

Peter took Galvorn in one hand and his knife in the other as they made their way out into the darkness. A cloudy night and not a single active street-light made for easy going through the dark. At the wall, there were lights aplenty, but all faced outward into the dark unknown, powered by generators that Peter suspected would drown out the sound of most anyone approaching from within the city.

They poisoned Justin. Why? How? At dinner? Or did it happen during my fight while they were watching us. Maybe they gave him a drink. He shook his head, the questions echoing through his mind over and over as he stepped carefully from one shadow to the next, his eyes well-adjusted to the dark.

His vision was better than ever, a side effect of his time fighting in the dark mists of his dreams, he suspected. *I've got to stop Jason. It doesn't matter why or how. He has to die.*

They snuck deeper into the city, closer and closer to Jason's abode. Peter felt a tap on his shoulder. He turned to face Simon, who whispered softly, "Jenni's inside. Corner of Broadway and Poplar."

Peter nodded. "She knows the layout well enough to get to the Pound?"

"Yeah, she's been studying a map of the city while waiting."

"Where'd she get that?"

"I didn't ask. But she knows the layout."

"All right, have her drop by the Pound, make sure she knows to whistle, and leave Hauch with Shawn and Gunter on guard duty, then rendezvous with us," Peter ordered.

"Yes, sir." Simon replied and began to input the message.

Moments later, they turned a corner, following loud music and lights spilling around the corner from the courthouse ahead. The courthouse was a towering red-brick building with broad white columns and enormous steps, typical of small Georgia towns.

The courthouse stood tall and proud, denying the abuse it endured at the hands of the Shattering, which left it with boarded windows and a crooked triangle at its top.

Enough light was there to illuminate the area around the building despite the covered windows. A single large, ruddy man sat outside on a bench by the door and exhaled a cloud of vape smoke. The rifle leaned against his bench, indicating he was supposed to be on guard duty.

Peter turned to his small group. "Jason's mine."

O'Cleary scowled but didn't protest.

"Breekie, what can you do here? I need to know what you've got up your sleeve before things get hot."

"Not much. I can deal with any warded armor. Cheekie and I warded yours some. Mine is better," he said, and thumped his armor lightly. "More charge. I can hammer too," he said with a grin, as he gave Foecrusher a small heft.

"Good, stay in the back then. Cover our rears." Then he looked to Simon and O'Cleary, and went on, "You heard him. If they've got any armor on, go for the boot knife kill."

They both nodded their understanding, with Simon's face a stoic statue and O'Cleary's slightly scarred face home to a savage grin.

"All right, O'Cleary, all yours."

O'Cleary inched forward for a better angle, and the grin on his face widened. Then he raised his pistol and fired. The large man on the bench convulsed, his vape falling out of his hand to land by his side. The last of its vapors leaked slowly out the back of his head. O'Cleary fired again, the shot took out a camera on the building's corner.

It gave no light to indicate it was active, but Peter was glad O'Cleary didn't ask whether or not to remove it. They waited for a moment in the shadows to see if anything changed. The building remained the same, like a major road under construction in Florida.

Peter gave the signal to move, and together they dashed across the light and stopped at the edge of the courthouse. They slid between the overgrown bushes that once made for a pleasant decoration and now served as a perfect place of concealment. *Takes a real idiot to make this their living space by choice — blind spots everywhere. Or just someone desperate to give off the appearance of power.*

Carefully they made their way around the side of the building and managed to find a fire exit mostly concealed by the bushes. The presence of fresh cigarette butts in the space between the door and the rest of the shrubbery told Peter all he needed to know. *They come out here to smoke. Of course, they do.*

Peter scrutinized the metal door. A rectangular pull handle rested under a standard circular lock. *If that's the case, the alarm has been disabled. We can wait for someone to come out for a smoke, or we can pick the lock.*

Peter signaled for them all to remain low and still. He removed a lock pick from his pocket, the same kit he never left home without, and stepped towards the lock. Just as he inserted the pick, he heard a noise from the other side of the door.

He locked eyes with Simon, who knew his meaning instantly. As the door pushed open, Peter rolled with it, letting it press him up against the wall as Simon moved forward.

From Simon's side, he heard a barfing sound and a grunt as the door pushed open. Peter slid out his boot knife and inserted the blade in the frame as he slowly closed the door, the edge of the knife left in place to stop the door from locking.

He then turned to see what Simon accomplished. A look of annoyance was plastered across Simon's face, and it was easy to see why. He'd caught the young, pale man as he came through the door and hunched over to vomit. Before the man had a chance to react, Simon grabbed him and put his hand over his mouth and a knife to his throat in a tight hold. This resulted in Simon being vomited on for the second time that evening.

He's barely eighteen, if that. The fellow stood there in Simon's vice-like grip, eyes the size of softballs, but he made no move to struggle or protest. Peter held a finger to his own lips. "If you try anything, you're dead. Got it?"

The wide-eyed boy nodded the best he could in Simon's grip. Peter looked to Simon, who almost eagerly drew his barf-covered hand away from the boy's mouth. Peter brought his boot knife away from the boy's throat, where it was drawing a trickle of blood.

The smell of alcohol spilled out of the boy's mouth with his words: "Aw, man. C'mon, dog, I ain't gonna rat. Please, man. I don't even like this gig. J-snip is tha worst. Uuugh," he moaned as one of his arm's jerked towards his waist.

A small spurt of blood sprayed on Peter from where a bullet passed through the boy's head and over Peter's shoulder.

Thump, came the sound of the bullet as it collided with a tree. Peter wiped the blood from his eyes and glowered at O'Cleary. *I didn't get a warning,* he thought.

"What? He was going for a weapon," O'Cleary whispered with feigned innocence.

"I could have stopped him," Simon chastised. "We don't know who's under Jason's influence or how bad. What's the point of saving everyone if we kill half of them in the process?"

"Avenging Justin is the point," Peter found himself saying. He shook his head slightly. "You've got a point, Simon, but we don't know who's under what influence, and odds are even without it, they're still going to see us as hostiles." Peter brought his hand to the door, anger mounted in his chest. "The boy's death is Jason's fault. The faster we get to Jason, the fewer bodies we have to drop. Ready?"

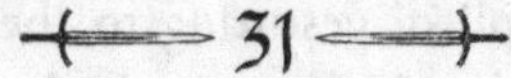

31

SELF DEFENSE

Shawn wiped the last of the tears off his cheek with the back of his hand. "So many people are dead. It doesn't make sense. We came to help. Why would someone do this?" he muttered to himself while he paced between the kennels and tried not to look at Justin's body.

From his seat on the ground, Gunter watched stoically. "Look, kid, running back and forth like a chicken with its head cut off isn't gonna bring him back."

Shawn paused his pacing. "Sorry."

Gunter shrugged. "Better get used to it. He's probably not gonna be the only one tonight. Hell, we probably won't make it through the night."

"What? Why would you say that?"

Gunter raised his hands in a noncommittal gesture. "I mean, think about it. They left us here because we'd just get in their way. Odds are something will go wrong, and then you and I are screwed. Get used to it, kid. Pretty much everyone you or I know is dead already. Why would we be any different."

"How long have they been gone?" Shawn inquired nervously. He didn't want to think about that possibility.

Gunter glanced at his watch. "About twenty minutes."

"You think they can do it? Kill him?"

Gunter toyed with his empty pack of cigarettes lazily, and took his time before responding, "Did you see the look in Peter's eyes?" he asked softly.

Shawn nodded. He kept seeing it in his mind's eye; pure rage, focused, refined, determined. "It was like he was looking past me, into my bones."

"Yeah. I think they'll be fine." He shrugged. "It's us I'm more worried about."

"Why? Do you think the guards will wake up?"

Gunter gave him a condescending look. "You think they left those guards alive? These guys are killers. Trained, professional killers," he said, giving his arms a rub. "It's cold in here. Let's head inside. I need to take a leak anyway."

"They said to stay here, though," Shawn protested.

"Yeah, here," Gunter replied, gesturing to the building. "They didn't say we have to stay back here with—" He stopped, glancing at where Justin lay, his jacket covering his face.

"Just come on," he said as he led Shawn into the human side of the building. Shawn went straight for the back of the desk. He plopped down in the chair there while Gunter made for the bathroom. The older man opened the door, flicked on the lights, and swore. Then he flicked the light off and made for the women's room, setting his pistol down on the desk.

"What?" asked Shawn, confused.

"I told you they wouldn't leave them alive," Gunter said dismissively as he entered the women's room. Then he stopped, turned back, and added, "Don't go in there."

Shawn set his blade on the desk and began to slowly spin in the chair. Then, while he span, he saw something that made him stop. "Lights!" A pair of headlights lit up the dark from outside in the parking lot, followed shortly by the sound of three doors slammed shut in a row.

"Gunter! Someone's here," he called softly and grabbed the gun off the desk before he ducked behind it. Outside there was a commotion, and Shawn heard yelling and gunfire. A second later, a man burst in loudly. "Michael! Jermaine! Where you at? There's a crazy dog and woman out here. They got Evan!"

Shawn watched the man's reflection in the mirrored sign that sat on the wall behind the desk. His face looked familiar, and after a moment, Shawn recognized him as James, one of Jason's lackeys who'd let them into the inner part of the city. James was grasping his right shoulder, the arm below it hung awkwardly.

"Come on, guys! I dropped my gun. They're still out there," he called as he turned and fiddled with the lock on the front door. Then Shawn saw his attention drawn to the women's bathroom, light shining under the door. *Oh, no.*

James glanced around frantically before catching sight of the knife on Shawn's desk. He stumbled forward to grab the blade with his good hand. The movement brought Shawn into his field of vision behind the desk.

"What the—" James managed to get out as he saw Shawn twist around. Shawn fell backward. He fired his pistol at the newcomer as he reached the floor: *Blam! Blam! Blam! Blam!*

He stopped. Some part of his brain warned him he might need the rest of the ammo as the man on the other side of the desk stumbled back, his face sheet white. His bloody hands clutched at his stomach, and he dropped the knife. His hand came away red, and he looked down at Shawn, his eyes full of tears.

"W-where am— Why?" he blubbered, then his eyes glazed over, and he fell. A second later, Gunter burst out of the bathroom wielding a plunger menacingly. "What?" he choked out, glancing down at the man dying on the floor. "Shawn, you okay?"

Gunter's words came to Shawn muffled and slurred. The world was blurry, spinning around him. He held onto the pistol for dear life, hoping it would steady him.

"Shawn. Give me the pistol, Shawn," came a voice from a blurry shape at his side.

He shook his head violently, he clung to the gun for dear life.

He heard banging at the front door, and Gunter disappeared from his view. Then he heard voices, mumbled, talking, murmuring confusing words he couldn't make out.

The words were interrupted by a loud bang.

But Shawn didn't care. All he could make out was that one word, "Why?", echoing in his mind.

Then he felt something wet and warm against his arm. Then something cold and wet nuzzled his hands. He opened his eyes, not realizing he'd squeezed them shut. A friendly set of brown eyes surrounded by fur greeted him.

"H-Hauch?"

The dog nuzzled his hands again, the barrel of the gun aimed at his head. Slowly, Shawn lowered it to his side, until it reached the floor. Hauch gave his face a big lick. Shawn saw blood-red teeth, and his heart stuttered for a moment. Hauch paused, tilted his head, and stared at him then stopped and laid his head in Shawn's lap softly. Shawn petted the dog gently.

After a second, he realized the voices were back, and he looked up. Gunter was helping Jenni into a seat. Her left leg was soaked in blood. "No, it's my fault. Shouldn't have gotten that close without double-tapping," Jenni said. "Shawn, you with us?"

Shawn nodded.

"Good. Next time aim for the chest. It's faster. Are you hurt?"

Shawn shook his head and continued petting Hauch.

"Good," said Jenni as she pulled out a broken radio and swore. "And there's the not good." Setting down the radio, she began to cut away at her pant leg, tearing it away and then ripping up the remaining sleeve.

"Listen, Gunter, I want you and Hauch to go find Peter and Simon. My radio is busted, and this cut on my leg is looking bad. Hauch will show you the way. Follow him closely. He'll keep you out of sight." She winced as she removed a tourniquet from her pack and began to apply it to her leg.

"Last I heard, they'd engaged. If it went well, it's over now. If not, better you're not here at least. Take that gun by Shawn," she ordered. "Should be a rifle in the parking lot too, and be careful. Got that?"

"Yeah. Stay safe," Gunter replied as he made for the door.

"One last thing," she called to him at the door. "If the worst happens, you tell Hauch *Zuhause*." Hauch's head perked up at this. "*Nein*, Hauch. *Kommen*."

Hauch rose slowly from Shawn's lap, giving him a soft nuzzle, and padded over to Jenni. "Good boy. *Begleiten* Gunter. *Finden* Peter."

Hauch wagged his tail eagerly, scurried over to Gunter, and followed him out the door.

EXECUTION

Peter dropped the unconscious woman he'd just incapacitated to the floor and signaled the others to move to breach the next room. They moved carefully toward a set of large wide-open double doors. Music blasted from within and covered the sound of their hurried footsteps.

They entered like the professionals they were and took in their surroundings before the crowd could realize they were there. A few quick shots muffled by music brought them to their enemies' attention, and the two men scrambled to return fire only to meet a quick end. People threw themselves in every direction except theirs. "Nobody move," Peter shouted as he searched the room for Jason.

The room froze. No one moved an inch. The speakers blared music, smoked, and sparked, never to be used again. Two bodies lay on the floor. Blood stained the carpet beneath them. *Five left. Four armed.* Peter searched eagerly through the courtroom-turned-party zone.

Fifteen men and women were strewn across the floor where they'd thrown themselves when SNW entered and had takken down two armed men and told the rest to put their hands up.

Four armed men stood with their hands raised in the air.

Peter spotted Jason. *There you are.*

Jason was at the back of the room by another door sitting in a chair. They locked eyes, and before Peter had a chance to fire, Jason yanked a young woman by the shirt in front of him to serve as a shield.

Coward. You're only delaying the inevitable.

"Put down your weapons," Jason commanded from his hunched position behind the woman. His loud voice had shifted almost imperceptibly and taken on a soothing quality. The shift was so subtle Peter doubted he'd have noticed it if not for his own strange instinct screaming at him that he was in danger when the man clutched his chain and opened his mouth.

Try it. I dare you.

Jason continued speaking. His sticky words clung to the inside of the ears and leaked into the crevices of the mind. The room's occupants were mesmerized; his words were oxygen, and they were short of breath.

"Put down your weapons and put your hands behind your heads," Jason continued.

Peter tore open the door he'd closed on his pain. The pain surged through his mind, washed away the words that pulled at him. The pain brought freedom and caused Jason's voice to change. It was no longer soothing. It was coarse and shouting, harsh and crazed.

"No," replied Peter, voice dripping with defiance as a cruel grin carved onto his face.

Jason's face contorted in confusion. With his hands raised, he turned to one of his men standing between him and the door. "Shoot them," Jason ordered, his voice brimming with rage.

The man spasmed and went for the revolver in his waistband.

O'Cleary fired. The gun's soft click was thunder in the silence. The bullet planted in the man's chest before he could draw his weapon. It knocked him back into the door — a door now soiled with his blood.

Jason turned back towards them, still holding the wobbly woman in front of him.

"Stop!" he screamed. "Why won't you obey?"

"Move," Peter ordered the men and women sprawled at his feet. They scurried out of his way as he marched towards Jason. Jason's face paled, and he scrambled quickly for the door as he kept the woman between himself and Peter. *I'll hamstring you, then slit your throat with my sword.*

Peter moved quicker, but there was too much in the way. Jason managed to throw himself out the door and drag the girl with him. Peter tore through the room. Scattered cups and plates crunched underfoot as he burst through the door. The girl was waiting for him on the other side of the door. The instant she saw him, she flung herself at him, nails raised to claw at his face.

Behind her, Jason was down the steps. His screams lashed out at the surrounding buildings and as he moved with all the speed his long legs could give him.

Peter sidestepped the woman, grabbed her, and brought her head into contact with the door frame with a thud. The blow was more forceful than he intended but had the effect he desired.

She dropped with a thud as the lights flickered on in the buildings around them.

Rage boiled over in his mind as Peter took aim and planted a bullet in the back of Jason's left leg, shattering his knee from behind. The blow sent him sprawling like a tree uprooted by an enormous blast of wind. He hit the road hard but kept moving as he yelled for help. "Get out here! Help me! They'll kill us all," he screamed violently.

Peter stalked forward, a wary eye on the buildings around him. His prey struggled forward, injured and weak. One by one, and then several at a time, doors opened and poured light into the street and illuminated the scene.

A pair of men were the first to emerge from one of the buildings closest, and Jason called to them desperately, "You! Get him!"

The pair shook as the words hit them, then together, they charged past Jason towards Peter.

Enough, Peter thought as he slid his pistol into its holster and drew Galvorn and his knife. Then he heard a voice behind him.

"Peter! It's not them," called Simon urgently.

Right, Peter thought, twirling Galvorn in his hand. It felt right. This is where the sword belonged, in his hand, ready to drink the blood of his enemies. *Kill them. It's self-defense. It'll make you stronger.* The thoughts echoed through his mind. Then, a calmer, controlled voice responded, *No. If you kill them, it would just make restoring peace here harder. People are watching. Once this is over, they'll know you had a choice. Drop the knife.* He did, letting the bone blade clatter onto the brick pavement behind him.

The younger of the two men reached him first, his youthful legs propelling him towards his fate more rapidly. Peter sidestepped the man's blow, and with a swipe of his leg, tripped him. He sent the man sprawling to the concrete, where he was forced to catch himself on his arms, one of which broke in the process.

Anger barely in check, Peter turned to meet his second assailant and found him brandishing a metal mop. Peter brought Galvorn up through the mop, which splintered apart. Then he followed through with a strike to the nose. The nose broke and knocked a now dazed man onto his rear. "Whuh?"

"No," he heard Jason cry from the ground a few steps away. Peter moved past the man who was sitting awkwardly on the ground holding his nose with a confused expression on his face.

Peter could feel the grin on his face. Rage mixed with pleasure as he drew closer and closer to his prey.

Peter grasped Galvorn with both hands as he looked down at his final victim, the gap finally closed between them. Jason clambered on hands and knees, trying desperately to pull himself backward.

It's no use. You're mine. Peter stepped closer, his shadow blanketed Jason back in the low light. Jason flipped over on his back to face him.

"No. No. No. Stop," Jason screamed with all his might as he threw his hands up defensively.

Peter felt the force of the order laced with magic. It was as though he'd been struck with a physical blow, and he felt himself take a step back. *Justin!* he screamed in his mind. His friend's smiling face filled his mind's eye as he brought the sword down, purging his mind of Jason's command by focusing on the pain in his own foot.

Galvorn met Jason's arm with bloody fury; severing muscle and bone a few inches below the elbow. The blood decorated the cool night air as the man's hand was torn away by the force of the swing. The blow cleared the last traces of fogginess from Peter's mind.

When Peter's vision refocused on Jason, he saw that more than just his number of intact appendages had changed. The man's face was devoid of color, and the necklace he wore was sizzling, melting into his neck, giving off the familiar smell of burned flesh, but Jason did not claw at it or scream.

He didn't even whimper at his severed hand. Peter stepped ever closer and saw blood leaking out the man's ears, and, eyes now empty, he rolled about in his head like marbles in a jar.

"Jason," Peter said forcefully. Jason gave no response other than a strange gurgle followed by bloody drool running down his chin. *What on Earth…?*

The lights around Peter were growing brighter, and he could hear approaching feet. Peter looked up and around and saw armed men with green bandanas around their left arms emerging into the area. *I have to kill him before it's too late, but this is just like before: no self-defense. If I kill him without a trial, everyone will know. They'll say I didn't have the right.*

His mind raced, weighing his options, trying to come to grips with the decision he knew he had to make. Then, a familiar voice called out to him.

"Captain Blair!"

Peter looked up from Jason's gurgling form, searching the growing number of men and women for who called his name. Then, he found him.

Gunter stood at the edge of the armed group, no sign of distress, barely out of the shadows, Hauch at his side. "What are you waiting for?" he cried through the darkness. "Do it!"

It was enough. Peter brought Galvorn down in a cruel arc. The blade passed through Jason's neck like paper and severed his connection with the mortal world. The night went silent for a moment.

The cold air stung Peter's eyes. He looked down at the blood filling the cracks in the concrete ground.

Breekie reached his side and bent down by the body. "Criske," Breekie murmured.

Then another voice cut through the dark of the night. "Out of the way. Coming through."

Peter looked up, bringing Galvorn into a defensive hold. He was surprised to see Caraticus pushing his way out of the nervous-looking crowd of fighters. He wielded a long metal spear with intricate swirling patterns along its shaft. Behind him, the group folded back in on itself.

Caraticus looked down at Jason's corpse then back up at Peter. A short man with hair and a short beard the color of fresh grain, who wore a green bandana, emerged at Caraticus' side.

Slowly, Caraticus rested the butt of his spear on the ground, then let go. It remained standing there, perfectly balanced. He placed a hand on the other man's chest, then whispered quietly to him as the blonde man's face flushed with anger.

After receiving a nod from the man, Caraticus walked towards Peter, a broad grin on his face.

"Looks like you didn't even need our help," he said warmly, extending a hand in congratulations. Peter lowered Galvorn. There was no sense of danger or warning energy coming from this man, so Peter took his hand and shook it.

"I told you," he called over his shoulder towards his followers. "I told you, plans never survive contact with reality." Caraticus' gaze drifted over to where Peter dropped his basilisk-bone dagger.

"Well, now, that is interesting," Caraticus said, stepping past Peter to retrieve the knife. "Tell me, Captain Blair, where does a modern man get hold of not only a Thalmein blade but also a basilisk fang dagger?"

Behind Caraticus, Peter could see O'Cleary fidgeting with his rifle. They were all there, ready to go toe to toe with this new threat if need be. Simon, however, hurried over to Gunter as Hauch traipsed to Peter's side.

But Hauch stopped a few feet short, tucked his tail between his legs, and gave Caraticus a strange growl.

Caraticus handed the dagger back to Peter and whispered, "You can tell me about it later." Then, as he ignored Hauch, he turned to the new fighters, his attention on the short man. "These are the folks I warned you about. I'm afraid Captain Blair has robbed you of your revenge, Oscar."

"I can see that," Oscar said, uncrossing his arms as he swaggered forward to meet Peter. He offered his free hand out to shake, the other hand grasping a round shield.

Peter accepted the handshake and found the man's grip far tighter than necessary. Oscar pulled himself a hair closer. His breath smelled like old bread. "Name's Oscar Scott, captain. I appreciate you taking care of that oaf," he continued, not releasing his grip. "I won't trade one bully for another though. This is my town, Captain Blair."

That's more like it. Peter squeezed back. "Don't worry. We're only stopping here on our way to Atlanta."

Scott's eyebrows shot up, he exchanged a look with Caraticus, and let Peter's hand go. "We have a lot to talk about then." He cursed. "If you'd just waited an hour, we'd have had this handled and let you go. Ah, well. I have some logistics to tend to. Shall we talk in the morning?"

"Absolutely," Peter replied.

Behind him, a man and woman stepped out of the crowd, now mixing with citizens, and began to collect Jason's body. After a short pause to watch Jason's corpse be carried off, the citizens began to disperse back into the buildings. Scott's fighters spread out, following orders.

Caraticus turned back to Peter. "Come," he said, as he hoisted his spear. "I have a place you all can rest safely until we can finish dealing with this in the morning. I'm glad you didn't agree to work for him. I wasn't looking forward to fighting you."

Peter nodded. "Thank you." Then he followed Caraticus' lead and added, "I'm glad we didn't have to fight either. That's a fancy spear you've got there."

"I find it useful. Where'd you get your sword?"

"An old dwarf gave it to me."

Caraticus smiled back. "Excellent. I got my spear from an elf."

REQUIEM IN A DREAM

There was no setting sun or rising moon to measure time in the place between worlds. Their surroundings changed only as Jadis seemed to will them to, and to that end, she only willed them to adjust for training, never for comfort. Peter's only way to track time was in actions. He counted the seconds it took to make each strike.

These seconds compiled into minutes, and those minutes into hours. And yet, he remained in the misty realm of his sleeping mind. Here he dueled, grew faster, more durable, and never tired. When they took breaks, it was only to discuss his ability or stretch.

Sometimes, they would exchange questions or even practice more mundane activities such as him tossing a knife under one arm to land in his other hand at a strange angle until the muscles had memorized the action.

Near as Peter could tell, he had been there for days. When he arrived this time, Jadis seemed almost pleased, assuring him that his actions had allowed them to make some real progress.

She was right. I'm improving, Peter thought. It was as natural as breathing now; always within his reach, but it only drained his energy when he acted upon it, allowed it to direct his movements. Not only that, but he had finally acclimated to the environment of this strange place. He still wasn't as fast as Jadis, but he no longer noticed the increased pressure that slowed his movements.

With a swift blow from Galvorn, Peter finished dispatching the last of the seven mist figures Jadis conjured up for him to fight all at once. When she saw he was finished, she sat down at the stone table which was always where she needed it.

"Your question," she said in her low silvery voice.

Peter joined her. *Killing lengthens my time here. I don't need to know any more about that yet. Oh, I know,* he thought, the question already formed on his lips.

"What is Galvorn made of?" The question offered no real tactical advantage but had been bothering him for some time. The sword felt unnatural. As much as it belonged in his hands, he could not shake the feeling there was more to it. What metal could endure what it did without dulling? What metal took on such a dark hue, impervious to scarring.

Jadis' still face gave more away now than before. Her steely aura was becoming easier for him to read.

"Blood," she said through clenched teeth.

"Blood? Like, from some faye creature?"

Jadis' eyes narrowed. Peter detected a subtle note of discomfort in her face.

"Blood and the same ore used to forge all Thalmein blades," she replied dismissively. It was clear something about the conversation made her uncomfortable.

There are more weapons like it then. Are they all bound to beings like her? Peter frowned. *Don't press her on it right now.* "Your turn."

Jadis didn't ask a question, though. Her eyes took on a faraway look, her vicious tenacity had evaporated.

A cold brush of air ran across Peter's face, and the ever-so-soft creak of the door to his room opening tore him from his sleep without so much as a goodbye. He simply felt and heard them and was awake. He cracked one eye open slowly. Whoever it was had stopped at the door, just outside the view of his barely open eye. Their dark silhouette was barely illuminated by soft morning light from the window.

Forget it, Peter thought, and sat up, drawing his sword from its place on the floor by his sleeping bag. He brought it in one fluid motion to point at the intruder at the door.

It was a vaguely familiar woman. She stepped closer and he got a better view. One side of her head was shaved while the other side-hung partially over her face. It was a bright green color; contrasting her blue eyes. It was the sunken state of her eyes and excess makeup that placed her name in his mind.

Marah. Why is she here?

She stood frozen in place, dressed in black skinny jeans with holes in the knees that looked self-made, a *Call of Duty* shirt, and shoes that looked like cheap combat boots peeled from one too many wet encounters. Peter saw no evidence that she was armed.

"Good morning, captain. Did you sleep well?" she said in a low voice.

"Better before the intrusion. What are you doing here?"

Marah brushed the bright hair from her face, a sultry look in her eye as she took a small step forward, running a finger aimlessly down her neck. "I came to thank you, Captain, for freeing us from that monster's hold."

"That's close enough," Peter said firmly. She paused in place. "You're welcome. Now get out."

"Would you stop pointing that sword at me?" she asked with a frown. Her eyes formed critical slits before she pushed the expression away with a smile.

Peter lowered the blade but kept it in hand.

Her smile widened. "There you go. You saved us, and you deserve to be thanked properly," she explained, shifting her weight gingerly off her left leg as she took a careful step forward. There was a familiar awkwardness to the movement. *She's injured.*

"I have no interest in anything you have to offer."

"You haven't heard what I have to—"

He cut her off, rising slowly from the sleeping bag. "From what I can tell from your stance, your right leg is bandaged under your jeans. Do you know what that tells me?"

Her expression didn't so much as flinch as she shrugged. "I have an injury?" she replied sarcastically. "I think you'd be hard-pressed to find anyone who wasn't injured during the Breaking."

"The Breaking was over a month ago. Your wound is more recent, and you're trying to hide it. Sure, it's possible it happened naturally. Maybe you didn't do it to yourself, but that's irrelevant."

"I don't see how—" she started.

"It's irrelevant because it means you went along with Jason's decisions."

Her eyes narrowed almost imperceptibly, and the corner of her smile twitched.

"I know pain canceled out his influence. In fact, for all I know, your influence on him led to the death of my friend, Justin," Peter said as he stepped out of the sleeping bag, white knuckles clenched around his sword. "So, I suggest you leave. I don't care for bullies, and I care even less for manipulative cowards."

Marah's relaxed demeanor melted away. Her expression reverted to its natural state of disdain. She stared down her nose and sneered. "If it wasn't for me, he'd have shot you all before you got to the wall. You owe me your life."

Peter met her eyes, searched her face, not sure what for. "I owe you nothing. Get. Out."

With a huff of breath from her nose, she turned and pushed open the door, which collided with a body on the other side. O'Cleary stepped back from where the door struck him, making room for her to exit. Upon seeing him, Marah paused and put a hand on his shoulder.

"I'm sorry," she said sweetly. "I didn't see you there," she added as she looked O'Cleary up and down. "I like your scar, soldier," she said, softly touching a scar on his cheek. "How'd you get it?"

"Longboarding," O'Cleary replied with a blank expression.

Marah drew her hand back and glared daggers at him. "Fine," she spat out and stormed off.

O'Cleary watched her go before turning to Peter, his expression one of great amusement. "She moves on quickly."

"She came to *thank* me."

O'Cleary raised an eyebrow. "Oh, I bet she did."

Peter's brow furrowed at this. "I told her to get out. You don't think she's…?"

"A stunner? In her own way. Don't you?"

"No. I was going to say dangerous. And you told me you got that scar in a bar fight."

"I did," O'Cleary replied, smirking.

Peter rolled his eyes. "That's not… You know what? Never mind. What's up?"

O'Cleary rubbed the back of his neck, a worried look on his face. "That guy Scott's ready to meet. He's got quite a scrappy crew with him too."

"Soldiers?" Peter asked, as he rifled through what he remembered about the town. It was all a bit of a blur after the dream; in fact, he felt different since he'd woken up. Lighter. It was only just now coming to him as he got ready for the day.

"Some probably, but I heard most of them are ex-convicts."

"Ex-convicts?" Peter glanced at the clock by the sleeping bag: *11:00* glowed in bright red numbers. *I slept longer than I should have.*

"Yup, seems like when his crew jumped ship here, they crossed paths with a prison. Apparently, the warden had locked everyone inside and left 'em to starve."

"And Scott let them go?" said Peter and slipped into a clean burgundy Henley shirt then adjusted Galvorn's sheath to rest at his hip.

"They were pretty reasonable, apparently. Starving can do that to a person," he explained with a far-off look.

Then, with a smile, Peter moved toward the door. "That, and they've all been fighting orks up in Atlanta since they left. Fighting monsters is therapeutic, I guess."

As they shut it behind them, O'Cleary's smile morphed into a confused expression. "Hold on. How did she…?"

"Know I was here?"

"Yeah," O'Cleary replied, his mouth slightly ajar as his lip curled in thought.

"Good question," Peter replied with a sigh. Last night when Caraticus left them in the office building right outside the town proper, he'd promised no one would know where they were. That, of course, hadn't stopped them resting in shifts.

Peter was still wary of the town despite the holistically thankful response they received. What's left of Jason's posse had run off or surrendered themselves the night before, but still, after Justin's demise, Peter had insisted on taking extra precautions. "You don't think Caraticus told her, do you?"

"Don't see why he would. If ya ask me, he didn't seem to like her."

As they made their way to the busy square where the fountain rested, Peter noticed the sizeable wooden head was gone. Additionally, he made a note of the increased number of well-armed, hard-eyed men and women that now walked about. After a moment, he caught sight of Breekie, Gunter, and Simon, who he approached.

"There you are, captain," Gunter said in a low voice once they'd come together.

"Jenni and Shawn?" Peter inquired.

"I have Jenni resting and practicing with a crutch," Simon replied. "Shawn decided to stay with her in case she needed anything. I think he's feeling a bit responsible for her injury."

Gunter scowled. "Wasn't the boy's fault."

"Nor was it yours," replied Simon. Peter had heard those words from him before.

"All right, Gunter, I'm not sure what else to do with you, so you might as well join us."

"Aw, gee willy, cap. Is that so?" Gunter mocked. "Don't forget, I am supposed to be keeping an eye on you."

"I look forward to hearing how I could have handled things better upon our return," Peter shot back sarcastically. *He's growing on me.*

"All right, what can you tell me about our meeting?"

"They have a dryad," Breekie chipped in eagerly.

"What?" Peter replied as he took slow steps toward the meeting place. He made sure to take their time getting there to learn as much as he could.

"Dah," Breekie repeated his head bobbing up and down, "is their ally."

Peter looked to Simon for clarification, but he only shrugged. Gunter, however, rose to the challenge. "The thing that was watching us at the barbecue site left the flowers warning us about this place. Scott's got one of those."

"Oh, right. What's this one look like?"

"She's like a tree person. Barky, tree-ish skin. Hair that looks like autumn, clothes made of leaves, weird eyes — they're all black, dark, and glowy."

"Like the thing Jason mounted in the fountain."

"Nyet, more person, less tree than treant. Not the same," Breekie almost interrupted with his correction. "I think their kind made the fog we went through, trying to keep people away from here."

Gunter raised his eyebrows. "Come to think of it, it hasn't been nearly as foggy since Peter took Jason out."

"All right, more importantly, what can you tell me about this guy, Scott," Peter said as he tried to get back on track.

"Oscar E. Scott," O'Cleary mocked. "I don't think he's a big fan of yours."

"Is that so?" Peter replied as he waved casually to a passing group of townsfolk on the street.

"Yeah, he doesn't seem too happy you killed Jason."

"He's still upset about that?"

"I would be," O'Cleary said with a shrug.

Peter laughed softly. "That, I believe. Well, if he expects me to apologize, it's not gonna happen. What about Caraticus? He seems helpful."

Gunter spoke up. "Not much to say we don't already know. He's well-liked by the town for bringing the strags in. He let Scott and his men in last night. Seems like they'd been planning this for a while."

Simon reinserted himself. "The townsfolk chose a man called Dory to speak for them. He's one of the ones who doesn't seem to like the way Caraticus and Scott handled things. He's the guy whose nose you broke last night."

"But he knows why I did?"

"Yeah, he's begrudging about it, but he's glad we dealt with Jason."

"Interesting. Thoughts, Ju—" Peter stopped. It dawned on him that he'd been about to ask a man who wasn't even there for his opinion. Peter's heart dropped as a flood of sorrow washed over him. The others tried to hide their winces, but it was too late. Their reactions only worsened the ache. Peter scowled. "Let's get this over with," he said as they made their way up the steps of the courthouse.

The scene within the courthouse was an odd one. The trash and bodies which scattered the floor the night before had been removed, and only bright red blood stains remained as a reminder that they were ever there. The windows had been opened wide and let in warm sunlight mixed with cold cleansing air.

A pair of rough-looking men pointed them into a courtroom adjacent to the one they'd chased Jason out of; wherein, they found an even stranger sight. A large poker table had been set up at the center of the room, and on it sat a tall pitcher of water and a plateful of some unfamiliar yet delicious-looking pink fruit. Seated around the table were three figures, and a fourth stood.

The fourth figure stood out the most, precisely as Gunter had described her. The dryad had a rectangular wooden build with green skin like a freshly carved stick that in places seemed to melt into the bark. A kaleidoscope of fall colored leaves that transitioned from yellow to orange to red, purple, and then back to yellow formed both her hair and her dress.

From her long, pointed ears hung small holly leaves with a single berry each, clearly an attempt at earrings. She was, without a doubt, a thing born of a tree in human form. Despite her wooden body, the most striking part of her appearance was her eyes. They were large orbs behind cat-like lids, they were dark, deep, and translucent. They glowed with tiny white sparks, which gave them the appearance of the night sky.

Seated beside the dryad was Oscar E. Scott. He was short but well-muscled and still head-and-shoulders above a dwarf. Other than a scraggly blonde beard and well-groomed head, there was nothing remarkable about his appearance other than a mouth of impeccably white teeth. His upper arms bore the same bandanas. On his back, the handle of his ax could be seen poking over his shoulder.

Sitting beside him was Caraticus, in a plain green t-shirt and jeans, his head still topped with a large beanie. His spear stood perfectly still at his side. Last of those gathered was the man, Dory, who Peter recognized from the day before only now with a broken nose and dark bags under his eyes. This man was as Southern as it got. His round head bore a well-kempt beard, a slowly receding hairline, and ruddy cheeks. He wore a flannel shirt and a camouflage baseball hat and spoke with the calm politeness of a man who knew all his neighbors by name.

"About time," said Scott as he made his way around the table. "You're late, Captain Blair."

"I apologize. Long night. Didn't realize we had a set start time," Peter replied as he extended a hand in greeting.

"Well, not knowing is hardly an excuse. You're still technically late. We have already begun." Scott took his hand and shook firmly. "Allow me to reintroduce myself. My name is Oscar E. Scott. I oversaw this town's fortifications post the Breaking," he added as he returned to his seat.

"I've already met the rest of you, and this," he said, motioning to the dryad who remained still as a statue as they approached and began to take their seats, "is Leuoradew."

Leuoradew bowed her head slightly. Her eyes, despite being hard to follow, were undeniably focused on Peter. Peter realized they were an incredibly deep brown, not black, as he'd been led to believe.

"Oh! Sundollops!" exclaimed Breekie delightedly as he stood in his chair to reach and snag one of the fruits on the table. "Finally, some familiar food," he mumbled as he bit into the fruit.

"Carrie was just informing me of your death toll from yesterday," Scott continued, holding up a hand proactively despite no one having moved to interrupt him. As they all sat, Gunter found himself left to stand awkwardly as there were no more chairs around the table or room to add one.

Scott frowned deeply. "I apologize for the lack of seating. This was the best we could find given the circumstances, and I did not expect you to show up with your entire platoon."

Gunter shrugged. "Technically, we didn't." With that, he went over to sit on one of the open windowsills and produced a fresh pack of cigarettes.

Scott eyed him and curled his lip. "I really wish you wouldn't, Mister Gunter. Orks and bandits are already present enough to send me to an early grave. I don't need lung cancer making it easier on them."

Gunter's face flushed red, but he gave no reply as he shoved the pack back into his pocket.

"Now, as I was saying," Scott continued as his fingers drummed on the table, "I understand that you did what you had to last night, and there were some casualties that technically might have been avoided, but there's no real way of knowing. What I am interested in discussing before moving on to more important matters are the rumors around Jason's death."

"I wasn't aware there were rumors," Peter said, as he reached out and took a fruit. "These safe for humans?"

"Of course. Please. Enjoy," Leuoradew said in a wispy voice, her gaze still focused on Peter, who was beginning to feel slightly uncomfortable. Then she went on without her lips moving. Her words now echoed in his mind. *Peter Blair, Avenger of the Arborous, Basilisk-Bane.* The soundless words made Peter's skin crawl.

Scott continued speaking at the same time, and his words overlapped with hers. "Yes. Apparently, there was smoke coming off him, and the smell of burning flesh before you oh-so dramatically beheaded him. Tell me, Captain Blair, do you have arcane abilities?"

The fruit in Peter's hand remained uneaten as he looked back and forth between the dryad and Scott. Neither of them made any sign they were going to acknowledge the strange overlap in their speech.

"Say again?" Peter said with furrowed brow to Scott as he bit into the fruit. A soft apple-like skin gave way to a tart pulp inside. He chewed for a moment, savored the new experience, then swallowed before he answered.

Scott sighed and repeated his question about Peter's ability.

"Not the kind that melts people, no," Peter replied once his mouth was empty.

"I can explain," interjected Breekie, who glanced at Peter while hesitantly raising his hand, but Breekie stopped when Peter shook his head ever so slightly, smiling softly.

Breekie went on, hand unraised. "Jason arcanized. Is when caster loses control of connection to arcane flow." Breekie shrugged. "He melted his brain."

"Intriguing," Oscar replied, "but you deflected my question, captain."

Peter drummed the fingers of his left hand as he examined the fruit in his right. "A bit, yeah. Nothing like Jason or Breekie here. It's really just a kind of a sixth sense."

O'Cleary gave Peter a confused look. "Do you mean more than normal, or are you just having the craic?"

Simon smiled slightly. "Is that why you've gotten faster?"

Peter shrugged. "Probably." *You could tell them about Jadis now. No, even with all we've seen, they'd think I was crazy if I mentioned Jadis. No need to start planting seeds of doubt.*

O'Cleary scowled. "You coulda said something about it," he murmured.

Scott raised an eyebrow. "Very well. On to the next item."

"Hold on," Peter countered. "I think it's only fair we get to ask a question, too."

Scott looked taken aback for a moment but shrugged and said, "I suppose. Proceed."

"Thanks," Peter quipped. "Just curious, why is the dryad here? And I don't just mean in the room. Why is she with you?"

"Technically that was—"

"Oh, for pity's sake, man. If you keep up like that, we'll be here all day," O'Cleary complained.

Scott's lips made a fine line. "Fine. She was sent by elvish general, Almurë, to help us deal with Jason. Satisfactory?"

Once again, Leuoradew spoke without moving her lips.

"Forces press around you from all sides; ancient magics, innumerable futures, and forgotten powers cling to your every step."

As before, the sensation of her words filled Peter with an unfamiliar sense of discomfort.

Peter met the dryad's unblinking gaze. *Why is he ignoring her interruptions? Am I imagining her talking? It's not the fruit. It started before that.* Still, he sat the remains of the fruit down on the table slowly and shook his head slightly before he spoke. "Sure," Peter replied as he scratched his beard. *What is going on?* "What's next on your list?"

"Yes," Scott replied. "As I was saying, it is important we establish leadership here now that we have created a power vacuum.

"Your blade is bound to dreams and shadows."

"Frankly, the way I see it, I should be in charge here, Captain Blair, are you listening?"

Peter blinked, realizing he'd matched the dryad's unblinking stare. "Yeah, sorry, but her interruptions are a little distracting."

Scott's brow furrowed in confusion. Caraticus' head whipped around though. His expression warped into a scowl at Leuoradew. "Are you speaking to him?"

She blinked once slowly and turned her gaze to Caraticus. In that brief moment, Peter found himself breathing a small sigh of relief.

"Yes," she said this time with moving lips.

Scott leered over at her. "Can't it wait? This is important." His surprisingly soft tone did not match the glare in his eyes.

Caraticus' own tone was not as gentle, nor was the expression of horror Peter noticed carved into Breekie's face. "This may be a first for you, Leuoradew, but I know you are aware that the same laws of divination are to be applied that would be among the elves," Caraticus said, his voice laced with a surprising steeliness.

Leuoradew nodded. "Of course. Apologies. Diviners are rare even among my own. His presence is… Exciting would be the best word in their tongue."

Scott's eyes went wide at this before his face fell into an even darker scowl.

Caraticus turned back to the table and tried unsuccessfully to take on a more amiable expression. "I'm sorry, Leuoradew has a rather unique arcane skill known as divination."

Breekie perked up at this; lowering his third fruit from his mouth, "That is good! Duelma Umindrabo will want to know about this," he said with a wide smile.

Caraticus' eyebrows rose, but he returned to silence.

Scott sucked on his teeth for a moment and said, "One of her abilities is a sort of telepathy. I'm sorry she was distracting you, Captain Blair, but I'd really like to—"

Peter's eyes jerked back to the dryad as he tried to gauge her blank expression.

Simon interrupted with a wave of his hand. "I'm sorry, Mister Scott, but are you telling us she can read minds?"

Dory added for the first time, his Southern accent coloring his words. "Now, hang on. I've already had one bad egg messing with my head. Don't need no talking plant reading my mind, too. That ain't right."

Scott shook his head. "No, no, it's not like that. She can't read thoughts, so to speak. It's more that she—"

"Are you serious! You expect us to believe a word you say? Breekie, is this anything like what Jason was doing?" O'cleary said.

Before Breekie had a chance to swallow and reply, Caraticus stood from his seat. The sudden movement drew the attention of everyone in the room.

"Calm yourselves. I realize this may be something of a shock, but the dryads are a peaceful race. And what Oscar said is true. Diviners do not read minds, although they can send thoughts to people and, in some cases, have them sent back." He raised his hands in a placating gesture. "This is nothing like Jason's ability, trust me. I have experience with her people. I very much doubt she'll be doing it anymore with how you've all reacted."

"I've had enough of your nonsense," Breekie bellowed in Dwarvish. His fists slammed the table as he pulled himself onto his chair to address Caraticus. "Do you really expect them to trust you when you conceal yourself from them?" Then, realizing what he'd done, he switched back to English and finished: "Tell them the truth, elf."

The room went silent as a graveyard. Everyone looked back and forth between Breekie and Caraticus, who stood bent over with fingers steepled on the table.

O'Cleary forced a laugh. "Breekie, now's not the time for jokes. He's clearly human. I mean, just—"

"That was not well mannered of you, dwarf," Caraticus said in a lilting language Peter surprisingly found himself able to understand.

Then the man blew a strange soft note out of his mouth as he raised a hand past his face, to his beanie, and pulled the hat off. His face changed ever so slightly; his features growing sharper, and his five-o'clock shadow disappearing.

Around his neck, the tightly bound braided necklace shifted, and it became clear it was made of eggplant-colored hair. His naked head bore short cut brown hair, and two prominent pointed ears protruded almost three inches from where they attached to his head. At his side, Dory jerked back in surprise. As a result, his chair almost tipped over.

"As usual, plans do not survive contact with reality," Caraticus mumbled to himself before he addressed the room. "I was only maintaining the minor illusion to make the rest of you more comfortable, but as Breekie has so graciously pointed out, and I suspect some of you may have already guessed, I am not human."

He took a deep breath. "My name is not Caraticus Whitaker either, although you may continue to call me such. It is Elborin Essërod, Slayer of Dumirgal Blacktooth, Valk of the ócom-véla under General Almurë." He paused. "And other titles which lack meaning to this room. I came here to get a measure of how your kind has changed during our absence."

Peter broke into laughter. After a full minute of tear-jerking mirth, he came to a stop, wiped a tear from his eye, and looked around.

"Well? Anyone else have anything they want to put out on the table? Any dragons or aliens in the room? Any shadows over my shoulder guiding my actions?"

No one replied. "No? Just an elf in disguise here to evaluate the human species? Well, given his eagerness to assist us after killing Jason, I'd say we're measuring up all right."

Peter gave Caraticus a slight bow. "I knew there was something odd about you — 'Got my spear from an elf.' He chuckled again then shook his head in amusement. "Sorry, Scott, back to your point. I think the question of who fills the power vacuum is moot."

Scott stared back at him, mouth ajar. Similar expressions were on Gunter and Dory's faces. "What? Do you want to talk about the mysterious stranger who turns out isn't a human? You all just accepted the Jean Grey tree. Why should a guy with pointy ears be more shocking? He's obviously not our enemy, and there's no denying he's a military man — sorry, elf. Whatever. My point is, I think, Elborin?"

Elborin nodded.

"I think Elborin will let us know if his unique heritage factors into anything we discuss here. And if not, I'm confident Breekie will call him on it," Peter added with a wink at Breekie, who sat with a smug smirk directed at the elf. Breekie nodded eagerly at the suggestion.

"Good, then can we please proceed? I, for one, want to know more about this elvish general you both mentioned," Peter said. A mumble of agreements and nods made their way around the table. "Faaantastic. As I was saying, the point is moot, Scott. I see no reason for anyone to remain here." Peter stood and removed what was left of the fruit from the plate then slid the empty plate closer to himself.

"We should send those not suited for combat back to Paragon." Peter pointed at the plate and placed three pieces of fruit on it. "Tighten defenses here, in Macon."

Peter placed his cup a bit ahead of the plate and placed fruit on two sides of it. "With a skeleton crew and then," he grabbed a napkin from the table, unfolded it and put the remaining fruits on it, "my team plans on proceeding to Atlanta."

Scott followed his actions and waited for him to finish. He and Elborin exchanged a look with raised eyebrows at the mention of Atlanta. "You want to abandon Macon? Why? What makes your city any better?"

Peter sat back in his chair and steepled his fingers in front of him. "Well, defenses for one. This place is a nightmare logistically and a target at that. Orks know we're here. Jason made that very clear."

Dory took a loud sip of water and cleared his throat. "And? We've got Scott's forces here and you. Any orks show up, we'll send 'em packing with their tails between their legs."

"Do orks have tails?" Gunter's question shot curiously from the side of the room.

"Not the ones I've seen," answered Scott with a chuckle.

Peter watched Scott. *Come on. You came back for a bloody reason.*

A frosty breeze passed through the room, giving everyone a slight shiver. "And winter is around the corner. Your generators can't last forever. We have stable power in Paragon," Peter added. "You can't stay here."

Scott's jaw worked as he gave it serious consideration. "No. We can't. There are too many monsters, and if Atlanta cannot be retaken…"

Peter's heart fluttered at those words. He'd been afraid of something like this, but he had hoped Atlanta would be in a better state than Paragon or Macon.

"What's to stop them just following us to Paragon?" Dory asked.

"Speed, for one. It took us a few days to get here, but it'll be quicker going back, even with more people," Peter replied. "Especially now that the strange fog seems to have lifted."

"That was my kind's doing," the dryad chimed in with a strange smirk.

Were they warning us? Or retaliating against Jason?

"That's a lot of women and children for even a day's travel. Is Paragon really that much better fortified?" Dory inquired.

"Yes," Peter said firmly. "And we've got some strong magic users there too. Doctor Walker, one of them, assured me that she's taken measures to ensure monsters are redirected away from the town."

Elborin perked up at this, "You have a caster powerful enough to cast a diversion ward over an entire city?" he asked, his eyes widening.

"Yes," replied Breekie. "Duelma Umindrabo Duridgrihulda is the most ancient and powerful dwarf I have ever met," he said puffing up his chest.

Elborin's eyes went wide, and he glanced between Peter and Breekie but kept his mouth tightly closed.

"If we're sending people back to Paragon, I'm going with them," chimed in Gunter from his spot on the windowsill. "You're not shipping me off to orks and monsters in Atlanta."

Peter fought the urge to roll his eyes. "You can do what you want, but I'm going to Atlanta."

"Now hold on, Cap, Scott just said there are enemy forces in that direction, which isn't even my point. We've gone way over our time budget. Paragon probably thinks we're dead, and if we keep pressing on away from the base, it won't be long until we are," O'Cleary countered. "We can't just go diving into more unknown enemy-occupied territory."

At Peter's left, Simon nodded. "He's right, captain. The plan was to be gone for a few days."

"Aye, we're almost double that," O'Cleary went on. "We already lost Justin. How much more are we gonna risk?"

"It's risky. I'm not saying it isn't," Peter said, nodded, and looked at Scott. "What's the state of Atlanta?"

Scott shook his head slowly, a faraway look in his eyes. "Not good. It's merged with an ancient elvish city. I don't understand how — maybe it grew out of the ground or something. It's unearthly." He paused and pulled some images from the back of his mind. "Tall stone walls all over. But the worst part? It's infested with orks. The entirety of what was once downtown, and more, is full of them and something else." He shook his head. The blood drained from his face. "That's just the city itself. There's the wandering groups of bandits — actual humans collecting people and trading them to the orks for God only knows what reason — between here and there."

Scott's lips pressed together as he clenched his jaw in frustration. "We lost some people when we got too close. Disappeared. Captured. Killed."

Scott looked at Elborin with a smile, "If it wasn't for Elborin and the elves, we'd have been massacred. He agreed to help us free Macon if some of us would help the elvish army retake the city afterward."

"How much did you map out between here and there?" Simon inquired.

"Plenty, enough to get close enough to see Atlanta and back. It's just dangerous, the closer you get."

Peter drummed his fingers on the table for a moment before he spoke back up. "Good enough for me. I still think we should go. Send civilians back to Paragon for now. You could leave some of your forces here in case things go poorly in Atlanta, and my men and I can join your return to Atlanta, Scott."

"What about your town? If they're doing as well as you say, could they send reinforcements to help us?" Elborin asked slowly. "We have sufficient forces to take the city, but the unfamiliar territory slows us down. Your people may not be used to how things have changed yet, but there are many still alive within the city that could use your help."

Peter bit his lip. *Reinforcements from Paragon? I'm sure most of SNW would be eager to help, but as for a sizable fighting force? Every bit would help, but we'd need to leave some forces intact. There's no way the council would go for it, though, coming from me.* "I can't guarantee any kind of reinforcements. They'll take in refugees, but beyond that…"

Simon glanced at Peter, his head slightly tilted, "Why don't we return to Paragon and make the case ourselves?"

Because if it comes from me, it'll be harder to convince them. Peter's jaw muscles worked as he chose his words. "Because every day we delay more of our countrymen die. Leefield, Alex, Ian, and the others could still be alive. We can't waste time where we could be helping."

"And if they aren't? If there's no one left to save?" said Simon.

Peter's lip curled at this like he'd smelled something rancid. "Then we go back, regroup, and figure out what's next." He shook his head. "Even if there's no one left, there's still equipment worth getting out."

"You gotta point there. If we could get into HQ, we'd have enough firepower for a small war," O'Cleary replied running a hand over his chin. "God bless the general's paranoia."

Peter held up a fist and started counting. "So, reasons to go to Atlanta are as follows — information, rescue, and equipment. I know it's a risk, and I won't force anyone to come. Honestly, it's probably a one-way trip, but I say we take it."

"Say no more. I'm in," replied O'Cleary.

"Someone's gotta stitch you up when it's over," said Simon with a shrug as Peter looked to the rest of the table.

"Umindrabo said follow you. I stay with you," said Breekie, stroking his beard.

Gunter stood from his relaxed lean at the window. "I'll make the case for reinforcements to the council. They'll be more receptive if it's not coming from SNW." He raised his shoulders almost to his ears. "Can't promise it'll do any good, though."

Peter smiled to himself. *I'll have to give him orders for Steven and William.*

Dory removed his hat and rubbed his temples, "You're crazy. You're all absolutely nuts. But if Scott says we should go to Paragon, we'll go. But I'm not going anywhere near Lanta. No sense risking more lives. Especially when those people could keep the rest of us alive."

"If I might?" Elborin asked. "Since it seems your minds are made up, I'll be returning with you, Captain Blair. What you know as Atlanta, I know as Vulacia. I can introduce you all to General Almurë and prepare you for battle against the orks and their weeping king."

An elvish general? That's reason enough to go. I'll ask him about the ork king later.

"Why didn't you say something sooner?" Peter said, throwing his hands up in exasperation.

"I wanted to see you form your own conclusions," Elborin replied. "I still have much to learn about your people."

Fair enough. Can't say I wouldn't have done the same.

"Well…" said Peter, trying to fill the silence as he considered what to say next, nodding absently. "Our priority is still reconnaissance… but this is good. All the more reason for Paragon to send reinforcements."

"Agreed," said Simon. "And your fighters as well, Scott."

The room's attention turned to Scott, who sat deep in thought. After a moment's hesitation, he cleared his throat and looked to Dory. "My men will escort Gunter and the rest of the town to Paragon. I will accompany Captain Blair and the rest of you to Atlanta. For now, we should keep our group small. If Paragon does send reinforcements, I'll instruct my forces to accompany them."

Cararticus' brow furrowed at this, a sour look in his eyes.

"I gave my word I would return with you, Elborin, or would you prefer Caraticus? I did not say my men would."

"The understanding was the latter," Elborin said. "Elborin is fine."

"Yes," Scott said. "Those willing will return with the Paragon reinforcements."

"Very well," Elborin said. His face stern as his eyes drifted over the group.

Interesting, Peter thought. "Fine. Jenni is injured, so she will return to Paragon. Gunter?"

"I'll keep her out of trouble," he replied sarcastically.

"Shawn will want to help her, which takes care of that," O'Cleary chimed in.

Peter stood, drumming his fingers on the table. "Good. Dory, let your people know they have twenty-four hours before departure. Bring only supplies and what is absolutely necessary."

"That's not a lot of time. Most aren't going to want to go," Dory countered.

"Then tell them Scott came back because there are more orks on the way, and there's a safer place. If they stay, they die," Peter said.

"I'll back you up," Scott added as he met eyes with Dory. "It's for their own good."

Dory frowned, released his hat from nervous fingers, and set it back on his head. "I still think y'all are nuts."

"You're probably right. Breekie, I think you should go with the Paragon group. I'd feel better if they had someone familiar with the arcane with them, and you can help convince Doctor Walker to back us up."

Breekie frowned. "I would go with you if you asked. Much more knowledge is gained by going forward, less by going back."

"I know, and you may rejoin us later, but for now, you're the only one I can trust to do this. I have a feeling we'll need her help."

Breekie thumped a fist on his chest. "Then it shall be done. I will see them safely to Paragon, then bring you powerful reinforcements."

"That's what I like to hear," said Peter as he clapped him on the shoulder.

"If you'll excuse me, I'd like to say a few farewells before departure," said Elborin, standing with the rest of them. Nods were exchanged around the table, and everyone began to gather themselves to leave. As everyone began moving away from the table, Elborin approached Breekie. "A word, Breekie, before you depart?"

Breekie looked to Peter, who shrugged. "You can catch up and update me when you two are done." *I don't like that. Wait. No, it's Breekie. Calm down, Peter. He'd tell me if there was something I need to know.*

Breekie pulled on his beard and walked with Elborin as Peter and the others made their way out.

"Where's Jenni? We need to update her," Peter said, turning to Simon.

"Follow me," Simon replied.

As they made their way to the door, Peter cast one last look over his shoulder at the dryad, and her voice entered his mind again. *"We will speak again soon, Peter Blair."*

Yeah, I have a feeling we will, Peter mused.

When they reached Jenni, they found she'd been busy teaching Shawn different orders in German for Hauch. They filled her in quickly on the plan.

"You, Gunter, Breekie, and Shawn will head back to Paragon. I want you to inform Doctor Walker, William, and Steven about what's happening. We'll need you to gather as many volunteers as possible to back us up. Let them know we'll have an army of elves backing us up, if that helps. Most importantly, though, there are people who need our help."

"You want Steven to remain at Paragon or follow you?"

Peter rubbed his beard contemplatively. "Have him stay. He'll have gotten on the council's good side by now, and it'll help to have you both there smoothing over the transition with all the newcomers. I'll have a list of orders for you before departure."

"Fine. I'll do it. It's better this way." Jenni sat down heavily, fidgeting with a silver ring on her right hand. "I'm going to find Justin's killer, Peter," she said softly, her scowl directed at the ground. Peter looked at her more closely, and made note of her dry, bloodshot eyes full of determination and rage.

"We killed Jason, Jenni. It's over," he replied.

"No." She shook her head, still twisting the ring. "No, not until I know for sure. It doesn't add up. Why poison Justin and leave the rest of you when he thought he had control?" she choked out. "There's something else going on, and Justin would want me to find out."

Peter sighed. "If you want to spend your time trying to track down the poison, so be it. As long as you promise me to wait until everyone is back safely before you make any enemies. You know my opinion on it, and I know you're smart enough to not cause any trouble doing it, but I want your word."

"You have it," she said as she grabbed his outstretched hand and shook it.

"Maybe while you're at it, see if my missing vial of venom turns up," Peter added.

"Maybe," Jenni replied, her scowl softening.

Behind her, Shawn shifted awkwardly. "I'm not going back to Paragon," the teenager mumbled so softly Peter wondered if the boy realized he'd said it out loud.

He turned to him. "Yes, you are," Peter said firmly.

"Why?" Shawn shot back, his voice rising. "What's the point? There's no one there for me. I have nothing to do there. I'm safer here with you," he exclaimed, his voice rising as he looked to O'Cleary for support.

"Do you really believe that?" Peter replied.

Shawn shrugged. "I, I don't know, but at least if I die out here with you, I'm dying for a reason."

Peter put a hand on Shawn's shoulder and lowered himself to Shawn's eye level. "Well said, but you can't come this time. You want to die for a cause? So be it. Train with Breekie every chance you get on the trip back to Paragon. That way, you can come with him when the time comes."

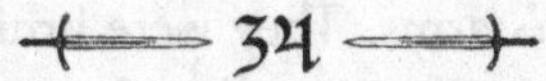

34

CONFESSIONS

Sarah watched Steven clamber to his feet, the same grin on his face as every other time she knocked him down. "I'd help you up, but I'd have to use magic to do it," she teased.

He chuckled. "What exactly did you just do to me?" he asked as he wiped the dirt off his arm.

"I increased the air between us."

Steven's eyes widened in surprise. "Be careful with that. I know the air is different from arcane energy, but… well, just be careful."

Despite the risks, he didn't even flinch when I asked if he'd be willing to spar with me. He must be right. I'll be extra careful with that.

"Want to take a break?" she asked. Steven glanced down at his watch. "Excellent idea," he replied, "That run was exhilarating," he added as he glanced around the field.

Men and women were gathered there where they sparred under the coaching of William and Cheekie. There was a new sense of urgency in these exercises; the news of Macon and Atlanta beyond sat heavily on the minds of all.

Those present were dressed in light armor made either from bits of basilisk or converted sports gear. As the drills progressed, William and Cheekie could be seen as they walked up and down the line, shouted instructions, and corrected mistakes.

Sarah and Steven had made sure to give the training grounds a wide berth. With Sarah's use of arcane energy in their sparring, she relied heavily on manipulating the earth, she did not want to disturb the others. As a result, the soil around them was damaged: large chunks of earth protruded from the ground, some of which reached Sarah's own height or higher. Sarah's use of earth for blocking or striking left behind a scarred circle of the land that took up forty feet of the field.

Steven's massive size was perfect for her training. It forced her to use small bursts of arcane manipulation. The practice was making her stronger; it increased her endurance, most importantly, as this allowed her to do more casting for longer without exhausting herself.

Sarah glanced at Steven's arms. They were bruised in a dozen places with purple and brown welts, some the size of her fist.

"Do you want me to help with your bruises?" she asked, her voice underscored with concern.

"No, they're just bruises. Your energy is best saved for bigger things," he replied warmly.

Thwack! Sarah winced at the sound of wood colliding with a skull. Then came a shrill scream, pulling Sarah's attention. In the bunch of trainees closest to them, a man lay on the ground, still as a doormat while one of the first responders on site rushed to his side.

Steven and Sarah made their way toward the able-bodied people gathered around the fallen man. As they drew closer, the crowd scattered backward to give the pair of them space. Hunched over the body was one of the medical students assigned to supervise these training sessions. "I'm sorry, there's too much blood. God, there's so much blood. I'm just a nursing student. There's nothing I can do. I'm not a surgeon," he protested desperately.

Oh, no, that's a lot of blood. Sarah found herself thinking as they reached the injured man.

He lay sprawled on the ground at an unnatural angle, with bright red blood pooled around his head, where it mixed with brown dirt and trampled ugly grass. The sight of it sent a wave of nausea through Sarah's gut.

"Crap," murmured Steven as he lowered himself to his knees next to the responder, where he began assessing the wound. "Don't worry, we've got it from here," he said to the man as Sarah guided the tall woman who'd dealt the blow back a few steps. "Lateral crack in his skull. Bleeding pretty bad," Steven called to Sarah.

"It's too late. W-we can't move him, and I'm not equipped to put a skull back together." The medic explained without even a glance up.

"Hold his head up for me," Sarah instructed as she stepped away from the other woman and slid her wand out from the leather holster on her hip that Steven designed for her.

"That's not a good idea. Like he said, we shouldn't move him," Steven said. His large hands removed a bandana from his pocket, which he used to clean around the wound.

"I'm telling you, it's too late," insisted the responder.

Steven looked up from the wound. "Then get out of the way," he commanded.

The man obeyed and muttered apologetically as he stood and backed away from the body.

"I'm sorry! I didn't mean to. He dodged into it," protested the tall woman.

Before things could escalate, William arrived at the scene, pushed his way through the group and barked orders. "Don't worry about him," William called out to the onlookers as he waved them back with both arms. "The medics will take care of him. Remember, if your ally goes down in battle, you keep fighting. You do not stop and stare. If you can, move your fight towards him if it means you can protect him. If you can't tell, then assume they're dead and focus on keeping yourself alive. Now go on! Back to it!" he ordered in a strained voice.

As the crowd slowly returned to their previous positions, William looked down at Sarah, Steven, and the responder. "Philip, let them handle this. You've done all you can," he commanded and pulled the responder farther back. *All he could? He didn't do anything!*

Philip shoved blood stained implements haphazardly into his bag. William placed a firm hand on his shoulder, and helped him to his feet to then guide him away. As they went Philip threw a worried glance over his shoulder back at the injured man.

As Sarah and Steven worked, the training resumed. Cheekie or William occasionally pulled a pair of fighters apart to demonstrate how they could improve.

Brushing the hair out of her face, Sarah addressed the remaining panicked woman, who she vaguely recognized from one of her college classes. "It's all right, Courtney. We've got this." Sarah felt the cold morning air slide across her face as she brought the point of her wand to the man's forehead. "Steven, describe the wound in detail to me."

"What are you doing?" Courtney said hoarsely, she didn't dare move from her spot in the trampled grass, obviously nervous of Sarah's presence. "I don't think he'd like you casting one of your spells on him."

Sarah blew air out of her nose as she tried to concentrate over the smell of sweat and the sound of clashing weapons. "I'm healing him, not putting a spell on him, and if I don't, he may not care about anything ever again," she exclaimed, her eyes locked with Steven's.

"It's a jagged four-centimeter crack in the skull. That's about all I can tell you with the way it's bleeding."

"Good enough. Ready?"

"Absolutely," Steven replied as he shifted to hold the man in place, his hands stained red with sticky warm blood.

"Okay, hold him still," she said calmly.

Sarah tapped into the arcane flow, guiding the energy as it coursed through her.

"Heal," she commanded the power. Her word led it through the wand into the man's skull. The energy slid over the skull. It glowed as it memorized the material and converted it. Blue light knitted into bone as the crack in the skull shrunk until gone and the bleeding was brought to an end.

Beneath the healed bone, the energy continued to do its work. It reconnected nerves and smoothed over the damage. The man was left with a bald spot among his thin gray and white hair.

A few seconds later, the man's eyes fluttered open. Confusion and fear made their home on his pale face. "I— What...? What happened?" he asked as he looked back and forth between Sarah and Steven. His eyes grew wide at the blood on Steven's hands as Steven sat him up.

It was then that Sarah finally recognized him. *The old man who couldn't remember my name. What's he doing out here training?*

"You dodged the wrong way and brought your skull into the path of your sparring partner's practice sword," Steven explained dryly as he rose from his knees where he whipped the blood off his hands. Once his hand was more or less clean, he offered it to the man and lifted him to his feet, where he stood there wavering back and forth.

"Speech seems all right," Steven commented and held up three fingers not far from the man's face. "How many fingers am I holding up?"

"Three," the man replied weakly. "I feel light-headed."

"You lost a substantial amount of blood. Now tell me when my fingers pass out of your vision. Can you remember your name?"

"Delford," the man replied as Steven tested his peripheral vision. "Now."

"Excellent, Mister Delford. So far so good. What day of the week is it?"

"Saturday?" the old man replied hesitantly.

"Correct." Steven handed him a bandana, and the man began to clean the blood from his skull, which left his hair a rusty pinkish color. "How do you feel?"

"Nauseous." Delford moved his hand around his head and searched for the wound. "It's gone? How did it— You... you cast a spell on me?" he asked in a panic, his face drained of what little color it had left.

"You can thank Miss Young for that," Steven said as he picked up the wooden practice sword Delford had dropped.

Delford looked skittishly back and forth between them, like a mouse cornered by a lion and an owl, not sure which to be more frightened of.

"Thank you," he managed to choke out. "P-please, don't tell anyone."

Sarah raised her eyebrows slightly. "I'm sorry, I couldn't catch that last bit," she said, her hands behind her back. *Great, he's embarrassed because he thinks it's witchcraft.*

"Please, don't tell anyone." He cast a look at the tall woman. "Courtney, please. If my daughter finds out I was injured, she won't let me go with them to Atlanta. She won't let me find my grandsons."

"That's what you're worried about?" the tall woman said with a furrowed brow and mouth agape. "What about all your talks about witchcraft? She just used her magic on you."

Delford glanced at Sarah, barely able to meet her eyes. "I was wrong. I must have been. Feeding the hungry? Healing the injured? She's doing God's work. She can't be a witch."

Courtney took a step back, her face pale as a sheet. "You said she's in league with the devil. Lord, help me, she's, she's…" The girl's mouth clamped shut, and she dashed away.

Delford winced, still unable to meet Sarah's eye, his face pale from loss of blood. "I'm grateful, thank you. I'm sorry for what I said before. If you'll excuse me, I think I need some rest." With that, the old man set off after the tall girl.

Sarah swallowed, not sure what to say. *I knew people were talking, but I never imagined I scared people this much. I'd prefer people think I'm doing miracles than witchcraft… but that could be almost as dangerous with the churches back on their feet. I wonder what* Doctor *Walker would think…*

Steven locked eyes with Sarah, but before he could speak, William rejoined them. Steven glanced at Sarah who had retreated into her own head space, so Steven greeted William.

"Thanks, Will. Looks like he'll be all right," Steven said happily.

"Good." William smiled then pointed to the edge of the field. "Looks like you've got company."

Steven turned and looked past where Sarah faced the trodden ground, deep in thought. "All right. Thanks again. I'll catch you later."

"Good luck," William replied as he redirected his attention to the drills.

"Hey, Firestick," Steven said teasingly as he walked over to Sarah, "we've got company," he added with a knowing look toward the edge of the practice field.

Sarah smiled weakly, her mind still troubled by the woman's words. She followed Steven's gaze to find Dr. Walker, Dr. Gibson, Al, and a fourth figure at a parking lot at the edge of the field.

A wave from Dr. Gibson was all it took to get the pair moving towards the parking lot.

Behind them, William's voice rang out instructions. "Your opponent is taller than you. Use this to your advantage. You have a lower center of gravity."

"Good morning, you two," called Dr. Walker jovially from a small crowd as they drew closer.

"Good morning," Sarah and Steven replied in unison.

"Glad you're here, Mister Thomas," Dr. Gibson said as he ran his thumb and forefinger over his mustache. "Still no news from Rory's scouting party, but the refugees from Macon should be arriving in an hour."

He nodded enthusiastically as he spoke. "I've already let Jessica know. She needs to finish recovering from her injuries before we will even consider sending her after Lieutenant Rory, if that's still her desire after what we heard from Captain Blair. I still can't believe only half of her scouting party made it back."

Steven's face wrinkled with concern. "An hour?"

"Indeed," Dr. Walker replied in her most professor-like voice.

Al interjected, "We've had a hectic day. Trying to help move in a baker's dozen of confused dwarves and debating how to respond to this call to arms and the incoming refugees…" He shook his head then grasped his left arm, making a pained expression.

"Are you all right?" Sarah asked, taking a step forward.

"Fine, Fine. Don't worry about me," he said with a grimace. "Just get weird pains now and then."

"You do know I am a physician, Mister Al," said Dr. Gibson.

"If you'd like, I can pray for it when we're done," Chimed in a slightly balding olive-skinned man with a clean face near the back of their group.

"Just Al is fine, Mister Mayor. Pastor Dylan, like I said, I'm fine," he insisted dismissively, still clinging to his arm. "Where was I? …Ah, yes," he said, finally releasing his grip on his arm. "As you know, the dog, Hauch, arrived with a handwritten letter from Captain Peter."

"It's pronounced Hauch," Steven corrected. "But we're very aware. Are we heading to the gate to meet them?"

Dr. Walker took Sarah by the elbow, pulled her to the back of the group, and waited there.

Sarah watched as Al, Steven, and the pastor continued on. Dr. Gibson stopped and turned to Sarah and Dr. Walker. "I was hoping you two would wait at the gate for these new arrivals. With how much your presence helped with the dwarves, and not really knowing what kind of mess Captain Peter is sending…" Dr. Gibson trailed off.

Dr. Walker smiled widely up at him. "Of course, Doctor Gibson, I expect you will be joining us as well."

Dr. Gibson nodded. "Yes. I think that would be prudent. But first, I must meet with the council to further discuss this request for reinforcements." He removed a tiny comb from his pocket and began combing his mustache as he spoke. "I'll do my best to convince them, but I just don't know…"

"Good, then why don't you go ahead to your meeting? Sarah and I will be along shortly. There a few things I'd like to discuss with her that I'm sure would only distract your already busy mind."

Mayor Gibson let out a relieved sigh. "Yes, thank you. We must see to a number of things if we really are about to gain a thousand or more mouths to feed, shelter, and clothe… Thank you," he said again, leaned down, and clasped the ancient woman's hands before he rushed off, looking like a man on the verge of a panic attack.

Dr. Walker and Sarah were now more or less alone as they made their way slowly to the small golf cart Dr. Walker relied on for transportation.

"How are our new friends?" Sarah asked. She was nervous as usual about whatever it was Dr. Walker wanted to talk to her about and a bit tired from the healing she'd done a few moments ago.

Dr. Walker waved a hand and rolled her eyes in mock exasperation as she carried herself forward on her cane. "They're a vexatious lot. Hard-headed and eager, though. Do me a kindness, and if they ask, do not tell them I made you your wands, else they'll all want some. In fact, best to keep them stowed away as much as possible when around them. Wouldn't want to embarrass Cheekie." She sighed deeply, like a whale coming up for air. "If it comes to it, though, I am sure they'll march to Atlanta with the rest."

Sarah nodded and quickly holstered the wand she'd tucked into the back of her belt.

"I'm not here to converse with you about my hard-headed kinfolk, though," she went on as she climbed shakily into the passenger side of the small vehicle. "No, Sarah, I am afraid I have some confessions to make, and I find myself convinced they are best made to you."

Sarah took her place in the cold driver's seat and started the small vehicle, then directed it towards the north gate. She waved good-bye as they passed Steven in the midst of an intense conversation between the pastor and Al.

I wonder what he thinks of Pastor Dylan. And why does she want to confess to me and not some of her own? As the cold air swirled around them, Sarah examined Dr. Walker. *Has she gotten even smaller?* She wondered. The woman already looked wrinkled and small but always stood strong and proud with her head held high.

The sight of Dr. Walker wracked with shivers in the small seat at her side reminded Sarah of the other healthy young dwarves. They were a sturdy, thick bunch, very unlike the Dr. Walker Sarah knew; a shriveled old woman who, despite her strength, grew frailer by the day.

"Does it have to do with my casting?" Sarah inquired, as she hoped it didn't.

"No, my confessions have little to do with you and your growth, dear woman," Dr. Walker replied. "Where to begin…" she murmured to herself as they rolled smoothly down the road.

"Criske," Dr. Walker murmured. "First things first. I apologize if this comes as a shock, although I doubt it will to one as keen as yourself, Miss Young. It would seem I am dying."

Sarah caught herself before she reflexively slammed on the brakes. She swallowed and nodded slowly. It made sense. "Why?" she choked out softly.

Dr. Walker smiled kindly. "Good question. Old age mostly, I suspect. I have lived far longer than any dwarf has the right. I have sustained myself with elvish coma methods, exercise, and good eating, but ultimately it was always some part of the Therin-Selu that sustained me, and now that it is gone, time is catching up with me, as it has done with so many of my friends before me."

Sarah knew it was true. She'd kept the thought of it at bay, but it lingered at the edge of her mind, pressed in, searched for validation. Now that she knew the truth, she felt a stew of emotions. Sorrow, relief, worry, fear, and doubt. They all swirled around in her mind.

"What happens when a dwarf dies?" she asked, hoping she'd shed a little insight on more than just what happens to dwarves.

Dr. Walker removed a chocolate bar from the folds of her robes and began to munch on it. "We are taken to the dwarf capital, encased in crystal, and added to the library of the dead."

She said it so matter-of-factly that it took Sarah a moment to realize she'd dodged the question. But before she could point it out, Dr. Walker spoke again. "I know that wasn't the answer you were hoping for, but I do hope you can indulge an old lady with her humor," she said with a twinkle in her eye.

"Of course," Sarah replied meekly.

"You were asking about the afterlife, though. I'm honestly surprised it took you this long to ask. I've never died, Sarah. I could tell you my thoughts on religion, but it is not my job to sway humanity in that regard. You must decide for yourself what you believe."

"That makes sense," Sarah replied disappointedly.

Dr. Walker went on. "My second confession has several parts, so do bear with an old woman should she digress."

Sarah stopped at a crosswalk to let a small family cross the street. "Of course, Duelma Umindrabo," she said respectfully.

"I have been preparing the world for the return of my kind for the last millennium." She tapped her cane on the floorboard softly. "There was opposition, which forced me to be more nuanced in my efforts over the last century."

"Opposition?" Sarah asked. The thought that anyone could oppose Dr. Walker if she set her mind to it filled her with dread.

"Yes, whatever one does in life, there is always opposition of one kind or another. That is a conversation for another time, though. I've had many dealings with opposition — cults, politicians, ignorance itself — that my journals could enlighten you on. Hopefully, most no longer pose a threat to us now that the Therin-Selu has ended."

Journals? She kept a record of her life? I have to read those, Sarah thought excitedly.

"It was my aging that warned me of the spell's unraveling. It began slowly, but after thousands of years without it, one notices the smallest changes quickly, so I set about building Paragon, gathering men and women who could prepare a place of knowledge and security in hopes that it could be a place of peace, where the faye and your own could come together in harmony. But my life has taught me peace cannot exist without warriors to defend it." She paused and swallowed the last of her chocolate eagerly.

"Here is my last major confession, Miss Young. It is a deed that I knew to be necessary but haunts me all the same as the grave draws nearer. I…" She took a deep breath, staring off into the distance as their cart came to a park at the north gate.

"I arranged the birth of a warrior, Hannah." She looked up to Sarah, meeting her confused look. "No, I am not her secret blood mother or anything so simple as that. I led her parents to one another. A cunning military man and a brilliant woman doctor with a military background — the perfect parental pairing for if my kind returned. I made sure they settled here in Paragon to raise their daughter." Dr. Walker reached back into her robes and removed another piece of chocolate and took a large bite.

"I thought I'd done all I needed. I fostered her interests, manipulated her influences from the sidelines, and guided events that defined her motivation all in hopes she would grow to be a warrior and the leader of this city your people needed when the time came." She let out a deep sigh. "But she died, saving her brother, Peter."

Sarah let out a soft gasp. *I didn't know he had a sister.*

"So, I was forced to repeat the process with him, as I knew time was running out, and it was too late to start over. If his sister couldn't be there, he had to be. But, before I knew it, the Shattering was upon us."

Dr. Walker took Sarah's hand as she helped her out of the cart.

"Then you appeared, Sarah. Just like Hannah's death — random, not according to plan, plain and ordinary, so very, very human, a woman whose existence I had no influence on. And it is you who presents the true power capable of defending your people, a connection to the arcane unlike any I have ever seen." She leaned heavily on her cane for a moment.

Stern eyes stared up at Sarah. "Do not misunderstand me. Peter Blair's gifts are extraordinary, but I fear he will not live long enough to fully realize them. There is too much of his sister's influence on him. That is why I have left him to his own devices and focused on you, my dear. The task of protecting humanity as they adjust to this old reality falls to you."

"Why are you telling me this about Peter?" Sarah asked as they moved slowly towards the gate.

"Because I fear I will not be able to tell him myself. Should he prove me wrong and return to help you, he needs to know so the two of you do not make my same mistakes. Prepare all that you can, but be open to the random happenings of the world. But most of all, so that you do not follow his and his sister's path," she said solemnly, leaning heavily on her cane as she took a trembling step forward.

"What path is that?" Sarah replied. "I don't understand."

"The path of the martyr. Peter's sister died to save his life, and I believe he desires a similar fate for himself. It is true some sacrifices must be made, Sarah. That is always the case. But I do not believe that is your fate," she said as they reached the gate.

It was a proper gate now, with two giant metal doors designed and fashioned by Cheekie and Steven with a little help from Sarah and Dr. Walker. They were three feet thick, large enough from side to side for a car to pass through easily, and sixteen feet tall. The only way to raise the gate was with a set of generators attached to a pair of chains that, when powered on, would pull the gate up from the ground.

Once it was up, metal bars were inserted from a position on the wall to hold it in place. It was an impressive structure, but, unfortunately, it was the only one to be completed. The three other entrances were now functioning as barricades rather than entry points until similar gates could be completed.

Shouldn't be too hard, though, now that those other dwarves are here, They all seem overjoyed to do as Umindrabo tells them after all, Sarah thought.

They waited there for an hour, after which they were joined by Dr. Gibson, Pastor Dylan, Al, and Steven.

"The council has agreed to take the refugees," Dr. Gibson said, his mustache looking frazzled despite his continuous maintenance of it. "But first, they must swear to keep the peace and agree to be separated."

"Separated?" Sarah asked as she jotted down what he said in her notebook.

"Yes, it was agreed that integration would be easier if we spread them throughout the town rather than clumping them all together."

"Like you did with the dwarves," Sarah said.

Dr. Gibson frowned. "Well, that was more their doing really, but yes, I suppose," he replied, his appearance like a hearty turkey two days from Thanksgiving. Together, they waited outside the gate, eager to present a welcoming image but not foolish enough to dismiss the guards above and behind them on the wall.

The sun hung halfway done with its daily toil above the cracked sky when the first group of travelers arrived; a ragged, dirty band of about fifty men and women. Many of them were lightly armed, but none were brandishing those weapons.

The ones who were unarmed carried or pulled large bags or boxes. At the front of the group was a frazzled looking Jenni. She was covered from head to toe in the grime of travel. Her clothes stuck to her skin or bunched uncomfortably all over.

The bandage on her leg was in desperate need of changing, yet despite the obvious pain it caused her to walk, she stayed a few paces ahead of the rest of her group. She was armed the same as when she'd left, but now even her weapons were dirty, her hair was a tangled mess, and her eyes were sunken and swollen from exhaustion. When she saw the gate, she quickened her pace, and almost ran despite her limp.

Steven rushed forward to meet her before she even made it to the gate, where he wrapped her in an enormous hug. Then, he pulled back to look at her, but did not let go of his hold on her. At last, he summoned the courage to ask the question which had been haunting him. "Who did we lose?" he said, the words unintentionally whispered.

Jenni's eyebrows curled in pain at his words. She swallowed, fought the surge of emotion that accompanied the reminder. "Justin," she said, her voice barely louder than Steven's.

Steven pulled her back into the hug and spoke softly. "Did you have a chance to talk to him before?"

Jenni shook her head and blinked back tears. "No, I wasn't even there when it happened, Steve. I— I didn't even get to be there for him when he went," she managed to choke out, gripped Steven's forearm, and signaled him to release her from the hug. He did, and she wiped her eyes with the back of her hand.

"Peter killed the bastard in charge, but it doesn't add up."

Steven nodded slowly, his own eyes wet with emotion, and took her hands in his and held them tightly. "We'll talk about that later. What orders did Peter send?"

"You are to remain here with a selection of essential personnel."

"Ridiculous, surely William can—"

"He said you'd say that. And he said to tell you he needs you here and that William and anyone else willing is to report to Atlanta. I'm to make sure you follow orders by any means necessary." She smiled wickedly. "Hauch is here already, isn't he?"

Steven smirked. "Fine, he knows what he's doing. I expect you'll get all hands on deck for SNW, at least. Can these newcomers be trusted?"

Jenni nodded and swallowed aggressively to clear her throat. "I hope so. Most of them are victims looking for safety. So, yes, I think so." She turned and motioned to Dory, who was standing with the rest of the group a few feet back from the gate. Dory made his way over to them at the same time Dr. Gibson, Dr. Walker, and Sarah reached them.

"Mister Mayor, this is Dory." Jenni introduced him with a hoarse voice.

"Dory Conners," the man said, extending a warm hand towards Dr. Gibson. "I know we sent ahead, but I wanted to thank y'all for making room for us. These sure are crazy times, ain't they?"

Dr. Gibson shook his hand eagerly. "Of course, Mister Conners. Now, there will be rules you all have to follow, but nothing extreme."

Dory nodded agreeably, but the reaction did not meet his eyes. "Sure thing. Y'all seem to be doing all right. We sure don't want to be messing that up."

Dr. Gibson's smile was friendly and hospitable. "Before I get to that, I do have to ask how many of you are there, and were you able to bring any supplies with you?"

"Fourteen hundred and seven. I expect two hundred or so of those are gonna turn around and go reinforce Captain Blair, though." He removed his red hat and scratched his head. "As far as supplies go, we brought as much food and gas as we could carry. Ain't much, but it's enough to feed us and help you for a bit till we figure something else out."

"That's good to hear," Dr. Gibson replied. "It is my understanding you've had some trouble with a magic user?"

Dory's face darkened, and he put his hat back on. "That's one way of sayin' it."

"Well, in the spirit of transparency, allow me to introduce Miss Sarah Young and Doctor Walker," Dr. Gibson replied, gesturing to the pair. "Our resident magic users who have done nothing but good for our small city."

"How y'all doin?" Dory asked, nodding curtly at them, and turned back to Dr. Gibson. "She a dwarf?"

"Yes, she is," Dr. Walker replied. "And she's not the only one. One of our scouting parties recently returned with a dozen or so others we have been sheltering. Before I can allow you and your people in, I need your word that you will do all in your power to help encourage peace between them and us."

Dory tapped his foot and nodded, the nod increased in intensity as it went on. "Yes, yes, of course. You have my word. People will be more scared of the young lady anyway. They're pretty warm to dwarves thanks to Breekie." He chuckled. "Fella's made himself rather popular during the trip."

Dr. Walker perked up at this. "Breekie has returned with you?"

"Yes, ma'am, and if you're the Umindrab-oh he keeps goin' on about, he's more eager to see you then a baby in a room full of puppies."

"Very good," Dr. Gibson said proudly. "Now, we won't ask you to hand over your weapons. Most of our own people are armed at all times themselves. If you come with me, I'll introduce you to our volunteers who will take any extra supplies, check everyone in, and escort them to where they'll be staying."

Dr. Gibson gave a wave to one of the men who looked down at them from the wall. The man waved back, and a moment later, the gate began to rise. It revealed three makeshift check-in booths set up on the other side and accompanied by a crowd of friendly faces of volunteers.

"I don't know if Captain Blair mentioned it, but we have a sort of council running things here, and they're all waiting to meet with your leaders. Is it just you?" Dr. Gibson went on as he led Dory over to where Al was already introducing himself to the crowd of newcomers.

"For now. What about them?" Dory referenced the group of a hundred men, women, and children that accompanied him.

"Al will oversee check-in. Your first group will be staying over on Carriage Hill Road, I believe. How far behind is your next group?"

"Should be here any minute. We tried to stay all together, but people move at their own paces."

The two of them then led the rest of the crowd over to sign in before they made their way to the council meeting. Shortly after, Jenni made her way in as well after Steven insisted things were under control and that she go get her leg looked at by a "proper doctor."

The next group arrived ten minutes later, led by a young woman with brightly dyed short hair and unnaturally green eyes, wearing a shirt with a faded white and orange circle. She peeled out of the crowd and approached Sarah and Dr. Walker, and eagerly introduced herself as Marah.

"Have you seen Mister Conners? I'm something of an unofficial second in command, and I'd like to talk to him about the logistics of getting everyone settled in," she asked warmly.

"He's in a meeting with the council," Steven replied. "But I don't think they're expecting anyone else."

"That's all right, are they at the courthouse or somewhere on campus?"

"The Posick building on campus. I can have someone show you—"

"That's all right. I know the campus," she replied casually before she strolled off.

Jenni watched her go with furrowed eyebrows. "What was up with her eyes?"

"Looked like colored contacts to me, then again, colors seem to be brighter for most people since the Shattering," Steven replied as he compared notes with Sarah on the number of arrivals. While this went on, another man supervised the exchange of supplies as people were welcomed into the city.

By two o'clock, the flood of people was streaming in at a steady speed. It was then that Gunter emerged from the river of arrivals, riding one of the dirt bikes they'd taken with them. He drove up to them hurriedly.

"Where is Mayor Gibson?" he demanded impatiently.

"Busy. Anything I can do for you, sir? The check-in line is over there," Steven replied with a friendly gesture.

Gunter gave him a cursory glance. "I don't need to check in. I'm Gunter Brown. I was assigned to supervise Captain Blair by the council."

"Oh, my mistake. I didn't recognize you, Mister Brown," Steven replied. Jenni stood from where she'd been sitting talking with Sarah and shuffled over. "Gunter, do you have a moment? I'd like to know what you're going to tell the council."

Gunter went rigid. "It's not really your business, is it?"

"It is as far as I'm concerned. I think you should have someone else with you there in case you try and twist the facts."

Gunter scowled. "Look, I may think Captain Peter is a grade-A jerk, but I know he does what he has to, and we'd be better off with him around. Speaking of, shouldn't you be gathering your SNW people to go back him up?"

"I was waiting for Breekie," Jenni replied, somewhat taken aback by the response she received from Gunter.

The man shrugged. "Do what you will, but I'll be insisting to the council we send whoever we can spare to back them up as soon as possible." He snapped his fingers. "Oh, yeah, Thomas, right? Is Lieutenant Rory with the council? Short, redheaded guy? His group should have been back days ago."

Steven shook his head, apologetically. "I'm afraid Lieutenant Effith's expedition has not returned or signaled us in any way."

Gunter paled a bit at this, then, without another word, made his way past them into the city.

Near the end of the day, the caravan began to slow to more of a trickle of small groups. It was then that Breekie and Shawn arrived, also mounted on the bikes they'd left on.

Shawn was dirty and covered in sweat with a plethora of fresh bruises and small cuts on his exposed skin, all contrasted by a broad grin. He made his way overeagerly, as he walked just a hair ahead of Breekie, whose face bore an equally enthusiastic grin, which was slowly replaced by a somber expression as he neared Dr. Walker. Shawn made a beeline for Jenni, who he pestered with questions about her leg and asked if there was anything she needed.

"I'm fine, Shawn. It's healing quickly. Are you all right?"

"Yes, ma'am, just some cuts and bruises. The captain said to train with Breekie, so that's what I've been doing."

"Dah," said Breekie, coming to a stop. "What his boney arms lack in strength he has in heart," he said, giving the boy a fist bump. "We will put meat on his bones soon, though," he added, then turned to Dr. Walker, and switched to Dwarvish.

"Deulma. Captain Blair, Basilisk-Bane, sent me to deliver my knowledge gained in accordance with your wisdom." He bowed respectfully before he continued. "Of greatest importance that you know, we met an elf with a purple braid wrapped around his neck, who requested I give a message to you."

"A Valk of the Véla?" Dr. Walker replied as her face lit up with curiosity. She placed a shaky hand on his shoulder as the humans gathered around her watched in confusion. "Quickly. Tell me what he had to say."

"General Almurë has been searching for the Duridgribuldam. He said if you are one of them, you must report at once to General Almurë as his forces gather outside Vulacia." As he said this, he handed over a small scroll.

Dr. Walker stood in silence, her lips moving soundlessly as she read over the scroll. Then she turned to Steven, a solemn expression on her wrinkled face. "Mister Thomas, gather what volunteers you can. I'm going to Atlanta."

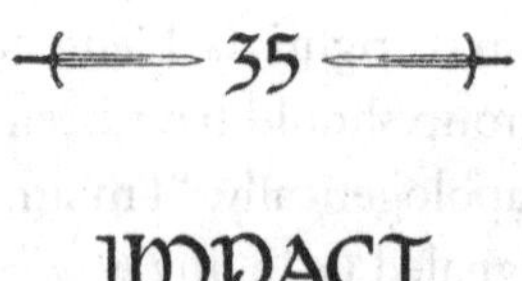

IMPACT

These things cost as much as your boots?" Elborin asked incredulously, as he held the name brand sunglasses up in front of his face.

"Some do," Peter replied. "These," he said as he pulled a pair out of the center console, "cost a hundredth of what that pair costs."

Elborin took the second pair of cheap plastic sunglasses. He put them on and then switched to the first pair. "But they accomplish the same thing. There is not substantial craftsmanship between… Why would you pay so much more?"

Peter shrugged. "I wouldn't. At least not for sunglasses like that. It's to attract others. Fancier things make some people more attracted to each other."

Elborin scowled. "Your kind always has strange notions of attraction. Collecting shiny things like birds," he added in a mumble to himself.

Behind them, in her seat, Leuoradew scowled even deeper than the elf. "I do not understand why one would hide any part of themselves from the glorious sun."

The other three had a quiet chuckle at this, much to her confusion, as they continued down I-75.

The closer they got to Atlanta, the more death and destruction they found. The ghostly wreckage that covered the road in a gory display of times gone by increased with every turn of the broken asphalt. Rotting corpses, either stripped of anything useful or picked down to the bone, could be found with minimal effort.

They were everywhere, trapped behind steering wheels or peeking out from under cars where they'd once thrown themselves in a desperate search for cover as the world broke around them. The road was void of human life or explanation in every direction one looked.

"There's a truck, and a rest stop about a mile ahead on our right," Peter said as he kept his eyes on the move. "Probably our best chance at siphoning more gas unless we want to stop in the middle of the road."

"I know the one," said Scott as he swerved the jeep around a flipped moving trailer with its contents spilled out onto the road's shoulder behind it. Toys and furniture strewn across the road served as a visceral reminder of mankind's suffering.

"Good, we'll make a stop there then," Peter replied as he scanned their surroundings. Several damaged buildings, trees aplenty, and a scattering of cars remained motionless under his scrutiny; nothing out of the ordinary. Peter's attention shifted to the upcoming bend in the road. "Slow it down. It'd be a good place for a—"

He was cut off by the sound of an enormous roar echoing through the surrounding trees, sending birds into flight from their perches.

Scott cursed, hit the brakes, and brought the jeep to a crawl. "Leuoradew?" he said over his shoulder. Leuoradew didn't reply. Peter glanced in the rearview mirror and saw that her eyes were shut tight, and she sat motionless, making her resemblance to a carving eerier. It was no surprise really with how she tended to interject herself into random points of conversation or withdraw from those same conversations erratically.

Simon and O'Cleary's jeep pulled up next to them, a battered green vehicle with the top removed like the one Peter sat in. The six of them were split between the two vehicles provided by Scott to make room for supplies: camping gear, plenty of gasoline, food, and water, all of which Scott insisted on. Peter glanced at the back of his jeep, where Elborin sat next to the dryad.

Elborin had abandoned any subtlety regarding inhumanity. His clothing was now replaced with charcoal gray armor, unlike anything Peter had ever seen. It shifted perfectly with Elborin's every movement, more like clothing than armor in that regard.

It was a fluid-like dark metal held together by a combination of dark leather woven into small, sleek metal scales. The armor itself was covered in intricate swirling shapes reminiscent of Celtic patterns, which, when stared at too long, seemed to force the looker to blink.

Another enormous roar shook the air around them.

"Elborin?" Peter said as he turned his attention to the bend in the road that formed their exit. He searched for a sign of approaching threats. "Any idea what we're up against?"

"No, but it's very close," Elborin replied with a shake of his head. *Jeeps could give us away, let's get a closer look.*

"Everyone out, weapons ready, we're moving on foot," Peter ordered as he hopped out of the jeep and drew Galvorn. "Could we take that around, Scott?" Peter asked and pointed to a road that curved to the right just before their road's left turn.

"Not without getting really close to an ork camp we passed on our way back," Scott replied as he drew the ax he kept strapped to his back and pulled a round battered shield from the rear of the jeep.

"Criske," Peter replied defeatedly. "Whatever it is, sounds like it's where we were going to refuel. We could just keep going and try siphoning on the road."

"No!" The word burst from Leuoradew's lips as she leaped from the jeep, the outcry gave them all a start. "Hurry! We're going to lose her," she exclaimed as she sprinted forward, dashing madly for the exit.

"Hold on!" Peter barked after the dryad, but the command had no effect as she continued forward. Elborin gave Peter an amused look as he also dashed forward before Peter had a chance to react. Peter scowled. "Simon, covering fire. O'Cleary, grab the fifty, might come in handy," he commanded before he lept after Leuoradew and Elborin, who'd already caught up to her, spear in hand.

Collectively, they hardly made a sound as they rushed forward along the pavement. The three of them cleared the corner moments later with Scott, Simon, and O'Cleary only a few steps behind.

Once around the bend, they came to a stop. The scene that greeted them sent rage pumping through Peter's blood. The Shattering's destructive effect here was undeniable. A few hundred feet down the broken road from them was a four-way stoplight that brought the four-lane highway together with a large truck stop on one side and a collection of fast-food restaurants on the other.

Warped, burned, and crushed metal spread across the four lanes formed a graveyard of vehicles. An upside-down school bus lay beneath the lights, a truck bending it in the middle where the crumpled hood had collided with it. Dozens of similarly wrecked vehicles brought the scene together in a strange chaotic tapestry.

The ruined traffic light farthest from them was where ten orks were spread haphazardly on and between the cars. Their skin varied in shades of gray and green underneath their bizarre conglomeration of armor and stolen clothes held together by duct tape and clasps. A dozen paces behind them, an eleventh ork in a single patchwork robe sat on an overturned truck with a chain in hand tethered to an enormous, almost hairless, bear.

Across from the orks, closer to Peter, stood five armed men with their backs to Peter in the middle of the road. Their weapons and armor were similar to what Scott's company wore; an awkward collection of misfit martial and modern weapons and armor not all that different from the orks.

The biggest difference between them was the humans knew how to wear human clothing and did not have it attached or hung awkwardly off other parts of clothing like the orks. This was the only semblance of unity among the humans. Directly behind the humans, a large leather bag lay on the ground tied shut with a rope, which squirmed and spasmed as whatever was inside tried to escape.

"I don't care what your crying king said," one of the humans was protesting to a disgruntled-looking ork. "And I don't care what he said his child needs to eat. The deal was one. Not three!"

"This isn't good. We should fall back," Peter whispered as he took another step, shoulder to shoulder with Elborin. At that moment, the scene changed. One of the orks raised a clawed hand and pointed accusingly at Elborin, yelling something at the man in front of him. The bear rose with a roar onto its back legs, and the bag tore open. The head of a small girl with enormous eyes and two tiny brown horns appeared first.

The strange little head was quickly followed by a body that couldn't have belonged to anyone older than six. As she sprang from the bag dressed in only an oversized brightly colored t-shirt, Peter spied a pair of furry, hooved legs. Then, the child burst towards them with unnatural speed.

Peter felt a pulse of commanding energy.

"Down!" he cried as he threw himself behind a sideways Suburban and took cover from the first round of gunfire as the group of men turned and opened fire on them.

Scott landed beside him with a series of curses. Beside him, Peter saw Elborin slide gracefully between a pair of SUVs. Leuoradew, though, did not take cover but resumed charging straight at the child as it zigzagged away from the men and almost tripped on its oversized shirt. The dryad's body shook as bullets tore into it, but the creature seemed barely fazed by the deadly metal. She continued to move forward, and Peter lost sight of her.

Another burst of gunfire echoed through the air as Peter drew his pistol. A few cars away, Simon returned fire, and Peter heard a scream of pain. *Gotta get closer to use the sword,* Peter thought as he searched for some kind of advantage.

Across from him, he saw a flipped Corolla, and one of its mirrors gave him a limited view of the men and orks on the other side of his cover. One of the five men was already down, presumably thanks to Simon. Another was struggling violently on the ground with one of the orks. Two were focusing their attention on Simon's location, and the last was reloading. Leuoradew, the child, and El-borin were out of sight.

Peter seized the opportunity. He rolled out from behind his cover and fired off four shots. The man in the middle of a reload collapsed. Peter's fourth bullet caught the man next to his first kill in the arm. The man dropped his gun and scrambled out of view. The last man on his feet swung his weapon in Peter's direction, but before he could fire, a spear burst out of his chest from behind as one of the orks impaled him with a cry that heralded the charge of the remaining orks.

Peter caught a flicker of movement to his left as Elborin burst from where he'd taken cover in a blur of deadly speed. "Guns are down," Peter called to Scott, who clambered onto the vehicle they'd been behind.

"Come on then!" Scott screamed at the orks as they continued to charge and weave in and out of cars to get closer.

Peter rushed forward to meet them, unsure of when Galvorn had replaced his pistol in his hands but glad that it had. Ahead, Elborin dispatched two orks with quick fluid thrusts from his spear, which moved with the speed of a striking snake. Peter met his first foe with a flying kick that took the creature by surprise as it attempted to flank Elborin.

The ork hit the ground hard, and a mangled shotgun was knocked out of his hand. Before the ork could react, Peter dyed its ragged semblance of clothing black with its own blood, as he shoved Galvorn through its chest into its spine.

Peter grinned down at the ork as it took its last few desperate gulps of air. From somewhere on the battlefield, he heard an ethereal wail that made his legs feel weak.

As Peter stood up, he heard a cry from Elborin.

"Drop!"

Peter obeyed as the energy pulsing through his veins pulled him back to-wards the ground. A second later, Elborin's silver spear passed the space he'd just occupied and crashed into the chest of the ork he'd sensed at his side.

A few yards away, he spied the dryad riddled with bullet holes that oozed amber sap. A strange purplish liquid covered her hands and arms, which she raised into the air.

Ahead of her, roots broke through the concrete beneath a pair of orks. The roots dove savagely into the legs of the orks, where they grew and expanded underneath the skin with supernatural speed until the ends of the roots burst out the heads and orifices of their victims in a gory display. But the dryad was on the move, vanished from Peter's sight.

Criske! That's horrifying! Don't piss her off!

Elborin was at Peter's side a second later, where he grabbed the spear from the ork's chest and rushed at Scott, who was fighting fiercely against a trio of orks who'd cut him off from Simon and O'Cleary.

They've got it, Peter thought as he rushed towards where the dryad disappeared into a maze of overturned vehicles. To his left, he heard the enormous bear roar and charge. Peter's connection to the arcane flow redirected his steps; it warned him of a different threat. He obeyed and narrowly dodged a war hammer meant for his head. The ork's weapon crashed into the underside of the overturned car beside Peter. The blow sent a burst of gasoline through the air and soaked Peter's coat.

Peter slid sideways and brought Galvorn up in an arc that severed the ork's arm at the elbow. It stumbled backward into the truck it came from. Peter followed its movement with a roar of his own.

The ork raised its remaining arm in an attempt to shield itself, but it wasn't enough, Galvorn plunged through the arm, drove it back and against the victim's chest as the sword pinned the monster to the door of the truck. Blood stained the white truck paint with oily black.

Peter yanked Galvorn back, and pulled the blade violently from the ork's chest, which sent the ork to the ground from where the sword was pinning it to the truck door.

Ahead of him, he heard the roar of a motorcycle coming to life.

"O'Cleary!" Peter cried out over his shoulder as he blocked a blow from another charging ork in a purple jersey. Over the cars around him, he saw the ork in the flowing patchwork robe on a motorcycle curve through a sea of vehicles strewn across the road away from them. "Shoot him," he screamed, the urgency in his voice scratching the cords of his throat. *Can't let any of them get away.*

Crackow! O'Cleary's rifle roared for the world to hear, loud enough to challenge the bear's roars as it rampaged. He let arcane energy guide his blows against his current opponent. Peter looked and saw the bike had flipped into the air above a Prius, no rider on its back.

Peter turned his attention back to his latest attacker. He took advantage of an opening, grabbed the ork by its collar, and smashed its head through a car window. Then, as he held the ork in place, he brought Galvorn's sharp pommel down on the back of the gray ork's exposed neck.

Another burst of warning energy brought Peter's head around in a whirl. The bear was changing direction. It charged straight for Peter and Elborin, whose back was turned as he battled one of the remaining orks.

Peter threw himself forward, the pulse of energy that warned him away ignored. He collided with Elborin. Together they were thrown behind a car out of the bear's path, but Peter lost hold of Galvorn in the process. The bear charged past, knocking vehicles aside as it searched for prey.

Peter hit the concrete hard and tasted blood in his mouth. Peter's enhanced reflexes rolled him onto his back, where he saw another leathery skinned ork, this one in a black and red jersey, standing over him. *No sword,* he managed to think as he yanked his pistol out with the intent to empty every round from the magazine in hopes it would stop the creature.

But Galvorn emerged from the ork's chest before he could pull the trigger. Blood trickled out of the orks mouth, and it collapsed forward as Galvorn was pulled back out. The orks' body landed next to Peter. The sword was in Simon's hand, soaked in black blood that gave the black metal of the blade a fluid appearance. Simon extended a hand and helped Peter to his feet.

"You good?" he asked as he handed the sword back to Peter.

"Yeah," Peter replied, taking Galvorn back eagerly. "Get to O'Cleary. Let's see if your rifle will work on that beast," Peter ordered, nodding to where the bear was battling the dryad and Scott as Elborin rushed past to back them up.

Simon nodded and disappeared between the cars. Peter looked down at the sword in his hand for a moment as thoughts swirled in his head.

Peter took a step back and surveyed the area. *How many left? I lost count. And where'd the child go?* It was nowhere to be seen. But then again, it was hard to search for anything with the bear, which stood sixteen feet high. Its original appearance was made more brutal by a now visible upside-down isosceles triangle branded into its chest and the blood oozing from its wounds, a darker shade of red than it had any right to be. It swiped violently at Scott, who barely managed to get out of the way of the enormous claws.

The chain bound to the beast's neck caught Scott in the shoulder as it swung wildly through the air and knocked the man sprawling across the ground.

Crackow! O'Cleary's rifle thundered a second time, and the bullet exploded through the bear's chest, taking the odd brand with it.

"Criske," Peter muttered Breekie's favorite curse word. *We could have maybe gotten away with one. We need to get out of here, fast.*

The bear teetered and collapsed onto the hood of an unfortunate Ford Fiesta. On the other side of its corpse, Peter saw Elborin leaping forward, rushing over and between cars in the direction of the motorcycle. Peter gave one more look around and found where O'Cleary lay flat on top of a van, carefully searching for another target.

Simon stood beside the van, his bone sword stained black with oily black blood. One of his sleeves was torn, and bright red blood was running down the side of his arm. *Good.* Peter moved forward to support Elborin.

"Careful, he's a warlock," Elborin muttered when Peter reached his side. Together, they made their way through the rubble and old carnage towards where the motorcycle had landed.

After a moment of cautious searching, they found what was left of the body. Elborin's eyes went wide, and he looked up at Peter as he bent down next to the corpse, of which little remained. The being's head was completely gone. Its blood-soaked robe was now a patchwork of unrecognizable cloth.

Peter saw a symbol in the back of its robe between the shoulders. At first glance, he'd mistaken it for a hole, but on closer inspection, the emblem was clearer: an upside-down isosceles triangle with an eye shape in the center and swirls coming out of the eye.

"How? This was a warlock. Your bullets shouldn't have been effective."

"We used bigger bullets," replied Peter. "We figured out last time, if you fire enough, they work. I don't know why yet, but I was curious if it was simply a matter of force."

"What do you mean?" Elborin asked without so much as a glance up as he removed a glove from one of the hands of the corpse. This revealed a symbol similar to the one branded on the bear's chest.

"One shot from that rifle generates more force than every round fired by Simon's M9. From what Breekie told me about wards and your armor, they're designed to cancel out kinetic energy from small projectiles. So, in theory, if we can produce enough kinetic energy…"

"You can overwhelm the ward," Elborin said. "Why didn't you just do that with all of them?"

"We've got limited ammo for his rifle. I wanted to save them for a desperate situation. We've got bigger guns and more ammo at HQ," Peter explained. "Didn't want this guy getting away to warn anyone after all. Speaking of, we need to move. We've made enough noise to bring everything in a two-mile radius down on us."

Elborin nodded his agreement as he continued to examine the body.

Sword still in hand, Peter began to make his way back towards the others, when he saw a movement beneath one of the cars. *Got you,* he thought savagely.

Peter bent down and grabbed the back of the man's boot and began to drag him out. The man did not come willingly, he flailed and cursed, as he was removed out from under the car. The commotion brought Scott rushing over, ax and shield raised, ready for more fighting. When Scott reached Peter, the other man was begging for his life, pinned to the ground with his hands behind his back.

"Please, no. Come on, you guys won already. I give up, man. I surrender. Come on, you gotta let me go. I didn't hurt nobody. Please…" he blubbered.

Before Scott had a chance to say anything, Peter was sliding Galvorn between the man's ribs, into his heart. The man gave a gurgling whimper and lay still.

Scott spat on the ground. "Good. Waste of oxygen, these bandits," he said with a huff before he returned to where the rest of them were gathered. Peter followed suit and emerged from the scattering of cars to find them all gathered in the opening under the stoplights. There, O'Cleary was helping Simon bandage his arm.

Simon looked up at Peter's approach and met his gaze with a raised eyebrow. "Something funny, captain?"

"No, why?" Peter replied.

"You're grinning," Simon explained.

Peter turned and looked at his reflection in the mirror. He barely recognized the face that looked back. It was covered in dark blood, sweat, and dirt. He shook his head and suppressed the grin. "I'm fine," he replied as he killed what was left of the smile. It was then that he noticed the child in Leuoradew's arms. A knot formed in Peter's throat as he saw the satyr child was covered in the same purple liquid all over the dryad's arms

"Is she…?" Those were the only words he could get past the knot in his throat. There was no need for the dryad to answer. The fact that Simon wasn't tending to the strange little girl's injuries was enough. Rage mounted in Peter's chest, where it pushed the knot out of his throat. He spun around, and before he realized what he was doing, glass was breaking around his fist, where he struck a car window. *I'm still too slow! Too weak! If I was faster, I could have dodged the gunfire and saved her.*

In the back of his mind, a small voice protested that such thoughts were ridiculous. The number of holes in the tree lady was enough evidence. Even if his reinforced coat had stopped some, and he'd been fast enough to dodge some bullets, it still wouldn't have been enough.

Behind him, he heard Simon asking Leuoradew to let him look at her wounds. "I don't know much, but perhaps I can help," he was saying.

"No," the dryad replied. "I will heal on my own. The child will not." The dryad began to carry the child towards a collection of trees off to the side of the road.

Elborin raised a hand to stop anyone from following her. Hot tears stained his cheeks as he cried openly. Even O'Cleary seemed uncharacteristically affected by the small creature's demise.

A scowl still etched on his face, Peter shook the glass from his glove and sat down to begin cleaning Galvorn off. *It doesn't matter,* he thought, unconvinced. *Everyone's fine, and I'll get a good training session out of this.*

"We should fuel up and get as far away from here as possible anyway," Peter said to the group standing around him in silence.

"Oscar, how much farther can we get in the jeeps?"

"A few miles if we don't refuel. Although, it might be better at that point to continue on foot," Scott replied.

"Simon, you good to move?" Peter asked calmly with an eye on his friend's wound as he sheathed his sword.

"Yes, just a through and through," Simon replied hesitantly, a strange look in his eyes as he watched Peter. "You sure you're okay, captain?"

"Better than ever, actually," Peter replied dismissively, adjusting the jacket to sit right with his sword and scabbard. "All right, once she's done, we get out of here before more trouble shows up," Peter ordered, unable to bring himself to look at the dryad as it buried the child among the trees.

There was silence among the men as they cleaned their wounds and weapons while they waited for the dryad to return. Once she finally did, her wounds miraculously healed, Peter spoke again. "We need to leave some kind of marker for our reinforcements. Scott's men will know to come this far, I assume, but from here on, it wouldn't hurt to leave some kind of trail. Any suggestions?"

Elborin looked to Leuoradew. "Can you leave a message among the trees?"

Leuoradew smiled sadly, her wooden teeth making the movement look strange. "It is done," she said proudly.

Peter looked around but saw no changes to their environment. He glanced quizzically at Elborin.

"Your Doctor Walker will know. If not her, then the dwarf, Breekie, will," he explained as they all clambered into the jeeps.

That night, they made camp under a partially collapsed overpass, sheltered from the cold and prying eyes. Once the food was distributed, Peter excused himself to the other side of their makeshift cave to "think."

There, Peter sat on the hood of an abandoned car half-buried in rubble and stared at Galvorn. A bit of cold food sat at his side, untouched as he sat deep in thought. *How many people are out there working with orks?*

The thought had been nagging him since their encounter. *I'll kill every last one of them I see.* As he sat there in the cold dark, he felt someone approaching, and he looked up, expecting Simon.

But it was Leuoradew walking over to him, her footfalls making a strange clunking on the broken concrete. *Glad she's on our side.*

Her strange eyes almost seemed to glow in the dark as she stared at him.

"Can I help you?" he asked, finally taking a few bites of cold food.

She tilted her head, leafy hair shifting over her bark-like skin. "Do you wish to help people, Peter Blair?"

Peter paused and lowered his food to his lap. "Of course, why do you ask?"

"You do not hesitate to kill your own kind," she replied as though her words explained her question. "Yet, the fawn's death troubles you."

"I'm a soldier. Before all this, my own kind were the only things I killed," Peter replied dismissively. Her unblinking stare made him uneasy. "The point has always been to protect kids. I don't care what kind of creature they are. A child is still a child."

"You kill your own kind to save your kind?" she asked curiously.

"Yeah. When I have to."

"Humans are a strange species."

"What? Dryads don't kill each other?"

"No," she said emphatically. "It is not so. Nor is it so for elves. I have heard it has happened among the dwarves, but I do not believe it."

Peter fidgeted with his food. "It's not like we like doing it. Most of us, at least. Sometimes you just don't have another choice."

"But you do. That is why you smiled after killing the man under the metal box. It is why you sit here alone."

Peter looked past her to where the rest of them were gathered in a small circle, talking. "I'm sitting alone because I like to have some time alone with my thoughts, not because I want to kill my companions."

Leuoradew finally blinked, slowly. *Why does she blink at all? Is she just mimicking human behavior?*

"I did not say you want to kill your friends, Peter Blair. I know little of humans, but I know you are different. Oscar Scott hates the men you call bandits. That is why he kills them. It is justice for what they did to him," she said. "What have they done to you, Peter Blair?"

"Nothing to me directly, but anyone who could treat a kid like that...." His knuckles grew white as he clenched a fist. "Anyone who sells or kills innocents deserves worse than death, but death is all I can give them for now."

She shook her head slowly. The leaves rustled softly. "You do not have hate in your eyes when you kill, Peter Blair." She took a step forward and brought her face closer to his. "No, I see the joy in your eyes when you kill. Joy, and something I do not yet recognize."

Peter cleared his throat and shifted back a bit where he sat. "Why the interrogation, Leuoradew?"

She smiled and raised a finger, which she tapped lightly beside her eye. "I am a diviner. I see futures. Many, constantly changing, futures full of possibilities. Yours, I can see only pieces of, Peter Blair. This is not how it should be."

Leuoradew's face took on an apologetic expression. "I know it is not right to see another's futures without their permission, but you are a diviner also, but not in the way I am. I was curious. We both see the arcane flow, how it bends, weaves, and effects all. I, with my mind, you with your body. All futures are in flux, but yours, Peter Blair — yours are a whirlwind of blood with so many choices I cannot see one from the other. I have only had a peek, Peter Blair, but I wish to see more."

Peter slid off the hood of the car and landed on his feet only a few inches from the wooden woman. "Are you telling me I could look into the future… I could see what happens tomorrow?" he asked eagerly.

"No," she said as she shook her head more quickly. "You are a diviner, but you are an *Antemáklasi*. You know only what is to happen as it affects the arcane flow directly around you. You do not see as I do, but there is more surety in what you see."

"And you need permission to look at my future any further?" Peter replied as he hid the disappointment from his voice.

"Yes. It is wrong for me to have seen what I have. I ask your forgiveness, Peter Blair, Avenger of the Arborous," she implored with a slight bow.

"First," Peter said, raising a finger. "What does Avenger of the Arborous mean?"

She raised one of her mossy eyebrows. "It is one of your titles. You earned it when you slew Jason, who struck down the great Gentleyew. And when Elborin buried Gentleyews remains outside the city, he was given the title Friend of the Arborous, for his kindness pleased us. It is why I knew you would come to the aid of Thimblehorn."

"Thimblehorn?"

"That was her name. Remember it well, Peter Blair.

"I see," Peter said, a familiar lump returning to his throat. After a moment of silence, he asked, "When I give my titles, should I include *Antemáklasi*?"

Her brow furrowed in mock concentration as she considered this. "You may if it is that which you desire to be known. It bears a heavy meaning though. Much will be expected of you should you use it."

"Good." Peter held up a third finger. "If I let you see my future, and tell it to me, is it set in stone?"

Leuoradew tilted her head. "There is no one future. I do not see your *future*, I see your futures. What could happen to you depends on your choices. It is always in flux, never certain. Like the heavens, it is immeasurable, dangerous to look at too closely, but beautiful all the same."

"You are forgiven for your intrusion." Peter scratched his beard as he replied. "But no. My future is mine and mine alone. And I would not have it alter my choices if I cannot know the end result for certain."

Leuoradew straightened, rising to her full height, then bowed slightly at the waist. "So be it, *Antemáklasi*, I shall not intrude upon your futures again," she said softly before she walked off to rejoin the others.

That night, Peter shifted about uncomfortably as he attempted to fall asleep, his mind troubled by what sleep would bring. As he tossed and turned, Thimblehorn's scared face troubled his thoughts, shifting into the terrified wide-eyed face of the man under the car.

His anxiousness was made worse as he saw that Simon was asleep before him. *Was Doctor Walker right? Is Jadis just a way for my subconscious to deal with stress?*

These questions and more bounced around his mind endlessly until, at long last, he drifted into a troubled sleep.

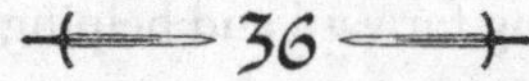

36

SIMON SAYS

Peter's eyes snapped open. He was back. He put his hands on the cold stone ground and rose. The mist swirled around him, shifting with every movement. *Good.* He wore the usual loose black garment. Galvorn stood embedded in the ground at his feet as always. The pressure in the room was different now, though. A few weeks ago, he wouldn't have expected to notice such a change, but he could feel it now.

"Stay back! What did you do to him?" a voice echoed through the fog. Simon was there, dressed in the same black clothes as Peter. His friend sat in the mist, his arms spread out behind him, palms to the stone, as though he'd been pulling himself backward.

Between the two of them stood Jadis, lean, muscled arms holding her sword pointed down menacingly at Simon's chest. *Why is he here?*

"Jadis!" Peter called out like an owner to an overly aggressive pet. But Jadis was no pet, and Peter was certainly not her owner. Her ears twitched at the name, but she did not pull the sword away from Simon. Rather, she jabbed at him. Simon tried to scramble back out of the way, but the blade buried in his arm.

Simon cried in pain as the blade cut flesh.

"Jadis, stop! He's a friend," Peter roared as he marched towards them, his words laced with fear and fury. Jadis whipped her head around and met Peter's gaze as he drew closer. The cold rage in her eyes unnerved him.

"Peter!" She spat his name like a vial curse, stomping towards him. "What is he doing here?" Her voice was barely in check, bordering on screaming.

Her fury caught Peter by such surprise that he took a reflexive step back.

Peter's eyes darted to where Simon was holding his wounded shoulder. "I don't know."

Simon looked down at his arm with a dazed expression. "I'm bleeding," he mumbled to himself before looking back at Peter. "Captain, what's going on?"

"What did you do with the sword," Jadis whispered to Peter through clenched teeth.

Peter ignored her, striding forward and helping Simon to his feet. "Simon, it's all right."

Simon shook his head slowly. "No, no, I'm not. I'd have woken up. This is far too lucid for a dream, and she stabbed me," he added, pointing at Jadis.

"Did you lose the sword, Peter?" Jadis demanded.

"No," Peter shot back, his mind swimming as he looked down at his friend's blood on his hands. "I... dropped it, just for a moment. Simon recovered it and used it to save me."

Jadis looked like a cornered, injured animal. Her eyes radiated malice and death. "You can't do this to me," she mumbled.

This isn't a dream. Did she bring Simon here? Is this some kind of test?

"Peter, where are we? Who is that?" Simon asked, pain dripping from his words.

She cut him. She's never cut me here. What happens if she kills him? Peter took a defensive step between his friend and the predatorial girl. "She's an ally, Simon," he said over his shoulder. "Jadis, we can figure this out. This could work to our advantage."

"No!" She cut him off before he could continue. "You have no idea what you've done. You've damaged the link," she shouted at him, pacing in front of them.

How do I know that's actually Simon? Maybe she's testing me. I have to make sure.

"Simon. What was the name of our first operation in SNW?" Peter said over his shoulder, still watching Jadis carefully, her yelling reduced to contemplative mumbling.

"Operation CALM. Why?" Simon replied.

"Because she wouldn't know." Peter looked closer at Simon, not sure what he was looking for. *Either he's really here, or this really is my subconscious.*

"Captain, what's going on? What is she? An elf?" Simon said.

Peter saw her lip curl ever so slightly at the word.

"No, something else. Jadis' been helping me train. I come here, and I get stronger."

Simon rose and took a step back, shaking his head, taking another step back from Peter. "You've been here before?"

Jadis froze. The sudden change in body language put Peter on high alert, her head slowly turned to face him. Her purplish eyes seared into him. "You have to kill him."

"What?" Peter replied reflexively as his brain caught up with the words. *If it's just a dream, he'll be fine. This could be a test. Maybe she wants me to prove myself before she teaches me more. But, if this isn't a dream…* Peter weighed the possibility as he looked over his shoulder at his friend. *He'd wake up, wouldn't he?*

Simon looked back and forth between them. "What's she talking about?" His eyes widened. "Oh my God, you're considering it?"

Peter took a step forward and paused, hand extended to Simon. "What? No! Of course not."

"You were," Simon shot back accusingly, not taking Peter up on his offer to help him up. "I saw it in your eyes. They went gray like they do. Don't lie to me, Peter."

Peter had never seen Simon like this before, but he couldn't blame him; being here for the first time was a terrifying experience. Simon took another step back and began to fall backward, his body tumbling towards the fog. But his body never made it to the ground; it hit the fog and vanished like a bubble popping but not leaving any sticky residue. He was simply gone, with no trace he'd been there are all.

Peter turned back to Jadis. "What was that? Where'd he go?" he demanded of Jadis, searching for something, he wasn't sure what, in her face, that would make sense of all this.

She scowled. "He woke up. The same thing happens to you," she said dismissively, shoving her sword into the stone ground.

"Is this another test?"

Jadis raised an eyebrow. "A test? You let someone else use Galvorn, and you think I'm testing you? Do you not remember what I told you would happen if you gave the sword away?" she shot back harshly, her anger rearing its ugly head again.

"So, I'll be disappearing soon?"

"Maybe." She shrugged again. "Time is different here. Your connection is stronger. You could both wake up at the exact same time, but you could have spent hours more here. Besides, you are used to this," she said with a sly smirk.

"What would killing him have done?"

She shook her head. She seemed back to her controlled self again. "No, it is my turn," she said, holding up four fingers. "Why did he use Galvorn?"

"I told you. I dropped it. A bear was charging me and Caraticus, and it got knocked out of my hand in the fall." *I need to wake up. I have to talk to Simon.*

She lowered a finger. "Were you not using your arcane?"

"I was."

She lowered another finger, an annoyed expression on her face. "Why did you not get out of the way?"

"It was going to hit him first. He didn't see it coming, so I had to help him."

She furrowed her brow. "Why?"

There's nothing I can do. I just have to wait it out. Peter ran a hand through his hair. "What?"

"Why did you have to help him?" Jadis repeated herself, lowering the last finger into a fist and striking a combat pose.

Peter mimicked the action, used to their conversations evolving into sparring. "Because if I didn't do something, he'd have died."

"And if you die, I have to start over," Jadis shot back, emphasizing her words with a strong right hook, which Peter barely managed to block.

"Start what over?" Peter replied, hoping to get an answer out of her while she was still high-strung, breaking her concentration just a little bit. She blocked his return blow without missing a beat but didn't answer his question.

Their blows sped up, without either of them managing to get the upper hand. "What do you do with him when you wake up?"

Peter faltered. It was barely a second, but it was enough. He suffered a hard blow to the chin for it, making his head spin. He planted his feet, regaining his balance, to get ready to start over like they always did when one got a blow on the other. But Jadis didn't stop. She hit him again, this time in the leg, bringing him down hard on his knee.

Peter embraced the flow of arcane energy, realizing he'd been ignoring its pull. He felt the next blow coming for the side of his head — a swift roundhouse kick. He flung his hand up, catching Jadis' foot before it could connect.

"I don't know," he spat out, striking the inside of her calf.

"Not an answer," she responded, giving him space. "Take this seriously. Every fight could be your last. Do not shirk your ability. What are you going to do?"

"Talk to him. Find out if he even remembers any of this. What would have happened if I'd killed him here?" Peter replied.

Jadis stalked over to where she placed her sword and pointed Peter towards Galvorn. Peter looked at the sword in confusion.

"Try it," she instructed as she gave her own blade a whirl. "He would have woken up, convinced this was nothing more than a bad dream. But now, because you hesitated again, you have to decide if he can live in the waking world, knowing what he does."

"He's my friend," Peter replied, taking hold of the sword. "I trust him." He gave the sword a pull, and to his surprise, it shifted. It didn't come out, but it moved.

He looked up at Jadis, who was grinning widely. "We are almost there. Are you sure he trusts you, though? After all, you have been consorting with demons in your sleep."

Peter hesitated. *What if he doesn't trust me?* "What happens when I can draw it?"

Jadis scratched the ground with the tip of her sword. "Then there is nothing more I can teach you here," she said with a guarded look in her amethyst eyes.

Peter woke with a familiar spasm. The cold air of reality stung his skin, the uneven ground beneath him pressing uncomfortably into the multitude of bruises covering his body. His hand flew to his sword, but he grasped only air and dirt.

Peter shot up into a sitting position, looking around for the blade, finding it at his left side, not his right where he thought he'd placed it last night. Gripping it, he glanced over at his companions.

They sat around a smokeless green fire made by Elborin. Elborin and Scott calmly were eating a small breakfast while O'Cleary quietly packed camp, and Leuoradew stood still as a statue farther back from the fire than the rest. All eyes were focused on Simon, who seemed to be telling the group a story.

"There was this strange fog everywhere, but no source of light, but I could see. It was almost as if the fog itself was providing the light. Above me, it was all dark, and as I looked around, I saw the captain lying in the mist, his sword buried in the ground at his feet." Simon brushed his hair behind his ears. "Then, this shape appeared out of the mist before I could get any closer to Peter."

He took a sip of water. "She had ash skin, pink eyes, white hair, and pointy ears just like you, Elborin," Simon said, gesturing towards the elf, who grinned and flicked softly at the tip of one of his ears.

"I'm flattered to have left an impression on your dreams," Elborin said with a smirk.

"Anyway, she was a tiny thing, but she came at me with this wicked, jagged, silver and black sword. Drove me back and knocked me down. I've never seen anything move that fast in a dream, and it felt so real."

Peter stood up and slowly made his way over towards the fire. Simon glanced up and continued his story. "Then you woke up, captain. Good morning. We were talking about the dreams we had last night. Apparently, dryads don't dream."

"I dreamt about a soft bed and a good beer," O'Cleary said. "You Americans can't make decent beer. That's about all you've missed so far, though."

"Don't let me interrupt then," Peter said hoarsely as he took a bit of food Elborin handed to him. "Did the creature have any strange markings, scars, or something like that?"

Simon's dark brown eyes stared intensely at Peter, watching him like a dog would a cat, uncertain of what to do with the creature, drawing a strange look from Elborin. Simon's eyes, though, remained on Peter, prodding him for answers.

"Yes, come to think of it. She had these thin scars on her fingers and face — almost surgical. She had a name too. You called it out. Ja-something. I'm not sure."

Peter locked eyes with him as he took a sip of cold water. *He remembers.*

"Janet?" Peter replied, coaxing Simon in the right direction.

"No," Simon said, not breaking his gaze. "That wasn't it."

"Hmmm, Janis? Janie? Jadis?"

"Jadis!" Simon said, snapping his fingers. "Yes, that was it. Well, she stabbed me, if I remember right," Simon said as he raised an eyebrow at Peter, who dipped his head ever so slightly in confirmation.

"Then what happened?" Scott said between mouthfuls.

"Then, I woke up," Simon said, still watching Peter, who shook his head, again ever so slightly.

"Seems like a normal enough dream to me, with all we've been going through lately," Scott asserted. "I dreamt about this show I used to watch when I was a kid. There was this girl with a scythe in it and—"

Simon stood gracefully, then interrupted. "Sorry, Scott, I think my bandage needs replacing, and I could use some fresh air. Captain, would you mind giving me a hand?" he asked as he made his way out of the makeshift cave.

Scott waved a hand dismissively.

Peter finished his food before donning his new jacket. Once ready, he grasped Galvorn by the sheath and followed Simon outside without a word to the others.

As Peter stepped into the sunlight and brisk morning air, he found Simon pacing in front of a pair of cars pressed together by the force of their crash.

Peter swallowed, not sure what to say. *Please, be real,* was the thought at the forefront of his mind. Simon saw him and stopped pacing, and just stood there watching him, shaking his head almost imperceptibly.

"What do you remember?" Peter asked in a low voice. *Please let it all be real.*

Simon let out a small huff of breath, then looked away from Peter up at the sky. "A stone room full of mist, Jadis attacking me, and then you were there, and it *knew* you, captain," he said, looking like a man walking on thin ice, afraid the wrong step would send him plunging into the freezing depths. "It hasn't faded like a normal dream. I remember every second. What is going on?"

"It wasn't just a dream," Peter replied, relief washing over him. "It was real. I've been there before."

Simon's hand went to his wounded arm, the bandage in clear need of replacement. Peter watched his eyes as they drilled into Peter's skull, desperate to find ground to stand on.

"You've really been there before?"

"Ever since Shadowfang, every time I use the sword, I fall asleep and end up there," Peter replied absently, still reeling from the confirmation that what he'd been experiencing was real. "Doctor Walker thought they were stress-induced, but you were there, so they must be real."

Simon took a step back, his eyes narrowing. "Why didn't you tell me?" he whispered.

It took Peter a moment to realize what his friend said, but when he did, he cackled as he brought a hand to his face. "Why do you think? Who would have believed me?" He gestured with the sheathed sword emphatically. "Doctor Walker didn't even believe me. For all I've known, she was right, and it's been my subconscious trying to deal with the stress."

"All the more reason to tell me," Simon shot back. "You've been thinking your subconsciousness wants me dead? That thing tried to kill me then wanted you to do it. That's not something you bottle up."

"What?" Peter replied, *Wants him dead? No, he's confused.* "No, it's not like that, I—"

"Peter, I'm a medical officer," Simon interrupted. "You've talked to me about what happened with your sister. If you thought this was subconscious, then I needed to know. I need to know if you're doubting your own mental state." Simon brought his hands to his temples. "And if you told me it was real, I would have believed you. Look around us. Only a fool thinks nothing is possible in times like this."

"This is *nothing* like what happened to Hannah," Peter shot back before continuing urgently, "Simon, listen to me. Let me explain before you say anything else."

Simon took a deep breath and crossed his arms, his face marred by a critical furrowing of his eyebrows.

"Jadis has been helping me, training me. Whether or not she was real didn't matter as long as I was getting stronger. You've all had enough to deal with without me telling you I saw some weird pointy-eared creature in my dreams with no way of proving to anyone that it was real."

Peter could feel his heart pounding faster and faster as he went on. "Even if you did believe me, you'd all have had doubts. It would have started eating away at you, making you question my decisions. We can't afford that right now. I've been learning, Simon — getting stronger, faster. She's strange, yes, but I have this under control."

Simon stood there, still as a rock buffeted by the sea, his eyes watching Peter like an injured animal, ready to strike at the first sign of hostility.

"You should have trusted me, Peter," he said in a voice heavy with thought. "If you really have this under control, then why was I brought into it?"

Peter's heart sank. *He's right. There's still too much I don't know about this,* he thought as he watched Simon take a few steps closer. *It doesn't matter, though. I can't stop now.*

"I saw it, that look in your eye you get, Peter. That cold, icy look you get before you kill. You thought about it. Is that why we're out here, Peter? Did she convince you after I woke up that I can't be trusted?" Simon asked, taking an aggressive step closer to Peter and the sword. "Because if that thing has got you that wrapped around its finger, we're all dead anyway."

"Simon, I'm not going to kill you. I never was. How could you even say that?" Peter cut back.

"You—" He stopped, whatever he was about to say imprisoned in his mind out of Peter's reach forever. Simon shook his head, mouth slightly ajar, hesitation in his eyes. "You haven't seen yourself since or been yourself since the Shattering, Peter."

"What's that supposed to mean?"

"You've changed, captain. You throw yourself from one conflict to the next, grinning like a maniac as you slaughter everything in your path. I thought it was just your way of trying to eliminate all threats, but it's more than that. You're not eliminating conflict. You're actively seeking it."

Peter flinched. "I'm doing what I have to. We haven't had a choice but to fight. We've been hounded by threats at every turn. If we don't get stronger, we die. How can you doubt that? You've seen the same horrors I have."

"Peter, do you really think there have been no other options?" Simon asked, looking aghast. "Even if there aren't, you don't even take time to consider anything other than killing. You don't believe me? What about the man you killed after the fighting earlier?"

"How do you—"

"Scott told me. He saw what happened."

"If we'd let him go, he could have brought others."

"You don't know that. That's my whole point," Simon shot back. "These are our countrymen. The same people we fought to protect. How long before you kill the wrong person?"

"I'm doing what I have to. We can't afford to take risks."

"Even if that's true, Peter, you're not doing this to avoid risks. You're doing it because you think it makes you stronger." Simon was almost shouting now. "What happens when there's no one left to kill? Or you pick a fight with something you can't handle? You live by the sword, you will die by the sword, captain."

"If that time comes, so be it," Peter replied firmly with a set jaw.

"For pity's sake, man, for all you know, you're consorting with a demon."

Jadis was right. There's no reasoning with him. He doesn't understand. Peter stared at Simon. His face struggled to hide the anger that burned in his eyes. *Wait for him, find a flaw in what he says next, and help him see why he's wrong.*

"Let me see the sword," Simon said, extending a hand.

Peter flinched. Caught truly off guard for the first time in days. "What? Why?"

"Just let me hold it for a moment, captain. Prove you still trust me."

The veins in Peter's arm bulged as he gripped the sword sheath tighter. *Even if he does try to use it on me, I can take him. I'm faster, and I need him to trust me.* After a moment, he tossed the sword to Simon, it flew through the air, caught easily by the doctor.

"It boggles me that you think you can trust that thing, captain," Simon said, looking down at Galvorn as he drew it from its sheath with an air of disdain. "Yes, she's made you stronger, faster than any human has a right to be. But you need to separate yourself from her. Peter, you have a choice you need to make." He drove Galvorn's blade into the ground between them.

"If you take that sword, you're telling me you trust that creature more than me. I beg you. Leave it where it is, we can turn it over to the elves, maybe they'll know something about her." Simon's words slashed into Peter's mind.

They might, but it's not worth the risk. I can't betray Jadis like that either.

Peter took a step forward without hesitating, and Simon's face fell. Ignoring the look on Simon's face, Peter drew Galvorn from the ground.

Simon just stood there staring, crestfallen, looking like a man who'd been kicked in the chest by a horse, all the air knocked out of him.

"You don't understand, Simon. She needs help just like we do. I'm helping her, and she's helping me. Besides, if Doctor Walker didn't know, why would the elves? Don't worry. I'm in control."

Simon's eyes narrowed. "Do you really believe that?"

Peter weighed his next words carefully. *If I don't, then I prove his point. If I do, he'll think maybe I'm crazy after all. So be it.*

"Yes. You're just going to have to trust me."

Simon took a step back, his face a mask of indifference. "I can't, captain. Not after this. You can't see what she's turning you into."

"What then? Are you going to leave and go back to Paragon?" Peter pushed back.

"No. I'm not going anywhere. We're on the verge of an alliance, and Atlanta needs help. I'm with you until this is done, but I do not trust you so long as you keep that sword, captain. I can't."

"So be it, but do me one last thing. You owe me that much."

"What?" Simon said, tossing Peter the sheath he'd been clutching in his hand.

"Don't tell the others. Not yet. No good would come of it."

Simon closed his eyes tightly and inhaled deeply through his nose. "Fine. But, captain, You're going to get us all killed."

37

CAFETERIA REFUGEES

Sarah finished putting her hair into the hairnet and pulled on the plastic gloves. *I hate how these things feel,* she thought as she lifted the lip of the glove and blew a small burst of air into it so the glove fit properly around her hand.

As she looked down, she saw her black tennis shoes were covered in red dirt from her morning sparring session with Steven. Sarah smiled at the memory of Steven's face as she'd knocked him off his feet; her first of what she hoped would be many victories against him.

Next, she donned a brown apron over her clothes and stored her useless glasses in her back pocket. *I'm early,* she realized when looking up at the clock in the makeshift changing room.

Her shift began in five minutes, so she decided to tidy up the room a bit more. The room previously served as a mailroom, but now that no mail was coming and going from the college, it was serving as a station for gearing up before working the food line.

As she made her way around the room picking up pieces of trash or knocked-over boxes of gloves, she realized she'd have to replace the pair she'd just donned and berated herself for the lack of foresight.

At least we have plenty of them, she thought as she picked up another small box of gloves. *Enough to last a decade, honestly. I wonder how long it would take to get to a point where we could make more. Maybe we don't even need more. We could come up with some kind of spell for clean-hand service, or enchant the gloves to degrade safely somehow.*

The soft tick above her from the clock was drowned out as a group of other volunteers entered the room and began to gear up. They greeted her politely but didn't let the greeting interrupt their conversation.

"I thought all the dwarves went with her though. That's what Joseph was telling me," a squat, middle-aged white woman with curly hair said to a brick-like college-aged African American man.

"Naw, that dude Cheekie and like three or four others stuck around." He carefully put a hair net over his bushy beard. "You know Joseph — always has to be the first with news. Don't matter how accurate it is."

An equally massive white man the same age chortled at this before launching into a complaint about his shift starting as Sarah slipped out the door.

I like this job. It's easier than practicing magic, and people don't recognize me as much in the hairnet.

As she walked towards her station, she quickly replaced her gloves after she put the old ones in her back pocket. The college cafeteria, recently converted into a food line structure rather than a set of different food stations, was as busy as always. One of the men, whose task was to punch meal tickets, waved her through before she was stopped by the shift manager.

Today's shift manager was Al, a familiar ruddy, round-faced man she'd met a few times before taking on the job. He looked up from a clipboard when she greeted him.

"Good morning, Al. How are you today?"

"Fine, how are you, Miss Young?" he replied distractedly.

"I'm good. Do you need me in the same spot as yesterday?" she asked politely.

Al's pen moved down along the keyboard until it came to a stop, and he checked something off. "Yes, ma'am. Only one scoop today. Just today, hopefully, we're reevaluating things based on what the Atlanta force took." He bit the inside of his cheek. "Don't let them try and tell you otherwise. Anyone has a problem, send them to me."

"Okay," Sarah replied. Then, as quickly as was permissible, she made her way through the shifting crowd to her spot in the food line. The young man assigned to the spot eagerly passed off a small ladle to her and departed without so much as a word. Sarah took up the position and began scooping a ladle of pasta into every plate on a tray presented to her.

She was painfully aware of the small size of the portion as almost each and every person she served looked down on it in disappointment. That look left her with a feeling of loneliness lingering in her mind as each hungry person moved along.

Fifteen minutes into the task, she began to notice that every once in a while, a man or woman in their early twenties to late thirties would see her and not offer up their tray for food. A few minutes later, a woman and her daughter approached her station, and when the child raised her tray, the mother's eyes went wide, and she pulled the child's tray back so violently that the tray's meager contents spilled to the floor.

The little girl's eyes grew wet and round as she looked between her mother and the spilled food. Her lower lip began to tremble, a herald of oncoming tears.

She can't be more than six. Poor thing. "Don't worry," Sarah began with her best attempt at a soothing voice as she made her way around to the front of the station. "We can get you some—"

"Stay away," the mother cried out in what sounded surprisingly like horror to Sarah. Sarah stopped, unsure what to do with her hands that she'd been aiming to grab the tray with, so she lowered them to her sides. She looked at the woman, who now stood protectively in front of her wide-eyed, wrinkly-browed daughter.

She was in her mid-thirties with a ragged bob haircut that looked several weeks past due for its usual trim and coloring. Her skin was sallow and sunken, and she was several pounds short of where she should have been. In contrast, her daughter seemed to be of normal weight with healthy, warm skin.

"It's okay. I was just going to pick up her tray," Sarah replied. *Why is it so quiet in here all of a sudden?* she wondered as she realized her reply was one of the only sounds in the room.

"No," the woman replied in a firm but fear-laced voice. "Please, please just leave us alone," she begged, as she kept an arm wrapped tightly around her daughter behind her.

Sarah's face wrinkled in confusion, but she took a step back. The woman's eyes remained focused on her, unblinking as they watched her every move as if she were a snake about to strike her child.

Then Al emerged from the crowd of people who'd frozen around the scene. "I'm sorry, y'all, is everything all right?" he began as he signaled for one of his assistants to start cleaning up the mess. "Come along now, ma'am. Let's find you and your daughter a place to sit down. We'll take care of your food now, don't you worry."

What was that all about? That lady looks like she's been starving herself to keep her child healthy but freaked out when I tried to help. I wasn't being aggressive. Maybe I look tired and angry, Sarah wondered as she made her way back around to her station and took in how unnaturally quiet everyone had grown.

The noise of the cafeteria was picking back up as Al ushered the mother and daughter away. Even so, there was still a strangeness to the sound around her. The oddity revealed itself as she looked down the line and saw plenty of people talking to each other and the folks serving their food. All of the talking ended just as they reached her station as if they were passing through a bubble of silence, which she stood at the center of.

Only a few minutes later, she heard Al's voice behind her. "Sarah."

She turned around quickly and put on a friendly smile. "Yes? Are the lady and her daughter all right?" she asked as Al, and another shorter man came into view.

"Yes, they're fine. Jere is just here to take over for you so you can go ahead and get something to eat." Al replied, but his eyes did not meet hers.

Did I do something wrong? "I've still got at least another half hour on my shift before my break," Sarah replied, confused by her face warming.

"Yes, I know. Mayor Doctor Gibson's here though, and he asked for you to join him. He's over by the old sandwich station," Al explained and still refused to meet her eyes.

Am I in some kind of trouble?

"Don't bother going back through the line though. He said he's already got your food," Al said and waved her along.

He must have gone through a different line. What's going on? Surely this isn't about the lady and her daughter. I didn't do anything wrong there. Maybe it's something else. Maybe something happened to Duelma Umindrabo. She fretted as she made her way around the serving tables and over towards where Dr. Gibson sat. At the table sat a woman with short, dyed hair, who Sarah recognized as one of the women who'd skipped her part of the food line.

Dr. Gibson greeted her with a broad smile, his mustache in a finer state than it had been in days. "Ah, Miss Young. Please, have a seat. I've seen to it that food was provided for you."

Sarah followed Dr. Gibson's hand and sat down at the end of the table between the two occupants. She glanced down at her food and felt the color partially drain from her face. There was clearly more food there than on any of the other plates she'd seen so far.

"Doctor Gibson, I don't know if they told you, but the food is being rationed due to the—"

The tall man stopped her with a wave of his hand. "I am very aware of the rationing being done until we reevaluate our supplies. I was the one who suggested it. I am also a medical professional. Doctor Walker instructed that I keep you well-fed, and I intend to do so. Obviously, this stays between us, of course," he said with a meaningful look at the woman across from him.

"If people were to complain, the blame is to be placed solely on me. Your protest regarding this decision is a credit to your character," he said as he ran his fingers over his mustache.

I don't want people to think I'm getting special treatment. If I am, they wouldn't just be thinking about it. I… I do find myself hungrier than usual today… Really, they're not feeding me so much as they're feeding my abilities… That feels dishonest, though, she thought as she took small bites of bland pasta and chewed thoroughly.

"Now, as to complaints. Sarah Young, this is Marah Reynolds. She is one of our Macon refugees," Dr. Gibson said in reference to the squat woman across from him. Sarah directed her attention to the woman's face. It was a plain face poorly hidden under more makeup than she'd seen since the Shattering. Marah's expression was guarded, and she offered Sarah an insincere smile in greeting.

"Marah is a popular choice among those from Macon as a representative council member while Mister Dory Langulb, who I believe you met, is off with the Atlanta force," Dr. Gibson explained quickly. "As you're aware, Sarah, the citizens of Macon, suffered quite a bit under the influence of a magic-capable man named Jason, correct?"

Both Sarah and Marah nodded.

"Good. Marah, would you please tell Sarah what you told me?"

Marah grimaced slightly. "Unfortunately, Sarah, due to the trauma suffered by most of us in Macon, quite a few of us are rather distrusting of anyone with magical abilities. You may have noticed a number of people avoiding taking food from you?"

Yes, you were one of them, Sara thought as she nodded.

"I see. Please don't hold that against them. I was asked to bring the situation up to Mayor Gibson, so here we are," Marah said and spread her arms in a manner that indicated things were out of her control.

"Now, Sarah. I asked you to join us because I wanted Marah to see the quality of your character so she can bear witness to it to her friends. That being said, you have as much a right to work here as anyone else, and the complaints of a few do not justify infringing on that right, in my opinion," Dr. Gibson said carefully with a measured look at Marah.

Sarah nodded slowly, still slowly finishing off the food provided for her. What it lacked in flavor it made up for in warmth. The bodies that filled the large room made up for the cold outside, but there was still something about warm food that scared away the lingering cold of the chilly outdoors.

"Given this information, Sarah, how would you like to proceed?" he asked as she neared completion of her food.

"Well…" Sarah said in an attempt to stall for time. "I've heard things are a little tense." She glanced at Marah and tried to read her expression but got nothing. "I like working at the food station… but I don't want anyone going hungry because of me."

"That would be their own fault," Dr. Gibson chipped in. "No one is denying them food."

"No… but they're scared. It's not their fault. I don't know what Jason did, or how he did it, or if it's even something I could do. Not that I'd want to. I'm just… I don't want to cause trouble." She struggled to find the right words.

"You seem like a sweet girl," Marah said as she set one of her hands on the table halfway towards Sarah. "I'm sure, given time, people would get used to you. I'm sure you don't *intend* any harm. Surely there's something better one with your talents could be doing than scooping food."

But I like it. It's calming, relaxing. Simple. Sarah felt a strange pang in her chest. "I… I could take a break from working here until things settle down a bit. Give people a chance to get used to me."

Marah nodded eagerly, a friendly smile plastered on her face. "Of course. If you'd be willing to do that, I'm sure it would go a long way. People would see you're a reasonable person."

Dr. Gibson frowned and shook his head ever so slightly. "I won't ask you to do that, Sarah. If that is what you want, very well, but I will back you up if you want to keep working here. It might do some good at first to distance yourself, but I think your actions speak for themselves."

"It's not a big deal. Everyone has to adjust these days. It's only fair if I do too," Sarah replied eagerly. "I can always devote my time to studying the books Doctor Walker left behind. There is quite a bit of material I haven't even scratched the surface of really."

"It's settled then," Marah began. "Mayor Gibson was right. You are a reasonable and kind girl, Sarah," she said with a smile. "I'm sure everyone will be over their paranoia in a heartbeat."

ALLURË

A day and a half after Simon and Peter's conversation, Elborin led their group through the outskirts of a forest only a few miles west of downtown Atlanta. The closer they drew to the city, the darker the sky got.

The only indication of their location was a damaged sign which read *W-stv-ew.* They'd left their vehicles at that sign, forced to continue on foot due to lack of gas and increased foliage. If not for their guide, they'd have been completely lost.

Above, thick rolling clouds congregated and blocked out the sun. Shattered, broken skyscrapers loomed in the distance. The space between them was impossible to judge accurately due to damage and overgrowth.

The now present forest showed no remorse for the buildings and roads it grew over. Peter felt unease settle under his skin as he became more and more lost. He and Scott were bringing up the rear of their group, with Elborin and the dryad out front while O'Cleary and Simon formed the middle.

They were well spread, sticking to cover, but Peter couldn't shake the sensation that crawled under his skin, like the lingering suspicion that a hand is running along the side of your bed in the dark of night.

But Elborin led them calmly ever forward between a set of overgrown buildings. The air here was thicker, but not unpleasantly so. No one else gave signs of nervousness, so Peter remained silent as they entered the small space between those green buildings.

After a few steps into the green gorge between the buildings, Peter came to a stop. Years of experience were screaming at him not to venture any farther.

This isn't right, he thought as he looked fervently around. The windows in the overgrown buildings were all broken, leaving their views unobstructed. At the end of the buildings, a collection of vines formed a wall, hiding what was on the other side. This was not a safe place to be.

The elf continued forward undisturbed without so much as a sideways glance. The space between the buildings was hardly big enough for two men to walk side by side, making it nearly impossible to move in the way combat demands. *I don't feel any warning, but this is a perfect spot for an ambush,* Peter thought, the sensation only compounded by his uncertainty as he studied the area for any signs of an ambush.

Peter's hand was frozen to his sword's handle as he slowly moved forward again. He did not want to draw it too soon and alert the shadows of his suspicion. The nervous sensation evolved into the feeling that he was being watched, haunted with hidden eyes every step.

They were halfway through the buildings, on a journey that felt like it was taking hours. But Peter still sensed no threat with his arcane awareness as they moved forward. Still, his neck hairs stood on end in defiance of his sixth sense. He looked ahead and saw O'Cleary and Simon beginning to slow down. *Good, it's not just me,* he thought as his hand pulled reflexively on Galvorn but was stopped when he felt something grip his wrist.

Elborin sensed their unease and turned back to face them. His eyes went to Peter's wrist and grasped it firmly in his grip. He gave a slight shake of his head and said in a quiet voice, with raised eyebrows, "Don't embarrass me, captain. You are my guests. You are in no danger here."

Peter released his sword hilt with an indigent look on his face. The elf smiled bemusedly in response.

"Come. We have arrived," he said as he stepped through the vines, which fell back into place behind him. Peter watched him go, still gripping the handle of his sword. The dryad followed the elf without hesitation, and Peter realized all that was left were his human companions. Scott and O'Cleary both eyed him strangely. Peter stepped to the front of the group. "Be ready," he ordered as he approached the vines.

Scott raised an eyebrow in Peter's direction, then shrugged, weapon in hand. O'Cleary's eyebrows wrinkled. "You all right, cap? You look shaken. Did you get enough sleep?"

"I'm fine, Brandon. Just tired. You're right. Haven't been sleeping well."

O'Cleary nodded slowly with a furrowed brow as he watched Peter. "All right, see you on the other side," he said with a grin.

Peter took a deep breath as he stepped into the vines. They were warm and heavy but allowed him to slip by easily enough. Upon exiting, he found they were in a small glade at the edge of a strangely conformist section of forest.

Through the openings in the trees, a dozen elves could be seen moving from one place to another. All were adorned in strange armor and equipped with a variety of spears, swords, bows, and arrows, and one was even holding a poleax.

They wore strange green-patterned cloth with small pieces of armor woven into it. Some wore thin helmets with slits down the side, which revealed distinct colored braids that ran along the slits. None were paying their emerging group the slightest attention. Instead, they carried on about their business. Their clothes reminded Peter of a blend of Roman and ancient celtic styles.

Peter's attention was drawn to O'Cleary as he exited the vines and began swearing good naturedly. Peter took a step back and grabbed O'Cleary by the shoulder. The man barely noticed, he was so occupied with a particularly clever curse at Elborin regarding what the elf could do with his fancy spear for not giving them a better sense of what to expect.

Elborin did not acknowledge the insult. He was too busy as he strode forward to meet a female elf that stood at the edge of the glade, clearly in wait for them. O'Cleary continued his good-natured derogatory comments about pointy-eared maniacs, despite not receiving a reaction.

Elborin stopped once he was a hair's breadth from the brown-eyed female elf with honey-gold hair and a red waterfall braid. Her armor was a deep green layered material, the same as Elborin's. She was a tad shorter than the elves moving through the trees, but she had a lean build.

Elborin greeted the female elf warmly in elvish. "Lúemeni, Mellonië."

"Lúemeni, Elborin," she replied with a voice like a mountain spring. Then she locked thumbs with him, pulling them together in an embrace that ended with their hands over their hearts and foreheads together. They stayed like this for a moment before pulling apart and releasing.

Elborin gave the female elf a peck on the forehead, and Mellonië reached up and ran a hand over Elborin's shaved head, smiling curiously. Then she glanced past him towards the rest of the party, which stood in awkward silence.

"What have you brought us, my Melisë?" she asked affectionately in English. The pet name remained in elvish, loud enough for the rest to hear.

Elborin grinned a warm mischievous expression. "A human Antemáklasi, with knowledge of Vulacia's changes. We should make haste to speak with General Almurë."

Mellonië's eyes widened. She looked at the newcomers more closely and tilted her head in greeting towards the dryad.

"An Antemáklasi?" she added with a smirk. "That will be of particular interest to General Fánagraw the Eighth."

"General Fánagraw is here as well?" Elborin replied with a large grin.

Mellonië's expression shifted to one of slight amusement. "Be on your way then. I shall see you soon. My seventh day approaches," she added in a low tone as she turned to the rest of them.

"Lúemeni, or Hello? Yes, hello warriors. Welcome to the war camp of General Almurë," she said with a gracious half bow. "I am Feniand Mellonië Essërod, Acairii to Elborin."

"Yeah, no idea what an Acairii is, but you are one beautiful lass," O'Cleary replied.

Mellonië furrowed her brow, concentrating, then whispered to Elborin, who whispered back and nodded. Then, grinning, Mellonië explained. "Wife. I am his wife."

O'Cleary's eyes widened for a moment. Peter feared he might try to draw attention to his comment by apologizing. Instead, the Irishman thumped Caraticus on the shoulder, which only brought confusion to both elves' faces.

Peter leaned slightly toward Leuoradew and whispered as Mellonië explained that Feniand was her rank, not her title to O'Cleary. "What's the proper greeting here?"

Leuoradew furrowed her brow, an act that made a strange noise but did not shift her gaze from the elves. "I do not know, Peter Blair," she whispered back.

Her expression is like a tree, unreadable, Peter joked to himself.

Peter repressed a smirk, took a step forward, and spoke. "Lúemeni, I'm Captain Peter Blair. I'm afraid your husband did not give us so much as a basic overview of your culture." He leered at Elborin. "Would have been nice before we arrived, Caraticus," Peter growled at the only familiar elf.

"It would have been, yes," Elborin shot back, still grinning like an older brother who'd just tricked his sibling into embarrassing themselves.

Mellonië rolled her eyes bemusedly and turned to Elborin. "Do give them some pointers, Caraticus." She said the name with a hint of amusement. "Almurë will not care, but the Blues will."

Leuoradew slid forward, plucked a leaf from her hair, and handed it to the elf-woman before she spoke. "It is good to see trees well cared for here. Root and branch tangle and lay about in chaos, but not here. Here the trees and their children are guided properly. Thank you for this."

Mellonië took the leaf and smiled. "The work of the arborous is always a blessing. Welcome back, Leuoradew," she said graciously.

Elborin nodded agreeably. "Come along, humans. There is still much to do before the day is done, and we must go speak to the generals. Leuoradew, you may join us or enjoy the forest and seek out your own."

Leuoradew looked around curiously for a moment before she placed herself behind Peter, which drew a strange look from Scott as he moved up to join the rest of them.

Only then did the discussion of generals fully dawn on Peter. He'd been so preoccupied with observing his surroundings and the elves' actions that their words slipped by without him taking in their meanings.

He cursed to himself. Generals? In this state? He became suddenly aware of the filthy, disheveled state of himself and his men. They were covered head to toe in injuries, dirt, and old blood. Their uniforms were in disarray, their hair unkempt, and their faces scruffy. *Hardly an acceptable appearance for meeting a foreign general.* But the elf was already on the move.

Peter thought back to the one time he'd met a general while serving in the Army. He'd known about it months in advance. His company had spent weeks cleaning leading up to the event, which was only a passing through for the high-ranking officer to make sure everything was perfect. It'd been a nightmarish exercise in perfectionism for a man who'd been gone an hour later. And now he was being taken before a pair of elvish generals, battle-weary and filthy. *I'd rather fight a dozen bulletproof orks by myself then do this.*

But there was nothing he could do. They fell into a double line, where Peter and Elborin walked shoulder to shoulder. Peter looked back over his shoulder. Scott carried on without a care in the world. In contrast, Simon was fidgeting to make himself more presentable. Bit by bit, he straightened this and that in a futile effort. No such attempts were made by O'Cleary; the Irishman was far too occupied with gaping at their surroundings.

Before Peter had a chance to ask if they could stop and clean themselves up a little, Elborin launched into explaining the does and don'ts of elvish culture. Around them, dozens of different types of trees formed an enormous, intricate spiral, each of which grew equidistant from the others in a turning pattern, surrounded by small foliage.

There was space between the trees that made a path of short soft grass, which sprung back up unharmed after receiving a footstep.

The patterned growth of trees was interrupted by the occasional opening into a small glade or clearing, many of which were occupied by elves who participated in one strenuous activity or another. What few buildings they saw were ignored by the trees, which grew through them regardless of their material. They never allowed the pattern to be disrupted. If not for these overgrown buildings and the occasional moss-covered vehicle scattered about, the place would have been unrecognizable as part of Atlanta's outskirts.

The strange collection of dirty travelers drew only passing glances as they traversed between orderly trees and tents toward the center of the busy camp. Peter found the lack of interest paid to them by the elves intriguing and noticed more attention was given to Elborin's shaved head and Leuoradew than any of the battered humans.

As he observed those present while they walked, Peter noticed that all the elves wore hair of varying length, though none nearly as short as Elborin's. Additionally, each and every one had a dyed braid of one kind or another, and the most prominent of these braids was a deep mossy green, but there was also a scattering of white and red braids.

"Do not sit in the company of those above your rank unless invited to do so. It is considered rude and arrogant," Elborin explained as they passed a glade full of elves who practiced what looked like an advanced form of calisthenics. Their flexibility and grace caused Peter's eyes to widen in surprise. It was evident upon closer observation that these people were at war. Many of the elves bore fresh injuries. Others were actively attending to dirty or damaged weapons and armor.

Elborin went on, "The greeting I exchanged with Mellonië is an informal one. A simple bow will do for most meetings, although I expect Almurë may go for a handshake. It seems like the type of thing he'd enjoy."

O'Cleary cleared his throat and asked, "What's the deal with the braids?"

Elborin's hand went reflexively to the braid tied around his neck. "Color denotes rank and braid specialization. Orks do not see color the way we do, so this way, our ranks are disguised."

"Fascinating, isn't it?" Scott muttered from the back.

"For example, Captain Blair would have a dark red, or perhaps even purple, braid, styled like my own. The rest of you would have green."

As they continued on, Peter noticed a strange hum as they moved farther into the camp. He realized it was singing — strange singing with no words, only notes, overlapping and mixing in a beautiful cacophony. High and low sounds harmonized and mixed with inhuman undulations and bravado. The sound both thrilled and terrified him.

"What's that singing?" Peter asked, as he tried to focus on it but was unable to discern where it came from.

Elborin's brow furrowed. "What sin— Oh. Of course, those are our casters practicing."

"Your magic users?" Peter clarified.

"Well, sort of. All elves are in tune with the arcane flow, but most of our warriors simply use that connection to strengthen their physical bodies. Our casters are the ones who focus on honing their connection into weaving more complex spells. They do this through song, whereas dwarves use tattoos, and humans often use speech."

"Wait, so all of you can cast, but only some of you do?" Peter replied, dumbfounded.

Elborin looked at him, nonplused. "You all have the ability to paint, do you not Peter? So why then do you choose to be a warrior rather than creating beautiful tapestries?"

Peter scowled. "That's hardly the same thing."

"No?" Elborin paused as he looked their group up and down. "Perhaps not to you. But you are bound by the constraints of time. We are not. We do not age lest we wish it, and even then, it is only a symbol of vanity which does not weaken us physically like your kind or the dwarves."

He smiled sadly as he stepped between a set of tents, with a nod at a passing elf in fresh armor. "Our time in this world only draws to an end by unnatural means. For this reason, many of our kind take time for granted. assuming they will get around to everything eventually. But I digress here. As we pass through this section of the camp, remain quiet. This is the place of the seventh day."

At this, they passed through an imperceptible sheen of shadow and entered a section of the camp void of movement or noise. Peter felt a shift in pressure, as if he'd gone up a mountain and swallowed, because his ears had popped. Here, their footfalls didn't make so much as a sound as they proceeded through the area. The only sounds Peter heard were the thumps of his heart and his own thoughts.

The tents here were more like cocoons, suspended in the trees, between and along branches overhead, with no ladders reaching down from them to give access. Despite this, the trees continued in their patterned fashion, many still overlapping with buildings and rubble.

There was noticeable darkness here, as though they were underwater. The light above waxed and waned as if it had pierced a veil of liquid.

At a distance, Peter saw a soft glowing blue light floating through the air towards them. As the blue light drew closer, he realized it was a pixy, a humanoid robin-sized creature with fluttering wings made of leaves giving off a translucent glow. The strange little being landed softly on Leuoradew's shoulder and seemed to whisper in her ear before it leapt off and fluttered away, only to disappear into the dark.

Moments later, they reached the center of camp, and as soon as they stepped out from under the suspended tents, Peter's ears popped again. Peter blinked rapidly as he tried to adjust to the shift in the light, which was restored to normalcy as he pulled at his earlobe to try and dismiss the uncomfortable sensation in his ear.

"Sorry about that. The place of the seventh day is where we take our long rests, and a spell is put over it to diminish sound and light so that sleep can go undisturbed."

Peter found his mind wandering back to the family dinner table years ago. His older sister explained the battle of San Jacinto to him as a proud mother set a hot casserole of poppy seed chicken on the table, and their dad poured drinks.

"Then, they caught them while they were napping," Hannah had exclaimed passionately as Peter listened in wonder.

"But what was their mistake?" Peter recalled their father asking with a twinkle in his eye as he winked at their mom.

Hannah hadn't even hesitated in her hasty reply. "They let the enemy generals escape."

Peter was snatched back to the present by a distant roaring, which did not make Elborin so much as flinch. Peter considered asking what it was, but it appeared they were closing in on their destination.

Ahead of them, at the center of the camp, was an enormous canopy supported by three large trees — a cedar, an oak, and a ginkgo — each towering over two hundred feet. The canopy material was white and seemed as light as silk but remained still and undisturbed even when breezes passed by.

Out to the side of the canopy stood a small squadron of savage-looking elves garbed in dark armor. They were huddled together in low conversation, but when Elborin got closer, they all nodded in acknowledgment towards him.

Were it a human camp, the canopy would have reached the ground and concealed the space's contents. The cover ended well above the heads of the tallest present, shadow casting a clear circumference over the meeting place; at the edge of which, a single guard was standing where an entrance to a tent would have been.

The guard was a young dark-skinned male elf with black dreadlocks and a simple white braid bound along the side of his head. He wore the same strange armored cloth as the rest and was brimming with idle energy as he watched their approach with curious brown eyes. Peter's attention was drawn away from him as a figure moved past him out of the shadow cast by the canopy.

A female elf stepped into full view as she moved towards their small knot of people. Her medium-length, ash-brown hair was pulled into a loose French braid on top of her head. Two smaller French braids dyed the same deep purple as Elborin's braid necklace ran across the right side of her head. It reminded Peter a bit of a feuxhawk, but was far too intricate to fully resemble one.

The dark cloth armor she wore was black, obviously tailored for fluidity. The small, layered pieces were woven together, shifting without hindering her movement. A long, open tunic-like garment fell over her garbed legs. Her toned right arm was bare just below the shoulder in stark contrast to her left, which was fully covered in a layered armor piece. On her back, a pair of thin swords rested comfortably in a single sheath.

After taking in her armor, Peter gave attention to her face. It was a warrior's face, lean and tight-lipped, beautiful with a brown freckle just below the left side of her lips. Her neck bore two harsh scars cutting from its center back around the left side.

O'Cleary muttered in a hushed voice behind him, "I'd ask her out for some craic, but I think she could break my arm with a look."

Her small, thoughtful, deep-set, almond-shaped, sea-glass, blue-green eyes were drawn to Elborin, focused on the short hair on his head. She changed her course from the squad of elves and approached Elborin.

"What happened to you?" she asked in elvish, her voice low, smooth, and calming, like a summer breeze.

"Lúemeni, Súmeriel. It was a necessary sacrifice," Elborin replied. "Is he well?" he asked and nodded toward the canopy.

Súmeriel let out a soft sigh, smiled weakly, and raised her arms emotively in a display of frustrated surrender. "He's obsessed with another human puzzle. Refuses to make a move on the city until we have a more sufficient understanding of the layout, or at least find one of the missing Duridgribuldam."

Elborin nodded. "I was afraid of that. Go ahead and prepare the ócom-véla. The child must be dealt with, and I've found a solution to convincing your father," he said, gesturing proudly at the group behind him.

"May Erúil guide your tongue," Súmeriel replied a bit sarcastically before she stalked off. Her movement reminded Peter of a wolf as he turned to watch her go and noticed a strange bone dagger sheathed at the small of her back.

Before Súmeriel could vanish into the camp, Elborin turned to them. "Wait here a moment," he instructed and disappeared into the canopy, leaving them under the curious watch of the guard.

"Well…" O'Cleary stretched the word and began looking around. "First time meeting a general for me, how about you lads?"

"Second," Peter replied shortly.

"Fourth," Simon replied.

"Fourth?" O'Cleary replied with wide eyes. He smirked. "What'd you muck up enough to get that much attention, Simon?"

Simon raised an eyebrow slightly. "Saved his nephew after taking a hit from an IED."

O'Cleary gave a soft whistle. "Aye, that'll do it."

A few minutes later, Elborin's head poked out from the canopy, and he motioned for them all to join him. The interior of the shadow was a single large room. The canopy roof was decorated by an enormous map of what looked like one country at first glance, but Peter quickly realized it was a massive continent surrounded by a body of water. Hundreds of cities and territories were listed in a language he couldn't even begin to decipher.

At the center of the map, the material changed to a mesh opening, which let in enough light to illuminate the center of the room, where a large dark wooden decagon table sat. On the table, seemingly carved from the same wood the table was made of, was an intricate model of a large city and the surrounding areas.

After a second, Peter recognized it as Atlanta. There were large unfilled open spaces in the map, but several familiar skyscrapers made the incomplete map of devastation more recognizable.

It was a strange sight to behold as it put into context the sheer magnitude of change the city had suffered. It was a more shocking sight than Peter expected. *It really looks like two different cities from different times were spliced together in a moment without rhyme or reason,* Peter thought as he examined the buildings, old and new, blended in disarray.

To Peter's left, sitting still in a small chair, was a male elf in a white leather kilt of the same fabric as the rest of the elves' armor, and a light, flowy gray shirt. There were no weapons on his person that Peter could see. He had almost the same ash brown hair as the female who'd just left, but his was sprinkled with gray and white. A violet braid ran along the right side of his head. His face bore a distinguished set of soft wrinkles and a pair of green eyes over a thin nose.

His fingers were steepled as he stared at a small colorful box on the edge of the table.

Elborin stepped forward and cleared his throat, gesturing at the seated elf. "This is General Almurë, Slayer of Aaepip, Scourge of Shadows, Siegemaster, First Wielder of the Thalmein Blade, Murinelar. General Fánagraw will join us soon."

Good. One general at a time, Peter thought as he breathed a small sigh of relief.

The general didn't so much as flinch. He simply sat there and stared at the Rubik's cube in front of him. After a moment of awkward silence, he stood slowly and picked the cube off the table. Despite his wrinkled face, there was nothing old about his physique or movement as he walked over to Peter, offering him the cube.

Oh great. He's testing me. I'm going to do it too slowly, or too quickly, and then get a lecture. Peter's heart sank as he took it and saw that while it was unsolved, it was not shuffled; rather, the colors were organized in a simple pattern repeated on each side. Peter looked back up at the general, but the elf's eyes remained focused on the cube in Peter's hands.

With a shrug, Peter gave the cube a few turns before the familiar pattern returned to him. Several turns and a few moments later, each side of the cube was a solid color. Accepting there was nothing he could do to stop whatever lesson he was about to be taught, Peter held it out towards the general. But Almurë did not take it. Rather, he finally looked Peter fully in the face.

"Open it," he said in a powerful yet friendly voice.

"Open it?" Peter replied, unsure he'd heard correctly, the cube in his hand still held out towards the general.

"Yes, open it. I've already done that, but it won't open," he said, his eyes narrowed at the cube.

"Sir, it doesn't open," Peter replied cautiously, he did not like how this was going at all. He felt strangely helpless, a feeling which he despised.

Almurë's brow furrowed, deepening his wrinkles. He scratched his forehead with a surprisingly smooth, strong hand. "What's the point then?" he asked, his voice giving off a sense of bewilderment. Then his eyes caught on Peter's sword, sheathed on his back, and went wide. "May I see that?" he said with a raised finger pointed at Peter's sword.

Peter hesitated as he set the cube on the table. The dozens of things that could go wrong if he handed over the sword rampaged through his mind. What if he has no intention of returning it?

"Captain Blair," Elborin prodded.

"Yes, sorry. Of course, general," Peter replied, drew the sword cautiously, and handed it begrudgingly, blade down, to the general.

The general took it and gave Peter a sideways sort of respectful bow with his head before turning and placing the blade in the light falling over the table. He sang a single high note, and the light from above increased. In this new light, Almurë examined the blade with cautious awe. "This is, without a doubt, a Thalmein blade," he muttered. "But, I have never heard of a black Thalmein blade."

Elborin shifted at this and took a step closer to get a better look himself.

Almurë's eyes went wide as they dawned with realization. "This blade is bound to the Therin-Selu." Elborin did not give a physical reaction, but there was a shift in the room's atmosphere as the silent elf to their right turned his head in a quick jerk towards them.

Almurë's attention shifted to Peter. "Valk Elborin, who have you brought into my presence?" he asked.

That doesn't sound good.

"This is Captain Peter Blair of SNW," O'Cleary said as he took a step forward and slapped Peter on the shoulder. Almurë raised his eyebrows at O'Cleary, and the Irishman took a step back, his hands raised in surrender.

"As he said, sir, this is Valk Peter Blair, Basilisk-Bane, Avenger of the arborous and an Antemáklasi.

"A human Antemáklasi wielding a black Thalmein blade bound to the Therin-Selu? Tell me, Captain Peter, what brings you here wielding a blade which should not exist?" he asked inquisitively. His voice did not threaten but demanded an answer be given.

Peter clenched and unclenched his right hand, eager to have the sword back before something went wrong. He swallowed, his throat uncharacteristically dry, as he focused on the general. "Death," Peter answered, his voice cold as steel, matching Almurë's critical stare.

Almurë raised an eyebrow a hairsbreadth. "Whose death?"

Peter frowned. "My people's, my enemies, and in due time my own."

Almurë's face remained indecipherable as he reexamined the blade in silence. Peter felt the ground shake slightly behind him as enormous footfalls approached. Peter looked up and saw a colossal silhouette approaching the canopy. "What on Earth…?"

Into the canopy strolled an enormous old polar bear, at least nine feet tall, walking on his hind legs. Small scars decorated his paws. One claw was missing from his left paw. He paused for a moment, his green eyes searching the room curiously as he looked over the terrified men. He wore an eggplant-purple braided hair collar around his neck. Seemingly satisfied with what he saw, he trundled forward, slightly bent from age. He stopped next to the general and plopped down on his backside with a large thud that knocked over a dozen pieces on the map.

Almurë reached over and scratched him under the chin, and then spoke to him in elvish. "Welcome back. Allow me to introduce General Fánagraw the Eighth," he added with an enormous grin in English.

General Fánagraw yawned, which revealed his enormous, immaculately clean teeth. Peter felt an itch in his hand where his sword should have been, but he sensed no danger from the massive bear.

Almurë returned to his previous line of thought as though the gigantic bear was perfectly ordinary. "Essërod would not have brought you if you were not capable or trustworthy. Erúil, guide me," he prayed. "What are your accomplishments? What I've seen of you humans these last few days has shaken my once steady confidence in your ability to survive."

It took Peter a moment to gather his thoughts as his eyes darted back and forth between the two generals. "Since the Shattering, I have been nearly eaten by a basilisk, nearly killed by a pair of overzealous dwarves, had my mind almost taken from me by an egotistical maniac…"

Peter paused and crossed his arms, his voice gaining confidence as he grew more comfortable with the relaxed atmosphere. "…fought dozens of orks, killed as many of my own kind, and survived a warlock and his enormous, cursed… bear," Peter added with a nervous glance at General Fánagraw, who he half expected to open his mouth and reply.

He ran a hand through his messy hair. "I have battled nightmares in the dark of night and the light of day. All in the pursuit of making this world safer for my kind. I have done this with that sword which you claim should not exist and with the help of these men and women with me. Before all this, I was a commander of an elite mercenary outfit that specialized in stealth operations with over a dozen successful missions carried out under my direct leadership."

Almurë still gave no indication of his thoughts. He simply asked softly, "You are familiar with the city, Valk Blair?"

"I knew it before it became this," Peter said, gesturing at the table. "And I intend to enter it to seek out my soldiers that may still be there."

Almurë grinned. "A proper answer. I'm sorry, my curiosity must be satiated before we discuss entering the city. By your clothes and tongue, you are a modern man, so where did you acquire your sword, and do you know its name?"

What is this obsession with Galvorn? What does he know that I don't? Does he know about Jadis? "Galvorn was given to me by an old dwarf. I know her as Dr. Walker, but her fellow dwarves referred to her as Duelma Umindrabo. But she said I should refer to her if need be as Umindrabo Duridgrihulda, last of the Duridgribuldam."

Almurë's jaw tightened at this. "Erúil's grace. Elborin did mention that to me," he said with a sly look at the short-haired elf.

Elborin smiled back, and the general continued.

"Liúre," the general swore. "To think one of the Duridgribuldam was so close all this time. Of course, I have dispatched riders to reinforce Elborin's letter to her, and it is of utmost importance that she reaches me with haste. She is the key to uncovering what has happened to cause all of this destruction."

"If all went to plan, she should be bringing us reinforcements from Paragon," Peter interjected.

"Yes, and they are also familiar with the city?" Almurë replied.

"Many will be."

"Elborin," Almurë said commandingly. "Select a few members of your Fardrim-Véla for infiltration, you will be accompanying Valk Blair into the city." He drummed his fingers on the table. "No, I take that back. Inform Folduin and Galamier they'll be accompanying you. They've done the most infiltrations and have been in contact with the human resistance."

Elborin brought a hand in a curve in front of his face in a strange form of salute. "I request Mellonië as well."

The general nodded, and Elborin departed.

"The resistance?" Peter asked, his curiosity heightened.

"Yes, there is a human faction in the city which has been holding out, but we have been unable to properly reinforce them."

"Do they have a stronghold, or are they rabbiting from one spot to the next?" Peter asked, taking a step closer to the table Almurë was examining.

"Rabbiting? Ah, a clever turn of phrase." Almurë knuckled his forehead and took a step around the table. He reached into one of his pockets and revealed a small notebook. He jotted down something in it while he chuckled to himself and then returned it to his pocket, his smile dropping slightly. "But, no, I believe the word best suited for it would be guerilla. Although, it would seem they are less combative than the word would imply. We know where the humans are, and it will hold for now, but there is strange ork activity here, which concerns me."

He pointed to what looked like a splice of the World of Coke and a large cathedral-like building, then he drew a circle in the air around the area. "For some reason, the orks do not like this area. They have it surrounded and don't seem to enter it. There may be humans there. I do not know." He tapped a finger on the structure. "I want you and your warriors to infiltrate with Elborin. Once there, I want you to determine what it is keeping them out and if we can utilize it when we strike."

Peter grinned fiercely. "Perfect." He pointed at a dark three-story building inside the circle Almurë drew in the air above the buildings. A pile of rubble from a fallen skyscraper lay in front of it, but it appeared mostly unaffected by the surrounding damage. "That building is mine. It contains supplies and weapons that could prove useful. It's a big part of why we came here."

Almurë replied in a firm voice, "I've seen your human weapons. They do not offer a significant enough advantage to risk attempting to gain access there.

They are insignificant when dealing with warlocks, of which these orks have plenty. Your assignment is information, not equipment."

Peter shook his head. "With respect, sir," Peter continued, addressing Almurë, "you haven't seen weapons like this. Trust me. You can ask Elborin. He'll confirm my claims."

The general eyed Peter critically, like a scout sizing up a high school athlete. After a moment, he spoke, while he handed Galvorn back to Peter, who fought the urge to snatch it.

"We will speak more of Galvorn and the Therin-Selu later. Your assignment is information. If you have an opportunity to seize these weapons, do so at Elborin's discretion. This is a test, Valk Blair. Is that understood?"

"Yes, sir," Peter said with a salute.

With a smile as though there was an inside joke only he understood, Almurë saluted back; a crisp response but with the wrong hand. "Ork vision is worst at dawn, so that is when you will move. You are dismissed, Valk Blair. My guard will see to it you are all properly equipped, and you will depart in the morning so there is time for rest."

He looked past Peter and locked eyes with Leuoradew. "Fair dryad, would you stay, that I may speak with you in wisdom?"

Leuoradew inclined her head softly in submission as the rest of them exited the tent and were escorted to rest and restoration before the next day's tasks.

— 39 —

THE RUINS OF ATLANTA

Peter woke up more rested than he'd felt since his adventure began. Eyes still closed, he felt something soft and small prod his nose. Peter opened his eyes slowly and saw that a tiny being, barely taller than his thumb, stood directly in front of his face.

He pulled back reflexively as the tiny anthropomorphic mushroom came into focus. It had two tiny ovular black eyes, no nose, and an almost imperceptible mouth. Its body and limbs were milky white.

As he watched, the mushroom raised two tiny arms, which were not long enough to even reach its brown and green cap, and turned its back on Peter before dashing off as quickly as its little legs could carry it towards the nearest tree. *Okay. Mushroom people are a thing. Why am I even surprised anymore?* With a resigned sigh, Peter sat up and looked around curiously.

Gray clouds hung low and motionless above the once great metropolis of Atlanta. Skyscrapers of glass and refined metal lay in shambles, and foreign stone structures, more ancient than the country itself, rose unhindered from the ground. They disrupted the city landscape like the sudden appearance of dozens of ant-mounds in a carefully manicured garden.

All of this was contained by a stone wall that cut through the city unbroken by human buildings, which it grew through like trees grow through a fence, and formed a strange alliance of old and new. The clouds made it impossible to tell what time it was, but the watch on Peter's wrist told him it was zero-four-fifty. The glade where they rested was bathed in a warm light coming from the center of his companions.

Peter rose from the soft grass and made his way over to the others. They were gearing up around a long wooden table with a lamp in the middle. *Some-*

one must have brought it during the night, Peter thought. Scott hefted a round new shield, getting a feel for the weight.

O'Cleary munched greedily on a piece of bread. O'Cleary caught his eye and waggled his eyebrows at him.

On the table sat a pile of human and elvish clothing. Bits and pieces of robes, black and red jerseys, suit pieces, a pearl necklace, and a strange scarf material that could only be elvish scattered across the table like a load of fresh laundry ready to be folded.

"Good morning, Peter." Elborin greeted him from across the table, as he tossed him a triangular piece of warm bread about the size of a potato. He caught it and brought the pastry to his mouth. Its warm sweet scent put his salivary glands into overdrive. The bread tasted as if made with a hint of honey and was firm but not overly so. It did not flake or crumble as he consumed it. Peter watched as the others did likewise. Behind the group, Elborin and a few elves stared curiously.

"Now that we're all awake," Elborin started seriously, "we have a long day ahead." He waved his hand over the clothes. "These are our disguises. Orks are scavengers — filthy things that collect and wear trophies from their victims. They're too lazy to bother to figure out how to wear them properly. The warlocks wear patchwork robes scrambled together from their trophies. Warlocks are rare, though, so only Galamier will be wearing a robe."

They must really hate these things, Peter thought as one of the elves sneered at Elborin's description. *His voice is practically dripping with disgust too.*

He pointed to a sleek female elf with olive skin and a waterfall braid wearing a patchwork robe with the hood pulled back. "As you can see, it's enough to cover most of her since there doesn't seem to be any standardization to the robes. The rest of us will just have to make it work with what we have. If we do get close to any orks, engage at my command. Until then, act as though Galamier is your superior. Understood?"

"Yes, sir," the humans replied.

"Good. Galamier specializes in illusion casting, so once we're closer, she'll be disguising our faces." Elborin donned a hoodie and sports jacket over his armor. Then, he pulled a misfitting horned helmet down over his ears. "The plan is to get close and figure out why they're all staying clear of that part of the city. It is imperative we do not get caught as we will be deep in enemy territory without reinforcements. Any questions?"

"Can we get our coats back? Your lads took them from us last night and didn't say what you were doing with them," O'Cleary inquired as he zipped up a pair of oversized, torn green jeans.

"Of course," Elborin said as he rounded on one of the elves in the group behind him. The elf nodded and stepped forward, a pile of jackets folded in his arms, which he distributed with the help of Elborin.

"Here you are. We've reinforced them. Our main source of armor is woven spider-steel, so we thought it wise to make some adjustments to your clothing. Do not worry, they will not be heavy, and they may save your life."

A memory dawned on Elborin's face, and he reached into a sack he'd placed on the table. From it, he withdrew a pair of dark bracers patterned with vines and straps, which allowed them to be over or under a jacket depending on the wearer's preference.

"These are for you, Valk Blair — a gift of the dryad as thanks for your defense of her kind," he said as he handed them to Peter. Peter took them in hand and found them to be as weightless as a leaf but made from a strange, deep brown wood that felt as hard as steel. "Wear them well. A gift from one such as her should not be ignored."

A gift from a prophetic tree... Does wearing them alter the future? Well, of course, it does somehow. No point in overthinking it. They're just like the sword — another tool for survival, Peter thought as he took the bracers.

Scott's head jerked up at this, his brow furrowed with frustration. "Oh, come on. I saved her life, and she barely thanks me, but you kill Jason and get a gift?" Scott spat out aggressively.

Peter gave him a sideways look, surprised by the sudden outburst. "Do you want them, Scott?" he asked in an attempt to placate the man's annoyance.

"No," Scott replied, embarrassed. "No, I don't want some second-hand gift. She obviously wants you to have them. Sorry, woke up in the middle of a sleep cycle," he explained, eager to shift the focus away from his outburst. They finished equipping themselves in the awkward silence that precedes a dangerous assignment. Once they finished, Elborin turned to Galamier.

"Lead the way," he commanded graciously. Galamier looked them over with a surprisingly kind expression before he led them out of the forest and to the edge of the city.

A large wall loomed ahead of them, melding with the ruins of Atlanta. Before they journeyed closer, the elf caster brought them all together, having them extend their palms. Once they did, Galamier sang a series of high notes that tickled on the edge of Peter's hearing. The song was like nothing any of the humans had ever heard. There were no distinguishable lyrics; just notes, which filled all humans present with a sense of wonder.

Peter felt a warm, stinging sensation wash over his face. He glanced around at the others, their faces disfigured to look like orks but still retaining their same bone structures enough to be recognizable. The elves' expressions were unfazed, but the men present exchanged looks of wonder disfigured by their altered faces. Peter glanced at a car window as they moved forward. The face that looked back at him was a monster's.

This would give me an edge fighting in the dark against humans, at least. Imagine seeing this in the dark. It'd scare almost anyone into a panic. As they drew closer to the wall, Folduin led them into a tall parking garage.

Once inside, he led them into the dark, where there were no lights to illuminate the path. Elborin gave a soft whistle, and a small orb of blue light appeared above their heads. It floated, translucent, illuminating their surroundings in a soft glow. This drew a curious exchange of glances from the humans but did not inspire words as they continued down — down until they reached the bottom floor of the damaged garage, where they found an opening into a series of pipes and tunnels.

There was no telling how much time passed in the dark of the tunnel, and Peter dared not set the light off on his watch. After what felt like hours, they reached a dark manhole. Folduin and Elborin set about shifting the manhole out of the way, and they all clambered through. Once through, Peter realized why no light was shining through the manhole cover.

They stood in the wreckage of a fallen skyscraper, in a room that rested sideways around them. "Watch your step." Instructed Galamier as she led them to an opening. They stepped outside into dawn. Peter felt grief wash over him like a tidal wave as he took in their surroundings up close and personal. They were within the walls of the city.

Around them was Atlanta, a city which weeks ago had hummed with industry, life, and human interaction, sewn together by planes, subways, and skyscrapers. It was now a desolate scattering of ruins. Peter could count the skyscrapers left standing on one hand, and of those, none remained undamaged.

The smell hit them next; a stink of rot, filth, and death that hung in the air. It permeated every inch of the city, from broken glass to bent steel. *Dad's heart would be broken if he could see this. Not to mention, Mom,* Peter thought in passing. There was no time for grief, though.

They moved forward, staying at a steady pace as they got closer to their true destination.

Around them, they saw vehicles scattered and piled about on every bit of broken road. There was no order to it, no universal destination as there seemed to be with all the abandoned vehicles leading away from the city. Here, the only unity among the vehicles was the chaos of their mangled, decaying forms. Their drivers sought one thing: escape.

Peter could see it all in his head. The chaos of civilians trying to escape from the madness as the city and sky broke around them, unleashing demons into their midst in the blink of an eye. Parents carried their children as buildings collapsed above them, many weakened by new structures, carved entirely out of enormous solid stones that had appeared out of nowhere in every direction.

Peter could hear the echoes of screams as they delved deeper into the city; screams so faint he could not distinguish whether they came from somewhere far off or were simply the imagined traces of lost souls that surrounded them or even his own fleeting imagination. Here, there were no burning pits to dispose of the dead. In fact, other than the occasional skeleton picked disturbingly dry, there were hardly any dead at all.

Peter thought back to his dream the night before. "If you can't figure it out, just grab an ork and torture the information out of it," Jadis had said after Peter voiced his concern about the mission.

"Torture doesn't get the truth. It just gets you what you want to hear," Peter countered. "It's not that easy."

Jadis shook her head emphatically. "I thought you humans had more grit than elves. But then again, you have no way of knowing this, do you?" She sighed. "Orks consider other races weaker than themselves. Power is the foundation of their society."

She seemed to glide like a ghost through the mist as she spoke. "They believe that if you can break them with pain, you have earned the truth. Elves do not have the stomach for this — something about it being immoral. It was the dwarves that discovered it, but even they consider it taboo. Orks do not break easily, after all," she added with a cruel grin. "Kill first, if you can. You are almost strong enough to help me now."

The tricky part isn't going to be catching one. It's going to be getting the Elves to let me torture it, Peter thought as they passed through the loose rubble of another collapsed office building. A few more steps, and he found himself reaching up to adjust his helmet, which kept sliding right to rest uncomfortably over his ear. *This is the worst,* he thought as he shifted the loose helmet back in place.

At least the elves don't care for it either, Peter chuckled to himself as he watched one of the elves named Folduin trying to adjust the bizarre conglomeration of clothing he was wearing. The elf's "get wild" shirt wouldn't stop sliding down his shoulders.

We could have pulled this off just as well without the extra layers, Peter thought. *At least up to this point. Still...* An uneasy feeling was beginning in his stomach as they drew closer and closer to their destination. Only Folduin could feign ork speech. *And he said that if he switched to English in a conversation, we'd have to fight their way out.*

After an hour of traveling in cautious silence, they came into view of their destination. By some miracle, the World of Coke and the Georgia Aquarium were still standing. *HQ is two blocks around the corner,* Peter realized as he moved up next to Elborin. "I haven't seen a single hostile, have you?"

"No," replied the elf, making no effort to hide the concern on his face as they stood in the shade of a gray stone building. "They could be anywhere too. In any building."

"I think we—" Peter stopped. A warning flash of energy shot through his bones. There was no impulsive jerk or dodge this time, but he knew the feeling well enough. *Danger.* He glanced about wildly, trying to discern what triggered it. *What in the world…? I don't see any — oh. Oh, no.*

He knew what it was. He could see Elborin's face — his real face — not hidden behind an ork illusion. Peter turned to the rest of them, human and elvish faces looking back at him. A chill ran down his spine. "Elborin, did she lift the illusion?"

"No, why would she—" Elborin replied as he turned back to meet his eyes. "Liúre," the elf swore. "Galamier, what's going on?" he asked, rounding on the female elf. But Galamier said nothing. Her eyes were wide with panic, her mouth was moving, and her throat was constricting, but no words or sounds issued forth.

She clawed desperately at her throat. Her fingers scratched it violently as though an invisible hand was wrapped around it. Mellonië reached out and grabbed her hands before she could do any lasting damage to herself. Galamier froze, still looking about like a wild animal trapped in a cage, then her eyes rolled back in her head, and her whole body went limp.

Folduin caught her in his arms and tossed her over his shoulder like a sack of potatoes in one smooth movement. "Warlock counterspell. A strong one," he murmured loud enough for others to hear.

A few blocks over, the raspy sound of an ork war horn split the air. "It's a trap," Peter yelled.

Behind him, O'Cleary was already scanning the area for enemies. "Cap, we're cut off. We've got hostiles coming in from three to nine o'clock. I see at least thirty. Three hundred meters out and closing."

We're too exposed here. "Move," Peter ordered, and they all broke into a sprint. "Elborin, we need to get to cover. If we can get to the headquarters, we might be able to hold out."

Elborin grimaced. "Very well. I can send a decoy, but the counterspell may hit me as well." He suggested as they darted in and around buildings towards the SNW HQ.

"Not worth the risk of dead weight, but it's your call," Peter replied as he drew his sword. They came around a corner and were met by three orks with brandished pikes. Peter took the head off one of the pikes with his sword. Following through, he grabbed the pike and yanked its owner forward into Galvorn. Elborin rammed his spear into the second ork's face. The third ork was dead before the other two; an arrow quivered in its throat from where Mellonië had placed it with her short bow.

Peter pulled Galvorn out of the ork and looked up. There *it is*, he thought as he saw the dark building only a hundred yards away on the other side of a collapsed tower.

Peter darted through the debris, a keen eye peeled for another encounter. He reached the building's entrance first. Dark thick glass windows reflected his surroundings back at him as he approached the right wall of the square and removed a glove from his right hand. As he reached the wall, a panel slid up in the glass with a small *woosh*.

"Thank God," Peter whispered as he placed his eyes on the biometric scanner. A second later, there was a whir and a click followed by a small green light. He pulled his eye back and saw a number pad appear on the scanner. He pressed eight then hit enter. There was the sound of heavy metal shifting, then the smooth black glass doors to his left slid open.

A wave of warm air rushed out to meet him and brought with it the nostalgic scent of SNW HQ, a scent like gunpowder, ink, and steel. Memories washed over him, full of faces and experiences, both joyful and sorrowful. They flashed through his mind and disappeared just as quickly.

Criske. That hit me harder than expected. I hope at least some of the men are here. Without looking back at the others, Peter stepped into the large open foyer.

The low light from outside was enough to illuminate the room. The interior was laid out like any other reception area, with one main exception. In the middle of the large room behind the reception desk sat an Abrams main battle tank on a raised mechanical platform. It was designed to be lowered into the base's garage, where maintenance could be performed or the vehicle could be traded out for another.

The tank stood there like a giant model. The enormous SNW logo painted on its front served as a reminder that this was without a doubt a place where warriors resided.

Peter came to a stop, throwing up an open hand, warning the others to do the same. The doors slid shut behind them, and the lights flicked on overhead. A whirring in the ceiling above was followed by a damaged synthetic voice:

"Confirm-m — *skrrt* — a-authorizationzz."

Peter tore the helmet off his head and let it fall to the floor as he directed his voice at the ceiling. "Captain Peter Blair. Authorization code 194294. Party of eight. Thermopylae protocol on standby," Peter said, each word enunciated carefully.

"Command — *zzitrk* — recognized. Reinstating-g." The doors behind them gave off a resounding *click*. This was followed by a series of thick, reinforced metal shutters that emerged from the floor and ceiling to bolster the doors and windows on both sides.

"Standby recognizzzed. Security measures increased-d-d. Two pending up-p-pdates. Insufficient platform power. You have one. One… One message, Captain Blair, marked u-urgent. Would you like to view it now?"

"Who's speaking?" Mellonië asked in a confused voice. "Is there a human caster here?"

"Oh-hoh, looks like the turns have tabled aye?" O'Cleary chuckled. "You lot aren't the only ones with a few tricks up their sleeves. Don't worry. Just the building's AI. It's not alive."

Peter ignored the conversation and addressed the system.

"Base, identify local users, and update me on Brucey's status."

"Bru— is fully mission capable. Last logged service —e days ago by Sergeant Alex Dan— Chan— head of engineering. No additional local users present."

Hope welled up inside Peter. *Alex survived. We may have reinforcements after all. System seems damaged though. There could be people here, and it's just malfunctioning.*

"Base, any other check-ins in the last week?" Peter asked, as he crossed his fingers absentmindedly.

"Negative. Y-you have a message marked urgent. Would you like to view it n-now?" the system sputtered robotically.

"Who's the message from?"

"Message is from Sergeant Chan — unclassified," the voice stuttered.

Peter turned back to the group. The elves, except the unconscious Galamier slung over Folduin's shoulder, looked about curiously for the source of the voice, obviously not satisfied with O'Cleary's explanation.

"We're safe for now, I think. They'd need a missile to get through that," Peter said. "Let's lay her down," he added, gesturing to a couch facing the smartboard on the wall labeled *Display One*.

"Base, play the message on display one," Peter ordered. His voice echoed softly in the large room.

A video lit up the display. In the video, a ruddy-faced man in helmetless bomb disposal gear sat in an office chair, his attention focused past the camera. The sudden appearance drew soft gasps from several of the elves, who looked on in confusion. The man in the video had bags under his eyes and a face so gaunt it looked like he hadn't slept in a month. *Just him?* After a few moments of staring past the camera with a glazed expression, he looked straight at it, speaking in a shaky, hoarse voice.

"Hey, Peter, if it's you. If anyone's still out there fighting this, it's you. I, uh…" He dragged both hands down his face as though the act would give him comfort. "It's been forty, uh, days, man… I, I didn't think it would end like this. I mean, fire and brimstone and all that. Sure. Everyone does. But, not like this. Not like this."

He's lost a lot of weight, Peter observed.

Alex's face twitched violently, but he didn't seem to notice. "I don't know what they hit us with. Hell, I don't know who hit us. The Russians, the Chinese, Korea, I, uh, I just don't know," he mumbled and stared blankly at the camera in silence a moment. "Whatever it is, it's turning people, man. Mutating them into monsters."

He moaned and suddenly slammed a fist on the table, shaking the camera. "I can't find any traces of bioweapons or radiation. Doesn't make sense. Maybe we weren't attacked. Maybe all this is just divine punishment. Lord knows we deserve it," Alex bumbled on. *He looks awful. He's in no shape to fight*, Peter thought as his attention remained riveted on the shell of the man his friend had become. "We flipped for it, Peter. It was Leeford's idea, and I lost."

Leeford's alive? Who else? Come on, give me more!

"Someone had to stay behind and hold down the fort. Don't let them in," Alex said. "Great idea. Just great. I've been here the whole time. Shouldn't have let them leave. Shouldn't have done it. Been waiting, trying to figure out. Just me. Just me," Alex sputtered.

Next to Peter, O'Cleary swore softly. "Ah, no, please don't let this be what I think it is."

On the screen, Alex froze like a squirrel trying to figure out what to do if you got any closer. He lurched forward suddenly too close to the camera and began to whisper. "I rigged the armory to blow, in case those monsters got in. They're e-eating people, you know. The ones that don't turn — hunting them down in the night and eating them. They're not even the worst of it. I've had drones scouring the city. There's something worse out there. A girl. Only got a glimpse of her. I don't know what she is, Peter, but she's even got the demons scared. They got her near the Marriot and those other hotels. It's all different n-now. There's a weird cathedral-like building molded in with them." Alex shivered and pulled back from the camera. "I figured it out after I lost the third drone. Uh, s-s-should have figured it out sooner."

Out of the corner of his eye, Peter saw Elborin exchange a look with Mellonië.

"I c-c-can't do it anymore, Peter. I don't have… anyone to hold on for… E-e-even if I did, they'd probably be dead." He paused. "I don't know why I'm even making this.

No, no, no, no. Come on, man. Don't say it. We're here. Please, don't.

"No one's gonna see it. You're as dead or turned as the rest of them anyway," Alex moaned as he put his head in his hands. Tears streamed down his cheeks now. "I'll leave the card key to the armory in the kitchen," he said between sobs.

"We're too late." Peter felt the realization sink into his chest, felt the hot tears well up in his eyes. He swallowed, forced himself to ignore the urge to cry. *You have to stay focused. We're too late. You failed. Move on. Your people here need you collected.*

"The code is forty-two. Just swipe the card and enter forty-two. One last joke between you and me, Peter." Alex bobbed his head wildly through the tears. "I can't let them in. You understand. C-c-can't let them in," he began babbling to himself. "I'm so sorry, guys, I can't. I can't do it anymore. I j-j-just want to sleep." He broke down into more tears. Then stood abruptly and nodded over-aggressively like a coked-up parrot. "I-I'll be in the freezer."

This time it was Peter who swore violently as the video continued playing.

"I'm sorry I can't do it anymore. I'm sorry. If I turn after, I'm sorry. I'll lock it in case that's how it works. I'm so s-sorry."

The video ended abruptly.

O'Cleary's cursing was muffled by the sound of him smashing a chair against the wall in a burst of frustration.

"Base, when was this recorded?" Peter asked after a deep swallow, fists clenched so tightly his knuckles popped.

"Three days ago," the synthetic voice replied, unfazed.

"Criske!" Peter's curse mixed with the flurry of swears spewing from O'Cleary. The elation he'd felt upon their arrival was gone, replaced by guilt and fury. *We came all this way and we're too late.*

"He couldn't have held out three more days?" Peter shouted in frustration, an outburst that drew an angry look from Simon.

"Calm down. It's not his fault. He had no way of knowing," Simon said in a firm, loud voice. "Besides, captain, we need a plan."

"Give me a second. I'm thinking," Peter replied.

"Do you think he had a point?" Scott asked the room.

"About what?" Replied O'Cleary through clenched teeth.

"What if we were hit with some kind of biological weapon, or radiation of some kind. All this could just be a mass hallucination. After all, the human brain is just chemicals, and they're easily influenced if you figured out how… I mean, if a hypnotist can make someone forget something, I'm sure scientists could make a weapon that would cause something like this."

"No," Simon interrupted. "There would be other side effects, those it didn't affect, inconsistencies."

"I'm talking about a government making a top-secret weapon here. I'm sorry, but some army medic is hardly qualified to just dismiss the possibility. Are you a cognitive psychologist too?" he said harshly.

"Enough," Peter interrupted. "It doesn't matter. Even if all this is a bizarre hallucination, it will take better people than us to figure that out and fix it. Our job is to do what we can with what we know. And right now, that means getting what we can from here and back to camp alive." He approached the display. *I need to figure out how much time we've got.* "Base, do we have any operational exterior cameras?"

"Three exterior camera— operational."

"Good. Display a live feed and alert me if any motion sensors are set off within a thirty-foot radius to the entrance."

"Confirmed," the voice replied, and the display pulled up three different video feeds of the outside. *Good.*

Elborin looked up from where he'd been whispering with Mellonië. Concern wrinkled his expression as he saw at least a dozen orks searching the rubble outside. "Are you sure we're safe here?"

"For now," Peter replied. "But I honestly don't know what those things out there are capable of, so we should get a move on." Peter ran a hand over his scruffy beard.

Insufficient platform power means we can't swap out the tank or get more vehicles. Peter clenched his jaw. *We can all fit, but it'll limit what we can take back. Prioritize firepower. We'll have to come back for more later.*

Peter turned to O'Cleary. "You remember where the kitchen is?"

O'Cleary gave him a weak smirk, his eyes bloodshot with rage. "Aye, 'course, I do."

"Good, head over there and grab the key card, then meet me at the armory."

"Captain." Simon inserted himself into the conversation. "What about Alex?"

Peter breathed deeply through his nose. "If he hadn't gone through with it, he'd have realized we were here already."

Simon scowled. "Not necessarily. He was obviously suffering from sleep deprivation. He could just be passed out somewhere."

Peter pursed his lips. "He could be. If you want to go looking for him, well, you saw the video. You know where to start. But if you find him in there, what then? We don't have time for a funeral, and we can't take a three-day-old corpse back with us."

Simon looked shocked. "We can't just leave him there. He deserves better than that."

"Then what do you want to do, Simon? If he'd held out three more days, we might've saved him. Just three days! But he didn't. We failed to get here in time. We were too late. I'm not wasting time on the dead, no matter how much I cared for them. Not when there are still living that can be saved. We can mourn later."

"There may not be a later, captain. You keep saying we'll mourn after, but when does this end? If we do not mourn him here and now, he may rot, forgotten in that freezer forever. The least we can do is pay our respects."

"Go on then. I'm not stopping you. But I'll be honoring his sacrifice by using what he left us to survive," Peter countered.

Eyes narrowed, Simon shook his head ever so softly and departed.

"O'Cleary," Peter said to the man who stood watching with a wide-eyed expression.

"Yessir?"

"When you get to the armory, don't bother with small things. For now, I want explosive rounds and more fifty cal ammo, and flashbangs, lots of flashbangs. Fit as much as you can on Brucey, we're taking her back."

O'Cleary's grin grew so large the top of his head threatened to fall off when he nodded.

"Caraticus, can Fouldin give him a hand?" Peter asked.

The elf nodded and stepped away from the unconscious female on the couch.

"Is she going to be okay?" Scott inquired as he stole a concerned glance at the pale elf.

"If we can get her back to camp, yes," Mellonië replied from where she knelt next to the other elf.

Elborin pulled Peter to the side as O'Cleary and Folduin made their way out. "Who is Brucey? We need to hurry. We still haven't gotten the information we came for, and it's only a matter of time before they figure out we're in here and bring a warlock."

"Agreed, but how do we know this wasn't all just a trap? Maybe they aren't scared of the area. They're out there searching for us after all." Peter gestured at the door. "That's Brucey," he said as he shifted his hand to point at the tank.

"You remove the option of stealth if you intend for us to take that vehicle out of the city. It puts us all at risk," Elborin countered.

"In case you forgot, we're surrounded."

"I did not forget, Peter, but I would like to be consulted before you decide to abandon our main objective."

"I'm not abandoning it. I have an idea."

"Then tell it to me sooner."

Peter fought to suppress his frustration. "We have a chemical here, something our military designed that forces people to tell the truth. I don't know if it'll work on orks, but it's worth a shot, and it's a lot less risky than trying to have a casual conversation. All we have to do is grab it and an ork on our way out of the city. And trust me, if we take the tank out, we won't have a problem finding an ork," Peter explained.

Elborin leered at him "How long have you been considering this, Captain Blair?"

"Truth serum and the tank?" Peter shrugged. "I've wanted the tank since I left Paragon. The truth serum idea came to me in a dream last night, but I didn't know what state this place would be in, so I didn't mention it."

"Very well. Where is the chemical?" Elborin conceded.

"I can get it now," Peter replied. "Anything else?"

"Best if we do not wait until dark. The orks have trolls and other, darker, beasts they release in the night that, unlike them, find the clouds to be insufficient cover."

Peter checked his watch. It was one in the afternoon.

"Scott, can you stay here and keep an eye out? I'll get updates if anything happens, but I'd like a set of living eyes on things," Peter said as he grabbed a radio out of a drawer behind the reception desk and began to tune it to his radio. "Here," he said and tossed it to the shorter man. Scott remained uncharacteristically quiet as he caught the radio and pulled a chair up next to the couch.

"Carrie, you're our first line of defense if those things get in before I get back," Peter said, confidently slapping the elf on the shoulder.

Peter's confident smile slipped as he made his way around the corner and picked up speed. *No sense taking our time. Too much to do.* Upon reaching the infirmary, he found Simon already there, his satchel restocked with medical supplies.

"Simon, do I need a code to get into the tongue loosener?" he asked as he searched the room for a syringe.

Simon's face was paler than usual and took on a curious expression. "That's one way of getting everyone to believe you about your dream," he replied in a low voice as he brushed a loose hair behind his ear.

That's an idea, Peter thought as he scratched at his head. "No, it's not for me. We're going to question an ork."

Simon's head went side to side, a motion he'd been repeating a lot lately. "We don't know enough about their biology to assume that would work," he replied as he stuffed a tube of something Peter couldn't make out into his bag.

"I know, but it's worth a try, and if it doesn't work, I have another idea, but I don't think the elves will approve."

"Care to share?" Simon asked as he made his way over to a cabinet and punched a code into the lock.

"I know what you're going to say, but I have it on *good* authority that torture works on orks."

Simon's jaw worked as he searched the cabinet. "Here. You'll be wanting ties too, I imagine," he said through a scowl as he handed Peter the bottle. "Strong ones."

"Those should be in supply, though." Peter paused. "Did you find him?"

Simon's face fell a few steps. "I did. Said a few words, shut his eyes for him."

"Good. I meant what I said earlier. When this is over, we'll bury Alex properly."

Simon didn't reply. He just continued to go through the room's supplies, where he found a second satchel and filled it. Peter watched him in silence for a moment. He tried to think of something to say but failed to find the right words.

Frustrated, Peter made his way back down to the lobby, where he found O'Cleary and Folduin loading supplies onto the tank.

"What have you got?" he asked.

O'Cleary looked over his shoulder at Peter with a guilty wince on his face. "Just the necessities, Cap."

"What is—"

O'Cleary turned, arms full of coffee he'd been about to pass up to Folduin, who now wore an equally sheepish expression.

"Dude. Really?" Peter asked, unable to hide his amusement.

"It was his idea," O'Cleary asserted. He nodded at Elborin as he passed the case off to the brown-haired elf on the tank. His face took on a warped smile at the accusation.

"Long as there's room for it," Peter replied. "You'll be riding top with me, O'Cleary. Be sure to have the MK-19 ready. We're gonna snag an ork on our way out."

"You don't want me running gunner?" O'Cleary said as he gestured with his thumb at the tank's barrel.

"Scott, do you have any military experience?" Peter inquired.

"Three years in navy munitions," Scott replied with a wince.

"Can you handle the gunner position?"

Scott looked up at the tank's barrel hesitantly.

"You'll make it work," Peter replied for him. "We'll only need it for clearing. Otherwise, I'd rather save it for later. O'Cleary on the mark gives us more maneuverability and reaction time since we're riding up top," Peter explained.

"The mark?" asked Elborin over his shoulder.

"That," Peter said as he pointed at the large black gun O'Cleary was fixing to the back of the top tank. "It's a grenade launcher. Should stop an ork even with armor."

"Yeah, how's it feel tah not be in the know?" O'Cleary shot out mockingly.

"Simon, you remember enough from your first tour to drive this thing?" Peter asked Simon as the dark-haired man approached.

Simon shook his head. "Maybe. But it'll be a bumpy ride."

"Bloody hell, we'll be a bunch of gowls by the end of dis," O'Cleary muttered, his accent brought out by his unique word choice.

"Elborin, I thought it would be best to have you, myself, and O'Cleary on the exterior," Peter said as the elf drew closer, and he tossed him a radio and headset. "That bit rests on your ears and the other on your neck like mine."

Elborin gave each of them a cursory look. "We should have a caster as well, but with Galamier still unconscious, I'm hesitant. Casting will be put on hold unless we have no other choice," he said as he donned the thin headpiece under his helmet. "That being said, Mellonië is an enhancer. At the very least, she could help me if I'm forced to cast any illusions."

Scott caught a radio and headset pair as Peter tossed it to him from by the display.

He gave it a puzzled look. "Where's the plug-in?"

Peter grinned. "You don't need one. Wireless bone conduction. State of the art."

"You guys got all the good stuff, don't you," Scott muttered as he turned back to the display.

"So, Scott on the gunner, Simon driving, and we stash the unconscious elf in the loader position and have O'Cleary working the commander slot."

"Leaving you and us on the exterior." A frown carved into Elborin's face as he took a step back and examined the tank. "Your call, Valk Blair," he said.

"No time for discussion," Scott shouted. "They figured it out," he said as he scooped the still unconscious female elf off the couch and rushed towards the tank. Behind him, on the display, one of the cameras went full-screen. Outside, a dozen orks were gathering a few yards outside of the entrance, preparing to charge.

"Gear up! Time to go!" Peter commanded as adrenaline began to pump into his veins, and he felt more alive than ever.

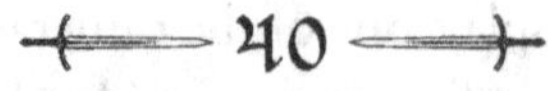

LETTERS

hat is it you want from life, Miss Young? I know it's probably not the kind of question you'd consider in the present times. Nevertheless, it is one you must answer for yourself. Do not put it off or think it will not change. Simply decide, for now. It is necessary. Otherwise, others will control and influence your actions until it is too late.

Sarah lowered the letter until her hands came to rest on the small table in front of her. *What do I want?* The question troubled her, or more accurately, her hesitation troubled her. *What* do *I want?* She repeated it to herself as if the second go would alter the meaning of the question. Regardless of what word she emphasized in her mind, the question remained the same.

I used to want to be a journalist. One that focused on reporting good news. Not that I wouldn't report bad news, but the news is always bad. I wanted to show people how things were good and getting better. So much for that. There's hardly any good news now, and it'll be a while before there's a need for journalists again.

Sarah folded the unfinished letter and stuck the remains of it in her pocket. Then her eyes drifted back to the two other envelopes on the old dwarf-woman's desk. The first was labeled *Peter Blair*, and the second *Last Will and Testament — Doctor Umindrabo Walker*.

"If I do not survive the coming days, I want you to take care of these for me." The little woman said before departing. "Yours, you may read as soon as the opportunity presents itself," she'd said with a familiar twinkle in her eye.

The opportunity came that evening when Sarah found herself alone in the doctor's office. They'd always stopped there for a warm drink at the end of the day to review what new things Sarah had learned. *It's funny how it seems so strange not to meet. Weird how we've only been doing this a few weeks, and it feels like longer than I've done anything in my life.*

Her gaze flitted over the diplomas hung all over the office. *I wonder how many more she has that she couldn't display… So much for my master's, even if I did live long enough to see universities return, would they still teach the same things? Would we just see them replaced with magic schools? No, that wouldn't work. Magic isn't that common in humans. I wish it was. This would be so much easier if there was a school. If I had teachers and other students to talk to…*

Sarah's eyes came to rest on one of the many PhDs on the wall, a fifty-year-old teaching degree. *What do I want…?* The words thrummed, alive in her mind. *I don't have to teach to establish one. I could start a school. Run it maybe. I'd still be able to give people good news. I could help people like me…*

She yanked the letter back out of her pocket and unfolded it gently in contrast to the speed with which she'd removed it. *I'm going to found a school! I should tell Steve. He'd probably make a great teacher. If he's good with kids, that is… Or teenagers? How old are humans when they manifest magic? I never asked Doctor Umindrabo that…*

She was halfway to the door when she realized what day it was and that Steven would be at the Forge, not HQ. *Dang. Would he be upset if I visited him while he's working on one of his projects? No, of course not. He'd probably be happy to see me. I can maybe help him with whatever he's working on. At the very least, I can help him stay awake. Not like he's been sleeping like a regular human being with all his tinkering. And if he's not there, it's only about a mile anyway.*

She went to put on a jacket over her hoodie and paused. *What was that?* she thought as she peered through the small window next to the low-handled front door. It was a dark night, around eleven, without the moon or streetlights on to push away the eerie blackness. Sarah finished donning her coat and scarf and opened the door quietly.

The door closed softly as she stepped out into the chilly fall night air. With cold hands, she locked the door behind her before stepping onto the university's cobblestone road. She made a mental note to one day find out how Dr. Walker got the university's permission to live on campus in a little house of her own design.

She slipped one of her wands out of her hoodie pocket and spoke softly: "Light." A small soft orb of light emerged from the tip of the wand and floated up to rest a few feet above her head. Behind her, she heard the sound of softly crunching leaves. Sarah spun around, wand held out defensively.

The soft light bathing the cobblestones around her in a forty-foot circumference revealed nothing. Adjusting her hold on the magic, she silently sent a tendril of light shooting off from the orb in the direction she'd heard the sound.

The tendril only lasted a split second before it faded out of existence, but it revealed nothing.

I should write my own language for spells, so others don't know what I'm casting when I say it… she thought, her mind already on the move, away from the idea that there was something else there.

She took a deep breath and let the cold air fill her. It stung her lungs and made her eyes water. She loved it. Most people she knew here in the South hated the cold. They complained about how it crept into their every crevice. But it made Sarah feel alive, especially when she fended it off with a warm blanket or cup of hot chocolate. *Mmm.*

Hot chocolate. There has to be some hot chocolate around here somewhere. Maybe the council is saving it for a special event…

Crunch.

The sound spun her around on her heel. Wand raised, she pointed back and forth between the buildings around her. There were dozens of shadowy places someone could have ducked into in the time it took her to turn. But once again, she saw nothing. *People have the right idea. It is kind of creepy out here at night.*

"Hello?" she called out in as friendly and quiet a voice as she could muster. "Is anyone there? I'm just going to see a friend, no need to hide in the dark."

No reply came from the shadows around her. The street was silent — unnaturally silent. Slowly, she turned back the direction she'd begun going, a little extra haste in her every step.

By the time she reached the Forge, she was almost jogging. Her footfalls crunched loudly against the pavement as her heart thundered. *You're okay. There's nothing there,* she told herself, but her rapid movement towards the doors to the Forge indicated that she didn't truly believe she was alone.

She could see light coming from inside, but when she reached the doors, she found them locked tight. *Thump. Thump. Thump.* She knocked loudly against the glass as she hoped someone was inside and they'd hear her over whatever work they were doing. No one came. The hairs on Sarah's neck stood on end with the sensation that she was being watched.

Knock. Knock. Knock. She tapped the glass once more. She listened but heard no response. There was no soothing call of "I'm coming" or "Be there in a minute."

Sarah was unable to shake the feeling that there were eyes on her. She reached out to her magic. Its calming presence filled her, heightened her senses and resolve. Calmly, she stretched out with it, felt out the inner workings of the door, exploring the mechanisms of the lock. She could see them in her mind's eye. All they needed was a little pressure…

"Open," she said softly, and there was an audible click. She tried the door again, and this time it swung outward and made room for her to enter. She did so and shut and locked it quickly as she stared through the glass into the empty darkness outside.

"Sarah?" a voice asked from behind her and made her jump. A yelp caught in her throat. She turned to face the voice and found a soot-covered Steven standing there with a befuddled look on his face. A dirty mask hung below his face and left the area around his mouth one of the only parts not tainted by soot.

"I could swear I locked that…" he began. "Are, are you all right? What brings you out so late on this frigid evening?" he asked with a still surprised yet friendly voice sprinkled with concern.

"I am now," she replied with a soft smile, as she tried to bring her breathing under control. Her neck felt hot beneath her scarf despite having only just escaped the chilly air. "And you did lock it. I couldn't tell if anyone was coming, but I saw the lights, so I used a bit of magic to unlock it," she explained shyly, a hint of guilt resting comfortably in her chest.

"Oh," Steven replied, "sorry about that. I was out back. I've been cleaning out the forges. First time in days I've been able to get Cheekie to take a break on the changes he's been making. And that required me presenting him with half a Britannica. Which won't last him much longer," he added with a mumble to himself. "Anyway, lock picking — I'll remember that as one of your new skills. Come on in," he said and waved for Sarah to follow him into the other room.

As Sarah followed Steven, she jumped right into what she'd wanted to talk to him about before he could begin pouring a typhoon of information into her lap about cleaning the Forge. "I figured out what I'm going to do with my life."

Steven chuckled softly. "At twenty-four? I'm not sure if that's early or late anymore," he said as he looked around the messy room for somewhere for them to sit.

His eyes came to rest on an equipment-covered table. Steven quickly pushed aside the tools to make room for her. "Given that life expectancy right now is in flux, early seems preferable to me. If you don't mind, I'm going to keep working while we talk. I've finished the worst of it, though, so I won't be in and out anymore."

Sarah squinted at him, but the tall man didn't see it. He wasn't avoiding looking at her. He was simply focused on cleaning his hands in a large wash station before putting the disaster zone of a room back together. *At least I'm not a distraction,* she thought with a hint of disappointment. "Well, I was going to be a journalist before all this, but that hardly seems reasonable anymore."

Steven nodded and shook the water off his hands. "You'd have made an excellent journalist. However, you may be right. It could be a time before we have need of journalists again. Then again, the news is always a thing. The return of journalism might not be as far away as you hypothesize."

"Well, the point is I have a *new* goal," Sarah replied in an attempt to coax Steven's curiosity.

"Let's hear it then," Steven said warmly as he began hanging a collection of hammers along the wall in order of size.

Sarah pursed her lips as she followed Steven's work. She watched as he hefted one heavy hammer after another. The large metal tools seemed like nothing more than a child's playthings in his hands.

"Sarah?" Steven said in the same busy tone he'd been using since her arrival.

Sarah's mind returned to their conversation. "I'm going to start a school for magic."

This got Steven's attention. He stopped mid-lift of a large crowbar. His focus deviated over his broad shoulders to give her a raised-eyebrow look. "A school for magic?" he repeated back to her.

His surprise caught her a little off guard. "Yeah, I want to found one," she replied defensively. "I don't want to teach so much. I mean, I will. I'm sure I'll need to some, especially at the beginning, but I want to run it more than teach."

Steven searched her expression, his round bottle-green eyes meeting her monolid tawny brown ones. He reached up and scratched his nose with a finger the size of a jumbo pencil. "You could teach too if you wanted. You're patient enough for it," he said as he returned to his task at hand and set down the crowbar.

"Maybe, but first, I have to master my own abilities before I can even start trying to set up a school," she said reluctantly. "And I'd have to find other human magic users. I doubt elves or dwarves would need a human's training."

Steven chewed on his lower lip. "Who knows. Maybe you'll be so good that even they come to you for teaching."

Sarah leered at him playfully. "Are you making fun of me?" she asked good-naturedly.

Steven raised both hands. "Not remotely. I wouldn't want to be turned into a newt," he said with a goofy grin.

Sarah crossed her arms as her stomach rumbled loudly.

"You should get something to eat," Steven commented. "I don't think we have any food here, and even if we did, I doubt it'd be worth your time."

Sarah looked out one of the Forge's square windows towards Dr. Walker's little house. She must have put on a worried face too, because Steven stopped re-racking tools.

"Sarah, is something wrong?" he asked. Concern laced his voice.

"I… Well… No, it's nothing. I just felt like I was being followed on my way here… I didn't see anyone, but I could swear something was watching me. And I'm alone in Doctor Walker's house. Which is fine. I don't mind being alone, but I'm just psyching myself out. Don't worry about it," she said urgently.

Steven's radio was in his hand as soon as she'd finished speaking. He spoke into it. "Someone get me Sergeant Jenni," he ordered.

No reply came that Sarah could hear, but then she noticed Steven was wearing an earpiece that bulged slightly under the bandana and protected his ears and hair. "I assumed she was asleep. The order to wake her up was implied," he said into his radio with a look of mild annoyance.

"You don't have to wake someone up," Sarah protested.

Steven's attention was on the radio. "Yes, I know what time it is. Gear up and report to the Forge. ASAP indeed." He looked down at Sarah. "No, just you. No, I'll explain when you arrive." He paused and seemed to listen for a second. "Sarah, is there a couch or spare bed at Doctor Walkers?"

"Both, but really, I'll be okay."

"Okay, update me with your ETA first chance," he said into the radio and returned his full attention to Sarah. "Sergeant Jenni is on her way. She'll be staying with you at Doctor Walker's and be working in a bodyguard capacity."

Sarah swallowed. *The girl from Peter's expedition…* "Steven, I really don't want to be a bother. It was probably just a stray cat or something. I'm fine, really," she countered.

Steven nodded as he walked over to a supply closet. His voice continued as he entered it, leaving the door ajar. "Most likely, you weren't being followed, but with Doctor Walker gone, you are our greatest resource other than Cheekie, who's abilities, while good for weapon-making, I suspect wouldn't be of much other use to us. The likelihood is irrelevant. After hearing Jenni's report on what happened in Macon and with what was going on in the cafeteria, I should have already assigned you protection." He reemerged with a black jacket in his arms.

"You… You heard about that?" she asked, unsure why his reference to it made a pit form in her stomach.

Steven grimaced. "Yes, and regrettably, I don't believe the feelings of hostility towards you are isolated to the Macon refugees." To himself, he mumbled, "I am a fool. I should have assigned you protection the instant Doctor Walker left."

"Hostility? They were scared. It's not that big a deal. No one was hostile," Sarah protested unconvincingly.

"No one was *openly* hostile, *yet*," Steven said. "Sarah… I know it's not… fair, but you have to be careful. We're operating as a refugee site. We're not screening the people we let in. That means we're letting in all kinds of people with different ideas and morals, or lack thereof. As well as things have been going, it's still dangerous. I'm convinced the only reason we haven't had more infighting is that everyone is afraid of what's out there, but the more comfortable people get, or hungry for that matter, the more they will begin to look for something to fear inside the wall." He sighed and offered her the jacket. "It's human nature."

"I will not be someone they fear," Sarah replied in a firmer voice than she expected as she refused the jacket. *I've spent enough of my own life in fear. I don't want to be the cause of it for someone else.*

"There may not be anything you can do," Steven replied with sad eyes but did not lower the jacket. "Try. By all means, try. It's my responsibility to keep you safe, and I'm going to do that the best way I know how, okay?"

Sarah took a deep breath through her nose. The smell of iron, soot, and sweat was strangely calming. *He's right. I can't found a school if I don't last long enough to master my own abilities. I have to do what I can not to scare people… but a little security won't hurt.*

"Okay," she replied reluctantly as she accepted the jacket and put it around her shoulders. Steve resumed his work in silence; not an awkward or uncomfortable silence, but a silence that accompanies deep thought and unresolved tension. After several minutes in which Sarah struggled to combat her tendency to overthink things, there was a knock at the front door. The sound freed her from her struggle, but Steven held up a hand to her before she could get up from her seat.

"Wait here. Stay low," he said in a quiet voice. An enormous pistol appeared in his hand, seemingly out of nowhere. *Did he have that on him this whole time? Probably. He is a soldier after all.*

Steven was only gone for a few seconds before Sarah heard him opening the door and greeting their guest.

"Sergeant Jenni Bashar, reporting for duty, sir," a voice began to Steven with what Sarah imagined was a crisp salute.

"At ease," Steven replied calmly. "Were you followed, sergeant?"

Jenni's voice seemed to stiffen. "No, sir. I didn't see anyone out and about on the way here either."

They came around the corner together a few seconds later, and Jenni started at the sight of Sarah. Despite her strange limp, she did not slow down. Instead, she matched pace with Steven. She approached in full uniform, with an unusual heat in her eyes.

She has really pretty skin, Sarah thought as the tired-looking woman got closer. It was not the tired look of one recently woken. Rather, her eyes bore the distinctive dark circles and puffiness of someone who hadn't slept well in days.

"Have you met Miss Young?" Steven asked casually.

"Not formally," Jenni said as she offered Sarah a handshake. Sarah accepted and found the woman's hand callused and warm with a firm grip.

"Sarah is stationed at Doctor Walker's old home on campus, are you familiar with it?"

Jenni's lips scrunched up at the side of her mouth as she considered. "The little brick building near the math building?"

"That's the one," Sarah replied eagerly.

"Why isn't she stationed at HQ? I believe she was before the… Macon mission." Jenni said, the word Macon caught in her throat.

"Doctor Walker insisted she'd be safe in her own home and that since Sarah was training under her, it made sense for her to reside there as well. Now that Doctor Walker has departed, I am assigning you bodyguard duties effective immediately. We can discuss the details later, but for now, consider her a priority-level-Eisenhower client," Steven explained quickly.

"If she's priority-level-Eisenhower, I'd like to request a change of location," Jenni replied with a solemn look.

"Request denied. This is a preliminary precaution, and I do not want to disrupt her studies or create the impression there is a valid threat."

Jenni's jaw stiffened as if she was biting down on something hard, but she nodded. "Understood," she said, then, after seeming to chew on the words for a minute, she asked, "Why's she in one of our jackets? She's a civilian."

"It's one of the modified ones," Steven offered.

"Lieutenant?" Jenni asked. Her face had taken on a slight pinkish hue.

Uh, oh, Sarah thought at the woman's tone.

"You know about the reinforced jackets, right? Yours is one of them," Steven replied in a confused tone.

"She's not SNW," Jenni repeated with an unexpected intensity.

"I realize that, Jenni, but those jackets are the closest thing to armor we have right now without outright putting her in armor, which is the last thing I want to do."

Jenni's face contorted as she tried to keep her expression in check. "Steven, I realize she's important, but she's a civilian. These jackets are for SNW members. You have to earn one of these. You don't just get one. We've buried people in these jackets. You have to earn them."

As she spoke, her voice grew louder, angrier, and sure of herself. "Listen, I understand the assignment. She's important. I get it. And I was willing to interrupt my investigation to come out here and see what you needed. But you can't. You can't just give her one of our jackets — not after we just buried Justin in one. We just buried him, and his killer is still out there. Why isn't anyone but me paying attention to that?"

"Jenni, it's a delicate situation. I understand why you're upset, but—"

"No! No, you don't! You don't get to just give one of our uniforms to some pretty girl because you've got a thing for her. They mean more than that. You know what I had to go through to get one of these — what we all did. And now you're just using it like a bouquet for your new girlfriend."

"Sergeant Bashar," Steven said in a deep rumbling voice, unlike anything Sarah had ever heard from him. He did not yell or raise his voice but straightened to his full height and for once put his size into his words. "I'm assigning you to this because of your unique situational awareness, which stems from the very background and experiences that you accuse me of having forgotten. That very experience convinced me to take you at your word that Justin's killer has not been brought to justice. I agreed with you. It is conceivable the poison was meant for Breekie. It makes sense someone would go after the only magical member of your party."

His words continued, unhindered. "*That* is why I am assigning you to Sarah. Because if Justin's killer is from Macon, they may be here now. And if they tried to kill Breekie, then Sarah could easily become a target, and, therefore, your proximity to her could bring you that much closer to Justin's killer."

He lowered his voice and took on a more soothing tone. "I want Sarah to have the jacket for her own safety. We do not have the luxury of using civilian armor, so it is the next best thing. In the future, do not accuse me of making emotionally based decisions when you do not have your own emotions in check, or I will be forced to reprimand you. Understood?"

Jenni's already fiery expression tightened. "Yes, sir," she replied, then turned on Sarah. "If you're going to wear it, at least wear it right. Not like some accessory," she snapped.

Sarah slid her arms into the jacket's sleeves, pushing her own reservations about it aside, she did not want to provoke Jenni's wrath or a similarly intense response from Steven by refusing Jenni's request. *I'll wear it when I have to...*

Besides, it's not like it's an ugly jacket… just a bit intimidating, she thought as she adjusted it over her hoodie.

"Good. Sarah, you should return and get some rest. We can talk more later," Steven instructed.

Talk more about the school or about your feelings? Sarah mused as she said goodnight and led Jenni back to the small domicile, where, instead of going to sleep, she spent the next few hours carefully examining her own feelings.

— 41 —

THE WEEPING KING

Thud. An ork crashed off the front door and careened away like a bouncy ball against a concrete sidewalk without leaving a scratch on the glass. The creature pulled back, a shocked expression above its crooked, broken nose. It tilted its head at the stain of dark blood smeared on the glass. Then, with a sneer, the ork bashed its jagged sword against the glass while he yelled in frustration back at the other orks. All this played out dramatically on the TV display in the lounge.

"Base und— attack. Thermopylae protocol enga-ged," the synthetic voice of the building informed those huddled within.

The tank hasn't started. Why hasn't the tank started?

"Simon?" Peter asked as he tried to keep his worry out of his tone like a proper officer.

"Hold on…" A moment later, the tank roared to life like a tiger with freshly conquered prey. "Got it," Simon called back over the radio as proudly as a young boy who just beat his father in checkers for the first time.

"Ready?" Peter asked the elves, and O'Cleary mounted the exterior of the tank with him. His eyes remained glued to the front entrance as he drew his sword and awaited their answers.

"May Erúil's hands guide us," replied Mellonië as she slipped off her extra layers of disguise and then notched an arrow into her silvery wooden bow.

"Base, open the front gate in ten seconds. When Brucey exits the building, engage final lockdown protocol," Peter ordered the AI.

"Confirmed," came the reply. "Ten… Nine…"

"Save that thing for an emergency," Peter instructed O'Cleary. The man scowled and replaced his MK-19 with naked steel, a lustful eye on the MK-19.

"S-ven."

"It's been a pleasure serving with you, cap," O'Cleary said with a mocking grin.

"F-ve."

"Wish I could say the same," Peter replied with a cruel glint in his eye.

"Thr-e."

"I don't think we're gonna make it," Elborin muttered loud enough for everyone to hear. This drew a murderous look from Mellonië, which only sparked a savage grin from the short-haired elf.

Peter glanced back to see the elf smiling sarcastically and tossing aside the blue hoodie he'd been wearing over his armor.

"One."

"Scott, don't fire the cannon unless I say."

"Zero. Front gate opening."

With a whir, the metal reinforcements returned to their places in the floor and ceiling and created an opening large enough for the tank and its occupants.

"Gun it," Peter roared. The tank lurched forward and obliterated the desk in their path and stopped abruptly. Then it roared forward again and blasted through the opening. On the other side, Mellonië was the first to make a kill. She launched two arrows in quick succession, each of which buried themselves in a different ork's surprised face.

Peter was next. He swiped Galvorn down over the side of the tank through a retreating ork and beheaded it as they passed out of the building. He turned and found Elborin impaling another of the orks through the shoulder then using the vehicle's momentum to hoist the creature onto the tank.

He doesn't waste any time. Peter ignored a warning pulse as he delivered a blow to the creature's head with his bracer. It worked, and the beast was rendered unconscious. However, the move left his head exposed, and Peter received a nasty cut an inch above his ear from the flailing claws of the ork. As the pain of the wound burned, and he felt the familiar sensation of warm blood begin to leak from his head. He met Elborin's gaze as the tank turned a corner.

The elf took his meaning, and his eyes darted to the wound. "You'll live," he assured Peter as O'Cleary handed Peter a set of restraints. Peter made quick work of securing the captured ork with metal zip-ties.

Behind them, Mellonië continued to fire arrow after arrow into orks as they emerged from the rubble all around. *They're all over the place,* Peter thought.

Elborin snagged a bandana from O'Cleary's arm and passed it to Peter, who glanced around and decided that at the moment, their speed and the height of the tank were enough defense. *Have to make this quick,* he calculated as he sheathed his sword and struggled against the wind to wrap the cloth around his wounded head to stop the blood.

Peter's heart raced harder than ever as he struggled to finish the task. He knew that every second wasted was a second of vulnerability for himself and his allies. After what seemed like minutes, he finished tying the makeshift bandage, and his hand brushed against his headset. *Oh no,* he thought as he realized the left side of his headset was damaged and might no longer relay his ally's words.

The realization came with a change in their surroundings. Orks and goblins: greener, small, leathery ork-like beings with broad toothy mouths and long spindly limbs. They were joined by trolls, and what looked like hyenas and other grotesque creatures Peter couldn't name. All swarmed together out of the ruins like ants when a stick is shoved into their home, who search desperately for the source of their disturbance.

"Cap, you know Atlanta better than me. How do we get out of here?" Simon's staticky voice came through the right side of his open-ear headphones.

Momentary relief splashed over Peter. "Take a left in five hundred feet. We need to get on Ivan Allen. It's the widest road," Peter ordered as he split a screaming goblin in half. Greenish-black blood spilled over the tank as both halves of the creature fell off. "We just have to get to the wall. Once we're there, we can find a way through. Copy?"

"Copy that," came the jumbled reply.

Beside him, O'Cleary opened fire with the MK-19 at a cluster of orks pushing vehicles together to form a blockade down the road ahead.

"*Ca-chunk-achunk-achunk,* sounded the weapon. The cacophony of noise mixed with the roar of air as it rushed by his ears and the screams of monsters all around them. The chaos forced Peter to yell to get Elborin to hear him. "Carrie! Is there a gate on this side of the wall?"

Elborin's spear slammed into the chest of charging ork riding on the back of an enormous, ugly, muzzled lizard. The force of the blow and the momentum of the tank yanked the ork from its seat and hurled it to the ground, where its screams were crushed as the beast charged blindly past them.

"One. But it's thick *aldreanic* wood. And a metal portcullis. We won't be able to crash through, and we won't have time to raise it," the elf replied as he narrowly reflected an incoming arrow.

"We'll get through. Just have to get there," Peter called back as the tank continued to push through and over the rubble that populated the city.

They rounded a corner, and Peter's eyes were drawn by a warning pulse to look up ahead. *Ambush. A pile of rubble lay ahead of them, blocking their path. Two dozen well-armed orks covered the area. At their center stood two imposing figures like adults among a crowd of teenagers.* The one on the left was a thin, twisted ork in a solid black robe with the hood pulled back.

This ork wore a somber expression on a wrinkled pale-green face. His eyes were an intelligent red, marked by age and with a singular tattered left eyebrow. A large, hooked nose sat over thin lips, which smiled with cruel intention. On his head, the dark, graying hair was pulled back in a tight braid, woven in mockery of the elves.

That's a commanding officer if I've ever seen one, Peter managed to think between defensive swipes of his sword.

At the thin ork's side stood another, six-foot, scar-covered, muscle-bound ork in a patchwork robe that bore only the triangle part of the same symbol. Strange lumps beneath the robe caused it to sit oddly on the ork's yellowish skin. This one was bald and bore a nasty scar down his forehead all the way to his chin.

"Liúre!" cursed Elborin.

"Is that the Weeping King?" Folduin called over the ruckus of noise, the fear in his voice unmissable. Peter felt a boost of confidence as the tank crushed a wounded ork under its powerful treads.

"And Gelsh the Unbreakable," Elborin replied with a hint of reluctant admiration.

They were waiting for us. Too bad for them we've got a tank, Peter thought as Simon slowed the tank down to a firing speed as they drew closer to the intimidating formation. Peter glanced around to make sure everyone was in a safe position. He reached out and pulled Elborin back, yelling an order as he did.

"Scott! Light 'em up," peter roared. "Cover your ears. Get behind the barrel!"

But the tank didn't fire.

Inside, Galamier sat up with a start. "What?" she managed to choke out before her chest was wracked with coughs. Nearby, Scott pulled himself out of his position on the gun to check on her. "It's all right, ma'am. We're on the way back," he said, sitting her up.

"What? No! You don't understand. It's a trap. All of it. They're using counterspell runes. He's planted them everywhere." She coughed. "He must have figured out how Dwarvish runes work," she exclaimed, her face pale with panic. "Where are Elborin and Folduin?"

"Up above. Don't strain yourself. You've been out for over an hour," Scott said.

"Scott, pay attention.! Captain said fire," Simon called over his shoulder, drawing Galamier's attention to the display.

Her face went even whiter. "That's him," she cried, surged to her feet, and shoved Scott. "Get out of my way. If they cast, they'll be killed," she shouted as O'Cleary slid down the ladder.

"Scott? What are you—" He was cut off as Galamier shoved past him to the ladder and clambered up it to get out the top of the tank. Scott half stumbled, half fell back into his seat. "Scott, fire!" Peter's voice roared over the headset he'd removed in his haste to attend to the elf.

"But Galamier is—"

With a curse, O'Cleary climbed into Scott's position, pushed the bearded man back and checked his aim before firing.

Boom! The tank fired as Galamier emerged. The tank lurched as a canister unloaded and sent eleven hundred ten-millimeter metal balls bursting forward in fire and flame at forty-five hundred feet per second. She was nearly thrown off by the blast. The sound tore at her eardrums, and she felt something rupture, but she wasted no time thinking about it.

As she turned, she was greeted by the sight of the Weeping King, unscathed, hand outstretched. Ten of his retinue were gone, dissolved into red mist by the power of the tank.

Galamier wasted no time. She could feel a runic trap beneath their strange vehicle. It pulled at her and corrupted her connection to the arcane flow. She saw Folduin and knew he was ready without having to say a word. She took hold of the magic and used it to create both light and sound.

She began with a large flash of light to blind the enemy, directed outward so as not to harm her own people. Next, she bent light around Folduin, conjuring a dozen copies of him, each of which shone with their own blinding light as they charged.

Folduin moved quickly, but it didn't matter. The specters evaporated as they passed over bloody pentagrams of orkish runes hidden under the rubble. In an instant, the true Folduin was exposed, a dozen paces from the first of the ork king's forces.

With a wave of his hand and a tear rolling from his eye, the Weeping King sent the bold elf tumbling through the air into a pile of ruins. The graying ork reached out and placed a hand on the shoulder of the taller ork next to him, and another tear ran down his cheek as his companion began to grow. Gelsh's own robe tore with the strain of the change of size, a joyful gleam in its eye.

The nine-foot Gelsh the Unbreakable, now fully disrobed, marched forward. The creature now wore only a ragged cloth around its waist. The lumps under where his robes tore away were revealed to be chunks of jagged metal blended with the beast's skin.

There was no time for Galamier to calculate; only time to react. The magic flowing through Galamier on instinct lurched. It filled her, boiling over, consuming her. She sensed a shift in the energy as she was no longer able to resist the counterspell set by her opponent, painted into the road beneath them. It didn't matter, though. This was the only way. With a melodic cry, distorted by her damaged hearing, she directed the energy.

As she did, she felt her connection to the arcane flow untether. Raw, unbridled energy ripped through her, tore her apart, atom by atom. Her body was crumbling out of existence with every millisecond, but her mind was still working overtime in one last-ditch effort to protect her allies. Unbridled arcane energy burst out, aimed to destroy the enemy commander with a massive *crackoom!*

The explosion tore the charging beast apart and echoed a split second later in the space Galamier once stood. Peter saw her go through tear-filled eyes as he lay, his back on the tank from the force of the first explosion. The second knocked him off the tank.

He hit the ground hard. The wind was knocked out of him in an instant, which made him feel like a hollow husk with an anvil on his chest. The elf above him had vanished with a shimmer, and a visible, shining shockwave arced around her for six feet. Peter swallowed, and warm blood ran down his throat as he tried to gather his senses. *Ow.* Every inch of his body hurt. His vision blurred as he tried to stay conscious.

Bit by bit, his vision cleared. The world still blurred and spun around him, accompanied by the familiar feeling of blood running out of one of his ears. Peter gasped for air and choked on more blood in the process. With an effort that felt equal to lifting a car, he rolled onto his side and spat the blood out in a desperate attempt to clear room for air to re-enter his lungs.

Get up. Get up! Get up! the energy in his veins screamed in chorus with his adrenaline as survival instincts battled the ache in his bones and chest.

Peter's brain tried to re-establish control over his limbs, but it still reeled from the overwhelming sensation of the aftershock and striking the ground. If his mind were a computer, it would have been aflame. Peter focused all his effort and squeezed his right hand. It met the resistance of Galvorn's handle. *Good, kept hold of the sword,* Peter managed to think as his thoughts tumbled about. *Who's alive?* was the next thought to gather into focus, anchored by the firm grip on his sword.

Noise. There was too much noise: screaming, roaring, gunfire, clashing blades, licking flames. It was everywhere. Peter tried to tune it out and focus on what he could see. *See past the pain and the blood.* He was reminded of how pain could overwhelm every one of his senses when there was enough of it.

Pain is just your body trying to keep you alive, Peter. His sister's words echoed in his mind, more meaningful now than when she'd spoken them the first time. They were their father's words, he knew, but it'd been Hannah who'd made him understand them.

He took control of the pain, pushed it to the back of his mind. The world seemed to slow around him. He noticed a bloody pentagram painted onto the ground beneath the tank, with the jagged runes that formed it glowing softly.

The ork in black robes raised a hand, and an ork behind him blasted a trumpet. At the sound of the trumpet, the area filled with silence. The creature spoke in a deep, smooth voice that reeked of control. "I am Draelic the Dread, First King of the Orkum. Surrender, hand over the elves, and you may go free, humans. This is not a negotiation. You have lost. If you continue to fight, you will be killed and devoured like all who oppose me. No metal box will be enough to save you."

Peter pulled himself to his feet with the aid of his trusty black blade, thrusting it into the bloody markings. The strange patterns sparked and began smoking; this gave Peter an idea.

Draelic raised a hand, and the orks all around them began to move in.

Out of the corner of his eye, Peter saw Folduin bursting from the ruins where he'd been thrown, Falchion in one hand, shield in the other. Folduin tore into the forward line of orks like a storm through an unfinished building, all pretense of peaceful resolution disintegrated.

Move, Peter felt the magic command. He obeyed and pulled his head back as quickly as he could. A jagged arrow passed in front of his face and bounced harmlessly off the tank treads beside him. The arrow drew Peter's gaze upward.

He saw Mellonië standing over Elborin, firing arrows with the speed of a hummingbird's wings into orks and goblins that came from every direction. O'Cleary was screaming something indiscernible from the top of the tank as he pumped lead into an ork that had made its way onto the tank until, at last, the bullets overwhelmed the beast's armor and emerged with a spray of black oily blood from the back of its head.

Folduin was at the front of the tank where he fended off a group of six orks. He cleaved their armor with his enormous broadsword. As he raged, his own bright blood oozed from multiple gruesome wounds to mix with the blood of his enemies.

Despite all the chaos, Peter was momentarily distracted as he noticed the elves' blood had a purplish hue in the same way the dwarves had bled brownish blood. The realization was quickly abandoned, though, as Peter was forced to block an incoming ax swung by one of the many attackers. Above him, he saw Scott emerge from the tank and mount the MK-19.

"Get back on," he and Scott roared in unison. A second later, the MK opened fire again and sent the oncoming orks scrambling for cover. *Where's the warlock?* Peter wondered as O'Cleary leaped off the tank's side and grabbed the still-unconscious body of the ork they'd secured.

*Must have been knocked off by the explosio*n. Peter rushed to his side, and together they hoisted the creature back on as Elborin and Mellonië covered them. The couple fought with the skill and grace of a pair of Olympic ice skaters.

There was no end in sight to the swarm of enemies, and Peter knew they couldn't keep this up. He caught a glimpse of the warlock moving slowly towards them out of the corner of his eye. "Simon, take us left. Down northside," he commanded over the commotion.

"Scott, keep the gun off the warlock, or he'll turn it on us."

Scott glanced in that direction and called his affirmative. A moment later, an arrow sprouted from Scott's shoulder and pulled a cry of pain from his lungs. Peter spun around and offered a hand to pull Elborin then Mellonië up onto the tank.

"Folduin, fall back," Elborin shouted to the other elf as he continued to cleave through his opponents. The tall elf held his ground as he shouted something Peter couldn't make out this close to the firing MK, and the elf's voice failed to come over the radio.

Behind Peter, O'Cleary dug desperately through the bags strapped to the top of the tank.

"Where's our caster?" Peter shouted to Elborin as he made his way to Scott, who continued to fire at the enemies. Peter reached the man, grabbed the arrow in his back, and cut it with his sword, leaving enough behind to grip.

"Pull it out," Scott screamed over the *tha-thunk-athunk* of the mark.

"I can't yet. You'll live," Peter yelled back. "Elborin, the caster?"

"Gone. We can't cast here. Get us away!"

Beneath them, the tank began to roll backward, towards the turn they'd barely passed.

"Heads down," O'Cleary roared for all to hear. At the moment before he complied, Peter saw O'Cleary chucking a pair of flash grenades in the warlock's direction. *I hope these things are as light-sensitive as the elves implied,* Peter thought as he turned away from the impending bang.

At the same time, Simon popped the tank's smoke canisters, which covered them in a cloud of gray.

My hearing is shot, Peter realized as he felt the tank swerve beneath him then pick up speed. *They're everywhere.* Peter swore. *We're not going to make it. There's no way. I have to find something — anything. How am I supposed to fight that thing? Focus, Peter. Take as many of them with you as you can.*

Peter held on tightly and blinked rapidly to clear the dust and sweat from his eyes. Despite the chaos, he searched for the broadsword-wielding elf, but Folduin was nowhere on the tank. Peter glanced back. He saw the elf falter while blocking a blow from one of the half dozen orks converging on him. His sword was knocked from his hand, and a moment later, a spear was lodged sickeningly into his chest.

"No!" Peter cried. At the same time, he saw an arrow fired from the back of the tank by Mellonië. The arrow tore through the air like a diving hawk, a rope tied to its back. It found its mark when it plunged into Folduin's back. Folduin was yanked off his feet. His stabber's body fell dead to the ground. Peter followed the line of the rope back to where Mellonië had tied it to the tank and was now reeling the tall elf in across broken terrain.

"You're killing him," Peter cried over the wind and battle.

"He was already dead," Elborin called back as he aided his wife in reeling in the dying soldier. But Draelic had appeared on the body, a cruel ax in his hand cutting through the rope.

"No!" Mellonië screamed as she lurched forward, but Elborin caught her and kept her from leaping or falling off the tank. Peter couldn't tell which; not with how the vehicle was lurching awkwardly as it weaved in and around the wreckage and between unfamiliar buildings, struggling to gain speed beyond thirty miles an hour.

"Cap, your six," O'Cleary cried out behind Peter. Peter swirled in place, sword raised to block the impending attack. The goblin that'd been hurled through the air at him split as the blade passed through it, and for a split-second, Peter thought he saw purple eyes reflected in his blade. *Jadis?* Peter wondered for a fleeting moment.

"You okay?" O'Cleary yelled as the tank slammed through a pair of vans. Ahead of them, the wall loomed, a colossal seemingly impenetrable barrier of thick stone that separated them from freedom.

"Yeah! Which way to the gate?" Peter called to Elborin over the sound of their screaming and roaring pursuers.

Elborin's head jerked around to give the wall a quick glance. He replied, "Left! We're almost there."

"Good. Simon, did you get that?"

"Yeah, working on it. We knocking down the gate?"

"That's the plan. Scott's on his way back down to you. Make sure he hears when I say to fire. My headset is damaged."

Peter sheathed Galvorn and grabbed one of the rifles they'd packed with them. Carefully, he braced it against his shoulder as he opened fire on the growing mass of orks, goblins, and other monstrosities that converged on them from all sides.

"Step on it, Simon. They're gaining on us. O'Cleary, back on the mark. Cover the front," Peter ordered as his bullets were met with mixed success. They cut down goblins more than orks, as they proved more effective against foes without armor, so he focused his fire on anything without armor that moved.

Mellonië's arrows proved more effective. They struck true against one target after another and killed what Peter's rifle could not. Those that made it closer thanks to steeds or placement were dealt with by the fluid blows of Elborin's spear.

The three of them fell into a pattern; a deadly combination that kept the tank from being overwhelmed as more and more enemies fell upon them like a summer's rain. But there was no end in sight to the mass of foes. *We're not gonna make it.*

They tore around a corner, which put a small distance between them and their pursuers for a moment as they found themselves at the wall. As they did, Scott's voice spoke into their ears over the radio.

"Brace yourselves."

Peter looked over his shoulder towards the front of the tank and saw the wall. Orks lined the ramparts, wonderfully exposed from this side of the wall. At the center of the monumental stone structure stood the gate. The gate was composed of an enormous blend of wood and metal in a thirty-by-thirty square. The chains above it hung loosely where they'd broken so that the gate could not be lowered, even if they did make it into the gatehouse above.

A guard of a dozen large orks in full armor who wielded pikes and other wicked long weapons stood between them and the grounded gate.

O'Cleary turned his gun on the ramparts, his spray of firepower sent orks flying in a series of powerful explosions as the gun traversed the ramparts. Mellonie fired an arrow towards the sky. Once the projectile reached the height of the wall, it burst into dazzling blue smoke. Seconds later, in the distance beyond the wall, a war horn sounded. *Almost there. Gotta breach the gate.*

"Get inside," Peter called out to the others. *We have to fire, but we're not all gonna fit.* O'Cleary slid himself into the inside of the tank without hesitation.

Mellonië looked to Elborin for confirmation. "I'm right behind you," he said as they passed under the shadow of another building. Peter grabbed a rope and began tying down the unconscious ork so it wouldn't be launched from the tank.

"Peter," Elborin called from where he stood at the top of the tank's ladder.

"Hurry," Peter shot back to Elborin as they neared the gate. He nodded and followed his wife.

Peter clambered over and closed the lid of the tank behind them.

"Fire," he ordered as he got low and placed his arms over his ears.

"But, capt—" Scott's voice came back.

"I said fire! I'll be fine. Don't stop until you're back to camp, Simon," he roared over the mic.

Whhiiir. The tank barrel shifted. Peter braced himself for the blast and then: *Kaboom!* The tank fired. Metal shrapnel from the shot barely missed Peter's head.

The orks in the tank missile's path were killed and blasted out of the way as the round thundered into the top right of the gate and created a fiery explosion.

The gate shifted awkwardly, but it wasn't enough. The tank barrel moved and fired again, striking the other top corner of the gate and portcullis with a powerful explosion as the tank lurched forward.

"That's it," Peter called in a voice he couldn't even hear. The gate teetered and began to fall outward, away from the wall. A moment later, they passed under the wall. The tank jerked as it crushed armored orks like bugs under its treads. Peter could feel blood oozing out of his ears. But it didn't matter. They'd made it. A familiar warning sensation drew Peter's attention to the side of the tank.

There, he saw a clawed green hand reaching over the other side of the tank. The hand was followed immediately by a large ork in full armor. It grinned at him, a mouth full of sharp yellow fangs.

"You're mine, manling," the ork taunted in its guttural language. The words twisted into something Peter could understand as they entered his damaged ears.

Galvorn was sheathed on his back, and Peter knew the rifle in his hands would be useless against this opponent from his armor. *Idiot,* he thought as he calculated what he had to do. Peter raised the rifle and threw it at the ork as hard as he could as they passed through the gate with a lurch.

The force of the gun striking was enough to knock the ork back off the tank. Unfortunately, with nothing to hold onto, the tank's lurch as it hit the gate on the ground knocked Peter for the second time that day from the vehicle.

This time, though, he saw it coming and rolled into the fall the way his father had taught him to. A second later, he sprang to his feet. He drew Galvorn in one swift motion, which followed into a blow, decapitating the ork he'd knocked off the tank.

There was no time to turn and run. In front of him, the gate lay in shambles around the eight orks that had survived the tank's onslaught and a half dozen goblins who bound forward on all fours, jaws wide in anticipation of feeding.

If I make a run for it, they'll catch me in the back. This is it. Good a spot as any to die, really, Peter thought as he raised Galvorn and gripped it with both hands as he let the magic he'd learned course through every inch of his being. He dispatched the goblins with ease as they hurled themselves, screaming through the air. Peter pivoted, swung, and stabbed with the grace of a leaf on the wind until no more goblins lashed out. But the goblins had served their purpose well, and in a moment, he was surrounded by greater foes. There was no time for thought. Only action.

Peter embraced the training he'd been undergoing in his sleep. He fell into familiar patterns of twisting, swinging, ducking, stabbing, and parrying as the energy directed. He used his opponents against one another whenever he could. He redirected spears into polearms and swords into spears as arcane energy mixed with old instincts and new tactics to keep him alive.

Galvorn cut through his enemies like threshing wheat, but still, they came. Black blood stained the ground and formed puddles. Still, they came. Peter felt a pike collide with his armored jacket where it bruised his ribs. He removed the blade from the pole, only to feel a spear scrape along his right calf.

Peter ignored the pain; there was no time for it. Still, in the recesses of his mind, he knew those were not his only injuries. The clang of metal on metal mixed with the smell of iron and defecation. The sound was a strange thing — a wild discord of screams and violence that clashed into a sort of incoherent music, which became a reminder that his heart still beat beneath it all.

Thump. Thump. Ca-thump. The sound grew louder. The earth thundered beneath his feet.

Peter fought on. The shaking ground was slippery below him as blood mixed with dirt to form mud. Every footfall splashed gore into the air. His strength was faltering. His body couldn't keep up with the overwhelming stimulus of warnings it received. He felt himself falling to the ground, knocked back by an enormous ork who wore black and red football gear over his armor.

This is it, Peter managed to think as he heard a threatening growl from his back left. He could only see the one ork through the blood and sweat on his face, but he knew he'd lost. They'd gotten around him; no magic or training would save him now.

The ork's polearm swung down in a cruel arc. Peter tried feebly to block it with his sword, but he was too slow, and the blade caught on the back of his gauntlet, sending a jolt of pain through his arm.

Gotcha! Peter thought in a final subversive maneuver of violent vindication. He sat forward, and stabbed with his sword, driving it upward into the creature's belly. The growling grew closer behind him, and a brown and black shadow burst into view as it grabbed the ork by its sword hand and splattered blood into Peter's eyes.

In his blind victory, he felt a new sensation. The ground shook like an earthquake around him and jostled him violently. Collapsing backward onto his back, Peter messily struggled to wipe the blood and sweat from his eyes with arms that shook almost as fiercely as the ground.

Peter managed to blink one eye free of the muck and raise his head a fraction to see what new horror was making the earth shake. It was no horror though. The elves were attacking. Thousands of warriors were charging past him. Strange elvish cavalry, accompanied by gigantic, armored bears were pushing through the ruined gate. Male and female elvish warriors were accompanied by tree-folk and other strange races; too many and too varied for him to put a name to in his state of exhaustion.

"*Töten*," a familiar voice screamed, and he felt the weight of the ork's blade pull away. The sound of clashing metal and screams multiplied exponentially, and suddenly Peter felt no immediate danger. He saw Jadis leaning over him for a split second, then he blinked, and the gray-skinned girl was gone.

What? Then strong hands grabbed him and pulled him to his feet and began dragging him backward. He wanted to fight back, to resist, but he was too weak. He felt a cloth pass over his face, and he blinked furiously to try and see as more tears filled his eyes.

Another familiar voice spoke. "Where'd the woman go? The dark shadowy one that was fighting back-to-back with him." The out-of-place but familiar sound of gunfire reached Peter's ringing ears.

"What are you talking about?" replied the first voice, which he now recognized belonged to a woman.

"I'm telling you, I saw a shadow. It looked like a woman with violet eyes behind him, and she was helping him," said the voice, and Peter realized it belonged to Shawn. "She vanished when we got close. How did you not see her?"

Peter finally managed to clear his vision and see what was going on. The elvish army was engaging the enemy, not a hundred yards ahead. At their backs were humans armed for conflict. Mixed in among them was a small gathering of dwarves, some of whom had to be dragged back by their companions rather than intentionally give ground with the elves.

Peter was being dragged back by Breekie, Gunter, Shawn, and Jessica. In front of him, Hauch stalked forward with ears flat and teeth around a bloody ork arm hanging from his mouth.

"Oh good, you're alive. You sure do know how to get yourself in trouble, don't you, cap. If you'd just held out a minute more, I'd be up there killing these scumbags instead of dragging your sorry butt," Jessica complained to him. Peter shook loose of their grips and regained his footing.

A flood of emotions washed over him: relief that he was alive and among friends, guilt for the lives already lost and those soon to join them, anger for being robbed of a hero's death, shame at the anger he felt —all mixed with absolute exhaustion and pain.

"I'm fine. Fall back. I can handle this," he replied as he barely managed to take a step toward the combat. His whole body was shaking, he realized.

Gunter grabbed him roughly by the shoulder. "Blair, you're injured. They can take the wall without you."

42

DARKSWORD

Peter?" O'Cleary repeated as he prodded the man in the shoulder. Peter winced and raised his head slowly from where he was cleaning an already immaculate blade. His bandages scraped against the inside of his freshly patched jacket. The strange daydream, where he saw Jadis sitting across from him, staring at him, melted away. He hadn't seen her in his dreams the past few nights, but now she seemed to haunt his shadows.

"What?" he replied harshly, tired of waiting for something to do. It'd been a day since he'd been dragged off the battlefield to be bandaged up. The elves had taken the gate and this side of the wall, and skirmishes were still ongoing, but Peter had been ordered to rest — an order which meant stewing in his own thoughts and wrestling with guilt. This made him irritable.

If O'Cleary was bothered by this, he gave no indication. "Here, eat up. You're shaking," he said patiently as he offered Peter a warm bread bowl.

Peter set the sword to the side and reached a hand up to take the food. The bread bowl was full of a thick warm stew, so thick it was almost porridge. Peter looked back up at O'Cleary with raised eyebrows.

"Mushroom stew – as good as my mom used to make, but not quite as good as her spaghetti," O'Cleary explained with a smile. "Should be cool enough by now. How'd the debriefing go?"

Peter eyed the soup suspiciously. *They wouldn't cook those little mushroom creatures, would they?* he wondered morbidly. *Eh, food is food, though. He's right. I should eat.*

"Thank you," Peter replied hesitantly before taking a slow sip of the savory stew. "Went well enough — reported what happened. Apparently, they have the city booby-trapped for elvish casters. That's what happened to Galamier," he explained between bites of savory mush. "We're going to discuss the ork prisoner soon."

"How're you feeling?" O'Cleary asked casually.

"Sore," Peter replied between bites of warm soggy bread. His cuts and bruises were mostly healed thanks to an elvish caster. "The spider silk stuff works. If I'd been wearing standard gear, I'd be dead or short a few limbs."

"Yeah, Scott said something similar. Looks like his shoulder is fine," O'Cleary replied before looking back toward the general's canopy.

Elborin emerged from the tent's shadow, his footsteps silent on the green grass. As he got closer, a set of dark blue dots painted lightly to the corner of his right eye became visible. He was accompanied by his wife, her hair unbraided, falling long and straight down to her shoulders. *She's been crying,* Peter realized.

O'Cleary excused himself quietly as the couple sat in the grass across from Peter. "It will be a few minutes before they're ready," Elborin explained. His eyes narrowed. "You seem troubled, Valk Blair. Let us help put your mind at ease before we meet to discuss our plans with the general."

He replied with a dismissive wave of his hand, "I don't like being here, not doing anything, especially while people are out there dying thanks to what I did in the city. It's disrespectful to them." He swallowed a lump in his throat. "And those we lost yesterday."

"You're mourning your own survival?" Mellonië replied with raised eyebrows.

"I— No," Peter fumbled to reply. "Never mind, I… You wouldn't understand, you're immortal."

"Immortal?" Elborin shot back, a surprising steel in his voice. "We are not immortal, Peter Blair. We may not succumb to age or natural ailments, but we die. Do you think Folduin and Galamier would have chosen to fight? To risk their 'immortal' lives if they were not prepared to die?"

"No," Mellonië answered for him. "They died as they wished to. They lived as they wished to."

"Then, why are you mourning them?" Peter's thought spilled out of his mouth before he could stop and think it through.

Elborin looked over at Mellonië with a soft kindness. "We will mourn them properly, as all the rest, when the battle is over. Being prepared to die does not take away from the pain of their loss. But I do not mourn their passing now."

Mellonië ran a hand through her hair. "I mourn the loss of Folduin's body. I failed him. I allowed his flesh to be taken. Who knows what evil may result from that? That is why I mourn."

"Do you mourn your own failure, Peter? Or are you wasting grief on things beyond your own control?"

Before Peter could answer, the canopy ahead of them opened, and an elf waved at them to approach.

"They're ready," Elborin said softly. "Are you, captain?"

Peter grimaced. "Yeah, I'll want to pick this up with you again later, Valk Carrie."

Elborin smirked at the nickname before rising and leading Peter into the canopy, leaving Mellonië behind.

Almurë sat at the table inside the canopy. Across from him was Dr. Walker, who, if Peter hadn't seen after her original transformation, he wouldn't have recognized. She'd aged even more in their time apart and now looked less like a healthy woman in her sixties and more like a sickly woman in her nineties.

But despite her rapid decline, the sparkling energy in the little old lady's eyes remained. She smiled fondly at Peter as he entered. On the table in front of her lay various sweet-looking pastries piled on a small plate.

"Doctor Walker, how are you?" Peter asked politely.

Dr. Walker sat back in her seat and gave Peter a slow nod. "Better than I deserve, Peter Blair. You have done well for yourself, it would seem."

To her side, Almurë wore a capricious expression, his eyes focused on her. Without turning to Peter, he spoke. "That you have, captain. Elborin confirmed your accounting and informed me that your actions saved his and Mellonië's lives. When offered the opportunity to preserve your own and the lives of your men at the cost of my soldiers, you did not even consider it."

And then you wasted it by sending your forces forward to save me, Peter thought.

"This has earned you my respect and gratitude," the general said.

Peter chastised himself: *I didn't do it for you. What is wrong with me? Calm down. Why am I being so hostile?*

"Hannah would be proud, Peter Blair," Doctor Walker said softly. The words felt like a sucker punch to his limbic system.

If she were alive… The thought of his sister sent a trickle of guilt through his stomach. A forgotten memory of his sister and a younger, healthier-looking Dr. Walker called to him from the back of his mind. *She knew my parents. She knew Hannah, before all this—* The train of thought was lost as the general spoke again.

Almurë went on, glancing down at a soft-looking blue notebook in front of him. "You mentioned earlier you believe you can extract more information from the ork you captured." He glanced at Peter, who gave no response. With a scribble in the notebook, he continued, "Never before has a living ork been brought into one of my camps, Captain Blair. There is no point. These creatures see pain suffered as a challenge, even a reward. It is one of the few things I respect about their race. Their obstinance has a certain charm. He will not give you information."

"I would at least like to try. Humans have come up with a few ways of making captives talk in the last century," Peter replied gruffly.

"I do not doubt your ingenuity or resolve, captain," Almurë replied. "A century is a blink to my people. I have been battling these creatures since before your family had a name. I have my doubts about this chemical of yours but am willing to test it. But what if it doesn't work?"

"Then I'll try more traditional methods," Peter replied, his mind distracted by thoughts of Hannah. *What would she do about Jadis?*

"You mean torture?" Elborin asked, his voice devoid of emotion.

"If that's what it takes," Peter responded distractedly, his mind trying to wrestle back the earlier thoughts of his sister and the old dwarf. *She knew all this was coming…*

"There has been some concern expressed regarding your mental well-being, captain." Almurë's eyes radiated controlled frustration as they flickered up from his notebook. "Your willingness to default to such barbarism would seem to bolster these concerns."

This snapped Peter out of his muddled thoughts as he shifted the gears of his mind into the defensive. "It is not a default response, sir. I have it on good authority such methods will work," Peter countered. *My mental well-being is fine.*

"Would this authority happen to be the being you see in your dreams?"

How does he…? Doctor Walker. Peter's eyes darted over to where the woman sat, her face devoid of tells as her eyes watched curiously. *Familiar eyes. No sense denying it if she told him. I should confront her. Wait. No. One wrong word, and for all I know, I could be locked up,* Peter thought as he broadened his vision onto the search for the safest escape route should it come to it.

The makeshift room had only cloth walls, so that gave him plenty of options. *I could cut through those in one swipe.* Elborin was standing to his back right. The general sat to his left, and Dr. Walker was seated across from him.

I could take Elborin if I have the drop on him. Luckily, the bear isn't here. I wouldn't make it out of the forest without a guide or a hostage. Even then, there's no accounting for magic. Who knows what the general is capable of.

"Deep breath, captain," Almurë said reassuringly, a hint of amusement in his eyes. "I do not believe you are losing your mind."

"I don't understand," Peter replied carefully. *I need to control my reactions better. What gave me away? My eyes,* he realized.

"What I need to know, and Umindrabo cannot seem to clarify for me, is whether or not these dreams of yours have any connection to your sword?" the general said softly as if speaking to an injured animal.

Peter glanced at Dr. Walker again. The dwarf seemed enraptured by the conversation. Her bright eyes observed the room as she continued to nibble quietly at the sweets in front of her. *Is this some kind of test? Hold on, why would he suspect the sword is connected to the dream? I didn't tell her about that, did I? Think Peter. Choose your words carefully.*

"I believe the being I see in them, an Eölin named Jadis, knows more about the sword than anyone I've met," Peter responded as he hoped to glean more information on what the elf knew.

The general steepled his fingers together and stared off into the distance for a time before speaking again.

"And this, Jadis, is the one who told you torture would work on an ork?" the general replied with characteristic curiosity.

"Yes. Do you know what an Eölin is? She has the same build as an elf," Peter said, trying to hide the eagerness in his voice.

The general shook his head slowly. "No. I have never heard of such a creature. Umindrabo?"

"My answer has not changed, Almurë. I'm not the one who entered the dream with him," the dwarf replied in a hoarse voice.

Simon! So, it's come to this then. Unable to contain himself, Peter let the question slip, barely keeping himself from shouting. "What did Simon tell you?"

Almurë's eyebrows rose, and he resumed jotting away in his notebook despite his gaze remaining fixed on Peter. "He expressed concerns to Valk Elborin that your chemical would be incompatible with ork biology and that you would resort to torture when it failed. He then cited a particularly disturbing dream he claims you shared with him."

What the hell? The torture bit I can at least respect. But my state of mind? When did he— It must have been while I was recovering, Peter thought as rage began to force its way through his mind.

"He says these dreams are why you believe torture will work and that he does not think you are mentally capable of further combat leadership," Almurë explained.

Peter focused on his anger, took control of it, and pushed it down and out of mind as he tried to think clearly. *Lying here won't do me any good.*

Watching Peter closely, the general went on. "I do not know you well, captain. so I feel it is important to clarify Simon confided in Elborin out of concern for your safety and the safety of others. An act of loyalty, not betrayal."

"Yes," Peter mustered despite his tightened chest.

"Keep in mind that Simon is under my protection and you are to do him no physical harm — not that you would. As a leader, I'm sure you can understand my caution."

"He was never in any danger from me," Peter replied carefully.

"Good. Now, has Jadis ever changed form in these dreams or demanded you swear any form of an oath?"

"No." *He must believe it. Why would he be asking all these questions if he didn't?* "She did say that no one would believe me if I tried to tell anyone about her," Peter explained.

"Indeed. An astute observation that has placed you in a rather strenuous position, it would seem."

"What do you know that I don't?" Peter asked.

"Less than I would like. There is too much in flux in our world as it is for me to explain with confidence. I have my suspicions about your dreamworld companion but none sufficient to act upon just yet," he said as he turned a page in his notebook, fingers pinched tightly to the ends of the sheet. "The next step of our attack on the city is already going to cost us thousands of lives. Anything we can do to reduce that number, I must consider." He sighed heavily. "You have my permission to extract information from the ork you captured by whatever means you deem necessary. Elborin will assist you—"

"Sir, I—" Elborin began to interrupt in a display of intense emotion but was quickly cut off by a dark, sullen look, from the general.

"Elborin will assist you. Only in that there is information he needs to know as well. He will not participate in any torture himself, and this will be done in private and seclusion, under his supervision. No one, not a single soul within my camp other than those here, is to know that this has occurred."

"The torture?" Peter asked.

"Yes. I would ask that you not even include your own people in the process."

"I will need the help of O'Cleary, at least," Peter replied.

The general's eyes narrowed. "If he helps you, he takes on the same risks as you."

"What risks might those be?" Peter asked, waiting for things to get worse as usual.

"If you do this and it fails to garner the results you believe it should, you will be banished from this camp and will be dead to my people."

Dead to them? Peter's brow furrowed. "I'm sorry?"

Almurë leaned forward and placed his hands on the table, and the power of his rank emphasized every word that followed.

"Torture is a wicked deed, and if my people were to find out you did this, especially without benefit, they would have you executed. I would not go unpunished either. They would not even stop to consider the implications of your dreams as I have. Are we understood?"

They'll slaughter orks like sheep, but the mere thought of torture is a capital offense?

"I understand. And if I am successful?"

"Then, you will have further gained my trust, and we will have more to go on when discussing your dreams," the general replied.

"Good. Can we return to business now that you've satiated your curiosity, Almurë?" Dr. Walker asked, her voice giving off a hint of irritation.

"In a moment, Duelma Umindrabo," the elf replied. "I am as eager as you to return to that discussion. I told you, I believe what is happening with Peter may help my understanding of your experiences, ancient one. We have precious little information. This could be linked to the absence of draconic influence on your Therin-Selu, which deeply worries me."

Dr. Walker pinched the bridge of her nose softly for a moment and waved a hand for the elf to go on.

Almurë gave the dwarf a look that was utterly lost on Peter. "Elborin, please escort Captain Blair to the prisoner. I understand your concerns, and believe me, I share them. But do trust me when I say I have a good reason I will be able to share with you later. Captain Blair, information on the child is my greatest concern."

Elborin stood tall and still as a statue, an internal debate raging behind his eyes. "Yes, sir. May Erúil guide us both."

How is Paragon? Peter felt compelled to ask the dwarf, but it seemed she already forgot he was in the room now that Elborin was making for the exit, so Peter followed him out from under the shade of a canopy and back to his friend.

An hour later, the three of them gathered in a small overgrown convenience store. Vines covered the windows, and most of the shelves lay in disarray. A blindfolded ork sat tied to a chair with an elvish rope placed in the middle of the building, directly under the only source of light pouring through a hole in the ceiling.

Next to the ork, O'Cleary stood and placed the tools Peter requested on a shelf. Elborin sat uncomfortably on a pile of shelves to Peter's left, a sour expression on his face.

Peter walked over to the shelf and picked up a blue can. "What's this?" he asked dramatically.

"Pepsi?" O'Cleary replied hesitantly. "You said to get soda instead of water, so the elves couldn't stop us."

"Hmm, well, given our purposes, I guess Pepsi is better for once," Peter replied before addressing the elf. "You sure no one will be able to hear anything?" he asked as he moved to undo the blindfold around the orks' eyes.

"Tested the spell myself. Whatever happens here, no sound of it will reach the outside." Elborin replied briskly.

"Good, now tell me what we need to know," Peter replied as the ork squinted, an expression of annoyed discomfort on his face as the light hit his eyes.

I need to get O'Cleary out of here, so he's not putting himself at risk. If he knows he'll do it regardless, Peter thought as he picked up the syringe from the HQ.

"Actually, O'Cleary, can you stand watch outside just in case?" Peter asked, and the man nodded back.

The Irishman gave the room a casual once over and walked toward the door. "I'd say holler if you need anything, but…" The rest of his joke never reached them as he exited the building.

"I speak," the ork cried desperately through a flurry of coughs as Peter stepped back, soda-drenched rag in hand. The orks words were slurred by his injuries and shortness of breath.

Peter tossed the rag onto the shelf and bent over the ork. He grabbed the creature by the back of the head and brought his face close to him.

"Say again?" Peter whispered in a low voice, applying pressure to one of the ork's ruined knees.

The beast winced. "I shpeak. You hurth good. Bethter than Chief Fhlug. Bruck is yoursh. Not Bruck of Fhlug, now Bruck of…" The ork's face struggled as he tried to remember a name he didn't know. "…Darksword. Bruck is now Bruck of Darksword."

Darksword? What's he talking about? Peter turned curiously to Elborin but did not loosen his grip on the ork's head. "What do we need to know first?" he asked.

Elborin rose from his seat and stalked closer to Peter with a sadistic smirk. "You're his chief now, Darksword. Ask him where the Weeping King is keeping the child."

"Well?" Peter asked Bruck.

Bruck glared back at the elf defiantly. "Elf not ork enough to break Bruck."

Peter glared at the ork, his eyes like a summer storm. "No. But I am." *Ork enough?* The thought made him angry. *But if it gets the beast to talk…*

Bruck tried to nod, but Peter's grip kept his head in place.

"Yesh. Bruck ish yoursh," he replied sincerely.

"Then answer the elf's questions."

Bruck's face contorted. A battle of contrasting ideas raged in his mind.

Peter watched curiously as the ork came to an expression that could have only been shame.

"The child ish in the tower," he replied dejectedly. "Bruck no go. Child shtrong. Drinks many crakeem. Darksword no go. Child ish evil."

"Crakeem?" Peter repeated to Elborin.

"Their word for casters," The elf replied distractedly. "Which tower?"

Bruck looked confused. "The tower," he repeated emphatically.

"Describe it, ork," Elborin said venomously, the word ork becoming a curse in the manner he spoke it.

"Tall. Glash and shtone. Tower is center. Part of old cashtle," the ork replied with effort.

"What did you mean when you said, 'Bruck is yours?' And why are you calling me Darksword?" Peter asked as Elborin jotted notes into a tiny notebook.

"Yer Bruck chief now. You more ork than old chief. Bruck heard you. Draelic want your shword. He call you Darksword."

What's that supposed to mean? How could Draelic have heard of me? Peter turned to Elborin. "Like a life debt?"

Elborin scowled. "That's what he wants you to think. These beasts aren't capable of loyalty. One of their 'rules' is that they should betray their chief if they can overpower them." He practically spat out the words. "I don't know how the Weeping King knew about you though. That is disturbing news."

"If chief is weak, need new chief. Orksh weak, orksh die," Bruck mumbled harshly. "Good chief no die. Get shtronger when he kill traitor. Even young ork know this. Elf ish weak. Draelic know many things elf do not."

Interesting. They're smarter than I thought, Peter thought. "So, your chief doesn't have to be an ork?"

Bruck sneered. "Orksh best chiefs. Orksh want orksh live."

"But you said I'm your chief now."

Bruck nodded emphatically. "You make pain good. You shtop when Bruck break. You good chief."

"See? There's no logic to it. If it was all just about who's stronger, they'd all obey us," Elborin taunted the ork.

Bruck convulsed against his ties. "Elvesh weak. Tiny littersh. Elvesh hate orksh. Orksh do not serve elvesh."

Elborin strode towards the ork, one hand reachign for his spear as he did, his whole body rigid.

I don't think so, Peter thought as he stepped between the two. "What are you doing?" he asked firmly, suspecting he already knew the answer.

"Out of the way. We have what we need. That thing needs to die."

"That can't be it," Peter replied. "The location of some child? There's got to be more we can learn."

"She's not just some child. She was a daughter of the elves. The orks stole her from us and forced her to drink the living arcane blood of another. Their *king* turned her into a living weapon. A yulmëar. She has been consumed by her hunger, and with every drop of arcane blood she consumes, she grows stronger. That's what we're dealing with, Captain Blair. Monsters who eat the flesh of those weaker than them and use blood-magic on children." Elborin's voice grew louder as his righteous fury mounted. "She has to be killed before she grows too strong for us. If she has to die, so do all of them."

"I understand. They've killed and probably eaten more of my people than I can count, but he's a prisoner. You can't just execute him when he's cooperating," Peter replied but refused to let his voice match the volume of the elf.

"He's an ork. Executing him is the best thing I can do for him. He's not going to be of any use after what you've done to him anyway. He's already dead," Elborin replied as he tried to push past Peter.

"Fine," Peter replied in a whisper, keeping a hand on the elf's shoulder. "Then let me do it. That way, if someone finds the body or asks questions, there's no way it can be connected to you." *And I shed more blood with Galvorn.*

Elborin pulled back, looking like he'd just been splashed in the face with cold water. Then he nodded, slowly. "Very well, Valk Blair."

Peter turned back to the ork still tied to its chair. The ork stared back defiantly despite his helpless, brutalized state as Peter drew his sword.

I don't have any options, might as well make use of the situation, Peter thought as he met the ork's gaze, unwavering.

"Any last words or prayers — say them now," Peter instructed the prisoner.

"Bruck does not pray. Bruck die well to man-ork Peter," the ork replied as he continued to struggle against his bonds. The calm in his voice contrasted the almost ritualistic fervor of his struggle.

I wonder how deep ork loyalty runs. Could I gather an army of orks if I broke each through torture? Or would I just have to break their leader? That would be a lot easier and less resource-consuming. Then again, a handful of loyal orks could be used to sabotage their ranks. But would they be more loyal to me, or preserve their own kind?

Peter placed one hand on the ork's chest and, with the other, drove Galvorn into Bruck's chest, where his heart would be. Blood began to slip from the creature's mouth, and as his eyes dimmed, he spoke his last words.

"Burn Bruck. Do not bury him to feed the weak wormsh."

Peter looked into Bruck's yellow eyes, saw a blue hint, and realized it was his own eyes reflecting back at him. Peter nodded, just enough for Bruck to see as he drew his last bloody breath.

OBSERVATION

Down the grass-covered broken road barely two miles away, Simon stood in a tent dressing the wound of a particularly stubborn man named Al.

At the back of the tent, seated on a small stool, Shawn watched Simon stitch up the man's bloody arm.

A scraggly mustache in desperate need of shaving sat on Shawn's face, which curved as Shawn smiled at the bigger man wincing.

"That's what you get for not letting them fix you," Shawn said as he enjoyed the man's obvious discomfort. After all, he'd practically dragged the man to see Simon after rescuing him from a pair of confused but equally stubborn healers.

"I told ya, boy, my uncle was a doctor, and his grandfather before him, and no pointy-ear or half-pint trickery is gonna mend my scratches," Al replied gruffly through clenched teeth.

"Done," Simon said quietly as he cut the thread off the needle.

Al glanced down at the wound, pursing his lips and nodding approvingly. "Ain't nothing that fairy folks coulda done better than that," he commented proudly as if the stitchwork on his arm was his own work.

"Don't sleep on that arm or use it any more than you have to," Simon explained. "It'll be a bit before the stitches are ready to come out — less time if you'd let those *fairy folks* speed up the healing."

Al scowled. "Ain't natural. I got no problem with them as people. Near as I can tell, this mess ain't their fault. But my body's human. I prefer it gets fixed by a human. Ya wouldn't have a plumber fix your truck is all."

"To each their own," Simon replied, bemused.

A moment later, the tent opened as a trio entered with a cold breeze and the smell of sweat.

Oh, man. This can't be good, Shawn thought as he observed the three new-comers whose backs towered over him. Even though they were now facing away, Shawn knew who these two women and this man were.

The man was William, SNW's combat training officer, a lean middle-aged Black man whose presence radiated military experience. Everyone who'd trained in Paragon knew him, and while they all trusted him, they also held a healthy amount of fear of him. The second member of the group was Jessica, another SNW officer. All Shawn knew about her was that she was bad-tempered, and she'd led one of the other three scouting groups which left Paragon.

What are they doing here? None of them look injured.

The third member of the group was Akena, the ex-police officer, made famous in Paragon for surviving Shadowfang at the cost of a leg — a leg that, according to rumor, was replaced with a bone carved by the dwarves from the very beast that took it.

The first two still wore their black SNW uniforms over their dark green leathers. Jessica's uniform was accented by the same frown that always darkened her face. Akena's green snake-leather vest with basilisk scale sleeves was visible.

She wore thick combat pants with knee guards and boots. At her hip rested one of the short bone blades the dwarves made so many of, and on her back sat a strange round shield that looked made using folded car metal and a hubcap.

None of them seemed to notice Shawn from his position at the back of the tent. He craned to get a better view of Akena's prosthetic leg poking out of a partially rolled-up pant leg. The white bone of the prosthetic was covered in a series of intricate, dwarven runes, which Shawn tried fruitlessly to decipher as he stared.

"You seen Peter or O'Cleary?" Jessica asked sharply.

"Peter was meeting the general last I heard. I think O'Cleary went to check on him," Simon replied as Al stood awkwardly.

"Do you mind giving us some privacy?" William asked Al, the firmness of his voice countering the freedom expressed in the question.

Al shrugged. "I 'spose," he said as he turned to grab his coat. During the movement, he met Shawn's eye and winked. A second later, Al was gone without so much as another look in Shawn's direction

Should I say something? Did Al's wink mean he wants me to stay? Shawn wondered, frozen in place by his fear of the consequences of moving. *Simon didn't forget me, did he? Is it eavesdropping if he knows I'm here?*

"I'd rather have this conversation with them here," William began once Al's footsteps faded away.

"Then why don't we?" Akena interjected as she sat in one of the strange curved wooden chairs. Akena reached down to scratch dirt out of the runes carved in her prosthetic foot. "It's more Captain Peter's business than anything else. They've got no right to do it any more than we do to talk about it without him."

"What exactly is—" Jessica began to shoot back.

"There's no harm explaining it to Simon," William interrupted. "Simon's known him longer than most of us, anyway. Maybe he can help break it to him."

"Is this the part where I ask what you're talking about, or do I just keep waiting for you to stop arguing?" Simon interjected.

"They're worried Peter won't be allowed to return to Paragon," Akena said.

Simon's eyes widened slightly, but he gave no other response.

Shawn's mouth dropped. *Why wouldn't the captain be allowed back? He's been out here, making things safer for everyone!*

William rubbed the back of his neck and sucked his teeth. "It's complicated. Some of the newcomers got involved with the council. Turns out, they weren't too crazy about what you guys pulled in their town. Most of them seem pretty grateful, but you know how it is. Disgruntled people speak the loudest."

"Peter agreed to a trial upon his return," Simon replied matter-of-factly.

"Yeah. And Mayor Gibson is gonna die on that hill. He keeps insisting the trial is the answer, but Peter never said anything about a trial for killing Jason," Jessica replied. "There's a growing sentiment that he's too dangerous to even give a trial after that."

"How many members on the council are supporting this? Surely Effith isn't."

"Effith's team never came back, Simon," Jessica replied.

The military guys who refused to take swords? What happened to them? Idiots should have listened to Peter and Doctor Walker, Shawn thought.

"My team almost didn't make it ourselves. There's more out here than big snakes and orks. I barely convinced anyone from my team to come — not after what we saw."

"What do you think, Akena? An outside opinion would be good," Simon asked as he offered her a used scalpel.

Akena took a deep breath and accepted the implement. The conversation was clearly taking a toll on her. "The focus is on Captain Peter. The rest of you are never even mentioned. Personally? I owe the man my life. Gunter hasn't stopped singing his praises," she explained as she used the scalpel to clean her foot.

"But there's this woman, Marah. She's loud, and people are listening to her. I don't know what we're gonna do. If we all show up at his back, it'll only strengthen her and her supporters' claim that Peter is dangerous."

Simon sat heavily with a wince.

Why would people be mad at Peter for killing Jason? He saved them? Shawn wondered as he kept his mouth clamped shut.

"And the longer we wait, the more difficult it becomes," Simon muttered.

"Exactly," William replied with a nod. "As I said, most people seem to support Peter, but almost all of the loud ones are here. And you know how unopposed voices tend to dominate public opinion."

"I say, screw' em. The captain's got as much a right to go back as anyone. More than most of them there," Jessica growled, her voice rising in frustration as she turned to begin pacing.

But she froze, eyes locked on Shawn. Not looking away from the boy, she spoke to Simon in a flat voice. "What's he doing here?"

Simon glanced dismissively at Shawn. "Listening, I imagine."

"Why didn't you say something when we sent Al out?" William said, his voice laced with curiosity rather than the anger which underscored Jessica's tone.

"Because unlike Al, Shawn has proven himself remarkably capable when he needs to keep his mouth shut. Case in point," Simon answered.

"He's a kid," Jessica replied, her face taking on a hint of red.

"Which means he has a unique perspective. One usually ignored. That much I've learned from Doctor Walker's decision to send him with us," Simon said.

IRP

Peter's training sword clanked across Shawn's knuckle. This drew a yelp of pain from the boy as he dropped his weapon.

"Ow," he mumbled, more as a statement of fact than a whine or plea for compassion. Shawn shook his hand up and down in the air, then brought it to his mouth and blew lightly on it.

"That won't help," Peter told him with a smirk as he bent down to pick up Shawn's weapon. "Try to isolate the pain."

Shawn's brows furrowed, and he stopped blowing and accepted the false blade reluctantly. "What do you mean, isolate it?" he asked.

Peter smiled to himself as the boy tried to ignore the red welt on his knuckles. "Pain is your body warning you of danger, right?"

"I think so," Shawn said as he raised the blade into a defensive hold Breekie had taught him.

"It's a chemical reaction in your brain. A response to negative stimulation is how Simon would say it." *Not that there are many things he won't say, apparently.* Peter continued with a coaxing tap on Shawn's blade. "As you were. Remember, the movement is in the elbows."

Shawn took a few test strikes at Peter, who blocked each effortlessly. "Good. Your grip is improving. Now, chemical reaction, control it," he ordered as he tapped the boy's other knuckles.

Shawn winced but maintained his grip on his weapon. "How?" he hissed out.

"Have you ever blocked out a memory?" Peter replied.

Shawn blinked. "Yeah. So, just put it out of my mind?"

"Exactly. It won't stop. You're distracting yourself from it. Weakening it. Turn it into energy. Redirect it at me."

"Peter," a familiar voice called over the clamor of training around them.

Peter looked over his shoulder to find the voice and received a blow across his right shoulder from a gleeful Shawn. *Oh, okay, you want to be a tough guy?* Peter thought humorously. He gave Shawn a steely look which froze the proud grin on the boy's face and replaced it with wide-eyed concern.

"Peter," the voice called again. Peter winked at Shawn then turned again. Finally, he spied Breekie making his way through sparring men, women, and elves, who'd all faded into the forested background while Peter fought with Shawn.

"Breekie," Shawn called out excitedly as Peter checked his watch.

Two hours until the big meeting. What's he doing here?

Shawn and Breekie met with a surprisingly complicated double high-five that led into a double low-five grip and ended in a double fist-bump.

When did they have time to learn that? Peter thought.

Once they were finished, Breekie turned to Peter, eyebrows raised expectantly as he extended a hand. Peter smacked it with a chuckle as he noticed the dwarf's cheeks were a good bit ruddier than usual.

"My friend, why you no visit my people?" Breekie asked with a suddenly somber expression.

Peter was caught off guard by the question. *Was I supposed to?* he wondered as he searched for a memory of any hint or invitation to do so.

Breekie's somber expression melted away to reveal coy amusement. "Is fine. You are busy man, dah?" Then his eyes narrowed slightly. "Buuut, now is good time, dah? O'Cleary, he is… enjoying our… before fight traditions."

"*Uh-oh*," Peter thought. It was plain by the dwarf's expression though that Peter's own face had communicated the thought.

"Nyet, is not bad. But perhaps would be wise for leader to see him?"

"Is there alcohol involved in these traditions?"

Breekie looked as if Peter had just spat in his face. "Dah," he managed to reply in a sputter.

"William," Peter called out over the training forces around him.

William was in the middle of conversing with an elf with a red braid when Peter called out to him. He quickly but politely excused himself and made his way over to Peter.

"Hey, captain, you didn't mention these guys use tri-blades for a lot of their weapons. You ever saw what those things do to a body? You can't stitch 'em back up. Downright inhuman."

"We're not fighting humans," Peter replied.

"Sure," William said with a frown. "Just saying, probably best if we stay on their good side. Anyway, what do you need?"

"O'Cleary's been partying with dwarves. Figured you might as well come with since it'll be time to meet with the general soon."

They made good time through the forest camp. The closer to the dwarves they got, the less they encountered elves. *If I didn't know better, I'd say they're avoiding the elves,* Peter mused as they neared their destination.

Peter heard the dwarf section of the camp before he saw it. Drums thundered rhythmically from deep within the building they'd taken up camp. The sound of the drums was soon joined by the familiar yet almost forgotten sound of partying. They rounded a bend in the trees. There, Peter spied a scattering of men, women, and dwarves of both genders around the front of a large grocery store covered in overgrowth.

Interesting choice of accommodation.

Peter braced himself as he noticed signs of feasting and drinking. While he didn't personally recognize any of the men or women there, he could feel their eyes on him. He ignored their whispers and side glances. Peter followed Breekie through where a set of sliding doors would have once stood and into the party within.

The scene was a curious one. Humans and dwarves were mingled about, exchanging stories, food, and drinks over the sound of drums. Drums sat at the far left of the building, played vigorously by a set of three dwarves. In front of them, space had been cleared for dancing.

This area currently contained six dwarves who did their utmost to teach thirty-odd humans how to perform a complex series of unified steps. While many of their students appeared eager to learn, it was clear a handful of rougher looking ones simply wanted to recreate the carnal grinding they were more familiar with.

But Peter had no time to watch and see how that would play out. He was forced to follow Breekie, who weaved in and out of the crowd that occupied the main space in front of him. After passing through their first cluster of people, Peter found that, somehow, he'd ended up with a drink in one hand and a chunk of greasy gray meat in the other.

He looked over his shoulder at his companions and found the same had happened to them, much to William's distress. The older, dark-skinned man quickly set his food and drink on an overturned stack of shelves before turning to snatch a tankard of liquid out of Shawn's hands. The boy's wide-eyed expression was replaced with a disappointed pout as William snatched the drink from his hand.

Next, they came to the center of the building where a gigantic hole sat in the ground to serve as a fire pit. There, they found four massive roasting lizards that Peter was reasonably certain were of the same species as the beasts he'd seen some of the orks riding within the city. The sight was enough to make his stomach rumble as the deliciously savory yet unfamiliar smell of the meat made his stomach growl.

A few dozen dwarves were gathered around this pit holding wooden tankards or plates of gray meat and colorful vegetables. The men all sported beards of varying lengths and decoration, and the women all had hair so long it fell well past their faces. Their jolly faces and warm greetings as Breekie led them past made it difficult to decline their food and drink offerings.

Relief washed over Peter as Breekie led them into a collection of rooms at the back of the large store. He was accustomed to crowds and parties, but the noise and overabundance of meaningless stimuli put him on edge. Here, the music and partying were quieter. It'd been cleared out and set up with couches and a dozen table and chairs, each occupied by dwarves and humans.

The dwarves all curiously and excitedly took notes as they were regaled with stories told by their new human friends. Stories ranged from a retelling of movie plots like *Star Wars* to the manufacturing process of marbles. There seemed to be no subject the dwarves didn't want to hear about.

It was here that they found a rosy-cheeked O'Cleary reclining in a deep brown leather couch pulled close to the fire. The Irishman has a large tankard in one hand, and his other hand draped over the shoulder of a smiling redheaded lady dwarf. She had a mug of her own, and her large green eyes stared at O'Cleary intensely.

Upon seeing them, O'Cleary surged to his feet. His grin threatened to separate his jaw from his head. The sudden movement nearly sent the little lady dwarf, tumbling back deep into the couch. Somehow, she kept her own drink aloft, and for a moment, Peter feared she'd be angry, but her smile only broadened.

"Peter," O'Cleary shouted, "there you are, you grouchy chancer. Now we can really crack on."

There's the accent. All it takes is a drop of alcohol or a boosted heart rate, Peter thought, bemused.

"Oi! Flint," O'Cleary called to one of the other dwarves. A surprisingly buff dwarf carving pieces of strange lizard on a plate looked up from his task, brow furrowed as if confused that someone would interrupt.

"That's Flint Rockwood," O'Cleary explained in a voice that Peter assumed'd was meant to be a whisper but failed spectacularly. "He's in charge of meals, and that includes drinking," the Irishman said fondly as the dwarf made his way over, cleaning his hands on a multi-pocket apron. The dwarf stopped at a large barrel on a table before reaching them, produced four tankards, and filled them to the brims before carrying them dexterously over to Peter's group.

When he spoke, Peter was surprised to hear no Russian accent in his mellow voice.

"Good. You found him. Welcome, Peter Blair," he said as he offered Peter a tankard. Peter hesitated a moment, but at a look from Breekie, he accepted the container of blue viscous liquid. Breekie was next to accept, but when the dwarf offered a drink to William, the man shook his head.

"I only drink water before a fight. Got a wife and kid to get back to," he explained politely. The dwarves exchanged a look. Then Flint shook his head. "No, we are not fighting now. Breekie has already done so with Peter, yes?"

"No, sorry," William replied. "I mean tomorrow's fight. The battle. We've actually got a meeting for it coming up, so maybe, Peter, it isn't a good idea to—"

But Peter already had the drink to his lips. It was cold, almost like a slushy. It was as if the liquid was stuck in a state of freezing yet still retaining syrupy liquidity. The taste was unlike anything Peter knew; both sour and sweet. The strange liquid instantly warmed his whole body once it passed his throat. He blinked as his head swam with the tingly sensation of just having swallowed a gulp of soda.

"No. None for Shawn either, he's just a kid." A flustered William was insisting much to Flint's dismay at offering Shawn a drink of his own. Before William could further offend or O'Cleary could further insist there was no harm in letting the boy try, Peter, stepped in.

"This is incredible, Rockwood. What's it made of?" The dwarf smiled, took a sip of the tankard he'd offered the now injured-looking Shawn, and offered the other spare to Breekie, who took it happily.

"A wonderful cave moss," the dwarf began to explain as Peter took another, more careful sip. The drink distracted him just a moment as it seemed to blend with the drums and the thumping of his own heart. This made for a surprising but pleasant stimulation of multiple senses.

But when his focus returned, he found that William was asking questions about making the strange drink while O'Cleary explained excitedly to Shawn how dwarf women would braid their hair into beards when going into battle so the enemy wouldn't know what they were up against.

Peter realized with a start that another dwarf had joined them and was greeting Breekie. *Maybe that's enough of this,* he thought as he lowered his tankard to his side. A warm fuzzy feeling radiated through his whole body.

Breekie turned to him, his ever-present grin as broad as ever.

"O'Cleary seems fine," Peter told the dwarf accusingly. "Unless you need me to have a word with him about his lady friend?" Peter asked cautiously as he watched O'Cleary pulling a helpless-looking Shawn over to the couch where the redheaded dwarf sat patiently sipping her drink.

"Nyet. Is fine," Breekie replied. "I must admit, though. You are busy, man, and there was more to me bringing you here than to check on your friend."

Peter felt himself tense slightly, his knees bending ever so slightly, the fuzzy sensation rushed from his brain. *Calm down. You're not in danger.*

"I asked him to bring you," The new dwarf explained. She looked, if she'd been human, to be a woman in her sixties. Her long black hair showed signs of graying, but her body was surprisingly lean and muscled. Peter noticed her hands and forearms were covered in scars with her runic tattoos beginning at the elbow.

"I am Due Aragurd Guldtuth," she said, her voice grandmotherly for a woman of her age, whatever that might be. "I did not want those pointy-ears to know I was speaking to you before the gathering. They're as suspicious as a mother owl."

"Due Gulduth will be our leader during the meeting and the battle tomorrow," Breekie explained with the use of the honorific.

"Not Doctor Walker?" Peter asked in an attempt to sound polite.

"Duelma Umindrabo is not well. She spends most of her time in the company of the pointy-ears' general. That leaves command to me," she explained. "I am the oldest of us here and with the most warfare experience."

I don't need your credentials, but thanks. "Okay, so what do you want with me?" Peter asked as he resisted the urge to bring his drink up for another draught.

"Breekie," she said the name strangely, and Peter got the sense she didn't particularly care for it. "Thought it would be wise to give you warning before the meeting. While some of my kind are indifferent, I do not much care for elves. I still remember how the father of elves tricked Firstbeard the Storied."

Breekie blinked slowly in annoyance.

"But," Guldtuth went on with a sigh, "this battle offers our people much knowledge." Her eyes twinkled at these words. "And we must purge the city of these orkish, runic abominations," she spat out.

"I see," Peter replied with concealed impatience. His eyes wandered over to where Shawn sat awkwardly on the couch next to a very loud and happy O'Cleary.

He'll be fine. Peter assured himself. *I've never seen that man hungover in all the time I've known him. I wish she'd get to the point, though. Dwarves really do like to talk.*

"Still, there is no need to let the elves know we're as eager as they are to take the city."

"I'm sorry, what?" Peter replied, unsure he'd heard the female dwarf correctly. Breekie grinned sardonically.

Guldtuth went on. "We're going to fight, but it'd be a shame not to make the elves sweat a little first. They're all worked up over those runes this Weeping King's got. Just a bit of fun, you see."

Peter couldn't believe his ears. The partying he understood. But this? It was so out-of-nowhere. A slow, amused puff of air from his nostrils was quickly followed by a mirthy chuckle. After a few seconds of almost crazed laughter, he managed to gain control of himself.

"And you want me to play along?" he asked as he wiped tears from his eyes. Both the dwarves nodded vigorously. "Why?"

Aragurd took a large bite of meat, which he chewed voraciously. "Would you like the whole history? Or just their most recent grievance."

Peter pursed his lips. He didn't like the look in the dwarf's eye when she suggested the whole history. "Most recent grieving?" he replied with a preemptive sip of his drink.

The dwarf looked disappointed but not surprised. Her eyes narrowed as she explained. "Most recently, they did not inform us of the orks' abominable use of our casting methods. They knew about it, and we have to hear it from your man, O'Cleary," she said with a gesture at the now singing Irishman.

"Fine," Peter replied with a wave of his hand. "I won't spoil your fun, but I hope you can understand I won't be participating myself."

Breekie continued, nodding enthusiastically. "Dah, is fine. Just do not worry for us. We have your back. This is the right phrase?"

"It is indeed," Peter replied as he finally took another sip of his drink, which he almost choked on when he saw William snatch yet another drink from Shawn's innocent clutches.

From there, Peter waited for the effects of his drink to slowly wash away as he observed in silence. The dwarves exchanged stories with O'Cleary, and William discussed brewing with their camp's musclebound cook.

Eventually, Shawn seemed to relax, but it was only after he'd gotten a bite to eat and Breekie insisted on showing all the dwarves their clever handshake. By the time Peter was ready to leave, the dwarves in the room were practicing the combination of slaps.

Before setting off for the gathering, Peter pulled Shawn aside. "Keep an eye on O'Cleary, will you? William, Breekie, and I have a meeting with the general. Just keep him out of trouble. Can you do that?"

The boy's grin faltered for a second, and he looked over at the older man half asleep on the couch.

"Yes, sir," Shawn replied. His right hand twitched into a well-meaning but poorly executed salute.

"Good, lad," Peter replied as he smacked the boy on the shoulder and moved over to Breekie. "Are you ready to go?"

Breekie's brow furrowed, and he looked at his wrist.

"What are you doing?" Peter asked, fearing he already knew the answer.

"This is what you do when you considering the time, dah?" the dwarf replied.

"Yeah, but I have a watch."

Breekie blinked, and his eyes narrowed. "You are safe here, see?" He gestured at O'Cleary, the man struggling to stay awake. "Is no need for watch."

Peter fought to keep his eyes from rolling. "No. A watch. A device for telling the time," he explained as he gestured at the black band around his wrist.

Breekie gave his beard an enthusiastic tug. "Your bracelet tells time? Oh," he nodded. "The glass — it reflects the sun. I see," he said with buzzed confidence.

Then it wouldn't work inside, you goofball, Peter thought but didn't have the heart to explain to the self-satisfied dwarf.

"We've got an hour. William and I are going to go ahead and head over so we aren't late."

Breekie shrugged. "I will be there soon," he said dismissively and chose to walk out of the back.

Upon returning to the main section of the store, Peter noticed the music had quieted and spied a small crowd louder than the main one. The familiar sound of blows being thrown came from within.

"We should probably check that out," Peter said to William in a resigned tone.

"Yeah, but I'm not getting shivved before a big fight, or at all for that matter," William replied.

"Shivved?" Peter asked as he steered toward the crowd.

"Yeah, that's Scott's crew. Half of 'em are convicts he let loose."

They began to shove their way through the press. *Oh, no. The hell is he doing now?* Peter thought as he saw Scott exchanging blows at the center of the group of jeering and cheering ruffians.

The short man had a black eye and bruised knuckles, and a few scrapes and bruises, but otherwise looked better than his opponent. He was a scrawny, mustachioed White man missing a number of his yellow teeth behind a busted purple lip. The two were breathing heavily and circling each other as sweat glistened on their skin despite the cool air.

Peter took a step forward to break up the fight but was stopped by William's hand on his shoulder and Breekie's on his wrist at the same time. "Sorry, cap," William started defensively when Peter wheeled on him. "That's a prison fight. You get involved, you'll get Scott killed and put us both in danger."

"And, you will anger my people," Breekie said with a nod to the crowd's enthralled dwarves. "Besides, I think he's got it," he added as he pointed to where Scott had knocked the meth-head to the ground. The visceral thump of fist against the soft flesh of face repeated as Scott turned the man's face into a bloody pulp, only stopping when his body had gone completely limp.

"I catch anyone else trying to deal, and it'll be more of the same," Scott cried out as he stood, and the blood on his fists dripped over his shoes. The crowd gave no reply, so Scott held up a hand, and an enormous bald man still wearing his prison jumpsuit around his waist stepped forward and dropped a large Ziplock bag full of white powder into Scott's outstretched hand.

In a dramatic gesture, Scott removed a pocketknife, gutting the bag and letting the white power pour onto the ground where he stamped it into the dirt. "I won't say it again. No hard drugs, and no trying to sell 'em to our allies." Then he stepped forward, yanked a drink from one of the onlookers, and finished it off in one gulp. Then he looked around with a bloody grin. "Well? Go on! It's a party, isn't it?"

A cheer went up from his crew. Meanwhile, the dwarves in observance all watched curiously and whispered excited questions to their human neighbors. Bit by bit, the crowd dispersed with soft whispers and left the barely breathing, beaten man on the ground where Scott had put him.

"You're just going to leave him there, aren't you?" William asked as Scott made his way to them.

"They'll learn better this way," Scott replied. "What do you want, Blair?"

"Not cocaine. That's for sure," Peter replied and raised his hands in mock surrender. "If you feel all right, you could walk with us to the briefing. It wouldn't hurt to get there early. I'd take a moment to clean yourself up, though."

Scott's jaw clenched for a moment. "What briefing?" the man asked irritably as he dabbed at a cut with a wet rag.

"General Almurë's briefing for the assault tomorrow," William explained hesitantly.

"No one told me anything about a meeting," Scott replied with a scowl.

Probably a good thing in your state, Peter thought, but William was still going.

The older man waved his hand dismissively. "Probably just an oversight with everything going on. You should come with us. Better to have extra people than too few, right?"

Scott nodded, still simmering.

Peter hid a scowl of his own. *Can't tell him not to come now, though. That'll just piss him off more. Hopefully, he doesn't mess things up.*

"Let's review," Peter suggested as they got closer to the general's pavilion. "Our priority is liberating and evacuating as many human survivors as possible. We'll need your help with that, Scott. Your men have more experience fighting these monsters than most of our forces."

Scott grunted acknowledgment. *Great. Off to a good start.* "I may need help convincing the elves to let us split our forces to escort civilians out of the warzone. Especially if it means taking dwarves with us."

"At least the dwarves won't be a problem," William commented and scratched the side of his jaw. "Speaking of elves, looks like she's here for us."

Mellonië was strolling towards them, back in uniform and her hair braided in that elven style. "Valk Blair," she said as she greeted them with a smile. Any traces of grieving gone. "Elborin said you'd be here early. He wanted me to introduce you to the Illuna. Come. They're already in the pavilion."

Inside the canopy were three important-looking elves standing hunched over the city. Each of them looked older than the average elf, with silvery blue hair pulled into waterfall braids. They walked with importance and wore long silver silky robes rather than the fluid cloth armor worn by the other elves.

"These three are Illuna Riniya, Illuna Thalanil, and Illuna Kueyr. There is no dwarf or human equivalent to their positions, so think of them as an extension of the general's will," Mellonië said quietly so as not to interrupt their discussion regarding the placement of siege weapons. Then, with a graceful smile, Mellonië exited the tent. This left the humans standing there awkwardly while the three elvish officers continued their discussion of tactics.

Having been on his feet all day, Peter took the lead and sat down. It was then that the elves finally seemed to notice them.

The tallest of the three, and the only male, Illuna Riniya, walked over and offered Peter a handshake. Peter stood and took it firmly as he met the elf's black eyes, the right of which had a long scar running from the eyebrow down to his jaw.

"Valk Blair, it is my understanding you have an amicable rapport with the dwarves?" he asked in elvish

His voice made Peter think of a leopard. *Oh, boy.* "I like to think so," he replied.

"Excellent. Then you're aware of their proclivity for considerable single-minded stubbornness."

"Sure…" Peter replied cautiously.

"We can depend on you to help convince them to work with us then?"

"Seems like that'd be best for everyone, yeah," Peter agreed.

That was enough for the three elves, and they returned to their strategizing.

This is going to be interesting, to say the least. Play along with the elves, play along with the dwarves, and make sure they agree to my plan. I'd rather just be in the middle of a fight.

Moments later, Peter's pondering was brought to a halt as a somewhat frazzled General Almurë entered the tent. The general was garbed in a loose, almost Roman-looking, robe and carried a set of notebooks tightly in his hands.

He was accompanied by his daughter, the fearsome-looking warrior, Súmeriel; the dryad, Leuoradew; and Elborin, whose necklace braid was now styled identically to the one which fell through the general's hair.

Did Elborin get some kind of promotion? Peter thought as the three took their places at the head of the table.

Peter's eyes made their way around the room, and he picked over the strange conglomeration of occupants as he waited for introductions to begin. Peter's hand found its way to his new necklace, a fang with brutal orkish runes carved into it. He'd taken the necklace for his own from Bruck's neck after killing him. He'd seen their kind wear human items like trophies and chose to respond in kind. The rough curve of the runes under his thumb made him feel powerful.

Peter refocused on his surroundings. All but two spaces at the table were occupied, but there were still more people under the canopy. There was no persiflage here. As Peter examined the group, he noticed that all faces present were as grim as the dark gray sky that hung above.

"Let us begin," the general commented distractedly as he set his books on the table and glanced around quickly. Then with pursed lips, he added, "Hold on, Captain Blair. I was only expecting you and one other officer to be in attendance."

Peter grimaced. "Yes, sir, this is my second in command; Lieutenant William Needs," Peter said as he pointed to his left. "And this is Commander Oscar Scott of the Wounded Company. He represents the forces gathered from Macon."

The general's eyes narrowed as he looked Scott up and down.

"Commander Scott's presence could be beneficiary, sir. He's a sufficient leader," Elborin said confidently without so much as a whisper.

"Very well," the general replied, the moment already a long-forgotten scene to him. He paused and tapped a finger on the table before shaking his head dismissively. "Where are the dwarves?"

As if on cue, the two dwarves strolled jovially into the canopy, cheeks pleasantly ruddy, but with no sway or clumsiness to their steps. They took their time taking their seats as they basked in the elves' silent judgment with each ponderous step to the table.

For a split second, Peter thought he glimpsed amusement in the general's tired eyes. His daughter, on the other hand, was making an effort not to smirk.

"Thank you for joining us, Breekie Fellhammer and Due Aragurd Guldtuth. Duelma Umindrabo sends her regrets that she is not well enough to attend."

"We are aware of our *Duelma's* situation. Were she at our capital, I expect her condition would be more favorable. I'm sure your healers are doing their best," replied Guldtuth as she pulled on the end of her hair, which she'd braided to form a beard.

Almurë ignored the retort and continued calmly. His voice took on a more focused, commanding tone that drew the attention of everyone in the room. "As many of you know, I do not care for wasted words. That said, Elborin will be taking my place as general for tomorrow's assault."

45

ACTIṆG GEṆERAL

The room was as silent as a graveyard. The Illuna elves exchanged looks of confusion while Elborin kept his face blank. At his side, Súmeriel 's face twitched in an expression Peter could only assume was more subtle amusement.

"What does Duelma Umindrabo have to say about this?" Aragurd asked. Her loud, demanding voice slaughtered the silence. "She would want to know of this cowardice."

Almurë smiled warmly, a surprisingly friendly reaction to what was just said. "Duelma Umindrabo's absence is why I am turning things over to Elborin. He is quite capable, and we have already discussed my plans to take back the city." Almurë's face took on a forlorn expression. "Were it not for Umindrabo's condition, I would direct the battle, but I am needed at her side."

"Are you a healer, General Almurë?" Aragurd replied firmly. "I was of the understanding that was your wife's profession, and yours was the more brutish job of leading armies. We may have to evaluate this change if we are to participate in this assault."

Here they go. I was hoping they weren't serious, but it looks like she's leaning into it.

"There was a time when we did both together, and I wish that she were here, but even with her help, there is no saving your Duelma, Aragurd. She is passing from this plane and wishes to leave with me her stories so they not be forgotten. May Erúil guide her body to the libraries of Craickor Whitebeard," Almurë replied heavily. "I do hope this does not alter your participation. It is her wish that you aid us, and your involvement will be pivotal in our success."

She's dying? Peter thought. *I knew she was sick, but we still need her help. She can't die. I need answers from her. How involved in my family's life was she?*

Aragurd clamped her mouth shut, and her face softened with a look of wonder as she bowed her head.

He played her like a fiddle. Did he know they were going to try something?

"General, this is not the time for your experimental tactic,." began Illuna Kueyr fervently. "With everything that is at stake now with what we are facing, your leadership and guidance is needed."

"Illuna Kueyr, you have served with me long enough to trust that I know what is most important. You will have my guidance and leadership, as I decided that Elborin should be the one to act in my stead. As Valk of the Fardrim-Véla, he is well suited to the task," Almurë explained firmly.

Fardrim-Véla, how did he put it…? Oh, right. They're basically the elvish version of us, but Doctor Walker can't be dying — not with all the resources at their disposal, can she?

"His qualifications are hardly the issue," interjected Illuna Thalanil, one of the female Illuna, with cat-like green eyes, thick eyebrows, high cheekbones, and a husky voice. She shook her head, and her silvery-blue waterfall braids almost shone in the light. "Deserving or not, he has not been appropriately selected for the rank of general. He has not undergone the trials of the position."

"Then consider this the trials," Almurë countered.

"If I may?" Peter interrupted.

Almurë's eyebrows raised, and he nodded his approval to Peter.

"I'm not familiar with your customs, and no disrespect to General Almurë, but in my opinion, Elborin isn't just as suitable a replacement. He's an improvement even better suited to lead this assault." Peter stroked his beard confidently. "Look at it this way, he has the most experience of anyone working with my men and Scott's as well as your own kind. He's the best suited to make calls that take the most advantage of this, frankly, unorthodox alliance."

"Seconded," Scott chimed in followed by a whisper. "Not that it matters."

Come on, dude, keep it together. Don't embarrass us in front of the faye.

"The Antemáklasi has a point," chimed in Illuna Kueyr. "Valk Elborin is exceptionally well suited to the task, but be warned, Almurë, his failure will count doubly as your responsibility should it occur."

"So long as it does the same when he succeeds," the general replied with a coy smile and began to gather his things.

"Is there anything we can do to help Doctor Walker?" Peter asked suddenly as Almurë stood to leave.

The general paused, reaching down to grab his notebook. Then he looked up from the table and spoke with a furrowed brow. "Take back the city," he said before departing from the canopy.

Once the general was gone, Elborin stood. "During our last incursion, we learned a great deal. First, that the ork war chief known as the Weeping King is unlike any orkish caster we've ever fought."

"The ability to unify multiple clans under one particularly powerful Warlock is not unheard of Elborin," replied Illuna Riniya, the male Illuna. His voice carried a challenge in it, strengthened by his authoritative presence and narrowed eyebrows.

"I realize this situation is unprecedented, Illuna Riniya, but having served under General Almurë, I would think you'd be used to the unprecedented," Elborin replied with a controlled tone and kept his face expressionless. "Unification was not what I was referring to, although we have not seen unification like this among the orks since the Garden Wars. There has been no sign of infighting at all."

Illuna, Mellonie said there's no human equivalent, and they're obviously high ranked, I really should have asked for a better explanation. What is their actual role?

"Well said, Valk… General Elborin," Riniya replied with a tilt of his head and folded hands. "The Illuna are here to serve you as we serve Almurë. You know this includes questioning your decisions to affirm your thoroughness. That said, my question was misplaced."

Elborin accepted the apology with a slight tilt of his head.

"*Ah-hem*, we may be few, but we remember when our people helped you to build Vulacia," Breekie chimed in after clearing his throat, a stoic expression on his face. "It was your kind that lost it, not us. We came because Duelma Umindrabo commanded it. We will fight as she commands, but we will not die recklessly."

Breekie went on as he curled a fist. "But if she dies, our duty will be to record what happens here, not to fight. Unless you can provide us with a better reason than cleaning up your mistakes, General Elborin."

Elborin raised an eyebrow and smirked. "You suspect there is more to this already, Breekie, don't you?"

Breekie shrugged. "We learned long ago in Eden that elves do not always share with us dwarves."

Elborin's face darkened at this. "We do not have time to debate history, Master Dwarf. You are correct, though, and had you been patient, you'd have known all the same." Elborin leaned forward and set his hands on the table. "The Weeping King has a yulmëar, a child, yulmëar."

"Criske," the dwarves gasped in unison, their mouths hanging open in shock. The air seemed to leave the room, chased out by the dark words Elborin uttered.

"An elf child?" Leuoradew asked, wide-eyed in a fearful voice.

Without looking in her direction, Elborin nodded but kept his gaze low to hide the tears which Peter saw slide down his cheeks.

"So?" Scott asked abruptly, his arms crossed tightly over his chest. "They have hundreds, maybe thousands, of human women and children."

Crap. Read the room and shut up, please.

All eyes turned to Scott. Expressions ranged from confused to angry as tears still lingered in the eyes of several elves.

"You must forgive him," Leuoradew interjected desperately. "He does not—"

"I don't need you apologizing for me." Scott cut her off rudely, his brow wrinkled with frustration. "I'm tired of not being in the loop. I was working with the elves weeks before Peter showed up. Now, what's the big deal with a *yulmëar*?" he asked, putting yulmëar in air quotes.

Maybe it was a mistake to bring him. He's been on edge since we arrived here, Peter thought as he watched Scott closely.

Leuoradew looked as offended as a tree person could but kept her lips sealed tightly.

"An abomination," Kueyr, a deep brown-skinned elf with golden eyes, said calmly from where she sat at Elborin's side. "A yulmëar is a user of the arcane that has eaten the living flesh of another arcane user."

"A magic cannibal?" Scott replied, unimpressed.

"Perhaps there is a better word in this tongue to help them understand," Kueyr said with a look to Elborin hopefully. "General Elborin, you're more familiar with their speech."

Elborin grimaced, his brow furrowed in thought. "A vampire," he said at last.

Scott chuckled. "So, what, we stab a piece of wood into its heart?"

The elves looked at each other with confused expressions. Even the dwarves were showing signs of discomfort at Scott's dismissive attitude.

"Preferably a sword, but, yes, a blow to the heart is the surest way to kill a yulmëar," Elborin replied rather than growing irritated.

Scott sneered. "If it's a child, that shouldn't be too hard."

"That's enough, Scott," William ordered firmly in his gruff voice, which echoed Peter's thoughts. "Shut up and listen before you embarrass yourself and us any further."

Scott's face went bright red, and he turned on William, both fists clenched at his sides. But Peter's voice struck him down: "Zip it," he commanded coldly.

Scott's gaze shifted to Peter. His nostrils flared and upper lip trembled as he tried to repress his sneer, but he did as he was told.

"Elborin?"

"Thank you, Peter," Elborin replied as he casted a disappointed glance at Scott. "As usual, your people seem to have twisted creatures from our time into something new. She is a vampire in the sense that she is a creature of the night that survives on blood, especially the blood of those with a connection to the arcane. Beings like her are incredibly powerful and unpredictable. They manifest differently depending on their race, but the fact that she is a child only makes her more dangerous."

The elves around the table all winced at the reminder of the creature's age.

"Normally, we would burn the city to the ground just to destroy one of her kind, but Almurë believes this is part of a pattern, that the Weeping King is part of something bigger. We've never seen an ork warlock abjurist before, much less one capable of controlling a yulmëar. Every time we've gained an advantage, he's brought her out and driven us back. He's been careful, meticulously making her stronger."

He shook his head wearily. "Thanks to Captain Blair, we know where he's keeping her. We have to kill her if we're going to take the city. Her and the Weeping King *must* be eliminated — all the more so now that we know he is combining orkish casting with runes like a dwarf."

"He did what?" Aragurd shouted, her face aghast as if this was the first she'd heard of the information.

They knew that? Wait? Did the elves not tell them? Oh, right — O'Cleary… I almost forgot, Peter thought as he remembered the dwarves' earlier warning.

"He's filled the city with runes, traps designed to untether a caster from their connection, killing them," Elborin replied calmly. "That is why we need your help, Aragurd. We know you are few, but you are all familiar with your casting methods."

That's it. That's why it was so easy to get in. That's why they're not guarding the walls better and why they fell back into the city quickly. They've turned it into Vietnam for magic users, Peter thought. *But why was my ability never affected? Is it because it's passive, or maybe it has to do with Jadis?*

"Why do we not have more reinforcements? Call upon the dwarves of the Icecrown Mountains. When the councils hear of this, they will send a flood of dwarves down upon the city the likes of which have not been seen since the fall of Eden," Aragurd insisted, her words reinforced by the enthusiastic bobbing of Breekie's head.

"The same reason we are not engaged in a full siege accompanied by two more elvish armies. We don't have time. Every day the child grows stronger, as do their defenses," Elborin countered. "We think Draelic is planning something, but we have no idea what."

And more humans die.

"But we know where the king is keeping her, and we've developed a plan to take back the city," Elborin said. "We must act before she is too strong to be contained, or Draelic figures out how to control her enough to use her as a weapon."

Aragurd pulled at the end of her faux-beard. "We must slay every ork warlock in the city. None can be allowed to escape, least of all this Draelic. We cannot under any circumstances allow these runes to spread to others."

The room went quiet as its members chewed on the information provided, weighed the risks and reasons for helping take back the city.

"It's a trap," Peter said calmly, looking over steepled fingers, "just like the one they set up for our infiltration. Except it's the whole city. That's why he's keeping the kid there — to draw us in," he continued as he leaned back in his chair. "That thing feeds on casters, and the city is full of traps designed to incapacitate casters." Peter paused, thinking. "What do elvish — no, what tactics does Almurë usually employ?"

Elborin's eyes narrowed. "Staggered, small groups taking major points one at a time."

"Has he fought the Weeping King before?" William asked in his deep voice as he ran a calloused hand over the stubble on his face.

Elborin looked to the trio of blue-braided elves. "Illuna Riniya?" he addressed the male elf with honey-colored skin and a scar connecting to his deep-set eyes full of knowledge and memory.

"That is a question for Illuna Thalani," he deflected.

Thalani's nose wrinkled slightly. Her face took on the far-off expression of someone deep in thought. After a moment, her eyes came back into focus, and she shook her head. "If he has, it was not as a chief. From what we can tell, Draelic the Dread, as he named himself to you, rose to power over the orks swiftly, almost instantaneously. But given he is old for their kind, I suspect he has been biding his time."

Elborin frowned, the corners of his mouth deepening. "Is it not unreasonable then to assume he has fought us before and simply eluded discovery?"

Thalani's lips formed a thin line, and she shook her head. "It is not, given how quickly they took the city. We already know he is one of the most intelligent warlocks we've ever encountered — probably a genius as far as orks are concerned. Liúre, if Gelsh the Unbreakable was serving under him... It's possible he's been around since the Garden Wars. Awan had many servants who escaped us after all."

Something about the name Awan struck Peter with a sense of discomfort, and he noticed William seeming to shift as well. It was as if the word lingered just outside of existence; it radiated an uncomfortable frequency the likes of which you stop hearing after you reach adulthood.

"You're not seriously suggesting this Weeping King was a disciple of Awan, are you? That'd make him truly ancient for his kind," Kueyr said, the horror evident in her voice.

Peter worked his jaw as he tried to get the strange ringing frequency to go away.

What is with that name? It's not Elvish or English.

"It's possible," Thalani said cautiously. "Have you ever heard of an ork weeping? Ork casters use rage. I've never heard of one capable of using other emotions to cast. That, and his title alone rings of Awan's influence, and we know Awan was capable of increasing many of his followers' longevity."

"Is all this history relevant to the upcoming battle?" Scott asked irritably, his own jaw working overtime.

Yes, of course, it is, Peter thought, then he leaned over to Scott. "Take it easy, or you can leave," he whispered in a low, threatning voice.

Then, Peter addressed the table. "If our foe has been watching from the shadows, they may be expecting the usual tactics, even if Almurë's tactics are as unorthodox as I've heard."

"What are you suggesting, Captain Peter?" Breekie asked with a broad grin.

"That we mix it up. Rather than sending in small groups, we spring all the traps at once. Put them on the defensive. All-out assault. Overwhelm the enemy." Peter pointed to the area where the humans of Atlanta were known to be holding out. "If the humans in the city have survived this long and can fight, we split our forces. Three-fourths hit where they expect it." He gestured at an enormous fortress near the center of the city. "The other fourth goes in behind, arm the surviving humans, and press the orks from behind."

Across the table, Súmeriel leaned forward to get a better view of the wooden map and entered the conversation for the first time. "Draelic will pull back. He'll want to protect the child. Here," she said, gesturing at a skyscraper Peter recognized as the Tesla Building, which now overlapped with some new elvish building.

"Perfect," Peter replied, nodding. "Do we have air support?"

"You mean, flyers?" Elborin asked, a twinkle in his eye.

"Yes, whatever that entails for you folks."

"Enough for my Ócom-Véla to get in," Súmeriel replied as she gazed at the table. "Not enough to support the main force, though. If we do get to the tower, a human Antemáklasi to help us navigate it would be wise. When we are done here, Valk Blair, I will need to see you fight."

See me fight? Hold on, she wants me to be part of the tower insurgence? I need to be on the front lines with my men.

"It's a very human way of doing it," Elborin mused as he ran a hand over the short hairs growing back on his head. "Almurë and I discussed a full-on assault, but it comes at great risk. Before our arrival, General Almurë was in contact with the surviving human's leader, a man named Leefield, but they did not possess the resources to support such an assault."

He's alive, Peter thought joyfully, his mind turning from the elf-woman.

William and Peter exchanged a look. "Do you know Leefield's last name?" Peter asked, enthused.

Elborin ran a finger over his nose, shaking his head. "No, he did describe him as having tattoos and a similar uniform to you and your men," he said, pointing at William's SNW uniform.

Peter grinned. "That's our Leefield," he said as William punched him proudly in the shoulder.

Elborin smiled. "Good. With your forces and the dwarves, we have enough to send a division in to evacuate the survivors then reinforce the main force," Elborin replied calmly. "They also said they have a helicopter. Not sure what that is, but the general was under the impression it was important."

How'd they get a chopper? It's gonna be a freaking news chopper probably. Still…

"If we're evacuating the stadium, that chopper could get me and a handful of others to the tower while William leads the rear assault," Peter exclaimed excitedly. "Scott could lead the forces we dedicate to getting those who can't fight out of the city."

Elborin looked at the dwarves. "We'll need the dwarves to split their forces between companies to deal with the runes. We'll send fewer casters with the humans to make our main assault more convincing. Aragurd, how many of your forces will be willing to aid us?"

Aragurd ground her teeth before she spoke, not eager to give up the ruse but aware the time had come. "All will be willing. If it takes every drop of dwarf blood we have, all traces of our casting marred by these mud-dwellers will be removed from the city. We are at your disposal, general."

"Captain Peter, we will need all of your forces to achieve this. Additionally, I will be assigning casters and a battalion of elves to reinforce you under your command," Elborin continued.

Peter nodded slowly. "We'll make the extraction. William will lead the assault. Scott will supervise the extraction." He glanced at Súmeriel. "Then I'll head for the tower."

The corner of Scott's mouth twitched. "I think my experience would be bet—" he began, stopped, and frowned. Then, through clenched teeth, he replied, "Yes, sir. I'll make sure not a single civilian is lost."

The rest of the meeting was spent dividing forces, planning routes, exchanging information on technology and magic, and fine-tuning the battleplan. Peter's mind wandered, thinking of the challenge ahead as he let others take the lead.

As the meeting concluded, Súmeriel made her way over to Peter where she extended her hand in greeting. Peter took it, reflexively going for a handshake at the same time that she went for an arm grip. Their callused hands met in a tangled mess in the middle before the elf let out a surprisingly loud laugh and let his hand go with a quick pump.

"Hah, sorry, Lúemeni, Antem — Valk Blair," she corrected herself halfway through. "I am Valk Súmeriel Almurë. Do you understand I need to know what you are capable of if you're going to join my assault?"

Peter nodded as he stood and straightened himself while the tent emptied out. "I do. I'd want to see a demonstration myself in your position."

Súmeriel's jaw flexed as she watched him carefully. "Elborin and Mellonië have both spoken of your bravery. Do you understand this fight is one we will not likely survive?"

Peter raised his eyebrows. "If I was only getting into fights I was likely to survive, I wouldn't be here, ma'am."

She smiled, the expression soft on her warrior-hardened face. "Meet me in the training glade in half an hour," she said then departed.

Peter entered the small clearing slowly, surprised to find it full of humans, elves, and dwarves alike all abuzz with discussion.

Almost everyone Peter knew was there, from Shawn to Elborin to Breekie. The only exceptions were the general and Doctor Walker. At the edge of his hearing, he picked up on the exchange of bets between humans and dwarves in excited speculation. *How did word spread this fast?*

Across from him stood the ash brown-haired elf, Súmeriel Almurë. She was a few inches shorter than him but lithe and toned. She carried herself with a unique intensity, the kind that comes with years of battle experience. *She is stunning,* Peter thought distractedly as he wiped the sweat on his hand through his now full beard. Elborin stood between them, a savage smirk slapped across his face.

Is this all really necessary? Peter wondered as he removed his coat and began to wrap it around Galvorn. Súmeriel raised her eyebrows, the freckled corner of her mouth slightly curled in amusement, which radiated from her voice as she asked, "What are you doing?"

Peter paused. The realization that the elf still wore full armor dawned on him.

"We're sparring, right?"

Súmeriel nodded. "Yes, but you'll need your weapon," she replied as she removed her sword and sheath with a quick tug and tossed them deftly to Elborin, who caught them with ease.

Peter hesitated, bundle in his arms. *If I keep it, I have the advantage, but she's testing me… Oh, what the hell,* he thought as he drew the sword and tossed the bundle to Elborin in a smooth motion. As Elborin exited the field to stand next to O'Cleary, Peter overheard him say, "My spear against your share of the coffee we brought back that he doesn't last a minute."

Without any kind of signal or warning, the fight began.

She came at him with a knife; a thin, curved, bone blade. Peter only managed to think one thing before his reflexes brought Galvorn up to block: *Criske.*

Súmeriel was a blur of movement, faster than his magically enhanced reflexes. As she struck at him, the difference in their experience became painfully obvious. Peter was reminded of his first encounter with Jadis, but instead of a small teenager in rags, this opponent was a full-grown warrior in armor. An all-too-familiar sense of dread settled into his stomach as he was forced into the defensive.

This was a warrior who'd been fighting for centuries. From her breathing to her strikes, every movement was a calculated step, honed by experience and practice. Seconds later, Peter was on the ground, Galvorn now in his opponent's grip, arced down through the air toward him.

Peter reacted on instinct. He jerked his basilisk-bone blade out from its place at the small of his back, the blade catching and deflecting Galvorn away from his chest. This gave him a moment to breathe, and he rolled back into a crouch and re-adjusted his grip on the dagger.

"Peter, don't!" Breekie roared in Dwarvish, and Peter remembered what his reflexes forgot. If he so much as scratched his opponent with this dagger, they'd die; skilled elf or not. *Idiot, you can't kill her. You need her, and if she can take your sword, she can take your knife,* he thought as he tossed the dagger aside. It landed silently in the grass to his right, far enough away to be out of the battle.

A strange look passed through his opponent's sea-glass green-blue eyes. Peter braced himself and raised his gauntleted arms in hopes this was why the dryad had given them to him.

But Súmeriel did not attack again. Rather, she drove Galvorn into the ground and stepped softly over to where Peter had tossed the dagger.

"Sorry. I didn't mean to—" Peter began to explain but stopped as the elf picked up his poisoned blade, her eyes carefully exploring it.

Her free hand touched lightly on the scar, which traveled down her neck. After a moment, she redrew her own dagger, which she'd sheathed during her attack. She held them side by side in her hands, then turned to Peter.

"Where did you get this?" she asked softly, a distant look in her eyes.

Forehead furrowed in befuddlement, Peter replied hoarsely, "The dwarves made it for me after I helped kill a basilisk called Shadowfang."

She looked at him again now. Her eyes examined him like a newly forged weapon she was seeing for the first time. Something about the look set off warning bells in the back of Peter's mind.

"You'll do, Peter Blair, Basilisk-Bane," she said quietly, and offered him the dagger. "Can you meet us atop the Weeping King's tower? Or will you need picking up?" she said with a mischievous glint in her eye.

Peter took his dagger back and sheathed it.

"I'll see you there," he replied confidently.

Not looking back, she turned and marched off into the trees.

I've got to get stronger, faster, Peter thought as he stepped forward to retrieve Galvorn. He was so deep in thought and berating himself that he failed to notice the oncoming milieu of people until he was already surrounded by familiar faces.

"You've gotten faster," was the first thing out of Shawn's mouth. "I've never seen people move like that. I don't know how you held out as long as you did."

This was followed by a harsh blow to Peter's thigh from Breekie's broad fist. Peter winced. Pain shot up his leg as he braced for the tirade he knew was about to follow.

"You short-bearded buffoon! What were you thinking? Just cause she's showing what a real fight looks like doesn't mean you try to kill her. An Ócom-véla and the general's daughter no less," he roared in Dwarvish. "I've got half a mind to take the black sword from you myself. I'd do it too if I wasn't scared you'd run me through with it now that you've learned how to fight." He finished with a large grin, hand raised for a high-five, which Peter reciprocated with a chuckle.

O'Cleary stomped his way through the crowd of friends and strangers and right up to Peter and planted a finger in his face. "Ya cost me my last cuppa joy, ya bloody idiot," he declared emphatically.

"You try fighting her next time," Peter shot back with a cackle.

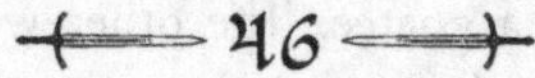

46

THE TUNNEL

The sting of cold air heralded even colder rain trapped in the clouds above. The smell of sweat, blood, and urine lingered stale in the air. It was all vaguely familiar to Shawn, like the pound in Macon multiplied by a thousand. But this was no night mission where they'd be in and out in a few hours. Even worse: this time, he was in the thick of it, not left behind to wait in terrified anticipation.

Mercedes-Benz stadium loomed on the horizon. Unfamiliar stone towers and parapets broke through its rough sides. Another building seemed to have grown partially through it, like how two trees are woven together, fighting for shared water and sunlight. The new tree distracted from the magnificence of the first with its own unique beauty.

They'd entered the city from the south, meeting no resistance at the wall, or any at all until they were deep within the city. A stew of anticipation, fear, excitement, rage, and hunger permeated the air. The heavy sensation was so sticky that when the enemy showed themselves, a breath of relief was felt throughout the army.

Shawn found himself confronted with the knowledge that if the worst happened, he might not even be remembered after this was over. If he died here, there was a chance his body would be eaten by his enemies and forgotten by the few people left alive who knew him, if any of them even survived.

This was a battle he knew could take days of bloody, face-to-face, gut-wrenching violence. *Not if everything goes to plan, of course,* Shawn found himself thinking. *But then again, when does anything ever go to plan? We're trying to infiltrate the city and rally the survivors who've been stuck there for weeks. I can't even begin to count the number of ways this could go wrong.* His thoughts were interrupted by the sight of a burned-out plane upside down in the road ahead where it must have crashed weeks ago. The sight filled him with a sense of dread as the charred remains reminded him of the burning pits back in Paragon.

Shawn glanced around from his position atop the tank, trying to clear his head of the flames and bones. There were two others with him. One was a short nervous-looking man with a goatee. The other was O'Cleary, garbed in his reinforced uniform. He sat and sang quietly to himself. Despite the drinking his friend had undergone, he seemed fine, maybe even better than fine. He looked refreshed, as if he'd finally had a full night's sleep after months without.

Breekie did mention the dwarf's alcohol didn't have the same after-effects as humans'. With no opportunity to further explore the idea, Shawn shifted his focus outward as he tried to familiarize himself with his surroundings and fellow fighters.

Their caravan of three thousand human soldiers from Macon and Paragon mixed well with the thousand elvish warriors accompanying them. They were split into units from there, which ranged in size from fifteen to thirty, primarily led by elvish officers.

Only a few humans were missing — volunteers familiar with Atlanta like Jessica, who'd gone with the larger elf company. There were so many of them, but Shawn couldn't help feel like they were only a small unit as they moved through the city's rubble.

Next to Shawn, the nervous-looking man cleared his throat. "I was a plumber, well, uh, I was going ta be," he said softly, the words almost lost to the sound of the battle ahead of them.

Shawn blinked and turned to the man. "What?" *Crap, he introduced himself to me earlier, and I forgot his name.*

"I was gonna be a plumber, before, ya know, all this," he repeated with a nod at their surroundings. "One year left in trade school. 'Snot a pretty job, but if I got me a girl, it'd provide," he continued distractedly.

Shawn set his gun down on the tank's warm metal surface. Then he set his palms on the metal before he pulled them back and rubbed his heated hands on his face to combat the cold.

"I was in high school," he replied simply, as he picked his weapon back up gingerly.

The goateed man's lip curled slightly. "And now we're both out here getting ready to be killed by monsters to save some strangers," he said bitterly.

"They're not strangers. I've got an aunt who lives up here."

"Lived," the man corrected. "You know what the odds are of someone you knew up here still being alive are?" he said in a hushed voice.

A scream of pain tore through the air somewhere up ahead.

The man pressed his rifle tightly against his chest. A pair of elves ran past the tank, swords drawn. A knot of human fighters trundled slowly after them, guns at the ready.

Shawn scowled. He did not enjoy where the conversation was going. "Do you?"

The man looked slightly puzzled by this as if he hadn't expected to be challenged on the point. "Well, no, but… but it can't be good," he replied as his eyes searched their surroundings desperately.

There was silence before the clopping of hooves signaled the approach of a pair of elves on horseback. They drew closer as they spoke in their soft lyrical language, which Shawn still was not sure why he understood.

"I'm not saying Elborin isn't capable, just that it's anomalous that General Almurë is busy talking to a dwarf instead of leading the attack himself," one of the elves with a white braid said. Shawn kept listening, interested in hearing what these soldiers had to say, rather than risk another awkward conversation with the skinny goateed man.

The elf went on, "And why are we working with these humans? Last I heard, the nearest humans were isolationist. Now we're working with humans to rescue more humans?"

The female elf riding next to him had a green braid and kept her mouth tightly shut as they moved down the broken road. In the distance, the sound of war horns both orkish, a deep roaring sound, and elvish, a high bellow, could be heard blaring over the chaotic battle for the city.

"There are children with the ones we're saving. Besides, whatever happened to the city, these humans were part of it, and they offered to help," the first elf's companion finally replied. "Also, their leader is an antemáklasi and a friend of the Arborous," she continued in a low voice. "I heard he lasted forty-five seconds in a duel with Súmeriel."

"I heard it was thirty, but she stopped because he fought like Sarma."

"Wouldn't you? Especially if he was wielding a cursed sword?"

"Who said his sword is cursed?"

"It's a black Thalmien blade. There's no such thing, so it has to be cursed," said the white-braided elf as they rode past the tank.

Up ahead, Shawn heard a murmur of voices pass down the line of soldiers followed by the tank rolling to a pause beneath him.

From his watchful spot higher and farther on the back of Brucey, O'Cleary cursed softly, one of his hands on the thin headset he wore beneath his helmet as he listened to some message Shawn couldn't hear. Then the Irishman leaped down off the tank. O'Cleary only made it a few steps before turning back to give Shawn an impatient look.

"Come on, boyo. Now that you're here, I'm not letting you outta my sight," he said gruffly.

Shawn clambered off the top of the tank with all the awkward grace a teenage boy could muster and quickly caught back up to O'Cleary, who didn't bother waiting.

"What about me?" said the confused-looking, goateed man.

"Stay at your post," O'Cleary ordered without a second glance at the man.

"O'Cleary, why aren't the dwarves spread through the ranks like the rest?" Shawn asked as they moved along the line of human and elf warriors standing at the ready, closer and closer to the front and the sound of battle.

"'Cause they're glorified magic minesweepers," O'Cleary answered as he made his way around a blackened Chevy.

"Oh… I thought it was because they don't get along with the elves."

O'Cleary glanced curiously back over his shoulder at Shawn. "Watch your step there," he instructed with a point at a pile of broken glass. "What do you mean they don't get along? Actually, never mind. Keep your voice down and your eyes up. We're nearing the front," he said as they arrived at a dwarf who stood a few feet outside the main force.

The dwarf was focused intently on a strange pattern painted on the ground in what looked like blood. As they passed her, a tattoo on the back of her hands lit up, glowing blue. As it did, the strange circle of bloody runes began to sizzle before fading out of existence. Once the sizzling came to an end, the dwarf wobbled a bit but was caught by the supporting hand of a woman Shawn recognized from Paragon but whose name he didn't know. She wasn't the only familiar face.

O'Cleary paused and exchanged a few words with Jessica, who was supervising the scene, before walking back over to Shawn. "Let's keep moving. We need tah get to the front."

As they moved forward, Shawn noted many familiar faces in the ranks of soldiers who stood at the ready. Among them was one of the grocers who'd always helped him and his mom carry their groceries to the car. Another was a man who he thought used to work at his dentist's office. Others he recognized as some of the men and women he'd seen in Macon while they ate with Jason.

The crowd was full of familiar, nameless faces, all cold with similar expressions of varying degrees of fear or anger. Many of them looked back at Shawn curiously. A few managed to smile; others nodded politely.

The elves, though, all looked at him the same, with a sort of friendly melancholy. One with a green braid even stepped out from the rank to approach him as they walked.

"Fána Shawn, hold a moment," he said in accented English. O'Cleary stopped, slowly, obviously eager to move along but curious as to what the elf wanted. He was tall, even for an elf.

"Here," he said as he handed Shawn a strange weapon. It was a long, thin, double-sided blade with a guarded hilt. Shawn holstered his gun, looking at the strange sword in awe. "I will trade you my sword for yours. It is of fine craftwork. I offer it to you as it will better suit your size than that short basilisk blade you carry now."

"How do you know my name?" Shawn replied. He was sure he'd never seen this elf before.

"We all know your name, young warrior. Even if you do not wear the braid of a Fána, your bravery is deserving of one," he said. His explanation drew nods from the nearby elves. "You would do me a great honor to make this trade."

"Are you sure? Yours is much nicer than mine," Shawn protested weakly, caught off guard by all the eyes trained on him.

"I am. Trust me, you do me a favor to give me a basilisk blade. I will be all the talk among my warriors to have received a gift from so young a warrior, and I will fight better as well knowing you are armed more to your build," the elf said warmly as they exchanged weapons.

"Thank you," Shawn said over his shoulder as O'Cleary set off again, a bit quicker than before. Shawn struggled to get the sword and sheath adequately secured to his belt as he rushed to catch up with O'Cleary as they were nearing the front. "What does Fána mean?" he asked the Irishman, in hopes he knew.

"Newbie, from what I can tell," O'Cleary was replying when suddenly he turned and side-tackled Shawn to the ground.

A few feet in front of him, a black arrow sliced through the air. As Shawn was falling, he flinched as he watched it sprout from the neck of one of the men in formation and send a spray of crimson blood droplets into the air. The world seemed to freeze for a moment. The man collapsed in a heap, his lips stained red with blood.

"Get down," someone screamed. But there was nowhere to take cover.

The elves moved. Like cogs in a well-oiled machine, they stepped forward in a line from their positions, where they raised large ovular shields. Suddenly, he was on his feet again, sandwiched between a pair of elves with shields in front of him. Adrenaline shot through Shawn's veins as he saw dark shapes moving on the top of a building to their right.

The twanging of bows mixed with a flurry of nearby gunfire. Movement to his right drew his attention, and he saw an elf lower an empty longbow and move out of O'Cleary's way. A second later, there were a series of thuds as the bodies of orks rained to the ground from four stories up.

"Platoon! Move up and clear the building," he heard Gunter order as a group of fifteen humans and five elves around him moved up to the building. They held in front of the door for a moment, tension building before the strike.

"Breach!" Gunter ordered, and the doors exploded inward before they all went rushing inside.

I wish we had some of those big tree people that are with the main force, Shawn thought as O'Cleary gave him a quizzical look.

"You all right?" O'Cleary asked calmly.

"Yes, sir."

"Good. Draw dat new sword of yours. We're near the front."

He was right. A moment later, they finally reached the front of the procession. Here, the forces broke from three vertical lines into their own individual units. An elf on horseback with a blue waterfall braid directed the whole affair with measured efficiency. The battle was now taking place only a few hundred yards ahead, but it sounded as though it was dying down.

Shawn was too short to see past the rows of armed men and women, but he could hear the crashing of blades and crack of gunfire ahead. Emerging from the shifting pile of soldiers preparing to move forward were three familiar faces — Peter, Breekie, and Simon — whose arms were stained with red blood, following close behind. Shawn fumbled as he tried to draw his sword. Fear and inspiration battled for control of his mind.

The sight of Peter brought back the memory from just the other day: Peter alone at the gate, where he fell upon the orks like a summer storm, his black blade rent flesh from body as he was overwhelmed by the enemy. He looked much the same now, as he made his way up a hill of rubble to a small building with a missing roof and damaged walls. Peter stepped carefully over a road sign for Ted Turner Drive crumpled on the hill.

Behind him, Breekie's hammer dripped grislily as his ever-present grin broke through his ample, round beard. Even Simon looked more frightening than usual; the red blood on his arms contrasted the dark blood that stained the clothes of his companions.

O'Cleary veered after them, and together they made their way up to a small hill of rubble. Behind the hill, a man in full SNW attire devoted his entire attention to a radio receiver. At the top, they strolled into a broken set of walls.

"Reporting for duty, cap," O'Cleary said.

In an effort to appear more soldier-like, Shawn stood straight and began a salute, but the familiar words of William on their way here from Paragon echoed in his head.

Never salute on the field of battle. We call that a sniper check, and it can get you and your officer killed. Shawn's hand halted awkwardly, halfway to his head. The strange spasm drew a raised eyebrow from O'Cleary. Shawn urgently pulled both his hands behind his back. *That was close. Need to be more careful.* He berated himself as he took in his surroundings.

Peter came to a stop in front of William, several elves, and a pair of dwarves. His black sword dripped oily blood onto the broken stones, his eyes as gray as the stormy clouds above. Something about him unnerved Shawn, but still, he admired the man's willingness to act.

There was no denying the man's change since Paragon. He was fiercer now. It was in the way he stood, as if he were still in the thick of combat, surrounded by opponents, where he waited for one of them to make the wrong move.

People may not like him, but at least he doesn't lead from the back.

Behind Peter stood Mellonië, her own armor stained with blood. Peter began to address O'Cleary as he cleaned the blood off his sword.

"According to Mellonië here, we're almost to the entrance. But it sounds like we're going to have to do some convincing," Peter said, irritated. "I want you and a few others to join me. She can get us close enough to make contact with the survivors and figure out our next step from there."

Boom! An explosion nearby rocked the ground beneath them, and everyone in the room flinched except for Peter. *Why didn't he flinch? He's a soldier. Even O'Cleary winced.*

"How are we getting past the enemy encirclement?" O'Cleary replied suspiciously as he straightened his stance.

"We have to take a tunnel," said Breekie proudly as he stepped forward and made his way over to stand by Shawn. His war hammer rested against his shoulder. His red-star-embroidered hat was covered by a blocky dwarven helmet. Shawn and Breekie fist-bumped, and Shawn grinned at the dwarf, who smiled back with twice the teeth.

"Breekie's coming with us in case there are traps," Peter added.

"Your tone makes me feel like I should be scared," Breekie said in a half-jesting tone.

"I will provide support as well," Mellonië said calmly as she stepped over to O'Cleary's side before Peter could reply to Breekie's jesting.

Peter scratched absently at his bloodstained beard hairs. "Good idea. With Simon, that makes five. You coming too, Shawn?" he asked as if he'd just seen Shawn for the first time.

"Lad's got good eyes. Wouldn't hurt to have them along, if he keeps them open and his mouth shut," Breekie interjected hopefully.

"All right, we need to get a move on. There could be hostiles anywhere in this godforsaken mess," Peter replied dismissively. "William, I want everyone to be ready to go at a moment's notice. You'll be working with Illuna Kueyr," he said with a motion to a tall elf with a blue waterfall braid.

Maybe I can ask him about the shadow woman… Shawn thought as Peter spoke to the other men and women gathered together. *He has to know about her, even if the others don't remember it. Unless that elf was right, and his sword is cursed…*

Once Peter was done giving instructions, they began making their way down the hill of debris toward the stadium as they followed Mellonië.

Suddenly, the radioman at the bottom of the hill dropped his receiver to the ground and ran like mad towards Peter. "Captain! Bravo two-six Romeo reports heavy resistance on Nelson Street. Orks have rallied and are preparing for another charge. Cannot raise two-six on the net. Please advise." Peter grimaced as he glanced between the front line and Mellonië as his hand went to his headset, and he said urgently, "Reese, you got that? Need you on our position ASAP." Shawn felt more than heard the familiar whine of Brucey as it moved down the street.

"Watch this," O'Cleary said with a grin as the tank rolled closer to the front line. The armored beast stopped short of the rubble, turret scanning the area for any unlucky orks. A metal hatch in Brucey's head groaned open, and a man in dirty digital camouflage popped out.

Shawn looked on from the position behind the rubble at the next row of buildings. A collapsed concrete parking garage left a ready-made no-man's-land for a city block. Nothing stirred. Even the regular bursts of rifle fire slacked off. The same dreaded anticipation Shawn felt on the ride returned in earnest.

All at once, a flurry of activity erupted onto the field as soldiers burst into the open space. They scrambled pell-mell across the broken ground toward his position, tripping over the uneven terrain the whole way.

Several hundred yards behind them, a mass of orks came charging with all manner of weapons brandished and accompanied by war cries that formed a pit in Shawn's stomach.

Everyone reacted in an instant: O'Cleary threw himself on the nearest rock and fired at the oncoming wave. William dropped to his knees to scream at the radio operator. Atop the tank, Reese thumbed his handset.

"Gunner, canister, troops, front right, three hundred meters, on my command!"

Behind the first few dozen orks, a truck-sized lizard burst onto open ground. Atop the beast rode an enormous ork in full spiky battle armor wielding a long mace. *That's the same thing the dwarves were eating yesterday. What'd they call them? Drakes? How do you fight something like that?* Shawn wondered from his place at O'Cleary's side. *It looks like a wingless dragon.*

The final straggler reached the line at that moment. Simon offered a bloody arm and yanked the man over the side of rubble being used as a ramshackle barricade.

Krakoom! The tank's cannon fired. The entire ground shook like the Shattering had come again. Shawn threw his hands to his ears. An instant later, a burst of black mist rose from the charging force.

When the mist cleared, only a handful of orks were still standing: the drake rider and four others. All of them wore the now familiar robes of warlocks, but none of the warlocks charged towards them. A strange note rose from the elves in the front line, like a chorus of vengeful angels. A series of fireballs burst out and forward, incinerating the few remaining orks as they struck.

Peter turned back towards Mellonië and the rest of them. "Let's go. They've got this."

They were then led into a long, flat, stone building half a mile ahead of the main force. The building was obviously not man-made, as it seemed to have been grown and carved out of a single stone. Once they'd passed through several damaged stone rooms full of unfamiliar curving furniture, they came to a strange sight. In the middle of the floor was a large manhole cover.

Mellonië bent over the manhole then knocked on it several times before she stepped back. The clang of something striking the other side of the metal circle made Shawn jump.

"Open it," Mellonië instructed with a commanding nature that caught Shawn a little off guard.

Together, O'Cleary and Breekie bent down and removed the manhole from its place. They were greeted by a dirty, bearded face full of rotting teeth with a smell to match. He looked up curiously at them, raised a hand, and motioned for them to join him as he spoke in words Shawn could not decipher from babble.

"C'monnw, wegonta geja tah shafety. Less yew ish de army?"

"Hurry Jebediah," Mellonië interrupted in a surprisingly soft voice. "Take us to Leefield. Thank you for your help."

Peter stopped before hopping in. His head tilted slightly as someone began to speak to him over his new open-ear headphones. Moments later, he turned back to the group.

"William says they've found a weak point in the barricade they can punch through and hold when we're ready to evacuate. The only problem is it's more southwest than we'd like," Peter informed the small party. Then he dropped down into the tunnel.

Jebediah nodded emphatically as he pursed his lips and offered Mellonië a withered helping hand. Once the rest of them were all crammed into the dark tunnel, like too many chocolates into a toddler's mouth, Mellonië spoke softly.

"We'll be going under the ork barricade. If Jebediah turns out his light, keep moving, silently, until he turns it back on. If he stops, you stop. Be careful," she said, then closed the manhole.

Shawn's heart thundered in his chest as he stared down into the gaping black hole. *You can do this. Come on. It's just a tunnel. You're with allies. You've got this.* Shawn continued trying to convince himself as he descended into the unknown.

Placing his war hammer gently on the ground, Breekie stooped to his knees in the tunnel. One of Breekie's tattooed runes on the back of his hand glowed blue as he placed his palms on the ground. Then, after the glow faded, a different rune lit upon his bare left shoulder. He nodded firmly then stood with a helping hand from Shawn.

"No rune traps," he said confidently.

Shawn watched Peter hunched over so as not to hit his head at the front of the group next to Jebediah, who was barely visible in the dim light coming in through the holes of the manhole cover above.

"Jebediah, we need you to get us inside as quickly as possible," Peter said.

The old man nodded vigorously. His lower lip quivered as he babbled something under his breath to himself then pointed at Peter's headset and shook his head violently.

"Yewsh goschta turn zat der oof," he managed to croak out.

With a scowl, Peter nodded and reached up to hold his finger in place until the small red light of his headset blinked out. With that, Jebediah set off down the tunnel in a scamper. They moved through the strange smooth tunnel in pairs side by side.

Shawn found it odd that despite the close quarters, he barely felt claustrophobic as they moved through the dark. In fact, for some reason, he felt less cramped down here than above. The main thing that bothered him in the tunnel was Jebediah. His smell lingered in the air with every step, and the wind-up flashlight he carried barely provided any light. Thankfully, the ground they strode on was smooth and consistent, making moving in the dark easy.

After they'd been going for about ten minutes, the light shut off and plunged them into darkness. Shawn froze on instinct, just for a second, unable to see more than a few inches in front of him. *Gotta keep moving. Can't stop here,* he told himself and kept walking.

Then he felt something bump into him from behind. Although soft, the sudden collision in the darkness caused Shawn's heart to almost explode in terror. His hand flew to his weapon rather than freezing in horror. *Oh God, please no. Oh, God.*

"Criske."

Oh, thank you, God. It's Breekie.

There was no other sound in the tunnel other than the soft patter of feet ahead. Outside though, he was sure he could still hear the distant roar of battle. He felt Breekie's hand on his shoulder, then it slid it down to his arm until the dwarf was holding his wrist.

"Don't slow down now, lad. Come on, we can't get left behind," the dwarf said in a firm whisper as he began to drag Shawn forward. Shawn obeyed, one hand on the hilt of his sword. The other, he pulled from Breekie's grip.

"I got this," he whispered back softly, and although he could not see the dwarf, he could feel the sense of approval that radiated from the bearded fellow.

How far do we have to go? he wondered as they continued down the strange tunnel. He heard the banging of feet from above, and both he and Breekie stopped and stood still, this time out of reflex rather than fear.

Guttural voices Shawn could not properly hear followed the sound of feet pounding above them. Although he couldn't make out the words, he knew for sure those voices belonged to orks; and something bigger than the orks, with steps that sounded like they belonged to a small elephant.

Slowly, but inevitably they resumed moving forward. Each step felt like it could be their last. This happened again two more times. Each time, they paused a moment before continuing on in silence, deeper into the dark. After what felt like hours to Shawn, the flashlight lit back up. The small soft light illuminated the tunnel ahead.

Another ten minutes were spent traveling in the light before they came to a dead end. Here, Jebediah pointed his soft light up at a large metal square with a single hole only about an inch wide in the bottom corner. The old man mumbled as he handed his light to Peter, whose hand he grasped to make sure he kept the light pointed up.

Then Jebediah fished a pen out of the folds of his overlapping clothes and pushed it up through the hole. There was a moment of resistance followed by light shining softly through the hole. Then there were more loud sounds — clanging and whirring — by something above the metal square.

Then the square rose. Shawn heard a click, and after a familiar whir that comes when someone starts a piece of machinery, they were all bathed in blinding white light.

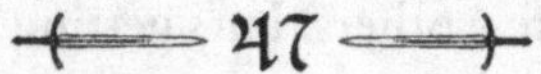

47

THE SHRINE IN THE STADIUM

Bright white light flooded the hole and illuminated the four towering figures that stood on all sides. Shawn's hand flew to his face as he blinked rapidly as he desperately tried to adjust his vision to see the silhouettes that stood menacingly above.

"Well, what have we here?" a firm male voice said as the light shifted out of their faces. As Shawn's eyes adjusted, he saw the four men more clearly; three armed with mismatched spears aimed in their direction and a fourth well-muscled man in football gear and metal armor leaning on a large war hammer. His right forearm bore a shaded geometric bear-head tattoo, and his left leg was heavily bandaged below the knee.

"You broke your glasses, didn't you, Leef," Peter accused, as the cold air from above contrasted the tunnel's warmth and stung Shawn's ears.

The broad man shifted awkwardly on his wounded leg and lowered the enormous industrial flashlight he'd been aiming at them. "I didn't break anything. Lost my contacts, sure, so no sense in risking my glasses too." Leefield shrugged. "No worries, boys. These fellas are our ticket to safety. You can relax. Oh, and it's Leefield, not Leef, no matter what he tells you."

"It's so good to see you, Lee," Peter said as a short ladder was lowered into the hole. Peter practically flew up the ladder and into the man's firm embrace. "About time something went right for us. What happened to your knee?"

Shawn barely heard him ask the question, he was so distracted by the sudden appearance of tears on Peter's smiling face. The smile wasn't one Shawn had seen from the man before. It held no malice or sarcasm, only genuine delight and relief.

Why's he crying? They look alike… same blue eyes, but the big guy's are friendlier. Who is this guy? Shawn wondered.

"It took a bit of an arrow. Nothing I couldn't handle," Leefield replied gruffly. "Hey there, O'Cleary, Simon. I can't believe you're alive."

"Barely," O'Cleary replied. "Any of the other lads make it, or is it just your sorry self?" he said as he shook hands with the broad man.

"Nah, Ian's here, and a few others. Ian's getting the chopper ready. Jebediah said you'd be bringing weapons."

"The weapons are with William and the rest of the force. Who else from SNW is here? What about Sabrina?" Peter replied. "Was she with you when it happened?"

Leefield shook his head heavily. "We've got a few from SNW — Tanner, Chris, Daniel, Abram, Courtney. No Sabrina. She was up visiting her parents. I was going to join her in DC, but my flight got delayed. Only reason I'm still here. Planes were falling like flies when it happened, Peter. But she'll be fine, her dad'll take care of her. They're probably better off than we've been," he said with the tone of someone who'd tried to convince themself of something they didn't fully believe.

We passed one of those planes on the way here — what was left of one, at least. Geez, I'd rather fight an ork than be in a crashing plane, Shawn thought as he helped Jebediah out of the hole. Once they were all out, Shawn looked around curiously. They'd come out in what looked like an old storage room with a concrete floor and walls. A metal door was the rooms' only exit.

Peter nodded with more compassion than Shawn expected from him. "I'm sure she is."

One by one, Leefield shook hands with them and introduced his own companions. His hands were large, rough, and warm, but his handshake was not so firm that it became painful. "I'm Leefield Vaughan. I'm actually Captain Blair's cousin. Glad to have you folks," the broad-shouldered man said eagerly, then he came to a stop at Breekie. An awed expression came over his face. "You — you're a dwarf, aren't you?"

Breekie smiled a tad condescendingly. "Dah, I am a dwarf. What's it to you and your tiny hammer?" he replied with feigned hostility.

Leefield smiled, wide but melancholic. "We had a strange humanoid ourselves," he said fondly.

Breekie's brow furrowed with concern. "Your tongue is strange. *Had?*"

Leefield nodded as his smile slipped. "Yeah, he, uh… He's not with us anymore. But if your kind is half as noble as he was, I'd take one of you over six men," Leefield said with a respectful nod at Breekie before stepping away.

Leefield moved over to the metal door and thumped it twice. "We're good here, Jerry," he called, and the door swung open. With a wave of his arm, he led them out of the small room. "You're lucky you had Jebediah. There are tons of tunnels under the city, and the orks have been using them to sneak around. I don't know how he figured that one out, but I'm glad he did."

That must be why he put out the light. I wonder how close we actually came to getting caught, Shawn thought as they emerged into one of the arena's white, windowless hallways. They passed through several barriers made out of whatever their builders could get their hands on: popcorn machines, tables, chairs, toilets, etc.

As they reached a set of escalators-turned-stairs, Peter spoke up again. "Is everyone ready to leave?"

Leefield's frown deepened. "That's where you come in. Some people need a bit of convincing. We've got some naysayers, especially this one guy, Joule, who are convinced leaving means we're dead."

As they made their way into the arena itself, Shawn's stomach turned. Large chunks of ceiling rubble lay scattered about the space, some embedded in the ground; others served as raised flat surfaces. But it was the smell of thousands of men, women, and children having gone weeks without proper plumbing that turned Shawn's stomach. *Not as bad as the burning pits,* he thought as he fought to keep his breakfast down.

"What have you been eating?" Shawn asked one of the men with a spear as they walked past a group of gaunt guards stationed outside an empty restaurant. As they passed a bend, the stadium's interior came into view, and he saw a large white stone building that covered the grassless field at the center. It stood tall, with parapets, a large open gate, and five towers that broke through the top of the stadium itself.

"Whatever we can," the man walking with them said dejectedly. "At first we were okay — lots of food to salvage from snack stands and restaurants. And then we found some strange dried fruit and vegetables when we got into the stone hold."

He gestured at the stone fortress. "The homeless population has helped though. The orks seem to ignore them for some reason. They've been able to get us supplies, a little bit at a time. It's thanks to them we got word you were coming."

The farther into the stadium they got, the more people Shawn realized were looking in awe at Breekie, who seemed relatively oblivious of the attention he was receiving.

"Do you at least have an exit point?" Shawn heard Peter demand while a pair of children pointed excitedly at Breekie. Their mother tried to calm them down and explain it was rude to point.

"Sorry, cuz, We didn't really build the defenses with the intention of leaving," Leefield replied.

"Why don't we take the tunnel?" Asked Shawn in an attempt to be helpful.

"Too slow. Too risky. That thing wasn't built for a mass exodus. If you cram this many people in that tight space, they'll be heard," Breekie replied dismissively.

"We've got a tank. It'll make an exit. We'll just have to make sure everyone is clear of where the exit is going," O'Cleary said nonchalantly.

"Hold on," Peter said, coming to a halt. "You've got weapons, but how have you not been overwhelmed? The orks outnumber you by thousands, and they've got warlocks. What's been keeping them out?"

Leefield leaned uncomfortably on his hammer, shaking his head slowly. "Kundo, the humanoid I mentioned earlier, did something that opened the stone-hold. Before that, he was keeping them out almost single-handedly."

"This Kundo, what was he?" Breekie asked eagerly.

Leefield sighed. "It's hard to explain. He was, this… enormous bearlike creature. Easily eight feet tall. This thing would make Thomas look small, Peter. And completely covered in bright plate mail. You could see his coarse brown hair sticking through where it connected. This was his," Leefield said as he hefted his weapon. "He had an enormous ax too. I could barely lift the thing myself, but he swung that thing like it was made of bamboo."

"Big and furry. Anything else?" Breekie pressed as he walked.

Leefield nodded. "Big bearlike claws, huge fangs, pointy almost dog-like ears. Looked kind of like the beast from that old Disney movie. He terrified the orks. It was strange."

Breekie shook his head. "I do not know this *fayemaia*. Did he tell you what he was?"

Leefield shook his head sadly. "We were just starting to understand him when he left us. We'd only just learned his name."

"Left you?" This time it was Peter asking.

"When he opened the doors, his armor all lit up like a beacon, and then he just vanished, armor and all. That's when the orks stopped coming near the stadium. They set up the barrier, yeah, but they won't come within a hundred feet of this place. Just the orks, mind you. Other things sometimes get closer in the night. We've lost too many people to those lizard things."

Leefield shuddered. "That's why people are scared to leave, they feel safe here. Even though we're running out of supplies," Leefield added and ground his teeth in frustration while he led them closer to the building. "Kundo's seen as something of a martyr now. That's why people are taking such notice of you."

Mellonië stopped at the entrance, where she looked up at elvish text written over the opening. Her forehead wrinkled with sorrow as a tear slid down her cheek. Shawn stopped next to her and placed a hand hesitantly on her forearm.

"Ma'am, are you all right?" he asked as gently as he could.

The elf blinked and stopped the tears flowing from her eyes but did not wipe them off her cheeks as they ran through her green war paint.

"This was Vulacia's Shrine of Memories. Kundo was its guardian. It is only opened once a century. It contains all the life songs of all who once came from this beautiful city. That is why the orks do not venture closer. They fear the vengeful spirits of my people." She swallowed. "Go on ahead. This is not a place I should be during a battle."

"You sure? I mean, if it's some kind of sacred elf tomb or something, I'm sure we could ask them to leave. I mean, maybe. I… uh…" Shawn fumbled to find a way to comfort the grief-struck elf.

Mellonië shook her head and smiled softly. "The doors are open for you. Their spirits welcome your people, offering them refuge. I must grieve in my own way, young one."

"I mean, I don't want to leave you alone out here. I could stay if you want. They don't really need me in there."

Mellonië tilted her head slightly while she muttered something under her breath, a far off look in her eyes. "Your kindness will be remembered, Shawn. Come, you will be my support in this place of mourning," she said, then took his arm and led him into the building.

Her skin is so soft… Wait. Stop. No, this is Elborin's wife. Her skin is not soft, Shawn thought in a panic as the elf-woman walked with him into the white stone Shrine of Memories. As Shawn's foot landed on the stone floor, he felt a surge of strange energy, almost like a static shock pulse through him. He was filled with an overwhelming sense of grief that would have frozen him in place if not for Mellonië.

Something about her touch soothed the grief, grounded him like an anchor in a storm. There was no time to figure out what brought the grief on in the first place; it only lasted a second before he was pulled forward by the elf's stride.

"It grows weak. The doors have been open for too long," he heard her mutter to herself.

The walls around them bore a strange, intricate pattern that, after a moment of staring, Shawn realized were some musical lyrics that covered every inch of the building's surface. There were no light fixtures anywhere. Instead, the entire building gave off its own soft light from ceiling to floor.

Both Peter and Breekie stood frozen in front of him as well. Tears flowed down their cheeks, their mouths slightly agape as they stared off into nothingness.

"Can you hear that?" Peter asked in a hoarse whisper. O'Cleary and Leefield stopped and looked back at them, confused expressions on their faces.

Shawn strained to hear, but his ears picked up nothing out of the ordinary.

"Hear what? Hey, are you okay?" Simon asked befuddled, voicing Shawn's thoughts for him, as Simon examined Peter critically as he walked back towards him.

"This place affects those in tune with the arcane flow differently," Mellonië explained as she led Shawn to the pair of them. She let go of his arm and gripped Peter's shoulder as she motioned with her head for Shawn to do the same. Shawn looked down at the dwarf, who was only a little shorter than himself.

Breekie's lips were moving silently as he stared blankly into the distance. Shawn reached out and grasped the dwarf by the shoulder. Breekie started as if he'd just woken from a dream.

"I, I… Songs… Songs of the dead. Crisking elvish sorcery," he said dispassionately as he wiped hurriedly at his face.

Peter said nothing. A strange cold look came over his face as he looked around at the walls as though they contained traps ready to spring at any moment.

"Come. Let us be done with this," Mellonië said and took Shawn's arm once again.

Leefield's brow furrowed, but he didn't question what had just occurred. Instead, he turned and led them into an enormous room full to the brim with several thousand people crowded in front of a round raised stage.

"Comin' through," Leefield called out unnecessarily, as men and women stepped aside at the sight of Breekie and their crew. This made room for Leefield to lead them to the front. "You're up. They're expecting you," he said to Peter, who seemed to have returned to his collected self.

Peter climbed up onto the stage and turned to face the crowd, then he stood there in silence and waited as the crowd quieted down.

"My name is Captain Peter Blair of SNW," he said in a commanding voice that echoed perfectly throughout the room. "We're here with an Elvish army led by General Elborin to help all of you evacuate the city."

"Where will we go?"

"Are you crazy? It's safe here!"

Voices called out from the crowd as Fear ran her cold fingers through the rows of people.

"I realize you're scared and tired, but you aren't safe. It is only a matter of time before the orks take this place or starve you out," Peter replied firmly. "I commend your bravery and resourcefulness in surviving here, but we have a place for you — a town we've built called Paragon, south of here, far from where our enemy grows stronger the longer we wait. You have one chance and one chance only to survive."

Peter's voice bore the weight of command. "Many have died today, and more are going to join them to get you out. Maybe me. Maybe you. Do not let their sacrifices go to waste by staying here and dying. My forces and the elves' will do our utmost to take back this city, and we need your help, those that are able. But for those incapable of fighting any longer, you *must* leave. It is your only option, and now is your only chance to do it."

The crowd stirred as the sound of thunder boomed hauntingly the distance.

"Come on… do something," Shawn muttered as the crowd seemed to mull over Peter's words.

"Perhaps I wasn't clear enough. Let me make this easier for you," Peter called over the crowd in a steely voice. "Anyone who stays *will* die. Gather what weapons you have. Anything else will only weigh you down. Those who are willing to fight, gather outside and report to Leefield. The rest of you spread the word and prepare to exit at the south gate."

The crowd flinched but slowly began to move like a school of fish away from an oncoming shark as they exited the building as if they were one being, when a man called out, "Kundo gave his life to let us in here!"

Breekie stormed the stage and took up a position next to Peter, the crowd's full attention on him. *What's he doing?* Shawn wondered.

"Kundo would have called you a bunch of half-witted, beardless, crisked fools if you let him die just to stay here and die," he yelled at them enough to be heard outside. "Now, do what Captain Peter said, and move it!"

The spell of complacency which had seemed to hang over the crowd was broken. Everyone began to move with a true sense of urgency.

Shawn began to follow the crowd, when O'Cleary's accented tone called out at him, "Oi! Lad, not you, you doser," he said as he waved Shawn over to where their group was gathering next to the stage.

He didn't give them a choice. He told them what they had to do, and they listened. How does he do that? Is it just his tone? Shawn wondered as he meandered back to the group.

"Interesting speech there, Peter. Didn't give them much wiggle room," Leefield commented as Peter rejoined them.

"Sun Tzu said to give your soldiers no option for escape, and they will prefer death to retreat. When there's no option other than to fight, people fight all the harder. I'd have preferred that, but most of you don't look fit for battle," Peter replied before putting his hand to his radio.

"William, go for breaching encirclement. From here, you'll be hearing from Simon on this end. You both know what to do," Peter ordered into his headset. As he spoke, a wiry, ginger-headed young man with a scraggly beard in an SNW uniform approached them.

He looks like a satyr. Shawn chuckled to himself as he imagined the man with a pair of goat horns.

"Hey, cap, Simon, O'Cleary. Good to see you," he said warmly. "You need anything from me, cap?"

"Ian, good. Is that chopper I saw on my way here operational?" Peter asked quickly.

Ian cleared his throat. "Uh-huh. Well, yeah, but it's only got about enough fuel for one flight."

"That's enough. You're dropping me off at the Tesla Building."

"Just you? It's no Blackhawk. I can't stress that enough."

"Me and the dwarf. Think you can handle it?"

Ian gave the dwarf a quick once over. "He'll fit. We could rig the gurney up to drop you both." He cleared his throat again and looked up at the dark sky. "Uh-huh. Yeah, I can do that. So long as you don't plan on landing. We need to go soon."

"Now hold on," Breekie interjected. "I'm nyet fan of heights. What's all this about flying?"

Peter grinned savagely. "Only way in buddy. You can close your eyes if you like."

"I… Look, long as it isn't a griffin. Those things don't like dwarves, Peter Blair."

"We're not taking an animal. We're talking about our flying machines. Trust me, it'll be worth the knowledge you'll gain to take back to your people," Peter said slyly.

Oh yeah, the most he's seen is cars, Shawn realized.

The dwarf pulled nervously at his long round beard before nodding his head in an attempt to convince himself of his decision to go. Next to him, Ian cleared his throat again.

"Is he all right?" Shawn whispered to O'Cleary.

"Aye. Aye, he is. He just does that. You'll get used to it," O'Cleary replied with his usual grin.

"As I was," Peter said loud enough to get the group's attention. "Ian, Breekie, and I are taking the chopper. O'Cleary, Simon, Mellonië, and Leefield, you're to oversee the evacuation. Any questions?"

Captain Peter is leaving us? The idea scared Shawn more than he expected.

"No, sir," the others replied in unison.

"Good. No dying. That's an order," Peter said emphatically before he, the ginger, and the dwarf made their way out ahead of the others.

"Wait, where are they going?" Shawn asked quietly when he realized he didn't know why they were leaving.

"Special assignment. Don't worry. He'll be all right," O'Cleary replied.

It's not him I'm worried about. It's nice having someone as scary as an ork on our side.

Simon turned to the remaining group. "Lee, go ahead and separate out the volunteers who are willing to help with the assault on the orks."

"Sure thing, Simon, but what's going on with Peter? Don't we need him here?" Leefield asked, his gaze in the direction Peter was departing.

"The captain has changed, Lee. He's going to help the elves deal with another threat. We probably won't see him again until this is over."

Frown plastered across his face, Leefield nodded. "All right, I'll see what we can do. We got weapons from here, but we'd have more volunteers if we had more weapons..." he replied.

"As soon as we rendezvous with the reinforcements, we will," Simon said coolly.

"O'Cleary, Mellonië, I need you to supervise the rear. Make sure everyone who's coming makes it out."

"An honorable assignment," Mellonië said with a slight tilt of her head.

Shawn shifted in place, but Simon seemed to have finished giving orders.

"Sir? What about me?" Shawn asked as he tried not to sound offended that he'd been overlooked.

Simon's eyes widened slightly. "Stay with O'Cleary. He may need your help."

Upon exiting the hauntingly beautiful elvish building, they found a crowd gathered outside. The crowd was split into two groups. The first and smaller group consisted mostly of the injured, old, and young.

All of the children in this group were gathered at its center, surrounded by a faction of well-armed men and women, who looked as though they belonged to the second group, which consisted of as many able-bodied adults as could wield a weapon. *There must be thousands of them,* Shawn thought as he looked around, *but so few children.*

Outside, over the growing rumble of thunder, they could hear the sounds of battle — the bellowing of horns and the occasional crash of cannon fire. Simon led them all to the south gate then had them gather to the side of it before giving an order over the radio.

Moments later, the sound of the allied tank firing echoed through the air, and the heavily fortified gate exploded inward and sent debris flying. *He knew just where to make them stand so they wouldn't be hit by anything,* Shawn noted as Simon began ushering the crowd towards the opening.

It was then that a man at the back began screaming at the top of his lungs as he booked it up the bleachers. "Stop! This is suicide! We've been safe here. If you go out, you'll die!" His screams seemed to unnerve the crowd, and half of them stopped while the other half began to move quicker. Panic threatened to take over the mass of terrified people.

Crap. Crap. Crap. Crap, Shawn thought as he tried to point people in the right direction. From somewhere on the other side of the crowd. Shawn heard Leefield call out, "Shut your fool mouth, Joule," to no avail.

Then he saw Simon pushing through the crowd towards the yelling man who now stood partially up the stadium's bleachers. He continued to move toward where the tall rotund man with slightly curly, dirty blonde hair, jowls, and wide-set eyes stood. As Simon reached Shawn, he spoke to him in a low voice without turning to him or breaking his stride.

"Make the children look away," Simon ordered as he pointed towards a small girl who clutched a floppy toy bunny in her arms. He then marched towards the source of the shouting.

Then Simon was past him. Shawn watched him for a moment and saw him pull a six-inch metal rod out of his satchel, which he attached to the end of his pistol and covered with the corner of his coat.

Shawn turned urgently and spied where the children were standing in confused silence. He made a dash for the area. He caught the attention of the man who seemed to be in charge of their protection.

"Turn the kids away," Shawn said loud enough for the man to hear them over the noise.

"Say what now, boy?" the man replied, an irritated look on his face as he looked past Shawn in the direction of Joule's yelling.

Shawn swallowed then thought about Peter and O'Cleary and the voices they used when giving orders. *Confident and firm, like there's no other option.* He straightened his back, standing as tall as he could and looked the man square in the eyes. "Turn the children around. *Now.* That's an order," he said in his most commanding voice, which only cracked a little.

The man flinched, glanced up at Simon as he broke through the crowd, nodded, and turned to the children, who he ushered to look towards the newly made exit.

"Their captain isn't even here. He doesn't even believe his own words. If it's so safe out there, why isn't he with us?" Joule continued to cry out. His words sent shivers of doubt through the crowd. The tension in the air was palpable as the crowd balanced on the edge of panic. Shawn listened above the noise of the mob and the gunfire. He focused his eyes on Simon.

Pfft. Pfft. Pfft. He could have sworn he heard the silenced gunshots, but it was impossible in the chaos. He did hear Joule's yelling stop though. Shawn saw Simon, one hand on the angry man's shoulders. His lips moved silently as he spoke into the man's dead eyes as he lowered him into the bleachers. Simon's gun was nowhere to be seen as he turned to address the crowd, but Shawn knew it was there. He'd seen the man's almost imperceptible spasm as Simon shot him.

He killed him, just like that. It's not just Peter. It's all his men. They're brutal. They really will do whatever it takes to keep us alive. The thought both thrilled and terrified him.

"Captain Peter is leaving for the front lines to face our enemy head-on while you escape. Keep walking. Don't run. Don't panic. Joule has decided to stay back and make sure the stadium is properly evacuated. Don't worry, we'll get you all out of here safely," he called soothingly to the crowd as he made his way towards them, leaving Joule's still and stoic corpse behind.

Leefield took charge from there. The tattooed man led them forth from the entrance towards the allied forces waiting for them on the other side. Meanwhile, men and women in police and firefighter uniforms directed the traffic of thousands of scared men, women, and children.

"Shawn! To me, lad," O'Cleary called out over the crowd. "We need to clear the stadium of stragglers."

Shawn converged with O'Cleary and Mellonië as the helicopter by the shrine rose steadily into the air, carrying Peter, Breekie, and Ian out of sight.

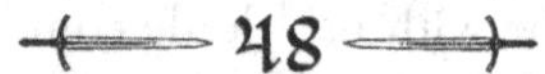

48

HOT CHOCOLATE

ot chocolate! The sweet, warm aroma hit Sarah's nose and made her mouth water joyously. She searched eagerly around the densely crowded meeting room for the source of the tantalizing scent. She spied a line along the side of the room that led to a small table where the drink was being carefully ladled into small cups. Too little, as far as she was concerned.

She did not take Jenni into consideration as she hurried through the crowd for the line. She weaved in and out of the men and women who stood around discussing the council's latest announcement.

"So, we've just completely abandoned the idea of things going back to normal, have we?" Sarah overheard a particularly plump woman with a large round purple hat say.

"I wouldn't say completely abandoned. More that we're taking steps to restore society," came a reply from a figure Sarah couldn't see.

"Restore it? By electing new members to an unconstitutional council?" replied another, nasally, voice.

"If you want to make comparisons to colonial-era documents, why not just consider the council to be a modern Continental Congress? It's what they're trying to be, near as I can tell."

The voices and their conversation faded away as Sarah joined the line for the warm sweet drink she craved. Sarah turned to see if Jenni was catching up and found her a hair's breadth away.

"Oh," Sarah said with a start, then smiled. "You're good. Are all SNW members that good at keeping up in a crowd?" Sarah asked, trying to make conversation and get on the woman's good side.

Jenni raised an eyebrow, unamused. "That was hardly an impressive maneuver. All SNW are trained in standard bodyguard techniques and practices, yes, and they are a cut above any other bodyguards you'll find. But like I said, sticking close to you in the crowd isn't all that impressive."

Jenni looked around. "Honestly, I was expecting a bigger turnout. This is hardly four thousand people. You'd think folks would be more interested in a decision like this."

Sarah's head bobbed in agreement. "It seems like a lot, though, doesn't it? All they did was tell us a few council members were stepping down to focus on some other areas, and some new ones were stepping in."

"Speaking of new," Jenni replied, a hungry look in her eye, "what do you think of that woman, Marah?" she asked in a surprisingly low tone.

Sarah took a step forward to make sure not to lose her spot in line as they spoke. "I don't know. I've only spoken to her once, and she seemed genuinely concerned with making sure the people from Macon integrated well."

"Well, she's coming this way," Jenni said in an even lower voice. Her eyes directed Sarah towards the woman as she approached.

"Good afternoon, Miss Young," Marah began in a loud, overfriendly voice. "How is our local magic… user? What would you call yourself? I am quite certain I heard you don't like being referred to as a witch. Warlock perhaps?" she continued in her loud voice as she closed in.

"You heard correctly," Sarah replied, caught a bit off guard. "Witchcraft is a far cry from the type of magic I use. If you have to give me a title, I suppose caster works, although I really don't think it's necessary."

Marah came to a stop within handshaking distance, a sour expression on her face as she got a full look at Sarah. Sarah wore her SNW jacket unbuttoned over a warm pine green sweater. She also wore a medium length black skirt, and long warm leggings that went into her boots. Her hair was pulled half up with one of the wands holding it into place.

Marah made a show of swallowing before speaking again. "I'm sorry. I didn't realize you were with *them*," she said. Disapproval colored her voice as she motioned at the jacket Sarah wore. "This will make things a bit more difficult, if I'm being frank with you, sweetie."

Sarah looked down at the jacket reflexively. "Oh, no. I'm not actually part of SNW," she protested, eager not to incur Jenni's wrath by way of the mix-up.

"She's wearing the jacket for her own protection," Jenni piped in to make sure there was no confusion.

Marah's gaze did not so much as flinch in Jenni's direction as the woman spoke. "Then why on Earth would you wear such a… controversial piece of clothing? I was under the impression you wanted to make our integration easier. Surely you realize that a majority of Maconites — I hope you are familiar with our moniker — feel that SNW's actions in our town were unwarranted and overly aggressive."

"This is the first I've heard of it actually. I really had no intention of offending anyone."

"Unwarranted and overly aggressive?" Jenni sputtered, the words coming at a delay caused by disbelief. "Your boyfriend poisoned one of our men," she shouted, which drew the attention of anyone not already listening.

Marah continued to ignore Jenni as if the woman simply did not exist. Sarah turned quickly, as she'd reached the end of the line, and accepted a small cup of steaming hot chocolate, which she thrust into Jenni's hands before she turned back and receiving a second cup.

"Well, now that you know, it will certainly make integration and trust more difficult to achieve. Surely you won't continue wearing it," Marah replied, thrown off guard by Sarah's investment in her beverage.

Sarah blew softly on her drink, sending warm sweet steam flowing outward. "I mean, honestly, Councilwoman Marah, if the Maconites — that's what you're calling yourselves, right?"

"Yes."

"If the Maconites — which, linguistically, seems like an antagonistic choice given we're trying to integrate everyone into Paragon here. If they can't accept that, like Jenni said, I'm wearing it for my own protection, then I really don't know what I can do," Sarah replied before taking a test sip of the hot chocolate. To her disappointment, she found it lacking chocolatey flavor.

Another council member arrived after pushing his way through the crowd toward Sarah, the short round woman named Fritz. "Miss Lese, Miss Young, your presence has been requested at the northern wall. There has been an incident, and Mayor Gibson asked me to see to it that you both make your way there as soon as possible. We have a car waiting outside if you'll please follow me," she instructed and left them without any time to ask questions or protest as she set off at a trundle for the main entrance.

A short, awkward car ride later, where Marah took shotgun, and Jenni stared daggers into the back of her skull, and they were at the wall. They quickly exited their vehicle. Sarah took care not to spill any of her precious warm brown liquid. Sarah took the same precautions as they made their way up the concrete steps littered with multicolored leaves.

Once at the top, she turned and saw the old woman struggle to make her way up the stairs behind Marah. Sarah set down her drink, met the old woman halfway down, took her arm, and supported her the rest of the way.

"These stairs need handrails and a wheelchair ramp installed as soon as possible," Marah mentioned offhand to them when they reached the top.

Handrails wouldn't hurt, but a wheelchair ramp? The wall is for defending the city, not sightseeing, she thought as she reached the top of the stairs. *Then again…* She reconsidered as the cacophony of colored leaves on the trees around the city came into view. Jenni stopped in front of her and followed her gaze.

"It's beautiful out there," Sarah said then took another sip of her drink. Jenni dragged her eyes away from the woods and looked at Sarah with bent eyebrows.

"How do you have anything left in that tiny cup? Mine was gone in a few sips?"

Sarah's eyes went wide, and she bit her lip lightly. She checked on the councilwoman a few steps ahead of them. Far enough. Then, with a twinkle in her eye, she brought the cup to her mouth again and whispered to Jenni, "Magic," before she followed the other women to where Steven, Mayor Gibson, and a third man stood clustered together around a set of orange cones and caution tape.

Sarah drew closer and recognized the worried looks on the faces of the two familiar men. Then she realized she'd been to this part of the wall before. A dawning uneasiness began to worm its way into her stomach with every step. *What happened?* She found herself running through a dozen possibilities in a heartbeat.

In his usual style, Mayor Gibson stepped forward to greet them with an outstretched hand, he took and shook each of theirs, even though he'd just seen them not half an hour ago at the ceremony. "I must apologize for leaving before the completion of your introduction, Miss Marah, but in a moment, you will see that it was with good reason."

He greeted the tough woman. "Ah, you must be Miss Jana Bashar. Am I pronouncing that correctly?"

"You are. Nice to meet you, sir," Jenni replied with genuine surprise. "I prefer to go by Jenni, if you don't mind."

Mayor Gibson nodded. "Of course, my apologies. Jenni, it is. I wanted to thank you personally for keeping an eye on our guardian angel. Speaking of, thank you for coming so quickly, Miss Young. I was hoping you could provide some insight into the seriousness of this. I do not know if it is dangerous or not," he said as he waved a broad hand towards the caution-taped area.

In the center of the tape and cones was the familiar glass etching of runes carved and enchanted by Dr. Walker only a week ago. But now, three black spray-painted lines marred the surface of the glass runes.

The lines were messy and broad without firm edges; clearly placed quickly. Regardless, they managed to cover all but one corner of the runes, concealing them from view.

"Mister Elijah here discovered this an hour ago during his rounds," Steven explained loud enough for all to hear. "He was understandably unwilling to touch it, but he says it could only have been placed during a short period when he was talking to one of the other watchmen on patrol, because it wasn't there when he began."

"That's right. Whoever did this was quick and didn't stick around," Elijah explained gruffly.

"So far, this is the only one where this has occurred," Steven added.

Sarah looked up at Elijah. He was dressed in warm civilian clothes and a skull cap, which no hair poked out off; and judging by its shape, he had no hair underneath. Something about his face was familiar but different. Sarah began to pick it apart quickly. She knew if she lingered, she risked staring.

Nose looks like it's been broken several times. Brown eyes, unremarkable eyebrows. Slight overbite. Where have I seen him before? …Thick sideburns but an otherwise weak patchy beard… Oh! He was at the Forge when Peter decided they were sending scouts. They almost got into a fight, didn't they?

"What do you think, Sarah? Is it safe?" Steven asked, redirecting her attention back to the sabotaged runes.

"I'm not sure. I don't understand why someone would paint over them. It might be a good idea to stand back." After everyone was a safe distance away, Sarah reached out and touched the runes' magic with her mind. She probed the energy within directly, trying to determine if the graffiti had affected the spells held by the runes.

The contact sent a warm pulse through her body. It invigorated her with the strength of a hundred cups of hot chocolate. A sudden urge came to her. *Hide it.* She felt her ears warm and a bit of blood rush to her cheeks. Her hair was standing on end all over her body. She blew a breath, which turned into steam in front of her shaking hands.

Everyone around her was staring, gawking with expressions that varied from amazement to concern. Their mixture of reactions jerked back and forth between her and the runes. Unsure what she'd done to warrant such a response, she glanced down at the runes and did a double take.

"What… What happened?" she asked, her voice laced with as much confusion as Mayor Gibson's expression.

"What do you mean, what happened? Did you not do that?" Councilwoman Fritz replied with a tilt of her head. The graffiti had melted away. No trace of it or the rune remained visible.

Eli had taken two full steps back. His eyes did not leave Sarah as one of his hands slid behind his back. Jenni took a step forward to place herself in front of

Sarah. Steven, meanwhile, bent down and ran his hand over the smooth blank concrete surface.

He looked up at Sarah, taking a moment to find the right words. "The whole thing started to glow purple, and then the concrete just… melted over the rest of it," he explained in bewilderment.

"It's still there. I can feel it. I wanted to hide it, but I didn't mean to do this." Sarah's eyes darted to Marah, whose attention was curiously focused on Elijah, not on her or the rune. *They don't need to know it was an accident,* she realized. *No one does. You can tell Steven later, but the last thing the rest of them need to know is that I didn't mean to do that.*

"I hid them. They're still perfectly safe. I doubt I or even a sledgehammer could do anything to damage them," Sarah stated boldly. "Sorry, I get a bit spacey for a few seconds after I cast sometimes," she lied better than she'd expected, courage mounting in her chest. "Whoever did this doesn't have the city's safety in mind."

"Agreed." Mayor Gibson's reply sent relief coursing through Sarah. "Although, this does present us with three questions. First, can this be done to the other three sets? Second, should it be done to them? And third, what, if anything, do we tell people?"

"Nothing. I'm sorry. I was not even aware of these runes or their purpose, and I think I prefer it that way, but now that I know they exist, I must ask, what do they do?" Marah replied, her gaze now directed at the hidden runes, a fearful expression carved on to her face.

"They conceal the city from monsters," Sarah replied after a nod from Mayor Gibson.

"Conceal?" Marah pressed for more.

"Well, it doesn't make us invisible. It just, sort of, redirects attention away from us. For most fayemaia, that is. It won't work on elves or dwarves. Might work on some orks though," Sarah tried to explain as she wished she had the notebook she'd written it all down in.

"And you created these… wards?" Marah replied?

Sarah shook her head enthusiastically. "Oh, no. No, I couldn't do anything like that. Not yet at least. Doctor Walker made them."

"Ah, I see," Marah replied with a nod. "And she told you that's what they do, right?"

"Yes," Sarah replied. She did not like the tone in the other woman's voice.

"So, we have no way of verifying that's what they actually do," Marah replied, an unsuitable eagerness poisoning her words.

"Now hold on," Steven began.

"Relax, commander," Marah stretched the second word strangely. "I am simply suggesting that the less of a deal we make of this, the better the Maconites will feel about it. In fact, personally, I would prefer that they are all removed entirely. However, I can see that you all would not agree to such a suggestion."

"You are correct," Mayor Gibson replied. "I understand your experience with magic has been traumatic, but believe me when I say that I knew Doctor Walker well before all this, and I trust her implicitly."

Marah shrugged. "It seems to me that this is a decision the whole council should be present for before instructing Sarah on how to proceed."

"Granted," Steven said, "but word travels quickly. Even if all here agree to silence, whoever did this will know. I recommend, for the time being, that we have Sarah hide the other runes to prevent further tampering."

"No," Marah replied simply.

Steven raised his eyebrows and looked to Mayor Gibson.

The older man ran his fingers over his salt and pepper mustache, sighing deeply. "Fritz, what do you think?"

The lumpy old woman pursed her lips. "For the time being, I agree with Commander Steven. Cover the other runes for now, and let us convene and discuss their fate as well as what to do with whoever did this," she replied seriously.

That's scary. Why is she scary?

"Surely, you don't mean to seriously punish someone for some harmless graffiti."

"Hardly harmless," Fritz replied. "Whoever did this must have known about the rune's purpose. That makes the act malicious at best."

"For now," Dr. Gibson interjected before the conversation could progress, "we take a vote. Given the circumstance, my own vote shall count as one, not two. Those in favor of leaving the remaining runes as is?"

Marah raised her hand and locked eyes with Fritz.

"Those in favor of concealing their locations for the time being?" The mayor asked. Fritz raised her hand and met Marah's eyes with a calm intensity. Her hand was soon joined in the air by the mayor. "The vote is two to one. Sarah, would you please see to it?"

"Yes, sir," Sarah replied before she took a final sip of hot chocolate.

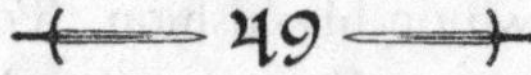

MISSION REPORT

In the warm folds of a grounded tent at the center of the elvish camp, Dr. Walker coughed again; a violent, wet, body-shaking cough. She was no longer able to stand. She was barely even able to sit up in the cot they'd made for her.

Dried fruits and pastries sat untouched on a platter next to the bed. Gathered in the room with the old dwarf were two of the elves' best healers, Laiex and Gilbella, as well as General Almurë, and the dryad, Leuoradew, who stood silently at the back of the tent.

"Go on. Enough. There are others who I have no doubt require your attention. There is nothing you can do for me. I am not ill, and I have suffered no injuries. Be gone. Tend to those your energies are not wasted on," Dr. Walker managed to say to the healers at her sides as she coughed frequently.

"Duelma Umindrabo, I—" Gilbella began.

"Can it, elf," Dr. Walker interrupted as she slouched back into her cot. "You know I'm right."

"Can it?" Almurë, with a befuddled expression, chipped in from where he sat cross-legged on the ground. "It's a human expression. It means shut up," the old dwarf replied harshly.

Almurë met the eyes of the two healers who stood helplessly by the bedframe. "Go on," he ordered, and they departed rather eagerly. Almurë began to rise from where he sat cross-legged next to her bed, but the dwarf put a hand out to stop him.

"Are you satisfied?" She coughed.

"Far from it. Is there anything else I can do to make this easier for you?" the general replied with raised eyebrows.

"Sit back down. I'm all right. Now, as I was trying to say before your healers interrupted us, do you understand — *cough* — how far humans have come?" she asked shakily.

"I do. Worry not, Duelma Umindrabo. I shall do my best to protect them," he replied as he sat back down on his cushion. "Focus, though. You must try. If we cannot save you, then we need you to remember. If you are the last of the Duridgribuldam, you are the only one with answers."

"I know that," Dr. Walker snapped back. "I have known that for a millennium. I have forgotten so much in my efforts to remember the casting. I don't know what happened to the other Duridgribuldam. I have outlived billions. I have been an educator, ruler, warrior, inventor, explorer. I have titles and degrees that you cannot even with your own longevity begin to understand. I have unraveled mysteries, toppled empires, established dynasties, ensured the very survival of humankind…" She broke into a fit of violent coughs that doubled her small frame over in her perch. When the coughing subsided, she took a moment to catch her breath.

"Despite all I have done, so much of what occurred during the casting remains beyond my knowledge. Alas, I only see haze in my mind's eye when I think on that day. My mind is drawn from it with every attempt to bring it to the forefront. Yet, as I grow weaker, the images sharpen. You've figured it out already, though. There is another layer to the Therin-Selu. Something else, hidden. Waiting for release."

"The black Thalmein sword you gave to the man, Peter, and the woman he sees — they must be connected."

Dr. Walker shook her head, breaking into yet another fit of coughing before she responded, "No. The sword is its own mystery. It was there when I woke in isolation. The girl is new."

"How can it not be connected? Shadowfang knew it was named Galvorn, yet we'd never heard of such a blade? Blair says the pale creature he saw knew its name too. They must be connected." He paused and shook his head softly, the purple feather at the end of his braid knocking against his shoulder.

"Basilisks are dracolearic. Perhaps he was not affected in the same way as the rest of us. Have there been any dragons sighted since your return, general?"

"Only dracolearic, drites, drakes, wyverns — none of the elder dragons. I hope whichever of them was involved in the casting will be able to explain what happened."

"There was no elder dragon at the casting."

Eyes narrowed, Almurë's voice was barely above a whisper. "You're telling me you cast a Therin-Selu without a dragon?"

"It was hardly my doing, I was little more than a novice at the casting," Umindrabo replied weakly.

"Then, we can be sure of nothing, Umindrabo."

"Then why are we wasting our time discussing it?" Dr. Walker countered as she took a raspy breath. "Einstein was right, that cocky nutjob. There are few things more relative than time. I'd grown used to an endless supply."

Almurë raised an eyebrow. "Perhaps you are more elf than dwarf now, my friend," he quipped with a small smile. "We discuss it because we must do what we can to fill in the blanks. The knowledge that we lack information is superior to total ignorance. I wish to plan for every conceivable outcome. In that way, I may prepare for inconceivable outcomes."

"And if it is the work of Awan and Cain or their disciples?" Dr. Walker said in a cold voice.

General Almurë's face paled at these words. "Then, Erúil protects us. But their names alone being utterable makes me think not. I am more concerned with the absence of the draconic. If they were uninvolved, where have they gone? And why not return?" His eyes narrowed, and his lips moved silently for a moment. "Is it possible that the eolin in Valk Blair's dreams is an elder dragon?"

The old dwarf chewed on her lip for a moment before replying slowly, "I do not know. It seems unlikely an elder dragon would take such a form."

Almurë frowned deeply.

Umindrabo shook her head. "It has been a long time, and my thoughts on them are addled by legend. If Peter Blair was being manipulated by a dragon, wouldn't there be side effects?"

"Liúre," the elf cursed. "My wife would know. The draconic is more her area of knowledge." He drummed his fingers against his leg. "I believe there would be physical side effects, though, starting with his eyes. I saw much sadness and burden in his eyes, but they were still those of a man. Even if he were speaking to a dragon, there is no guarantee said dragon would be an enemy."

Dr. Walker convulsed as she tried to keep from coughing. "Peter is not our only ally among the humans. There's a girl back in Paragon. Her name is Sarah. She's unlike anything I've seen, Almurë. An enhancer well on her way to mastery."

"Then why did you leave her in the city and not bring her with you?" Almurë asked, having resigned himself to Dr. Walker's seemingly random pattern of conversation.

"She's not ready. She has much to learn. Besides, Paragon needs her."

"And she is to learn these things on her own? Is she as young as Peter?"

"By your standards. I've forgotten what being young means. I've been old for so long, and humans have such a fleeting existence," Dr. Walker said as she clutched tightly with boney hands to a pillow. Pain painted her an unpleasant profile.

"You intended to replace Peter with her as their leader," Almurë said in a moment of realization.

"Peter himself was a replacement for his own sister. She was meant to be the one to lead humanity when the spell broke, but she was killed in an accident protecting Peter. It was all very heroic."

"Was she your first herald for humanity?"

"Yes. At least, in terms of your return. I brought her parents together. Both of them are brilliant, with skills and knowledge ideally suited for what was coming. As I extrapolated though, Hannah died, and I was left with the son. He was weaker. Thankfully, his sister's death became his driving force." She coughed violently for a full minute.

"I should have known the deformities they'd developed were a side effect of the Therin-Selu," she mumbled to herself before returning to normal speaking volume. "But still, even with all I've done to prepare him, he's nothing compared to what Sarah has the potential to be for humanity," Dr. Walker managed to wheeze out along with a self-deprecating laugh.

"You use their children like pawns but demand that I protect them. Is your time spent among them responsible for such a human way of thinking?" the general said with a hint of disdain.

"Do not speak to me of pawns and hypocrisy, Almurë. I have not forgotten what your kind was willing to do when the flooding came. Or the billions who would have survived if your kind were willing to strike a final decisive blow to the orks when you had the chance at the First Breaking of the Land," Dr. Walker replied scornfully.

"We will not speak of genocide in my camp, Umindrabo. No matter what you have endured, I will not tolerate it," Almurë said as he clenched a fist and seethed with controlled anger.

"So be it." Dr. Walker waved a shaky hand dismissively. "I can feel it even now. I am slipping. Let my final words not be ones of conflict. Listen, and I will tell you of mankind's great accomplishments in your absence. If my deeds cast doubt on my methods, let their stories speak for them."

50

SÚMERIEL

T he helicopter lurched to the side as the pilot slammed the controls with all the panicked skill he could muster. Outside the helicopter, a giant winged two-legged lizard careened past. Mounted on the creature's back, an ork desperately tried to regain control as it lost altitude.

In the helicopter, Peter held on with one hand for dear life as he did not trust the tie which secured him to the aircraft. As carefully as he could, he pulled away from his position at the open door and threw himself into a seat.

"Air support! Backup of any kind needed! William, can you read me?" Ian yelled into his headset. Across from Peter, Breekie sat strapped in and pale-faced, fingers clutching at his seat.

"We've got some kind of flying lizards up here," Ian called over his headset.

"Wyvern! Left!" screamed Breekie with all his might.

Ian slammed the controls and yanked the helicopter through the air. The maneuver gave Peter a quick glimpse of the battle that raged below.

The orks were clashing with the elves on what was left of Centennial Olympic Park Drive, an enormous elvish fortress that served as their main base. Trolls, drakes, orks, goblins, and other monsters Peter didn't have names for held their ground against elves, war bears, dwarves, treefolk, humans, and what Peter thought were centaurs. In a way, he found it beautiful. The blend of structure and chaos ever-present on the battlefield filled Peter with a sense of belonging. That was where he was supposed to be.

Below, spells flew back and forth on both sides. The spells ranged from bursts of radiant energy to blasts of icy shrapnel as casters fought back and forth for the advantage. Another swerve of the helicopter tore Peter's line of sight away before he could determine if William's forces were inbound or fighting their own battle.

"The hell?" Ian shouted as something dark surged past the newschopper from above and collided with one of the wyverns.

"Get us out of here," Peter cried. As Ian attempted to course-correct, Peter searched the air and spotted the second wyvern. It was slightly smaller than the first, and it climbed in the air towards them while its rider brandished a cruel-looking sword.

Jump, a small voice in the back of his mind whispered. *Go on. He'll meet you, head-on. Kill him and take the wyvern.* Peter realized his hand was on the latch of his seatbelt, ready to tear it off the instant the moment was right.

But before Peter could act on the thought or give it further consideration, a black alicorn dove past him from the clouds above. Mounted on its back was an elf wielding a savage pike. The wyvern roared a challenge, to which the elf responded by hurling the pike deep towards the roaring wyvern's mouth. Then they disappeared out of sight.

The helicopter climbed higher. The growing storm buffeted the small chopper as it barely stayed under control. Peter leaned back and looked at Breekie, whose face was an unpleasant shade of pale green accented by tightly shut eyes.

Peter focused on the expression in an effort to keep his own mind off the hundreds of feet of open air, which beckoned to them from below.

He looks like a seasick walrus. I shouldn't be here. I'm useless here. We need to land so I can at least get into the fight rather than sit up here waiting to die. He turned his vision to the cockpit. Past Ian, he could see through the windshield to their destination. The Tesla Building blended with ancient elvish structures.

The human building was only a few years old and designed to withstand an earthquake. Its most notable feature was the twenty floors of transparent glass solar panels, designed to independently power the building.

But a single earthquake was nothing compared to the Shattering. While the building still stood, its special glass was now either covered in grime or broken entirely. The building was now a dark shell of its former self, with a strange black stone cathedral grown out of its side like a tumor.

Another landmark ruined, Peter thought with a frown.

"Captain, are those what I think they are?" Ian asked over his headset, drawing Peter's attention from the building. Up ahead, diving out of the clouds above were ten more dark alicorns with enormous wings, ridden by more elves in their unique armor, all as black as the horses they rode upon.

He strained to hear if their casting could be heard, carried over the winds, but the sound of the helicopter and wind drowned out the sound of haunting elvish casting.

"That's backup," he shouted to Ian with a useless gesture towards where the alicorn were circling, as two more appeared from below, gore dripping from their horns.

"Mister Dwarf, we're almost there. You ready?" Ian called back to Breekie.

"Dah. Just get me out of this thing," Breekie cried out gravely. The deep bass of his voice seemed small compared to the thrum of the helicopter.

The first alicorn landed lightly atop the building, and a lithe figure dismounted with a vaguely familiar intensity highlighted by a flash of lightning from the clouds above.

There she is, Peter thought as the chopper rose higher into the air, climbing over the top of the building.

"Captain, there's no way you'll be able to rappel in this. The wind's going to toss you around like a paper bag," Ian shouted over the noise, his voice almost lost to a clap of thunder.

"We'll make it," Peter replied dismissively.

"Peter, this is suicide," Ian protested as the helicopter fought against the growing storm.

"Trust him. We'll make it," called Breekie from his seat, eyes squeezed tightly but barely open.

Ian cleared his throat. His face hardened in concentration as more wind assaulted the chopper.

"Just get us over it. I'll take care of the rest. Once we're out, put this thing down near MLK and Chapel. You should be able to see the Wounded Company and the rest of the evac crew there," Peter ordered between claps of thunder.

"Look, there's a landing pad," Ian shouted, pointing below. "But there's no telling what the building integrity is like. It's a risk, I know, but it could work," Ian explained.

If this thing goes through the roof, it could kill everyone.

"Not worth the risk. How low can you get to it without landing?" Peter asked as the helicopter hovered shakily over the drop zone, barely managing to stay in place.

"Close enough to survive the fall. But, captain, one good blast of wind, and you'll be free-falling off the side."

"I've got a trick to handle the timing. Just tell me when you're low enough," Peter ordered.

Ian didn't respond. He was too focused on flipping switches and piloting the vehicle closer and lower to the drop.

"Almost there," Ian called. Peter was already out of his seat and strapping Breekie to himself. "Ready!"

Peter finished securing Breekie. He grabbed a gurney and threw it out the open door to test the wind. It fell through the air, then was caught by a buffet of wind that snapped the line taut. After a few moments, it stilled itself and began to slacken. *It's now or never,* he could practically hear his sixth sense whispering to him.

With a loose grip on the rope and a tight grip on Breekie, Peter leaped from the chopper down towards the landing pad six feet below.

The rope slowed his fall as it ate away at his glove. They landed hard, but he rolled to lessen the impact. As quickly as he could, Peter detached the dwarf from his side and cut the rope, which released it from the chopper.

Breekie rolled over slowly so his face pressed against the rooftop and celebrated his reunion with a solid surface.

Almost immediately, Ian pulled the helicopter away, and it disappeared down the side of the building. *Careful, Ian. Don't fly too low. Who knows what else they've got down there,* Peter thought but did not dare step closer to the edge of the building and watch his friend depart.

"Lúemeni, Valk Blair, you got your people out?" Súmeriel asked as she approached him. Her expression indicated genuine concern. Behind her, half her unit was spread across the roof, and the other half was attempting to calm the alicorns prancing nervously in place.

"Yes," Peter replied as he turned his attention to the elf. She was dressed in her usual cloth-like black armor, but now with black war paint spread over her eyes visible from within her curved, almost spartan, elvish helmet.

Something about her gaze made Peter feel like she was staring into his thoughts. *She might be. Can't tell these days. Keep your head clear.* He shifted his gaze so he was looking past her and focused in on one of the alicorns as he responded, "William's unit should be moving in on our position now while the Wounded Company gets the civilians out." Peter drew his sword. "This feels wrong. Why would Draelic keep the creature here? Why wouldn't he keep it in that fortress we passed?"

"It's too dangerous to be kept with their main forces. There's an ancient elvish library overlapping with the base of this tower. That's where he'll have her. I don't have time to explain, but it makes sense," she replied. "We should move. They may already know we're coming," she said calmly. "Remember, you're here to help us navigate and avoid traps. Your ability may help us kill Draelic, but do not try to fight the yulmëar. It will kill you," she explained, her voice like sharp steel. Everything about her radiated calm control.

Kill whatever you can get your sword into, Jadis' voice seemed to echo at the back of his mind.

"Yes," Peter replied.

"Good. You, the dwarf, and I are taking point," Súmeriel said as she led them towards an elevator.

"That thing isn't going to work," Peter said as they neared it.

"Is it sealed with a spell?" one of the elves in the group asked as he scrutinized the elevator doors and found no handle or runes.

"Nope. Just doesn't have power," Peter said as he tapped one of the buttons pointlessly. "The cart itself is probably at the bottom of the chute. You guys brought some rope, right?" Peter asked as he took Galvorn, pushed the tip of the sword between the doors, and used it to pry them open. It took a moment, but the doors slid apart lazily and revealed a dark cavernous drop.

"Nyet. Nyet, not again," Breekie, who'd just caught up with them, protested weakly as he took a step back from the opening. "No more falling."

Peter sheathed his sword reluctantly and removed a small flashlight from one of his pockets. He clicked it on and pointed it at the ground so the red glow didn't shine off the top of the tower. Then, with one hand on the side of the elevator opening, he leaned in and lit up the chute. The red light reflected off the metal walls for a distance. Inside, Peter found no sign of the cart; only a dark drop and loose cables.

"This chute won't go all the way to the bottom floor. How much rope have you got? Should only be a few floors until we can take the stairs or find another set of chutes," Peter explained as he turned back to Súmeriel. He found that in the time it took him to examine the chute and say all this, the elves had already finished setting up two lines of rope, which they held ready to toss into the chute.

"Felhammer, do you sense any rune traps?" Súmeriel asked Breekie.

Breekie scowled. Then he lowered himself so to lie flat on the roof. There, he cautiously placed his right hand on the elevator chute, a soft blue glow emanating from the fresh tattoo on his hand. Then he shook his head, crawling back and getting to his feet. "None... That is suspicious."

"Valk Blair, do you have another one of those?" she asked Peter as she pointed at the small inactive flashlight Peter was twiddling between his fingers.

Peter nodded and reached into his pocket for the spare he always carried. "It's not magic, so it shouldn't set anything off," he explained as he handed it to her.

"I assumed as much," Súmeriel replied coyly as she took the small flashlight and accidentally clicked it on and blasted herself in the eyes. She clicked it back off with a deft motion and blinked to restore her vision as she slipped it into the folds of her armor. Peter hid a grin, the surprised wide-eyed look on her face when the light hit her etched into his memory.

"If they know we're coming, we have two options. More of this, and risk an enemy slipping past us and cutting the line, or taking the stairs and having to potentially fight our way down fifty or so flights," Peter said as the elves checked the ropes. At a look from Súmeriel, one of the elves opened her mouth and waved a hand. This conjured a soft red ball of light inside the chute.

Peter's brow furrowed as he turned off his flashlight. *I thought they had to sing to cast,* he thought as he and Súmeriel were handed ropes to secure themselves. Peter looked around as he secured the line. He caught sight of one of the elves he knew was called Marcelia. She moved her lips in silence. *Their sleeping area,* Peter realized. *How does that not activate traps?* he pondered as he fastened his rope, giving it a tug to be sure it was tight.

Súmeriel tapped her leg lightly a few times then began her descent into the chute.

Was that a quirk, or is she doing something? I can't tell with these people, Peter thought as he did his best to step softly into the elevator. He realized that as they descended, his footfalls were like thunderclaps compared to the silent way Súmeriel made her way down the chute.

Accompanied by the glowing red orb, they continued downward until Súmeriel came to a stop at the third set of elevator doors they reached. When Peter caught up seconds later, she looked to him and nodded at the door. Blood pounded in his ears. Peter drew Galvorn and inserted it between the new set of doors. Then he waited a moment to see if there was any flash of warning magic.

None came, so he leaned into the sword and forced the doors apart to reveal their first challenge. Curled into a massive heap of scales and muscles at the edge of the room by a set of enormous broken windows was a wyvern. Peter's breath caught in his throat as he spied the truck-sized beast, its body immobile. *It's asleep. We're not in danger.* His mind offered him the excuse for not seeing it coming. Not eager to redirect his focus, he looked over at the elf.

A small smile curled the edge of her lip, and she pulled herself up off the ledge and onto her feet in one fluid motion. Her sword remained sheathed as she turned and grabbed Peter by the back of the collar.

It took every shred of self-control Peter had not to cry out, as an instant later, he was being yanked up into the room. He knew she was strong, but the easy suddenness of her hoisting him made his heart skip in surprise.

Súmeriel walked over to the stoic wyvern and drew her blade silently. Peter wasn't sure whether to follow or not. The creature still hadn't noticed their presence. Then Peter's heart dropped straight into his stomach.

The elf had just slapped the creature's haunch with the flat of her blade.

"Criske!" The curse sprang involuntarily from Peter's lips as he jerked his sword up into a defensive hold.

But the creature didn't move. In fact, the only thing that moved in the room was the elf, as she shook with silent laughter while walking back over to their ropes. She gave them both two quick tugs, then turned back to Peter. "It's dead," she commented. Her smile shifted the freckle tucked below the left side of her lips.

"I gathered," Peter replied as he tried to lower his sword nonchalantly.

Súmeriel's grin showed no sign of widening as the rest of their team headed into the room. Peter occupied himself in the interim by examining the wyvern. As he reached the creature's front, he found a hole, roughly the size of a microwave, had been burrowed into the beast. He examined it with his flashlight and, to his surprise, found that something had eaten the creature from the inside out and left behind only scales and bones.

How is it still sitting like this? he wondered at the eerie sight. But it was only the first of many mysteries in the tower that would remain unsolved.

They continued their descent. They climbed through holes in the floor, what few stairs remained, and back in and out of elevator shafts. The building had been ravaged from top to bottom. Each new level greeted them with a different horrifying display of gore, destruction, and filth.

They passed through three rooms where the windows had been broken and everything shoved out to be replaced with grotesque displays of bones organized into some strange barbaric shrines. Of the three, Peter was certain one was only composed of children's bones. Whether they were ork or human children, there was no time to tell.

For several floors, they found rooms covered in unenchanted orkish runes drawn in blood and other fouler bodily fluids. The closer they got to their destination, the more Peter's stomach turned, and unease settled into his bones. It wasn't until they were down to the twentieth floor that they began to encounter living creatures. The sense of relief Peter felt upon finding the living after so much death evaporated almost instantly.

There's something wrong with them, Peter realized as they cut down their sixth ork in two floors. These creatures' movements were strange, jerky, and unnatural. Their eyes rolled or jerked about chaotically; no trace of the intelligence Peter had come to expect from the beasts. These creatures made the savagery he'd grown accustomed to with the orks seem natural and controlled.

The mania of these monsters was juxtaposed by the silent ferocity with which the elves tore through floor after floor of opponents. They executed each ork they fell upon with surgical precision. The process was a familiar one to Peter, and he quickly fell into a rhythm with them.

Peter's fist crashed into another ork's throat. The blow crushed its windpipe and brought water to the being's yellow eyes as it stumbled back towards the broken window behind it. *Die.* Peter followed the blow with a powerful kick, which knocked his foe off its feet.

The creature fell, impaled on the jagged chunks of glass that made up the remainder of the room's large window. There was no scream of pain from the ork, though, as one might expect. He'd lost count of how many of them he'd killed in the last hour.

They'd been fighting for the last six floors. They pushed ever downward and forward, and took one group of screeching, spasming orks down after another as silently as they could. This was familiar, stealth, silent steps; a knife in the side and out the front of the throat. Peter took a step closer but did not sense any other danger.

It didn't take their group long to fall into a cohesive rhythm, a rhythm especially strong between himself and Súmeriel. She matched his every move-ment with calculated precision as though they'd practiced it a hundred times. Looking down, Peter saw an elvish arrow jutting from the ork's throat. It had killed him before he hit the glass. *Criske. That was my kill.*

"Careful," Súmeriel hissed in a low voice. "If he'd screamed or gone out the window, they'd know we're here."

I had him. He wasn't going out the window, and that's why I struck him in the throat, Peter thought but nodded in agreement, his lips pursed. "I can't shake the feeling we're walking into a trap," he whispered back through clenched teeth to the elf as the others fell in around them. "This has been too easy."

Súmeriel raised an eyebrow. "We have a long way yet to go. You'll know if we are walking into an ambush before anyone else," she said, unfazed by the idea.

It's more than that, though. The lower we get, the more I get this strange rotting feeling in my stomach.

"How will we know where they're keeping the girl?" he asked to distract himself from the growing sense of unease.

"Merilinor is a diviner," she said, her words aimed at a particularly freckled dark-skinned elf in their company. "He'll know when we're close because of the effect a yulmëar has on the arcane flow," Súmeriel replied. "That, or Fellhammer will sense runes being used to keep her in place."

I'm out of my depth here. I don't know the layout for this elvish building we're going in, Peter thought as he glanced over at the black stone surface of the other structure, which overlapped with the inside of the tower.

"You want me to stay on point?" he asked.

"Yes," Súmeriel said distractedly as one of the elves with a waterfall braid walked up to her.

"The Weeping King is on his way. Elborin's attack was successful," Feniand said in a low confident tone.

"We need to move now," Súmeriel said, already in position at the front of their formation. "This will be easier if we can get to her before he gets here. Hurry, the entrance should be this way," she explained as she led them through a series of offices that followed the curve of the elvish building. As they moved, Peter shivered with a growing sensation someone was breathing on his neck. This further unnerved him.

After cutting through a slab of drywall, they found themselves on a stone walkway sloping downward, carved along the smooth stone of the elvish structure.

"We're close," Elorin, a shorter elf with a blue waterfall braid, said loudly enough for them to hear.

At a signal from Súmeriel, Breekie approached the wall cautiously and placed a hand on the cold hard stone as though it might burn him. With a deep breath, the dwarf concentrated, the rune on the back of his hand glowing with soft blue light. "Nothing on the door. It's not even locked," he said as air escaped him in a huff of relief.

What door? Peter wondered as he searched the stone for some outline of an entrance.

"Good. They may not know about it then. Weapons ready. Remember, no active casting, and whatever happens, kill the yulmëar," Súmeriel said, unflinching, then stepped forward and placed her hand sideways on the wall so that only her palm touched the stone surface. The walls and floor shook as an opening appeared in the wall in front of Súmeriel.

Oh, great. Magic passageways.

They entered through the opening slowly, one at a time. The cold of the room instantly set off goosebumps across Peter's skin. *It's freezing in here.* Bit by bit, they made their way single file through a thin downward sloping stone passageway. *Magic doors and hidden passages — what I'd give to be clearing an armed Russian base right now,* Peter grumbled to himself as they reached the end of the slim corridor.

Súmeriel gave the group a look. Her furrowed brow and clenched jaw told them it was time. Her free, unarmored arm rose and held up three fingers. From his position, inches from her side, Peter noticed a rune tattoo hidden just inside of where her armor ended on her shoulder. *I thought she had armor on that arm earlier. When did she lose it?*

The thought bounced around his mind. He saw the ruin began to glow a soft red as she raised her arm. The skin around the tattoo darkened, like a pen point bleeding onto the paper around it. The darkness continued down her arm until it reached the tips of her fingers seconds later. *Did her arm just coat itself in metal?* Peter thought as she repeated the motion she'd used on the first door, and the wall in front of them slid open with a *woosh* and revealed the interior of the building.

The glowing red orb hovered over them illuminated the room; the only source of light. Inside were four tall intricately carved pillars that connected the pristine marble floor to the vaulted ceiling. At the back of the room, to their left, were a set of simple stone doors. To their right, a pair of thick intricately carved wooden doors twice Peter's height led out of the room. Between these two sets of doors was a room full of scattered debris and bones.

Broken bones of all shapes and sizes lay scattered across the floor or in piles. Worse, among the bones were orkish runes drawn in blood, scattered about the room, as well as smears too messy to have been part of a drawing or rune. Peter took it all in. The rotten dread in his stomach from the warning of arcane energy sent a wave of nausea over him.

For a moment, he thought he might vomit; not in response to the smell or the gory spectacle, but for his refusal to obey every tingling sense of magical energy within him that screamed at him to run, that begged him to run as far and fast away from here as he could.

As the orb of red light rose towards the center of the room, Peter saw a shape hanging from a pillar. He took a cautious step forward. It was a person, hanging upside down from their ankles in the air from a wooden bar. His ragged frame was covered in hundreds of cuts, which bled slowly down the body past the barely recognizable face of Folduin.

No! Why? Peter followed the blood as it dripped slowly into a small plastic turtle sandbox wherein sat a second figure:

A little girl, no more than eight years old, with skin so pale it seemed to glow red with the orb.

It was hard to tell, though. She was covered in dirt and gore. Her hair was a tangled, short mess of knots and clumps. She was dressed in rags, and sat with her legs crossed below the elf's dangling body with her head tilted back and jaw wide.

Horror washed over Peter as he realized she was letting blood fall drip by drip into her maw. *That must be the—*

The girl's head jerked around unnaturally and revealed hungry red eyes with white slitted pupils in the center of blood-red irises that covered the rest of the eyes. Her eyes looked straight at him as her face broke into a gruesome bloody-fanged smile, the likes of which would have made the devil himself squirm in fear. Peter immediately recognized her for what she was: *a vampire.*

The child raised a wicked finger and pointed it at the glowing orb, the room's only source of light, and it blinked out of existence and plunged the room into inky blackness.

Run! Every fiber of Peter's body screamed in terror.

51

SEPARATION ANXIETY

S hawn kicked absently at a piece of rubble as he strolled forward, O'Cleary at his side. They emerged out into the sloped rubble outside of the stadium and onto a battlefield.

The scene in front of them was divided into three sections. The evacuees and two battle lines. Shawn had no frame of reference for the forces laid out before him. O'Cleary or Peter might have known at a glance how many thousands made up the waves of beings in front of him, but Shawn had no idea.

There's so many, he marveled as the scope and sound of the battle crashed into him.

The sound of beeping trucks and engines added a strange rhythm to the cacophony of roaring soldiers, screaming children, and the dying. The chaos had a strange order to it though, at least from where he stood. As he looked out over it, he saw the elvish forces — elves, dwarves, men, treefolk, bears, and creatures he didn't have any name for clashed with the enemy. Goblins, orks, enormous lizards, hippos, wyverns, and all manner of nightmares were held back as his allies refused to give ground and endanger the refugees.

A line of mismatched old vehicles still capable of running stretched out from the stadium to the back of the armed forces. A few feet away, Mellonië was helping a young girl into the back of one of those trucks. Leaning against the same truck's side was a bearded Gunter, armored and covered in grime, a watchful eye focused on the ongoing battle.

"Any more?" Shawn called to the elf over the calamity.

"Only the souls of the temple," Mellonië replied with a melancholy smile. "And their work is done."

Gunter's face lit up in a relieved smile as Shawn drew closer.

"Thank god you're alive! Ready to get out of here?" Gunter shouted, his hand resting on the truck door.

Shawn raised his voice in kind. "Hey, Gunter, good to see you, but I think I'm supposed to stay with these two."

A familiar frown found Gunter's face. "We already split while you were clearing the stadium. We're the tail end of Scott's evac here. William's going to push to break through the enemy so they can reinforce Elborin's assault as soon as we've gone a safe distance," Gunter blurted, "This is only a fraction of the main fight."

Shawn swallowed. The idea that the main forces were nowhere to be seen was a heavy one. The weight of the situation mounted as he saw the caravan of civilian vehicles under Scott's protection had already begun to move slowly away. Gravel crunched under the weight of their tires as they left behind the broken remains of the parking lot.

"O'Cleary?" he asked, his voice not as deep a chord as he would have liked. *We'll get left behind,* Shawn thought as Gunter stood impatiently by the truck. He couldn't help but ask one of the questions at the front of his mind. "What do we do now?"

O'Cleary and Mellonië exchanged a look; one he'd seen before on his parents' faces. It meant they weren't sure what to say but didn't want to admit it.

"William is getting ready to make the push. We need to decide quickly. We can't stay here," O'Cleary explained. "We can head back the way we came with Gunter or join the main assault."

Mellonië frowned as she looked over at the rolling sea of battle. "We do not have a squadron to rendezvous with. How familiar are you with the city, O'Cleary?"

O'Cleary scowled and shook his head. "Much as we Irish like to say we're the fifty-first state, I've only been here a half dozen times, and that was before this," he said with a gesture to the ruins around them.

"Then perhaps out is our safest option," Mellonië said with a subtle glance towards Shawn.

Shawn felt a scowl of his own form on his face. "I'm here to fight," he said in the bravest voice he could muster, his hands still clutched around his pistol and sword hilt.

Gunter shifted awkwardly and looked down at a watchless wrist none-too-subtly.

"You have done more than your fair share of risking your life already. Is that not how your people do things — your fair share?" Mellonië replied soothingly.

Shawn's brow wrinkled as he concentrated on finding an impressive answer. "Maybe, but if I leave — if we leave — someone else might not do their fair share and get someone else killed." *That didn't make sense, you idiot.*

Mellonië nodded. "That would not be your fault."

"No… but wouldn't it? I'm alive. I can do more," Shawn protested. "My dad always said the only time you should fight is if someone else needs protecting."

"Well said, Shawn," Mellonië said with a smile. "O'Cleary, do you have qualms with pressing forward?"

"Only that I'll be the only one who knows the songs I sing while we do," O'Cleary said as he checked the magazine in his rifle.

"Good luck," Shawn said to Gunter as he slammed the truck door shut a little harder than necessary.

"You too, kid," Gunter said as he met Shawn's outstretched fist with his own. "Y'all be careful," he added begrudgingly then clambered into the front of the truck.

O'Cleary began to sing loudly as they moved towards the back of their own forces at a slow jog. By the time they caught up with the rear, a company of about 250, the main body, had broken the enemy line and begun the push deeper into the city. Mellonië spoke to an elvish officer with a red side braid, and then the three of them took up a position on the left flank of the group.

A short while later, they found themselves in the middle of a ruined parking lot where a large metal falcon statue lay out of place on its side. As he walked, a pungent moist reek with a faint repulsive sweetness to it leached its way into Shawn's nostrils. He gagged. The stench conjured images of the burning pit to his mind. He searched for the source of the smell.

Out of the corner of his eye, Shawn saw rubble shift to their left. Then the screams began. In the midst of the sudden outburst of noise, he thought he heard Mellonië cry out in a horrified voice, "Troll!"

But the word mixed with other cries:

"Ambush!"

"Bellow us!"

"Aaeeiiyyyeee!"

"They're everywhere!"

"Look out," Shawn cried to O'Cleary, who'd squared up to his right, weapon raised. O'Cleary turned. The warning was accompanied by the sound of breaking concrete and as the earth shifted in front of them.

Shawn watched in horror as a large grotesque clawed hand burst through the surface of the street. Debris spewed in all directions with a loud *crack* as concrete gave way to the monster. It's sudden arrival almost at their feet drove Shawn and the older man apart. He barely heard O'Cleary curse as the man scrambled backward towards the broken falcon.

The falling rubble gave way to a massive, broad, stone-colored troll with mossy green hair that pulled itself out of the earth with hairy tree-trunk sized arms. His thick clawed fingers left dents in the concrete it gripped. Bent car parts and metal signs decorated the beast, who wore a large green pendant accompanied by a mismatched attempt at armor. Two long flat ears hung out from under a helmet that barely covered the top of the troll's head.

Its face bore a broad nose, and short tusks jutted from a lower jaw full of large ugly teeth. This all on a head that sat on the front of the beast and gave it a hunchback appearance. The creature gave off a deep, rocky roar at the sight of them. Its stink permeated the air even worse now that it was in the open.

A dozen arrows sprouted from the troll's arm before it was free of the rubble, but there was no way to tell who from. The organized force of mismatched races and creatures had become a storm of violence.

Orks and every other nightmare they were facing clashed with their allies all around them. They'd sprung up from countless holes and cut them off from the main forces.

That, or we got left behind, Shawn considered from his semi-catatonic state in front of the enormous monster. It was the first clear thought he'd had in the few seconds it had taken for the world to go mad with blood and death.

Another arrow glanced off the troll's enormous crumpled green road-sign helmet. The arrows only angered the troll. It turned, roared, and hurled a chunk of jagged rubble that pulverized a cluster of elves and orks. One of the elves barely dodged and was hurtled towards Shawn.

Behind the elf, Shawn spied a small group of orks as they clambered out of another hole. Their horrible screeches rent the air as they came.

The sight of their jagged fangs tore Shawn from his stupor, and he slid deftly behind a crumpled car, where he took a deep breath to steady his shaking hands. *Gotta help. People are dying. Gotta stay near O'Cleary.*

"Down," he heard Mellonië call out as she appeared at his side, where she unleashed one arrow after another into the troll. "Don't worry about the orks! Focus on the troll," she shouted in elvish to someone Shawn couldn't make out over the chaotic din of destruction.

Guns boomed. Swords clashed against armor. Arrows slapped into flesh. Men and monsters screamed and shrieked.

She's right. We need to stop the big thing, Shawn realized as he ducked around from behind his cover and fired at one of the orks moving his way. The bullet caught the ork in the arm, and it gave a wail.

"I hit it," Shawn said to himself in a moment of joy.

The feeling shriveled away as the ork caught sight of Shawn and began to charge faster towards him. That ork was followed by two more, drawn towards his gunfire away from dead human opponents.

"Aw, criske," Shawn mumbled. Then, he breathed like O'Cleary and so many others had taught him, planted his feet, and fired more rounds into the first ork. *Bang! Bang! Bang!*

It worked. The ork stumbled to a stop a few feet in front of him, collapsed forward, and dropped an ax and broken elvish shield. Shawn continued shooting. Bullets streaked through the air towards the other two charging orks as they drew closer, unintimidated by the gunfire. One shot found its mark and downed a second ork. With his fallen companions around him, the third ork ducked behind a bulldozer, narrowly dodging Shawn's shots.

A harmless *clink* and locked slide told Shawn his pistol was empty, so he holstered the gun and clumsily drew his sword. Then, he stooped to snatch the shield from where it had landed at his feet.

The last ork was on him seconds later. Shawn brought the broken crescent-shaped shield in front of him to block a mace blow. The clash of the mace against the shield sent painful shockwaves through Shawn's arm. He backstepped for space and noticed his opponent's left arm was bleeding.

The ork let him go. It had realized too late that it was a mistake to give the boy breathing room and tried to correct itself, but the movement caused it to stumble forward. Its boot landed clumsily and slipped on the blood of Shawn's first victim.

The ork faltered and careened forward. Shawn saw his opening and stepped forward to shove his sword into the ork's exposed neck above its chest plate with a *shhhllk*. The weight of the ork around the sword pulled at Shawn's grip, so he yanked it back out before the creature could fall. But there was no time to watch in horror as the life left the ork's eyes.

That was too close. You can't miss shots like that.

"Help O'Cleary!" Mellonië called as she continued to stay just out of range of the rampaging troll as it swung a mangled light pole around like a club. Mellonië danced around the troll. She led it here and there. Its light pole smashed against the ground around her without coming close to hitting.

All the while, she sank arrows into it, which only seemed to further infuriate the beast. Vehicles crumpled like paper cups if they found themselves between the troll and his prey. It crushed anything and anyone else in its path. Ally or enemy; it made no difference.

Shawn looked about desperately for O'Cleary amid the chaos. *Be okay. Please, be okay.* He spotted O'Cleary a dozen yards away in a fight with two screaming orks at once, several vanquished opponents already scattered on the ground around him. O'Cleary's white sword slung oily black blood through the air as he parried and struck, his rifle abandoned for close-range combat.

Without stopping to think, Shawn charged, shield up, at O'Cleary's opponents. He dodged and weaved in and around the sea of deadly obstacles. Arrows, swords, spears, and claws tore apart flesh and the air around him until the charge brought him to his destination.

His sudden weight knocked the creature off balance as he slammed into it from the side and bounced off. Despite failing to incapacitate its target, the blow created an opening that O'Cleary used to decapitate the other ork.

Shawn stumbled back in pain. Looking down, he realized he'd received a cut to his shoulder. Shawn gritted his teeth against the burning in his shoulder and raised his jagged shield and barely blocked a long dagger.

There was a sickening crunch, and the weight of his foe's weapon disappeared. Shawn lowered his shield half an inch and saw O'Cleary standing over the now dead ork on the ground. Shawn's brow wrinkled as he noticed pebbles that bounced on the ground around the ork.

What?

Thud. Thud. Thud.

They both turned and saw the troll. The creature, having abandoned trying to catch the elf, had set its sights on smaller pickings.

Thud. Thud. Thud. Its enormous feet pounded the ground in warning as it towered toward them. Everything in its path fled. For a split second, Shawn was reminded of a porcupine, as he noticed all the arrows poking from its skin, but the image was quickly chased from his mind by fear.

Somebody stop it! I can't fight that thing, Shawn thought in a panic as he looked around wildly for a place to take cover. As he searched, he spied O'Cleary's fallen rifle against a collapsed car a few yards away.

"Rifle," Shawn choked out through a dry throat and hoped it was enough for O'Cleary to catch his meaning as the young boy took off towards the weapon.

O'Cleary understood. He drew his pistol and began firing at the troll's eyes. Meanwhile, Shawn dashed towards the weapon. The adrenaline pounded through his veins. A man spun past him, an arrow embedded in his skull like an antenna.

"Come on, you bloody beast," O'Cleary roared, doing his best to draw the troll's attention while he ducked behind the falcon statue for cover.

The distraction was enough. The troll ignored Shawn and continued towards O'Cleary, who yelled a challenge. Mellonië was in close pursuit, but with her arrows proving ineffective, Shawn doubted she'd be able to help O'Cleary in time. He barely reached the rifle as the troll tore a wing from the statue, which forced O'Cleary to scurry the other way.

Okay, okay, okay. Gotta shoot it, Shawn coached himself as he tumbled youthfully to the ground and took the rifle in both hands. *Holy crap, this thing is massive. How has he been carrying it around so much?* He made sure it was ready to fire, just like O'Cleary had shown him. As he looked up, he saw the troll now wielded a crumpled falcon wing in addition to the light pole.

O'Cleary scrambled, a look of scared desperation in his eyes as he threw himself from one piece of cover to the next without respite.

The troll tore through cars, rubble, and anything O'Cleary put between them. He seemed barely slowed by the arrows Mellonië continued to plant in his skin — arrows she was running out of.

They'd managed to pull the creature away from the thick of the fighting, but if they couldn't stop it soon, it wouldn't take long for it to return to the dumpster fire of a battle.

Bit by bit, the troll gained on the Irishman, a slower target than the spry elf.

Mellonië tried to get closer, tried to draw the creature's attention, but the beast's fury was focused on O'Cleary. Its wild, unpredictable swings kept her from taking advantage of its distraction for a closer attack.

Shawn took another deep breath as he tried to mimic O'Cleary's actions from back when he'd sniped the orks in Macon. But one of the rifle's bipods had been broken clean off. He looked about for something to prop it on, he spied a car mirror and door embedded in the ground close by. As quickly as he could, he got low and braced the weapon's barrel in the groove between the mirror and door. Then, sitting awkwardly on the ground, he braced the rifle against his shoulder and aimed it at the creatures back.

Come on. Bring him closer, the boy prayed as he tried to line up the shot. O'Cleary caught sight of Shawn and pivoted to the left. Whether to get out of the line of fire or draw the troll into it, there was no time to know.

Shawn's heart pounded in his chest like an out-of-control train. Everything else became a blur. *Come on, come on, you got this,* he chanted to himself as he released a breath and pulled the trigger.

The gun jerked, almost leaping out of his grip as it thundered, sending an enormous bullet streaking through the air. It gave off a bang so loud it made

Shawn dizzy as his ears succumbed to a burst of pain. A cloud of debris from the barrel swirled around him, filling his eyes with tears. Blinking his eyes clear, he was filled with horror. The troll still stood, unfazed. Strange green smoke rose from the now cracked amulet on its neck. It turned towards him with an angry scowl, tusks trembling with rage.

Did I miss? Shawn thought in a panic as he realized it was about to come for him. The troll let out a roar, or at least Shawn thought it did; the massive open jaws and flying spittle definitely looked like a roar. But all he could hear was a painful ringing. Mouth clamping shut, the troll raised its weapons high and charged.

Shoot it again, you idiot! his mind screamed at him. Taking an involuntary step back, he realized he'd risen reflexively to his feet, and there was no time to brace the rifle now. With shaking arms, he pointed the Barrett at the incoming troll and pulled the trigger again.

The shot reverberated through his whole body as the gun knocked him off his feet and flew out of his hands. This time, the sound of the rifle firing was muffled by his unrecovered eardrums. *I'm dead,* he thought as he hit the ground and saw stars, his eyes shutting against the pain.

It's gonna kill me. I don't want to see it, Shawn managed to think as his body screamed for him to regain the air knocked from his lungs. He could taste blood; salty and iron.

The stars continued sparking behind his closed eyelids. Tears filled his eyes at the pain from his ears, pain he thought was surely about to end, replaced by even worse pain, then death. But he didn't want the troll's face to be the last thing he saw.

His thoughts swirled, spinning wildly about, disjointed. One thought took center stage. *Death.* He was about to die.

There was something peaceful about the realization. Perhaps it was the thought of finally getting some rest. Or the idea that he might see his parents again. This thought brought his parents' faces to the front of his mind.

His mother, her smile, was always followed by warm food and deep, soothing hugs. He could smell her sweet scent, like blueberry muffins. His dad, with his specialty cologne he loved so much, grinned down at him like he did whenever he woke him up with good news.

"I'm coming, Mom. I'm sorry, Dad. I tried. I really tried. I did my best," he said aloud, the words barely reaching his ears.

His dad's lips moved in a silent reply. A strange white patch mixed into his hair on the top of his head, drawing Shawn's attention. Something was wrong. *Dad didn't have a white spot. Wait, I'm still alive. Why am I still alive?*

Shawn's eyes popped open. His vision was still blurry, but he could see O'Cleary and Mellonië's battered frames standing over him. A giant lopsided grin was plastered across O'Cleary's face. A smaller, more controlled smile graced Mellonië's mouth.

Shawn blinked again, not believing his eyes.

"It… it got you guys, too?" he said, tears rolling involuntarily down his cheeks even as he realized how silly the question was, the question not reaching his own ears.

Mellonië said something, her lips moving lightly, but Shawn couldn't hear it. All he could hear was a growing ringing. Shawn smacked the side of his head, instantly regretting it.

"I can't hear you. My ears really hurt," he said aloud. He must have, at least, because they both flinched.

O'Cleary turned and seemed to ask Mellonië something, the corners of his mouth battling to suppress a laugh at the confused expression on the boy's face.

"What?" Shawn yelled from where he lay in the rubble.

O'Cleary threw a finger in front of his lips. *Probably telling me to shut up,* Shawn realized, clamping his lips closed.

Mellonië leaned down over Shawn, placing her hands over his ears. Shawn lay motionless, watching the elf's lips continue to move, but no sound came out. *I almost died before getting my first kiss,* he thought.

Shawn realized he'd said it out loud when the elf raised an amused eyebrow at him. Shawn's tan cheeks pinkened, and, for a moment, he wished the troll had gotten him. As his mind blanked on a way to save himself from the embarrassment, he felt a warm pulse from Mellonië's hands and heard a pop, which brought the ringing and most of the pain to an end.

Mellonië spoke again, close to his ear. "Can you hear me?" he managed to make out, although it was muddled like she was speaking through a thick wall.

"Barely," he replied, then clenched his jaw as she winced. "Sorry," he apologized more softly.

She took a step back and spoke again.

Shawn bit his lip. He could tell she was asking a question by the pitch but couldn't make out the words. "Everything's muffled," he explained, tapping at his ear.

Mellonië scowled where she stood, said something muffled to O'Cleary, then looked around.

Despite the muffled sound in his ear, he was glad he could hear again, at least well enough to not blabber his thoughts aloud. It reminded him of being half asleep with people talking in the other room. He could hear their tone but couldn't properly discern the words themselves.

"Thanks," Shawn replied and winced as pain burst from his jaw into his brain.

O'Cleary stepped forward and placed a hand on his shoulder. Then he pointed to his own jaw and moved it around. Shawn got the idea and moved his jaw and felt another pop, then the pain left in his jaw subsided to a dull ache.

O'Cleary said something friendly from the smile on his face as Mellonië continued to cast her eyes around, and the man helped Shawn to his feet. Once he was upright, he saw the troll not twenty feet away, lying motionless on the ground.

Mellonië began salvaging arrows from the troll's corpse.

O'Cleary ordered something, pointing to Shawn's gun on the ground. A lecturing tone followed.

Probably telling me to be more careful with my weapons. "Yes, sir."

O'Cleary smiled proudly, mouthing, "Good Job," or maybe saying it out loud; Shawn couldn't tell. Either way, he felt the warmth of pride color his cheeks. Even though it was muffled, he made that much out.

O'Cleary asked something, finger pointed at the wound on Shawn's arm, which was no longer bleeding. Shawn glanced down at the cut, then prodded it lightly. "Ow," he said, wincing. The pain of touching the wound, though, paled in comparison to the eye roll he caught O'Cleary give him. O'Cleary let him go and bent down to collect his weapons. Shawn's hand closed around his pistol. He felt a strange, faint, shaking below.

"I think… I think I'm okay," he said, holstering the empty weapon.

The parking lot was full of fresh corpses. Dozens of orks, men, and women lay scattered around the giant mutilated metal falcon statue. How it got there in the first place was a mystery, but now it stood, bent and battered, like a headstone that heralded the deceased. The tens of large holes in the ground had the highest numbers of bodies.

Shawn felt sick as he glanced hesitantly at the bodies. A pit formed in his stomach as he searched the faces for one he was familiar with, or for any sign of life. *There are so many.* A look of grief on Mellonië's face drew Shawn's gaze to a pair of burned corpses that must have belonged to elves. *There should be more. Where are the rest of them?*

Unsure of what to say to the elf, he moved on, with no faces that he could put a name to. Just as the pit in his stomach began to release, he saw him — the would-be-plumber from the tank. His stomach was torn open from some cruel blow; his still-open eyes stared blankly up at the sky.

I... I don't even remember his name, Shawn thought. He bent down to search his pockets for a wallet with some identification so he could at least absolve himself of the guilt of not remembering the dead man's name. Then he noticed the man's hand was trembling.

How is he alive? He's not breathing. How is he— Oh. He stopped. Then he looked up to see a mortified look on O'Cleary's face. The shaking was coming from below. Mellonië was at his side before Shawn could blink. Shawn watched her lips moving, a look of panicked fear plastered across her face. "Go!" He recognized the shape of the word on her lips as she put an arrow to the bowstring.

"What's going on?"

The question was answered as the elf loosed the arrow over Shawn's shoulder. Shawn's head whipped around, and he saw an ork collapse back into the troll's tunnel behind him.

O'Cleary and Mellonië exchanged charged muffled words. O'Cleary waved his arms dramatically as the elf shook her head, countering with a calm expression.

What's going on? Are there more coming? Shawn watched their lips as closely as he could, but he was only able to make out the now familiar word "orks."

O'Cleary raised a hand and pointed down the road in the direction they'd been heading at a crashed 747, which lay largely intact on its side.

Mellonië nodded slowly in response and motioned Shawn forward, a tight-lipped expression on her face as she kept a watchful eye, looking past Shawn.

O'Cleary leaned in close, speaking urgently, but Shawn was unable to make anything out. All he could hear was muffled gibberish — the final word he more felt than heard as the Irishman pushed him lightly forward. Following the push and Mellonië's lead, Shawn dashed towards the plane.

As he ran, he watched his feet so they didn't strike anything and give him away. His sprint looked clumsy in comparison to the fluid sliding of the elf's run. Every step Shawn took was matched by three thunderous beats of his heart. With every second, he fought the urge to turn his head, to glance at the creatures he was running so desperately to avoid, to see if they'd noticed them, to see if they were preparing to attack, to see if the Irishman was keeping pace.

He kept his eyes facing their destination. The urgency of Mellonië's movements served as a reminder that they were not alone. A cool breeze caressed their skin, sending a shiver through Shawn as it traced the sweat on his skin in the cold air. The elf reached the plane first, where she stopped and turned back to face Shawn, motioning for him to hurry.

Shawn didn't slow down, sliding to a stop next to the crashed plane moments later.

Mellonië explained something, her eyes narrowing, but the thundering of Shawn's heart made it impossible for him to decipher what she was trying to tell him.

Shawn followed her gaze back the way he'd come but saw nothing. Then the realization hit him.

"Where's O'Cleary?" he whispered urgently. The scrawny man was nowhere to be seen.

Mellonië's lips told him nothing when they moved.

Over the muffled ringing, Shawn heard something new: a sound that shot fear up his spine, cutting through the muffled world.

"Arrgrrowwgh!"

Mellonië cursed. He could tell by the way her brows furrowed.

Shawn fought the urge to run back for O'Cleary. The look in Mellonië's eyes told him if he did, he was dead. He could already feel sharp jagged claws and teeth ripping at his flesh.

She ordered something briskly, leaning down and making a step of her hands.

I can't reach up there even if she boosts me, Shawn thought as he looked at the side of the plane.

"Now!" Mellonië's lips formed the order clearly. Then she looked meaningfully down at her interlocked hands.

She's the boss, Shawn thought as he grabbed her shoulders to boost himself into her hands. A second later, he was airborne, tossed as easily as a father tosses his infant child. If not for the plane solidly beneath him, Shawn would have flailed about. But as it was, he landed with a painful thud on his side by the door of the plane. A moment later, the elf landed lightly next to him.

She ordered him down, pointing into the plane as she opened the hatch. He obeyed, scrambling in with all the haste his spindly arms could manage.

Right behind him, Mellonië dropped into the plane, closing the door behind her as she went.

Inside the plane, Shawn looked at the elf in confusion. "What are you doing? O'Cleary's still out there," he said, doing his best to keep from yelling. *Was he trying to tell me his plan at the end? Did I miss something important? What was he saying before he told me to go?*

The elf clamped a hand over his mouth. Her eyes were only inches away from his face screaming at him to be quiet.

Shawn's lips stilled as he obeyed. Mellonië drew her hand back slowly then led him past the skeletons in their seats, deeper into the plane.

As they clambered through the plane, Shawn paused at a strange sound at the edge of his fuzzy hearing. *Is that singing?* he wondered, the faint lyrical words indiscernible. *Boom!* The sound of gunfire somewhere nearby drowned out the song. *O'Cleary! They found him. He's still out there. We need to help him!*

The rate of gunfire increased as it moved away from them. The sound of roaring monsters pursued the sniper farther and farther into the distance. *Come on, O'Cleary.*

52

THE NIGHTMARE CHILD

Peter stood with his back braced against the cold stone pillar. Galvorn was raised defensively in front of him, gripped so tightly in both hands that he could count the straps of leather that wrapped its handle. Desperately, he tried to quiet his out-of-control breathing.

Don't move. Don't move. Don't move, Peter thought as his heart beat a rhythm he was sure could be heard by all in the dark room. Over the pounding of his heart, he could hear a cacophony of screams, breaking bones, and crashing weapons.

Warm blood slid down his chin from his split lip. He fought the urge to spit, not knowing what he might hit in the dark if he did.

Flashlight! The thought tore through his mind like a bullet through paper. *Why isn't she using the one I gave her? She could be dead… Come on, you coward, you need light.* They *need light!*

But his hand refused to release his sword. He couldn't bring himself to reach into his pocket. *There's no guarantee it will work, and the click could give you away, then what if it does work? That thing will tear you apart,* a small voice whispered to him from the dark crevices of his mind. *Hide. There's still a chance you can get out of here.*

Every fiber of Peter's being screamed at him to run. Flee. Find an exit. Make an exit. Just escape. *Get out! Get out! Get out!* But he knew it was too late.

No. Peter focused on denial as he tried to calm himself, to wrest control of his mind from the panic which pervaded it. He breathed in slowly, focusing, clearing his mind of the terror and dread. Peter opened his eyes. Then he closed them.

Nothing. He tried blinking. Nothing. It was so dark, all he could see were strange colors, which seemed to tease the edge of his vision in search of light in the pitch black. *Am I blind?*

The answer to his question was swift and terrifying. One of the elves exploded in a blast of blinding arcane energy and a scream, not fifteen feet to his right. The blast illuminated the room for half a second. A curse slipped out of his mouth as a piece of armor careened past his face and his environment plunged back into darkness.

Concentrating, he reviewed what he'd seen at that moment, but there was nothing new from where he stood braced against the pillar, which stood between him, the rest of the elves, and hopefully the child.

At least I'm not blind, Peter thought, and he used the realization as a foothold to finally wrest control of his mind from the panic brought back by the explosion.

The faint sound of something scurrying passed overhead stood Peter's hair on end.

Come on, coward. Whether you die or not, go down fighting. Hannah wouldn't hide like this. At last, one of his hands broke free from the sword and found his small flashlight in the pocket of his jacket. Carefully, he ran his fingers over it until he found the front, which he aimed down at the floor. Then, his thumb braced against the button, and he clicked it on.

Light blossomed into the room. Shadows spread, as all went quiet other than the moans of the injured. Peter braced himself and turned around the pillar to reveal the horrifying scene around him. At least three of the elves were dead, as far as he could tell from the fresh body parts strewn throughout the room. Breekie lay on the ground only a few feet from him, where he cursed up a storm in Dwarvish as he struggled with something in his hands.

Peter looked closer and saw the dwarf trying to reattach his left hand, which hung limply by a piece of flesh from the end of where his forearm had turned into splintered, bloody bone. The blood gushing from his wound covered his remaining hand and made him lose hold of it. The sight made Peter's scarred chest ache.

Peter found the elves as he pulled his gaze away from the gory sight. In the center of the room was Súmeriel braced together with the other elves in a defensive circle. The previously untouchable, hardened, elite elvish warriors were all bearing savage wounds.

Panic threatened to seize Peter's mind again. It was driven back, though, as a voice reached his ears.

"Keep the light on," Súmeriel cried out to Peter, who had no intention of turning it off.

The vampire child was nowhere to be seen, but Peter could feel her there, watching, preparing to strike.

Help him, or he dies too, the voice in Peter's head demanded as he looked down at Breekie. *I'll get killed helping him,* the same voice countered. "No, no death is nobler than one that saves a life," Peter whispered his father's words to himself. Then, with all the speed he could muster, Peter rushed towards Breekie and angled the beam of light around the room as he moved. When he reached the dwarf, he grabbed him and began dragging him back. He stepped over a headless elf torso and leaned the dwarf against a pillar.

Peter bent down, and his knee grew wet with blood on the floor. "Breekie! Get it together," he half-shouted, half-whispered at the dwarf who was staring, dumbfounded at his gruesome injury and prattling in Dwarvish, "Criske. She — she tore it off, Peter. She just tore it off."

"Súmeriel!" Peter yelled out to Súmeriel. "Take this," he shouted and hurled the flashlight towards her. She caught it with ease and passed it to one of the other elves, then carefully reached into the folds of her armor and removed her flashlight, this time without blinding herself. Together, the two of them immediately began flicking beams of light around the room in search of their opponent.

Peter knelt by the dwarf's side to get a better look at the grotesque wound. The hairs on his neck stood on end as he let his guard down. Despite the flickering lights, Peter was able to see where the flesh around the bone was torn away. The injury was so severe that it had left nothing for the dangling hand to be reattached to. *I need to remove the arm before he bleeds to death.*

"Hey, Breekie, look at me. Focus. Come on, Fellhammer," he said as he grabbed the dwarf by the beard to try and get his full attention. "Can you heat up my sword?" Peter asked as clearly as he could, the sound of violence resuming behind him.

"Are you crazy? Get your crisked hand out of my beard," Breekie replied, speaking nothing but Dwarvish. "If I cast in here, I'm gone."

As the dwarf protested, Peter grabbed his arm just above the elbow and brought his sword down. The blade carved through the flesh and bone with a *shlick,* and the ruined remnants fell to the ground.

"Criske!" the dwarf cursed with all his might, his words rolling into a tirade of Dwarvish too fast and angrily for Peter to understand. Hurriedly, Peter turned, searching for something to bind the wound. His attention fell on the mutilated elvish torso.

Reaching out, he grabbed the corpse by the arm and slid it closer. Once he had it, he used Galvorn to remove a sliver of cloth. Then, turning back around, Peter set Galvorn down and took the fabric in both hands to tie off the wound.

"Play dead," he whispered to the dwarf, who, judging by the pale skin of his face, wasn't far off. Breekie nodded and reached out weakly for his hammer with his remaining hand. Peter grabbed the handle of it and handed it to the dwarf, who, once he had a firm grip, slumped in place so quickly Peter wondered if he might have, in fact, just died.

Reflexively, he went to grab the dwarf's wrist to check for a pulse but was cruelly reminded that there was no wrist to check when he grazed the bandaged stump. Luckily, Breekie winced, and thus eliminated the need to check for a pulse.

You've done what you can. Time to move on.

Peter rose from his place at the dwarf's side and noticed a heater-shield on the ground a few feet away. He did not stop to consider where it came from, but instead snatched it up with his left arm. Then, sword and shield in hand, he carefully approached the encirclement of elves. "Súmeriel, what's the plan?" he asked forcefully.

"Keep the lights on. We need to trap her if we're going to have a chance of killing her. She doesn't like the light, but that'll wear off. The dwarf? We need him to get rid of these runes."

"Badly injured," Peter replied then felt a burst of warning energy. He turned on a dime and threw the shield up in front of him, barely managing to block the broken femur that'd been thrown at him with the force of a cannonball. Peter felt the collision in his bones but managed to remain standing. But when he brought the shield down, the child was nowhere to be seen. He felt a sudden warmth on the side of his neck and brought a hand up to touch it. It came away red and sticky.

Not deep enough to be life-threatening, but not good. The thought came to him with an ounce of relief.

From a different direction, a dark ball of shadow slammed into one of the elves. Rather than stopping, it kept going. Peter watched in horror. He was not fast enough to stop it, as the child dragged the now bloody elf with it into the shadows, which left behind a smear of blood.

"We've got to corner her and finish her before she picks us off or Draelic gets here," Súmeriel warned.

The enormous room with its piles of bones, freezing temperatures, and still air made the search as tedious as it was terrifying. Those still alive were none too keen on splitting up to cover more ground. So they went, pillar by pillar, searching for their opponent. Peter's eyes jerked towards the ceiling, where he scanned the dark. *Something moved up there, like a spider. Please don't let there be giant spiders too.*

He signaled Súmeriel with a wave of his hand to light the area up, but by the time the lights flickered over the space, it was empty. A moment later, they caught sight of the child slipping quickly behind a pillar closer to the ground.

Before Peter could react, Súmeriel, Merilinor, and two other elves were leaping past him, weapons raised as they charged the pillar's right side.

There it is. Push the left side of the pillar, Peter coached himself and took a step forward, but a strange *ca-clunk* behind him made him pause.

"Oh, no," he heard one of the elves let slip. Peter pivoted. A sense of dread welled up inside his stomach and compounded into dismay as he realized what was happening.

Reinforcements.

The enormous carved wooden doors leading into the room burst open and brought with them a woosh of warm putrid air and light, which illuminated the foyer in all its gory splendor.

At the opening to the doors was Draelic, the Weeping King, having come from the battlefield himself. A fresh severed elvish head clutched by the hair was in one hand, a cruel spiked battle-ax in his other. At his sides were a pair of orkish warlocks.

The remaining elves between the door and Peter reacted with inhuman speed as they fell into a staggered defensive formation before the doors could come to a stop.

Draelic paused mid-stride. A look of genuine surprise was on his face as he realized what he was seeing. The shock melted away, replaced by rage. Without a word, the warlocks at his side charged. Their bodies stretched and grew with each step, their muscles pulling at their robes tight against their skin. By the time they were halfway to the elves, the pair of hulking behemoths were large enough to go toe to toe with a grizzly.

"Hold them off," Súmeriel cried in elvish as she and two others moved in on the child.

Peter caught a glimpse of it as it slurped greedily on an elvish corpse tucked away in the shadows of the back right corner of the room.

The elves between him and the door charged to meet the warlocks. Mid-charge, they split in two directions and drew the warlocks away from each other. Each step from the elves was made with calculated precision, contrasting the erratic flailing of the gargantuan orks.

Peter was left standing directly in Draelic's path. "No, sure, that's fine. I'll fight him myself," Peter murmured as the ork marched into the room. He was an intimidating specimen; tall, lean, and uniformed in combat robes rather than the piles of trophies worn by most orks.

As the ork moved closer, his eyes widened with horror. Drealic raised a hand and dropped the severed head, and in a voice dripping with anguish, he cried out, "Littlefang, retreat!" The words sprung from his mouth and rang with what sounded to Peter like genuine concern.

He's worried about that thing; not scared of it like the rest of us, Peter realized. The look of abject horror plastered across the orks face reminded Peter of a father seeing their toddler walk into traffic. The accompanying tears rolling down his leathery green cheeks only further unnerved Peter. They'd told Peter why he did it, but the sight of an ork crying in the heat of battle still unsettled him.

Peter trusted his ability and the distance between him and the ork enough to glance back and see that the smaller doors at the back of the room were open. The child, which was now locked in violent combat with Súmeriel and her reinforcements, saw the opening. As quickly as a snake, she scurried into the room with familiar, incredible speed.

The elves were in close pursuit, rushing through the doors as they closed, but only two made it through before the doors, moved by some invisible force, crashed shut behind them with a resounding *thud*. One of the elves collided with the doors as they slammed. They knocked him clear off his feet and left Súmeriel and Merilinor alone in the room with the vampire-child.

Peter felt a familiar sting of warning energy and whipped his head back around, backstepping and raising the shield in one fluid movement.

Clang! Draelic's ax met his shield in a violent clash. Automatically, Peter countered by stabbing forward with Galvorn, but the ax was already slipping off the shield to brush the sword aside. With a backstep, Draelic tossed the cruel weapon back and forth between clawed hands. He looked Peter up and down slowly, searching for an opening or sign of weakness.

I can't keep this up, Peter realized as the ork spun into another attack. Peter felt no warning energy this time, but his eyes and natural instincts were warning enough, and he managed to block the ax with Galvorn.

Why didn't I sense that?

The ork's eyes widened as Peter's defense gave him a full view of Galvorn.

"Where did you get that?" he hissed at Peter in surprisingly articulate English as their weapons met again. The ork leveraged his height as he tried to push Galvorn back towards Peter with his ax. Peter adjusted his grip and brought the sword and ax downward, sliding to the side in the process to expose the ork's fury-filled face. Peter introduced his shield to the ork's nose, then pulled back to avoid a wild swing of the ax.

The ork reeled back, arms flailing for balance, and spat black blood. *Now!* Peter thought as he stabbed forward. But the ork recovered before Peter's blow could reach him. Galvorn was batted away from his chest with the length of the ax. Peter struck again but was blocked.

Then Drealic stopped and stood still, his ax floating through the air as he tossed it back and forth between his hands, but he did not push the attack. Instead, he straightened his back and spoke in a controlled voice as though he and Peter were sitting down at a table for coffee. "Listen to me, human. Did the elves give you that black blade?"

Peter fought to get better footing as he searched for a way to use his surroundings. *I can't overpower this guy. Find another option,* Peter told himself as he sidestepped and circled the ork, who responded in kind. Peter pushed the attack, trying to force his opponents back against a pillar.

"No," he replied in an effort to keep the king's attention.

"Then, where? Where did you get it?" Draelic repeated, louder now, an emotion Peter couldn't quite place coloring his words. Peter gave no reply, staying light on his feet as he looked for a sign of weakness from the ork. *Come on — a cut, a bruise, anything I could use to slow him down.*

"Listen to me. It is important. Tell me where you got that sword."

Peter took a swing, a careful test of the ork's reflexes to gauge how he responded. Draelic leaned back out of the way of the attack rather than raising his weapon this time.

"The elves are lying to you, manling. Using you."

Peter swung again, fast enough this time to force the king to bring his ax up in a block.

"Listen to me. Do you know who I am, boy? I am Draelic, the Weeping King, first of his line. I possess knowledge beyond your imagination or the foolishness of the elves. How did you come upon Galvorn, the Bloodsword? Answer me! That blade will get us all killed. Are you mute?"

Is he scared? It's not of me. The sword? Find a way to use that.

"Nah," Peter replied with a step forward and blade raised menacingly, "just sick of hearing your name." He pushed forward, a flurry of furious swipes driving the ork back towards one of the pillars.

But Draelic was a king worth his title. He met each of Peter's blows with the same savage intensity, speed, and strength. He countered some strikes before Peter could make them and dodged others with inches to spare.

Peter could feel it at the edges of his muscles. He'd been fighting for too long. His arms felt heavy, sluggish even, despite the speed at which they tore through the air. *I'm running out of time,* he realized as they continued to trade blows.

Draelic seemed to grow angrier. His reactions became quicker and more precise, rather than wilder.

Not good. He's mirroring my pattern. They said he was an abjurist. Does that mean he's canceling out my magic? Peter thought as the ork blocked a blow before Peter even realized he was going to make it.

Draelic now began to gain the upper hand. His blocks changed to counters; his counters followed into more attacks as he began to push Peter back towards the pillar where Breekie rested.

Don't use magic to strike — just to defend. I can't keep this up. Gotta find a way to end this.

The din of clashing weapons and violent deaths around them continued to grow louder. Peter saw one of the orks fall, cut to ribbons by the elves, several of whom he'd struck down first. There was no time to focus on the others, though, as Peter settled into the flow of combat.

Peter reached out for his connection to the arcane flow, but the warnings that came with it were overwhelming, and he almost faltered. The ork sensed his hesitation and pressed the attack, so Peter went with it. He continued to fall back as the shield he bore grew weak on his arm under the flurry of blows. *Clang!* Sword met ax, again and again.

"You're going to get everyone killed, you fool," the ork roared, then his voice switched back to being calm. The one-eighty in tone was disturbing. "Put the sword down! I can help you. Man and ork have allied before — why not again?"

Peter ignored his offer and instead forced Draelic into a series of defensive blows as he fell back. *Almost to the pillar. Almost.*

He blocked another blow and sidestepped to put the pillar to Draelic's left as the ork followed through with his next attack.

As he pushed towards Peter, he stepped over the dwarf's severed hand on the ground at his feet.

Now!

At the foot of the pillar, Breekie's eyes snapped open. With his one good hand, the dwarf raised and swung Foecrusher with all his strength.

The hammer thundered through the air as it came crashing into Draelic's left leg with a sickening *ker-crunch.*

The Weeping King let out a shriek as the hammer obliterated his knee.

Peter seized the moment. With a final burst of energy, he battered the ax out of the way with his shield and swung Galvorn up in a cruel arc through the ork's stomach and chest. *Got you,* he thought as a strange shimmer emanated through the air.

Draelic's ax clattered to his side. His arms clutched his chest, blood glowing with energy gushing forth. Desperately, he tried to hold himself together with his bare hands. "No, no, no, no, no, no! It's too soon," he cried.

The hell? Why is it glowing? Peter wondered for a split second.

The cut along the ork king's chest sparked with energy as the ork fell. He collapsed in a heap onto the ground.

In the chaos, Peter didn't notice the ork's black blood floating around him in the air, sparking into red and purple energy that winked in and out of existence. He was too focused on shoving his black blade into the ork's chest with both hands. Blade and ork met the ground and the wound pinned him there. Peter's gaze locked on Draelic's eyes, a twisted laugh trapped in his own chest as the rock's malevolent eyes wrestled with the call of death.

Before Peter could break into a cackle of triumph or even attempt to, he was thrown back, torn from his accomplishment and his weapon by some unseen blow. A moment later, he found himself in a tangle of limbs with Breekie. Desperately, he tried to untangle himself, to get free, back to his weapon.

Galvorn's red jewel glowed with a bright light refracted off the sparking blood that somehow floated in the air around them, which Peter noticed for the first time as he struggled to his feet. Time slowed in the way it always does in moments of catastrophe.

The sparkling blood swirled around the blade that still pinned Draelic's dying body to the ground. Small lances of red and purple lightning shot from the jewel in the sword's pommel and drew the blood towards the sword, where it ceased to resemble blood and transformed into pure energy. The energy crackled up and down the blade to form a line of electricity in the air six feet high.

A glowing gouge in reality appeared.

Arcane warnings of danger spiked and coursed through his veins, where they stole what little energy Peter had left. He was paralyzed by exhaustion, wonder, and fear. He wanted to flee, but he knew if he left the sword, he was as good as dead. Even so, his muscles refused to obey him. He stood there, frozen, and watched helplessly as the magic schism of red and purple energy continued unabated.

His heart thundered in his chest. The rest of the room's violence faded into a distant thrum. For a solitary instant, everything else went quiet. Whether by the schism's power or the instinct of those present, there was no knowing. Then, there was a roaring clap of thunder as red and purple lightning tore up from the blade and crashed through the ceiling forty feet above.

Peter was hurled through the air by a shockwave that sent elves and orks alike flying off their feet. Red lightning splintered the air around the sword and formed a crackling and hissing break in reality behind it.

Galvorn was unmoved, with no sign of damage or movement as colorful sparks leaped off the blade.

Peter hit the ground hard. The edges of his vision blurred. Exhaustion overtook him. *What's going on?* He realized he was losing consciousness.

Behind the sword, the rift began to widen into a twenty-foot-wide hole in reality. It revealed blackness and a gray fog spilling out from the outline of jagged red energy.

A door was open that led into a world of cold gray stone, darkness, and fog. Into the world from Peter's dreams.

Something moved in the fog just out of sight. A familiar silhouette moved towards the sword. Mist swirled around the shape and drew closer to Peter's waking world. Scar-covered fingers grasped at the air as the figure, still shrouded in fog, pushed through an invisible web of energy. The hand grabbed Galvorn by the blade, gripping tightly and pulling.

Jadis?

To Peter's surprise, no cut appeared on the hand, and no inhuman blood slid along the metal. Slowly, the hand was followed by an armored arm, then a torso. The fog melted away as Jadis slipped into the world.

Stop her! Peter's mind yelled to him to move, but his body refused to obey his commands.

Inch by inch, she appeared, fog slipping away to reveal she was now garbed in full armor, a jagged sword in her other hand. She clung to Galvorn's blade like it was the only piece of driftwood in a stormy sea. The instant the last of her emerged, the portal clapped shut behind her with a loud crack. She stood there, naked blade in hand, dark ragged armor mirroring the cruel grin spreading across her face.

What have I done? Peter wondered in a final moment of confirmation that shot a wave of fear through his body.

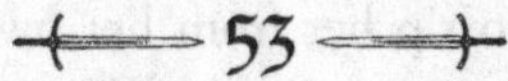

THE DUELMA AND THE DRYAD

Don't invade the minds of the fayeleager. It is invasive. They feel it the way we feel if termites infest our skin. They do not like it, Leuoradew reminded herself. It was rare she thought back on past conversations. Remembering was not her responsibility; she was young. Remembering was the work of older woodlings, but it seemed important to the fleshlings. She wasn't sure why it mattered to her now, but it did.

Leuoradew experienced the world aging and changing around her. She always did. All of her kind did. Few sensed it as intensely as her though, or were as curious about the whys and hows of it all. Most were content to sit and enjoy the change rather than question it.

But not her; especially now. This was different from the usual, natural curving flow of magic. She could see it: a tempest of ethereal energy invisible to the naked eye that swirled around where Dr. Walker lay in the tent, across from where the elf stood.

She knew it was wrong. She knew she shouldn't, that it was termites in the skin; a violation in the eyes of all the fayeleager. Not to mention dangerous. She could be lost, untethered. But she had to know. She had to understand the tempest in the same way she had to have water and sunlight. So, despite it all, Leuoradew looked into Dr. Walker's mind.

At first, it was like touching the mind of one of the elder trees whose job it was to remember a harrowing, powerful experience she remembered well. All saplings were impressed upon by the elder trees as part of a treefolk coming-of-age ceremony, and Leuoradew was no exception.

But that sensation quickly shifted. Stepping into the dwarf's mind was surreal in the same way, touching the minds of all flesh beings was surreal. Their way of thinking was so confined by their perception of time and individualism.

It was more than that though. This time, it was more akin to being dropped into a forest of burning redwoods.

Everything around her was being consumed as the magic raged. The magic here was strong, more forceful than anything she'd ever felt before, and wrong. The raw power threatened to rip her from her own form root and stem. But Leuoradew was stubborn. She refused to lose her sense of identity.

This was wrong. This was very wrong. This was not how ethereal energy was meant to behave. *You have to understand,* the dryad told herself.

Looking into one's mind always varied according to their arcane ability. Weaker casters could only share impressions and images; whereas, strong diviners could even share conversations. She'd shared her mind with her own kind for years. They all experienced the same things, desired light and drink, cared for the weaker saplings around them, and tended to the physical needs of the trees, the bushes, the air. They were a forest, all connected — all growing together.

Here, it was different. The dwarf's mind was not a forest. She did not share the same desires as the dryad, the treefolk, and the foliage.

She was conscious, individualistic, and enormous. But most striking of all was the dwarf's emotion. Dryads did not feel emotion. They feigned it to put fleshings at ease, but none truly experienced it. They had instincts, of course. When many trees burned or were felled before their time, it was unnatural, and therefore wrong. Orks were unnatural creatures, twisted forms of themselves that broke and ruined the forest without care for its restoration. Her kind fought them for this. Not because they feared death, but because their task was to preserve what was natural. It had always been this way; none had questioned why or how this was their task. It merely was their nature.

This was not so for the dwarf. Here in Umindrabo's mind, the dryad saw this. Emotion battled with ethics. It struggled with the good and evil of her actions, weighed not by whether they were natural or not, but by something else. Leuoradew didn't know what. She had no context for it or even the idea that she lacked context.

She tried to focus, to see through all the overwhelming emotion. It colored every sense, every sight. It flooded over her. Entering this being's mind was like sinking deep into an ocean, but the sea was made of emotion, populated by strange thoughts and focus. It was unfamiliar, clouded, and overbearing. There was a madness about it; a burning madness which consumed the floods of emotion.

There was more magical energy here than there was mind. Leuoradew could feel pieces of the dwarf's spirit somewhere in the swirling insanity, just out of reach. Desperate to understand, Leuoradew forced her way through the heat and smoke of burning energy.

She searched for shelter from the flames of the madness in the woman's mind. She found one as she came into contact with the remnants of the essence of Dr. Walker's sanity. She reached out, and their minds clung to each other as the storm raged around them.

Then, it dawned on her. She recognized the pattern and ferocity of the ethereal storm. It was the Therin-Selu, the powerful spell which tore them all from the Earth. This spell was raw, ethereal energy; a blend of all casting methods: divination, enhancement, abjuration, illusion, transfiguration. Somehow, the spell was here, connected to the dwarf's mind, intrinsically linked to her very existence.

But before Leuoradew could absorb and understand the connection, memories burst back into Dr. Walker's mind like lightning; bright, violent, and blinding. The dwarf convulsed, both physically and mentally.

In the physical world, the sight of this brought the general to her side. Leuoradew could see him twice, as she saw through her own eyes and the eyes of the dwarf. But he was a faraway image; translucent, barely there at all.

The elf faded away as the dwarf's eyesight abandoned her, banished by images that continued to careen in and out of her mind. In the realm of the mind, Leuoradew watched in earnest, tried to understand as she peered through time with the dwarf.

She was there a millennium ago, seeing through the eyes of Umindrabo, but it was as though the entire world was being seen through the sheen of a waterfall, distorted. Together they looked and saw that they stood in a cold room of towering rune-covered stones. Smooth arches full of blazing arcane energy surrounded them on all sides.

The tempest of magic swirled around her, a million times more powerful. Here it was given physical and visible shape, outside the stones and within the arches. Bright red, purple, blue, green, and all other colors, brilliant with crackling energy, formed the Therin-Selu. Here Umindrabo was young, and she could see it in her hands and her reflection in the smooth stone. She could feel it in the painless movement of her joints.

There was no time to revel in youth, though. They saw Galvorn, wielded by a tall gray male being with short ragged white hair that was stained with blood along the sides. He was a being of a forgotten race now remembered. The black blade in his hand swung hatefully through the air, carving through the dwarf's fellow Duridgribuldam as they stood, frozen in place by their casting. Arcane energy tore out of their hands and open mouths into the arches on all sides.

Together, they remembered the horror of the blade cleaving powerful wards and counterspells like lilies in a field. They remembered a girl; small, covered in cruel scars, not much younger than Umindrabo at the time. Then, the terrible man's face towered into view, and everything snapped into focus.

They saw him for what he was: one of the Eölin. *So few flesh people, all barely distinguishable from one another when compared to the vast multitudes of the arborous,* they thought together. His name eluded the dwarf even then, but she knew him to be a legendary blacksmith, and thus, so did the dryad.

They remembered her thrusting her hands into the raging tempest of raw magical energy flowing around them. They remembered the exhilaration as time itself and unbridled power passed through her, leaving her by way of her hands. Then, as the magic tore through them, they were torn back to the present.

Together, somewhere far away, they heard the general calling to her, shaking her, trying to bring her back. But it was too soon, and they could not leave now.

In the present, Dr. Walker felt Leuoradew's presence and clung to her like a robin to a branch in a hurricane.

Together, they pushed back the smaller tempest of energy. They tried to master it. The dwarf grounded herself in the dryad's mind. Perched there, she reached out and tried to pluck the memories from the storm. She strove in earnest as the events of a hundred lifetimes ago sprouted in her mind and ripped it apart like roots through concrete. Holding tightly, Umindrabo dragged the dryad's mind with her back into the memories.

There, they saw the blacksmith drop the sword. The blade stabbed into the ground. Yet he pushed towards them through the force of the spell, the last of the Duridgribuldam slain behind him. The Therin-Selu tore at her mind across time as Leuoradew saw the dwarf embrace it again, redirected it, focused it on the blacksmith, on his daughter, on their entire race. Yet still, he came; he pushed ever closer as ethereal red and black lighting shredded his clothes and armor. As he forced his way forward, he whispered unfathomable, inaudible words in the din of chaos.

The dryad watched in horror as Umindrabo willed the Eölin not to be. She felt the command as they wilted away in front of her, yet even as he began to slip away, out of existence, the blacksmith continued towards them with unbending rage and hatred in his violet eyes. Even now, the heat in his gaze burned like an inferno as he was wrenched from existence.

Behind him, the girl reached out. Her translucent fingers wrapped tightly around the black sword-like roots to the soil in a storm, clinging to it for dear life. She began whispering; something dark and powerful beyond their hearing. Their eyes met hers. They were large and full of fear as they drilled into Umindrabo's soul, piercing so thoroughly that Leuoradew could have sworn the child saw her too.

Then the girl vanished with her father from sight and memory. Left behind were the sword, the dead, the dwarf, and the dryad as the tempest that was the Therin-Selu crashed down around them and cut Umindrabo off for a millennium from all she once knew.

"Umindrabo!" General Almurë called out. His strong hands were on the tiny ancient dwarf's shriveled shoulders. Umindrabo's sight came back, weak and blurred, as she tried looking up at the elf through a waterfall of tears. She knew it was ending. She no longer felt Leuoradew's mind. Their connection was severed, but the dryad had taken something with her; a small piece of the dwarf's mind had grafted onto hers.

Umindrabo felt the world around her melt away as she took in shallow breaths, rich with a life which she could not grasp. *I have to warn them*, she thought as her mind strayed further and further from her body. She could feel the dryad at the edge of the tent, eyes and mouth agape, the creature was dumbfounded by what she'd foolishly witnessed. *She can't retain it. I must warn them.*

Umindrabo knew she only had strength for a single word as her body and mind withered away. Somewhere in her crumbling mind, she found humor in this. Billions of words spoken, learned, and forgotten, and now she was left with only enough energy for one last utterance. *Might as well make it a long one.* The echoes of her consciousness laughed to one another. Her thoughts slipped apart, never to be seen again.

Umindrabo tried to bring the blur of the elvish general into focus, but it was useless. Her eyes were no longer hers to command. White was filling the edges of her vision. She could feel her soul slipping from her body. So, she whispered one final parting word and hoped it would be enough to preserve what she left behind. The dwarf hoped it would help the dryad retain what she saw, one last hint to decipher.

"Nàrsidian." With that, there was an enormous clap of thunder from within the city.

At that moment, as all things do in the end, Umindrabo Duridgrihulda, last of the Duridgribuldam, the binder of worlds, Allfriend, last of the faye no longer, a dwarf of exceptional magical talent, PhD, passed from the mortal world.

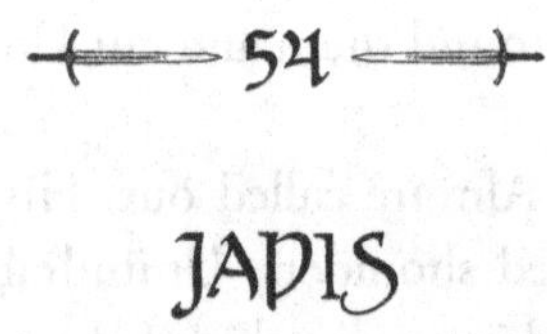

54

JADIS

As an ancient dwarf took her last living breath, a young eölin took her first breath of Earth's air in thousands of years.

At last, Jadis thought irritably as fresh air stung her lungs. She sucked more air in enthusiastically, trying to rid herself of the overwhelming sensation that she'd just been pulled through a wall of static electricity. The feeling permeated every fiber of her being, thrummed with the excitement of blood returning to muscle after too much pressure. It was all she experienced for what felt like an eternity.

The seconds ticked by, and bit by bit, the effects of her return subsided. Her senses came back under her control. Her vision returned to normal first. Blurred blackness melted away as fluid seemed to sweat from her eyes. Once her eyes drained, the world quickly came into focus.

The first thing she noticed was Galvorn. She held it at eye level, where she clutched the bare blade in her hand. The sharp metal did not cut her skin. *Of course not,* she thought in a quickly fading outburst of disgust at her own weakness for forgetting, even for a moment, and at the sword itself for its origin.

As she looked around, she found her surroundings all too similar to the ones she'd escaped when last on Earth — dark walls and ruins on all sides, the floor filled with the dead and dying. The most significant difference here was the absence of the Therin-Selu. No swirling, all-powerful energy could be seen.

She blinked. There was something else; something about her vision still felt strange. She blinked again, tried to discern what it was that felt so off. Then it hit her. *Blood.*

Not the presence of it, or the abundance of it in the room. No, even Jadis' time spent in a world without it had not desensitized her to so familiar a substance. No, it was the color — the way the rich redness blended into its surroundings.

There was so much of it; rusty dried blood, smooth dark fresh blood, the brown tint of dwarf blood, the sheen of black ork blood, and the scattering of purple-tinted but still red elvish blood. There was color everywhere; in the decorated braids of dead and injured elves and in the strange clothing of the orks. There was even color hidden among the shadows; the green and brown of moss creeping through the cracks. She'd gone so long without it. In her dark world of gray so long, she'd forgotten what it felt like for color to grace her eyes.

A familiar shiver slid across her skin. The icy fingers of the wind served as a sharp reminder of her freedom. In her home out of time, there was no breeze or fluctuation of temperature. There, she was cold. But there was warmth here, emitting from light not bound to smog. She could feel it beating down on her, thrumming from all around. The world was not stagnant. A breeze was inherently imbued with variance, bringing with it warmth or cold.

Here, the wind was alive. Bodies, light, blood — they all gave off heat. Still and cold as the room was, it paled in comparison to the nothingness that had been Jadis' prison. She could feel the warmth radiating around her, pushing back against the cold, and struggling to stay alive.

Her sense of smell struck her like a battering ram. The room was full of an overwhelming cacophony of scents. The dominant smell in the room was undeniably death. There was no getting around it — the stench radiated from every direction, new, old, and stages in between. Yet even though it offended her nostrils, she breathed in deeply. Discerning the rancid complexity of it, appreciating the variety of layered scents. It blended the sweat of many races, the iron of blood, the putridity of excrement, the subtle hints of broken wood and old stone.

On the heels of the smell came taste. Dominating the air was the taste of bitter iron. There was no time to linger on the salty bitterness of it. No, there would be more time to experience taste later, she realized as her hearing took focus, arriving in pops and bursts.

The moaning of the injured washed over her. She drank it in, reveling in the weakness it represented. She knew pain. She knew the sounds the living made when their insides were torn out. The gasping of lungs too weak to take in more air was all-too-familiar to her. It filled her with confidence — the injured made for easier targets.

All around her were corpses and unconscious warriors. She smirked. *Who were these weaklings to think they'd earned the right to express pain? They did not know pain. They did not deserve the ability to express pain. They have not endured what I endured, nor could they,* she thought. She listened for something to distract from the groans. She heard the din of combat, close and far. Close was the thudding of blows and cracking of furniture on the other side of closed wooden doors.

Distant was the sound of clashing armies and explosions, the zing of spells, the music of elvish casting. Cries of rage, mourning, cruel joy — they all echoed through the air, bouncing and reverberating off walls into her ears.

It was staggering. Jadis felt her mind trying to panic, threatening to switch off to hide away from it all. It was so much. Blades clashing, breathing, fluids oozing along the floor, groans of pain, violence in the distance. The taste of iron. Excrement. Colors. Cold. Warmth. Blood. Death.

It threatened to trample her like a charging army. In fact, if not for Peter's regular appearances these last few weeks, she realized, she might have been overwhelmed by the sheer complexity of it all.

No. I am not some weak child.

She clamped her eyes shut, breathed deeply, just for a moment. She sealed herself off from as much as she could, just like she'd learned to do with pain. She escaped to a part of her far, far away. Bit by bit, the waves weakened, and the flow of sensory stimulation faded to more of a steady stream, present and unavoidable, but manageable.

Think. You are here now. What needs to be done first to keep you here and keep you alive. Eliminate all threats. Find the dwarf and kill her before she finds and kills you. No! More immediate than that. What threats are now?

Looking down, she was met with the bloodstained grin of an orkish warlock, his bloody hand gripping her ankle weakly. Blood pooled around him from where the sword she gripped pinned him to the rough floor. He opened his mouth to speak. His broken voice invaded her ears in a raspy whisper.

"I know you," he cackled with feigned disappointment. "If you're here, he's not far behind. Heh-heh-heh. I told those Awan-loving fools they were wrong."

Jadis sneered and tore Galvorn violently from his chest and doubled her killing prowess with the second blade.

The sword's weight felt good in her hand. Gravity was weaker here, which meant she was faster. She glowered down at the ork. He was dead. What little time he had left was cut short when she removed the blade. Despite that, she was ready to hasten his demise should he so much as tighten his grip on her.

"Wait. Please," The ork managed to slur out through a blood-filled mouth. He let go of her leg in a motion of surrender. "Please, save the yulmëar. Save Littlefang," he begged as he convulsed in pain. "Her elfling name was Rava. It has power over her." He coughed a wet, pathetic sound. "Your father can use her," he begged. "Tell him she is a gift from King Draelic." Draelic pleaded.

How does he know? No one should know about him, Jadis thought as she smirked and leaned down close to the ork so it could hear as she whispered back, "No," while stabbing Galvorn slowly into Draelic's neck. A look of confused despair adorned his face as his severed head tumbled to the floor.

She bent down and rifled through the ork's corpse, searching for anything useful. Her hands slid over something soft in the folds of his armor. She pulled it out and found it was a simple brown leather notebook wrapped in a plain cord. *Strange. Orks are not known for their reading. This could be useful.*

Slowly, she undid the binding and opened the soft folds of the book. On the first page, signed in orkish script, one sentence was written: *Draelic, the Weeping King.*

A journal, Jadis realized while flipping through the pages. *Too hard to read now. Look at it later,* she thought as she slid it into the folds of her tattered dress. *I need to get out of here. A yulmëar is too dangerous, too big a risk… But, if the name has power over her, she could be useful…*

She stood from where she'd knelt over the ork. She saw a dwarf eyeing her curiously, his pale, sunken face contrasting his dark round beard. *Orks, a dwarf, an elfling — what has that stupid human gotten me into?* Before she could address the dwarf, though, she heard the rising of bodies.

Threats? The yulmëar, whoever is fighting it. The dwarf is too wounded to pose a threat. Elves. She realized the bodies on the ground between her and the large open doors belonged to living elves. *Can't go that way.*

She turned her back to the door as the elves strewn through the room recovered from the aftershock of her arrival. *A crisked yulmëar. Of course, there is a crisked yulmëar. If I get control of it, I can use it as a distraction.* Stealthily, she stalked forward, past a dead elf, and put herself on the other side of a pillar.

Then she caught sight of Peter strewn on the ground in front of her not far from a pair of small doors in the back wall. *Is he alive?* Carefully, she slid forward and squatted by the immobile human. There was a gash in his head that bled slowly. Unsure why she was doing it, she wiped at the blood with her thumb to redirect the flow away from his eye. Then her fingers went to his throat, pressing against it for a sign.

Pulse is steady. He is alive. What do I do with him? She pondered this for a moment then made up her mind. *Focus. Find the yulmëar.* She stepped away from Peter and made her way to the doors at the back of the room. Then she cracked them open and stepped inside in one fluid moment.

Wham! An elvish body struck the door next to her as she shut it behind her. Jadis didn't even flinch at the collision. She looked over at the elf's bloodied, limp body sliding down the door leaving behind a bloody trail. When it came to rest on the ground, it rolled over, and she saw that his throat was torn out. *Found it,* she thought sadistically.

Jadis turned away from the elf, and to her surprise, she found she was in a library full of scrolls and leather bound books. All were illuminated by two softly glowing arcane lanterns. Four other lanterns were shattered, broken, and scattered around the room among damaged books, scrolls, tables, and blood; casualties of a battle that still raged. A female elf with ash brown hair with a purple braid clashed viciously with the nightmare child.

Liúre, she's a kid. He did not say she was just a kid. Fighting an Ócom-Véla Valk? This was a mistake. Too many variables, the voice in her head warned. But she saw no exit other than the doors she'd come in through. *So young. Almost as young as…*

Her lips formed a thin line as she considered her options. *If I run, it kills her, then Peter, and it has my scent now. It'll come after me, too. liúre,* She swore again. *Why couldn't he have made the final kill at a better time?*

Meanwhile, a brutal blow from the child sent the elf into a shelf of books next to Jadis, which gave her a glimpse of the elf's face. There was something familiar about it. *She'd probably been there during one of her father's trips to Gino-lore,* she thought as she recalled the trips bitterly, trips in which she was always instructed not to speak or kill so long as they were in the city. She hated the city and its rules.

No rules here, Jadis thought, eyes locking with Rava's, who was more a living skeleton than a little elvish girl. Jadis froze, just for a moment. She saw herself reflected in the creature's glowing red eyes.

Rava hissed and raised her thin, bloodstained, clawed hands aggressively. The little monster rushed forward, passing over where one of the elf's twin blades lay on the ground. Jadis was left with one option: fight. *Do not worry. I will not let them use you anymore, little one.*

To Jadis' right, the sound of broken wood and clattering books signaled the female elf's rise. The elf shook herself off and looked back and forth between Jadis and the yulmëar. With hard metal arm defensively in front of her, she took a menacing step towards Jadis, a thin broken blade raised readily in the air.

The child might not be the biggest threat in the room, after all, Jadis thought at the sight of the warrior elf adorned in her black armor. Jadis barely managed to dodge out of the way as the creature slammed into the doors, her claws drove into the wood.

Then again… She let out a sigh of exasperation.

"Sword!" the elf called out. *That broken blade won't do her much good, and I do not need two swords.* She looked down at Galvorn and her own blade in her two hands. *I can disarm her against me and rearm her against our mutual foe in one move.* Then, without so much as a greeting, Jadis flung Galvorn to the elf. Súmeriel caught it easily by the hilt. The look on her face darkened for a moment, then she reengaged Rava without hesitation.

Jadis focused. She did not dare take her eyes off the yulmëar even for a second. The child tore herself from the door and retreated back a few feet. Jadis and the elf countered as they moved in opposite circles around the grisly vampire child.

Rava's gaze flitted back and forth between her opponents like a tiger hounded by two wolves.

"Flank," Jadis ordered curtly to the elf. *I have to free her from this hell.*

The elf grimaced but made no reply. She adjusted her grip on the sword and passed it from a bare metal hand to her gauntleted hand.

In that instant, the child shot forward and slashed out at Jadis as she hurled through the air. Her claws were long deadly daggers thirsty for more blood.

Jadis deflected the blow. The flat of her blade clashed with claws. She sidestepped and let the child slam into another bookshelf.

"Rava!" Jadis cried out to the child, who flinched, ever so slightly at the name. "Heed your name!"

The child's head shook, like a dog whose ears are being harassed by a fly. Her face spasmed, trying to express every negative emotion at once.

"She's gone," the elf replied for the girl. "All she has left is hunger."

There is still a part of her left. There is always a little bit left fighting, Jadis thought but knew it was too late; there was no saving her now. A flinch was not enough for the name to make a difference. The only freedom left for this girl was death.

Head and heart. Her father's voice echoed in Jadis' memories, lectured her even now. *Only three creatures can survive without one or the other, but none without either.* Rava leaped forward, a dark streak of lightning in the low glow of the lantern, but Jadis' sword was lightening of its own and blocked the onslaught of slashing claws in a thunderous crash.

The gray-skinned warrior used the weaker gravity to her advantage and moved faster than she'd ever moved before. Jadis was no prey to be devoured. She was the predator. She'd killed before; this was no different. It didn't matter if it was a little girl forged into a weapon. Rava was nothing more than another obstacle in the way of her survival.

Jadis' free hand whipped out and snatched Rava's wrist. The creature's loose skin made for a weak grip. The elf saw her and moved as precisely as she'd hoped. The child, furious at the touch, leapt back to escape the hold. The movement broke the thin bones in her wrist with the force of her retreat, right towards the elf.

Jadis let her go. It was exactly the reaction she wanted.

As the child hurled away from her, her wrist knitted itself back together with unnatural speed, and she was met by the cold touch of the elf's blade.

Súmeriel swung again, eager to follow the thrust of the blade across the creatures back with decapitation. But the yulmëar was too quick. It dodged Súmeriel's swing, going for the elf's neck.

Súmeriel caught the child's open mouth on her black metal arm. The unpleasant sound of teeth scraping against metal shrieked through the air. Then to both Súmeriel and Jadis' horror, there was a loud *crack,* and the fangs sunk into the metallic skin.

Súmeriel cried out in pain and swung her arm wildly out so it crashed into a bookshelf, where it broke the yulmëar's hold.

With a scream, Rava kicked out with both feet and struck the elf in the chest, which launched her backward out of range and into a rubble pile.

Jadis moved in and tried to stab Rava through the side, but the little monster was still too fast. It slid back and slammed into a stone wall. Jadis barely had time to react as the yulmëar's legs braced against the wall and launched her towards Jadis.

Jadis caught her with her sword. The black and silver blade buried itself in the small chest of the child and burst out through her back. The force of the collision knocked Jadis on her back in a pile of books. Her sword suspended the monster in the air above her, but she maintained her grip.

Rava did not die like most things in that position would, though. She didn't even bleed from the wound in her chest. She just kept coming. Her clawed hands gripped at the blade of the sword and opened bloodless cuts as she pulled herself forward. The child crawled down the length of the sword closer and closer to Jadis, fangs gnashing violently, spraying blood and spittle everywhere.

"Rava, be still," she tried commanding the child, but the words were useless. *He lied to me, you fool. Of course, he did. Now you die,* she heard her father's voice echo in the back of his mind.

"No!" she yelled and threw a hand up to catch the child's face in her fingers to slow the beast's descent. Then, a sharp pain shot through her left pinkie at the second knuckle. The child's head reared back and took the skin and muscle off Jadis' finger with it.

"Aaaaeeeyyaaagghh!"

The elf was there just as the child's claws began to scrape across Jadis' face. Thin razor blades carved red lines in her gray skin. Súmeriel reached them like a raging storm, swinging the black sword with murderous intent.

Galvorn tore through the child's neck, severing the head from the body. Rava wailed even as the head barely missed Jadis and fell to the floor — not a scream of pain or fear, but a haunting, bone-chilling cry of relief, which poured from her fanged mouth as it rolled across the floor.

Suspended above Jadis, the child's body convulsed and began twisting and shriveling. Purple ethereal energy sparked from the edges of where the sword pierced her and spread like the slow burn of sparks on paper. Bit by bit, the sparks rolled over the pale bloodstained skin and burned it away. Once the skin was gone, only a dried-out, mummified husk remained for a moment, then it crumbled into dust in the air around Jadis.

Galvorn came to a stop a few inches from Jadis' own neck. In the seconds it took for the child to become nothing but dust, the sword stayed there. Even when the dust had settled, Súmeriel did not raise the sword. Instead, she twisted it so the tip prodded Jadis' neck. *That won't work,* Jadis thought victoriously as she fought to keep her expression neutral.

One of the elf's boots rested on the flat of Jadis' silver and black blade and pinned it to the uneven floor. *Liúre. Doesn't matter if she cannot cut me, if I cannot cut her.* The elf did not move for a time. Rather, she stood there menacing Jadis unceremoniously among the pile of dusty remains.

"Explain yourself, Eölin," she ordered. Her battered appearance lent more to her ferocity than her voice. "Why are you here? Are you an ally of Draelic? Is that how you knew the child's name?"

Jadis sized her up. The elf was the taller of the two, which gave her better reach. She was a few years physically older with toned muscles that spoke to her physical prowess. *As fast as me, if not faster. Hand is a risk.* On top of that, Jadis could feel exhaustion knocking on her door.

She looks worn to the bone, too. I could try it. There are no witnesses. She would die a hero. No, too risky. There is no exit, and the other elves are outside. Take your time. You have the advantage. She does not know Galvorn cannot cut you.

Jadis let go of her own sword, peeling her fingers out from under it, but did not relax her tensed muscles. "Side effect of the Therin-Selu. I am the only one of my kind to make it out," she replied. *So far.* "I do not know Draelic, but the ork caster gave me her name, thinking I was his ally. He was fatally mistaken."

A realization came over the elf's face. "The antemáklasi's visions," she said in a hushed voice.

"Yes, Peter Blair helped free me. We should see to him and the others," Jadis suggested, eager to have the sword far from her neck and hoping the remainder of the elves' allies would distract her.

The elf drew the sword back and gave Jadis room to rise but did not put it away or remove her boot from Jadis' sword. "I am Súmeriel Almurë. Do you know where you are?"

Will she remember my name if I tell her now that I'm here?

"Home. That is all that matters. I am Jadis, Lúemeni Súmeriel," she lied.

"Lúemeni Jadis," the elf replied. Her eyes narrowed slightly as she spoke the name. Then she gestured Jadis towards the door with her cracked metal arm.

"Does that hurt?" Jadis asked to try to distract the elf with her own pain so Jadis could find an escape.

Súmeriel looked down at the dark metal skin on her arm, frowning. "A bit. I've used this spell to block war hammers, halberts, arrows — nothing has ever even scratched it until now." She adjusted the arm, looked it over, followed the cracks with her eyes. "I will have to leave it until I can find a dwarven transfigurer," she muttered to herself.

Jadis glanced at her sword on the ground. "My sword?" she said and let the question hang in the air.

Súmeriel raised her eyebrows and gestured towards the doors with her own sword. A scowl on her face, Jadis opened the doors with little effort. Behind her, the elf sheathed her sword and retrieved Jadis' weapon.

I am going to kill her. Through the doorway, bright light poured into the room as the doors opened and revealed an arcane lantern hanging in the center of the pillared hall. Jadis winced as pain coursed through her from her damaged finger.

"Let's go," Súmeriel prompted from behind her, Jadis' sword now doing the menacing.

"I won't be your prisoner," Jadis replied, letting her defiance show in her voice as she met the elf's eyes.

"Call yourself what you want, but you will do as I say for now," the elf replied, not bothering to sugarcoat the situation.

"Then, as your prisoner, I request healing for my injury before proceeding," she replied as she tried to buy time to find a way out as she showed the elf her bleeding hand.

Súmeriel's eyes darted back and forth between hers. "We have a healer who can help. Now, come."

Jadis' eyes continued darting around the room, looking for anything else of potential use. As she searched, she spied a familiar book under the rubble near a ruined desk.

It cannot be, she thought as she pulled the book out. An all-too-familiar black symbol was on the front; a downward-facing triangle, overlapping with an eye and three curling spindles beginning at the center of the eye and breaching out in curls from each side of the triangle.

She knew its contents. She knew it did not belong in an elvish library and that if the elves found it, they would burn it and scatter the ashes in a river. *Come back for it.* Jadis' eyes snapped back to the elf, then turned and strode out the door.

Jadis exited the library and saw Peter rising shakily to his feet. An idea struck her, and she surged forward to help him up. The elf's surprise escaped in a warning behind her.

"Hey!"

Jadis caught him by the arm to help him balance. Peter flinched away from her touch as the muscles in his arms tightened, as if he expected her to attack him. After what felt like an eternity of him watching her through cold angry eyes, he spoke in an icy voice. "Simon isn't going to be happy to see you. How did you get here?" he demanded, then his eyes snagged on her injury. "You're hurt?"

"It is complicated, and barely," Jadis replied snidely as she reached around his side to try to steal his dagger.

Peter caught her hand by the wrist before she could remove the blade from the sheath. "Let go," he growled softly. Jadis' eyes narrowed, but she released her grip.

Peter released his hold on Jadis in return and turned to Súmeriel as she approached, a hint of hesitation in his voice. "You can see her, too, right?" he asked.

"Yes, Valk Blair, I see the eölin. She is no illusion," Súmeriel replied patiently. "Step away from him," the elf commanded Jadis.

Peter noticed the blades in Súmeriel's hand and extended a hand to her for his black blade. The elf consented and passed Galvorn back to him.

"What's going on?" he asked, looking back and forth warily between the two nonhumans.

"Nothing," Jadis replied as she clenched her empty fists. She didn't like the way he had angled his sword and dagger between them.

"I don't trust her," Súmeriel replied.

"What happened? Where's the vampire kid?" Peter asked with a hint of apprehension in his voice as he began to look around the room.

"Dead. We killed it," Súmeriel responded with a glance at Jadis.

"And you don't trust her," Peter replied contemplatively as his grip on his sword tightened.

"Until I know more, no. I do not. This is a wicked place. I would not trust my own father if I found him here," Súmeriel replied.

Peter nodded. "Fine. But there's still fighting to be done. If we leave her unarmed, we might as well go ahead and kill her."

No! What is he doing? she thought in horror. Her eyes darted around for any sort of weapon.

Súmeriel bit the inside of her cheek softly then nodded. "So be it. She is your responsibility. You're more suited to the task if she tries something any-way," she said, then snagged a well-made elvish bastard sword from where it lay on the ground. Once her new weapon was secure in hand, she tossed Jadis' sword back to her.

They are not going to kill me. Why? What does he get out of helping me? It does not matter. Deal with your injuries. Find advantages.

"Do you have bandages?" Jadis asked as politely as she could, the words still sprinkled with sarcasm.

Súmeriel nodded agreeably before moving off toward the remaining five elves, each of whom bore fresh wounds of their own and were giving Jadis strange looks.

Peter took a step closer to Jadis and spoke in a low voice only she could hear, sword and dagger still naked in each of his hands. "I owe you for the training and the intel on torturing orks, but we humans have a saying — *you're on thin ice.* If you cross me, I might not be able to beat you one on one, but I can keep you busy long enough for the elf to get involved. Understood?"

Jadis felt a smirk teasing the edge of her lips. *Good. He has some steel in him after all. Play along.* She nodded.

"Was going for my dagger really necessary?" he asked, his voice suddenly tired as exhaustion melted away some of the firmness in him.

"I do not like to be unarmed," she replied flatly.

Peter turned to watch the elves, his gaze lingering on Súmeriel as she bent down next to one of the fallen. "She knows what you are, doesn't she?"

"Yes, but I do not think the elf remembers forgetting," Jadis replied conde-scendingly, "which means this is not over."

Peter grimaced. "We have a lot to talk about when this is over then."

Jadis gave no reply, as they were being joined by the dwarf with the full, round black beard. Bandaged arm hanging in front of him, the dwarf hobbled over next to Peter, keeping his eyes on Jadis, speaking the human tongue. "Quick thinking there. I owe you one, Peter."

Peter glanced at the dwarf, his attention still on Jadis. "You paid me back when you took out that crying monster's legs."

The dwarf's lips peeled back, and he chuckled in acknowledgment. Then his voice shifted to address Jadis in Dwarvish. "I am Breekie Fellhammer, and I would duel you to know you Eölin, but I am far too injured." He raised his now bandaged stump to indicate the injury. "My curiosity shall wait. Give me your name, and let us depart to finish cleansing this city of orks."

"Jadis," she replied. "You will slow us down."

"Bah!" Breekie replied gruffly. "If Peter intends to continue to fight, I will not see my ork-king-slaying brother do it alone. This is less than a flesh wound," he declared, as he waved his stump emphatically. "I need only one hand to wield FoeCrusher, and by my beard, I have one."

"Are the rest of your companions this obstinate?" Jadis asked Peter with a scowl. *We're wasting time. There's still a battle out there. I can hear it.*

"At least. His obstinance is just more concentrated since it travels a shorter distance," Peter replied while removing his jacket, then fiddled with a strange black box.

Peter's hand shot to his ear, a faraway look came over his face, and then a savage grin broke free of his somber expression. Jadis heard soft speech coming from the strange device resting around his ears.

He spun around and called out to Súmeriel, "Communications are back. William says the ork command structure is breaking down, and they're retreating." The grin darkened as more words were whispered in his ear. "They're falling back underground."

He is different here. More sure of himself, Jadis thought as she watched Peter closely. *More dangerous. Not dangerous enough, though. I can kill him if I have to.*

An almost forgotten pain rumbled and clawed through her stomach. *Hunger. I am hungry,* she realized. The sensation struck her oddly.

She looked down at the dwarf. "Before we go, do you have food?" she asked calmly. "Something sweet?"

AFTERMATH

The sun shone through the cracks in the sky, blending with the fires burning throughout the city, creating an orangish glow in the air. For all appearances, they'd won the battle. The sporadic sounds of combat could still be heard but were growing fainter with each passing minute.

Somewhere, someone was crying. Skirmishes still broke out here and there when orks or other foul beasts were caught hiding above ground. Despite the complaints and urging of the few dwarves present, neither man nor elf dared venture underground yet.

Shawn stumbled over uneven ground as he was led by his elvish companion through their main forces towards an unknown destination.

He saw Mellonië differently now, he realized. He felt almost scared of her, having seen her ferocity in battle firsthand over the last few hours.

They moved slowly through the crowd, giving way to vehicles or the injured every dozen or so steps. As they paused to let a pair of men pass by with a woman on a stretcher, Shawn looked up from the crowd at their surroundings. It was then that he caught sight of the Tesla Building, barely recognizable with the strange black stone cathedral sticking out of its side.

Shawn tried to take in as much as he could. His eyes darted about their surroundings, lingering on a broken overpass. Despite the gore around it, green vines grew out from the concrete, spreading along the broken bridge.

His staring broke as an elf yanked a spear from the ground. It was one of many bearing human and ork heads in a gory display scattered about in this area. It was strange seeing the already decomposing heads. They seemed to be mocking the corpses of the recently deceased being tended to by a small group of men and elves. Some of them went about gathering the spiked trophies, tossing them into one of the many burning fires here and spread throughout the city.

They were putting humans and their own kind on spikes? Why? he wondered, then bumped into a broad bald man with a well-trimmed beard. Shawn winced as one of the edges of the broken shield he carried poked his hip. "Sorry," he said louder than he should have and received a glower from the man who kept moving.

My hearing is still whack. Maybe there's a healer that can fix it, he mused while he continued to follow Mellonië through the crowd. Everything was still a bit muffled, but he could hear well enough to follow a conversation if he was close and focused.

He spied a series of medical tents set up in the shade of a collapsed tower. Elvish healers, nurses, and emergency responders, including a blood covered Simon, rushed in-between patients.

Breaking away from the female elf, Shawn pushed his way out of the crowd and in-between the tents. There, he caught sight of the gory truth of battle — hundreds of wounded men and women; legs crushed beyond repair, limbs missing, horrific burns, cuts that would only stop bleeding once there was no more blood to bleed.

A nauseating sense of déjà vu swept over him. The rubble, death, and blood filled his mind with images of Paragon in the days and hours following the Shattering. The sight of a woman writhing as a pair of nurses tried to patch a monstrous bite mark made with two sets of teeth in her side made him feel lightheaded. Most people don't realize how much blood is in the human body. Shawn had a sense for it, but he still hadn't gotten used to it. He hoped he never would.

Is this just the world we live in now? he thought as he took a deep breath, steadying himself. *This is no time to be queasy. Find a way to help.*

"Simon," he called out as the man rushed past him into a neighboring tent. The man either didn't hear him or ignored him, so Shawn followed him into the tent. Shawn's regret was instantaneous as he was struck by the smell of burned flesh and excrement mixing with sweat and blood.

Simon stood over the body of a large man with a cut running down his face from left ear to his lip. Shawn's nausea was chased away by dread as he noticed a dozen other deep cuts on the man.

"How can I help?" he heard himself saying in too loud a voice.

Simon didn't so much as look up from his work. "Even the elves have given up on this one, so unless you're a renowned surgeon…" he replied enthusiastically.

"No, but—"

"Then, if you have any medical experience, we have hundreds of other patients that need tending to," the doctor interrupted.

"I—"

Simon looked up at last, and Shawn saw that he hadn't even known who he was talking to. "You. You can get out of the way," he stated flatly.

Before Shawn could respond or even turn to exit, two newcomers entered the canopy. Peter looked like the bloody ghost of his former self. The only parts of him not covered in blood or grime were his eyes — crazed eyes that looked right through Shawn as if he were a window they were deciding whether or not to break.

The second figure did not look half so crazed. She didn't need to; her ragged armor and scar-covered ashen skin gave her all the appearance of a ghost. She moved with the calculated silence of a stalking cat, maintaining a position at Peter's back and side that seemed to use him as her own personal shield.

For a brief moment, Shawn wondered if he was the only one who'd seen her and her suspicious expression. Simon's reaction dismissed that notion thoroughly.

"What is she doing here?" he demanded loudly, the first traces of anger Shawn had ever heard from him highlighted by the tensing in his body language.

A strange grin broke across Peter's face. The unexpected reaction to Simon's displeasure made Shawn uneasy from his position between the two men.

"Don't worry. It's not a dream this time," Peter said, pointing to a shallow cut on the side of his neck.

"Get her away from me," Simon lashed out, causing Peter to take a reflexive step back; a step perfectly mirrored by the strange lady. *No,* Shawn realized. *Girl. She looks about the same age as me.*

Shawn followed Peter's eyes to Simon, whose face bore a fierce expression. The dark-haired man now watched the ashen girl. The expression softened for a minute as his gaze darted between the two of them.

Simon pursed his lips for a second. "Captain, you should sit. You need to rest."

"I'm fine," Peter replied dismissively.

"Peter, I don't have time for this," Simon started to implore.

Peter's eyes darkened. "I'm fine, Simon. I'll rest when this is over," he said flatly and exited the tent, the strange companion at his side.

Unsure what else to do, Shawn followed the captain out. Trying to catch up with him as he weaved effortlessly through the crowd.

"Captain, I killed a troll," he blurted out in an effort to get the man's attention, but Peter didn't acknowledge him. It was as if the man was in a daze. It dawned on Shawn that he wasn't the only one. The realization came to him as he noticed the same vacant expression on several other men and women milling about aimlessly, their eyes focused on nothing. Up ahead, a truck was stuck in mud as a skinny man in a green jersey and a short man in a ragged polo struggled to move it.

What's everyone doing? He felt frustration mature into an inexplicable anger. The anger seized his chest, tightening it, searching for an outlet which he gave it.

"What are you doing?" he shouted at the nearest traumatized fighter, a short round man with a scraggly black beard. Black-beard blanched, freezing like a child caught in a forbidden act. A very different effect was had on Peter, who came to a stop then looked back at Shawn curiously, the glazed-over expression in his eyes clearing.

Shawn wasn't sure why, but this just made him angrier. He began barking orders to the short man and the other dazed fighters. "Help them! They're struggling to do something important, and you're all just stumbling around like a bunch of stupid toddlers," he shouted, fueling the fire in his voice. The zombie-like survivors obeyed lazily and were joined by Peter, who braced himself beside Shawn against the truck, pushing it with his shoulders. Riding high on his frustration, Shawn snapped at the gray girl. "You, too!"

The girl made no effort to join them. She simply raised a white eyebrow and replied flatly, "I do not take orders from children."

But the cutting comment was left unaddressed as the truck found solid ground and lurched forward, almost throwing Shawn into the mud from which it escaped. A helping hand from Peter, though, saved him from a mud bath. Shawn rounded on him, yanking himself out of the man's grip, the movement still governed by the anger in his gut.

But then he saw Peter's face, and the anger drained out of him as quickly as it had arrived, subsequently substituted by a sudden, strong sonder. *Grow up, Shawn. People are hurt and tired, not ignoring you or out to get you.*

Peter looked him up and down. "Good job. Come on," he instructed, turning back into the crowd, which they maneuvered through for a few more minutes.

Finally, they broke from the crowd, and Shawn saw Peter heading towards an elvish canopy under which a small group stood huddled around a table. There were several injured elves, as well as William, Breekie, Elborin, and Mellonië, their backs to the broken overpass.

Every one of them looked like a disaster survivor, covered head to foot in filth, blood, and wounds, some shaking from exhaustion but refusing to sit down. Despite their haggard appearances, Shawn felt comfort in their presence. Slinking awkwardly forward, Shawn slipped into their conversation.

"Unlike the elves, we took heavy casualties, especially Scott's forces," Shawn heard William explain.

"How many of us?" Peter asked in a low growl.

"Allan is MIA. Last anyone saw, he was being backed down an alley by a pack of goblins and with only a quiver of arrows and a broken bow left."

Peter squeezed his eyes shut for a moment, pinching the bridge of his nose. "If I know Allan, he made it out. Any confirmed KIA from SNW?"

"The only one confirmed so far is Ian, who took a volley of arrows covering a retreat half an hour after putting down the chopper. Poor guy must have saved a dozen lives." Peter winced hearing this, and William made a poor crucifix in the air before he continued. "Plenty of injuries to go around too."

"Does Cassandra know?" Peter asked with a pained expression.

"She was with him when he passed," William replied.

"Good." Peter did a double take when he noticed the newcomers join the gathering. His gaze flitted back and forth between Mellonië and Shawn before moving behind them into the ranks of soldiers.

"Where's O'Cleary?" he asked as if waiting for his rugged friend to emerge smiling from the crowd.

Mellonië altered her stance and cast a subtle look in Shawn's direction. *I wasn't supposed to notice that.*

"We got separated, trying to catch up with the main forces," she explained in a soothing tone.

Peter's eyes narrowed, a storm brewing beneath the surface. "William?"

William shook his head. "I've heard nothing. If he caught up injured, he didn't find me, but you know him. That doesn't mean anything."

Peter nodded curtly. "We tried to get him on the radios?"

"His radio was busted," Shawn chipped in to be helpful.

Mellonië winced and shook her head ever so slightly. "No. It wasn't."

Peter's jaw worked beneath cold eyes before he spoke. "What do you mean? Was it broken or not? He wouldn't go into the field with it if it was."

Mellonië brushed her hair back to reveal an SNW headpiece and produced a small radio from her pocket.

What? Shawn wondered. *When did she get that?*

"It was never damaged. He told the boy it was to try to get him to go with Scott's group. When O'Cleary realized there was a chance we'd be separated, he gave it to me and told me to make sure Shawn was returned safely," Mellonië explained as she avoided Shawn's dumbfounded expression.

It's my fault. I knew it was my fault. Shawn found himself staring at the ground as it threatened to spin. *No. Deep breath. Get yourself together,* he told himself as he peeled his eyes from the ground.

Peter cursed. "He'll turn up," he added with a glance at Breekie, who held the bandaged stump of his right hand in his left.

Woah, he lost a hand. How's he still grinning? I don't know if I could ever smile again if I lost a hand.

Breekie caught him staring and waggled his eyebrows before mouthing, "We're going to have to make a new handshake."

With a smirk, Shawn stifled a snicker. Unsure of what to do next, Shawn approached Jadis. He didn't want to suffer the embarrassment of a rejected handshake, so he kept his hands firmly at his sides. He came to an awkward stop to Jadis' left and stood there for a moment as he tried to think of what to say to the girl ignoring him.

Is she an elf? She looks like an elf? he wondered. *I haven't seen any young elves.*

"Hi. I'm Shawn. Are — are you…" he inquired hesitantly. *…an elf?* he added in his mind, afraid to actually ask.

The girl's eyes snapped towards him, raking him up and down with an unamused expression that seemed at home on her face. "No. Leave me alone, manling."

She's got purple eyes. Manling? Is that an insult? That sounds like an insult, Shawn thought as the group around him continued with their conversations regarding the ended battle and what came next.

Having failed to make a new friend, Shawn once again found himself unsure what to do, so he resumed looking around, and he paused his unfocused search when he saw Akena. The tall woman was engaging in an exciting conversation with Peter's female elf-friend with the purple braid. The elf was grinning and pointing at the scar on her neck with a bandaged arm. Meanwhile, Akena tore away the tattered remains of a shoe, which no longer adequately supported her prosthetic foot.

As he watched the excited exchange, something at the corner of his vision moved. Desperate for anything to distract his thoughts from O'Cleary, he followed the movement. It was coming from under the collapsed overpass. Something was emerging from behind the rubble.

A tall figure stepped into view as it cut down a scout at the edge of the camp. Shawn stepped forward, trying to get a better line of sight. The figure dragged something behind it. It was an ork, eight feet tall, covered head to toe in spiked armor. He carried an enormous double-sided battle-ax in one hand. In the other, he clutched the black jacket of a man he dragged effortlessly along behind him.

"No," the boy whispered as he took another slow step forward, drawing closer to Peter, who was cleaning his sword and listened to the discussion.

The approaching figure passed closer to one of the low-burning fires; the flames melted away the shadows that barely concealed them. Between Shawn and the beast, Peter raised Galvorn and, having cleaned it, began to sheath the blade on his back. A warning cry came out from someone in the crowd behind them, and Shawn took another step forward and passed Peter.

"No," Shawn said aloud, which drew the crowd's already divided attention. The thought echoed through Shawn's mind as a white patch of hair became visible in the mess of brown hair of the man being dragged towards them.

"No!" Shawn cried out, a scream of anguish drawing the full attention of all around. He charged the figure with a newfound energy.

The enormous ork came to a stop only a few hundred yards away and called out, "Is this your sacrifice, humanity?" in guttural English as he tossed O'Cleary forward in front of him. "Is this the best you can do?" The warrior challenged them as he waved his wet ax about menacingly.

Shawn heard movement behind him, and suddenly Peter tore past him, sword unsheathed.

The ork took a step toward where O'Cleary lay and raised his weapon with both hands preparing to behead the man.

A floodgate of fury tucked deep within Shawn welled over and burst like a dam. He felt it surge, searching for an escape, the world around him turning red. Hot, boiling rage strained against every fiber of his being, searching erratically for an outlet. Ahead of him, Peter collapsed into a heap.

Shawn didn't see what brought the warrior down. He was too distracted by the energy as he sped past Peter's crumpled form. It was too much. His malice was burning him, hurting him. The anger screamed and lashed out. Shawn realized he was only holding his tattered shield as he hurled towards the beast.

"Stop!" Shawn cried out at the pain and his foe. The word tore through his throat and out into the world, where it struck the enormous ork. The creature was pinned in the air, frozen in space by an invisible force. The ork trembled slightly, the cruel ax mid-swing.

Then Shawn reached him. He crashed into the beast, undeterred by the danger it posed to him. Irate beyond verbal expression, he plunged the spiked corner of his shield into the ork's armor and sent them both tumbling to the ground.

The ork landed on its back but still did not move a muscle, Shawn's five-foot-seven frame crouched on his chest. Shawn yanked the shield back and rended it from the armor as black blood filled the air. Untempered, he brought it back down with a sickening *sclunch* as he buried it in the creature's exposed neck.

Again: *Sclunch.*

Again: *Sclunch.*

Again: *Sclunch.*

Again: *Sclunch.*

Again: *Sclunch.*

Over and over, he struck until, at last, he heard the *ting* of shield against concrete. Only then did he let the shield clatter to the ground.

Shawn felt hot tears carve through the dirt on his checks. Then three strong hands grabbed him, hoisted him up and back, enveloped him in a warm embrace. He recognized the sweet aroma of Mellonië and the musk of Breekie as he buried his face in the dwarf's surprisingly soft beard. His whole body shook, succumbing to his weeping as they held him there, tight and warm in their embrace.

Shawn pulled his face out of the beard to get air. A nauseous sensation in his stomach met with a warm heat on the back of his neck and spread across his body like lava down a hillside. Shawn's head came to rest on Breekie's shoulder, and he saw Peter stumble forward on trembling legs. No spear or arrow marked his body, but he bore fresh scrapes and bruises.

He must have collapsed from exhaustion. The disheveled warrior clattered onto the ground where O'Cleary lay only a few feet away at the edge of the broken overpasses shadow.

"Brandon," Peter choked out, his voice barely audible to Shawn. "Come on, man," Peter said as he clambered forward and looked the Irishman up and down in horror.

O'Cleary lay motionless on the ground, covered head to toe in dozens of lacerations. One arm hung awkwardly, broken at his side. Chunks of his legs were missing, and a wound on his forehead was still slowly oozing blood.

"Medic!" Peter screamed with all his might, the word ripping from his throat. "Get a medic here!"

Shawn watched as Peter coughed violently between cries for a medic. Hot tears carved their way down Shawn's blood-stained cheeks.

Peter looked up from his old friend and locked eyes with Shawn still wrapped in Mellonië and Breekie's embrace.

Peter's face was a painting of blood, sweat, and tears, interrupted by bleary gray eyes. Shawn felt as if they cut through him into his soul, and he felt a pain in his chest. The sound of footfalls heralded the arrival of savage-looking elves who formed a protective barrier around the group.

Peter's gaze left Shawn and looked down at the bloody hand he clasped in his grip.

"We got him. He's all right," Shawn heard Peter mumble before yelling, "Medic! Simon where are you?" over his shoulder again with a look away from his friend's battered face. Peter's head shook almost imperceptibly, and he muttered something Shawn couldn't hear. Shawn tried to think of what to do, but his brain felt full of molasses. There was nothing he could do.

Shawn felt Mellonië's grasp relax and let go, but Breekie did not follow suit. It was then that he realized the dwarf was speaking to him. But Shawn wasn't paying attention to the dwarf. He was listening to Peter, straining to hear something that might restore hope for his friend.

"Come on, man, it's going to be all right. You've been through worse than this," Peter murmured down at the unmoving man. "Come on, you have to earn your ring still. We have to take you back to Paragon," he continued as he struggled to remove a black ring from his own hand without letting go of his friend's hand.

Simon appeared across from Peter, hands already digging through his open medical satchel. He stopped his searching and placed his fingers on O'Cleary's throat. Simon's pale face hardened. Simon shook his head slightly and gave Peter a look, which dropped Shawn's heart into his stomach. *No.*

Peter laid O'Cleary's hand at his side as he muttered to himself, his voice full of rage and grief. Peter paused and swallowed desperately. While he continued speaking to himself, Simon pulled a long syringe from his bag and stabbed it into the man's chest. O'Cleary's body spasmed briefly but didn't move more than that.

Peter struck the ground with his first. "No. No. No," Shawn heard him repeating over and over.

Then Súmeriel arrived, an elvish healer in tow. Urgently, the healer knelt down by Simon and joined him in examining O'Cleary. As the healer began to examine O'Cleary, Peter froze. No words or even breaths escaped him as he sat there on his knees still as a statue.

It seemed to take minutes, but in actuality, a few seconds later, the elvish healer stood from where he'd knelt with one hand on O'Cleary's leg. He shook his head with a forlorn expression.

No, please, no. He can't be dead, Shawn begged no one in particular.

"I'm sorry. I was too late. There's nothing I can do," he heard the elf's shrill voice say.

Simon ignored the elf as he tore open O'Cleary's shirt and began chest compressions. Blood soaked his hands from the pressure that pushed it out of the man's countless wounds.

Peter turned his back to Shawn's friends and rose, arms trembling with clenched fists. More tears streamed down Shawn's face; he was unable to look away as Peter approached the elf. Then Peter struck him, fist connecting fully with the healer's jaw, and sent him stumbling back as Peter took a menacing follow-up step towards him.

"Peter!" Súmeriel cried out. But Peter didn't seem to hear it. He took another threatening step forward, his body language screaming for violence.

Súmeriel stepped over O'Cleary and Simon. She wrapped her strong, steely arms around Peter in a tight bear hug, which stopped his momentum.

"Not another. It's my fault. Not again," Peter begged through sobs. Slowly, almost gracefully, the elf lowered him, still trembling, to the ground. Once she brought his knees to the torn concrete, Súmeriel loosened her grip and twisted him carefully until he came to rest on his back.

"Be still, Peter Blair. Look to the sky to grieve." she said in a firm, calming voice as she sat on her knees by his side.

There, Peter lay, his shaking hands clutching his hair he stared blankly up into the sky, while the world moved on around them both.

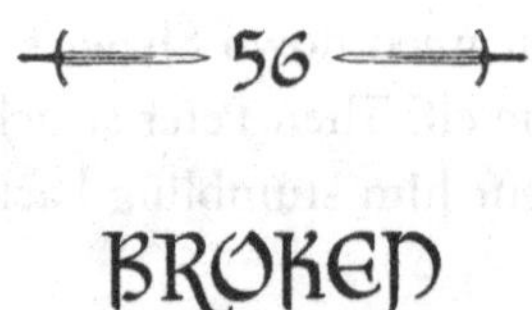

BROKED

I wish they'd stop that dreadful singing," Peter groaned. His words formed clouds in the frosty air of the freezer. He brought his hands to his mouth and blew on them to warm them up. "All I've heard is mournful singing since…" He trailed off as he looked down at the unzipped body bag containing O'Cleary's corpse.

Even through the walls of the freezer, he could still hear it. The sound of it reverberated through every inch of the city; heartfelt lamentations carried the voices of sorrowful elves. There was no escaping the music within the city's walls. It drenched everything and pulled forth tears from anyone whose mind was left to wander or whose hands were idle.

Three days of singing. Singing that sounds like the dead themselves are saying farewell, Peter thought. "You'd have loved it," he said aloud, his words underlined by the tick of his watch in the quiet of the cold room. "People keep trying to talk to me, Brandon," he confided in the corpse, "but I don't have anything to say. They all have questions. Are you okay? What's next? Are we safe?" He shook his head.

"I don't have answers. I failed. I wasn't strong enough. I'm never strong enough anymore." He pressed his nose against his clenched hands to warm it. He squeezed his eyes shut just for a moment to hide away in the darkness. *What was that song you taught me — the one you made me swear to sing if you didn't know if your body would make it home? How did it go?*

Softly he began to sing, his voice barely loud enough to hear himself. His words heated his hands by his mouth. "'Long long ago,' said the fine young maiden. 'Long long ago,' this proud young maiden declared…" he sang. Then, from behind him, a faint voice joined him for the second verse, harmonizing with his own.

"There was war and death, pestilence and famine. Our wains did starve, by village, river, and tree." Peter stopped, but the singing went on, and grew louder, closer. He opened his eyes slowly.

"And their screaming tears— they broke the very heavens. 'My four blue streams ran dark with their blood,' said she."

The song was coming from inside the room, directly behind him. Peter turned, slowly, inch by inch towards the all-too-familiar voice softly singing the Irish tune. A bead of sweat ran down Peter's spine as he brought the singer into view.

"'What have I now?' said the fair young maiden. 'What have I now?' this strong young maiden did say."

O'Cleary stood only four feet away. His pale skin was still decorated in fresh open wounds. None of the wounds bled as they should have. The wounds around his heart were close and deep enough that no one could survive them. O'Cleary's face contorted with a wide lopsided smile.

"No," Peter choked out. He looked back to where O'Cleary's body was resting in the body bag on the slab behind him. The bag was empty.

Peter rounded on the smiling corpse. He was still there, a wide, terrible grin full of sharp teeth plastered across his face. The grin began to melt away, replaced by a scowl.

"Let me go," O'Cleary said in a raspy voice. "I want tah go home — home to my green fields. Why are you keeping me here?" he demanded angrily, his accent as thick as when he'd first met Peter.

Peter took a step back and bumped into the table. O'Cleary's head tilted unnaturally, then the dead man took a menacing step forward. "Let me go," he demanded harshly.

"No. Who…? What are you?" Peter managed to rasp, his hands clinging to the cold slab behind him.

"You know who I am, cap," O'Cleary said menacingly, his eyes empty and milky.

Peter felt his way along the slab with his bare hands until he found the edge. Then, he let go and retreated back towards the freezer door.

"They fought, and they died," O'Cleary sang in a croaking voice. "So many died, Peter. But not you. You never die."

Peter reached the door. His shoulders slammed into it as he refused to turn his back on the haggard version of his friend, which staggered towards him.

O'Cleary's cracked lips formed a broken circle, and a ragged whistle was ushered forth. Peter felt for the small button in the freezer door. He found and pushed it as O'Cleary drew closer. Peter fell out of the freezer as the door opened behind him.

He landed on his rear and scooted backward until he was clear of the door. The instant he was clear, he kicked the door shut. Then he rose quickly and braced against the door, which he expected to shudder as O'Cleary collided with it, but the collision didn't come.

Jadis looked up at him from where she sat silently on one of the empty countertops. Her strange notebooks she'd been carrying around rested in her lap.

"Jadis, did you hear singing?" Peter asked urgently.

Jadis raised an eyebrow sarcastically. "Do you not?" she asked, the sound of the elves perpetual mourning faint in the distance.

"No, no. Not that. From in there?" Peter asked as he pointed with his thumb at the freezer he still leaned against.

Jadis shook her head hesitantly. "No… Why?"

"Come here," Peter said as he gestured her over and stepped hesitantly away from the door.

Clearly exasperated, Jadis clapped her book shut and made her way over to the freezer. Without explanation, Peter opened the door to the freezer and stepped back.

Jadis didn't flinch. She stared blankly into the freezer then looked back at Peter.

"Why am I looking in the freezer, Peter?" she asked as her voice took on a curious note.

Peter didn't reply. He was staring over her head at the table, which still contained the sealed body bag of O'Cleary.

"He… moved," Peter managed to reply. "He got up and sang…"

Jadis turned around to face him. She was a good bit shorter than he was, so he was forced to take his eyes off the corpse to meet her gaze.

Their eyes met, and hers searched his cynically. "He is dead, Peter," she replied.

"I know. But Brandon moved. He spoke to me," Peter replied, hand still on the open door.

Jadis' frown deepened as she closed the entrance to the fridge. "Are you sure?"

"Yes," Peter replied urgently.

"I believe you," Jadis replied with her back to him. "But, Peter, he is dead."

"Then why…?" Peter trailed off. He took a step away from the freezer and winced when one of the bruises on his side bumped the counter. *I'm losing my mind…*

"When did you last leave here?" Jadis asked.

"Three days ago," Peter replied absentmindedly. "I'm not crazy."

"I know. You should go outside. Get some air. You are being haunted," she replied calmly. "You are not the first, and you will not be the last. Get over it."

Haunted? A ghost. Of course. Why wouldn't ghosts be real, too? Peter nodded. "Yes."

She took the lead, and a minute later, Peter exited the stairs into the now tankless foyer. He took a deep breath to collect himself as he looked at the damaged glass doors of HQ. He pushed the ghostly image of O'Cleary from his mind as he stepped into the chilly fall air.

I need a distraction from this singing. Constant, unfollowable, undulating caroling fills the soul with sorrow, he thought as he stepped out of the damaged front doors of the SNW HQ into the surrounding, torn remnants of the city. No real purpose was in mind other than to find something to do. There were years' worth of restoration that needed doing, but the elves were focused on repairing the city's defenses first.

Whatever they decided about cohabitation, this place isn't going to be safe for a while yet, Peter told himself as he slowed his pace and listened for the doors closing automatically behind him. After they shut, he continued aimlessly forward, the crunch of his footfalls matched by Jadis' careful steps.

Wherever I go, she follows like a shadow. She's never invasive, but always present, watching everything I do with those wary, analytical eyes or reading from those books. What am I going to do with her? he wondered while he strolled past a semi-collapsed coffee shop.

Is she my responsibility? She isn't a child, she's older and more durable than me, even if she does look like a teenager. But she doesn't seem to have anywhere to go. The elves don't even seem to remember forgetting her species existed. Maybe Doctor Walker would. Fat lot of good that does me, though.

Peter paused at a crossroad, unsure which way to go. He turned to look at Jadis. He was greeted by an unamused expression from the eölin.

"Súmeriel came by earlier," she said suddenly.

Peter felt a pang of guilt in his chest. He hadn't spoken to her since O'Cleary's death. In fact, he hadn't spoken to anyone since then; not even during the funeral they'd thrown for O'Cleary, Alex, Ian, and the rest of the battle's casualties. *It's my fault they're dead. I shouldn't have left them. I should apologize to her too. She lost more than I did. I reacted like a child.*

"What did she want?" Peter asked after swallowing.

"For me to talk to the general now that he has done his grieving," she replied matter-of-factly.

Peter nodded. *Maybe he'll know something about why they can't remember forgetting her,* he thought. There were still so many questions.

"Do you want to go now?" Peter asked the white-haired girl.

Jadis ran the fingers of her right hand methodically along the scars on the outside of her left hand and knuckles. She stopped when she reached the bandage on her pinkie. "No, not yet. There are some things we should discuss first," she said as they moved through the city.

Peter slowed his pace. "Very well."

"There is an eölin, like me. A blacksmith named Nársidian. I think he anchored himself to something before our race was struck by the Therun-silu. As far as I can tell, he is trapped for now, but I suspect the Weeping King was part of a cult trying to free him."

Peter's jaw clenched. *A cult? You've got to be kidding me. I thought we were done.*

"And you need help finding the anchor and freeing him before the cult can?"

Jadis shook her head slowly, eyes focused on some distant memory. "No. No, we have to stop him from escaping. Even if It means none of the rest of my race being freed."

"That seems… harsh," Peter probed as he hoped for some insight into the strange girl.

"If they free him…" She shook her head. "Peter, he is the reason for all of this." She gestured at the ruins all around them. "He attacked the *duridgribuldam.* He is the reason the spell took so long to unravel. I thought I was the only one who survived. But this…" She pulled out a small leather notebook. "This was Draelic's. His cult, the disciples of Awan, think they have found a way to free their master. They are wrong. The blacksmith has them fooled. He is the one they are going to free."

Peter ran a thumb over the point of Galvorn's pommel. His mind reeled at the idea that one person could be solely responsible for the deaths of billions. Something dark coiled around Peter's heart and sank its claws into his chest. *One man. No, not a man. Whatever he is, he's responsible for all this. For the deaths of billions. He's the reason so many of my friends had to die. O'Cleary. Alex. Ian. Justin. Doctor Walker. Galamier. Folduin. And so many others I can help avenge.*

"What do you need from me?"

The idea that she needed anyone's help seemed to irritate her like a fire ant bite to the toe. "The elves do not trust me."

"But you need their help to stop him and this cult?" Peter said.

Jadis scowled and replied through gritted teeth, "Yes."

"And you need my help to get their help," Peter said with a smirk.

Jadis' scowl turned into a sneer. "Yes. Even if you are too weak to handle the deaths of your allies," she said harshly.

Peter's eyes narrowed, but he did not rise to the bait. "If you want my help convincing them to take you seriously, you might want to be nicer."

"The cult will be enough to convince them," Jadis replied dismissively.

"Then what do you need me for?"

Jadis winced. "I… am not diplomatic."

Peter stifled a laugh. "And you think I am?"

Jadis shrugged. "No, but they have listened to you before."

"Fine. I'll help you with the elves before I go home," he replied.

As they turned a corner and came into view of the elvish stronghold at the center of the city, they saw an enormous stone elvish fortress sat at the center of the elvish portion of the city's layout. A fortress that, if the orks had chosen to hold, would have made taking the city much more difficult. But orks cared more for size than defensibility, which was why they'd chosen the Tesla Building as their main base.

As they came within a stone's throw, Peter spied a familiar group of shapes depart from the front entrance. The group split in half a moment later. One half walked in the opposite direction, the other towards Peter.

Gunter's dense frame walked at the front of the second group. Behind him, William, Simon, Shawn, and Jessica walked in step. Scott and a few of his officers were making their way as a separate group towards a set of parked cars.

Gunter caught sight of Peter and Jadis approaching and called out, "Peter, we should talk," as he picked up his pace to meet them.

"Gunter, maybe we should—" Simon began, but Gunter rounded on him and began to walk backward.

"No. He's here. I'm not putting this off," Gunter snapped as they reached him. "Good grief, captain, you look terrible."

Peter scanned the group as he crossed his arms. "Can't it wait?"

"I'm afraid, captain, I agree with Gunter. It would be best if it was discussed ASAP in the present company so a proper solution can be reached," William replied.

Peter raised his eyebrows and turned to match pace with them. Jadis gave him a dirty look and fell in a few paces behind the group as they walked back the way the two of them had come.

"Here's the thing, captain," Gunter said as he adjusted his stance awkwardly. "There are some concerns about your safety if you return to Paragon."

"I still say that's bull crap," Jessica interjected, but she quickly bit her tongue at a steely look from William.

"To be perfectly candid, Peter, we're concerned that after what happened in Macon, you won't get a fair trial if you return with us to the city," Simon added, then raised his hands in surrender. "I know. It's a bit much. But there are people who don't agree with how you handled Jason, and when that's added to what happened before we left…"

"I gave them my word I'd return and stand trial," Peter replied in a firm tone.

"Yes," William responded. "For what happened before you left. Not for what happened after. We just think you should give it some time. Time for things to settle down."

Gunter kicked at a piece of rubble. "What they aren't telling you, Captain Peter, is that there's more. Things are tense back home. Some of the folks from Macon have openly spoken out against you and want what happened there added to your list of crimes."

William shook his head. "You're right, but it's only a few, and Doctor Gibson will never agree to that."

"Maybe not," Gunter replied, "but there's even mutterings of people calling Miss Young a witch. You know Sarah, the sweetest girl alive?" Gunter continued. "You'd be surprised what some people don't say when they see that uniform of yours, William."

Jessica reinserted herself into the conversation. "If they think that little princess of ours is a witch, imagine what they say when they find out you summoned the demonic-looking chick from your dreams," she said with a leer back at Jadis.

"That's not what happened. She's not a demon," Shawn began.

"Doesn't matter," Jessica replied. "Word's already spread, Everyone has their own story, and there's no way to control that narrative at this point."

Simon sighed. "It's not just that, Peter. There are those here who are concerned for your mental health, especially after you struck that elf-healer."

Shawn chimed in, "But Súmeriel said hitting the healer was a perfectly human reaction—"

"Now is not the time for you to speak, Shawn," William interrupted. "Besides, it's more than that. Those who oppose him will use whatever they can against him, and given the precarious state of things, this is not an ideal point for setting precedent. Personally," he went on with a sideways look at Simon, "I think the council be damned. You did what you had to, and they have no right to put you on trial."

"Agreed," Jessica said emphatically. "We can handle a few naysayers."

"I'm simply suggesting a short time away from conflict — time to rest," Simon replied defensively. "Give things a chance to cool down." Simon stopped and gave Peter an inquisitorial look. "Captain, are you all right?" he asked cautiously.

They don't want me to go back. My own friends don't trust me anymore, Peter thought.

William spoke again. "Ultimately, captain, it is entirely your decision to make. I'll support you either way. We just wanted you to be aware of the circumstances before you made plans."

"If you're going back, cap, I'll have your back too," Gunter added through gritted teeth.

"Peter?" Simon asked again, as the look of concern on his face deepened.

Peter nodded slowly, a faraway look in his eyes. Then he said flatly, "I saw O'Cleary earlier."

"That's good," Simon replied hopefully. "I was going to stop by and see him when I got back."

"No," Peter explained. "I mean, that's how it started. But he got up, he sang, and then he spoke to me."

Simon's look of concern was tinged with anger, but he continued to speak calmly. "Peter, when was the last time you slept?"

"Jadis thinks he's haunting me," Peter went on. "Figured I'd tell you in case you saw him too."

"You haven't slept, have you?" Simon asked with a step closer to Peter. "Peter, you *need* sleep."

Peter shook his head. "It was real, Simon."

Simon stopped moving toward him, and his eyes took on a dark look. "Really, Peter? Really? What sounds more likely, that your grief-stricken and sleep-deprived mind is hallucinating, or that your friend is haunting you? Why would O'Cleary haunt you, Peter?"

"Jadis said—"

"I don't care what Jadis said!" Simon shouted back. "I'm your doctor. Your friend. I've known you for years. I've sat by for weeks while you destroy your body, because I know what you're capable of. Because I trust you." He stopped, just for a moment, to regain his composure. "You have to trust me back, captain. You can't do this anymore. You need to rest. Look at you. You're killing yourself."

William placed a hand on Simon's shoulder. "Luu," he said in a warning tone.

I'm fine, Peter repeated to himself as he adjusted his grip on his sword. *Why should I go back to Paragon at all? Simon or someone else will just tell them I'm cra-*

zy. Paragon's safe, isn't it? If they don't want me to go back, what's the point? There's still plenty of orks that need killing here. Going back would be a waste of time.

Gunter took a step forward, hands raised in a placating gesture. "Captain, you do look like you've been hit by a steamroller. Maybe you should stay here, get some rest. Meet up with the rest of us before heading back to Paragon?" he suggested.

There's nothing for me to do there. Tell them you'll stay and rest. You can hunt down the rest of the orks, help finish clearing the city. They aren't going to stay and check, Peter told himself.

"Sir, I think—" Shawn began, but William cut him off with a harsh whip of his head. Shawn clamped his mouth shut, a flash of anger burning in his eyes.

He's picked up some fire. Peter nodded distractedly and released his sword handle, which he didn't remember grabbing. "I'll stay. Get some rest. You're right," he said as he nodded calmly and stepped through their midst. "Oh, what about Scott's forces?" he asked as he turned back to them as Jadis walked around the group.

"Some are going all the way with us to Paragon. Some are returning to Macon to set up an outpost," William explained. "I'll detail it all in the report before we set out tomorrow."

"Good," Peter replied. "I need time to think," he said as they made their way back into HQ. Before he reached the stairs, he turned back to them and asked, "Shawn, I heard you killed a troll. Is that true?"

Shawn started. "Y-yes, sir."

Peter nodded, his eyes moving from one of the others to the next, meeting each of their stares. "Any of you kill a troll?" he asked calmly. They all shook their heads in their own way. Gunter himself got a slight grin.

"I see. Get Shawn a uniform. He's earned it," he ordered, then made for his room.

Jadis was left in the hall as Peter shut the door firmly behind him and paused. He could still hear the haunting, wailing songs of the elves. His eyes came to rest on a folded SNW uniform jacket on his bed at the back of the room. The jacket had been repaired but the familiar black fatigue with a snowflake patch surrounding an assault rifle on the shoulders was torn in half on the right shoulder.

He took a cautious step closer and picked it up. He saw that it bore the dwarf modifications — bits of Shadowfang scales — and as it unfolded in his hands, he saw the elvish reinforcement to its lining.

When did this get here? he wondered as he looked it over. Then he spied the tag on the inside, which read *O'Cleary* in the man's familiar scratchy writing.

The jacket was in surprisingly good shape, given the injuries the man had endured, with only a handful of cuts and tears, none of which compromised its integrity as armor.

Maybe I really am being haunted, Peter thought as he sat down on the bed, the jacket clutched in his hands.

What do I do with this? Ordinarily, we'd bury him in it. But it's valuable armor at this point. I could give it to Shawn. It would be better than a standard-issue one. He held it up in front of him. *No, it's too long for him. I could wear it… Maybe that's what he wants, why he put it here. Can ghosts do that? Was it him? It wasn't some kind of cruel prank. No one would have had time to pull it off. Maybe it's just a coincidence.*

He lowered the jacket. *Maybe Simon's right. Maybe I am losing it… No… No. I'm fine. Tired, that's all. They're all just not adjusting to the new world we live in as quickly. They haven't been as exposed to it as I have.*

He pulled Galvorn off his back and lay the sword down at his side. *Can I trust Jadis? She hasn't lied to me yet, as far as I know. Then again, if she did, would I be able to know? If the elves can't remember forgetting her, how do I know… No, you can't function like that, Peter. You can't question every little thing. Focus on what you do know. You're not going back to Paragon. If Jadis is telling the truth about this blacksmith, you have to help her. If not, I'll burn that bridge when I cross it. She says we need the elves' help. If it was up to me, I'd take Elborin and Súmeriel. She's a warrior too, and at least she's been straight with me since the beginning.*

What would Hannah do? he thought as he glanced at a family photo he'd snagged from his father's office on the dresser across from the bed. *She'd have told everyone about Jadis from the start probably. What about dad? I wonder how he's doing. Did England get hit as hard as us? He'd probably head back to Paragon to face the music. But there's no guarantee I'll get that far.*

Okay. That settles it. Get the elves to help Jadis. Then you'll be free to help clean up the city on your own — no putting anyone else in harm's way. Peter yawned. *They're right that I need sleep, at least.*

The next morning, Peter rose early, donned his weapons, and put on O'Cleary's jacket. With his own coat tossed over his arm, he descended the stairs. As Peter exited into the foyer, he saw Shawn in almost full uniform — dark gray shirt tucked into black pants over black boots — but he was missing the jacket.

Shawn straightened at the sight of Peter. "Good morning, captain," he said with an almost perfect salute.

"At ease, Shawn," Peter replied. "Where's your jacket?"

Shawn winced. "They're trying to find one in my size, sir."

Peter smirked. "They won't, and any they do find won't be as strong. Here," he said, tossing the bronze-skinned boy the jacket in his arms. Behind Shawn and William, some of the others emerged from the kitchen. "Take care of it. You won't find more like it."

Peter exited the HQ, where he was promptly joined by Jadis. *As usual. Always around.* Together they returned to the fort, where they made their way inside, unmolested by the guards. A few steps into the cold stone building, he turned a corner and bumped into a short, bearded figure. Peter managed to catch his balance as the dwarf stopped. The abrupt shift in speed sent a scroll falling from the dwarf's bundle.

"Breekie? Where are you going in such a hurry?" Peter asked as he scooped the scroll up and placed it back on the others in the dwarf's arms.

"Ah, Peter Blair, good. I worried the grief had taken you. That would not do," he said hurriedly. "I am taking these maps. Us dwarves are heading back to Paragon with you, then taking Duelma Umindrabo home, but we have to figure out how we get home first, dah?" Breekie explained.

"Ah, well, go on then," Peter replied and stepped out of the dwarf's way. Breekie scampered off without another word as he clutched the scrolls tightly.

"Dwarves," Jadis muttered harshly under her breath.

A few more turns down thick stone halls led them into the general's new command center. The setup was so identical to the one in the forest canopy that it was as if the general had teleported himself and his belongings. Six tall windows hung open, letting in a cool breeze and plenty of light. To the left, Leuoradew stood, eyes shut, as still as the houseplant by one of the room's broad windows.

Peter greeted the highest-ranking officer in the room, who sat at the head of his war table with a pile of papers in front of him. "Lúemeni General Almurë."

Almurë waved a hand dismissively at the mention of his name. From the creases in his brow, Peter could tell he was deep in thought. A second later, Almurë waved Peter forward, still not looking up. In one hand, the general continued to stir a steaming mug of liquid.

Peter strode up to the intricate wooden table. The grown wooden map of the city had been altered to match the city's current state.

Seated with Almurë were Elborin and Súmeriel. Each wore new bird feathers in their braids. Sumeriel's feather was black with a streak of dark blue and hung from the end of her braid. Elborin's braid still hung around his neck, now with a purple and white feather.

Peter came to a stop and stood at attention. "General, this is Jadis," he said as the ancient girl came to a halt at his side, "the being I spoke of from my dreams."

"Lumeni," Súmeriel said calmly with a hint of annoyance, the kind only a daughter can show for their father, yet her voice remained smooth as ever. A collection of familiar-looking braids hung at her side from her belt. Peter noticed a set of deep blue dots painted lightly near the corner of her right eye.

Almurë's gaze rose slowly from where he'd been staring at the detailed map in front of him. His eyes wrinkled with confusion as they came to rest on Jadis. He stared, unabashedly at the girl, as he traced her scars with his eyes.

"Did you know about her kind's existence?" Peter inquired.

"That's a strange question to ask, isn't it," Almurë replied. "Especially of your own ally whom we've discussed."

"When we discussed her, you said you knew nothing about a species called eölin," Peter replied as he tried to keep the accusation out of his voice.

Almurë set down his mug and steepled his fingers. "Interesting. I have known of the eölin since they came to be. Although, I have noticed that since the Therin-Selu broke, none have made themselves known until we found Jadis. Not altogether surprising. They are a rather… insular people."

They don't remember then, Peter thought, and, unsure what to say, let silence pervade the room. Peter watched as Jadis meandered over to a platter of sweets on a desk near where the dryad stood.

Almurë continued to watch her with a perturbed expression. "Jadis… This is a human name, is it not?" he asked.

Jadis' ever-present frown deepened as she took one of Dr. Walker's leftover donuts from their plate on the desk at the dryad's side. She bit into it as she mulled over her words.

After swallowing, she replied, "It is. I gave it to Peter because I feared my own name would not be retainable with the Therin-Selu still active."

The dryad's eyes opened slowly and focused on the gray girl standing at the table beside her. Other than this, though, Leuoradew remained motionless.

"Shall we give it a try then now that you have escaped?" the general asked. "A truly remarkable feat, I might add."

Typical. Absolutely typical. Why can't anyone just use their actual name? I should be used to this by now, Peter thought as he waited for the eölin to make a decision. *I'm going to stab the next faye or person I meet who introduces themselves with an alias.*

Jadis sighed, looking for all the world like a cornered animal. "Isilmë." Behind her, Leuoradew shifted for the first time since they'd entered the room.

"Interesting — meaning moonlight. Curious that I can retain your name, but you do not give the name of your parents," the general replied.

Jadis' gaze flickered to Peter for half a second. *She was right. They don't trust her.*

Jadis replied to the elf, "Umindrabo locked our race, our very existence, out with the casting. My parents are dead. Their names would hold no meaning to you."

Why did Doctor Walker lock her entire race out?

"Unlike them, I was able to ground myself with Galvorn—"

"And when circumstances were similar enough to when it was cast, you were able to cross back over. Brilliant," the general interrupted, almost giddy. "If my theories are correct, then it is possible to return. Yet there must be a remnant yet if I cannot retain more than your given name, and as Valk Blair suggests, I did not remember your kind even existed until I saw you, and now that I have seen you, I don't recall forgetting."

"How very clever of you," Isilmë replied gruffly. "I suspect there will be more attempts to break older Therin-Selus."

"How? How do you know this?" Elborin's raspy voice interjected with a doubtful tone while he set down his warm drink. "I'm sorry, but you've been trapped in the Therin-Selu. You said yourself when we spoke the other day that your only real access was through Peter and the occasional vision."

Jadis raised an eyebrow. "Because of this." She produced a medium-size red leather-bound book, which she tossed to General Almurë.

He caught it eagerly and stared down at it with a shocked expression.

Elborin asked harshly, "Where did you get this?"

"Draelic's study. "

"Is that a blood book?" Súmeriel asked.

A blood book?

"Yes, and it explains the yulmëar… Liúre," the general swore. "Valk Blair, my daughter, has spoken on your behalf. You trust this eölin?"

Peter took his time replying. For a moment, he reveled in Jadis' growing discomfort, an act of small revenge for the weeks of beatings she'd inflicted on him in his dreams.

"She's been honest with me so far. If nothing else, she believes she's in danger, which is enough of a motivator for me."

The general tapped his finger slowly against the table. "That will have to suffice for now."

Leuoradew spoke suddenly. "The blacksmith must not be allowed to return to the land of the living."

All eyes turned to look at the wooden woman, but she spoke no more.

"Curious," the general muttered. "That is the first she's spoken since Doctor Walker's passing, and it's gibberish."

He grabbed a large cloth napkin from the table and wrapped it around the book. "Isilmë, would you be willing to come back to the capital with me to discuss these things there? What I can do to pursue this cult is limited here, and I need to return so that I might report and see to this city's restoration."

Isilmë gave Peter a furtive look. "No. I am not going anywhere near the elvish capital."

"Do you have any way of tracking the cult you mentioned?" Peter chimed in.

Jadis looked up from where she'd been ingesting pastries. "Not now. I have an idea, but I need help translating parts of Draelic's journal," she replied.

This got Elborin's attention. He sat forward abruptly. "The Weeping King was writing a journal?"

Jadis gave Peter an accusatory scowl then produced another book, this one small and brown. She threw this one over to the general as well.

Almurë's eyes grew wider with every page he eagerly flit through. "Is there no way I can convince you to return to the capital with me?" he asked in elvish without looking up from the pages.

"No," Jadis answered back briskly in the same tongue. "The journal may reveal how Draelic mimicked Dwarvish rune casting. I expect it has to do with the cult."

"Do you plan to go after these cult members?"

Jadis' scowl deepened. "Yes."

After a moment of quiet, disturbed only by the turning of pages, the general said, "Daughter, I am needed at the capital, and I intend to send Elborin and Mellonië as ambassadors to Paragon. I want you to assist Isilmë in her hunt. She will need an elf's assistance to navigate our territory safely."

"She can come only if Peter Blair does," Jadis interjected.

A small smile teased the edge of Peter's mouth. *That's it.*

Elborin nodded. "That is his decision, not mine. If the cult is connected to this new use of runes by the orks, then the dwarves will want to be involved," he commented.

"I know just the dwarf," Peter replied. "When do we leave?"

"As soon as you're rested, I've found what we need here," the general said. "I assume then you are not returning to Paragon."

"No," Peter replied. "I don't think I will."

PARAGON

Sarah stared down at the crowd in disbelief. It was a small group of only thirty to forty people, a number certainly not representative of the city as a whole, but even so, there were more of them than she could have dreamed. *These are just the ones brave enough to show up, too. Who knows how many agree with them but didn't want to participate.*

As anxious thoughts harassed her mind. She examined the protestors' signs again. One sign bore the word *magic* with a circle and line crossing it out. Another simply said *No* with a drawing of a pointy ear next to it. A third clearly read, *Cast out the casters*. The rest were much the same.

As one, the crowd stepped forward, closer to the wall. A skinny woman made her way to the front and began to lead them in a slow chant. As she turned to face the wall, Sarah recognized her as Mrs. Norman, the woman whose son's scouting party still hadn't returned. She was a woman who'd been very vocal in not only her opposition to the council itself but also to the idea of bringing in any refugees.

Hers wasn't the only familiar face. Sarah recognized the large mole above the left eye belonging to the woman from the cafeteria who'd refused her help.

"No faye. No way. No faye. No way," they chanted in unison.

Oh, no. Sarah thought as her heart pounded faster in her chest. *Doctor Umindrabo will be furious.*

From their place on the wall, Sarah saw Al scooting out from where he'd been stationed at the gate. He approached the group hurriedly and waved his arms in a shooing motion.

Sarah turned to see how Dr. Gibson and the council members reacted. As she did, she caught Marah rolling her eyes at the protesters and felt a pang of anger towards the woman from deep in her chest. *This is serious. People are getting irrational about all the magic. Why'd they have to do this now with the Elvish dignitaries almost here? I mean, I know why it's obviously intentional. But it's so foolish.*

Dr. Gibson wasted no time. He excused himself from the council and made his way down the stairs and towards the crowd. He moved quickly but gave off no sense of urgency in his gait. The rest of the council seemed unsure what to do as they looked back and forth between the empty road outside the city and the crowd below.

In the end, they split, half following Dr. Gibson, including Donna Meents and Councilwoman Fritz, while the other half lingered on the ramparts. Marah stayed with the second group, to Sarah's surprise. *She seems more like the type to go confront them.*

Sarah turned to Steven and found that his eyes were looking everywhere but at the crowd and the council.

"What's wrong?" she whispered. The worry lines on his forehead made her concerned that something else might be going on.

He shook his head almost imperceptibly to acknowledge he'd heard her but did not respond. His eyes continued to scan their surroundings. After a few tense moments of searching, he stepped away from those gathered on the ramparts and spoke into his radio.

Sarah was torn. She wanted to know what Steven was up to, but she also wanted to know how Dr. Gibson was going to address the crowd. *If they're upset about more faye and magic, I'd probably only make them more irrational,* she decided.

So, she stepped over to where Steven, in full SNW uniform, was already clipping his radio back to his belt. With each step, she could feel Marah watching her. *She's probably worried I'll do something to antagonize them — or worse, Steven will.*

Somewhere deep inside, Sarah felt the urge to draw her wand and blast the woman off the wall. It'd be easy, like swatting a fly. All she'd need to do was point and speak. She brushed the thought aside. The very idea of it made her queasy.

Steven gave her a weak smile while he spoke into the radio before lowering and addressing her. "You okay? Seeing that can't be easy for you, and you look ready to kill someone," he said with a gesture towards the crowd.

"I'm fine," she replied. "They're just scared."

Steven scowled. "Fear makes people stupid. Stupid people get smart people killed."

"True…" Sarah replied hesitantly. She'd never seen him this worked up before. "Are… are *you* okay?" she asked carefully.

Steven braced his knuckles against his chin and cracked his neck. "Indeed. Sorry, just being cautious. This reminded me of something that happened on tour."

"Oh?" Sarah replied.

"Yeah. It was only my second operation with Peter. A terror cell we were sent to take care of used a protest as a distraction to set off a bomb. Then, when our backs turned to focus on the bomb, they blew up the protestors," he explained with a faraway look in his eyes. "We lost four men."

"That's horrible," Sarah replied in a hushed tone. "So, you were checking to make sure this wasn't a distraction?"

"Still checking," Steven replied as he tapped the radio. "Looks like Doctor Gibson might have a handle on this though. Listen."

Sarah moved to the edge of the rampart and watched the crowd below. She focused on Dr. Gibson's voice as it echoed off the walls. *Where did they get the supplies to make those signs?* she wondered for a split second.

"I understand your grievances. I do. But now is neither the time nor the place to present them," the mustached man explained calmly. "Please, return to your homes."

"We have a right to be here. We have a right to protest," a man called from the crowd.

"Of course," Dr. Gibson replied firmly. "Mister?" he asked the man's name with surprising formality.

The short, balding man with thick glasses and a stern expression blinked; put off guard by Gibson's congeniality. He adjusted his tweed jacket before he spoke. "Eangl. Edward Eangl," he replied while he ran his right thumb and forefinger up and down the bridge of his nose.

"Mister Eangl, no one denies your right to be here, but please think. Consider your timing. If you do fear these newcomers, would it not be better to avoid offending them?"

"Our timing is clearly intentional, Mister Mayor. How can we expect to protect the people of this town if we let in the very things that threaten it?" Eangl replied emphatically.

A movement to the left drew Sarah's focus away from Dr. Gibson. Marah was pushing her way out of her group, towards her and Steven. Sarah glanced at her half-shaved head as she got closer. The shaved hairs had been dyed a deep purple. *I can only imagine what mom would have to say about that. 'It must be nice to be able to wear whatever you want. It does look convenient, though, other than the dye, at least. Who has time to dye hair right now?'*

Marah came to a stop within whispering range, her gaze focused on Steven with barely an acknowledging nod towards Sarah.

"Mister Thomas, are you going to have your men arrest these protesters?" she said in almost a shout.

Steven raised both eyebrows. "Excuse me?" he replied, dumbfounded.

"I asked if you're going to have your men arrest them?" she insisted as she waved her arms dramatically. Her voice lowered only a tiny bit. "I cannot allow you to take such actions."

Steven crossed his arms. "Look, I don't know how you did things in Macon, but around here, people still have their constitutional rights. I can't just have thirty-eight people arrested for signs and chanting."

Marah's hands went to her hips, her eyes bulging. "As a council member, I order you to have your men stand down," she said in a shockingly controlled voice compared to the look on her face.

Steven uncrossed his arms and put his hands slowly in his pockets. "I'm telling you my men aren't trying to arrest anyone yet," he replied simply.

Marah's jaw worked as she ground her teeth and turned to Sarah. "Miss Young."

Sarah's eyes widened in surprise. "Yes?"

"If Commander Steven or any of his men make a move to arrest these protesters, I want you to use any forces at your disposal to stop them," she said slowly, emphasizing every word.

Sarah looked at Steven. *I can't believe this.*

Steven's brow furrowed, and he shook his head.

"I, uh— That… won't be necessary," she replied. Her voice squeaked a little as she turned back to Marah. Something about the woman was starting to scare her.

Marah's eyes narrowed as she seemed to pick Sarah apart piece by piece with them. When she spoke again, her voice was low and threatening. "Good. The last thing we need right now is totalitarian action," she declared then turned to march down the stairs of the wall.

Steven's radio was at his mouth before Marah got halfway down the stairs. "This is Commander Thomas. No one is to take any action against these pro-testors unless myself or Doctor Gibson give a direct order, is that understood?"

Confirmations came back over the radio. Below, Dr. Gibson met Marah between where he'd addressed the protestors at the bottom of the stairs. The crowd dispersed behind him. Sarah yanked her notebook open and followed Marah's path down to where Al stood between the stairs and the gate.

"How did he get them to leave?" she asked, eager to make a note of what she'd missed.

Al scratched the back of his neck. "He just told 'em there were only a pair of ambassadors coming and promised to have a town hall meeting in the morning to discuss their concerns."

Sarah blinked. "That's it?"

"Yarp, apparently. Somehow they got the idea we were taking in a bunch of elvish refugees or something. Don't see the issue with that myself, if it were the case. We've got plenty of room," he mumbled.

"We're bringing in refugees from Atlanta, just like with Macon. Maybe they got it confused?" Sarah hypothesized.

"Maybe," Al said with a shrug.

Sarah returned to the top of the ramparts, where she watched eagerly over the organized road below. Vehicles were spread out on either side of the road, staggered to make approaching more difficult. They'd been moved out of the way for this special event.

A few feet away, the council stood with their backs to Sarah and Steven. Dr. Gibson, Mrs. Lucia, and their newest member, Marah, engaged most outspokenly in a quiet discussion. Marah's harsh gaze occasionally slid out of the huddle to transfix suspiciously on Steven. However, Steven did an excellent job of ignoring the gaze, though Sarah suspected he hadn't noticed it at all.

I don't get it. What's her problem with Steven? Must be a SNW thing, Sarah thought as she mentally reviewed their few brief encounters. She couldn't think of anything he'd done to garner the woman's disdain, but she wasn't always with him. Sarah brushed at some dust that had found its way onto her dress and looked back at the road.

In the corner of her eye, she could see the enormous skull of Shadowfang attached carefully to the wall above the gate. Sarah didn't like it. Not just the skull itself, but the decision to place it on the wall. *I get it, after hearing about what happened in Macon. And I know it's intimidating, even without the teeth, but who's going to see a basilisk skull and think this place looks safe?*

"They're taking their sweet time, aren't they?" Steven said as he stepped up next to her. His voice providing a welcome distraction from Sarah's train of thought.

"Yeah, I'm a little nervous, to be honest," Sarah replied as she resisted the urge to look over at where she'd hidden Dr. Walker's rune.

"You don't look nervous. You look good. Very pretty dress," Steven said in a soft tone.

Sarah felt a hint of blush warm her cheeks in the cold autumn air. "Thank you," she replied as she fidgeted with the wand in her notebook, twisting it in and out of its compartment.

She glanced up at Steven, glad they'd been able to get their feelings out in the open. He was wearing his SNW uniform, which he'd gone so far as to iron from the looks of it. "You look nice too. Putting your best foot forward for the elvish dignitaries?"

Steven smirked and gave a soft sigh. "I was going to say it's not every day you get to meet representatives from an unfamiliar intelligent species, but…"

Sarah chuckled softly. "You've got a point there. If Cheekie's to be believed, and I suspect he is, there are hundreds more out there." After a moment of quiet, she added. "Where is he, by the way?"

Steven rolled his eyes. "At the Forge. He said there's still work to do, and he isn't stopping it for some *crisking* elves," he explained with air quotes.

"Oh," Sarah replied, then after a moment asked, "What do you think they'll be like?"

"The elves? According to reports, a warrior people. Pointy ears. Colored braids. Nothing like Santa's workshop," Steven said with a soft smile.

Sarah chuckled. "If they were, you know, Santa elves, this would be a lot less stressful. Hey, look," she said as she pointed over the wall.

Down the road, a man on a bike pedaled towards them. The familiar frame of Rick Gardiner quickly came into focus.

Steven brought a radio to his mouth. "This is Thomas checking in. Over."

After a moment, a familiar voice came back over the radio. "Hey, Thomas. This is William. Sorry about the delay. I was checking in with your scouts. Our first section is about five minutes out at our current pace. Over."

"Good to hear your voice, William. Any idea why there's an Aussie biking towards me like a mad man? Over," Steven replied.

"No idea. Over," William replied over the radio.

It took Rick a few minutes to reach the wall despite his speed. Once he arrived at the open gate, he was ushered through it and up the ramparts. Sarah watched as his scrawny form came to a halt at the top of the stairs. There, he leaned back with two hands braced against his lower back and gulped in air.

He's gonna fall if he's not more careful, Sarah thought as she and Steven approached Rick.

"Give… me… a second," he gasped out between breaths.

Sarah and Steven exchanged a puzzled look as neither of them had spoken to him yet. Steven produced a water bottle and offered it to the panting man, who took it eagerly. The shuffling of feet alerted them to the incoming council members.

They approached in a bunch, gathered together like a flock of penguins led by a walrus. At least that was the image Sarah saw. After all, Dr. Gibson was a good head-and-shoulders taller than the rest with an increasingly long but still immaculate mustache.

"Mister Gardiner, are you all right?" he said with a cocked eyebrow.

Rick nodded vigorously and gave a thumbs-up as he glugged down water.

He sighed and recapped the bottle. "Do we have a recycling box up here?" he asked, looking around.

"Mister Gardiner, please," Dr. Gibson replied, placing a hand on his shoulder to guide him from the edge of the stairs then taking the bottle from him. "Why the hasty return?"

"Ah, well, they're almost here," he replied with a broad smile as though it were the best news anyone could ever hear.

Everyone else exchanged confused looks as Dr. Gibson ran a finger over his mustache. "Is that all?"

"Yeah," Rick said with a glance at his watch. "Should be about twenty minutes or so."

Dr. Gibson sighed deeply, and Sarah suppressed a giggle at the look of exhaustion on the man's face. "Are you sure there isn't anything else?" he asked, his mustache deepening his frown.

"No, sir. Everything seemed just about fine to me," Rick replied in his strange blend of Australian and Southern dialects.

"Mister Gardiner, you are aware we have radios?" the mayor asked, carefully concealing his frustration, but before Dr. Gibson could hear a reply from Rick, something else drew his attention.

"Sarah," Steven called softly. She turned and found him motioning her to the front of the wall. "They're here," he exclaimed, the excitement in his voice escaping.

Sarah joined him at the edge of the ramparts just in time to see the fleet of ragged old vehicles led by an enormous semi-truck toting a tank crest the road's distant hill.

"They brought Brucey," Steven exclaimed joyfully.

"Who's Brucey?" Sarah asked as she silently counted the number of approaching vehicles. She searched eagerly among the faces for familiar shapes and silhouettes.

"That's what SNW named the tank. I know, it's a little silly, but trust me, it was the lesser of several evils," he explained with a wink.

Sarah glanced back down at her notebook, and then another question struck her. "Why did you put your hands in your pockets?"

"What? Steven replied as he tore his gaze away from the incoming envoy.

"When Marah was accusing you of planning to arrest the crowd, you uncrossed your arms and put them in your pockets," Sarah explained.

"Ah," Steven said as he ran a hand down his face and stretched his jaw. "Well, I'm kind of a big dude. I didn't want people to think I was trying to threaten her, so I adopted a more neutral posture."

"It seemed to make her madder," Sarah countered with a hint of amusement, as she made notes in the margins of her notebook.

"It does that. But people usually take the side of the person with his hands in his pockets over the person yelling. Peter taught me that, actually," he said bemusedly. "Weird. I don't see him on Brucey. Maybe he's driving." A pair of small binoculars made their way to his face from his pocket.

"Ahem," a voice said from behind them.

Hesitantly, Sarah looked back to see who it was, eager to borrow Steven's binoculars when he'd satiated his curiosity. Dr. Gibson stood a respectful distance back, hands clasped behind his back, his mustache in a state of minor distress. Sarah's body followed the turn of her head, and she smiled welcomingly.

"Doctor Gibson! What can I do for you?" she asked politely.

Dr. Gibson brought one of his large hands around and offered it affectionately. Sarah shook it. His warm brown hand enveloped her small white digits, providing them a momentary respite from the cold.

"First of all, I wanted to apologize for that embarrassing display just a moment ago, Miss Young. I understand things are stressful enough as is, and the last thing I want is for you to feel uncomfortable, especially with all you've done for us," he began.

Sarah smiled weakly back, not really wanting to think about the protestors or the implications of them.

"Secondly," the doctor continued, "I have yet another favor to ask." His face darkened. "And, a bit of bad news, unfortunately."

Sarah tensed slightly. The idea of doing any magic this close to actually capable casters, especially after the surprise protest, scared her.

Dr. Gibson gave her a comforting smile. "My request is nothing difficult, dear. I simply was hoping you would join me in greeting the elvish ambassadors. I believe it would be pertinent for relations with these new people to include someone familiar with their arts."

"Oh…" Sarah stalled to think. "Well, if you think it's a good idea. They'll have Doctor Walker to introduce them though. I'm sure you don't need me."

"Therein lies the bad news, I'm afraid," Dr. Gibson replied with a downcast face.

No, Sarah protested silently. Her mind made the connection her heart feared.

"I'm afraid I just received a report…" Dr. Gibson continued.

No.

"…that unfortunately Doctor Walker has passed away."

Sarah felt struck in the chest and buried in rubble all within a fraction of a section. Her head felt surprisingly light, though, despite the crushing weight on her chest that pulled her towards the earth.

A firm hand grasped her shoulder, pulled her up and out of the panic. The hand on her shoulder held her in place, kept her from tumbling back out. She took a slow breath, deep and deliberate.

Between calming breaths, she pushed away her tears. There would be plenty of time for those later. *You can do this. You need to do this. They need you to do this.*

"Are you all right, Sarah?" Steven's voice came from close by.

Don't be afraid. Sarah nodded, convincing herself it was the truth. "Yes. Let's see what the new world has brought us."

EPILOGUE

Snow fell softly over what was once the state of Georgia. No more than a soft dusting collected on the armor of the small band of orks moving along the overgrown back road. Their boots crunched lightly as they left faint impressions along the ground. It was the only sounds to be heard as the snow quieted the earth.

Their quick marching left behind tracks that would be quickly covered. This resulted in little evidence they'd ever been there. The orks had no idea that the white crystals falling from the sky were a rare occurrence in this part of the world, nor did they know of the three figures waiting in ambush ahead.

Peter stared down at Galvorn. Black blood slid down the blade's length and gave the sword a fluidic appearance. A drop of the blood splashed onto his ash-coated boots and ran down the length of it, growing smaller until none of it reached the ground. Peter twisted his wrist, turning the sword over in his hand.

Galvorn felt heavy for once, like it wanted to pull him into the ground. He switched hands, and the sensation dissipated. Peter sighed through his nose, directing his attention away from the sword. His eyes wavered over the four ork corpses scattered around the campfire at his feet.

The fifth being in a hooded cloak lay face down in the mud to Peter's left. Jadis was kneeling beside the figure, where she rifled through its clothes. *Human*, Peter realized as he watched the red blood around the being's head mix with the mud. Not that it mattered. *Whoever they were, they'd been in league with these dead orks. Why else would they have been sitting peacefully with them?*

Peter heard Súmeriel's strangely comforting voice from behind him: "No warlocks."

It'd been easy. They hadn't seen it coming. They'd barely even put up a fight; it happened so quickly. The three of them were falling into sync, he realized. They each had their own unique way of killing, each as efficient as the other.

Peter pulled out a bandanna from his pocket and began to clean his blade. He watched it closely, his dark reflection in the metal. *Who's wielding who here?* he wondered.

Shawn burst into the main room of SNW's headquarters in Paragon, the gift clutched in one hand behind his back. He didn't have to search for long before he spied Breekie. The dwarf was sitting in a corner by the fire. Much to Shawn's surprise, Akena's leg rested in the dwarf's lap. Determined to be nonchalant, Shawn relaxed his shoulders and strolled over slowly, but despite his best effort to appear casual, he failed in a way only a teenager could.

Breekie didn't look up from the work he was doing on the foot as Shawn got closer. Still focused on the foot, Breekie raised his hands — well, hand. One hand was simply a screwdriver attached to the stump where his hand had been. The dwarf removed the screwdriver and reached over to the short table next to him.

On the table was Breekie's *handoleer*, as Shawn liked to call it — a bandoleer of different hands, or tools, which could attach to the modified stump of Breekie's hand. As Shawn watched awkwardly, Breekie traded the screwdriver for a scalpel. Shawn hadn't asked who'd designed the prosthetic or where the dwarf acquired it, but that didn't stop his fascination with the device.

Shawn came to a stop a few steps from the fire, hands clenched tightly on the surprise hidden behind him as he waited impatiently for Breekie to finish. Breekie finally glanced up at Shawn, and a grin made its way onto his face.

"Come to wish me well before I leave?" Breekie asked in a friendly tone while still tinkering away with the bone prosthetic.

"I thought you weren't leaving until tomorrow?" Shawn replied, a bit surprised.

"Dah, dah. I forget, you humans make your good-byes as short as the word. We dwarves prefer to have our good-byes last days if we can," Breekie replied much to Akena's waning silent annoyance. "Weeks, if possible, so that when all the celebrating is said and done, you've almost forgotten we're leaving."

"Would you focus? I'd like to get on with my foot," Akena interjected. The berating was emphasized by a playful kick from her other foot, which made poor Breekie grimace.

"That does sound like fun," Shawn replied while trying to hide a smirk at his friend's misfortune, "but I brought you something for your handoleer, if that makes up for it," he explained as he produced the green dinosaur-head snapper.

Breekie's eyebrow skyrocketed, and Shawn proceeded to dramatically reach out with the toy and begin gnawing at one of Breekie's large ears with the dinosaur's plastic mouth.

Breekie's grin broke back through the thick black of his beard. He guffawed. "Is perfect, thank you, Shawn. Come have seat."

Akena threw up her hands. "I give up. You can fix my leg, and then maybe I'll finish," she said while she lifted her leg and set her false foot on a stool in front of Breekie's seat by the fire.

The movement forced Shawn to step over it in order to reach a chair. Once he had his seat, Breekie pulled back from Akena's foot.

"Dah, is done," he said proudly.

While Akena pulled back her foot and began to test her weight on it, Shawn handed over the dinosaur.

"Ah-hah! That's much better. Thank you," she said as she gleamed down at her basilisk-bone prosthetic. "That elf was rather impressed with it, by the way. Not sure if I mentioned that."

"Dah, dah. I did not forget. Súmeriel hates basilisk as much as you," Breekie replied as he sat forward and removed the scalpel currently slotted into the attachment over his stump. Then he reached over carefully and set the scalpel on the table with the bandoleer.

He slowly removed an attachable magnifying glass from the belt and inserted it into his hand slot. "I know of her. Did you know she is a basilisk-bane herself?" he added as he inched forward to get a closer look at the foot.

It didn't take Jenni long to reach the memorial outside the city's gates. The enormous amber slab full of bones decorated in vines and flowers was a beautiful sight. She walked along the edge and read over the list of names carved elegantly into the amber's surface until she found the name she was here to read.

Justin Lewis. More recent than most of the names but not as recent as those that followed. Many of those were written for the casualties of the Battle for Atlanta. Jenni knelt down next to the memorial and produced from her satchel a pair of beers: her last two Killians; Justin's favorite. She opened one and took a sip before opening the second and pouring it onto the ground in front of her. Jenni hated the taste of beer, but she finished the bottle. She let the warmth of alcohol do battle with the cold air.

"I'll find whoever did this, Justin. I know they're here somewhere," Jenni said softly. "I can feel it." Then she sat alone in the cold and cried to herself for a time.

In Dr. Walker's old home, Sarah stood in front of a fireplace and stared down at the letter addressed to Peter that she'd thrown into it. As the flames licked up the paper and ink, she felt a sense of unease about her decision to destroy it.

Steven dug through a stack of papers behind her for anything useful, not entirely sure what he was looking to find.

A loud, jarring knock echoed from the front door and pulled Steven from his treasure hunt. Much to his amusement, Sarah did not so much as budge from in front of the fire. *She probably didn't even hear it,* he thought fondly to himself as he stood carefully from the too short chair.

Steven paused and stretched his cramped muscles. The stretching was heralded by more aggressive knocking. *She locked the door again; probably a wise decision,* Steven thought as he made his way through the room to the door.

"Hold your horses," Steven called out as he scowled and reached the peephole and saw he'd have to stoop to use it. He elected to ignore it as he opted to open the door without seeing who was on the other side. Cold air rushed into the room, and Steven was greeted by Simon. Behind Simon, he made out a scared-looking middle-aged man with a small, limp body in his arms.

"Sarah?" Simon asked, short of breath.

Steven didn't hesitate as she opened the door wider and ushered them in, then closed it quickly behind them so as not to lose more heat.

"What's going on?" Sarah said as she at last turned from the fire. She reached up and brushed her glasses involuntarily as she looked to Simon for an explanation. Then she saw the man with the bundle of child in his arms.

"Here. Lay her down on the couch," she said as she pulled the blanket she wore off her shoulders to lay over the unconscious form as the man laid the child down.

"I think she's a magic-user," Simon said calmly. "There was an accident. Her mother was burned pretty badly. I've dealt with that but she won't wake up. I was hoping you could help somehow."

"Please, ma'am. I can't lose another child. She was only trying to help. He didn't mean to hurt Rebecca," the man blubbered and clung to his daughters still hands.

Sarah was already reaching for her wand. "Steven, there's a clear orb in the kitchen. Fetch it for me, would you?" she said to the large man, who moved without further prodding.

"The mother is stable, but I want to get back and check her more closely. The girl has been unconscious since they brought her to me," Simon explained quickly, already on his way to the door.

Sarah nodded then called out to Simon. "Bring the mother here. If you can't figure out what else is wrong with her. Maybe I can help. Send someone to wake up Elborin and Mel." *But first, I have to help this child learn before they hurt someone else.*

Sarah took a shallow breath through her nose. The warm smell of books filled her nostrils. *Is this what being the head of a school will be like? Constantly floundering with the unknown while children depend on me?* Sarah reached out with magic. *So be it.*

As Simon emerged onto the cold street, he caught a glimpse of Jenni as she walked briskly in from the south gate's direction. She nodded at him as she wrapped her coat snugly around herself, and her brown hair fluttered in the chilling breeze of the late afternoon.

Being a member of the city's council had its perks. Marah liked perks; especially the privacy of her own apartment in all the chaos that was the city and its refugees. More came every day. Most sought Paragon, desperate for a safe place to stay. Others looked for work, and still others came simply because they had nowhere else to go.

They would be safe here, so long as they followed her rules. After all, she'd seen both sides of the coin, hadn't she? Who was more qualified to lead and protect these people than her? *People don't want to follow,* she told herself. *They want to be led without knowing it.* She smiled to herself as she made her way around her desk and turned to face the pair.

She hid the sneer. She felt her lips forming. *What I wouldn't give to have Jason's power back. Look at these two. Her with her suburban-mom haircut, and him with his try-hard haircut. Still… They've done well so far.*

"Did anyone see you come in?" she asked. *It'll be easier if we keep this between us for now.*

"No," the bald man replied. "What's this about?"

"I brought you both here to discuss a certain Miss Sarah Young," Marah replied with a fake smile as she took a seat, "and what her presence here means to the safety of this city."

TO BE CONTINUED

THANK YOU FOR READING!

As a small indie book, every page read helps! But so do reviews! If you liked, loved, or hated this book please leave a review wherever possible! Amazon, Audible, Etsy, Goodreads, all help! And if you want to post anything on social media about the book we find most of our readers that way! Don't hesitate to tag Mikel Melwasul regardless of how much you liked or disliked what you read. We want to hear from you and learn how we can improve our story in future novels.

Book two of The Galvorn Saga; *Paragon Attrition* is coming soon! And keep an eye out for our short story collection in the world of Paragon; *Paragon Apocrypha*, or our southern-gothic horror novella that reveals what happened to Lt. Rory; *Paragon Odyssey!*

If you enjoyed this, you may enjoy some other works by indie authors! Check out:

The Song Of Thyssia by S.J. Stiles
Corrupted Tides by S.M. Campbell
Flipside by Leumas Llewtnac
The Wingbreaker by Megan G. Mossgrove
The Adventures of Hemera Nyx in The Galaxy of the Future! By RSK
Remnant by K.R. Solberg & C.R. Jacobson
Armitage by Atlas Creed
Voices of the Void by Patrick Leitzen
The Shards of Etherious - Arisen by Colin JD Crooks
The Guardian's Speaker Series by Katherine E. Wibell
Beta by M.T. Zimny
Or if you want more suggestions reach out to us at
mikelmelwasul@gmail.com!

ABOUT THE AUTHOR

Mikel Melwasul does not exist. He is the amalgamation of the minds of three-ish individuals who conspired to write together. If you encounter him in the wild, that is most likely his "avatar" "Mik" whose body he "shares". There's also a chance it's "Dave" who he pilots less often.

If you encounter them both at the same time, run.